HAUNTED AMERICA

Star-Spangled
Supernatural Stories
Selected by Marvin Kaye
with Saralee Kaye

DOUBLEDAY BOOK & MUSIC CLUBS
GARDEN CITY, NEW YORK

Quality Printing and Binding by
Berryville Graphics
P.O. Box 272
Berryville, VA 22611 USA

Contents

THE EAST

THE SOUTH

OTHER BOOKS BY MARVIN KAYE

Devils & Demons
Ghosts
Masterpieces of Terror and the Supernatural
13 Plays of Ghosts and the Supernatural
Weird Tales™: The Magazine that Never Dies
Witches & Warlocks

HAUNTED AMERICA

INTRODUCTION

The Lively Ghost of Liberty

Haunted America? Can spectres still clank their chains in a nation that boasts atomic submarines, computers, fiber optics, intercontinental superhighways, spaceships, satellite TV and videotape recorders?

Ten years ago when I edited my first Doubleday anthology, *Ghosts: A Treasury of Chilling Tales Old and New,* the answer was definitely Yes. A decade later, ghosts are paradoxically more alive than ever in American literature, films, TV and even (especially?) the banner headlines of supermarket checkout-counter newspapers.

This widespread fascination with the supernatural is a comparatively recent American cultural phenomenon. In the down-to-earth 1940s, critics and teachers thought fantasy fiction marginally prurient or at best, "kid stuff"—an echo of that Puritan pragmatism our country needed to survive the Depression and the Second World War. In the ethnocentric 1950s, when Cold War paranoia equated the study of hard science with patriotism, imagination became even more gravely suspect, while the display of a liberal social conscience was almost tantamount to treason.

But after that tragic Friday afternoon of November 22, 1963, when President John F. Kennedy was assassinated, our country was plunged into a national identity crisis in which both gapped generations displayed distressingly similar uniform-wearing conformist mentalities. As I wrote in the introduction to *Ghosts* in 1980, "America was ripe—spiritually and practically—for a rebirth of faith and its 'flip side,' superstition. An explosion of fundamentalism, back-to-Jesus movements, Hare Krishna and Reverend Moon demagoguery was matched by a new interest in vampirism, satanism, demonic possession."

Historically, fantasy and horror literature tends to flourish during eras of repression and strife. Today, as the world enters the final decade of the twentieth century, democracy is dramatically reshaping the Communist sector and at least one criminal emperor has been deposed, but our nation's still beset by hunger and homelessness, cancer and new diseases, escalating taxes and conservative politicians whose knowledge of the American Constitution does not appear to include the hallowed principle of the separation of church and state. In such a cultural ferment, fantasy is virtually a spiritual necessity.

AMERICA AFTER DARK

Once I found tales of devils, ghouls, monsters, werewolves, witches and vampires frightening, but time has diluted their potency; they are offshoots of a dualistic theology that has wrought great harm on the human mind and spirit. But ghost stories still chill me. As I stated in my own haunted-house novels, *A Cold Blue Light* (written in collaboration with Parke Godwin) and *Ghosts of Night and Morning*, it is not necessary to believe or, for that matter, disbelieve in survival after death to accept the proposition that certain houses may be haunted. I have had a few too many strange experiences in my life (especially the summer I spent acting in the Edinburgh Theatre Festival) to deny the possibility.

While something of a sequel to *Ghosts*, *Haunted America* has its own distinctive flavor. The phantoms flitting through these pages are all—pardon the expression—homebodies chiefly created by American authors; they appear and vanish exclusively on native soil. In the earlier volume, a couple of revenant bloodsuckers were included, but not in this collection. Death himself drops in a couple of times, and there are a few anomalous supernatural entities (Frank Belknap Long's elemental is one), one resurrected Egyptian and a couple of out-and-out fakes. The determining test in these cases was the word "haunted." As long as the bogeys in question frequented some recognizably American locale, they qualified for these pages, but as my friend Ellen Asher, editor in chief of the Science Fiction Book Club, put it, "Itinerant vampires need not apply."

I have as often as possible chosen pieces set in actual towns and cities of the U.S.A. Though it was not possible to find a ghost story for every one of the fifty states, there is a generous assortment of tales from every major geographical sector of the country. For the sake of reference, the fifty states were preliminarily divided into five regions, as follows:

NEW ENGLAND: Connecticut, Maine, Massachusetts, New Hampshire, Rhode Island, Vermont.

THE EAST: Delaware, Maryland, New Jersey, New York, Pennsylvania.

THE SOUTH: Alabama, Arkansas, Florida, Georgia, Kentucky, Louisiana, Mississippi, North Carolina, South Carolina, Tennessee, Virginia, West Virginia.

THE WEST: Alaska, Arizona, California, Colorado, Hawaii, Idaho, Montana, Nevada, New Mexico, Oklahoma, Oregon, Texas, Utah, Washington, Wyoming.

THE MIDWEST: Illinois, Indiana, Iowa, Kansas, Michigan, Minnesota, Missouri, Nebraska, North Dakota, Ohio, South Dakota, Wisconsin.

The above order varies in one respect from the arrangement in the *Rand McNally Road Atlas* that I used as a reference guide. For some inexplicable reason that indispensable traveler's companion places Delaware and Maryland in the South, which is neither geographically nor historically accurate. I have put them back in the East where they belong. The District of Columbia might have posed a placement problem, but the closest any story in this collection comes to being set in Washington is Henry Kuttner's "We Are the Dead," which takes place in Arlington National Cemetery across the Potomac in Virginia. In the Appendix, D.C. has its own separate heading.

The arrangement of the five subsections follows the development of America itself, beginning with New England, the Eastern states and the South, moving to the West (with a side excursion into the Pacific) and ending in the Midwest. It might have made geographical and historical sense to put the West last, but I always reserve the closing spot for my own personal favorite. This time, Larry Siegel's "Another Chance for Casey" fits the definition, so our excursion across *Haunted America* follows the perimeter before proceeding into the nation's heartland.

A popular feature of my earlier ghost anthology was a list of allegedly haunted houses and sites in nineteen American states. I have revised and expanded it and include it in the present volume as the Appendix, "The Midnight Tourist's Guide to Haunted America." Many places named there may be visited by the general public.

—MARVIN KAYE
Manhattan, January 1990

HAUNTED AMERICA

NEW ENGLAND

Our spectral journey begins, appropriately enough, where the Pilgrims landed in the *Mayflower*. Begun in 1620 when Massachusetts, our second oldest colony, was first settled, New England is the birthplace of presidents, the American Revolution and such important early writers as Ralph Waldo Emerson and Henry David Thoreau. But it is also the home of the Puritan witch trials and H. P. Lovecraft's redoubtable Miskatonic University, an institution of higher learning that surely boasts the greatest unexplained student mortality rate in the annals of American education.

Forbidden knowledge and superstition lurk among the quaint rolling hills and seaside vistas of Connecticut, Maine, Massachusetts, New Hampshire, Rhode Island and Vermont, where the traveler encounters constant reminders of those hardworking Yankees who faced the future with clear heads but still kept their fingers firmly crossed after dark.

In this section, Salem-born writer Nathaniel Hawthorne's sense of sin and expiation casts a long shadow. Most of the following stories hinge on the corruptive force of secret wickedness.

EDITH WHARTON

The Triumph of Night

EDITH WHARTON *(1862–1937), born Newbold Jones in New York, is generally remembered as the author of such satirically cosmopolitan novels as* The Age of Innocence, The House of Mirth *and* Hudson River Bracketed, *but she also penned many ghost stories, as well as what may be America's greatest "conte cruelle,"* Ethan Frome, *set on a New England farm. "The Triumph of Night" is an atmospheric sermon about sin masquerading as righteousness. It takes place in New Hampshire near the town of Northridge, which, though not on the map, might be Northfield, a village some twenty miles north of the state capital, Concord, that plays annual host to New England's largest quilting festival.*

It was clear that the sleigh from Weymore had not come; and the shivering young traveler from Boston, who had counted on jumping into it when he left the train at Northridge Junction, found himself standing alone on the open platform, exposed to the full assault of nightfall and winter.

The blast that swept him came off New Hampshire snowfields and ice-hung forests. It seemed to have traversed interminable leagues of frozen silence, filling them with the same cold roar and sharpening its edge against the same bitter black-and-white landscape. Dark, searching and swordlike, it alternately muffled and harried its victim like a bullfighter now whirling his cloak and now planting his darts. This analogy brought home to the young man the fact that he himself had no cloak, and that the overcoat in which he had faced the relatively temperate air of Boston seemed no thicker than a sheet of paper on the bleak heights of Northridge. George Faxon said to himself that the place was uncommonly well-named. It clung to an exposed ledge over the valley from which the train had lifted him, and the wind combed it with teeth of steel that he seemed actually to hear scraping against the wooden sides of the station. Other building there was none: the village lay far down the road, and thither—since the Weymore sleigh had not come—Faxon saw himself under the necessity of plodding through several feet of snow.

He understood well enough what had happened: his hostess had forgotten that he was coming. Young as Faxon was, this sad lucidity of soul had been acquired as the result of long experience, and he knew that the visitors who can least afford to hire a carriage are almost always those whom their hosts forget to send for. Yet to say that Mrs. Culme had forgotten him was too crude a way of putting it. Similar incidents led him to think that she had probably told her maid to tell the butler to telephone the coachman to tell one of the grooms (if no one else needed him) to drive over to Northridge to fetch the new secretary; but on a night like this, what groom who respected his rights would fail to forget the order?

Faxon's obvious course was to struggle through the drifts to the village, and there rout out a sleigh to convey him to Weymore; but what if, on his arrival at Mrs. Culme's, no one remembered to ask him what this devotion to duty had cost? That, again, was one of the contingencies he had expensively learned to look out for, and the perspicacity so acquired told him it would be cheaper to spend the night at the Northridge inn, and advise Mrs. Culme of his presence there by telephone. He had reached this decision, and was about to entrust his luggage to a vague man with a lantern, when his hopes were raised by the sound of bells.

Two sleighs were just dashing up to the station, and from the foremost there sprang a young man muffled in furs.

"Weymore? No, these are not the Weymore sleighs."

The voice was that of the youth who had jumped to the platform—a voice so agreeable that, in spite of the words, it fell consolingly on Faxon's ears. At the same moment the wandering station lantern, casting a transient light on the speaker, showed his features to be in the pleasantest harmony with his voice. He was very fair and very young—hardly in the twenties, Faxon thought—but this face, though full of a morning freshness, was a trifle too thin and fine-drawn, as though a vivid spirit contended in him with a strain of physical weakness. Faxon was perhaps the quicker to notice such delicacies of balance because his own temperament hung on lightly quivering nerves, which yet, as he believed, would never quite swing him beyond a normal sensibility.

"You expected a sleigh from Weymore?" the newcomer continued, standing beside Faxon like a slender column of fur.

Mrs. Culme's secretary explained his difficulty, and the other brushed it aside with a contemptuous "Oh, *Mrs. Culme!*" that carried both speakers a long way toward reciprocal understanding.

"But then you must be—" The youth broke off with a smile of interrogation.

"The new secretary? Yes. But apparently there are no notes to be answered this evening." Faxon's laugh deepened the sense of solidarity which had so promptly established itself between the two.

His friend laughed also. "Mrs. Culme," he explained, "was lunching at my uncle's today, and she said you were due this evening. But seven hours is a long time for Mrs. Culme to remember anything."

"Well," said Faxon philosophically, "I suppose that's one of the reasons why she needs a secretary. And I've always the inn at Northridge," he concluded.

"Oh, but you haven't, though! It burned down last week."

"The deuce it did!" said Faxon; but the humor of the situation struck him before its inconvenience. His life, for years past, had been mainly a succession of resigned adaptations, and he had learned, before dealing practically with his embarrassments, to extract from most of them a small tribute of amusement.

"Oh, well, there's sure to be somebody in the place who can put me up."

"No one *you* could put up with. Besides, Northridge is three miles off, and our place—in the opposite direction—is a little nearer." Through the darkness, Faxon saw his friend sketch a gesture of self-introduction. "My name's Frank Rainer, and I'm staying with my uncle at Overdale. I've driven over to meet two friends of his, who are due in a few minutes from New York. If you don't mind waiting till they arrive I'm sure Overdale can do you better than Northridge. We're only down from town for a few days, but the house is always ready for a lot of people."

"But your uncle—?" Faxon could only object, with the odd sense, through his embarrassment, that it would be magically dispelled by his invisible friend's next words.

"Oh, my uncle—you'll see! I answer for *him!* I dare say you've heard of him—John Lavington?"

John Lavington! There was a certain irony in asking if one had heard of John Lavington! Even from a post of observation as obscure as that of Mrs. Culme's secretary the rumor of John Lavington's money, of his pictures, his politics, his charities and his hospitality, was as difficult to escape as the roar of a cataract in a mountain solitude. It might almost have been said that the one place in which one would not have expected to come upon him was in just such a solitude as now surrounded the speakers—at least in this deepest hour of its desertedness. But it was just like Lavington's brilliant ubiquity to put one in the wrong even there.

"Oh, yes, I've heard of your uncle."

"Then you *will* come, won't you? We've only five minutes to wait," young Rainer urged, in the tone that dispels scruples by ignoring them; and Faxon found himself accepting the invitation as simply as it was offered.

A delay in the arrival of the New York train lengthened their five minutes to fifteen; and as they paced the icy platform Faxon began to see why it had seemed the most natural thing in the world to accede to his new acquaintance's suggestion. It was because Frank Rainer was one of the privileged beings who simplify human intercourse by the atmosphere of confidence and good humor they diffuse. He produced this effect, Faxon noted, by the exercise of no gift but his youth, and of no art but his sincerity; and these qualities were revealed in a smile of such sweetness that Faxon felt, as never before, what Nature can achieve when she deigns to match the face with the mind.

He learned that the young man was the ward, and the only nephew, of John Lavington, with whom he had made his home since the death of his mother, the great man's sister. Mr. Lavington, Rainer said, had been "a regular brick" to him—"But then he is to everyone, you know"—and the young fellow's situation seemed in fact to be perfectly in keeping with his person. Apparently the only shade that had ever rested on him was cast by the physical weakness which Faxon had already detected. Young Rainer had been threatened with tuberculosis, and the disease was so far advanced that, according to the highest authorities, banishment to Arizona or New Mexico was inevitable. "But luckily my uncle didn't pack me off, as most people would have done, without getting another opinion. Whose? Oh, an awfully clever chap, a young doctor with a lot of new ideas, who simply laughed at my being sent away, and said I'd do perfectly well in New York if I didn't dine out too much, and if I dashed off occasionally to Northridge for a little fresh air. So it's really my uncle's doing that I'm not in exile—and I feel no end better since the new chap told me I needn't bother." Young Rainer went on to confess that he was extremely fond of dining out, dancing and similar distractions; and Faxon, listening to him, was inclined to think that the physician who had refused to cut him off altogether from these pleasures was probably a better psychologist than his seniors.

"All the same you ought to be careful, you know." The sense of elder-brotherly concern that forced the words from Faxon made him, as he spoke, slip his arm through Frank Rainer's.

The latter met the movement with a responsive pressure. "Oh, I *am:* awfully, awfully. And then my uncle has such an eye on me!"

"But if your uncle has such an eye on you, what does he say to your swallowing knives out here in this Siberian wild?"

Rainer raised his fur collar with a careless gesture. "It's not that that does it—the cold's good for me."

"And it's not the dinners and dances? What is it, then?" Faxon good-humoredly insisted; to which his companion answered with a laugh: "Well, my uncle says it's being bored; and I rather think he's right!"

His laugh ended in a spasm of coughing and a struggle for breath that made Faxon, still holding his arm, guide him hastily into the shelter of the fireless waiting room.

Young Rainer had dropped down on the bench against the wall and pulled off one of his fur gloves to grope for a handkerchief. He tossed aside his cap and drew the handkerchief across his forehead, which was intensely white, and beaded with moisture, though his face retained a healthy glow. But Faxon's gaze remained fastened to the hand he had uncovered: it was so long, so colorless, so wasted, so much older than the brow he passed it over.

"It's queer—a healthy face but dying hands," the secretary mused: he somehow wished young Rainer had kept on his glove.

The whistle of the express drew the young men to their feet, and the next moment two heavily-furred gentlemen had descended to the platform and were breasting the rigor of the night. Frank Rainer introduced them as Mr. Grisben and Mr. Balch, and Faxon, while their luggage was being lifted into the second sleigh, discerned them, by the roving lantern gleam, to be an elderly grey-headed pair, of the average prosperous business cut.

They saluted their host's nephew with friendly familiarity, and Mr. Grisben, who seemed the spokesman of the two, ended his greeting with a genial—"and many many more of them, dear boy!" which suggested to Faxon that their arrival coincided with an anniversary. But he could not press the inquiry, for the seat allotted him was at the coachman's side, while Frank Rainer joined his uncle's guests inside the sleigh.

A swift flight (behind such horses as one could be sure of John Lavington's having) brought them to tall gateposts, an illuminated lodge, and an avenue on which the snow had been leveled to the smoothness of marble. At the end of the avenue the long house loomed up, its principal bulk dark, but one wing sending out a ray of welcome; and the next moment Faxon was receiving a violent impression of warmth and light, of hothouse plants, hurrying servants, a vast spectacular oak hall like a stage setting, and, in its unreal middle distance, a small figure, correctly dressed, conventionally featured, and utterly unlike his rather florid conception of the great John Lavington.

The surprise of the contrast remained with him through his hurried dressing in the large luxurious bedroom to which he had been shown. "I don't see where he comes in," was the only way he could put it, so difficult was it to fit the exuberance of Lavington's public personality into his host's contracted frame and manner. Mr. Lavington, to whom Faxon's case had been rapidly explained by young Rainer, had welcomed him with a sort of dry and stilted cordiality that exactly matched his narrow face, his stiff hand, and the whiff of scent on his evening handkerchief. "Make yourself at home—at home!" he had repeated, in a tone that suggested, on his own part, a complete inability to perform the feat he urged on his visitor. "Any friend of Frank's . . . delighted . . . make yourself thoroughly at home!"

II

In spite of the balmy temperature and complicated conveniences of Faxon's bedroom, the injunction was not easy to obey. It was wonderful luck to have found a night's shelter under the opulent roof of Overdale, and he tasted the physical satisfaction to the full. But the place, for all its ingenuities of comfort, was oddly cold and unwelcoming. He couldn't have said why, and could only suppose that Mr. Lavington's intense personality—intensely negative, but intense all the same—must, in some occult way, have penetrated every corner of his dwelling. Perhaps, though, it was merely that Faxon himself was tired and hungry, more deeply chilled than he had known till he came in from the cold, and unutterably sick of all strange houses, and of the prospect of perpetually treading other people's stairs.

"I hope you're not famished?" Rainer's slim figure was in the doorway. "My uncle has a little business to attend to with Mr. Grisben, and we don't dine for half an hour. Shall I fetch you, or can you find your way down? Come straight to the dining room— the second door on the left of the long gallery."

He disappeared, leaving a ray of warmth behind him, and Faxon, relieved, lit a cigarette and sat down by the fire.

Looking about with less haste, he was struck by a detail that had escaped him. The room was full of flowers—a mere "bachelor's room," in the wing of a house opened only for a few days, in the dead middle of a New Hampshire winter! Flowers were everywhere, not in senseless profusion, but placed with the same conscious art that he had remarked in the grouping of the blossoming shrubs in the hall. A vase of arums stood on the writing table, a cluster of strange-hued carnations on the stand at his elbow, and from bowls of glass and porcelain clumps of freesia bulbs diffused their melting fragrance. The fact implied acres of glass— but that was the least interesting part of it. The flowers themselves, their quality, selection and arrangement, attested on someone's part—and on whose but John Lavington's?—a solicitous and sensitive passion for that particular form of beauty. Well, it simply made the man, as he had appeared to Faxon, all the harder to understand!

The half hour elapsed, and Faxon, rejoicing at the prospect of food, set out to make his way to the dining room. He had not noticed the direction he had followed in going to his room, and was puzzled, when he left it, to find that two staircases, of apparently equal importance, invited him. He chose the one to his right, and reached, at its foot, a long gallery such as Rainer had described. The gallery was empty, the doors down its length were closed; but Rainer had said: "The second to the left," and Faxon, after pausing for some chance enlightenment which did not come, laid his hand on the second knob to the left.

The room he entered was square, with dusky picture-hung walls. In its center, about a table lit by veiled lamps, he fancied Mr. Lavington and his guests to be already seated at dinner; then he perceived that the table was covered not with viands but with papers, and that he had blundered into what seemed to be his host's study. As he paused Frank Rainer looked up.

"Oh, here's Mr. Faxon. Why not ask him—?"

Mr. Lavington, from the end of the table, reflected his nephew's smile in a glance of impartial benevolence.

"Certainly. Come in, Mr. Faxon. If you won't think it a liberty—"

Mr. Grisben, who sat opposite his host, turned his head toward the door. "Of course Mr. Faxon's an American citizen?"

Frank Rainer laughed. "That's all right! . . . Oh, no, not one of your pin-pointed pens, Uncle Jack! Haven't you got a quill somewhere?"

Mr. Balch spoke slowly and as if reluctantly, in a muffled voice of which there seemed to be very little left, raised his hand to say: "One moment: you acknowledge this to be—?"

"My last will and testament?" Rainer's laugh redoubled. "Well, I won't answer for the 'last.' It's the first, anyway."

"It's a mere formula," Mr. Balch explained.

"Well, here goes." Rainer dipped his quill in the inkstand his uncle had pushed in his direction, and dashed a gallant signature across the document.

Faxon, understanding what was expected of him, and conjecturing that the young man was signing his will on the attainment of his majority, had placed himself behind Mr. Grisben, and stood awaiting his turn to affix his name to the instrument. Rainer, having signed, was about to push the paper across the table to Mr. Balch; but the latter, again raising his hand, said in his sad imprisoned voice: "The seal—?"

"Oh, does there have to be a seal?"

Faxon, looking over Mr. Grisben at John Lavington, saw a faint frown between his impassive eyes. "Really, Frank!" He seemed, Faxon thought, slightly irritated by his nephew's frivolity.

"Who's got a seal?" Frank Rainer continued, glancing about the table. "There doesn't seem to be one here."

Mr. Grisben interposed. "A wafer will do. Lavington, you have a wafer?"

Mr. Lavington had recovered his serenity. "There must be some in one of the drawers. But I'm ashamed to say I don't know where my secretary keeps these things. He ought to have seen to it that a wafer was sent with the document."

"Oh, hang it—" Frank Rainer pushed the paper aside: "It's the hand of God—and I'm as hungry as a wolf. Let's dine first, Uncle Jack."

"I think I've a seal upstairs," said Faxon.

Mr. Lavington sent him a barely perceptible smile. "So sorry to give you the trouble—"

"Oh, I say, don't send him after it now. Let's wait till after dinner!"

Mr. Lavington continued to smile on his guest, and the latter, as if under the faint coercion of the smile, turned from the room and ran upstairs. Having taken the seal from his writing case he came down again, and once more opened the door of the study. No one was speaking when he entered—they were evidently awaiting his return with the mute impatience of hunger, and he put the seal in Rainer's reach, and stood watching while Mr. Grisben struck a match and held it to one of the candles flanking the inkstand. As the wax descended on the paper Faxon remarked again the strange emaciation, the premature physical weariness, of the hand that held it: he wondered if Mr. Lavington had ever noticed his nephew's hand, and if it were not poignantly visible to him now.

With this thought in mind, Faxon raised his eyes to look at Mr. Lavington. The great man's gaze rested on Frank Rainer with an expression of untroubled benevolence; and at the same instance Faxon's attention was attracted by the presence in the room of another person, who must have joined the group while he was upstairs searching for the seal. The newcomer was a man of about Mr. Lavington's age and figure, who stood just behind his chair, and who, at the moment when Faxon first saw him, was gazing at young Rainer with an equal intensity of attention. The likeness between the two men—perhaps increased by the fact that the hooded lamps on the table left the figure behind the chair in shadow—struck Faxon the more because of the contrast in their expression. John Lavington, during his nephew's clumsy attempt to drop the wax and apply the seal, continued to fasten on him a look of half-amused affection; while the man behind the chair, so oddly reduplicating the lines of his features and figure, turned on the boy a face of pale hostility.

The impression was so startling that Faxon forgot what was going on about him. He was just dimly aware of young Rainer's exclaiming: "Your turn, Mr. Grisben!" of Mr. Grisben's protesting: "No—no; Mr. Faxon first," and of the pen's being thereupon transferred to his own hand. He received it with a deadly sense of being unable to move, or even to understand what was expected of him, till he became conscious of Mr. Grisben's paternally pointing out the precise spot on which he was to leave his autograph. The effort to fix his attention and steady his hand prolonged the process of signing, and when he stood up—a strange weight of fatigue on all his limbs—the figure behind Mr. Lavington's chair was gone.

Faxon felt an immediate sense of relief. It was puzzling that the man's exit should have been so rapid and noiseless, but the door behind Mr. Lavington was screened by a tapestry hanging, and

Faxon concluded that the unknown looker-on had merely had to raise it to pass out. At any rate he was gone, and with his withdrawal the strange weight was lifted. Young Rainer was lighting a cigarette, Mr. Balch inscribing his name at the foot of the document. Mr. Lavington—his eyes no longer on his nephew—examining a strange white-winged orchid in the vase at his elbow. Everything suddenly seemed to have grown natural and simple again, and Faxon found himself responding with a smile to the affable gesture with which his host declared: "And now, Mr. Faxon, we'll dine."

III

"I wonder how I blundered into the wrong room just now; I thought you told me to take the second door to the left," Faxon said to Frank Rainer as they followed the older men down the gallery.

"So I did; but I probably forgot to tell you which staircase to take. Coming from your bedroom, I ought to have said the fourth door to the right. It's a puzzling house, because my uncle keeps adding to it from year to year. He built this room last summer for his modern pictures."

Young Rainer, pausing to open another door, touched an electric button which sent a circle of light about the walls of a long room hung with canvases of the French Impressionist school.

Faxon advanced, attracted by a shimmering Monet, but Rainer laid a hand on his arm.

"He bought that last week. But come along—I'll show you all this after dinner. Or *he* will, rather—he loves it."

"Does he really love things?"

Rainer stared, clearly perplexed at the question. "Rather! Flowers and pictures especially! Haven't you noticed the flowers? I suppose you think his manner's cold; it seems so at first; but he's really awfully keen about things."

Faxon looked quickly at the speaker. "Has your uncle a brother?"

"Brother? No—never had. He and my mother were the only ones."

"Or any relation who—who looks like him? Who might be mistaken for him?"

"Not that I ever heard of. Does he remind you of someone?"

"Yes."

"That's queer. We'll ask him if he's got a double. Come on!"

But another picture had arrested Faxon, and some minutes elapsed before he and his young host reached the dining room. It was a large room, with the same conventionally handsome furniture and delicately grouped flowers; and Faxon's first glance showed him that only three men were seated about the dining table. The man who had stood behind Mr. Lavington's chair was not present, and no seat awaited him.

When the young man entered, Mr. Grisben was speaking, and his host, who faced the door, sat looking down at his untouched soup plate and turning the spoon about in his small dry hand.

"It's pretty late to call them rumors—they were devilish close to facts when we left town this morning," Mr. Grisben was saying, with an unexpected incisiveness of tone.

Mr. Lavington laid down his spoon and smiled interrogatively. "Oh, facts—what *are* facts? Just the way a thing happens to look at a given minute. . . ."

"You haven't heard anything from town?" Mr. Grisben persisted.

"Not a syllable. So you see. . . . Balch, a little more of that *petite marmite*. Mr. Faxon . . . between Frank and Mr. Grisben, please."

The dinner progressed through a series of complicated courses, ceremoniously dispensed by a prelatical butler attended by three tall footmen, and it was evident that Mr. Lavington took a certain satisfaction in the pageant. That, Faxon reflected, was probably the joint in his armor—that and the flowers. He had changed the subject—not abruptly but firmly—when the young men entered, but Faxon perceived that it still possessed the thoughts of the two elderly visitors, and Mr. Balch presently observed, in a voice that seemed to come from the last survivor down a mine shaft: "If it *does* come, it will be the biggest crash since '93."

Mr. Lavington looked bored but polite. "Wall Street can stand

crashes better than it could then. It's got a robuster constitution."

"Yes; but—"

"Speaking of constitutions," Mr. Grisben intervened: "Frank,
are you taking care of yourself?"

A flush rose to young Rainer's cheeks.

"Why, of course! Isn't that what I'm here for?"

"You're here about three days in the month, aren't you? And
the rest of the time it's crowded restaurants and hot ballrooms in
town. I thought you were to be shipped off to New Mexico?"

"Oh, I've got a new man who says that's rot."

"Well, you don't look as if your new man were right," said Mr.
Grisben bluntly.

Faxon saw the lad's color fade, and the rings of shadow deepen
under his gay eyes. At the same moment his uncle turned to him
with a renewed intensity of attention. There was such solicitude
in Mr. Lavington's gaze that it seemed almost to fling a shield
between his nephew and Mr. Grisben's tactless scrutiny.

"We think Frank's a good deal better," he began; "this new
doctor—"

The butler, coming up, bent to whisper a word in his ear, and
the communication caused a sudden change in Mr. Lavington's
expression. His face was naturally so colorless that it seemed not
so much to pale as to fade, to dwindle and recede into something
blurred and blotted out. He half rose, sat down again and sent a
rigid smile about the table.

"Will you excuse me? The telephone. Peters, go on with the
dinner." With small precise steps he walked out of the door
which one of the footmen had thrown open.

A momentary silence fell on the group; then Mr. Grisben once
more addressed himself to Rainer. "You ought to have gone, my
boy; you ought to have gone."

The anxious look returned to the youth's eyes. "My uncle
doesn't think so, really."

"You're not a baby, to be always governed by your uncle's
opinion. You came of age today, didn't you? Your uncle spoils you
. . . that's what's the matter. . . ."

The thrust evidently went home, for Rainer laughed and
looked down with a slight accession of color.

"But the doctor—"

"Use your common sense, Frank! You had to try twenty doctors to find one to tell you what you wanted to be told."

A look of apprehension overshadowed Rainer's gaiety. "Oh, come—I say! . . . What would *you* do?" he stammered.

"Pack up and jump on the first train." Mr. Grisben leaned forward and laid his hand kindly on the young man's arm. "Look here: my nephew Jim Grisben is out there ranching on a big scale. He'll take you in and be glad to have you. You say your new doctor thinks it won't do you any good; but he doesn't pretend to say it will do you harm, does he? Well, then—give it a trial. It'll take you out of hot theaters and night restaurants, anyhow. . . . And all the rest of it. . . . Eh, Balch?"

"Go!" said Mr. Balch hollowly. "Go *at once,*" he added, as if a closer look at the youth's face had impressed on him the need of backing up his friend.

Young Rainer had turned ashy pale. He tried to stiffen his mouth into a smile. "Do I look as bad as all that?"

Mr. Grisben was helping himself to terrapin. "You look like the day after an earthquake," he said.

The terrapin had encircled the table, and been deliberately enjoyed by Mr. Lavington's three visitors (Rainer, Faxon noticed, left his plate untouched) before the door was thrown open to readmit their host.

Mr. Lavington advanced with an air of recovered composure. He seated himself, picked up his napkin and consulted the gold-monogrammed menu. "No, don't bring back the filet. . . . Some terrapin; yes. . . ." He looked affably about the table. "Sorry to have deserted you, but the storm has played the deuce with the wires, and I had to wait a long time before I could get a good connection. It must be blowing up a blizzard."

"Uncle Jack," young Rainer broke out, "Mr. Grisben's been lecturing me."

Mr. Lavington was helping himself to terrapin. "Ah—what about?"

"He thinks I ought to have given New Mexico a show."

"I want him to go straight out to my nephew at Santa Paz and stay there till his next birthday." Mr. Lavington signed to the butler to hand the terrapin to Mr. Grisben, who, as he took a second helping, addressed himself again to Rainer. "Jim's in New York now, and going back the day after tomorrow in Olyphant's private car. I'll ask Olyphant to squeeze you in if you'll go. And when you've been out there a week or two, in the saddle all day and sleeping nine hours a night, I suspect you won't think much of the doctor who prescribed New York."

Faxon spoke up, he knew not why. "I was out there once: it's a splendid life. I saw a fellow—oh, a really *bad* case—who'd been simply made over by it."

"It *does* sound jolly," Rainer laughed, a sudden eagerness in his tone.

His uncle looked at him gently. "Perhaps Grisben's right. It's an opportunity—"

Faxon glanced up with a start: the figure dimly perceived in the study was now more visibly and tangibly planted behind Mr. Lavington's chair.

"That's right, Frank: you see your uncle approves. And the trip out there with Olyphant isn't a thing to be missed. So drop a few dozen dinners and be at the Grand Central the day after tomorrow at five."

Mr. Grisben's pleasant grey eye sought corroboration of his host, and Faxon, in a cold anguish of suspense, continued to watch him as he turned his glance on Mr. Lavington. One could not look at Lavington without seeing the presence at his back, and it was clear that, the next minute, some change in Mr. Grisben's expression must give his watcher a clue.

But Mr. Grisben's expression did not change: the gaze he fixed on his host remained unperturbed, and the clue he gave was the startling one of not seeming to see the other figure.

Faxon's first impulse was to look away, to look anywhere else, to resort again to the champagne glass the watchful butler had already brimmed; but some fatal attraction, at war in him with an overwhelming physical resistance, held his eyes upon the spot they feared.

The figure was still standing, more distinctly, and therefore more resemblingly, at Mr. Lavington's back; and while the latter continued to gaze affectionately at his nephew, his counterpart, as before, fixed young Rainer with eyes of deadly menace.

Faxon, with what felt like an actual wrench of the muscles,

dragged his own eyes from the sight to scan the other countenances about the table; but not one revealed the least consciousness of what he saw, and a sense of mortal isolation sank upon him.

"It's worth considering, certainly—" he heard Mr. Lavington continue; and as Rainer's face lit up, the face behind his uncle's chair seemed to gather into its look all the fierce weariness of old unsatisfied hates. That was the thing that, as the minutes labored by, Faxon was becoming most conscious of. The watcher behind the chair was no longer merely malevolent: he had grown suddenly, unutterably tired. His hatred seemed to well up out of the very depths of balked effort and thwarted hopes, and the fact made him more pitiable, and yet more dire.

Faxon's look reverted to Mr. Lavington, as if to surprise in him a corresponding change. At first none was visible: his pinched smile was screwed to his blank face like a gaslight to a whitewashed wall. Then the fixity of the smile became ominous: Faxon saw that its wearer was afraid to let it go. It was evident that Mr. Lavington was unutterably tired too, and the discovery sent a colder current through Faxon's veins. Looking down at his untouched plate, he caught the soliciting twinkle of the champagne glass; but the sight of the wine turned him sick.

"Well, we'll go into the details presently," he heard Mr. Lavington say, still on the question of his nephew's future. "Let's have a cigar first. No—not here, Peters." He turned his smile on Faxon. "When we've had coffee I want to show you my pictures."

"Oh, by the way, Uncle Jack—Mr. Faxon wants to know if you've got a double?"

"A double?" Mr. Lavington, still smiling, continued to address himself to his guest. "Not that I know of. Have you seen one, Mr. Faxon?"

Faxon thought: "My God, if I look up now they'll *both* be looking at me!" To avoid raising his eyes he made as though to lift the glass to his lips; but his hand sank inert, and he looked up. Mr. Lavington's glance was politely bent on him, but with a loosening of the strain about his heart he saw that the figure behind the chair still kept its gaze on Rainer.

"Do you think you've seen my double, Mr. Faxon?"

Would the other face turn if he said yes? Faxon felt a dryness in his throat. "No," he answered.

"Ah? It's possible I've a dozen. I believe I'm extremely usual-looking," Mr. Lavington went on conversationally; and still the other face watched Rainer.

"It was . . . a mistake . . . a confusion of memory. . . ." Faxon heard himself stammer. Mr. Lavington pushed back his chair, and as he did so Mr. Grisben suddenly leaned forward.

"Lavington! What have we been thinking of? We haven't drunk Frank's health!"

Mr. Lavington reseated himself. "My dear boy! . . . Peters, another bottle. . . ." He turned to his nephew. "After such a sin of omission I don't presume to propose the toast myself . . . but Frank knows. . . . Go ahead, Grisben!"

The boy shone on his uncle. "No, no. Uncle Jack! Mr. Grisben won't mind. Nobody but *you*—today!"

The butler was replenishing the glasses. He filled Mr. Lavington's last, and Mr. Lavington put out his small hand to raise it. . . . As he did so, Faxon looked away.

"Well, then—all the good I've wished you in all the past years. . . . I put it into the prayer that the coming ones may be healthy and happy and many . . . and *many*, dear boy!"

Faxon saw the hands about him reach out for their glasses. Automatically, he reached for his. His eyes were still on the table, and he repeated to himself with a trembling vehemence: "I won't look up! I won't. . . . I won't. . . ."

His fingers clasped the glass and raised it to the level of his lips. He saw the other hands making the same motion. He heard Mr. Grisben's genial "Hear! Hear!" and Mr. Balch's hollow echo. He said to himself, as the rim of the glass touched his lips: "I won't look up! I swear I won't!—" and he looked.

The glass was so full that it required an extraordinary effort to hold it there, brimming and suspended, during the awful interval before he could trust his hand to lower it again, untouched, to the table. It was this merciful preoccupation which saved him, kept him from crying out, from losing his hold, from slipping down into the bottomless blackness that gaped for him. As long as the problem of the glass engaged him he felt able to keep his seat, manage his muscles, fit unnoticeably into the group; but as the glass touched the table his last link with safety snapped. He stood up and dashed out of the room.

IV

In the gallery, the instinct of self-preservation helped him to turn back and sign to young Rainer not to follow. He stammered out something about a touch of dizziness, and joining them presently; and the boy nodded sympathetically and drew back.

At the foot of the stairs Faxon ran against a servant. "I should like to telephone to Weymore," he said with dry lips.

"Sorry, sir; wires all down. We've been trying the last hour to get New York again for Mr. Lavington."

Faxon shot on to his room, burst into it, and bolted the door. The lamplight lay on furniture, flowers, books; in the ashes a log still glimmered. He dropped down on the sofa and hid his face. The room was profoundly silent, the whole house was still: nothing about him gave a hint of what was going on, darkly and dumbly, in the room he had flown from, and with the covering of his eyes oblivion and reassurance seemed to fall on him. But they fell for a moment only; then his lids opened again to the monstrous vision. There it was, stamped on his pupils, a part of him forever, an indelible horror burnt into his body and brain. But why into his—just his? Why had he alone been chosen to see what he had seen? What business was it of *his*, in God's name? Any one of the others, thus enlightened, might have exposed the horror and defeated it; but *he*, the one weaponless and defenceless spectator, the one whom none of the others would believe or understand if he attempted to reveal what he knew—*he* alone had been singled out as the victim of this dreadful initiation!

Suddenly he sat up, listening: he had heard a step on the stairs. Someone, no doubt, was coming to see how he was—to urge him, if he felt better, to go down and join the smokers. Cautiously he opened his door; yes, it was young Rainer's step. Faxon looked down the passage, remembered the other stairway and darted to it. All he wanted was to get out of the house. Not another instant would he breathe its abominable air! What business was it of *his*, in God's name?

He reached the opposite end of the lower gallery, and beyond it saw the hall by which he had entered. It was empty, and on a long table he recognized his coat and cap. He got into his coat, unbolted the door, and plunged into the purifying night.

The darkness was deep, and the cold so intense that for an instant it stopped his breathing. Then he perceived that only a thin snow was falling, and resolutely he set his face for flight. The trees along the avenue marked his way as he hastened with long strides over the beaten snow. Gradually, while he walked, the tumult in his brain subsided. The impulse to fly still drove him forward, but he began to feel that he was flying from a terror of his own creating, and that the most urgent reason for escape was the need of hiding his state, of shunning other eyes till he should regain his balance.

He had spent the long hours in the train in fruitless broodings on a discouraging situation, and he remembered how his bitterness had turned to exasperation when he found that the Weymore sleigh was not awaiting him. It was absurd, of course; but, though he had joked with Rainer over Mrs. Culme's forgetfulness, to confess it had cost a pang. That was what his rootless life had brought him to: for lack of a personal stake in things his sensibility was at the mercy of such trifles. . . . Yes; that, and the cold and fatigue, the absence of hope and the haunting sense of starved aptitudes, all these had brought him to the perilous verge over which, once or twice before, his terrified brain had hung.

Why else, in the name of any imaginable logic, human or devilish, should he, a stranger, be singled out for this experience? What could it mean to him, how was he related to it, what bearing had it on his case? . . . Unless, indeed, it was just because he was a stranger—a stranger everywhere—because he had no personal life, no warm screen of private egotisms to shield him from exposure, that he had developed this abnormal sensitiveness to the vicissitudes of others. The thought pulled him up with a shudder. No! Such a fate was too abominable; all that was strong and sound in him rejected it. A thousand times better regard himself as ill, disorganized, deluded, than as the predestined victim of such warnings!

He reached the gates and paused before the darkened lodge. The wind had risen and was sweeping the snow into his face. The cold had him in its grasp again, and he stood uncertain. Should he put his sanity to the test and go back? He turned and looked down the dark drive to the house. A single ray shone through the trees, evoking a picture of the lights, the flowers, the faces grouped about that fatal room. He turned and plunged out into the road. . . .

He remembered that, about a mile from Overdale, the coachman had pointed out the road to Northridge; and he began to walk in that direction. Once in the road he had the gale in his face, and the wet snow on his moustache and eyelashes instantly hardened to ice. The same ice seemed to be driving a million blades into his throat and lungs, but he pushed on, the vision of the warm room pursuing him.

The snow in the road was deep and uneven. He stumbled across ruts and sank into drifts, and the wind drove against him like a granite cliff. Now and then he stopped, gasping, as if an invisible hand had tightened an iron band about his body; then he started again, stiffening himself against the stealthy penetration of the cold. The snow continued to descend out of a pall of inscrutable darkness, and once or twice he paused, fearing he had missed the road to Northridge; but, seeing no sign of a turn, he ploughed on.

At last, feeling sure that he had walked for more than a mile, he halted and looked back. The act of turning brought immediate relief, first because it put his back to the wind, and then because, far down the road, it showed him the gleam of a lantern. A sleigh was coming—a sleigh that might perhaps give him a lift to the village! Fortified by the hope, he began to walk back toward the light. It came forward very slowly, with unaccountable zigzags and waverings; and even when he was within a few yards of it he could catch no sound of sleigh bells. Then it paused and became stationary by the roadside, as though carried by a pedestrian who had stopped, exhausted by the cold. The thought made Faxon hasten on, and a moment later he was stooping over a motionless figure huddled against the snowbank. The lantern had dropped from its bearer's hand, and Faxon, fearfully raising it, threw its light into the face of Frank Rainer.

"Rainer! What on earth are you doing here?"

The boy smiled back through his pallor. "What are *you*, I'd like to know?" he retorted; and, scrambling to his feet with a clutch on Faxon's arm, he added gaily: "Well, I've run you down!"

Faxon stood confounded, his heart sinking. The lad's face was grey.

"What madness—" he began.

"Yes, it *is*. What on earth did you do it for?"

"I? Do what? . . . Why I. . . . I was just taking a walk. . . . I often walk at night. . . ."

Frank Rainer burst into a laugh. "On such nights? Then you hadn't bolted?"

"Bolted?"

"Because I'd done something to offend you? My uncle thought you had."

Faxon grasped his arm. "Did your uncle send you after me?"

"Well, he gave me an awful rowing for not going up to your room with you when you said you were ill. And when we found you'd gone we were frightened—and he was awfully upset—so I said I'd catch you. . . . You're *not* ill, are you?"

"Ill? No. Never better." Faxon picked up the lantern. "Come; let's go back. It was awfully hot in that dining room."

"Yes; I hoped it was only that."

They trudged on in silence for a few minutes; then Faxon questioned: "You're not too done up?"

"Oh, no. It's a lot easier with the wind behind us."

"All right. Don't talk any more."

They pushed ahead, walking, in spite of the light that guided them, more slowly than Faxon had walked alone into the gale. The fact of his companion's stumbling against a drift gave Faxon a pretext for saying: "Take hold of my arm," and Rainer obeying, gasped out: "I'm blown!"

"So am I. Who wouldn't be?"

"What a dance you led me! If it hadn't been for one of the servants happening to see you—"

"Yes; all right. And now, won't you kindly shut up?"

Rainer laughed and hung on him. "Oh, the cold doesn't hurt me. . . ."

For the first few minutes after Rainer had overtaken him, anxiety for the lad had been Faxon's only thought. But as each laboring step carried them nearer to the spot he had been fleeing, the reasons for his flight grew more ominous and more insistent. No, he was not ill, he was not distraught and deluded—he was the instrument singled out to warn and save; and here he was, irresistibly driven, dragging the victim back to his doom!

The intensity of the conviction had almost checked his steps. But what could he do or say? At all costs he must get Rainer out of the cold, into the house and into his bed. After that he would act.

The snowfall was thickening, and as they reached a stretch of the road between open fields the wind took them at an angle, lashing their faces with barbed thongs. Rainer stopped to take breath, and Faxon felt the heavier pressure of his arm.

"When we get to the lodge, can't we telephone to the stable for a sleigh?"

"If they're not all asleep at the lodge."

"Oh, I'll manage. Don't talk!" Faxon ordered; and they plodded on. . . .

At length the lantern ray showed ruts that curved away from the road under tree darkness.

Faxon's spirits rose. "There's the gate! We'll be there in five minutes."

As he spoke he caught, above the boundary hedge, the gleam of a light at the farther end of the dark avenue. It was the same light that had shone on the scene of which every detail was burnt into his brain; and he felt again its overpowering reality. No—he couldn't let the boy go back!

They were at the lodge at last, and Faxon was hammering on the door. He said to himself: "I'll get him inside first, and make them give him a hot drink. Then I'll see—I'll find an argument. . . ."

There was no answer to his knocking, and after an interval Rainer said: "Look here—we'd better go on."

"No!"

"I can, perfectly—"

"You shan't go to the house, I say!" Faxon redoubled his blows, and at length steps sounded on the stairs. Rainer was leaning against the lintel, and as the door opened, the light from the hall flashed on his pale face and fixed eyes. Faxon caught him by the arm and drew him in.

"It *was* cold out there," he sighed; and then, abruptly, as if invisible shears at a single stroke had cut every muscle in his body, he swerved, drooped on Faxon's arm, and seemed to sink into nothing at his feet.

The lodgekeeper and Faxon bent over him, and somehow, between them, lifted him into the kitchen and laid him on a sofa by the stove.

The lodgekeeper, stammering: "I'll ring up the house," dashed out of the room. But Faxon heard the words without heeding them: omens mattered nothing now, beside this woe fulfilled. He knelt down to undo the fur collar about Rainer's throat, and as he did so he felt a warm moisture on his hands. He held them up, and they were red. . . .

V

The palms threaded their endless line along the yellow river. The little steamer lay at the wharf, and George Faxon, sitting in the verandah of the wooden hotel, idly watched the coolies carrying the freight across the gangplank.

He had been looking at such scenes for two months. Nearly five had elapsed since he had descended from the train at Northridge and strained his eyes for the sleigh that was to take him to Weymore: Weymore, which he was never to behold! . . . Part of the interval—the first part—was still a great grey blur. Even now he could not be quite sure how he had got back to Boston, reached the house of a cousin, and been thence transferred to a quiet room looking out on snow under bare trees. He looked out a long time at the same scene, and finally one day a man he had known at Harvard came to see him and invited him to go out on a business trip to the Malay Peninsula.

"You've had a bad shake-up, and it'll do you no end of good to get away from things."

When the doctor came the next day it turned out that he knew of the plan and approved it. "You ought to be quiet for a year. Just loaf and look at the landscape," he advised.

Faxon felt the first faint stirrings of curiosity.

"What's been the matter with me, anyway?"

"Well, overwork, I suppose. You must have been bottling up

for a bad breakdown before you started for New Hampshire last
December. And the shock of that poor boy's death did the rest."

Ah, yes—Rainer had died. He remembered. . . .

He started for the East, and gradually, by imperceptible degrees, life crept back into his weary bones and leaden brain. His
friend was patient and considerate, and they traveled slowly and
talked little. At first Faxon had felt a great shrinking from whatever touched on familiar things. He seldom looked at a newspaper and he never opened a letter without a contraction of the
heart. It was not that he had any special cause for apprehension,
but merely that a great trail of darkness lay on everything. He had
looked too deep down into the abyss. . . . But little by little,
health and energy returned to him, and with them the common
promptings of curiosity. He was beginning to wonder how the
world was going, and when, presently, the hotelkeeper told him
there were no letters for him in the steamer's mailbag, he felt a
distinct sense of disappointment. His friend had gone into the
jungle on a long excursion, and he was lonely, unoccupied and
wholesomely bored. He got up and strolled into the stuffy reading room.

There he found a game of dominoes, a mutilated picture puzzle, some copies of *Zion's Herald* and a pile of New York and
London newspapers.

He began to glance through the papers, and was disappointed
to find that they were less recent than he had hoped. Evidently
the last numbers had been carried off by luckier travelers. He
continued to turn them over, picking out the American ones first.
These, as it happened, were the oldest; they dated back to December and January. To Faxon, however, they had all the flavor of
novelty, since they covered the precise period during which he
had virtually ceased to exist. It had never before occurred to him
to wonder what had happened in the world during the interval of
obliteration; but now he felt a sudden desire to know.

To prolong the pleasure, he began by sorting the papers chronologically, and as he found and spread out the earliest number,
the date at the top of the page entered into his consciousness like
a key slipping into a lock. It was the seventeenth of December: the
date of the day after his arrival at Northridge. He glanced at the
first page and read in blazing characters: "Reported Failure of

Opal Cement Company. Lavington's Name Involved. Gigantic Exposure of Corruption Shakes Wall Street to Its Foundations."

He read on; when he had finished the first paper he turned to the next. There was a gap of three days, but the Opal Cement "Investigation" still held the center of the stage. From its complex revelations of greed and ruin his eye wandered to the death notices, and he read: "Rainer. Suddenly, at Northridge, New Hampshire, Francis John, only son of the late . . ."

His eyes clouded, and he dropped the newspaper and sat for a long time with his face in his hands. When he looked up again he noticed that his gesture had pushed the other papers from the table and scattered them at his feet. The uppermost lay spread out before him, and heavily his eyes began their search again. "John Lavington comes forward with plan for reconstructing company. Offers to put in ten millions of his own—The proposal under consideration by the District Attorney."

Ten millions . . . ten millions of his own. But if John Lavington was ruined? . . . Faxon stood up with a cry. That was it, then—that was what the warning meant! And if he had not fled from it, dashed wildly away from it into the night, he might have broken the spell of iniquity, the powers of darkness might not have prevailed! He caught up the pile of newspapers and began to glance through each in turn for the headline: "Wills Admitted to Probate." In the last of all he found the paragraph he sought, and it stared up at him as if with Rainer's dying eyes.

That—*that* was what he had done! The powers of pity had singled him out to warn and save, and he had closed his ears to their call, and washed his hands of it, and fled. Washed his hands of it! That was the word. It caught him back to the dreadful moment in the lodge when, raising himself up from Rainer's side, he had looked at his hands and seen that they were red. . . .

NATHANIEL HAWTHORNE

The White Old Maid

NATHANIEL HAWTHORNE (1804–1864) was born in Salem, Massachusetts, where his own magistrate ancestor, John Hathorne, persecuted witches, so it is understandable that a brooding obsession with sin, suffering and expiation invests Hawthorne's fiction, which includes the masterful novels The Scarlet Letter and The House of the Seven Gables. The latter was described by H. P. Lovecraft as "New England's greatest contribution to weird literature." The following symbolic ghost story, first printed in 1835 in New-England Magazine and included in the expanded 1842 edition of the author's Twice-Told Tales, is set in an unnamed New England town.

The moonbeams came through two deep and narrow windows, and showed a spacious chamber richly furnished in an antique fashion. From one lattice the shadow of the diamond panes was thrown upon the floor; the ghostly light, through the other, slept upon a bed, falling between the heavy silken curtains, and illuminating the face of a young man. But, how quietly the slumberer lay! How pale his features! And how like a shroud the sheet was wound about his frame! Yes; it was a corpse, in its burial clothes.

Suddenly, the fixed features seemed to move with dark emotion. Strange fantasy! It was but the shadow of the fringed curtain waving betwixt the dead face and the moonlight, as the door of the chamber opened and a girl stole softly to the bedside. Was there delusion in the moonbeams, or did her gesture and her eye betray a gleam of triumph, as she bent over the pale corpse—pale as itself—and pressed her living lips to the cold ones of the dead? As she drew back from that long kiss, her features writhed as if a proud heart were fighting with its anguish. Again it seemed that the features of the corpse had moved responsive to her own. Still an illusion! The silk curtain had waved, a second time, betwixt the dead face and the moonlight, as another fair young girl unclosed the door, and glided, ghost-like, to the bedside. There the two maidens stood, both beautiful, with the pale beauty of the dead between them. But she who had first entered was proud and stately, and the other a soft and fragile thing.

"Away!" cried the lofty one. "Thou hadst him living! The dead is mine!"

"Thine!" returned the other, shuddering. "Well hast thou spoken! The dead is thine!"

The proud girl started, and stared into her face with a ghastly look. But a wild and mournful expression passed across the features of the gentle one; and weak and helpless, she sank down on the bed, her head pillowed beside that of the corpse, and her hair mingling with his dark locks. A creature of hope and joy, the first draft of sorrow had bewildered her.

"Edith!" cried her rival.

Edith groaned, as with a sudden compression of the heart; and removing her cheek from the dead youth's pillow, she stood upright, fearfully encountering the eyes of the lofty girl.

"Wilt thou betray me?" said the latter, calmly.

"Till the dead bid me speak, I will be silent," answered Edith. "Leave us alone together! Go, and live many years, and then return, and tell me of thy life. He, too, will be here! Then, if thou tellest of sufferings more than death, we will both forgive thee."

"And what shall be the token?" asked the proud girl, as if her heart acknowledged a meaning in these wild words.

"This lock of hair," said Edith, lifting one of the dark, clustering curls that lay heavily on the dead man's brow.

The two maidens joined their hands over the bosom of the corpse, and appointed a day and hour, far, far in time to come, for their next meeting in that chamber. The statelier girl gave one deep look at the motionless countenance, and departed—yet turned again and trembled ere she closed the door, almost believing that her dead lover frowned upon her. And Edith, too! Was not her white form fading into the moonlight? Scorning her own weakness she went forth, and perceived that a Negro slave was waiting in the passage with a wax-light, which he held between her face and his own, and regarded her, as she thought, with an ugly expression of merriment. Lifting his torch on high, the slave lighted her down the staircase, and undid the portal of the mansion. The young clergyman of the town had just ascended the steps, and bowing to the lady, passed in without a word.

Years, many years, rolled on; the world seemed new again, so much older was it grown since the night when those pale girls had clasped their hands across the bosom of the corpse. In the interval, a lonely woman had passed from youth to extreme age, and was known by all the town as the "Old Maid in the Winding Sheet." A taint of insanity had affected her whole life, but so quiet, sad, and gentle, so utterly free from violence, that she was suffered to pursue her harmless fantasies, unmolested by the world, with whose business or pleasures she had nought to do. She dwelt alone, and never came into the daylight, except to follow funerals. Whenever a corpse was borne along the street in sunshine, rain, or snow; whether a pompous train of the rich and proud thronged after it, or few and humble were the mourners, behind them came the lonely woman in a long white garment which the people called her shroud. She took no place among the kindred or the friends, but stood at the door to hear the funeral prayer, and walked in the rear of the procession, as one whose earthly charge it was to haunt the house of mourning, and be the shadow of affliction, and see that the dead were duly buried. So long had this been her custom that the inhabitants of the town deemed her a part of every funeral, as much as the coffin pall, or the very corpse itself, and augured ill of the sinner's destiny unless the "Old Maid in the Winding Sheet" came gliding, like a ghost, behind. Once, it is said, she affrighted a bridal party with her pale presence, appearing suddenly in the illuminated hall, just as the priest was uniting a false maid to a wealthy man, before her lover had been dead a year. Evil was the omen to that marriage! Sometimes she stole forth by moonlight and visited the graves of venerable Integrity, and wedded Love, and virgin Innocence, and every spot where the ashes of a kind and faithful heart were moldering. Over the hillocks of those favored dead would she stretch out her arms, with a gesture, as if she were scattering seeds; and many believed that she brought them from the garden of Paradise; for the graves which she had visited were green beneath the snow, and covered with sweet flowers from April to November. Her blessing was better than a holy verse upon the tombstone. Thus wore away her long, sad, peaceful, and fantastic life, till few were so old as she, and the people of later generations wondered how the dead had ever been buried, or mourners had endured their grief, without the "Old Maid in the Winding Sheet."

Still years went on, and still she followed funerals, and was not yet summoned to her own festival of death. One afternoon the great street of the town was all alive with business and bustle, though the sun now gilded only the upper half of the church spire, having left the housetops and loftiest trees in shadow. The scene was cheerful and animated, in spite of the somber shade between the high brick buildings. Here were pompous merchants, in white wigs and laced velvet; the bronzed faces of sea captains; the foreign garb and air of Spanish creoles; and the disdainful port of natives of Old England; all contrasted with the rough aspect of one or two back settlers, negotiating sales of timber from forests where axe had never sounded. Sometimes a lady passed, swelling roundly forth in an embroidered petticoat, balancing her steps in high-heeled shoes, and courtesying with lofty grace to the punctilious obeisances of the gentlemen. The life of the town seemed to have its very center not far from an old mansion that stood somewhat back from the pavement, surrounded by neglected grass, with a strange air of loneliness, rather deepened than dispelled by the throng so near it. Its site would have been suitably occupied by a magnificent Exchange or a brick block, lettered all over with various signs; or the large house itself might have been a noble tavern, with the "King's Arms" swinging before it, and guests in every chamber, instead of the present solitude. But owing to some dispute about the right of inheritance, the mansion had been long without a tenant, decaying from year to year, and throwing the stately gloom of its shadow over the busiest part of the town. Such was the scene, and such the time, when a figure unlike any that have been described was observed at a distance down the street.

"I espy a strange sail, yonder," remarked a Liverpool captain. "That woman in the long white garment!"

The sailor seemed much struck by the object, as were several others who, at the same moment, caught a glimpse of the figure that had attracted his notice. Almost immediately the various topics of conversation gave place to speculations, in an under-tone, on this unwonted occurrence.

"Can there be a funeral so late this afternoon?" inquired some.

They looked for the signs of death at every door—the sexton, the hearse, the assemblage of black-clad relatives—all that makes up the woeful pomp of funerals. They raised their eyes, also, to the sun-gilt spire of the church, and wondered that no clang proceeded from its bell, which had always tolled till now when this figure appeared in the light of day. But none had heard that a corpse was to be borne to its home that afternoon, nor was there any token of a funeral, except the apparition of the "Old Maid in the Winding Sheet."

"What may this portend?" asked each man of his neighbor.

All smiled as they put the question, yet with a certain trouble in their eyes, as if pestilence or some other wide calamity were prognosticated by the untimely intrusion among the living of one whose presence had always been associated with death and woe. What a comet is to the earth was that sad woman to the town. Still she moved on, while the hum of surprise was hushed at her approach, and the proud and the humble stood aside, that her white garment might not wave against them. It was a long, loose robe, of spotless purity. Its wearer appeared very old, pale, ema-ciated, and feeble, yet glided onward without the unsteady pace of extreme age. At one point of her course a little rosy boy burst forth from a door, and ran, with open arms, toward the ghostly woman, seeming to expect a kiss from her bloodless lips. She made a slight pause, fixing her eye upon him with an expression of no earthly sweetness, so that the child shivered and stood awestruck, rather than affrighted, while the Old Maid passed on. Perhaps her garment might have been polluted even by an infant's touch; perhaps her kiss would have been death to the sweet boy within a year.

"She is but a shadow," whispered the superstitious. "The child put forth his arms and could not grasp her robe!"

The wonder was increased when the Old Maid passed beneath the porch of the deserted mansion, ascended the moss-covered steps, lifted the iron knocker, and gave three raps. The people could only conjecture that some old remembrance, troubling her bewildered brain, had impelled the poor woman hither to visit the friends of her youth; all gone from their home long since and forever, unless their guests still haunted it—fit company for the "Old Maid in the Winding Sheet." An elderly man approached the steps, and, reverently uncovering his gray locks, essayed to explain the matter.

"None, madam," said he, "have dwelt in this house these fifteen years agone—no, not since the death of old Colonel Fenwicke, whose funeral you may remember to have followed. His heirs, being ill agreed among themselves, have let the mansion-house go to ruin."

The Old Maid looked slowly round with a slight gesture of one hand, and a finger of the other upon her lip, appearing more shadow-like than ever in the obscurity of the porch. But again she lifted the hammer, and gave, this time, a single rap. Could it be that a footstep was now heard coming down the staircase of the old mansion, which all conceived to have been so long untenanted? Slowly, feebly, yet heavily, like the pace of an aged and infirm person, the step approached, more distinct on every downward stair, till it reached the portal. The bar fell on the inside; the door was opened. One upward glance toward the church spire, whence the sunshine had just faded, was the last that the people saw of the "Old Maid in the Winding Sheet."

"Who undid the door?" asked many.

This question, owing to the depth of shadow beneath the porch, no one could satisfactorily answer. Two or three aged men, while protesting against an inference which might be drawn, affirmed that the person within was a Negro, and bore a singular resemblance to old Caesar, formerly a slave in the house, but freed by death some thirty years before.

"Her summons has waked up a servant of the old family," said one, half seriously.

"Let us wait here," replied another. "More guests will knock at the door, anon. But the gate of the graveyard should be thrown open!"

Twilight had overspread the town before the crowd began to separate, or the comments on this incident were exhausted. One after another was wending his way homeward, when a coach—no common spectacle in those days—drove slowly into the street. It was an old-fashioned equipage, hanging close to the ground, with arms on the panels, a footman behind, and a grave, corpulent coachman seated high in front—the whole giving an idea of solemn state and dignity. There was something awful in the heavy rumbling of the wheels. The coach rolled down the street, till, coming to the gateway of the deserted mansion, it drew up, and the footman sprang to the ground.

"Whose grand coach is this?" asked a very inquisitive body.

The footman made no reply, but ascended the steps of the old house, gave three raps with the iron hammer, and returned to open the coach door. An old man, possessed of the heraldic lore so common in that day, examined the shield of arms on the panel.

"Azure, a lion's head erased, between three flower-de-luces," said he; then whispered the name of the family to whom these bearings belonged. The last inheritor of his honors was recently dead, after a long residence amid the splendor of the British court, where his birth and wealth had given him no mean station. "He left no child," continued the herald, "and these arms, being in a lozenge, betoken that the coach appertains to his widow."

Further disclosures, perhaps, might have been made, had not the speaker suddenly been struck dumb by the stern eye of an ancient lady who thrust forth her head from the coach, preparing to descend. As she emerged, the people saw that her dress was magnificent, and her figure dignified, in spite of age and infirmity —a stately ruin but with a look, at once, of pride and wretchedness. Her strong and rigid features had an awe about them, unlike that of the White Old Maid, but as of something evil. She passed up the steps, leaning on a gold-headed cane; the door swung open as she ascended—and the light of a torch glittered on the embroidery of her dress, and gleamed on the pillars of the porch.

After a momentary pause—a glance backward—and then a desperate effort—she went in. The decipherer of the coat-of-arms had ventured up the lowest step, and shrinking back immediately, pale and tremulous, affirmed that the torch was held by the very image of old Caesar.

"But such a hideous grin," added he, "was never seen on the face of mortal man, black or white! It will haunt me till my dying day."

Meantime, the coach had wheeled round, with a prodigious clatter on the pavement, and rumbled up the street, disappearing in the twilight, while the ear still tracked its course. Scarcely was it gone, when the people began to question whether the coach and attendants, the ancient lady, the specter of old Caesar, and the Old Maid herself, were not all a strangely combined delusion, with some dark purport in its mystery. The whole town was astir, so that, instead of dispersing, the crowd continually increased, and stood gazing up at the windows of the mansion, now silvered by the brightening moon. The elders, glad to indulge the narrative propensity of age, told of the long-faded splendor of the family, the entertainments they had given, and the guests, the greatest of the land, and even titled and noble ones from abroad, who had passed beneath that portal. These graphic reminiscences seemed to call up the ghosts of those to whom they referred. So strong was the impression on some of the more imaginative hearers, that two or three were seized with trembling fits, at one and the same moment, protesting that they had distinctly heard three other raps of the iron knocker.

"Impossible!" exclaimed others. "See! The moon shines beneath the porch, and shows every part of it, except in the narrow shade of that pillar. There is no one there!"

"Did not the door open?" whispered one of these fanciful persons.

"Didst thou see it, too?" said his companion, in a startled tone.

But the general sentiment was opposed to the idea that a third visitant had made application at the door of the deserted house. A few, however, adhered to this new marvel, and even declared that a red gleam like that of a torch had shone through the great front window, as if the Negro were lighting a guest up the staircase. This, too, was pronounced a mere fantasy. But at once the whole multitude started, and each man beheld his own terror painted in the faces of all the rest.

"What an awful thing is this!" cried they.

A shriek too fearfully distinct for doubt had been heard within the mansion, breaking forth suddenly, and succeeded by a deep stillness, as if a heart had burst in giving it utterance. The people knew not whether to fly from the very sight of the house, or to rush trembling in, and search out the strange mystery. Amid their confusion and affright, they were somewhat reassured by the appearance of their clergyman, a venerable patriarch, and equally a saint, who had taught them and their fathers the way to Heaven for more than the space of an ordinary lifetime. He was a reverend figure, with long, white hair upon his shoulders, a white beard upon his breast, and a back so bent over his staff that he seemed to be looking downward continually, as if to choose a proper grave for his weary frame. It was some time before the good old man, being deaf and of impaired intellect, could be made to comprehend such portions of the affair as were comprehensible at all. But, when possessed of the facts, his energies assumed unexpected vigor.

"Verily," said the old gentleman, "it will be fitting that I enter the mansion-house of the worthy Colonel Fenwicke, lest any harm should have befallen that true Christian woman whom ye call the 'Old Maid in the Winding Sheet.'"

Behold, then, the venerable clergyman ascending the steps of the mansion, with a torch-bearer behind him. It was the elderly man who had spoken to the Old Maid, and the same who had afterward explained the shield of arms and recognized the features of the Negro. Like their predecessors, they gave three raps with the iron hammer.

"Old Caesar cometh not," observed the priest. "Well I wot he no longer doth service in this mansion."

"Assuredly, then, it was something worse, in old Caesar's likeness!" said the other adventurer.

"Be it as God wills," answered the clergyman. "See! my strength, though it be much decayed, hath sufficed to open this heavy door. Let us enter and pass up the staircase."

Here occurred a singular exemplification of the dreamy state of a very old man's mind. As they ascended the wide flight of stairs, the aged clergyman appeared to move with caution, occasionally standing aside, and oftener bending his head, as it were in salutation, thus practicing all the gestures of one who makes his way through a throng. Reaching the head of the staircase, he looked around with sad and solemn benignity, laid aside his staff, bared his hoary locks, and was evidently on the point of commencing a prayer.

"Reverend sir," said his attendant, who conceived this a very suitable prelude to their further search, "would it not be well that the people join with us in prayer?"

"Welladay!" cried the old clergyman, staring strangely around him. "Art thou here with me, and none other? Verily, past times were present to me, and I deemed that I was to make a funeral prayer, as many a time heretofore, from the head of this staircase. Of a truth, I saw the shades of many that are gone. Yea, I have prayed at their burials, one after another, and the 'Old Maid in the Winding Sheet' hath seen them to their graves!"

Being now more thoroughly awake to their present purpose, he took his staff and struck forcibly on the floor, till there came an echo from each deserted chamber, but no menial to answer their summons. They therefore walked along the passage, and again paused, opposite to the great front window through which was seen the crowd, in the shadow and partial moonlight of the street beneath. On their right hand was the open door of a chamber, and a closed one on their left. The clergyman pointed his cane to the carved oak panel of the latter.

"Within that chamber," observed he, "a whole lifetime since, did I sit by the death-bed of a goodly young man, who, being now at the last gasp—"

Apparently there was some powerful excitement in the ideas which had now flashed across his mind. He snatched the torch from his companion's hand, and threw open the door with such sudden violence that the flame was extinguished, leaving them no other light than the moonbeams, which fell through two windows into the spacious chamber. It was sufficient to discover all that could be known. In a high-backed oaken armchair, upright, with her hands clasped across her breast, and her head thrown back, sat the "Old Maid in the Winding Sheet." The stately dame had fallen on her knees, with her forehead on the holy knees of the

Old Maid, one hand upon the floor and the other pressed convulsively against her heart. It clutched a lock of hair, once sable, now discolored with a greenish mold. As the priest and layman advanced into the chamber, the Old Maid's features assumed such a semblance of shifting expression that they trusted to hear the whole mystery explained by a single word. But it was only the shadow of a tattered curtain waving betwixt the dead face and the moonlight.

"Both dead!" said the venerable man. "Then who shall divulge the secret? Methinks it glimmers to and fro in my mind, like the light and shadow across the Old Maid's face. And now 't is gone!"

OGDEN NASH

Victoria

OGDEN NASH *(1902–1971) is best known for his rhythmically outrageous light verse, but the following cautionary fable is a rare Nashian foray into ironic prose. "Victoria" (also known as "The Three D's") takes place in a Massachusetts girls' school a little too close to Salem, where all those witches were hanged.*

Victoria was an attractive new girl at the Misses Mallisons' Female Seminary—such an attractive new girl, indeed, that it is a pity she never grew to be an old girl. Perhaps she would have, if the Misses Mallison had established their seminary a little closer to Newburyport—or at least a little farther from Salem.

Victoria was good enough at games and not too good at lessons; her mouth was wide enough to console the homely girls and her eyes bright enough to include her among the pretty ones; she could weep over the death of a horse in a story and remain composed at the death of an aunt in the hospital; she would rather eat between meals than at them; she wrote to her parents once a week if in need of anything; and she truly meant to do the right thing, only so often the wrong thing was easier.

In short, Victoria was an ideal candidate for The Three D's, that night-blooming sorority which had, like the cereus, flourished after dark for many years, unscented by the precise noses of the Misses Mallison.

So felt The Three D's, so felt Victoria, and the only obstacle to her admission lay in the very title of the club itself, which members knew signified that none could gain entrance without the accomplishment of a feat Daring, Deadly, and Done-never-before. Victoria was competent at daring feats, unsurpassable at deadly feats, but where was she to discover a feat done-never-before?

Of the present membership, Amanda had leaped into a cold bath with her clothes on, Miranda had climbed the roof in her nightgown to drop a garter snake down the Misses Mallisons' chimney, Amelia had eaten cold spaghetti blindfolded thinking it was worms, and Cordelia had eaten worms blindfolded thinking they were cold spaghetti. What was left for Victoria?

It was Amanda who, at a meeting of the Steering Committee, wiped the fudge from her fingers on the inside of her dressing gown and spoke the name of Eliza Catspaugh.

"Who was she?" asked Miranda, pouring honey on a slice of coconut cake.

"A witch," said Amanda.

"She was burned," said Amelia.

"Hanged," said Cordelia.

"And she couldn't get into the churchyard, so they buried her in the meadow behind the old slaughterhouse," said Amanda.

"The gravestone is still there," said Amelia. "Oh, bother, the cake's all gone! Never mind, I'll eat caramels."

"There's writing on it, too," said Cordelia, who was not hungry, "but you can't read it in the daytime, only by moonlight."

"I'd forgotten how good currant jelly is on marshmallows," said Amanda. "The Three D's must tell Victoria about Eliza Catspaugh."

Late next evening Victoria took her pen in hand. *Dear Father and Mother*, she wrote, *I hope you are well. I am doing well in algebra but Miss Hattie is unfair about my French ireguler verbs. I am doing well in grammar but Miss Mettie has choosen me to pick on. Dear Father, everybody elses Father sends them one dollar every week. I have lots of things to write but the bell is wringing for supper. Lots of love, your loveing daughter, Victoria.*

Victoria knew that in ten minutes Miss Hattie Mallison would open the door slightly, peer at the bed, murmur, "Good night, Victoria, sweet dreams," and disappear. It took Victoria seven minutes to construct a dummy out of a mop, a nightgown, and several pillows and blankets. As she lowered herself to the ground she heard the door open, heard Miss Hattie's murmur, heard the door close.

The soaring moon ran through Victoria as she marched, as she skipped, as she pranced toward the old slaughterhouse. She had for company her high moon-spirits and her long shadow—the shadow which was a Victoria that no Miss Mallison could ever cage. "No girl has ever had a taller, livelier companion than my shadow," thought Victoria, and she breathed deeply and spread her arms, and her shadow breathed with her and spread crooked arms up the walls and across the roof of the slaughterhouse.

The moon grew brighter with each burr that Victoria struggled against on her way across the meadow that had been abandoned to burrs, the meadow where no beasts fed, the meadow where Victoria's shadow strengthened at each proud and adventurous step.

Where the burrs grew thickest, where her loyalty to The Three D's wore the thinnest, she came upon the gravestone. How hard the moon shone as Victoria leaned against the crooked slab, perhaps to catch her breath, perhaps to stand on one foot and pluck the burrs off. When the stone quivered and rocked behind her, and the ground trembled beneath her feet, she bravely remembered her purpose: that at midnight, in the moonlight, she was to prove herself a worthy companion of Amanda and Miranda, Amelia and Cordelia. Unwillingly she turned, and willfully she read the lines which the rays of the moon lifted from the stone so obscured by rain and moss.

Here Waits
ELIZA CATSPAUGH
Who touches this stone
on moonlight meadow
shall live no longer
than his shadow.

The job of memorizing was done, the initiation into The Three D's handsomely undergone. "Gracious, is that all there is to it?" thought Victoria, and set out for the seminary.

It was natural that she should hurry, so perhaps it was natural that she did not miss the exuberant shadow which should have escorted her home. The moon was bright behind Victoria—who can tell how she forgot there should have been a shadow to lead the way?

But there was no shadow—her shadow had dwindled as she ran, as though Victoria grew shorter, or perhaps the moon grew more remote. And if she did not miss her shadow, neither did she hear or see whatever it may have been that rustled and scuttled past her and ahead of her.

"I hope my dear little dummy is still there," thought Victoria as she climbed through the window. "I hope Miss Hattie hasn't been unfair and shaken me."

She tiptoed across the room in the dark to the bed and bent to remove the dummy. But as she reached down, the dummy, which was no longer a dummy, reached up its dusty fingers first. . . .

H. P. LOVECRAFT

The Terrible Old Man

H. P. LOVECRAFT *(1890–1937), a native of Providence, Rhode Island, was America's most important contributor to* Weird Tales *magazine. August Derleth and Donald Wandrei founded Arkham House Publishers in order to collect Lovecraft's fiction in permanent volume form, including such popular stories as "The Rats in the Walls," "The Music of Erich Zann," "The Dunwich Horror" and "The Outsider." The following rare Lovecraftian excursion into black humor is set in the fictional New England town of Kingsport, a place that reappears along with "the terrible old man" in a later HPL tale, "The Strange High House in the Mist."*

It was the design of Angelo Ricci and Joe Czanek and Manuel Silva to call on the Terrible Old Man. This old man dwells all alone in a very ancient house in Water Street near the sea, and is reputed to be both exceedingly rich and exceedingly feeble; which forms a situation very attractive to men of the profession of Messrs. Ricci, Czanek and Silva, for that profession was nothing less dignified than robbery.

The inhabitants of Kingsport say and think many things about the Terrible Old Man which generally keep him safe from the attentions of gentlemen like Mr. Ricci and his colleagues, despite the almost certain fact that he hides a fortune of indefinite magnitude somewhere about his musty and venerable abode. He is, in truth, a very strange person, believed to have been a captain of East India clipper ships in his day; so old that no one can remember when he was young, and so taciturn that few know his real name. Among the gnarled trees in the front yard of his aged and neglected place he maintains a strange collection of large stones, oddly grouped and painted so that they resemble the idols in some obscure Eastern temple. This collection frightens away most of the small boys who love to taunt the Terrible Old Man about his long white hair and beard, or to break the small-paned windows of his dwelling with wicked missiles; but there are other things which frighten the older and more curious folk who sometimes steal up to the house to peer in through the dusty panes. These folk say that on a table in a bare room on the ground floor are many peculiar bottles, in each a small piece of lead suspended pendulum-wise from a string. And they say that the Terrible Old Man talks to these bottles, addressing them by such names as Jack, Scar-Face, Long Tom, Spanish Joe, Peters and Mate Ellis, and that whenever he speaks to a bottle the little lead pendulum within makes certain definite vibrations as if in answer. Those who have watched the tall, lean, Terrible Old Man in these peculiar conversations do not watch him again. But Angelo Ricci and Joe Czanek and Manuel Silva were not of Kingsport blood; they were of that new and heterogeneous alien stock which lies outside the charmed circle of New England life and traditions, and they saw in the Terrible Old Man merely a tottering, almost helpless grey-beard, who could not walk without the aid of his knotted cane and whose thin, weak hands shook pitifully. They were really quite sorry in their way for the lonely, unpopular old fellow, whom everybody shunned, and at whom all the dogs barked singularly. But business is business, and to a robber whose soul is in his profession, there is a lure and a challenge about a very old and very feeble man who has no account at the bank, and who pays for his few necessities at the village store with Spanish gold and silver minted two centuries ago.

Messrs. Ricci, Czaneck and Silva selected the night of April eleventh for their call. Mr. Ricci and Mr. Silva were to interview the poor old gentleman, whilst Mr. Czanek waited for them and their presumably metallic burden with a covered motor car in Ship Street, by the gate in the tall rear wall of their host's grounds. Desire to avoid needless explanations in case of unexpected police intrusions prompted these plans for a quiet and unostentatious departure.

As prearranged, the three adventurers started out separately in order to prevent any evil-minded suspicions afterward. Messrs. Ricci and Silva met in Water Street by the old man's front gate, and although they did not like the way the moon shone down upon the painted stones through the budding branches of the gnarled trees, they had more important things to think about than mere idle superstition. They feared it might be unpleasant work making the Terrible Old Man loquacious concerning his hoarded gold and silver, for aged sea-captains are notably stubborn and perverse. Still, he was very old and very feeble, and there were two visitors. Messrs. Ricci and Silva were experienced in the art of making unwilling persons voluble, and the screams of a weak and exceptionally venerable man can be easily muffled. So they moved up to the one lighted window and heard the Terrible Old Man talking childishly to his bottles with pendulums. Then they donned masks and knocked politely at the weather-stained oaken door.

Waiting seemed very long to Mr. Czanek as he fidgeted restlessly in the covered motor car by the Terrible Old Man's back gate in Ship Street. He was more than ordinarily tender-hearted, and he did not like the hideous screams he had heard in the ancient house just after the hour appointed for the deed. Had he not told his colleagues to be as gentle as possible with the pathetic old sea-captain? Very nervously he watched that narrow oaken gate in the high and ivy-clad stone wall. Frequently he consulted his watch, and wondered at the delay. Had the old man died before revealing where his treasure was hidden, and had a thorough search become necessary? Mr. Czanek did not like to wait so long in the dark in such a place. Then he sensed a soft tread or tapping on the walk inside the gate, heard a gentle fumbling at the rusty latch, and saw the narrow, heavy door swing inward. And in the pallid glow of the single dim street lamp he strained his eyes to see what his colleagues had brought out of that sinister house which loomed so close behind. But when he looked, he did not see what he had expected; for his colleagues were not there at all, but only the Terrible Old Man leaning quietly on his knotted cane and smiling hideously. Mr. Czanek had never before noticed the color of that man's eyes; now he saw that they were yellow.

Little things make considerable excitement in little towns, which is the reason that Kingsport people talked all that spring and summer about the three unidentifiable bodies, horribly slashed as with many cutlasses, and horribly mangled as by the tread of many cruel boot-heels, which the tide washed in. And some people even spoke of things as trivial as the deserted motor car found in Ship Street, or certain especially inhuman cries, probably of a stray animal or migratory bird, heard in the night by wakeful citizens. But in this idle village gossip the Terrible Old Man took no interest at all. He was by nature reserved, and when one is aged and feeble one's reserve is doubly strong. Besides, so ancient a sea-captain must have witnessed scores of things much more stirring in the far-off days of his unremembered youth.

EDWARD D. HOCH

The Problem
of the Pilgrims
Windmill

*The prolific past president of the Mystery Writers of America, EDWARD D.
HOCH often flirts with the supernatural in his Simon Ark murder mysteries,
which the following tale resembles. In it, Dr. Sam Hawthorne, retired
country physician, tells of "one of the strangest crimes I ever encountered" at
the fictional Pilgrim Memorial Hospital in Northmont, which could be
Northford, Connecticut; Northbridge, Massachusetts; Northvale, New
Hampshire; or one of the New England Northfields in Massachusetts, New
Hampshire or Vermont—take your pick. "The Problem of the Pilgrims
Windmill" is concerned with one of the wickedest ghosts still haunting
America—racial prejudice.*

Dr. Sam Hawthorne filled the glasses and settled back in his chair.
"This time I promised to tell you about what happened when we
opened the new Pilgrim Memorial Hospital in Northmont, back
in March of 1929. I'd been practicing medicine in the town for
seven years by that time, and the idea of a hospital all our own was
something to fill me with wonder and delight. Dr. Bob Yale,
who'd come to Northmont the year before the hospital opened,
landed a job on their staff. I was offered one myself, but I told
them I wanted to keep on bein' a plain old G.P. As it turned out,
though, I was summoned to the hospital before it had been open
a week, to investigate one of the strangest crimes I ever encoun-

tered. It was like something Mister Chesterton might have written about, and if he had I suppose he would have called it *The Devil in the Windmill.* . . ."

On March fourth (Dr. Sam continued) Herbert Hoover was inaugurated as the 31st President of the United States. On the following day Pilgrim Memorial Hospital opened its doors for the first time. It was located just outside of town on land that had belonged to the Collins family for generations. When they donated the land for a hospital there was only one stipulation—the old Dutch windmill on the property should remain standing.

People are always startled to see windmills in New England, but there are still a few around. You pass one on Cape Cod, on the road to Provincetown, and I think the one at Northmont is still standing, too. When people passing through town asked about Northmont's windmill they were usually reminded that the Pilgrims had come to America by way of The Netherlands, and the *Mayflower*'s companion ship, the *Speedwell,* actually sailed from The Netherlands before being forced to turn back. I suppose that had something to do with the Collins family windmill being called the Pilgrims windmill, though to tell the truth it wasn't built till the middle of the 19th Century and had mighty little to do with Pilgrims.

Anyway, it looked right nice standing there in front of Pilgrim Memorial Hospital. Its four wooden vanes still turned slowly when the wind blew, even though the mill was no longer in use. Inside was a good-sized room where an exhibit of Northmont history had been prepared. The building itself was made of fieldstone, which helped to give it an aged look that might have dated back to Pilgrim times. Some of the windmill's gears and wheels were still in place overhead, and I glanced up at them as I toured the place with my nurse April and half a hundred other honored guests.

"Was this place ever used as a mill?" I asked her.

"I guess so, long before I was born." She grinned at me. "Folks say Randy Collins's pa hid a fortune in gold somewhere in the windmill, but no one was ever able to find it."

"If you believe that story I'll tell you the one about the little green men. Randy Collins isn't the sort who'd give anything away that belonged to him. When he donated the land and this wind-mill, he was darn sure there was no gold or anything else around."

"I suppose you're right," she agreed. We passed through the historical exhibit and left the windmill, starting up the curving driveway to the hospital itself. It was a low two-story brick build-ing that had a wide front and two wings on the back. Some folks had snorted at the idea of an eighty-bed hospital in Northmont, but the town planners figured you had to build for tomorrow's needs and there was no doubt the region was growing. Of course all the beds weren't in use yet, so they'd opened with a limited staff of doctors and nurses—but even here there was a problem, and as April and I approached the hospital's main entrance I saw the problem standing in the doorway to greet us.

His name was Lincoln Jones, and he was the first black doctor the people of Northmont had ever seen.

It was not a good time for blacks in the north or the south. The Ku Klux Klan was once again active and I'd heard about a cross burning just a month earlier in another part of the state. But Lincoln Jones was a good doctor, a young man who specialized in children's illnesses. There weren't too many specialists around in those days, and I figured we were mighty lucky to have him in Northmont.

Dr. Bob Yale was standing at Lincoln Jones's side to greet us. "Welcome to Pilgrim Memorial, Dr. Sam. How's it look?"

"The windmill exhibit was fine. Now I'm looking over the hospital."

"You know Dr. Jones?"

I shook hands with the black man. He was tall and handsome, probably in his early thirties like me. "We met briefly the other day but we haven't had a chance to talk. I hope you'll find the community to your liking, Dr. Jones."

He smiled. "I guess you'd better be calling me Lincoln. I think we'll be working close a lot of the time."

"I hope so." Then, while Lincoln Jones chatted with April, I took Bob Yale aside. "Any more trouble about him, Bob?"

"Nothing we can't handle here. The hospital administrator, Dr. Seeger, had a few telephone calls complaining about a black doctor. You know the sort. But I think it'll blow over."

I nodded and walked on with him across the hospital lobby. It was tastefully decorated with a few landscape paintings, and there was an admissions desk that made the place look like a hotel lobby. I recognized bald-headed Dr. Seeger standing behind it. Seeger was around 60, a businessman first and a doctor second. I didn't much like him but I had to admit he'd been mainly responsible for getting Randy Collins to donate the land for the hospital.

"What do you think of it, Dr. Sam?" he asked.

"I think you're off to a great start. A place this size, you'll be able to treat patients from three counties."

Seeger laughed without mirth. "We'll have to if we want to cover the overhead. This is an expensive place to run, and it's even more expensive with eighty empty beds."

Randy Collins and his wife Sara Jane came down the stairs from the second floor. Seeing Randy was no treat—his big broad-shouldered figure and glowering face were familiar sights at the town council meetings where he'd been known to argue half the night over some minor resolution. But Sara Jane was indeed a treat. She was slim and cool and lovely, a honey-blonde with never a hair out of place. I could have looked at her all day and dreamed of her all night. They were familiar figures on whatever small social scene Northmont possessed.

Randy was a man in his early forties, conservative and set in his ways. "Can't say I approve of all your new gadgets," he told Seeger, "but then I don't have to approve. I only donated the land."

"Let me show you our operating room," Dr. Seeger said, leading him off down the first-floor corridor.

"Operating rooms aren't for me," Sara Jane decided, lingering close to me. She was a good ten years younger than her husband, and that along with her fresh openness had led to the usual small-town rumors. Some of the older women had even called her a "flapper," a word they'd discovered from reading the magazines of the day.

"Me neither," I agreed. "I'm just a country doctor."

Suddenly she tugged on my arm. "Damn! There's Isaac Van Doran and I don't want to see him!"

I steered her down a corridor before Van Doran could spot us.

He was a muscular if slow-witted young man who ran Northmont's only gas station. Tongues had been set wagging when he'd been seen once riding in Sara Jane's roadster, but she insisted later he was only checking out her steering wheel.

"What have you got against Van Doran?" I asked with a smile.

"He and Randy don't get along. When Randy goes in there for gas they hardly talk."

"And you don't want to upset your husband."

"Well, Randy is very good to me." She fluttered her lashes as she said it, and I decided she'd been seeing too many moving pictures. Next thing I knew she'd be pulling a whiskey flask out of her stocking top.

We'd reached the end of the corridor and turned back. I could see there was some sort of commotion in the lobby and I wondered what the trouble was. "It's probably my husband," Sara Jane said with a resigned sigh, but we quickly saw that it wasn't.

A shabbily dressed woman, whom I recognized as Mabel Foster from up on Hill Road, had confronted Dr. Jones and was pointing a knobby finger at the black doctor. "You get rid of this man!" she screeched. "He's in league with the Devil! If he stays here Satan himself will come!"

Her words sent a chill down my spine, not for Lincoln Jones or for the coming of Satan but only for this poor deranged creature. I'd treated her off and on over the years, listening calmly to her claims of psychic power. But now, confronting our new black doctor, the hatred of generations had come boiling to the surface.

Luckily for everyone, April moved quickly to her side, comforting her with murmured reassurance as she moved her out the door. Dr. Seeger tried to laugh it off. "Did you put her up to that, Randy?" he asked Collins.

"Hardly!" Sara Jane's husband answered, visibly shaken. "Too bad something like that had to spoil the opening. Let's hope Mabel's psychic powers are all in her imagination."

"I'm sure they are," Lincoln Jones said with a smile. "Things like that don't disturb me, and I trust they won't disturb anyone else. It's something I learned to live with a long time ago."

April came back in after a bit. "I managed to get her in her carriage and headed for home," she said. "That woman should be locked away, Dr. Sam."

"Sometimes she's as sane as the two of us. I wish I was better equipped to help her."

We left the hospital shortly after that. I never did get up to the second floor that day, but it didn't matter. Within a week I'd be spending a great deal of time there.

The call came late on Sunday night, close to twelve. Pilgrim Memorial Hospital had been open five days by that time, but the word around town was that it had yet to admit its first patient. A pregnant farm wife had delivered her baby at home, as she had on three previous occasions, and a man who broke his leg had insisted on being driven to the old hospital in the next county because, he said, they knew him there.

So I was a bit surprised to hear Bob Yale's voice on the line, summoning me with something close to panic. "You'd better come over to the hospital mighty quick, Sam. We need you here."

"What's happened?" I asked. "A train accident?" It was the first thing that popped into my head.

"A fire. I'll tell you when you get here."

Winter had delivered a late blow that night, and about an inch of snow covered the ground. That wasn't too unusual for the tenth of March, but we'd been spoiled by a relatively mild season and I'd thought we'd seen the last of the snow. When I reached the hospital I saw lanterns in the road and the town's fire truck pulled up by the Pilgrims windmill. The building itself didn't appear damaged, and the vanes with their canvas covering were turning slowly in the night breeze.

Bob Yale came running up to my car and I saw that his hands and arms were bandaged.

"What happened to you?" I asked.

"Burned myself. Not serious."

"You're the hospital's first patient!"

There was no humor on his face when he replied. "No, I'm not. Randy Collins was badly burned. We don't know if he'll live."

"Randy! What's been happening here?"

His face reflected the flickering red glow from the firemen's lanterns. "I was coming off duty about an hour ago, and as I went out to my car I saw a flash of light through the window of the windmill. It looked like a fire and I walked out to investigate. I thought some kids might have gotten in there, and I saw a single set of footprints in the fresh snow leading to the door."

As he talked we moved through the crowd of firemen and hospital staff to the door in question. I saw Dr. Seeger come out of the building, stepping nimbly over a fire hose. "Hello, Sam. Is Bob filling you in on what happened?"

I said he was, and for the first time the thought struck me that I wasn't here as a doctor. Seeger and Yale had phoned me because of something else—some mystery they couldn't explain. "What about Collins?" I asked Bob.

"I heard him scream before I reached the door. I pushed it open and saw him standing in the center of the room, covered with flames."

"The room was on fire?"

"Not the room—just Randy Collins. He staggered around, smashing the glass on some of the historical display cases. I was close to panic myself. There was nothing to wrap him in, to smother the flames. Finally I just grabbed him and yanked him out the door and rolled him in the snow. There was nothing else I could do."

"That was a brave act," I told him.

"Brave or foolish. That's how I burned my arms."

"Is he up at the hospital now?"

Bob Yale nodded. "We had to give him a sedative. The burns on his body are terrible."

"Did he say anything?"

"Just one word—Lucifer. He kept repeating it."

"Lucifer. He must have remembered what old Mabel Foster said about the devil."

I looked around at the inside of the windmill. The floor in the center of the room was badly scorched, and there was evidence that Randy's flailing body had set fire to some of the display cases as well. But the firemen had extinguished it quickly. The stone walls of the mill were undamaged, of course. I stepped carefully around some broken glass from the display cases and peered up toward the high ceiling. There was enough lantern light to make out the wind shaft and gears—and enough light to see that no one was hiding up there. I thought I saw a tiny piece of something red, but I couldn't be sure. "I checked with Dr. Seeger, who was in charge of the exhibit. He assured me nothing inflammable was left inside."

"What do the firemen think?"

Bob Yale shrugged. "They don't know either. He just caught fire."

The room had been wired with electric lights for the exhibit, but no one had thought to turn them on. I flicked the switch now and the bulbs lit. "It's not the electrical wiring," I said.

"One fireman thought he smelled gasoline."

I frowned. "Do you think someone tried to kill Collins by burning him to death?"

"I'd think that except for one thing."

"What's that?"

"There were no other footprints in the snow, Sam. Randy Collins was alone in this windmill when it happened."

We waited at the hospital until Dr. Jones finished dressing Collins' burns as best he could. Then he came into the corridor to talk with us. "I thought you specialized in children's illnesses," I said.

"I treated a few burn cases in children. Seeger figured I was the burn expert on the staff."

"Will he pull through?"

Lincoln Jones ran a hand through his thick black hair. "It's in the hands of the Lord now. But I'm hoping he'll make it."

"Is he conscious?" I asked. "Could I talk to him?"

"He's heavily sedated but he was talking a bit. I'll give you one minute with him if it's absolutely necessary." He wagged a finger at me to emphasize the point. "Not a second more—he's my patient!"

I entered the room and stood by the bed, looking down at the burned man. Randy Collins must have sensed my presence because he opened his eyes. "Dr. Sam . . ." His voice was barely a whisper.

"What happened to you, Randy? What happened at the windmill?"

"I . . ."

"You kept saying *Lucifer*."

"Driving by . . . saw light in the windmill . . . flickering light like a fire . . . went in and . . . it was the Devil, Dr. Sam . . . just like that woman said . . . a ball of flame just enveloped me . . ."

Lincoln Jones tapped me on the shoulder. "Sorry, Sam. Your minute's up. Let him sleep now."

Randy Collins closed his eyes and I followed Jones out of the room. Sara Jane was in the corridor, her eyes swollen with tears. "What happened to him? Will he be all right?"

Yale filled her in on what little he knew. Then she turned to me again. "What happened to him, Sam?"

I could only hold out my hands helplessly. "We just don't know, Sara Jane. We just don't know."

By Wednesday Randy Collins had recovered enough to have visitors, and Lincoln Jones was grinning broadly as he studied the chart at the end of the bed. "You're out of danger, Mr. Collins. You're going to live."

Collins shifted his gaze from the black doctor to me and asked, "What about my face, Sam? And my skin?"

"They can do amazing things these days. As soon as you're strong enough Dr. Jones plans to send you by ambulance to a hospital in Boston that specializes in burn cases. They'll use plastic surgery and skin grafts to make you as good as new."

"I'll be like this for years!"

"But consider the alternative," Jones pointed out. "If Bob Yale hadn't rushed in to save your life, we'd be burying you today."

"How are his hands?"

"Not as bad as yours. You were both lucky there was snow on the ground."

"Have you remembered anything else about the fire?" I asked.

"Seems like I've told it a hundred times around. It was a ball of fire floating there, just enveloping me. All I could think of was Mabel Foster's predictions of Satan." He glanced pointedly at Lincoln Jones.

"Well, the Devil's not going to drive me away from this job," Jones responded. "I've seen the Devil wearing a white sheet and delivering a speech, and that didn't scare me. I guess a ball of fire doesn't scare me either."

During those first days when he could have visitors, it seemed that half of Northmont trooped out to the hospital to see Randy Collins. While Sara Jane hovered near his bed, most of the town council put in an appearance and even Sheriff Lens drove out to pay a visit. We hadn't needed his services yet because no one could figure out if there'd been a crime or not. If there was a criminal involved—one who'd tried to murder Randy Collins—he'd have had to be invisible.

"Think somebody slipped one of them there infernal devices into his pocket?" Sheriff Lens asked as we left the hospital building and strolled down toward the windmill.

"Without his knowing it? That's hardly possible, Sheriff. Besides, he insists the fireball was already inside the place when he entered it."

"Don't they keep it locked at night?"

"It was left open because of the exhibit. There was nothing to steal here."

We went inside and I saw that the fire damage had not been repaired since Sunday night. The floor was still scorched and broken glass still littered the area. Something caught my eye and I stooped to pick it up. It was a thick piece of curved glass.

"What's that, Doc?" Sheriff Lens asked.

"Just a piece of glass. This place should be swept out before someone cuts himself."

"Who's in there?" a voice called suddenly from outside. I walked to the doorway and saw it was Isaac Van Doran.

"Just us, Isaac—the sheriff and me."

"Thought it might be that devil Randy seen," Van Doran said with a chuckle.

"What brings you out here?"

"Come to visit him. That's the least I can do."

I was surprised by that. "Didn't know you two were all that friendly."

"Hell, we're not enemies. He's been a customer of mine for years—him and Sara Jane both. It's good business to come see him."

I knew Sara Jane had gone home for lunch and I wondered if

Isaac had purposely chosen a time when she wouldn't be there. We watched him walk up to the hospital and Sheriff Lens asked, "What do you make of him, Doc? Think maybe he tried to kill Randy so's he could run off with Sara Jane?"

"You've been listening to the town gossip too much, Sheriff. If Van Doran had tried to kill him I'm sure Randy Collins wouldn't be covering it up."

"Then you believe this devil business?"

"I don't know. But I think it's time I called on Mabel Foster."

I was driving along the highway toward Mabel's place on the hill when I happened to spot her horse and buggy. I wondered where she was going and decided to follow along at a short distance. It wasn't easy making the car run that slow but I managed—and I was rewarded for my patience when I saw her turning into the driveway of the Collins house. A few snow flurries were just beginning to fall.

I parked down the road and went the rest of the way on foot, arriving just in time to see Mabel Foster confronting Sara Jane at the front door. "I warned them all—I warned them and they laughed at me! Now your husband is on his bed of pain—and that won't be the end of it!"

"Get away from here!" Sara Jane screamed. "I'll call the police!"

Mabel made a pass with her fist as I hurried up to grab her. "Time to go home," I told her quietly.

"Let go, Dr. Sam! Let go!"

But I managed to get her back to her buggy. "You've got to behave, Mabel, or people will want to lock you away."

"The Devil will guide me! Satan is my master!"

"And it was Satan that burned Randy Collins?"

"Of course! I warned you all it was coming!"

"Why Collins?"

"Don't you see? Because he donated the land for the hospital!"

"And who will be burned next?"

"Seeger!" She almost spat out the name. "He's the one who hired the black doctor—Seeger is next!" She raised her buggy whip and I thought for an instant she would strike me. But her target was the horse's back and the blow galvanized him into action. Horse and buggy took her down the road with the snow flying around her.

I walked back to the doorway where Sara Jane stood. She was trembling so bad she had to hold the door for support. "God, she frightened me half to death! I'm so glad you came by, Dr. Sam. Come in and have some coffee."

"You need something to calm you down."

"Do you think she tried to kill Randy? To make her crazy prediction come true?"

"I doubt if she'd be capable of it."

Sara Jane poured two cups of coffee and then nervously picked up a box of friction matches to light a cigarette. Not many women in Northmont smoked, but for Sara Jane it was part of her flapper image.

"If someone did try to kill Randy, they might try again at the hospital."

Her words reminded me of something. "Isaac Van Doran came to visit him this noon. Did you know that?"

She shook her head. "I only see Isaac at his station. Those stories about us were foolish."

"I'm sure they were." I finished my coffee and stood up. "I have to be going. I was on my way over to see Mabel Foster but I guess I've seen her now."

"If you go back to the hospital tell Randy I'll be over in a little while."

I didn't go back to the hospital right away, though. I had my own patients to consider, and April was waiting for me back at the office with a sheaf of phone messages. It was late afternoon before I returned to Pilgrim Memorial. Bob Yale told me they'd admitted two more patients that morning—a broken leg and an appendix case—but neither was a patient of mine. People in the surrounding towns were beginning to realize that the new hospital was open at last, and I had no doubts about its future.

"How are your arms?" I asked, because I hadn't seen him that morning when I chatted with Sheriff Lens.

He patted the bandages. "Coming along. I'm going to unwrap them in a day or so and see if the air will help them heal faster. It's more a nuisance than anything else."

Sara Jane was visiting with Collins, so I didn't disturb them.

Instead I went down to Seeger's office on the ground floor. He looked up from a mass of paperwork as I entered. "Hello, Sam. What can I do for you?"

I told him about my encounter with Mabel Foster and her threat against his life. "That woman should be locked up," he muttered. "But thanks for the warning. I won't go anywhere near the windmill—or any fireplaces, for that matter."

"How's the hospital coming?"

Seeger shrugged. "Three patients, with another coming in tomorrow. I've no doubt some people are staying away because of Lincoln Jones, but I think they'll come around sooner or later. We have a good hospital here, with modern equipment, and that's what will win them over."

I left Seeger's office and spent some time chatting with a couple of nurses. Then I decided it was time to be on my way. Though the days were growing longer as spring approached, it was still dark before six o'clock in mid-March, and I turned on my headlights as I drove out of the parking lot. In their searching beams I caught a sudden glimpse of someone by the side of the road near the windmill. It wasn't till I was some distance away that I realized it had been Isaac Van Doran.

I slowed the car and made a U-turn in the road. By the time I returned to the spot, Van Doran had disappeared. There was no place he could have gone except into the windmill. Though much of the earlier snow had melted, the few flurries earlier in the day still clung to the grass. There was enough for me to trace his footprints leading up to the windmill door. I saw no other prints nearby.

Then, almost at once, I heard the scream. It was the drawn-out scream of a man who might have been falling from a great height —falling all the way to Hades itself. I burst through the door into an inferno of flame. Isaac Van Doran lay in the middle of it, trying to rise from the floor, stretching out his hand toward me. This time the flames were not confined to the body but seemed to fill the windmill's interior, shooting high into the mechanism above.

I tried to beat at the flames with my coat, but it was useless. With his dying screams still in my ears I was forced to retreat before the fire.

The town's fire engine came again, and Seeger and Bob Yale ran down from the hospital with some of the nurses. The whole scene could have been a duplicate of Sunday evening's, except this time there was no survivor. When the flames had finally been extinguished, they wrapped the blackened remains of Isaac Van Doran in canvas and carried the body away. Then the rest of us trooped up to the hospital and went into Seeger's office. "We'd better report this to Sheriff Lens," Seeger said, reaching for the telephone.

"As what? Another unexplained accident?" I asked.

Bob Yale looked at me. "You were there, Sam. What do you think it was?"

"I'm damned if I know. We've had two fires, with one man badly injured and another dead. Both men were alone when it happened. Randy Collins entered the windmill because he thought he saw a glow of some sort. We don't know why Van Doran went in."

"You saw no one else around?"

I shook my head. "There were only Van Doran's footprints going in. And anyone hiding inside from earlier in the day would surely have been consumed by those flames. We have to face it— both men were alone in that windmill when they suddenly caught fire for no apparent reason."

"Did Van Doran manage to shout anything as he was dying?" Yale asked me.

"Just screams. If he thought it was the Devil he didn't say so."

Sheriff Lens drove out and talked to us, then went to look over the windmill as best he could in the dark. The electric wiring, undamaged in the first fire, was burnt out now, and everyone agreed a better inspection could be made in the morning. I went home to bed and dreamed of Isaac Van Doran's final moments in the fire, screaming and reaching out his hand toward a salvation I could not give him.

In the morning I drove back to the hospital. I parked my car in the gravel lot, and as I started down the hill toward the windmill, Lincoln Jones intercepted me. "There's something I thought you'd want to know," he said.

"About last night?"

He nodded. "I gave Van Doran's body a cursory examination before it was removed. The man had a broken leg."

"What?"

"A compound fracture of the left tibia."

"You couldn't be mistaken?"

"The bone was protruding through the skin."

"I see. Why are you telling me this?"

"Because you said he walked into the windmill. He couldn't have, with that leg. You must have seen someone else."

I considered that. "Or Van Doran broke his leg after he was inside."

"During the fire? It was a pretty bad break to get from just falling down."

"Anyway, thanks for the information. It may be a big help." I left him and continued down the hill.

Sheriff Lens was already on the scene, standing in the doorway. After this second fire the wooden floor was almost burned through in spots, and the display cases for the exhibits were all but consumed. Even the windmill mechanism above our heads was charred and unmoving. The wind shaft on which the outside vanes revolved had become jammed in the fire, freezing the blades in position. "Like a cross to keep away the Devil," Sheriff Lens observed, and his words surprised me. I'd never known him to be a particularly religious man.

"I want to go up there," I said, standing in the doorway and pointing above our heads at the blackened gears.

"What for?"

"Van Doran died with a broken leg. If he walked in here by himself he must have broken his leg here, in the instant the fire started. When I heard him scream I had the impression he might have been falling. Maybe I even heard him hit the floor without realizing it. And if he fell, it was from up there."

Sheriff Lens grunted. "I got another idea. The body was pretty badly burned, wasn't it?"

"Yes."

"Maybe Van Doran had injured someone else, broken his leg. When he saw you coming he returned here and set fire to the body, then managed to escape out one of the windows. The dead man might not be Van Doran at all."

"You've been reading those mystery novels again, Sheriff. There was only one set of prints coming in here. And I saw his face clearly in the flames before he died. I even dreamed of it last night. Besides, I would have seen anyone trying to climb out a window, even that high one over the wind shaft."

"Then the thing's impossible, unless you're telling me he committed suicide."

"I'm not telling you anything of the sort. But I do want to climb up there and take a look."

We got a ladder from the hospital groundskeeper and carried it over between us.

Sheriff Lens snorted as I lifted it into position. "If you need a ladder to get up there, Doc, how in hell you figger Van Doran got up there—flew?"

"He could have stood on one of the display cases." I went halfway up the ladder until I was within reaching distance of the blackened central wind shaft. Certainly nothing was hidden up here, and there was no sign of what had caused the fire. But over to one side, at the edge of the charred area, I did find something of interest.

A tiny piece of—what? rubber?—half melted from the heat and stuck to the wood. The unmelted part was red, which earlier had attracted my attention. But I couldn't for the life of me figure out what it had been. Had the killer hung from the roof by a giant rubber band that snapped him up out of sight when the fire started? No, I'd as soon believe in the Devil as in that idea.

I came back down the ladder. "Any luck, Doc?"

"Not much," I admitted.

"What now?"

"Let's go up to the hospital."

Bob Yale was in Seeger's office and he was just hanging up the telephone as we entered. "Mabel Foster's at it again. She was down in the town square creating a disturbance, warning people the Devil has come to Northmont. One of your deputies picked her up, Sheriff, and he's bringing her out here."

"Don't know what in hell we'll do with her," Seeger muttered.

I walked to the window and stared out at the windmill. "How's Collins coming along?"

"He was filling rubber balloons with small quantities of gasoline from a glass jug. The balloons were attached to a long fuse wound around the wind shaft up above. The gasoline ignited, breaking the jug and setting fire to his clothes. The wind shaft was turning at the time, and lifted some of the gasoline-filled balloons up out of the way of the fire."

"Why would Collins want to burn down the windmill?" Dr. Seeger asked, clearly unconvinced.

"He didn't want to burn the whole windmill," I explained. "Look out at it now, with those four vanes frozen in position. Sheriff Lens said it looked just like a cross, and it does. Randy Collins was going to burn a giant cross in front of this hospital because you hired a black doctor."

Lincoln Jones never looked up at my words. He kept on ministering to his patient as if none of this concerned him. Collins just lay there with his eyes closed as I hurried on. "The day the hospital opened and we had that scene with Mabel Foster, Seeger asked you, Randy, if you put Mabel up to it. Sara Jane wondered, too, if you were causing the disturbance. Even though they spoke in jest, I should have known from that—and from your conservative reputation—where you stood on hiring a black doctor at Pilgrim.

"The Ku Klux Klan has been active near here, burning crosses and so forth. Whether you're an active member or merely a KKK sympathizer, it must have struck you as fitting that the canvas-covered vanes of your windmill could be set afire for a cross burning. So you got a gallon jug of gasoline from Isaac's station. The idea, I suppose, was to attach the gasoline-filled balloons to the vanes of the windmill as they turned, then light the fuse and scoot away while the balloons burst and that flaming gasoline spread itself over the canvas. You were filling the balloons, letting the turning wind shaft carry them up above your head, when the accident happened."

"What about this business with the Devil?" Sheriff Lens asked.

"When it first happened, Randy didn't use the words *Devil* or *Satan.* He said *Lucifer,* though no one else including Mabel Foster used that name. Once he knew what he was saying, Randy's talk was of the Devil and fireballs. He didn't mention Lucifer any more either. But if he didn't mean the Devil when he first said it, what else could *Lucifer* have meant? What else is Lucifer a name for? Common friction matches.

"They're still called Lucifers by some people, and I know Randy used them because I saw a box at his home. He was simply telling us that a friction match accidentally ignited and caused the fire. But when he came to his senses and decided on a coverup— he changed Lucifer to the Devil."

"But Collins hasn't left his hospital bed," Bob Yale protested. "How was he able to kill Isaac Van Doran?"

"When I figured what must have happened to Randy, the rest was easy. After the first fire I found a piece of thick curved glass— not from the flat display cases, more like from a glass jug. That helped me, same as finding bits of rubber today helped me make a good guess about the balloons. If Randy brought the gasoline out in a glass jug, where'd he get it from? Only from Isaac Van Doran, who operates the town's only gas station.

"So what happened a few days after the fire, when Collins could have visitors? Van Doran comes to see him, at noon when Sara Jane's not around. How come, when the men have always been cool to one another? Because Van Doran knows damn well that Randy burned himself up somehow, with that gallon jug of gasoline he bought at Isaac's station." I turned to the man in the bed. "Van Doran came to blackmail you, didn't he, Randy?"

The eyes were still closed, but after a moment's silence he spoke. "Yeah, he wanted money. Said he'd tell them I was probably setting a fire with the gas. I told him where he could get money."

The scorched lips twisted into a sort of smile.

"Of course!" The final piece of the puzzle dropped into place. "The old stories about money hidden in the windmill! You told him the money was there—where? In little balloons full of gold dust? Something like that, I suppose. You knew the fire hadn't consumed the gasoline-filled balloons already wrapped around the wind shaft. You knew you had to get rid of them somehow, before the gasoline leaked through or they were otherwise discovered. Because if they were found, everyone would realize what you were trying to do.

"So here was Van Doran presenting himself at your hospital

bed. A man you already disliked because of the rumors about him and your wife. A man threatening blackmail. What better way to destroy the last evidence of your disastrous mistake? I suppose you told him where the money was supposed to be, told him to light a match or take a candle so he didn't need to turn on the windmill lights.

"Van Doran worked around gasoline every day, so he probably didn't even catch the odor of it when he climbed up there and lit his match. The fumes would have ignited, or one of the balloons would have burst. Whatever happened, Van Doran was immediately enveloped in flames and fell screaming to the floor, breaking his leg as he did so. Isaac Van Doran, and the evidence of the first fire, were destroyed together."

Sara Jane reached out her hand toward the man in the bed. "I can't believe it. Tell them it isn't true, Randy! Tell them!"

But he didn't say anything at all. He just lay there on the bed with his eyes closed, as if he couldn't stand the sight of the black doctor who was ministering to his wounded flesh.

"It was an odd sort of murder case," Dr. Sam Hawthorne continued, "difficult to prove in a court of law, since Randy Collins was helpless in a hospital bed at the time the victim died. They never did bring it to trial, but I guess he suffered enough anyway, what with all the operations to rebuild his body after the fire. They took him off to Boston and he never did come back, and I hear tell that Sara Jane finally left him and married someone else. It was the last of the trouble over Lincoln Jones, though, and over the years he proved to be one of the most popular doctors on the Pilgrim staff."

Dr. Sam got to his feet, leaning heavily on his cane. "Sorry you haven't time for another—ah—small libation. But come by again and I'll tell you about the boat on the lake, and our own miniature version of the *Mary Celeste* mystery."

HENRY JAMES

The Romance of Certain Old Clothes

Boston, capital of the Bay State of Massachusetts, is the setting of the
following trio of eerie stories. "The Romance of Certain Old Clothes,"
published in 1865 in Atlantic Monthly, *is the first ghost story by* HENRY
JAMES *(1843–1916), a New Yorker who became a British subject a year*
before he died. James, one of the few Victorian novelists still popular today,
wrote several important novels, including The Ambassadors, The
American, The Bostonians, Daisy Miller, The Golden Bowl, Portrait of a Lady, Washington Square *and* The Wings of the Dove, *as*
well as a number of ghost stories, the most famous being the oft-dramatized
"The Turn of the Screw."

Towards the middle of the eighteenth century there lived in the
Province of Massachusetts a widowed gentlewoman, the mother
of three children, by name Mrs. Veronica Wingrave. She had lost
her husband early in life, and had devoted herself to the care of
her progeny. These young persons grew up in a manner to reward her tenderness and to gratify her highest hopes. The first-
born was a son, whom she had called Bernard, after his father.
The others were daughters—born at an interval of three years
apart. Good looks were traditional in the family, and this youthful
trio were not likely to allow the tradition to perish. The boy was of
that fair and ruddy complexion and that athletic structure which

in those days (as in these) were the sign of good English descent
—a frank, affectionate young fellow, a deferential son, a patroniz-
ing brother, a steadfast friend. Clever, however, he was not; the
wit of the family had been apportioned chiefly to his sisters. The
late Mr. Wingrave had been a great reader of Shakespeare, at a
time when this pursuit implied more freedom of thought than at
the present day, and in a community where it required much
courage to patronize the drama even in the closet; and he had
wished to call attention to his admiration of the great poet by
calling his daughters out of his favourite plays. Upon the elder he
had bestowed the romantic name of Rosalind, and the younger
he had called Perdita, in memory of a little girl born between
them, who had lived but a few weeks.

When Bernard Wingrave came to his sixteenth year his mother
put a brave face upon it and prepared to execute her husband's
last injunction. This had been a formal command that, at the
proper age, his son should be sent out to England, to complete
his education at the university of Oxford, where he himself had
acquired his taste for elegant literature. It was Mrs. Wingrave's
belief that the lad's equal was not to be found in the two hemi-
spheres, but she had the old traditions of literal obedience. She
swallowed her sobs, and made up her boy's trunk and his simple
provincial outfit, and sent him on his way across the seas. Bernard
presented himself at his father's college, and spent five years in
England, without great honour, indeed, but with a vast deal of
pleasure and no discredit. On leaving the university he made the
journey to France. In his twenty-fourth year he took ship for
home, prepared to find poor little New England (New England
was very small in those days) a very dull, unfashionable residence.
But there had been changes at home, as well as in Mr. Bernard's
opinions. He found his mother's house quite habitable, and his
sisters grown into two very charming young ladies, with all the
accomplishments and graces of the young women of Britain, and
a certain native-grown originality and wildness, which, if it was
not an accomplishment, was certainly a grace the more. Bernard
privately assured his mother that his sisters were fully a match for
the most genteel young women in the old country; whereupon
poor Mrs. Wingrave, you may be sure, bade them hold up their
heads. Such was Bernard's opinion, and such a tenfold higher

"Better," Seeger said. "I think we can move him to Boston by the first of next week."

"His spirits are good," Yale added, confirming the diagnosis.

"The fire damaged your windmill," I said. "It doesn't turn any more."

"We can get that fixed," the hospital's director assured me.

I remembered something that Sheriff Lens had said. I had to think about it for a few moments, sorting it out in my mind, but then I was certain. "I know who did it," I told them.

"What?"

"I know who caused Randy Collins' injuries and then murdered Isaac Van Doran."

"Not the Devil?" Dr. Seeger asked with a slight smile.

"No, not the Devil. It was a very human killer." I started for the door. "Where's Lincoln Jones now?"

Yale glanced at the wall clock. "Probably up with Collins, changing the dressing on his burns."

"I'm going up there," I said, and though I didn't tell them to, the others trailed along.

Sara Jane was seated next to her husband's bed as we entered the room. Dr. Jones looked up from his task of spreading salve over the burned flesh and said, "I really don't know if it's good to have so many people in here at once."

"This is very important," I said. "I want to explain who caused Van Doran's death and how it was done."

Sara Jane came forward in her chair. "Was it the same person who did this to my husband?"

"Yes."

"Who was it?"

I leaned over the bed. "Shall I tell them, Randy? Shall I tell them who did this terrible thing to you and Isaac?"

"It was Satan," he rasped. "The Devil."

I shook my head. "No, it was only the Devil that dwells within each of us. You set fire to yourself, Randy. It was an accident, of course, but it was no accident when you sent Isaac Van Doran out to his death last evening."

They were all trying to talk at once, but it was Sara Jane's voice I heard above the rest. "What do you mean he set fire to himself? How could that be?"

more either. But if he didn't mean the Devil when he first said it, what else could *Lucifer* have meant? What else is Lucifer a name for? Common friction matches.

"They're still called Lucifers by some people, and I know Randy used them because I saw a box at his home. He was simply telling us that a friction match accidentally ignited and caused the fire. But when he came to his senses and decided on a coverup— he changed Lucifer to the Devil."

"But Collins hasn't left his hospital bed," Bob Yale protested. "How was he able to kill Isaac Van Doran?"

"When I figured what must have happened to Randy, the rest was easy. After the first fire I found a piece of thick curved glass— not from the flat display cases, more like from a glass jug. That helped me, same as finding bits of rubber today helped me make a good guess about the balloons. If Randy brought the gasoline out in a glass jug, where'd he get it from? Only from Isaac Van Doran, who operates the town's only gas station.

"So what happened a few days after the fire, when Collins could have visitors? Van Doran comes to see him, at noon when Sara Jane's not around. How come, when the men have always been cool to one another? Because Van Doran knows damn well that Randy burned himself up somehow, with that gallon jug of gasoline he bought at Isaac's station." I turned to the man in the bed. "Van Doran came to blackmail you, didn't he, Randy?"

The eyes were still closed, but after a moment's silence he spoke. "Yeah, he wanted money. Said he'd tell them I was probably setting a fire with the gas. I told him where he could get money."

The scorched lips twisted into a sort of smile.

"Of course!" The final piece of the puzzle dropped into place. "The old stories about money hidden in the windmill! You told him the money was there—where? In little balloons full of gold dust? Something like that, I suppose. You knew the fire hadn't consumed the gasoline-filled balloons already wrapped around the wind shaft. You knew you had to get rid of them somehow, before the gasoline leaked through or they were otherwise discovered. Because if they were found, everyone would realize what you were trying to do.

"So here was Van Doran presenting himself at your hospital

bed. A man you already disliked because of the rumors about him and your wife. A man threatening blackmail. What better way to destroy the last evidence of your disastrous mistake? I suppose you told him where the money was supposed to be, told him to light a match or take a candle so he didn't need to turn on the windmill lights.

"Van Doran worked around gasoline every day, so he probably didn't even catch the odor of it when he climbed up there and lit his match. The fumes would have ignited, or one of the balloons would have burst. Whatever happened, Van Doran was immediately enveloped in flames and fell screaming to the floor, breaking his leg as he did so. Isaac Van Doran, and the evidence of the first fire, were destroyed together."

Sara Jane reached out her hand toward the man in the bed. "I can't believe it. Tell them it isn't true, Randy! Tell them!"

But he didn't say anything at all. He just lay there on the bed with his eyes closed, as if he couldn't stand the sight of the black doctor who was ministering to his wounded flesh.

"It was an odd sort of murder case," Dr. Sam Hawthorne continued, "difficult to prove in a court of law, since Randy Collins was helpless in a hospital bed at the time the victim died. They never did bring it to trial, but I guess he suffered enough anyway, what with all the operations to rebuild his body after the fire. They took him off to Boston and he never did come back, and I hear tell that Sara Jane finally left him and married someone else. It was the last of the trouble over Lincoln Jones, though, and over the years he proved to be one of the most popular doctors on the Pilgrim staff."

Dr. Sam got to his feet, leaning heavily on his cane. "Sorry you haven't time for another—ah—small libation. But come by again and I'll tell you about the boat on the lake, and our own miniature version of the *Mary Celeste* mystery."

HENRY JAMES

The Romance
of Certain
Old Clothes

*Boston, capital of the Bay State of Massachusetts, is the setting of the
following trio of eerie stories. "The Romance of Certain Old Clothes,"
published in 1865 in* Atlantic Monthly, *is the first ghost story by* HENRY
JAMES *(1843–1916), a New Yorker who became a British subject a year
before he died. James, one of the few Victorian novelists still popular today,
wrote several important novels, including* The Ambassadors, The
American, The Bostonians, Daisy Miller, The Golden Bowl, Portrait of a Lady, Washington Square *and* The Wings of the Dove, *as
well as a number of ghost stories, the most famous being the oft-dramatized
"The Turn of the Screw."*

Towards the middle of the eighteenth century there lived in the
Province of Massachusetts a widowed gentlewoman, the mother
of three children, by name Mrs. Veronica Wingrave. She had lost
her husband early in life, and had devoted herself to the care of
her progeny. These young persons grew up in a manner to reward her tenderness and to gratify her highest hopes. The first-
born was a son, whom she had called Bernard, after his father.
The others were daughters—born at an interval of three years
apart. Good looks were traditional in the family, and this youthful
trio were not likely to allow the tradition to perish. The boy was of
that fair and ruddy complexion and that athletic structure which

in those days (as in these) were the sign of good English descent
—a frank, affectionate young fellow, a deferential son, a patroniz-
ing brother, a steadfast friend. Clever, however, he was not; the
wit of the family had been apportioned chiefly to his sisters. The
late Mr. Wingrave had been a great reader of Shakespeare, at a
time when this pursuit implied more freedom of thought than at
the present day, and in a community where it required much
courage to patronize the drama even in the closet; and he had
wished to call attention to his admiration of the great poet by
calling his daughters out of his favourite plays. Upon the elder he
had bestowed the romantic name of Rosalind, and the younger
he had called Perdita, in memory of a little girl born between
them, who had lived but a few weeks.

When Bernard Wingrave came to his sixteenth year his mother
put a brave face upon it and prepared to execute her husband's
last injunction. This had been a formal command that, at the
proper age, his son should be sent out to England, to complete
his education at the university of Oxford, where he himself had
acquired his taste for elegant literature. It was Mrs. Wingrave's
belief that the lad's equal was not to be found in the two hemi-
spheres, but she had the old traditions of literal obedience. She
swallowed her sobs, and made up her boy's trunk and his simple
provincial outfit, and sent him on his way across the seas. Bernard
presented himself at his father's college, and spent five years in
England, without great honour, indeed, but with a vast deal of
pleasure and no discredit. On leaving the university he made the
journey to France. In his twenty-fourth year he took ship for
home, prepared to find poor little New England (New England
was very small in those days) a very dull, unfashionable residence.
But there had been changes at home, as well as in Mr. Bernard's
opinions. He found his mother's house quite habitable, and his
sisters grown into two very charming young ladies, with all the
accomplishments and graces of the young women of Britain, and
a certain native-grown originality and wildness, which, if it was
not an accomplishment, was certainly a grace the more. Bernard
privately assured his mother that his sisters were fully a match for
the most genteel young women in the old country; whereupon
poor Mrs. Wingrave, you may be sure, bade them hold up their
heads. Such was Bernard's opinion, and such a tenfold higher

degree, was the opinion of Mr. Arthur Lloyd. This gentleman was a college-mate of Mr. Bernard, a young man of reputable family, of a good person and a handsome inheritance; which latter appurtenance he proposed to invest in trade in the flourishing colony. He and Bernard were sworn friends; they had crossed the ocean together, and the young American had lost no time in presenting him at his mother's house, where he had made quite as good an impression as that which he had received and of which I have just given a hint.

The two sisters were at this time in all the freshness of their youthful bloom; each wearing, of course, this natural brilliancy in the manner that became her best. They were equally dissimilar in appearance and character. Rosalind, the elder—now in her twenty-second year—was tall and white, with calm gray eyes and auburn tresses; a very faint likeness to the Rosalind of Shakespeare's comedy, whom I imagine a brunette (if you will), but a slender, airy creature, full of the softest, quickest impulses. Miss Wingrave, with her slightly lymphatic fairness, her fine arms, her majestic height, her slow utterance, was not cut out for adventures. She would never have put on a man's jacket and hose; and indeed, being a very plump beauty, she may have had reasons apart from her natural dignity. Perdita, too, might very well have exchanged the sweet melancholy of her name against something more in consonance with her aspect and disposition. She had the cheek of a gipsy and the eye of an eager child, as well as the smallest waist and lightest foot in all the country of the Puritans. When you spoke to her she never made you wait, as her handsome sister was wont to do (while she looked at you with a cold fine eye), but gave you your choice of a dozen answers before you had uttered half your thought.

The young girls were very glad to see their brother once more; but they found themselves quite able to spare part of their attention for their brother's friend. Among the young men their friends and neighbours, the *belle jeunesse* of the Colony, there were many excellent fellows, several devoted swains, and some two or three who enjoyed the reputation of universal charmers and conquerors. But the homebred arts and somewhat boisterous gallantry of these honest colonists were completely eclipsed by the good looks, the fine clothes, the punctilious courtesy, the perfect elegance, the immense information, of Mr. Arthur Lloyd. He was in reality no paragon; he was a capable, honourable, civil youth, rich in pounds sterling, in his health and complacency and his little capital of uninvested affections. But he was a gentleman; he had a handsome person; he had studied and travelled; he spoke French, he played the flute, and he read verses aloud with very great taste. There were a dozen reasons why Miss Wingrave and her sister should have thought their other male acquaintance made but a poor figure before such a perfect man of the world. Mr. Lloyd's anecdotes told our little New England maidens a great deal more of the ways and means of people of fashion in European capitals than he had any idea of doing. It was delightful to sit by and hear him and Bernard talk about the fine people and fine things they had seen. They would all gather round the fire after tea, in the little wainscoted parlour, and the two young men would remind each other, across the rug, of this, that and the other adventure. Rosalind and Perdita would often have given their ears to know exactly what adventure it was, and where it happened, and who was there, and what the ladies had on; but in those days a well-bred young woman was not expected to break into the conversation of her elders, or to ask too many questions; and the poor girls used therefore to sit fluttering behind the more languid—or more discreet—curiosity of their mother.

II

That they were both very fine girls Arthur Lloyd was not slow to discover; but it took him some time to make up his mind whether he liked the big sister or the little sister best. He had a strong presentiment—an emotion of a nature entirely too cheerful to be called a foreboding—that he was destined to stand up before the parson with one of them; yet he was unable to arrive at a preference, and for such a consummation a preference was certainly necessary, for Lloyd had too much young blood in his veins to make a choice by lot and be cheated of the satisfaction of falling in love. He resolved to take things as they came—to let his heart speak. Meanwhile he was on a very pleasant footing. Mrs. Wingrave showed a dignified indifference to his "intentions," equally remote from a carelessness of her daughter's honour and from that sharp alacrity to make him come to the point, which, in his quality of young man of property, he had too often encountered in the worldly matrons of his native islands. As for Bernard, all that he asked was that his friend should treat his sisters as his own; and as for the poor girls themselves, however each may have secretly longed that their visitor should do or say something "marked," they kept a very modest and contented demeanour.

Towards each other, however, they were somewhat more on the offensive. They were good friends enough, and accommodating bedfellows (they shared the same four-poster), betwixt whom it would take more than a day for the seeds of jealousy to sprout and bear fruit; but they felt that the seeds had been sown on the day that Mr. Lloyd came into the house. Each made up her mind that, if she should be slighted, she would bear her grief in silence, and that no one should be any the wiser; for if they had a great deal of ambition, they had also a large share of pride. But each prayed in secret, nevertheless, that upon *her* the selection, the distinction, might fall. They had need of a vast deal of patience, of self-control, of dissimulation. In those days a young girl of decent breeding could make no advances whatever, and barely respond, indeed, to those that were made. She was expected to sit still in her chair, with her eyes on the carpet, watching the spot where the mystic handkerchief should fall. Poor Arthur Lloyd was obliged to carry on his wooing in the little wainscoted parlour, before the eyes of Mrs. Wingrave, her son, and his prospective sister-in-law. But youth and love are so cunning that a hundred signs and tokens might travel to and fro, and not one of these three pairs of eyes detect them in their passage. The two maidens were almost always together, and had plenty of chances to betray themselves. That each knew she was being watched, however, made not a grain of difference in the little offices they mutually rendered, or in the various household tasks they performed in common. Neither flinched nor fluttered beneath the silent battery of her sister's eyes. The only apparent change in their habits was that they had less to say to each other. It was impossible to talk about Mr. Lloyd, and it was ridiculous to talk about anything else. By tacit agreement they began to wear all their choice finery, and to devise such little implements of conquest, in the way of ribbons and top-knots and kerchiefs, as were sanctioned by indubitable modesty. They executed in the same inarticulate fashion a contract of fair play in this exciting game. "Is it better so?" Rosalind would ask, tying a bunch of ribbons on her bosom, and turning about from her glass to her sister. Perdita would look up gravely from her work and examine the decoration. "I think you had better give it another loop," she would say, with great solemnity, looking hard at her sister with eyes that added, "upon my honour!" So they were for ever stitching and trimming their petticoats, and pressing out their muslins, and contriving washes and ointments and cosmetics, like the ladies in the household of the vicar of Wakefield. Some three or four months went by; it grew to be midwinter, and as yet Rosalind knew that if Perdita had nothing more to boast of than she, there was not much to be feared from her rivalry. But Perdita by this time—the charming Perdita—felt that her secret had grown to be tenfold more precious than her sister's.

One afternoon Miss Wingrave sat alone—that was a rare accident—before her toilet-glass, combing out her long hair. It was getting too dark to see; she lit the two candles in their sockets, on the frame of her mirror, and then went to the window to draw her curtains. It was a gray December evening; the landscape was bare and bleak, and the sky heavy with snow-clouds. At the end of the large garden into which her window looked was a wall with a little postern door, opening into a lane. The door stood ajar, as she could vaguely see in the gathering darkness, and moved slowly to and fro, as if some one were swaying it from the lane without. It was doubtless a servant-maid who had been having a tryst with her sweetheart. But as she was about to drop her curtain Rosalind saw her sister step into the garden and hurry along the path which led to the house. She dropped the curtain, all save a little crevice for her eyes. As Perdita came up the path she seemed to be examining something in her hand, holding it close to her eyes. When she reached the house she stopped a moment, looked intently at the object, and pressed it to her lips.

Poor Rosalind slowly came back to her chair and sat down before her glass, where, if she had looked at it less abstractedly, she would have seen her handsome features sadly disfigured by jealousy. A moment afterwards the door opened behind her and her sister came into the room, out of breath, her cheeks aglow with the chilly air.

Perdita started. "Ah," said she, "I thought you were with our mother." The ladies were to go to a tea-party, and on such occasions it was the habit of one of the girls to help their mother to dress. Instead of coming in, Perdita lingered at the door.

"Come in, come in," said Rosalind. "We have more than an hour yet. I should like you very much to give a few strokes to my hair." She knew that her sister wished to retreat, and that she could see in the glass all her movements in the room. "Nay, just help me with my hair," she said, "and I will go to mamma."

Perdita came reluctantly, and took the brush. She saw her sister's eyes, in the glass, fastened hard upon her hands. She had not made three passes when Rosalind clapped her own right hand upon her sister's left, and started out of her chair. "Whose ring is that?" she cried, passionately, drawing her towards the light.

On the young girl's third finger glistened a little gold ring, adorned with a very small sapphire. Perdita felt that she need no longer keep her secret, yet that she must put a bold face on her avowal. "It's mine," she said proudly.

"Who gave it to you?" cried the other.

Perdita hesitated a moment. "Mr. Lloyd."

"Mr. Lloyd is generous, all of a sudden."

"Ah no," cried Perdita, with spirit, "not all of a sudden! He offered it to me a month ago."

"And you needed a month's begging to take it?" said Rosalind, looking at the little trinket, which indeed was not especially elegant, although it was the best that the jeweller of the Province could furnish. "I wouldn't have taken it in less than two."

"It isn't the ring," Perdita answered, "it's what it means!"

"It means that you are not a modest girl!" cried Rosalind. "Pray, does your mother know of your intrigue? does Bernard?"

"My mother has approved my 'intrigue,' as you call it. Mr. Lloyd has asked for my hand, and mamma has given it. Would you have had him apply to you, dearest sister?"

Rosalind gave her companion a long look, full of passionate envy and sorrow. Then she dropped her lashes on her pale cheeks and turned away. Perdita felt that it had not been a pretty scene; but it was her sister's fault. However, the elder girl rapidly called back her pride, and turned herself about again. "You have my very best wishes," she said, with a low curtsey. "I wish you every happiness, and a very long life."

Perdita gave a bitter laugh. "Don't speak in that tone!" she cried. "I would rather you should curse me outright. Come, Rosy," she added, "he couldn't marry both of us."

"I wish you very great joy," Rosalind repeated, mechanically, sitting down to her glass again, "and a very long life, and plenty of children."

There was something in the sound of these words not at all to Perdita's taste. "Will you give me a year to live at least?" she said. "In a year I can have one little boy—or one little girl at least. If you will give me your brush again I will do your hair."

"Thank you," said Rosalind. "You had better go to mamma. It isn't becoming that a young lady with a promised husband should wait on a girl with none."

"Nay," said Perdita, good-humouredly, "I have Arthur to wait upon me. You need my service more than I need yours."

But her sister motioned her away, and she left the room. When she had gone poor Rosalind fell on her knees before her dressing-table, buried her head in her arms, and poured out a flood of tears and sobs. She felt very much the better for this effusion of sorrow. When her sister came back she insisted on helping her to dress—on her wearing her prettiest things. She forced upon her acceptance a bit of lace of her own, and declared that now that she was to be married she should do her best to appear worthy of her lover's choice. She discharged these offices in stern silence; but, such as they were, they had to do duty as an apology and an atonement; she never made any other.

Now that Lloyd was received by the family as an accepted suitor, nothing remained but to fix the wedding-day. It was appointed for the following April, and in the interval preparations were diligently made for the marriage. Lloyd, on his side, was busy with his commercial arrangements, and with establishing a correspondence with the great mercantile house to which he had attached himself in England. He was therefore not so frequent a visitor at Mrs. Wingrave's as during the months of his diffidence and irresolution, and poor Rosalind had less to suffer than she had feared from the sight of the mutual endearments of the young lovers. Touching his future sister-in-law Lloyd had a perfectly clear conscience. There had not been a particle of love-making between them, and he had not the slightest suspicion that he had dealt her a terrible blow. He was quite at his ease; life promised so well, both domestically and financially. The great revolt of the Colonies was not yet in the air, and that his connubial felicity should take a tragic turn it was absurd, it was blasphemous, to apprehend. Meanwhile, at Mrs. Wingrave's, there was a greater rustling of silks, a more rapid clicking of scissors and flying of needles, than ever. The good lady had determined that her daughter should carry from home the genteelest outfit that her money could buy or that the country could furnish. All the sage women in the Province were convened, and their united taste was brought to bear on Perdita's wardrobe. Rosalind's situation, at this moment, was assuredly not to be envied. The poor girl had an inordinate love of dress, and the very best taste in the world, as her sister perfectly well knew. Rosalind was tall, she was stately and sweeping, she was made to carry stiff brocade and masses of heavy lace, such as belong to the toilet of a rich man's wife. But Rosalind sat aloof, with her beautiful arms folded and her head averted, while her mother and sister and the venerable women aforesaid worried and wondered over their materials, oppressed by the multitude of their resources. One day there came in a beautiful piece of white silk, brocaded with heavenly blue and silver, sent by the bridegroom himself—it not being thought amiss in those days that the husband-elect should contribute to the bride's trousseau. Perdita could think of no form or fashion which would do sufficient honour to the splendour of the material.

"Blue's your colour, sister, more than mine," she said, with appealing eyes. "It's a pity it's not for you. You would know what to do with it."

Rosalind got up from her place and looked at the great shining fabric, as it lay spread over the back of a chair. Then she took it up in her hands and felt it—lovingly, as Perdita could see—and turned about toward the mirror with it. She let it roll down to her feet, and flung the other end over her shoulder, gathering it in about her waist with her white arm, which was bare to the elbow.

She threw back her head, and looked at her image, and a hanging tress of her auburn hair fell upon the gorgeous surface of the silk. It made a dazzling picture. The women standing about uttered a little "Look, look!" of admiration. "Yes, indeed," said Rosalind, quietly, "blue is my colour." But Perdita could see that her fancy had been stirred, and that she would now fall to work and solve all their silken riddles. And indeed she behaved very well, as Perdita, knowing her insatiable love of millinery, was quite ready to declare. Innumerable yards of lustrous silk and satin, of muslin, velvet and lace, passed through her cunning hands without a jealous word coming from her lips. Thanks to her industry, when the wedding-day came Perdita was prepared to espouse more of the vanities of life than any fluttering young bride who had yet received the sacramental blessing of a New England divine.

It had been arranged that the young couple should go out and spend the first days of their wedded life at the country-house of an English gentleman—a man of rank and a very kind friend to Arthur Lloyd. He was a bachelor; he declared he should be delighted to give up the place to the influence of Hymen. After the ceremony at church—it had been performed by an English clergyman—young Mrs. Lloyd hastened back to her mother's house to change her nuptial robes for a riding-dress. Rosalind helped her to effect the change, in the little homely room in which they had spent their undivided younger years. Perdita then hurried off to bid farewell to her mother, leaving Rosalind to follow. The parting was short; the horses were at the door, and Arthur was impatient to start. But Rosalind had not followed, and Perdita hastened back to her room, opening the door abruptly. Rosalind, as usual, was before the glass, but in a position which caused the other to stand still, amazed. She had dressed herself in Perdita's cast-off wedding veil and wreath, and on her neck she had hung the full string of pearls which the young girl had received from her husband as a wedding-gift. These things had been hastily laid aside, to await their possessor's disposal on her return from the country. Bedizened in this unnatural garb, Rosalind stood before the mirror, plunging a long look into its depths and reading heaven knows what audacious visions. Perdita was horrified. It was a hideous image of their old rivalry come to life again. She made a step toward her sister, as if to pull off the veil and the flowers. But catching her eyes in the glass, she stopped.

"Farewell, sweetheart," she said. "You might at least have waited till I had got out of the house!" And she hurried away from the room.

Mr. Lloyd had purchased in Boston a house which to the taste of those days appeared as elegant as it was commodious; and here he very soon established himself with his young wife. He was thus separated by a distance of twenty miles from the residence of his mother-in-law. Twenty miles, in that primitive era of roads and conveyances, were as serious a matter as a hundred at the present day, and Mrs. Wingrave saw but little of her daughter during the first twelvemonth of her marriage. She suffered in no small degree from Perdita's absence; and her affliction was not diminished by the fact that Rosalind had fallen into terribly low spirits and was not to be roused or cheered but by change of air and company. The real cause of the young lady's dejection the reader will not be slow to suspect. Mrs. Wingrave and her gossips, however, deemed her complaint a mere bodily ill, and doubted not that she would obtain relief from the remedy just mentioned. Her mother accordingly proposed, on her behalf, a visit to certain relatives on the paternal side, established in New York, who had long complained that they were able to see so little of their New England cousins. Rosalind was despatched to these good people, under a suitable escort, and remained with them for several months. In the interval her brother Bernard, who had begun the practice of the law, made up his mind to take a wife. Rosalind came home to the wedding, apparently cured of her heartache, with bright roses and lilies in her face and a proud smile on her lips. Arthur Lloyd came over from Boston to see his brother-in-law married, but without his wife, who was expecting very soon to present him with an heir. It was nearly a year since Rosalind had seen him. She was glad—she hardly knew why—that Perdita had stayed at home. Arthur looked happy, but he was more grave and important than before his marriage. She thought he looked "interesting"—for although the word, in its modern sense, was not then invented, we may be sure that the idea was. The truth is, he was simply anxious about his wife and her coming ordeal. Nevertheless, he by no means failed to observe Rosalind's beauty and splendour, and to note how she effaced the poor little bride. The allowance that Perdita had enjoyed for her dress had now been transferred to her sister, who turned it to wonderful account. On the morning after the wedding he had a lady's saddle put on the horse of the servant who had come with him from town, and went out with the young girl for a ride. It was a keen, clear morning in January; the ground was bare and hard, and the horses in good condition—to say nothing of Rosalind, who was charming in her hat and plume, and her dark blue riding coat, trimmed with fur. They rode all the morning, they lost their way, and were obliged to stop for dinner at a farmhouse. The early winter dusk had fallen when they got home. Mrs. Wingrave met them with a long face. A messenger had arrived at noon from Mrs. Lloyd; she was beginning to be ill, she desired her husband's immediate return. The young man, at the thought that he had lost several hours, and that by hard riding he might already have been with his wife, uttered a passionate oath. He barely consented to stop for a mouthful of supper, but mounted the messenger's horse and started off at a gallop.

He reached home at midnight. His wife had been delivered of a little girl. "Ah, why weren't you with me?" she said, as he came to her bedside.

"I was out of the house when the man came. I was with Rosalind," said Lloyd, innocently.

Mrs. Lloyd made a little moan, and turned away. But she continued to do very well, and for a week her improvement was uninterrupted. Finally, however, through some indiscretion in the way of diet or exposure, it was checked, and the poor lady grew rapidly worse. Lloyd was in despair. It very soon became evident that she was breathing her last. Mrs. Lloyd came to a sense of her approaching end, and declared that she was reconciled with death. On the third evening after the change took place she told her husband that she felt she should not get through the night. She dismissed her servants, and also requested her mother to withdraw—Mrs. Wingrave having arrived on the preceding day. She had had her infant placed on the bed beside her, and she lay on her side, with the child against her breast, holding her husband's hands. The night-lamp was hidden behind the heavy

curtains of the bed, but the room was illumined with a red glow
from the immense fire of logs on the hearth.

"It seems strange not to be warmed into life by such a fire as
that," the young woman said, feebly trying to smile. "If I had but
a little of it in my veins! But I have given all *my* fire to this little
spark of mortality." And she dropped her eyes on her child.
Then, raising them, she looked at her husband with a long, pene-
trating gaze. The last feeling which lingered in her heart was one
of suspicion. She had not recovered from the shock which Arthur
had given her by telling her that in the hour of her agony he had
been with Rosalind. She trusted her husband very nearly as well
as she loved him; but now that she was called away forever she felt
a cold horror of her sister. She felt in her soul that Rosalind had
never ceased to be jealous of her good fortune; and a year of
happy security had not effaced the young girl's image, dressed in
her wedding-garments, and smiling with simulated triumph. Now
that Arthur was to be alone, what might not Rosalind attempt?
She was beautiful, she was engaging; what arts might she not use,
what impression might she not make upon the young man's sad-
dened heart? Mrs. Lloyd looked at her husband in silence. It
seemed hard, after all, to doubt of his constancy. His fine eyes
were filled with tears; his face was convulsed with weeping; the
clasp of his hands was warm and passionate. How noble he
looked, how tender, how faithful and devoted! "Nay," thought
Perdita, "he's not for such a one as Rosalind. He'll never forget
me. Nor does Rosalind truly care for him; she cares only for
vanities and finery and jewels." And she lowered her eyes on her
white hands, which her husband's liberality had covered with
rings, and on the lace ruffles which trimmed the edge of her
nightdress. "She covets my rings and my laces more than she
covets my husband."

At this moment, the thought of her sister's rapacity seemed to
cast a dark shadow between her and the helpless figure of her
little girl. "Arthur," she said, "you must take off my rings. I shall
not be buried in them. One of these days my daughter shall wear
them—my rings and my laces and silks. I had them all brought
out and shown me today. It's a great wardrobe—there's not such
another in the Province; I can say it without vanity, now that I
have done with it. It will be a great inheritance for my daughter

when she grows into a young woman. There are things there that
a man never buys twice, and if they are lost you will never again
see the like. So you will watch them well. Some dozen things I
have left to Rosalind; I have named them to my mother. I have
given her that blue and silver; it was meant for her; I wore it only
once, I looked ill in it. But the rest are to be sacredly kept for this
little innocent. It's such a providence that she should be my
colour; she can wear my gowns; she has her mother's eyes. You
know the same fashions come back every twenty years. She can
wear my gowns as they are. They will lie there quietly waiting till
she grows into them—wrapped in camphor and rose-leaves, and
keeping their colours in the sweet-scented darkness. She shall
have black hair, she shall wear my carnation satin. Do you promise me, Arthur?"

"Promise you what, dearest?"

"Promise me to keep your poor little wife's old gowns."

"Are you afraid I shall sell them?"

"No, but that they may get scattered. My mother will have them
properly wrapped up, and you shall lay them away under a
double-lock. Do you know the great chest in the attic, with the
iron bands? There is no end to what it will hold. You can put them
all there. My mother and the housekeeper will do it, and give you
the key. And you will keep the key in your secretary, and never
give it to any one but your child. Do you promise me?"

"Ah, yes, I promise you," said Lloyd, puzzled at the intensity
with which his wife appeared to cling to this idea.

"Will you swear?" repeated Perdita.

"Yes, I swear."

"Well—I trust you—I trust you," said the poor lady, looking
into his eyes with eyes in which, if he had suspected her vague
apprehensions, he might have read an appeal quite as much as an
assurance.

Lloyd bore his bereavement rationally and manfully. A month
after his wife's death, in the course of business, circumstances
arose which offered him an opportunity of going to England. He
took advantage of it, to change the current of his thoughts. He
was absent nearly a year, during which his little girl was tenderly
nursed and guarded by her grandmother. On his return he had
his house again thrown open, and announced his intention of

keeping the same state as during his wife's lifetime. It very soon came to be predicted that he would marry again, and there were at least a dozen young women of whom one may say that it was by no fault of theirs that, for six months after his return, the prediction did not come true. During this interval, he still left his little daughter in Mrs. Wingrave's hands, the latter assuring him that a change of residence at so tender an age would be full of danger for her health. Finally, however, he declared that his heart longed for his daughter's presence and that she must be brought up to town. He sent his coach and his housekeeper to fetch her home. Mrs. Wingrave was in terror lest something should befall her on the road; and, in accordance with this feeling, Rosalind offered to accompany her. She could return the next day. So she went up to town with her little niece, and Mr. Lloyd met her on the threshold of his house, overcome with her kindness and with paternal joy. Instead of returning the next day, Rosalind stayed out the week; and when at last she reappeared, she had only come for her clothes. Arthur would not hear of her coming home, nor would the baby. That little person cried and choked if Rosalind left her; and at the sight of her grief Arthur lost his wits, and swore that she was going to die. In fine, nothing would suit them but that the aunt should remain until the little niece had grown used to strange faces.

It took two months to bring this consummation about; for it was not until this period had elapsed that Rosalind took leave of her brother-in-law. Mrs. Wingrave had shaken her head over her daughter's absence; she had declared that it was not becoming, that it was the talk of the whole country. She had reconciled herself to it only because, during the girl's visit, the household enjoyed an unwonted term of peace. Bernard Wingrave had brought his wife home to live, between whom and her sister-in-law there was little love as you please. Rosalind was perhaps no angel; but in the daily practice of life she was a sufficiently good-natured girl, and if she quarrelled with Mrs. Bernard, it was not without provocation. Quarrel, however, she did, to the great annoyance not only of her antagonist, but of the two spectators of these constant altercations. Her stay in the household of her brother-in-law, therefore, would have been delightful, if only because it removed her from contact with the object of her antip-

athy at home. It was doubly—it was ten times—delightful, in that
it kept her near the object of her early passion. Mrs. Lloyd's sharp
suspicions had fallen very far short of the truth. Rosalind's sentiment had been a passion at first, and a passion it remained—a
passion of whose radiant heat, tempered to the delicate state of
his feelings, Mr. Lloyd very soon felt the influence. Lloyd, as I
have hinted, was not a modern Petrarch; it was not in his nature
to practice an ideal constancy. He had not been many days in the
house with his sister-in-law before he began to assure himself that
she was, in the language of that day, a devilish fine woman.
Whether Rosalind really practised those insidious arts that her
sister had been tempted to impute to her it is needless to inquire.
It is enough to say that she found means to appear to the very
best advantage. She used to seat herself every morning before the
big fireplace in the dining room, at work upon a piece of tapestry,
with her little niece disporting herself on the carpet at her feet, or
on the train of her dress, and playing with her woollen balls.
Lloyd would have been a very stupid fellow if he had remained
insensible to the rich suggestions of this charming picture. He
was exceedingly fond of his little girl, and was never weary of
taking her in his arms and tossing her up and down, and making
her crow with delight. Very often, however, he would venture
upon greater liberties than the young lady was yet prepared to
allow, and then she would suddenly vociferate her displeasure.
Rosalind, at this, would drop her tapestry, and put out her handsome hands with the serious smile of the young girl whose virgin
fancy has revealed to her all a mother's healing arts. Lloyd would
give up the child, their eyes would meet, their hands would touch,
and Rosalind would extinguish the little girl's sobs upon the
snowy folds of the kerchief that crossed her bosom. Her dignity
was perfect, and nothing could be more discreet than the manner
in which she accepted her brother-in-law's hospitality. It may
almost be said, perhaps, that there was something harsh in her
reserve. Lloyd had a provoking feeling that she was in the house
and yet was unapproachable. Half-an-hour after supper, at the
very outset of the long winter evenings, she would light her
candle, make the young man a most respectful curtsey, and
march off to bed. If these were arts, Rosalind was a great artist.
But their effect was so gentle, so gradual, they were calculated to

work upon the young widower's fancy with a *crescendo* so finely shaded, that, as the reader has seen, several weeks elapsed before Rosalind began to feel sure that her returns would cover her outlay. When this became morally certain, she packed up her trunk and returned to her mother's house. For three days she waited; on the fourth Mr. Lloyd made his appearance—a respectful but pressing suitor. Rosalind heard him to the end, with great humility, and accepted him with infinite modesty. It is hard to imagine that Mrs. Lloyd would have forgiven her husband; but if anything might have disarmed her resentment it would have been the ceremonious continence of this interview. Rosalind imposed upon her lover but a short probation. They were married, as was becoming, with great privacy—almost with secrecy—in the hope perhaps, as was waggishly remarked at the time, that the late Mrs. Lloyd wouldn't hear of it.

The marriage was to all appearance a happy one, and each party obtained what each had desired—Lloyd "a devilish fine woman," and Rosalind—but Rosalind's desires, as the reader will have observed, had remained a good deal of a mystery. There were, indeed, two blots upon their felicity, but time would perhaps efface them. During the first three years of her marriage Mrs. Lloyd failed to become a mother, and her husband on his side suffered heavy losses of money. This latter circumstance compelled a material retrenchment in his expenditure, and Rosalind was perforce less of a fine lady than her sister had been. She contrived, however, to carry it like a woman of considerable fashion. She had long since ascertained that her sister's copious wardrobe had been sequestrated for the benefit of her daughter, and that it lay languishing in thankless gloom in the dusty attic. It was a revolting thought that these exquisite fabrics should await the good pleasure of a little girl who sat in a high chair and ate bread-and-milk with a wooden spoon. Rosalind had the good taste, however, to say nothing about the matter until several months had expired. Then, at last, she timidly broached it to her husband. Was it not a pity that so much finery should be lost?— for lost it would be, what with colours fading, and moths eating it up, and the change of fashions. But Lloyd gave her so abrupt and peremptory a refusal, that she saw, for the present, her attempt was vain. Six months went by, however, and brought with them new needs and new visions. Rosalind's thoughts hovered lovingly about her sister's relics. She went up and looked at the chest in which they lay imprisoned. There was a sullen defiance in its three great padlocks and its iron bands which only quickened her cupidity. There was something exasperating in its incorruptible immobility. It was like a grim and grizzled old household servant, who locks his jaws over a family secret. And then there was a look of capacity in its vast extent, and a sound as of dense fullness, when Rosalind knocked its side with the toe of her little shoe, which caused her to flush with baffled longing. "It's absurd," she cried; "it's improper, it's wicked"; and she forthwith resolved upon another attack upon her husband. On the following day, after dinner, when he had had his wine, she boldly began it. But he cut her short with great sternness.

"Once for all, Rosalind," said he, "it's out of the question. I shall be gravely displeased if you return to the matter."

"Very good," said Rosalind. "I am glad to learn the esteem in which I am held. Gracious heaven," she cried, "I am a very happy woman! It's an agreeable thing to feel one's self sacrificed to a caprice!" And her eyes filled with tears of anger and disappointment.

Lloyd had a good-natured man's horror of a woman's sobs, and he attempted—I may say he condescended—to explain. "It's not a caprice, dear, it's a promise," he said—"an oath."

"An oath? It's a pretty matter for oaths! and to whom, pray?"

"To Perdita," said the young man, raising his eyes for an instant, but immediately dropping them.

"Perdita—ah, Perdita!" and Rosalind's tears broke forth. Her bosom heaved with stormy sobs—sobs which were the long-deferred sequel of the violent fit of weeping in which she had indulged herself on the night when she discovered her sister's betrothal. She had hoped, in her better moments, that she had done with her jealousy; but her temper, on that occasion, had taken an ineffaceable fold. "And pray, what right had Perdita to dispose of my future?" she cried. "What right had she to bind you to meanness and cruelty? Ah, I occupy a dignified place, and I make a very fine figure! I am welcome to what Perdita has left! And what has she left? I never knew till now how little! Nothing, nothing, nothing."

This was very poor logic, but it was very good as a "scene." Lloyd put his arm around his wife's waist and tried to kiss her, but she shook him off with magnificent scorn. Poor fellow! he had coveted a "devilish fine woman," and he had got one. Her scorn was intolerable. He walked away with his ears tingling—irresolute, distracted. Before him was his secretary, and in it the sacred key which with his own hand he had turned in the triple lock. He marched up and opened it and took the key from a secret drawer, wrapped in a little packet which he had sealed with his own honest bit of blazonry. *Je garde,* said the motto—"I keep." But he was ashamed to put it back. He flung it upon the table beside his wife.

"Put it back!" she cried. "I want it not. I hate it!"

"I wash my hands of it," cried her husband. "God forgive me!"

Mrs. Lloyd gave an indignant shrug of her shoulders, and swept out of the room, while the young man retreated by another door. Ten minutes later Mrs. Lloyd returned, and found the room occupied by her little step-daughter and the nursery-maid. The key was not on the table. She glanced at the child. Her little niece was perched on a chair, with the packet in her hands. She had broken the seal with her own small fingers. Mrs. Lloyd hastily took possession of the key.

At the habitual supper-hour, Arthur Lloyd came back from his counting-room. It was the month of June and supper was served by daylight. The meal was placed on the table, but Mrs. Lloyd failed to make her appearance. The servant whom his master sent to call her came back with the assurance that her room was empty, and that the women informed him that she had not been seen since dinner. They had, in truth, observed her to have been in tears, and, supposing her to be shut up in her chamber, had not disturbed her. Her husband called her name in various parts of the house, but without response. At last it occurred to him that he might find her by taking the way to the attic. The thought gave him a strange feeling of discomfort and he bade his servants remain behind, wishing no witness in his quest. He reached the foot of the staircase leading to the topmost flat and stood with his hand on the banisters, pronouncing his wife's name. His voice trembled. He called again louder and more firmly. The only sound which disturbed the absolute silence was a faint echo of his

own tones, repeating his question under the great eaves. He
nevertheless felt irresistibly moved to ascend the staircase. It
opened upon a wide hall, lined with wooden closets, and termi-
nating in a window which looked westward, and admitted the last
rays of the sun. Before the window stood the great chest. Before
the chest, on her knees, the young man saw with amazement and
horror the figure of his wife. In an instant he crossed the interval
between them, bereft of utterance. The lid of the chest stood
open, exposing, amid their perfumed napkins, its treasure of
stuffs and jewels. Rosalind had fallen backward from a kneeling
posture, with one hand supporting her on the floor and the other
pressed to her heart. On her limbs was the stiffness of death, and
on her face, in the fading light of the sun, the terror of something
more than death. Her lips were parted in entreaty, in dismay, in
agony; and on her blanched brow and cheeks there glowed the
marks of ten hideous wounds from two vengeful ghostly hands.

DONALD A. WOLLHEIM

Bones

Modern does not always mean new. New York author-editor-publisher
DONALD A. WOLLHEIM *appropriately sets "Bones" in a decaying neigh-*
borhood of Boston, where one visitor from Vermont flees in horror from
nocturnal goings-on at the Museum of Natural Sciences.

The Museum of Natural Sciences was not very far from the place
where he was staying, so Severus found himself striding briskly
through the dim, winding streets that night. He had come to
Boston on a visit, renewed acquaintances with learned men with
whom he had exchanged knowledge in years past; thus the letter
he had received in this morning's mail inviting him to a private
demonstration this night.

It was not a pleasant walk; already he was beginning to regret
not having taken some other means of transportation. The buildings were old and loomed darkly over the narrow streets. Lights
were few; for the most part, they came from flickering, dust-
encrusted lamp posts of last century's design. Large moths and
other nocturnal insects fluttered over their surfaces, added their
moving shadows to the air of desolation which hung about these
ways.

The moon was behind clouds that had streaked across the
autumn skies all day and now blocked out the stars. The night

about him was warm with that touch of unexpected chill which comes in autumn. Severus shuddered more than once as a wandering breeze slithered across his face unexpectedly around some dreary corner. He increased his pace, looked more suspiciously about him.

Boston, the oldest section of the city. Antique brick buildings dating back to the Revolution, some much farther. Dwelling places of the best families of two centuries ago. Now steadily advancing progress and life had left them derelict as upon deserted shores. Old, three- or four-story structures, narrow tottering dirty red-bricked houses with yawning black windows that now looked out through filth-encrusted panes upon streets and byways that served to shelter only the poorest and most alien section of the city's people. Forgotten, the district imparted its despair and overhanging doom to the man who walked its ways that night.

Half conquered by the smell of the antique houses, the subtle vibrations of past generations still pervading his spirit, Severus came at last out of the narrow streets into the open square where stood the museum.

The change surprised him. Here all was open. The dark, cloud-streaked sky loomed down overhead with a closeness that appalled him for a moment. The white marble façade of the structure glistened oddly in his view. It stood out, the cleanliness of it, as something exceedingly out of place, as something too new, too recent to have any right here. Its neo-Grecian designs were horribly modern and crude for the eighteenth-century blocks that surrounded it.

He walked swiftly across the open square, up the wide stone steps to the entrance of the building. Quickly he thrust open the small side door, hurried through as if to escape the thoughts of forgotten streets outside.

How futile such hopes in a museum! He realized that the instant the door was closed. He stood in a dark hall, lit dimly by one bulb above the entrance, another one at the opposite end of the main passage. And at once his nostrils were assailed by the inescapable odor of all such institutions—age!

The musty air rushed over his body, took him into its folds.

The silence assailed his ears with a suddenness that all but took his breath away. He looked about, trying to catch his bearings. Then he ventured a step, walked rapidly across the large chamber, down a wide corridor opening off it. Not a glance did he cast from side to side. The looming shadows of indescribable things were enough for him. His imagination supplied the rest. Unavoidable glimpses of shadowy sarcophagi and grotesquely carven idols sent great cold chills thrilling down his spine.

Up a narrow staircase, a turn to the right. At last he was at the room set aside for the night's demonstration. He stood a moment trying to catch his breath and regain composure. Then he pushed the door open, stepped inside.

A bare room with scarcely any furnishings. About seven or eight other men were there. In low tones they greeted him, drew him over to their circle. All were standing; there were no chairs in the room. A couple of small instrument racks and the main object was all.

The room was dominated by a long, low table upon which rested a six-foot bundle of dull gray cloth like a giant cocoon. Severus stared at it a moment, then recognized it as an Egyptian mummy removed from its coffin case. It obviously awaited unwinding.

So this was what he'd been invited to, he thought, wishing he hadn't been so friendly to the Egyptologists attached to this particular museum.

Glancing around, Severus took note of the others present. He was surprised to recognize one as a medical doctor highly esteemed at a city hospital. The doctor indeed seemed to be one of the active participants in what was about to take place, for he wore a white smock that indicated action.

Bantling, the Egyptologist, held up a hand for silence.

"Most of you know what is about to take place tonight. Therefore I will merely outline it for your convenience and for the one or two who know nothing about it." He nodded to Severus and smiled.

"This object, as you have all surmised, is an Egyptian mummy. But it is, we hope, different from all other such mummies previously examined.

"According to our painstaking translation of the hieroglyphics of the sarcophagus whence this body came, this marks an attempt of the priesthood of the IVth Dynasty to send one of their number alive into the lands to come. The unique part of it, and that which occupies us tonight, is that this priest did not die, nor was his body in any way mutilated. Instead, according to the inscriptions, he was fed and bathed in certain compounds that would suspend, indefinitely, the actions of his body cells. He was then put to sleep and prepared for a slumber very like death, yet not true death. In this state he could remain for years, yet still be reawakened to walk again, a living man.

"In brief, and using modern terminology, these people of what we call ancient times, claim to have solved the secret of suspended animation. Whether or not they did is for us now to determine."

Severus felt himself grow cold as this knowledge penetrated his being. The past had indeed reached out to the present. He would witness this night the end of an experiment started thousands of years before. Perhaps he himself would yet speak to and hear speak an inhabitant of this lost age. Egypt, buried these hundreds of centuries, Egypt aged beyond belief—yet, a man of that time-lost empire lay here in this very room, in the North American city of Boston.

"3700 B.C." he heard someone remark in answer to an unheard question.

Severus raised his eyes from the object on the table, let his gaze fall upon the window and what was revealed through it. Some of the clouds had cleared away and the cold, bright stars shone through. Far-off flickering spots of light that must surely have shown upon Ancient Egypt as coldly. The very light just passing through his cornea may have originated in the time when this thing upon the table was about to be plunged into Life-in-Death.

Far off, the dull clanging of a church bell drifted into the room. "Buck up, old man." A hand patted Severus' shoulder as an acquaintance came over to him. "It isn't as bad as it looks. Why that fellow will be as hale as any of us before the night is out. You'll think he's just a new immigrant."

Bantling and an assistant were even now engaged in unwrapping the mummy. Rolls and rolls of old, crumbling cloth were carefully being unwound from the figure on the table. Dust of death and ages now filled the air. Several coughs were heard; the door was opened on the dark passage outside to let the air change.

A gasp as at last the windings fell away. The body now lay entirely uncovered. Quickly, quietly, the wrappings were gathered together and piled in a receptacle while all crowded about to observe the Egyptian.

All in all, it was in a fine state of preservation. The skin was not brownish; it had not hardened. The arms and legs were still movable, had never stiffened in rigor mortis. Bantling seemed much pleased.

With horror Severus noted the several grayish-blue patches on parts of the face and body which he recognized without asking as a kind of mold.

Dr. Zweig, the physician, bent over and carefully scraped off the fungoid growths. They left nasty reddish pitted scars in the body that made Severus feel sick. He wanted to rush out of the room, out of the building into the clean night air. But the fascination of the horrible kept his glance fixed in hypnosis on the gruesome object before him.

"We are ready," Dr. Zweig said in a low voice.

They began to bathe the body with a sharp-smelling antiseptic, taking off all remaining traces of the preservatives used.

"Remarkable how perfect this thing is," breathed the physician. "Remarkable!"

Now at last the way was open for the work of revival. Large electric pads were brought out, laid all over the body, face and legs. Current was switched into them; the body surface was slowly brought up to normal warmth.

Then arteries and veins were opened, tubes clamped to them running from apparatus under the table. Severus understood that warm artificial blood was being pumped into the body to warm up the internal organs and open up the flow of blood again.

Shortly Dr. Zweig announced himself ready to attempt the final work toward actually bringing the now pliant and vibrant corpse to life. Already the body seemed like that of a living man, the flush of red tingling its skin and cheeks. Severus was in a cold sweat.

"Blood flows again through his veins and arteries," whispered the Egyptologist. "It is time to turn off the mechanical heart and attempt to revive his own."

A needle was plunged into the chest, a substance injected into the dormant, thousands-of-years-old cardiac apparatus of the body. Adrenaline, Severus assumed.

Over the mouth and nostrils of the former mummy a bellows was placed, air forced into the lungs at regular periods. For a while there was no result. Severus began fervently to hope that there would be no result. The air was supercharged with tension, horror mixed with scientific zeal. Through the chamber, the wheeze of the bellows was the only sound.

"Look!"

Someone cried out the word, electrifying all in the room of resurrection. A hand pointed shakily at the chest of the thing on the table. There was more action now; the chest rose and fell more vigorously. Quietly the doctor reached over and pulled away the face mask and stopped the pumps.

And the chest of the Egyptian still moved, up and down in a ghastly rhythm of its own. Now to their ears became noticeable an odd sound, a rattling soft wheezing sound as of air being sucked in and out of a sleeping man.

"He breathes." The doctor reached out and laid a finger on the body's wrists. "The heart beats."

"He lives again!"

Their eyes stared at what had been done. There, on the table, lay a man, a light-brown-skinned, sharp-Semitic-featured man, appearing to be in early middle age. He lay there as one quietly asleep.

"Who will waken him?" whispered Severus above the pounding of his heart.

"He will awaken soon," was the answer. "He will rise and walk as if nothing had happened."

Severus shook his head, disbelievingly. Then . . .

The Egyptian moved. His hand shook slightly; the eyes opened with a jerk.

Spellbound they stood, the eyes of the Americans fixed upon

the eyes of the Ancient. In shocked silence they watched one another.

The Egyptian sat up slowly, as if painfully. His features moved not a bit; his body moved slowly and jerkily.

The Ancient's eyes roved over the assembly. They caught Severus full in the face. For an instant they gazed at one another, the Vermont man looking into pain-swept ages, into grim depths of agony and sorrow, into the aeons of Past Time itself.

The Egyptian suddenly wrinkled up his features, swept up an arm and opened his mouth to speak.

And Severus fled from the room in frightful terror, the others closely following. Behind them rang out a terrible, hoarse bellow, cut off by a gurgling which they barely heard. The entire company, to a man, fought each other like terrified animals, each struggling to be the first out of that museum, out the doors into the black streets and away.

For there are parts of the human body which, never having been alive, cannot be preserved in suspended life. They are the bones, the teeth—strong in death, but unable to defy the crushing millennia.

And when the Egyptian had moved his body and opened his mouth to speak, his face had fallen in like termite-infested wood, the splinters of fragile, age-crumbled bones tearing through the flesh. His whole body had shaken, and, with the swing of the arm, smashed itself into a shapeless mass of heaving flesh and blood through which projected innumerable jagged fragments of dark gray, pitted bones.

MARY E. WILKINS FREEMAN

The Vacant Lot

In the preceding story, a Vermonter had an unpleasant time of it in Boston, but not half so bad as the Townsend family, who left their old home in Vermont to move in next door to "The Vacant Lot." Though no Townsend Center exists, the Rand McNally Road Atlas *shows a Thetford Center not too far from Barre, Vermont; one wonders whether it ever had a tavern similar to the Blue Leopard mentioned in the following tale by* MARY E. WILKINS FREEMAN *(1852–1930), a lifelong New England resident who at one time is said to have served as secretary to Oliver Wendell Holmes.*

When it became generally known in Townsend Center that the Townsends were going to move to the city, there was great excitement and dismay. For the Townsends to move was about equivalent to the town's moving. The Townsend ancestors had founded the village a hundred years ago. The first Townsend had kept a wayside hostelry for man and beast, known as the "Sign of the Leopard." The signboard, on which the leopard was painted a bright blue, was still extant, and prominently so, being nailed over the present Townsend's front door. This Townsend, by name David, kept the village store. There had been no tavern since the railroad was built through Townsend Center in his father's day. Therefore the family, being ousted by the march of progress from their chosen employment, took up with a general

country store as being the next thing to a country tavern, the principal difference consisting in the fact that all the guests were transients, never requiring bedchambers, securing their rest on the tops of sugar and flour barrels and codfish boxes, and their refreshment from stray nibblings at the stock in trade, to the profitless deplenishment of raisins and loaf sugar and crackers and cheese.

The flitting of the Townsends from the home of their ancestors was due to a sudden access of wealth from the death of a relative and the desire of Mrs. Townsend to secure better advantages for her son George, sixteen years old, in the way of education, and for her daughter Adrianna, ten years older, better matrimonial opportunities. However, this last inducement for leaving Townsend Center was not openly stated, only ingeniously surmised by the neighbors.

"Sarah Townsend don't think there's anybody in Townsend Center fit for her Adrianna to marry, and so she's goin' to take her to Boston to see if she can't pick up somebody there," they said. Then they wondered what Abel Lyons would do. He had been a humble suitor for Adrianna for years, but her mother had not approved, and Adrianna, who was dutiful, had repulsed him delicately and rather sadly. He was the only lover whom she had ever had, and she felt sorry and grateful; she was a plain, awkward girl, and had a patient recognition of the fact.

But her mother was ambitious, more so than her father, who was rather pugnaciously satisfied with what he had, and not easily disposed to change. However, he yielded to his wife and consented to sell out his business and purchase a house in Boston and move there.

David Townsend was curiously unlike the line of ancestors from whom he had come. He had either retrograded or advanced, as one might look at it. His moral character was certainly better, but he had not the fiery spirit and eager grasp at advantage which had distinguished them. Indeed, the old Townsends, though prominent and respected as men of property and influence, had reputations not above suspicion. There was more than one dark whisper regarding them handed down from mother to son in the village, and especially was this true of the first Townsend, he who built the tavern bearing the Sign of the Blue Leop-

ard. His portrait, a hideous effort of contemporary art, hung in the garret of David Townsend's home. There was many a tale of wild roistering, if no worse, in that old roadhouse, and high stakes, and quarreling in cups, and blows, and money gotten in evil fashion, and the matter hushed up with a high hand for inquirers by the imperious Townsends who terrorized everybody.

David Townsend terrorized nobody. He had gotten his little competence from his store by honest methods—the exchanging of sterling goods and true weights for country produce and country shillings. He was sober and reliable, with intense self-respect and a decided talent for the management of money. It was principally for this reason that he took great delight in his sudden wealth by legacy. He had thereby greater opportunities for the exercise of his native shrewdness in a bargain. This he evinced in his purchase of a house in Boston.

One day in spring the old Townsend house was shut up, the Blue Leopard was taken carefully down from his lair over the front door, the family chattels were loaded on the train, and the Townsends departed. It was a sad eventful day for Townsend Center. A man from Barre had rented the store—David had decided at the last not to sell—and the old familiars congregated in melancholy fashion and talked over the situation. An enormous pride over their departed townsman became evident. They paraded him, flaunting him like a banner in the eyes of the new man.

"David is awful smart," they said; "there won't nobody get the better of him in the city if he has lived in Townsend Center all his life. He's got his eyes open. Know what he paid for his house on Boston? Well, sir, that house cost twenty-five thousand dollars, and David he bought it for five. Yes, sir, he did."

"Must have been some out about it," remarked the new man, scowling over his counter. He was beginning to feel his disparaging situation.

"Not an out, sir. David he made sure on't. Catch him gettin' bit. Everythin' was in apple-pie order, hot an' cold water and all, and in one of the best locations of the city—real high-up street. David he said the rent in that street was never under a thousand. Yes,

sir, David he got a bargain—five thousand dollars for a twenty-five-thousand-dollar house."

"Some out about it!" growled the new man over the counter.

However, as his fellow townsmen and allies stated, there seemed to be no doubt about the desirableness of the city house which David Townsend had purchased and the fact that he had secured it for an absurdly low price. The whole family were at first suspicious. It was ascertained that the house had cost a round sum only a few years ago; it was in perfect repair; nothing whatever was amiss with plumbing, furnace, anything. There was not even a soap factory within smelling distance, as Mrs. Townsend had vaguely surmised. She was sure that she had heard of houses being undesirable for such reasons, but there was no soap factory. They all sniffed and peeked; when the first rainfall came they looked at the ceiling, confidently expecting to see dark spots where the leaks had commenced, but there were none. They were forced to confess that their suspicions were allayed, that the house was perfect, even overshadowed with the mystery of a lower price than it was worth. That, however, was an additional perfection in the opinion of the Townsends, who had their share of New England thrift.

They had lived just one month in their new house, and were happy, although at times somewhat lonely from missing the society of Townsend Center, when the trouble began. The Townsends, although they lived in a fine house in a genteel, almost fashionable, part of the city, were true to their antecedents and kept, as they had been accustomed, only one maid. She was the daughter of a farmer on the outskirts of their native village, was middle-aged, and had lived with them for the last ten years. One pleasant Monday morning she rose early and did the family washing before breakfast, which had been prepared by Mrs. Townsend and Adrianna, as was their habit on washing-days. The family was seated at the breakfast table in their basement dining-room, and this maid, whose name was Cordelia, was hanging out the clothes in the vacant lot. This vacant lot seemed a valuable one, being on a corner. It was rather singular that it had not been built upon. The Townsends had wondered at it and agreed that they would have preferred their own house to be there. They had, however, utilized it as far as possible with their innocent, rural disregard of property rights in unoccupied land.

"We might just as well hang out our washing in that vacant lot," Mrs. Townsend had told Cordelia the first Monday of their stay in the house. "Our little yard ain't half big enough for all our clothes, and it is sunnier there, too."

So Cordelia had hung out the wash there for four Mondays, and this was the fifth. The breakfast was about half finished—they had reached the buckwheat cakes—when this maid came rushing into the dining-room and stood regarding them, speechless, with a countenance indicative of the utmost horror. She was deadly pale. Her hands, sodden with soapsuds, hung twitching at her sides in the folds of her calico gown; her very hair, which was light and sparse, seemed to bristle with fear. All the Townsends turned and looked at her. David and George rose with a half-defined idea of burglars.

"Cordelia Battles, what is the matter?" cried Mrs. Townsend. Adrianna gasped for breath and turned as white as the maid. "What is the matter?" repeated Mrs. Townsend, but the maid was unable to speak. Mrs. Townsend, who could be peremptory, sprang up, ran to the frightened woman and shook her violently. "Cordelia Battles, you speak," said she, "and not stand there staring that way, as if you were struck dumb! What is the matter with you?"

Then Cordelia spoke in a fainting voice.

"There's—somebody else—hanging out clothes—in the vacant lot," she gasped, and clutched at a chair for support.

"Who?" cried Mrs. Townsend, rousing to indignation, for already she had assumed a proprietorship in the vacant lot. "Is it the folks in the next house? I'd like to know what right they have! We are next to that vacant lot."

"I—dunno—who it is," gasped Cordelia.

"Why, we've seen that girl next door go to mass every morning," said Mrs. Townsend. "She's got a fiery red head. Seems as if you might know her by this time, Cordelia."

"It ain't that girl," gasped Cordelia. Then she added in a horror-stricken voice, "I couldn't see who t'was."

They all stared.

"Why couldn't you see?" demanded her mistress. "Are you struck blind?"

"No, ma'am."

"Then why couldn't you see?"

"All I could see was . . ." Cordelia hesitated, with an expression of the utmost horror.

"Go on," said Mrs. Townsend, impatiently.

"All I could see was the shadow of somebody, very slim, hanging out the clothes, and . . ."

"What?"

"I could see the shadows of the things flappin' on their line."

"You couldn't see the clothes?"

"Only the shadow on the ground."

"What kind of clothes were they?"

"Queer," replied Cordelia, with a shudder.

"If I didn't know you so well, I should think you had been drinking," said Mrs. Townsend. "Now, Cordelia Battles, I'm going out in that vacant lot and see myself what you're talking about."

"I can't go," gasped the woman.

With that, Mrs. Townsend and all the others, except Adrianna, who remained to tremble with the maid, sallied forth into the vacant lot. They had to go out the area gate into the street to reach it. It was nothing unusual in the way of vacant lots. One large poplar tree, the relic of the old forest which had once flourished there, twinkled in one corner; for the rest, it was overgrown with coarse weeds and a few dusty flowers. The Townsends stood just inside the rude board fence which divided the lot from the street and stared with wonder and horror, for Cordelia had told the truth. They all saw what she had described—the shadow of an exceedingly slim woman moving along the ground with upstretched arms, the shadows of strange, nondescript garments flapping from a shadowy line, but when they looked up for the substance of the shadows nothing was to be seen except the clear, blue October air.

"My goodness!" gasped Mrs. Townsend. Her face assumed a strange gathering of wrath in the midst of her terror. Suddenly

she made a determined move forward, although her husband
strove to hold her back.

"You let me be," said she. She moved forward. Then she recoiled and gave a loud shriek. "The wet sheet flapped in my
face," she cried. "Take me away, take me away!" Then she
fainted. Between them they got her back to the house. "It was
awful," she moaned when she came to herself, with the family all
around her where she lay on the dining-room floor. "Oh, David,
what do you suppose it is?"

"Nothing at all," replied David Townsend stoutly. He was remarkable for courage and staunch belief in actualities. He was
now denying to himself that he had seen anything unusual.

"Oh, there was," moaned his wife.

"I saw something," said George, in a sullen, boyish bass.

The maid sobbed convulsively and so did Adrianna for sympathy.

"We won't talk any about it," said David. "Here, Jane, you
drink this hot tea—it will do you good; and Cordelia, you hang
out the clothes in our own yard. George, you go and put up the
line for her."

"The line is out there," said George, with a jerk of his shoulder.

"Are you afraid?"

"No, I ain't," replied the boy resentfully, and went out with a
pale face.

After that Cordelia hung the Townsend wash in the yard of
their own house, standing always with her back to the vacant lot.
As for David Townsend, he spent a good deal of his time in the lot
watching the shadows, but he came to no explanation, although
he strove to satisfy himself with many.

"I guess the shadows come from the smoke from our chimneys,
or else the poplar tree," he said.

"Why do the shadows come on Monday mornings, and no
other?" demanded his wife.

David was silent.

Very soon new mysteries arose. One day Cordelia rang the
dinner-bell at their usual dinner hour, the same as in Townsend
Center, high noon, and the family assembled. With amazement
Adrianna looked at the dishes on the table.

"Why, that's queer!" she said.

"What's queer?" asked her mother.

Cordelia stopped short as she was about setting a tumbler of water beside a plate, and the water slopped over.

"Why," said Adrianna, her face paling, "I—thought there was boiled dinner. I—smelt cabbage cooking."

"I knew there would be something else come up," gasped Cordelia, leaning hard on the back of Adrianna's chair.

"What do you mean?" asked Mrs. Townsend sharply, but her own face began to assume the shocked pallor which it was so easy nowadays for all their faces to assume at the merest suggestion of anything out of the common.

"I smelt cabbage cooking all the morning up in my room," Adrianna said faintly, "and here's codfish and potatoes for dinner."

The Townsends all looked at one another. David rose with an exclamation and rushed out of the room. The others waited tremblingly. When he came back his face was lowering.

"What did you . . ." Mrs. Townsend asked hesitatingly.

"There's some smell of cabbage out there," he admitted reluctantly. Then he looked at her with a challenge. "It comes from the next house," he said. "Blows over our house."

"Our house is higher."

"I don't care; you can never account for such things."

"Cordelia," said Mrs. Townsend, "you go over to the next house and you ask if they've got cabbage for dinner."

Cordelia switched out of the room, her mouth set hard. She came back promptly.

"Says they never have cabbage," she announced with gloomy triumph and a conclusive glance at Mr. Townsend. "Their girl was real sassy."

"Oh, father, let's move away; let's sell the house," cried Adrianna in a panic-stricken tone.

"If you think I'm going to sell a house that I got as cheap as this one because we smell cabbage in a vacant lot, you're mistaken," replied David firmly.

"It isn't the cabbage alone," said Mrs. Townsend.

"And a few shadows," added David. "I am tired of such nonsense. I thought you had more sense, Jane."

"One of the boys at school asked me if we lived in the house next to the vacant lot on Wells Street and whistled when I said 'Yes,' " remarked George.

"Let him whistle," said Mr. Townsend.

After a few hours the family, stimulated by Mr. Townsend's calm, common sense, agreed that it was exceedingly foolish to be disturbed by a mysterious odor of cabbage. They even laughed at themselves.

"I suppose we have got so nervous over those shadows hanging out clothes that we notice every little thing," conceded Mrs. Townsend.

"You will find out some day that that is no more to be regarded than the cabbage," said her husband.

"You can't account for that wet sheet hitting my face," said Mrs. Townsend, doubtfully.

"You imagined it."

"I *felt* it."

That afternoon, things went on as usual in the household until nearly four o'clock. Adrianna went downtown to do some shopping. Mrs. Townsend sat sewing beside the bay window in her room, which was a front one in the third story. George had not got home. Mr. Townsend was writing a letter in the library. Cordelia was busy in the basement; the twilight, which was coming earlier and earlier every night, was beginning to gather, when suddenly there was a loud crash which shook the house from its foundations. Even the dishes on the sideboard rattled, and the glasses rang like bells. The pictures on the walls of Mrs. Townsend's room swung out from the walls. But that was not all: every looking-glass in the house cracked simultaneously—as nearly as they could judge—from top to bottom, then shivered into fragments over the floors.

Mrs. Townsend was too frightened to scream. She sat huddled in her chair, gasping for breath, her eyes, rolling from side to side in incredulous terror, turned toward the street. She saw a great black group of people crossing it just in front of the vacant lot. There was something inexpressibly strange and gloomy about this moving group; there was an effect of sweeping, wavings and foldings of sable draperies and gleams of deadly white faces; then they passed. She twisted her head to see, and they disappeared in the vacant lot. Mr. Townsend came hurrying into the room; he was pale, and looked at once angry and alarmed.

"Did you fall?" he asked inconsequently, as if his wife, who was small, could have produced such a manifestation by a fall.

"Oh, David, what is it?" whispered Mrs. Townsend.

"Darned if I know!" said David.

"Don't swear. It's too awful. Oh, see the looking-glass, David!"

"I see it. The one over the library mantel is broken, too."

"Oh, it is a sign of death!"

Cordelia's feet were heard as she staggered on the stairs. She almost fell into the room. She reeled over to Mr. Townsend and clutched his arm. He cast a sidewise glance, half furious, half commiserating at her.

"Well, what is it all about?" he asked.

"I don't know. What is it? Oh, what is it? The looking-glass in the kitchen is broken. All over the floor. Oh, oh! What is it?"

"I don't know any more than you do. I didn't do it."

"Lookin' glasses broken is a sign of death in the house," said Cordelia. "If it's me, I hope I'm ready; but I'd rather die than be so scared as I've been lately."

Mr. Townsend shook himself loose and eyed the two trembling women with gathering resolution.

"Now, look here, both of you," he said. "This is nonsense. You'll die sure enough of fright if you keep on this way. I was a fool myself to be startled. Everything it is is an earthquake."

"Oh, David!" gasped his wife, not much reassured.

"It is nothing but an earthquake," persisted Mr. Townsend. "It acted just like that. Things always are broken on the walls, and the middle of the room isn't affected. I've read about it."

Suddenly Mrs. Townsend gave a loud shriek and pointed. "How do you account for that," she cried, "if it's an earthquake? Oh, oh, oh!"

She was on the verge of hysterics. Her husband held her firmly by the arm as his eyes followed the direction of her rigid pointing finger. Cordelia looked also, her eyes seeming converged to a bright point of fear. On the floor in front of the broken looking-glass lay a mass of black stuff in a gruesome long ridge.

"It's something you dropped there," almost shouted Mr. Townsend.

"It ain't. Oh!"

Mr. Townsend dropped his wife's arm and took one stride toward the object. It was a very long crepe veil. He lifted it, and it floated out from his arm as if imbued with electricity.

"It's yours," he said to his wife.

"Oh, David, I never had one. You know, oh, you know I— shouldn't—unless you died. How came it there?"

"I'm darned if I know," said David, regarding it. He was deadly pale, but still resentful rather than afraid.

"Don't hold it; don't!"

"I'd like to know what in thunder all this means?" said David. He gave the thing an angry toss and it fell on the floor in exactly the same long heap as before.

Cordelia began to weep with racking sobs. Mrs. Townsend reached out and caught her husband's hand, clutching it hard with ice-cold fingers.

"What's got into this house, anyhow?" he growled.

"You'll have to sell it. Oh, David, we can't live here."

"As for my selling a house I paid only five thousand for when it's worth twenty-five, for any such nonsense as this, I won't!"

David gave one stride toward the black veil, but it rose from the floor and moved away before him across the room at exactly the same height as if suspended from a woman's head. He pursued it, clutching vainly, all around the room, then he swung himself on his heel with an exclamation and the thing fell to the floor again in the long heap. Then were heard hurrying feet on the stairs and Adrianna burst into the room. She ran straight to her father and clutched his arm; she tried to speak, but she chattered unintelligibly; her face was blue. Her father shook her violently.

"Adrianna, do have more sense!" he cried.

"Oh, David, how can you talk so?" sobbed her mother.

"I can't help it. I'm mad!" said he with emphasis. "What has got into this house and you all, anyhow?"

"What is it, Adrianna, poor child," asked her mother. "Only look what has happened here."

"It's an earthquake," said her father staunchly; "nothing to be afraid of."

"How do you account for *that?*" said Mrs. Townsend in an awful voice, pointing to the veil.

Adrianna did not look—she was too engrossed with her own terrors. She began to speak in a breathless voice.

"I—was coming—by the vacant lot," she panted, "and—I—I had my new hat in a paper bag and—a parcel of blue ribbon, and —I saw a crowd, an awful—oh! a whole crowd of people with white faces, as if—they were dressed all in black."

"Where are they now?"

"I don't know. Oh!" Adrianna sank gasping feebly into a chair.

"Get her some water, David," sobbed her mother.

David rushed with an impatient exclamation out of the room and returned with a glass of water which he held to his daughter's lips.

"Here, drink this!" he said roughly.

"Oh, David, how can you speak so?" sobbed his wife.

"I can't help it. I'm mad clean through," said David.

Then there was a hard bound upstairs, and George entered. He was very white, but he grinned at them with an appearance of unconcern.

"Hullo!" he said in a shaking voice, which he tried to control. "What on earth's to pay in that vacant lot now?"

"Well, what is it?" demanded his father.

"Oh, nothing, only—well, there are lights over it exactly as if there was a house there, just about where the windows would be. It looked as if you could walk right in, but when you look close there are those old dried-up weeds rattling away on the ground the same as ever. I looked at it and couldn't believe my eyes. A woman saw it, too. She came along just as I did. She gave one look, then she screeched and ran. I waited for some one else, but nobody came."

Mr. Townsend rushed out of the room.

"I daresay it'll be gone when he gets there," began George, then he stared round the room. "What's to pay here?" he cried.

"Oh, George, the whole house shook all at once, and all the looking-glasses broke," wailed his mother, and Adrianna and Cordelia joined.

George whistled with pale lips. Then Mr. Townsend entered.

"Well," asked George, "see anything?"

"I don't want to talk," said his father. "I've stood just about enough."

"We've got to sell out and go back to Townsend Center," cried his wife in a wild voice.

"Oh, David, say you'll go back."

"I won't go back for any such nonsense as this, and sell a twenty-five-thousand-dollar house for five thousand," said he firmly.

But that very night his resolution was shaken. The whole family watched together in the dining-room. They were all afraid to go to bed—that is, all except possibly Mr. Townsend. Mrs. Townsend declared firmly that she for one would leave that awful house and go back to Townsend Center whether he came or not, unless they all stayed together and watched, and Mr. Townsend yielded. They chose the dining-room for the reason that it was nearer the street should they wish to make their egress hurriedly, and they took up their station around the dining-table on which Cordelia had placed a luncheon.

"It looks exactly as if we were watching with a corpse," she said in a horror-stricken whisper.

"Hold your tongue if you can't talk sense," said Mr. Townsend.

The dining-room was very large, finished in oak, with a dark blue paper above the wainscoting. The old sign of the tavern, the Blue Leopard, hung over the mantel shelf. Mr. Townsend had insisted on hanging it there. He had curious pride in it. The family sat together until after midnight and nothing unusual happened. Mrs. Townsend began to nod; Mr. Townsend read the paper ostentatiously. Adrianna and Cordelia stared with roving eyes about the room, then at each other as if comparing notes on terror. George had a book which he studied furtively. All at once Adrianna gave a startled exclamation and Cordelia echoed her. George whistled faintly. Mrs. Townsend awoke with a start and Mr. Townsend's paper rattled to the floor.

"Look!" gasped Adrianna.

The Townsends with one accord rose and huddled together in a far corner; they all held to each other and stared. The people, their faces gleaming with a whiteness of death, their black robes waving and folding, crossed the room. They were a trifle above mortal height, or seemed so to the terrified eyes which saw them. They reached the mantel-shelf where the signboard hung, then a black-draped long arm was seen to rise and make a motion, as if plying a knocker. Then the whole company passed out of sight, as if through the wall, and the room was as before.

Mrs. Townsend was shaking in a nervous chill, Adrianna was almost fainting, Cordelia was in hysterics. David Townsend stood in a curious way at the sign of the Blue Leopard. George stared at him with a look of horror. There was something in his father's face which made him forget everything else. At last he touched his arm timidly.

"Father," he whispered.

David turned and regarded him with a look of rage and fury, then his face cleared; he passed his hand over his forehead.

"Good Lord! What *did* come to me?" he muttered.

"You looked like that awful picture of old Tom Townsend in the garret in Townsend Center, Father," whimpered the boy, shuddering.

"Should I might look like 'most any old cuss after such darned work as this," growled David, but his face was white. "Go and pour out some hot tea for your mother," he ordered the boy sharply. He himself shook Cordelia violently. "Stop such actions!" he shouted in her ears, and shook her again. "Ain't done nothin' wrong, have ye?"

Then Cordelia quoted Scripture in a burst of sobs and slaughter.

"Behold, I was shapen in iniquity; and in sin did my mother conceive me," she cried out. "If I ain't done wrong, mebbe them that's come before me did, and when the Evil One and the Powers of Darkness is abroad I'm liable, I'm liable!" Then she laughed loud and long and shrill.

"If you don't hush up," said David, but still with that white terror and horror on his own face, "I'll bundle you out in that vacant lot whether or no. I mean it."

Then Cordelia was quiet, after one wild roll of her eyes to him. The color was returning to Adrianna's cheeks; her mother was drinking hot tea in spasmodic gulps.

"It's after midnight," she gasped, "and I don't believe they'll come again tonight. Do you, David?"

"No, I don't," said David conclusively.

"Oh, David, we mustn't stay another night in this awful house."

"We won't. Tomorrow we'll pack off bag and baggage to Townsend Center, if it takes all the fire department to move us," said David.

Adrianna smiled in the midst of her terror. She thought of Abel Lyons.

The next day Mr. Townsend went to the real estate agent who had sold him the house.

"It's no use," he said, "I can't stand it. Sell it for what you can get. I'll give it away rather than keep it."

Then he added a few strong words as to his opinion of parties who sold him such an establishment. But the agent pleaded innocent for the most part.

"I'll own I suspected something wrong when the owner, who pledged me to secrecy as to his name, told me to sell that place for what I could get, and did not limit me. I had never heard anything, but I began to suspect something was wrong. Then I made a few inquiries and found out that there was a rumor in the neighborhood that there was something out of the usual about that vacant lot. I had wondered myself why it wasn't built upon. There was a story about its being undertaken once, and the contract made, and the contractor dying; then another man took it and one of the workmen was killed on his way to dig the cellar, and the other struck. I didn't pay much attention to it. I never believed much in that sort of thing anyhow, and then, too, I couldn't find out there had ever been anything wrong about the house itself, except as to the people who lived there were said to have seen and heard queer things in the vacant lot, so I thought you might be able to get along, especially as you didn't look like a man who was timid, and the house was such a bargain as I never handled before. But this you tell me is beyond belief."

"Do you know the names of the people who formerly owned the vacant lot?" asked Mr. Townsend.

"I don't know for certain," replied the agent, "for the original owners flourished long before yours or my day, but I do know that the lot goes by the name of the old Gaston lot. What's the matter? Are you ill?"

"No; it's nothing," replied Mr. Townsend. "Get what you can for the house; perhaps another family might not be as troubled as we have been."

"I hope you are not going to leave the city?" said the agent, urbanely.

"I am going back to Townsend Center as fast as steam can carry me after we get packed up and out of that cursed house," replied Mr. David Townsend.

He did not tell the agent nor any of his family what had caused him to start when told the name of the former owners of the lot. He remembered all at once the story of a ghastly murder which had taken place in the Blue Leopard. The victim's name was Gaston and the murderer had never been discovered.

THE EAST

Massachusetts, birthplace of President John Adams, may claim itself the nursery of American freedom with some justification, but Pennsylvanians rightly style their commonwealth the cradle of liberty, and not only because the Declaration of Independence was signed in Philadelphia. When William Penn accepted "a tract of land in America, north of Maryland, west of the Delaware and northward as far as plantable" as settlement of a debt that Charles II of England owed the Penn family, Penn established the first stronghold of religious freedom in the New World. The Quaker colonists lived peacefully side by side in "Penn's Woods" with native Indians, as well as Dutch, English, Germans, Irish, Scots, Swedes, Swiss and Welsh settlers.

It is understandable, then, that the liberal spirit (sic) dominates the following mid-Atlantic-state ghost stories. Highborn spectres hobnob skull to skull with patriots, artists and ruffians—an immigrant breed that cast away its old allegiances to become the first true Americans.

THE EAST

MARK TWAIN

A Curious Dream
Containing a Moral

MARK TWAIN *(1835–1910), the pseudonymous Samuel Langhorne Clemens, was born in Florida and raised in Hannibal, Missouri. In his earlier years he apprenticed to a printer and for about five years worked as a pilot on the Mississippi River. Eventually Twain came east and did a stint as a newspaper publisher in Buffalo, New York, before penning his series of comic masterpieces that includes* The Adventures of Tom Sawyer, Huckleberry Finn, A Connecticut Yankee in King Arthur's Court *and many others. In 1869, shortly before marrying Olivia Langdon, Twain used a loan from his father-in-law to buy a share in the Buffalo* Express, *which he edited and contributed to for several years. "A Curious Dream," which appeared in the April 30 and May 7, 1870, issues of that newspaper, is indeed curious: partly editorial, partly social satire—an echo of that strain of mordant humor that characterizes Twain's later writings.*

Night before last I had a singular dream. I seemed to be sitting on a doorstep (in no particular city perhaps), ruminating, and the time of night appeared to be about twelve or one o'clock. The weather was balmy and delicious. There was no human sound in the air, not even a footstep. There was no sound of any kind to emphasize the dead stillness, except the occasional hollow barking of a dog in the distance and the fainter answer of a further dog. Presently up the street I heard a bony clack-clacking, and guessed it was the castanets of a serenading party. In a minute more a tall skeleton, hooded, and half-clad in a tattered and mouldy shroud, whose shreds were flapping about the ribby lattice-work of its person swung by me with a stately stride, and disappeared in the grey gloom of the starlight. It had a broken and worm-eaten coffin on its shoulder and a bundle of something in its hand. I knew what the clack-clacking was then; it was this party's joints working together, and his elbows knocking against his sides as he walked. I may say I was surprised. Before I could collect my thoughts and enter upon any speculations as to what this apparition might portend, I heard another one coming—for I recognized his clack-clack. He had two-thirds of a coffin on his shoulder, and some foot- and head-boards under his arm. I mightily wanted to peer under his hood and speak to him, but when he turned and smiled upon me with his cavernous sockets and his projecting grin as he went by, I thought I would not detain him. He was hardly gone when I heard the clacking again, and another one issued from the shadowy half-light. This one was bending under a heavy gravestone, and dragging a shabby coffin after him by a string. When he got to me he gave me a steady look for a moment or two, and then rounded to and backed up to me, saying:

"Ease this down for a fellow, will you?"

I eased the gravestone down till it rested on the ground, and in doing so noticed that it bore the name of "John Baxter Copmanhurst," with "May 1839," as the date of his death. Deceased sat wearily down by me, and wiped his os frontis with his major maxillary—chiefly from former habit I judged, for I could not see that he brought away any perspiration.

"It is too bad, too bad," said he, drawing the remnant of the shroud about him and leaning his jaw pensively on his hand. Then he put his left foot up on his knee and fell to scratching his ankle bone absently with a rusty nail which he got out of his coffin.

"What is too bad, friend?"

"Oh, everything, everything. I almost wish I never had died."

"You surprise me. Why do you say this? Has anything gone wrong? What is the matter?"

"Matter! Look at this shroud—rags. Look at this gravestone, all battered up. Look at that disgraceful old coffin. All a man's property going to ruin and destruction before his eyes, and ask him if anything is wrong? Fire and brimstone!"

"Calm yourself, calm yourself," I said. "It *is* too bad—it is certainly too bad, but then I had not supposed that you would much mind such matters, situated as you are."

"Well, my dear sir, I *do* mind them. My pride is hurt, and my comfort is impaired—destroyed, I might say. I will state my case—I will put it to you in such a way that you can comprehend it, if you will let me," said the poor skeleton, tilting the hood of his shroud back, as if he were clearing for action, and thus unconsciously giving himself a jaunty and festive air very much at variance with the grave character of his position in life—so to speak—and in prominent contrast with his distressful mood.

"Proceed," said I.

"I reside in the shameful old graveyard a block or two above you here, in this street—there, now, I just expected that cartilage would let go!—third rib from the bottom, friend, hitch the end of it to my spine with a string, if you have got such a thing about you, though a bit of silver wire is a deal pleasanter, and more durable and becoming, if one keeps it polished—to think of shredding out and going to pieces in this way, just on account of the indifference and neglect of one's posterity!"—and the poor ghost grated his teeth in a way that gave me a wrench and a shiver—for the effect is mightily increased by the absence of muffling flesh and cuticle. "I reside in that old graveyard, and have for these thirty years; and I tell you things are changed since I first laid this old tired frame there, and turned over, and stretched out for a long sleep, with a delicious sense upon me of being *done* with bother, and grief, and anxiety, and doubt, and fear, for ever and ever, and listening with comfortable and increasing satisfaction to the sexton's work, from the startling clatter of his first spadeful on my coffin till it dulled away to the faint patting that shaped the roof of my new home—delicious! My! I wish you could try it to-night!" and out of my reverie deceased fetched me with a rattling slap with a bony hand.

"Yes, sir, thirty years ago I laid me down there, and was happy. For it was out in the country, then—out in the breezy, flowery, grand old woods, and the lazy winds gossiped with the leaves, and the squirrels capered over us and around us, and the creeping things visited us, and the birds filled the tranquil solitude with music. Ah, it was worth ten years of a man's life to be dead then! Everything was pleasant. I was in a good neighborhood, for all the dead people that lived near me belonged to the best families in the city. Our posterity appeared to think the world of us. They kept our graves in the very best condition; the fences were always in faultless repair, head-boards were kept painted or whitewashed, and were replaced with new ones as soon as they began to look rusty or decayed; monuments were kept upright, railings intact and bright, the rosebushes and shrubbery trimmed, trained, and free from blemish, the walks clean and smooth and gravelled. But that day is gone by. Our descendants have forgotten us. My grandson lives in a stately house built with money made by these old hands of mine, and I sleep in a neglected grave with invading vermin that gnaw my shroud to build them nests withal! I and friends that lie with me founded and secured the prosperity of this fine city, and the stately bantling of our loves leaves us to rot in a dilapidated cemetery which neighbors curse and strangers scoff at. See the difference between the old time and this—for instance: Our graves are all caved in, now; our headboards have rotted away and tumbled down; our railings reel this way and that with one foot in the air, after a fashion of unseemly levity; our monuments lean wearily, and our gravestones bow their heads discouraged; there be no adornments any more—no roses, nor shrubs, nor gravelled walks, nor anything that is a comfort to the eye; and even the paintless old board fence that did make a show of holding us sacred from companionship with beasts and the defilement of heedless feet, has tottered till it overhangs the street, and only advertises the presence of our dismal resting-place and invites yet more derision to it. And now we cannot hide our poverty and tatters in the friendly woods, for the city has stretched its withering arms abroad and taken us in, and all that remains of the cheer of our old home is the cluster of lugubrious forest trees that stand, bored and weary of a city life, with their feet in our coffins, looking into the hazy distance and wishing they were there. I tell you it is disgraceful!

"You begin to comprehend—you begin to see how it is. While our descendants are living sumptuously on our money, right around us in the city, we have to fight hard to keep skull and bones together. Bless you, there isn't a grave in our cemetery that doesn't leak—not one. Every time it rains in the night we have to climb out and roost in the trees—and sometimes we are wakened suddenly by the chilly water trickling down the back of our necks. Then I tell you there is a general heaving up of old graves and kicking over of old monuments, and scampering of old skeletons for the trees! Bless me, if you had gone along there some such nights after twelve you might have seen as many as fifteen of us roosting on one limb, with our joints rattling drearily and the wind wheezing through our ribs! Many a time we have perched there for three or four dreary hours, and then come down, stiff and chilled through and drowsy, and borrowed each other's skulls to bale out our graves with—if you will glance up in my mouth, now as I tilt my head back, you can see that my head-piece is half full of old dry sediment—how top-heavy and stupid it makes me sometimes! Yes, sir, many a time if you had happened to come along just before the dawn you'd have caught us baling out the graves and hanging our shrouds on the fence to dry. Why, I had an elegant shroud stolen from there one morning—think a party by the name of Smith took it, that resides in a plebeian graveyard over yonder—I think so because the first time I ever saw him he hadn't anything on but a check-shirt, and the last time I saw him, which was at a social gathering in the new cemetery, he was the best dressed corpse in the company—and it is a significant fact that he left when he saw me; and presently an old woman from here missed her coffin—she generally took it with her when she went anywhere, because she was liable to take cold and bring on the spasmodic rheumatism that originally killed her if she exposed herself to the night air much. She was named Hotchkiss —Anna Matilda Hotchkiss—you might know her? She has two upper front teeth, is tall, but a good deal inclined to stoop, one rib on the left side gone, has one shred of rusty hair hanging from the left side of her head, and one little tuft just above and a little forward of her right ear, has her under jaw wired on one side where it had worked loose, small bone of left forearm gone—lost in a fight—has a kind of swagger in her gait and a 'gallus' way of going with her arms akimbo and her nostrils in the air—has been pretty free and easy, and is all damaged and battered up till she looks like a queensware crate in ruins—maybe you have met her?"

"God forbid!" I involuntarily ejaculated, for somehow I was not looking for that form of question, and it caught me a little off my guard. But I hastened to make amends for my rudeness, and say, "I simply meant I had not had the honor—for I would not deliberately speak discourteously of a friend of yours. You were saying that you were robbed—and it was a shame, too—but it appears by what is left of the shroud you have on that it was a costly one in its day. How did—"

A most ghastly expression began to develop among the decayed features and shrivelled integuments of my guest's face, and I was beginning to grow uneasy and distressed, when he told me he was only working up a deep, sly smile, with a wink in it, to suggest that about the time he acquired his present garment a ghost in a neighboring cemetery missed one. This reassured me, but I begged him to confine himself to speech thenceforth, because his facial expression was uncertain. Even with the most elaborate care it was liable to miss fire. Smiling should especially be avoided. What *he* might honestly consider a shining success was likely to strike me in a very different light. I said I liked to see a skeleton cheerful, even decorously playful, but I did not think smiling was a skeleton's best hold.

"Yes, friend," said the poor skeleton, "the facts are just as I have given them to you. Two of these old graveyards—the one that I resided in and one further along—have been deliberately neglected by our descendants of to-day until there is no occupying them any longer. Aside from the osteological discomfort of it —and that is no light matter this rainy weather—the present state of things is ruinous to property. We have got to move or be content to see our effects wasted away and utterly destroyed. Now, you will hardly believe it, but it is true, nevertheless, that there isn't a single coffin in good repair among all my acquaintance—now that is an absolute fact. I do not refer to low people who come in a pine box mounted on an express wagon, but I am talking about your high-toned, silver mounted burial-case, your monumental sort, that travel under black plumes at the head of a procession and have choice of cemetery lots—I mean folks like the Jarvises, and the Bledsoes and Burlings, and such. They are all about ruined. The most substantial people in our set, they were. And now look at them—utterly used up and poverty-stricken. One of the Bledsoes actually traded his monument to a late bar-keeper for some fresh shavings to put under his head. I tell you it speaks volumes, for there is nothing a corpse takes so much pride in as his monument. He loves to read the inscription. He comes after awhile to believe what it says himself, and then you may see him sitting on the fence night after night enjoying it. Epitaphs are cheap, and they do a poor chap a world of good after he is dead, especially if he had hard luck while he was alive. I wish they were used more. Now, I don't complain, but confidentially I *do* think it was a little shabby in my descendants to give me nothing but this old slab of a gravestone—and all the more that there isn't a compliment on it. It used to have

GONE TO HIS JUST REWARD

on it, and I was proud when I first saw it, but by-and-by I noticed that whenever an old friend of mine came along he would hook his chin on the railing and pull a long face and read along down till he came to that, and then he would chuckle to himself and walk off, looking satisfied and comfortable. So I scratched it off to get rid of those fools. But a dead man always takes a deal of pride in his monument. Yonder goes half-a-dozen of the Jarvises, now, with the family monument along. And Smithers and some hired spectres went by with his a while ago. Hello, Higgins, good-bye, old friend! That's Meredith Higgins—died in '44—belongs to our set in the cemetery—fine old family—great-grandmother was an Injun—I am on the most familiar terms with him—he didn't hear me was the reason he didn't answer me. And I am sorry, too, because I would have liked to introduce you. You would admire him. He is the most disjointed, sway-backed, and generally distorted old skeleton you ever saw, but he is full of fun. When he laughs it sounds like rasping two stones together, and he always starts it off with a cheery screech like raking a nail across a window-pane. Hey, Jones! That is old Columbus Jones—shroud cost four hundred dollars—entire trousseau, including monument, twenty-seven hundred. This was in the spring of '26. It was enormous style for those days. Dead people came all the way from the Alleghanies to see his things—the party that occupied the grave next to mine remembers it well. Now do you see that individual going along with a piece of a head-board under his arm, one leg-bone below his knee gone, and not a thing in the world on? That is Barstow Dalhousie, and next to Columbus Jones he was the most sumptuously outfitted person that ever entered our cemetery. We are all leaving. We cannot tolerate the treatment we are receiving at the hands of our descendants. They open new cemeteries, but they leave us to our ignominy. They mend the streets, but they never mend anything that is about us or belongs to us. Look at that coffin of mine—yet I tell you in its day it was a piece of furniture that would have attracted attention in any drawing-room in this city. You may have it if you want it—I can't afford to repair it. Put a new bottom in her, and part of a new top, and a bit of fresh lining along the left side, and you'll find her about as comfortable as any receptacle of her species you ever tried. No thanks—no, don't mention it—you have been civil to me, and I would give you all the property I have got before I would seem ungrateful. Now this winding-sheet is a kind of a sweet thing in its way, if you would like to—No? Well, just as you say, but I wished to be fair and liberal—there's nothing mean about *me*. Good-by, friend, I must be going. I may have a good way to go to-night—don't know. I only know one thing for certain, and that is, that I am on the emigrant trail, now, and I'll never sleep in that crazy old cemetery again. I will travel till I find respectable quarters, if I have to hoof it to New Jersey. All the boys are going. It was decided in public conclave, last night, to emigrate, and by the time the sun rises there won't be a bone left in our old habitations. Such cemeteries may suit my surviving friends, but they do not suit the remains that have the honor to make these remarks. My opinion is the general opinion. If you doubt it, go and see how the departing ghosts upset things before they started. They were almost riotous in their demonstrations of distaste. Hello, here are some of the Bledsoes, and if you will give me a lift with this tombstone I guess I will join company and jog along with them—mighty respectable old family, the Bledsoes, and used to always come out in six-horse hearses, and all that sort of thing fifty years ago when I walked these streets in daylight. Good-by, friend."

And with his gravestone on his shoulder he joined the grisly procession, dragging his damaged coffin after him, for notwithstanding he pressed it upon me so earnestly, I utterly refused his hospitality. I suppose that for as much as two hours these sad outcasts went clacking by, laden with their dismal effects, and all that time I sat pitying them. One or two of the youngest and least dilapidated among them inquired about midnight trains on the railways, but the rest seemed unacquainted with that mode of travel, and merely asked about common public roads to various towns and cities, some of which are not on the map now, and vanished from it and from the earth as much as thirty years ago, and some few of them never *had* existed anywhere but on maps, and private ones in real estate agencies at that. And they asked about the condition of the cemeteries in these towns and cities, and about the reputation the citizens bore as to reverence for the dead.

This whole matter interested me deeply, and likewise compelled my sympathy for these homeless ones. And it all seeming real, and I not knowing it was a dream, I mentioned to one shrouded wanderer an idea that had entered my head to publish an account of this curious and very sorrowful exodus, but said also that I could not describe it truthfully, and just as it occurred, without seeming to trifle with a grave subject and exhibit an irreverence for the dead that would shock and distress their surviving friends. But this bland and stately remnant of a former citizen leaned him far over my gate and whispered in my ear, and said:—

"Do not let that disturb you. The community that can stand such graveyards as those we are emigrating from can stand anything a body can say about the neglected and forsaken dead that lie in them."

At that very moment a cock crowed, and the weird procession vanished and left not a shred or a bone behind. I awoke, and found myself lying with my head out of the bed and "sagging" downwards considerably—a position favorable to dreaming dreams with morals in them, maybe, but not poetry.

NOTE. —The reader is assured that if the cemeteries in his town are kept in good order, this Dream is not levelled at his town at all, but is levelled particularly and venomously at the *next* town.

ROBERT BLOCH

The Man Who Collected Poe

The death of America's greatest macabre writer, Edgar Allan Poe, was tragic and mysterious. According to The Oxford Companion to English Literature, *he died "five days after having been found semi-conscious and delirious from alcohol, heart failure, epilepsy, or a combination of these" and was buried in Baltimore, Maryland. In the following slyly parodistic story,* ROBERT BLOCH, *author of* Psycho, *"Yours Truly, Jack the Ripper," "Enoch," "The Sorcerer's Apprentice" and many other weird tales, speculates on the dream of all true book lovers to own a complete and unabridged collection of their favorite author.*

During the whole of a dull, dark, and soundless day in the autumn of the year, when the clouds hung oppressively low in the heavens, I had been passing alone, by automobile, through a singularly dreary tract of country, and at length found myself, as the shades of the evening drew on, within view of my destination.

I looked upon the scene before me—upon the mere house, and the simple landscape features of the domain—upon the bleak walls—upon the vacant eyelike windows—upon a few rank sedges —and upon a few white trunks of decayed trees—with a feeling of utter confusion commingled with dismay. For it seemed to me as though I had visited this scene once before, or read of it, perhaps, in some frequently rescanned tale. And yet assuredly it could not be, for only three days had passed since I had made the acquaintance of Launcelot Canning and received an invitation to visit him at his Maryland residence.

The circumstances under which I met Canning were simple; I happened to attend a bibliophilic meeting in Washington and was introduced to him by a mutual friend. Casual conversation gave place to absorbed and interested discussion when he discovered my preoccupation with works of fantasy. Upon learning that I was traveling upon a vacation with no set itinerary, Canning urged me to become his guest for a day and to examine, at my leisure, his unusual display of memorabilia.

"I feel, from our conversation, that we have much in common," he told me. "For you see, sir, in my love of fantasy I bow to no man. It is a taste I have perhaps inherited from my father and from his father before him, together with their considerable acquisitions in the genre. No doubt you would be gratified with what I am prepared to show you, for in all due modesty, I beg to style myself the world's leading collector of the works of Edgar Allan Poe."

I confess that his invitation as such did not enthrall me, for I hold no brief for the literary hero-worshipper or the scholarly collector as a type. I own to a more than passing interest in the tales of Poe, but my interest does not extend to the point of ferreting out the exact date upon which Mr. Poe first decided to raise a mustache, nor would I be unduly intrigued by the opportunity to examine several hairs preserved from that hirsute appendage.

So it was rather the person and personality of Launcelot Canning himself which caused me to accept his proffered hospitality. For the man who proposed to become my host might have himself stepped from the pages of a Poe tale. His speech, as I have endeavored to indicate, was characterized by a courtly rodomontade so often exemplified in Poe's heroes—and beyond certainty, his appearance bore out the resemblance.

Launcelot Canning had the cadaverousness of complexion, the large, liquid, luminous eye, the thin, curved lips, the delicately modeled nose, finely molded chin, and dark, weblike hair of a typical Poe protagonist.

It was this phenomenon that prompted my acceptance and led

me to journey to his Maryland estate which, as I now perceived, in itself manifested a Poe-esque quality of its own, intrinsic in the images of the gray sedge, the ghastly tree stems, and the vacant and eyelike windows of the mansion of gloom. All that was lacking was a tarn and a moat—and as I prepared to enter the dwelling I half expected to encounter therein the carved ceiling, the somber tapestries, the ebon floors, and the phantasmagoric armorial trophies so vividly described by the author of *Tales of the Grotesque and Arabesque.*

Nor, upon entering Launcelot Canning's home was I too greatly disappointed in my expectations. True to both the atmospheric quality of the decrepit mansion and to my own fanciful presentiments, the door was opened in response to my knock by a valet who conducted me, in silence, through dark and intricate passages to the study of his master.

The room in which I found myself was very large and lofty. The windows were long, narrow, and pointed, and at so vast a distance from the black oaken floor as to be altogether inaccessible from within. Feeble gleams of encrimsoned light made their way through the trellised panes, and served to render sufficiently distinct the more prominent objects around; the eye, however, struggled in vain to reach the remoter angles of the chamber or the recesses of the vaulted and fretted ceiling. Dark draperies hung upon the walls. The general furniture was profuse, comfortless, antique, and tattered. Many books and musical instruments lay scattered about, but failed to give any vitality to the scene. Instead they rendered more distinct that peculiar quality of quasi recollection; it was as though I found myself once again, after a protracted absence, in a familiar setting. I had read, I had imagined, I had dreamed, or I had actually beheld this setting before.

Upon my entrance, Launcelot Canning arose from a sofa on which he had been lying at full length, and greeted me with a vivacious warmth which had much in it, I at first thought, of an overdone cordiality.

Yet his tone, as he spoke of the object of my visit, of his earnest desire to see me, and of the solace he expected me to afford him in a mutual discussion of our interests, soon alleviated my initial misapprehension.

Launcelot Canning welcomed me with the rapt enthusiasm of

the born collector—and I came to realize that he was indeed just that. For the Poe collection he shortly proposed to unveil before me was actually his birthright.

Initially, he disclosed, the nucleus of the present accumulation had begun with his grandfather, Christopher Canning, a respected merchant of Baltimore. Almost eighty years ago he had been one of the leading patrons of the arts in his community and as such was partially instrumental in arranging for the removal of Poe's body to the southeastern corner of the Presbyterian Cemetery at Fayette and Green Streets, where a suitable monument might be erected. This event occurred in the year 1875, and it was a few years prior to that time that Canning laid the foundation of the Poe collection.

"Thanks to his zeal," his grandson informed me, "I am today the fortunate possessor of a copy of virtually every existing specimen of Poe's published works. If you will step over here"—and he led me to a remote corner of the vaulted study, past the dark draperies, to a bookshelf which rose remotely to the shadowy ceiling—"I shall be pleased to corroborate that claim. Here is a copy of *Al Araaf, Tamerlane and other Poems* in the 1829 edition, and here is the still earlier *Tamerlane and other Poems* of 1827. The Boston edition, which, as you doubtless know, is valued today at $15,000. I can assure you that Grandfather Canning parted with no such sum in order to gain possession of this rarity."

He displayed the volumes with an air of commingled pride and cupidity which is ofttimes characteristic of the collector and is by no means to be confused with either literary snobbery or ordinary greed. Realizing this, I remained patient as he exhibited further treasures—copies of the *Philadelphia Saturday Courier* containing early tales, bound volumes of *The Messenger* during the period of Poe's editorship, *Graham's Magazine,* editions of the *New York Sun* and the *New York Mirror* boasting, respectively, of *The Balloon Hoax* and *The Raven,* and files of *The Gentleman's Magazine.* Ascending a short library ladder, he handed down to me the Lea and Blanchard edition of *Tales of the Grotesque and Arabesque,* the *Conchologist's First Book,* the Putnam *Eureka,* and, finally the little paper booklet, published in 1843 and sold for 12½¢, entitled *The Prose Romances of Edgar A. Poe;* an insignificant trifle containing two tales which is valued by present-day collectors at $50,000.

Canning informed me of this last fact, and, indeed, kept up a running commentary upon each item he presented. There was no doubt but that he was a Poe scholar as well as a Poe collector, and his words informed tattered specimens of the *Broadway Journal* and *Godey's Lady's Book* with a singular fascination not necessarily inherent in the flimsy sheets or their contents.

"I owe a great debt to Grandfather Canning's obsession," he observed, descending the ladder and joining me before the bookshelves. "It is not altogether a breach of confidence to admit that his interest in Poe did reach the point of an obsession, and perhaps eventually of an absolute mania. The knowledge, alas, is public property, I fear.

"In the early seventies he built his house, and I am quite sure that you have been observant enough to note that it in itself is almost a replica of a typical Poe-esque mansion. This was his study, and it was here that he was wont to pore over the books, the letters, and the numerous mementos of Poe's life.

"What prompted a retired merchant to devote himself so fanatically to the pursuit of a hobby, I cannot say. Let it suffice that he virtually withdrew from the world and from all other normal interests. He conducted a voluminous and lengthy correspondence with aging men and women who had known Poe in their lifetime—made pilgrimages to Fordham, sent his agents to West Point, to England and Scotland, to virtually every locale in which Poe had set foot during his lifetime. He acquired letters and souvenirs as gifts, he bought them, and—I fear—stole them, if no other means of acquisition proved feasible."

Launcelot Canning smiled and nodded. "Does all this sound strange to you? I confess that once I, too, found it almost incredible, a fragment of romance. Now, after years spent here, I have lost my own objectivity."

"Yes, it is strange," I replied. "But are you quite sure that there was not some obscure personal reason for your grandfather's interest? Had he met Poe as a boy, or been closely associated with one of his friends? Was there, perhaps, a distant, undisclosed relationship?"

At the mention of the last word, Canning started visibly, and a tremor of agitation overspread his countenance.

"Ah!" he exclaimed. "There you voice my own inmost conviction. A relationship—assuredly there must have been one—I am morally, instinctively certain that Grandfather Canning felt or knew himself to be linked to Edgar Poe by ties of blood. Nothing else could account for his strong initial interest, his continuing defense of Poe in the literary controversies of the day, and his final melancholy lapse into a world of delusion and illusion.

"Yet he never voiced a statement or put an allegation upon paper—and I have searched the collection of letters in vain for the slightest clue.

"It is curious that you so promptly divine a suspicion held not only by myself but by my father. He was only a child at the time of my Grandfather Canning's death, but the attendant circumstances left a profound impression upon his sensitive nature. Although he was immediately removed from this house to the home of his mother's people in Baltimore, he lost no time in returning upon assuming his inheritance in early manhood.

"Fortunately being in possession of a considerable income, he was able to devote his entire lifetime to further research. The name of Arthur Canning is still well known in the world of literary criticism, but for some reason he preferred to pursue his scholarly examination of Poe's career in privacy. I believe this preference was dictated by an inner sensibility; that he was endeavoring to unearth some information which would prove his father's, his, and for that matter, my own, kinship to Edgar Poe."

"You say your father was also a collector?" I prompted.

"A statement I am prepared to substantiate," replied my host, as he led me to yet another corner of the shadow-shrouded study. "But first, if you would accept a glass of wine?"

He filled, not glasses, but veritable beakers from a large carafe, and we toasted one another in silent appreciation. It is perhaps unnecessary for me to observe that the wine was a fine old Amontillado.

"Now, then," said Launcelot Canning. "My father's special province in Poe research consisted of the accumulation and study of letters."

Opening a series of large trays or drawers beneath the bookshelves, he drew out file after file of glassined folios, and for the space of the next half hour I examined Edgar Poe's correspondence—letters to Henry Herring, to Dr. Snodgrass, Sarah

Shelton, James P. Moss, Elizabeth Poe—missives to Mrs. Rock-
wood, Helen Whitman, Anne Lynch, John Pendleton Kennedy—
notes to Mrs. Richmond, to John Allan, to Annie, to his brother,
Henry—a profusion of documents, a veritable epistolary cornu-
copia.

During the course of my perusal my host took occasion to refill
our beakers with wine, and the heady draught began to take effect
—for we had not eaten, and I own I gave no thought to food, so
absorbed was I in the yellowed pages illumining Poe's past.

Here was wit, erudition, literary criticism; here were the mud-
dled, maudlin outpourings of a mind gone in drink and despair;
here was the draft of a projected story, the fragments of a poem;
here were a pitiful cry for deliverance and a paean to living
beauty; here were a dignified response to a dunning letter and an
editorial pronunciamento to an admirer; here were love, hate,
pride, anger, celestial serenity, abject penitence, authority, wonder, resolution, indecision, joy, and soul-sickening melancholia.

Here were the gifted elocutionist, the stammering drunkard,
the adoring husband, the frantic lover, the proud editor, the
indigent pauper, the grandiose dreamer, the shabby realist, the
scientific inquirer, the gullible metaphysician, the dependent
stepson, the free and untrammeled spirit, the hack, the poet, the
enigma that was Edgar Allan Poe.

Again the beakers were filled and emptied.

I drank deeply with my lips, and with my eyes more deeply still.

For the first time the true enthusiasm of Launcelot Canning
was communicated to my own sensibilities—I divined the eternal
fascination found in a consideration of Poe the writer and Poe the
man; he who wrote Tragedy, lived Tragedy, was Tragedy; he who
penned Mystery, lived and died in Mystery, and who today looms
on the literary scene as Mystery incarnate.

And Mystery Poe remained, despite Arthur Canning's careful
study of the letters. "My father learned nothing," my host confided, "even though he assembled, as you see here, a collection to
delight the heart of a Mabbott or a Quinn. So his search ranged
further. By this time I was old enough to share both his interest
and his inquiries. Come," and he led me to an ornate chest which
rested beneath the windows against the west wall of the study.

Kneeling, he unlocked the repository, and then drew forth, in rapid and marvelous succession, a series of objects each of which boasted of intimate connection with Poe's life.

There were souvenirs of his youth and his schooling abroad—a book he had used during his sojourn at West Point—mementos of his days as a theatrical critic in the form of playbills, a pen used during his editorial period, a fan once owned by his girl-wife, Virginia, a brooch of Mrs. Clemm's; a profusion of objects including such diverse articles as a cravat stock and—curiously enough —Poe's battered and tarnished flute.

Again we drank, and I own the wine was potent. Canning's countenance remained cadaverously wan—but, moreover, there was a species of mad hilarity in his eye—an evident restrained hysteria in his whole demeanor. At length, from the scattered heap of curiosa, I happened to draw forth and examine a little box of no remarkable character, whereupon I was constrained to inquire its history and what part it had played in the life of Poe.

"In the *life* of Poe?" A visible tremor convulsed the features of my host, then rapidly passed in transformation to a grimace, a rictus of amusement. "This little box—and you will note how, by some fateful design or contrived coincidence it bears a resemblance to the box he himself conceived and described in his tale, *Berenice*—this little box is concerned with his death, rather than his life. It is, in fact, the self-same box my grandfather Christopher Canning clutched to his bosom when they found him down there."

Again the tremor, again the grimace. "But stay, I have not yet told you of the details. Perhaps you would be interested in seeing the spot where Christopher Canning was stricken; I have already told you of his madness, but I did not more than hint at the character of his delusions. You have been patient with me, and more than patient. Your understanding shall be rewarded, for I perceive you can be fully entrusted with the facts."

What further revelations Canning was prepared to make I could not say, but his manner was such as to inspire a vague disquiet and trepidation in my breast.

Upon perceiving my unease he laughed shortly and laid a hand upon my shoulder. "Come, this should interest you as an *aficionado* of fantasy," he said. "But first, another drink to speed our journey."

He poured, we drank, and then he led the way from that vaulted chamber, down the silent halls, down the staircase, and into the lowest recesses of the building until we reached what resembled a dungeon, its floor and the interior of a long archway carefully sheathed in copper. We paused before a door of massive iron. Again I felt in the aspect of this scene an element evocative of recognition or recollection.

Canning's intoxication was such that he misinterpreted, or chose to misinterpret, my reaction.

"You need not be afraid," he assured me. "Nothing has happened down here since that day, almost seventy years ago, when his servants discovered him stretched out before this door, the little box clutched to his bosom; collapsed, and in a state of delirium from which he never emerged. For six months he lingered, a hopeless maniac—raving as wildly from the very moment of his discovery as at the moment he died—babbling his visions of the giant horse, the fissured house collapsing into the tarn, the black cat, the pit, the pendulum, the raven on the pallid bust, the beating heart, the pearly teeth, and the nearly liquid mass of loathsome—of detestable putridity from which a voice emanated.

"Nor was that all he babbled," Canning confided, and here his voice sank to a whisper that reverberated through the copper-sheathed hall and against the iron door. "He hinted other things far worse than fantasy; of a ghastly reality surpassing all of the phantasms of Poe.

"For the first time my father and the servants learned the purpose of the room he had built beyond this iron door, and learned what Christopher Canning had done to establish his title as the world's foremost collector of Poe.

"For he babbled again of Poe's death, thirty years earlier, in 1849—of the burial in the Presbyterian Cemetery—and of the removal of the coffin in 1874 to the corner where the monument was raised. As I told you, and as was known then, my grandfather had played a public part in instigating that removal. But now we learned of the private part—learned that there was a monument and a grave, but no coffin in the earth beneath Poe's alleged resting place. The coffin now rested in the secret room at the end of this passage. That is why the room, the house itself, had been built.

"I tell you, he had stolen the body of Edgar Allan Poe—and as he shrieked aloud in his final madness, did not this indeed make him the greatest collector of Poe?

"His ultimate intent was never divined, but my father made one significant discovery—the little box clutched to Christopher Canning's bosom contained a portion of the crumbled bones, the veritable dust that was all that remained of Poe's corpse."

My host shuddered and turned away. He led me back along that hall of horror, up the stairs, into the study. Silently, he filled our beakers and I drank as hastily, as deeply, as desperately as he.

"What could my father do? To own the truth was to create a public scandal. He chose instead to keep silence; to devote his own life to study in retirement.

"Naturally the shock affected him profoundly; to my knowledge he never entered the room beyond the iron door and, indeed, I did not know of the room or its contents until the hour of his death—and it was not until some years later that I myself found the key among his effects.

"But find the key I did, and the story was immediately and completely corroborated. Today I am the greatest collector of Poe—for he lies in the keep below, my eternal trophy!"

This time I poured the wine. As I did so, I noted for the first time the imminence of a storm; the impetuous fury of its gusts shaking the casements, and the echoes of its thunder rolling and rumbling down the time-corroded corridors of the old house.

The wild, overstrained vivacity with which my host harkened, or apparently harkened, to these sounds did nothing to reassure me—for his recent revelation led me to suspect his sanity.

That the body of Edgar Allan Poe had been stolen—that this mansion had been built to house it—that it was indeed enshrined in a crypt below—that grandsire, son, and grandson had dwelt here alone, apart, enslaved to a sepulchral secret—was beyond sane belief.

And yet, surrounded now by the night and the storm, in a setting torn from Poe's own frenzied fancies, I could not be sure. Here the past was still alive, the very spirit of Poe's tales breathed forth its corruption upon the scene.

As thunder boomed, Launcelot Canning took up Poe's flute, and, whether in defiance of the storm without or as a mocking accompaniment, he played; blowing upon it with drunken persistence, with eery atonality, with nerve-shattering shrillness. To the shrieking of that infernal instrument the thunder added a braying counterpoint.

Uneasy, uncertain, and unnerved, I retreated into the shadows of the bookshelves at the farther end of the room, and idly scanned the titles of a row of ancient tomes. Here was the *Chiromancy* of Robert Flud, the *Directorium Inquisitorum*, a rare and curious book in quarto Gothic that was the manual of a forgotten church; and betwixt and between the volumes of pseudoscientific inquiry, theological speculation, and sundry incunabula I found titles that arrested and appalled me. *De Vermis Mysteriis* and the *Liber Eibon*, treatises on demonology, on witchcraft, on sorcery moldered in crumbling binding. The books were old, but the books were not dusty. They had been read—

"Read them?" It was as though Canning divined my inmost thoughts. He had put aside his flute and now approached me, tittering as though in continued drunken defiance of the storm. Odd echoes and boomings now sounded through the long halls of the house, and curious grating sounds threatened to drown out his words and his laughter.

"Read them?" said Canning. "I study them. Yes, I have gone beyond grandfather and father, too. It was I who procured the books that held the key, and it was I who found the key. A key more difficult to discover, and more important, than the key to the vaults below. I often wonder if Poe himself had access to these selfsame tomes, knew the selfsame secrets. The secrets of the grave and what lies beyond, and what can be summoned forth if one but holds the key."

He stumbled away and returned with wine. "Drink," he said. "Drink to the night and the storm."

I brushed the proffered glass aside. "Enough," I said. "I must be on my way."

Was it fancy or did I find fear frozen on his features? Canning clutched my arm and cried, "No, stay with me! This is no night on which to be alone; I swear I cannot abide the thought of being alone, I can bear to be alone no more!"

His incoherent babble mingled with the thunder and the echoes; I drew back and confronted him. "Control yourself," I counseled. "Confess that this is a hoax, an elaborate imposture arranged to please your fancy."

"Hoax? Imposture? Stay, and I shall prove to you beyond all doubt"—and so saying, Launcelot Canning stooped and opened a small drawer set in the wall beneath and beside the bookshelves. "This should repay you for your interest in my story, and in Poe," he murmured. "Know that you are the first, other person than myself, to glimpse these treasures."

He handed me a sheaf of manuscripts on plain white paper; documents written in ink curiously similar to that I had noted while perusing Poe's letters. Pages were clipped together in groups, and for a moment I scanned titles alone.

"The Worm of Midnight, by Edgar Poe," I read, aloud. *"The Crypt,"* I breathed. And here, *"The Further Adventures of Arthur Gordon Pym"* —and in my agitation I came close to dropping the precious pages. "Are these what they appear to be—the unpublished tales of Poe?"

My host bowed.

"Unpublished, undiscovered, unknown, save to me—and to you."

"But this cannot be," I protested. "Surely there would have been a mention of them somewhere, in Poe's own letters or those of his contemporaries. There would have been a clue, an indication, somewhere, some place, somehow."

Thunder mingled with my words, and thunder echoed in Canning's shouted reply.

"You dare to presume an imposture? Then compare!" He stooped again and brought out a glassined folio of letters. "Here —is this not the veritable script of Edgar Poe? Look at the calligraphy of the letter, then at the manuscripts. Can you say they are not penned by the selfsame hand?"

I looked at the handwriting, wondered at the possibilities of a monomaniac's forgery. Could Launcelot Canning, a victim of mental disorder, thus painstakingly simulate Poe's hand?

"Read, then!" Canning screamed through the thunder. "Read, and dare to say that these tales were written by any other than

Edgar Poe, whose genius defies the corruption of Time and the Conqueror Worm!"

I read but a line or two, holding the topmost manuscript close to eyes that strained beneath wavering candlelight; but even in the flickering illumination I noted that which told me the only, the incontestable truth. For the paper, the curiously *unyellowed* paper, bore a visible watermark; the name of a firm of well-known modern stationers, and the date—1949.

Putting the sheaf aside, I endeavored to compose myself as I moved away from Launcelot Canning. For now I knew the truth; knew that, one hundred years after Poe's death a semblance of his spirit still lived in the distorted and disordered soul of Canning. Incarnation, reincarnation, call it what you will; Canning was, in his own irrational mind, Edgar Allan Poe.

Stifled and dull echoes of thunder from a remote portion of the mansion now commingled with the soundless seething of my own inner turmoil, as I turned and rashly addressed my host.

"Confess!" I cried. "Is it not true that you have written these tales, fancying yourself the embodiment of Poe? Is it not true that you suffer from a singular delusion born of solitude and everlasting brooding upon the past; that you have reached a stage characterized by the conviction that Poe still lives on in your own person?"

A strong shudder came over him and a sickly smile quivered about his lips as he replied, "Fool! I say to you that I have spoken the truth. Can you doubt the evidence of your senses? This house is real, the Poe collection exists, and the stories exist—they exist, I swear, as truly as the body lying in the crypt below!"

I took up the little box from the table and removed the lid. "Not so," I answered. "You said your grandfather was found with this box clutched to his breast, before the door of the vault, and that it contained Poe's dust. Yet you cannot escape the fact that the box is empty." I faced him furiously. "Admit it, the story is a fabrication, a romance. Poe's body does not lie beneath this house, nor are these his unpublished works, written during his lifetime and concealed."

"True enough." Canning's smile was ghastly beyond belief. "The dust is gone because I took it and used it—because in the works of wizardry I found the formulae, the arcana whereby I could raise the flesh, recreate the body from the essential salts of the grave. Poe does not *lie* beneath this house—he *lives!* And the tales are *his posthumous works!*"

Accented by thunder, his words crashed against my consciousness.

"That was the end-all and the be-all of my planning, of my studies, of my work, of my life! To raise, by sorcery, the veritable spirit of Edgar Poe from the grave—reclothed and animate in flesh—set him to dwell and dream and do his work again in the private chambers I built in the vaults below—and this I have done! To steal a corpse is but a ghoulish prank; mine is the achievement of true genius!"

The distinct, hollow, metallic, and clangorous, yet apparently muffled reverberation accompanying his words caused him to turn in his seat and face the door of the study, so that I could not see the workings of his countenance—nor could he read my own reaction to his ravings.

His words came but faintly to my ears through the thunder that now shook the house in a relentless grip; the wind rattling the casements and flickering the candle flame from the great silver candelabra sent a soaring sighing in an anguished accompaniment to his speech.

"I would show him to you, but I dare not; for he hates me as he hates life. I have locked him in the vault, alone, for the resurrected have no need of food nor drink. And he sits there, pen moving over paper, endlessly moving, endlessly pouring out the evil essence of all he guessed and hinted at in life and which he learned in death.

"Do you not see the tragic pity of my plight? I sought to raise his spirit from the dead, to give the world anew of his genius— and yet these tales, these works, are filled and fraught with a terror not to be endured. They cannot be shown to the world, he cannot be shown to the world; in bringing back the dead I have brought back the fruits of death!"

Echoes sounded anew as I moved toward the door—moved, I confess, to flee this accursed house and its accursed owner.

Canning clutched my hand, my arm, my shoulder. "You cannot go!" he shouted above the storm. "I spoke of his escaping, but did you not guess? Did you not hear it through the thunder—the grating of the door?"

I pushed him aside and he blundered backward upsetting the candelabra, so that flames licked now across the carpeting.

"Wait!" he cried. "Have you not heard his footstep on the stair? *Madman, I tell you that he now stands without the door!*"

A rush of wind, a roar of flame, a shroud of smoke rose all about us. Throwing open the huge, antique panels to which Canning pointed, I staggered into the hall.

I speak of wind, of flame, of smoke—enough to obscure all vision. I speak of Canning's screams, and of thunder loud enough to drown all sound. I speak of terror born of loathing and of desperation enough to shatter all my sanity.

Despite these things, I can never erase from my consciousness that which I beheld as I fled past the doorway and down the hall.

There without the doors there *did* stand a lofty and enshrouded figure; a figure all too familiar, with pallid features, high, domed forehead, mustache set above a mouth. My glimpse lasted but an instant, an instant during which the man—the corpse—the apparition—the hallucination, call it what you will—moved forward into the chamber and clasped Canning to his breast in an unbreakable embrace. Together, the two figures tottered toward the flames, which now rose to blot out vision forevermore.

From that chamber, and from that mansion, I fled aghast. The storm was still abroad in all its wrath, and now fire came to claim the house of Canning for its own.

Suddenly there shot along the path before me a wild light, and I turned to see whence a gleam so unusual could have issued—but it was only the flames, rising in supernatural splendor to consume the mansion, and the secrets, of the man who collected Poe.

WASHINGTON IRVING

Guests from Gibbet Island

WASHINGTON IRVING (1783–1859) was born in New York, the son of a rich British businessman who supported the American Revolution. The young Irving studied for the law but soon turned to writing essays and fiction that was sometimes amusing, sometimes eerie, including such gems as "The Legend of Sleepy Hollow," "Rip Van Winkle," "The Adventure of the German Student," "The Devil and Tom Walker" and the following flavorful tale of phantom pirates. Gibbet Island still exists in New York harbor. It is the place where countless European refugees first set foot in America: the U.S. Immigration Service station on Ellis Island.

Whoever has visited the ancient and renowned village of Communipaw may have noticed an old stone building of most ruinous and sinister appearance. The doors and window-shutters are ready to drop from their hinges; old clothes are stuffed in the broken panes of glass, while legions of half-starved dogs prowl about the premises, and rush out and bark at every passer-by; for your beggarly house in a village is most apt to swarm with profligate and ill-conditioned dogs. What adds to the sinister appearance of this mansion, is a tall frame in front, not a little resembling a gallows, and which looks as if waiting to accommodate some of the inhabitants with a well-merited airing. It is not a gallows, however, but an ancient sign-post; for this dwelling, in the golden days of Communipaw, was one of the most orderly and peaceful of village taverns, where public affairs were talked and smoked over. In fact, it was in this very building that Oloffe the Dreamer, and his companions, concerted that great voyage of discovery and colonization, in which they explored Buttermilk Channel, were nearly shipwrecked in the strait of Hell-gate, and finally landed on the island of Manhattan, and founded the great city of New Amsterdam.

Even after the province had been cruelly wrested from the sway of their High Mightinesses, by the combined forces of the British and the Yankees, this tavern continued its ancient loyalty. It is true, the head of the Prince of Orange disappeared from the sign, a strange bird being painted over it, with the explanatory legend of "DIE WILDE GANS," or, The Wild Goose; but this all the world knew to be a sly riddle of the landlord's, the worthy Teunis Van Gieson, a knowing man, in a small way, who laid his finger beside his nose and winked when anyone studied the signification of his sign, and observed that his goose was hatching, but would join the flock whenever they flew over the water, an enigma which was the perpetual recreation and delight of the loyal but fat-headed burghers of Communipaw.

Under the sway of this patriotic, though discreet and quiet publican, the tavern continued to flourish in primeval tranquillity, and was the resort of true-hearted Nederlanders, from all parts of Pavonia, who met here quietly and secretly, to smoke and drink the downfall of Briton and Yankee, and success to Admiral Van Tromp.

The only drawback on the comfort of the establishment was a nephew of mine host, a sister's son, Yan Yost Vanderscamp by name, and a real scamp by nature. This unlucky whipster showed an early propensity to mischief, which he gratified in a small way by playing tricks upon the frequenters of the Wild Goose: putting gunpowder in their pipes, or squibs in their pockets, and astonishing them with an explosion, while they sat nodding round the fireplace in the bar-room; and if perchance a worthy burgher from some distant part of Pavonia lingered until dark over his potation, it was odds but young Vanderscamp would slip a brier under his horse's tail as he mounted, and send him clattering along the road, in neck-or-nothing style, to the infinite astonishment and discomfiture of the rider.

It may be wondered at, that mine host of the Wild Goose did not turn such a graceless varlet out of doors; but Teunis Van Gieson was an easy-tempered man, and, having no child of his own, looked upon his nephew with almost parental indulgence. His patience and good nature were doomed to be tried by another inmate of his mansion. This was a cross-grained curmudgeon of a negro, named Pluto, who was a kind of enigma in Communipaw. Where he came from, nobody knew. He was found one morning after a storm, cast like a sea-monster on the strand, in front of the Wild Goose, and lay there, more dead than alive. The neighbours gathered round and speculated on this production of the deep; whether it were fish or flesh, or a compound of both, commonly called a merman. The kind-hearted Teunis Van Gieson, seeing that he wore the human form, took him into his house, and warmed him into life. By degrees, he showed signs of intelligence, and even uttered sounds very much like language, but which no one in Communipaw could understand. Some thought him a negro just from Guinea, who had either fallen overboard, or escaped from a slave-ship. Nothing, however, could ever draw from him any account of his origin. When questioned on the subject, he merely pointed to Gibbet Island, a small rocky islet which lies in the open bay just opposite Communipaw, as if that were his native place, though everybody knew it had never been inhabited.

In the process of time, he acquired something of the Dutch language—that is to say, he learnt all its vocabulary of oaths and maledictions, with just words sufficient to string them together. "Donder en blicksem!"—thunder and lightning—was the gentlest of his ejaculations. For years he kept about the Wild Goose, more like one of those familiar spirits, or household goblins, we read of, than like a human being. He acknowledged allegiance to no one, but performed various domestic offices, when it suited his humour: waiting occasionally on the guests; grooming the horses, cutting wood, drawing water; and all this without being ordered. Lay any command on him, and the stubborn sea-urchin was sure to rebel. He was never so much at home, however, as when on the water, plying about in skiff or canoe, entirely alone,

fishing, crabbing, or grabbing for oysters, and would bring home
quantities for the larder of the Wild Goose, which he would throw
down at the kitchen door, with a growl. No wind nor weather
deterred him from launching forth on his favourite element: indeed, the wilder the weather, the more he seemed to enjoy it. If a
storm was brewing, he was sure to put off from shore; and would
be seen far out in the bay, his light skiff dancing like a feather on
the waves, when sea and sky were in turmoil, and the stoutest
ships were fain to lower their sails. Sometimes, on such occasions, he would be absent for days together. How he weathered
the tempest, and how and where he subsisted, no one could
divine, nor did anyone venture to ask, for all had an almost
superstitious awe of him. Some of the Communipaw oyster-men
declared they had more than once seen him suddenly disappear,
canoe and all, as if plunged beneath the waves, and after a while
come up again, in quite a different part of the bay; when they
concluded that he could live under water like that notable species
of wild duck commonly called the hell-diver. All began to consider him in the light of a foul-weather bird, like the Mother
Carey's Chicken or stormy petrel; and whenever they saw him
putting far out in his skiff, in cloudy weather, made up their
minds for a storm.

The only being for whom he seemed to have any liking was Yan
Yost Vanderscamp, and him he liked for his very wickedness. He
in a manner took the boy under his tutelage, prompted him to all
kinds of mischief, aided him in every wild harum-scarum freak,
until the lad became the complete scapegrace of the village; a
pest to his uncle, and to everyone else. Nor were his pranks
confined to the land: he soon learned to accompany old Pluto on
the water. Together these worthies would cruise about the broad
bay, and all the neighbouring straits and rivers; poking around in
skiffs and canoes; robbing the set nets of the fishermen; landing
on remote coasts, and laying waste orchards and water-melon
patches; in short, carrying on a complete system of piracy, on a
small scale. Piloted by Pluto, the youthful Vanderscamp soon
became acquainted with all the bays, rivers, creeks, and inlets of
the watery world around him; could navigate from the Hook to
Spitting-devil on the darkest night, and learned to set even the
terrors of Hell-gate at defiance.

At length, negro and boy suddenly disappeared, and days and weeks elapsed, but without tidings of them. Some said they must have run away and gone to sea; others jocosely hinted that old Pluto, being no other than his namesake in disguise, had spirited away the boy to the nether regions. All, however, agreed in one thing—that the village was well rid of them.

In the process of time, the good Teunis Van Gieson slept with his fathers, and the tavern remained shut up, waiting for a claimant, for the next heir was Yan Yost Vanderscamp, and he had not been heard of for years. At length, one day, a boat was seen pulling for shore, from a long, black, darkish-looking schooner, that lay at anchor in the bay. The boat's crew seemed worthy of the craft from which they debarked. Never had such a set of noisy, roistering, swaggering varlets landed in peaceful Communipaw. They were outlandish in garb and demeanour, and were headed by a rough, burly ruffian with fiery whiskers, a copper nose, a scar across his face, and a great Flaunderish beaver slouched on one side of his head, in whom, to their dismay, the quiet inhabitants were made to recognize their early pest, Yan Yost Vanderscamp. The rear of this hopeful gang was brought up by old Pluto, who had lost an eye, grown grizzly-headed, and looked more like a devil than ever. Vanderscamp renewed his acquaintance with the old burghers, much against their will, and in a manner not at all to their taste. He slapped them familiarly on the back, gave them an iron grip of the hand, and was hail fellow well met. According to his own account, he had been all the world over; had made money by bagsful; had ships in every sea, and now meant to turn the Wild Goose into a country-seat, where he and his comrades, all rich merchants from foreign parts, might enjoy themselves in the interval of their voyages.

Sure enough, in a little while there was a complete metamorphose of the Wild Goose. From being a quiet, peaceful Dutch public-house, it became a most riotous, uproarious private dwelling; a complete rendezvous for boisterous men of the seas, who came here to have what they called a "blow out" on dry land, and might be seen at all hours, lounging about the door, or lolling out of the windows; swearing among themselves, and cracking rough jokes on every passer-by. The house was fitted up, too, in so strange a manner: hammocks slung to the walls, instead of bedsteads; odd kinds of furniture, of foreign fashion; bamboo couches, Spanish chairs; pistols, cutlasses, and blunderbusses, suspended on every peg; silver crucifixes on the mantelpieces, silver candlesticks and porringers on the tables, contrasting oddly with the pewter and Delf ware of the original establishment. And then the strange amusements of these sea-monsters! Pitching Spanish dollars, instead of quoits; firing blunderbusses out of the window; shooting at a mark, or at any unhappy dog, or cat, or pig, or barn-door fowl, that might happen to come within reach.

The only being who seemed to relish their rough waggery was old Pluto; and yet he led but a dog's life of it; for they practised all kinds of manual jokes upon him; kicked him about like a football; shook him by his grizzly mop of wool, and never spoke to him without coupling a curse by way of adjective to his name, and consigning him to the infernal regions. The old fellow, however, seemed to like them the better the more they cursed him, though his utmost expression of pleasure never amounted to more than the growl of a petted bear, when his ears are rubbed.

Old Pluto was the ministering spirit at the orgies of the Wild Goose; and such orgies as took place there! Such drinking, singing, whooping, swearing; with an occasional interlude of quarrelling and fighting. The noisier grew the revel, the more old Pluto plied the potations, until the guests would become frantic in their merriment, smashing everything to pieces, and throwing the house out of the windows. Sometimes, after a drinking bout, they sallied forth and scoured the village, to the dismay of the worthy burghers, who gathered their women within doors, and would have shut up the house. Vanderscamp, however, was not to be rebuffed. He insisted on renewing acquaintance with his old neighbours, and on introducing his friends, the merchants, to their families; swore he was on the look-out for a wife, and meant, before he stopped, to find husbands for all their daughters. So, will-ye, nill-ye, sociable he was; swaggered about their best parlours, with his hat on one side of his head; sat on the good wife's nicely waxed mahogany table, kicking his heels against the carved and polished legs; kissed and tousled the young *vrouws;* and, if they frowned and pouted, gave them a gold rosary, or a sparkling cross, to put them in good humour again.

Sometimes nothing would satisfy him, but he must have some of his old neighbours to dinner at the Wild Goose. There was no refusing him, for he had the complete upper hand of the community, and the peaceful burghers all stood in awe of him. But what a time would the quiet, worthy men have among these rake-hells, who would delight to astound them with the most extravagant gunpowder tales, embroidered with all kinds of foreign oaths; clink the can with them; pledge them in deep potations; brawl drinking-songs in their ears; and occasionally fire pistols over their heads, or under the table, and then laugh in their faces, and ask them how they liked the smell of gunpowder.

Thus was the little village of Communipaw for a time like the unfortunate man possessed with devils, until Vanderscamp and his brother merchants would sail on another trading voyage, when the Wild Goose would be shut up, and everything relapse into quiet, only to be disturbed by his next visitation.

The mystery of all these proceedings gradually dawned upon the tardy intellects of Communipaw. These were the times of the notorious Captain Kidd, when the American harbours were the resorts of piratical adventurers of all kinds, who, under pretext of mercantile voyages, scoured the West Indies, made plundering descents upon the Spanish Main, visited even the remote Indian Seas, and then came to dispose of their booty, have their revels, and fit out new expeditions, in the English colonies.

Vanderscamp had served in this hopeful school, and, having risen to importance among the buccaneers, had pitched upon his native village and early home, as a quiet, out-of-the-way, unsuspected place, where he and his comrades, while anchored at New York, might have their feasts, and concert their plans, without molestation.

At length the attention of the British Government was called to these piratical enterprises, that were becoming so frequent and outrageous. Vigorous measures were taken to check and punish them. Several of the most noted free-booters were caught and executed, and three of Vanderscamp's chosen comrades, the most riotous swashbucklers of the Wild Goose, were hanged in chains on Gibbet Island, in full sight of their favourite resort. As to Vanderscamp himself, he and his man Pluto again disappeared, and it was hoped by the people of Communipaw that he had fallen in some foreign brawl, or been swung on some foreign gallows.

For a time, therefore, the tranquillity of the village was restored; the worthy Dutchmen once more smoked their pipes in peace, eyeing, with peculiar complacency, their old pests and terrors, the pirates, dangling and drying in the sun, on Gibbet Island.

This perfect calm was doomed at length to be ruffled. The fiery persecution of the pirates gradually subsided. Justice was satisfied with the examples that had been made, and there was no more talk of Kidd, and the other heroes of like kidney, On a calm summer evening, a boat, somewhat heavily laden, was seen pulling into Communipaw. What was the surprise and disquiet of the inhabitants, to see Yan Yost Vanderscamp seated at the helm, and his man Pluto tugging at the oar! Vanderscamp, however, was apparently an altered man. He brought home with him a wife, who seemed to be a shrew, and to have the upper hand of him. He no longer was the swaggering, bully ruffian, but affected the regular merchant, and talked of retiring from business, and settling down quietly, to pass the rest of his days in his native place.

The Wild Goose mansion was again opened, but with diminished splendour, and no riot. It is true, Vanderscamp had frequent nautical visitors, and the sound of revelry was occasionally overheard in the house; but everything seemed to be done under the rose; and old Pluto was the only servant that officiated at these orgies. The visitors, indeed, were by no means of the turbulent stamp of their predecessors; but quiet, mysterious traders, full of nods, and winks, and hieroglyphic signs, with whom to use their cant phrase, "everything was smug." Their ships came to anchor at night, in the lower bay; and, on a private signal, Vanderscamp would launch his boat, and, accompanied solely by his man Pluto, would make them mysterious visits. Sometimes boats pulled in at night, in front of the Wild Goose, and various articles of merchandise were landed in the dark, and spirited away, nobody knew whither. One of the more curious of the inhabitants kept watch, and caught a glimpse of the features of some of these night visitors, by the casual glance of a lantern, and declared that he recognized more than one of the free-booting, frequenters of the Wild Goose, in former times; whence he concluded that

Vanderscamp was at his old game, and that this mysterious merchandise was nothing more nor less than piratical plunder. The more charitable opinion, however, was that Vanderscamp and his comrades, having been driven from their old line of business, by the "oppressions of Government," had resorted to smuggling to make both ends meet.

Be that as it may: I come now to the extraordinary fact, which is the butt-end of this story. It happened late one night, that Yan Yost Vanderscamp was returning across the broad bay, in his light skiff, rowed by his man Pluto. He had been carousing on board of a vessel, newly arrived, and was somewhat obfuscated in intellect by the liquor he had imbibed. It was a still, sultry night; a heavy mass of lurid clouds was rising in the west, with the low muttering of distant thunder. Vanderscamp called on Pluto to pull lustily, that they might get home before the gathering storm. The old negro made no reply, but shaped his course so as to skirt the rocky shores of Gibbet Island. A faint creaking overhead caused Vanderscamp to cast up his eyes, when, to his horror, he beheld the bodies of his three pot companions and brothers in iniquity dangling in the moonlight, their rags fluttering, and their chains creaking, as they were slowly swung backward and forward by the rising breeze.

"What do you mean, you blockhead!" cried Vanderscamp, "by pulling so close to the island?"

"I thought you'd be glad to see your old friends once more," growled the negro. "You were never afraid of a living man; what do you fear from the dead?"

"Who's afraid?" hiccupped Vanderscamp, partly heated by liquor, partly nettled by the jeer of the negro; "who's afraid? Hang me, but I would be glad to see them once more, alive or dead, at the Wild Goose. Come, my lads in the wind!" continued he, taking a draught, and flourishing the bottle above his head, "here's fair weather to you in the other world; and if you should be walking the rounds tonight, odd's fish! but I'll be happy if you will drop in to supper."

A dismal creaking was the only reply. The wind blew loud and shrill, and, as it whistled round the gallows and among the bones, sounded as if they were laughing and gibbering in the air. Old Pluto chuckled to himself, and now pulled for home. The storm burst over the voyagers, while they were yet far from shore. The rain fell in torrents, the thunder crashed and pealed, and the lightning kept up an incessant blaze. It was stark midnight before they landed at Communipaw.

Dripping and shivering, Vanderscamp crawled homeward. He was completely sobered by the storm; the water soaked from without having diluted and cooled the liquor within. Arrived at the Wild Goose, he knocked timidly and dubiously at the door, for he dreaded the reception he was to experience from his wife. He had reason to do so. She met him at the threshold, in a precious ill-humour.

"Is this a time," said she, "to keep people out of their beds, and to bring home company, to turn the house upside down?"

"Company?" said Vanderscamp meekly; "I have brought no company with me, wife."

"No indeed! they got here before you, but by your invitation; and blessed-looking company they are, truly!"

Vanderscamp's knees smote together. "For the love of Heaven, where are they, wife?"

"Where?—why, in the blue room upstairs, making themselves as much at home as if the house were their own."

Vanderscamp made a desperate effort, scrambled up to the room, and threw open the door. Sure enough, there at a table, on which burned a light as blue as brimstone, sat the three guests from Gibbet Island, with halters round their necks, and bobbing their cups together, as if they were hob-or-nobbing, and trolling the old Dutch free-booter's glee, since translated into English:

> For three merry lads be we,
> And three merry lads be we;
> I on the land, and thou on the sand,
> And Jack on the gallows-tree.

Vanderscamp saw and heard no more. Starting back with horror, he missed his footing on the landing-place, and fell from the top of the stairs to the bottom. He was taken up speechless, and either from the fall or the fright, was buried in the yard of the little Dutch church at Bergen, on the following Sunday.

From that day forward, the fate of the Wild Goose was sealed. It was pronounced a *haunted house*, and avoided accordingly. No one inhabited it but Vanderscamp's shrew of a widow, and old Pluto, and they were considered but little better than its hobgoblin visitors. Pluto grew more and more haggard and morose, and looked more like an imp of darkness than a human being. He spoke to no one, but went about muttering to himself; or, as some hinted, talking with the devil, who, though unseen, was ever at his elbow. Now and then he was seen pulling about the bay alone, in his skiff, in dark weather, or at the approach of nightfall; nobody could tell why, unless on an errand to invite more guests from the gallows. Indeed, it was affirmed that the Wild Goose still continued to be a house of entertainment for such guests, and that, on stormy nights, the blue chamber was occasionally illuminated, and sounds of diabolical merriment were overheard, mingling with the howling of the tempest. Some treated these as idle stories, until on one such night—it was about the time of the equinox—there was a horrible uproar in the Wild Goose, that could not be mistaken. It was not so much the sound of revelry, however, as strife, with two or three piercing shrieks, that pervaded every part of the village. Nevertheless, no one thought of hastening to the spot. On the contrary, the honest burghers of Communipaw drew their nightcaps over their ears, and buried their heads under the bedclothes, at the thoughts of Vanderscamp and his gallows companions.

The next morning, some of the bolder and more curious undertook to reconnoitre. All was quiet and lifeless at the Wild Goose. The door yawned wide open, and had evidently been open all night, for the storm had beaten into the house. Gathering more courage from the silence and apparent desertion, they gradually ventured over the threshold. The house had indeed the air of having been possessed by devils. Everything was topsy-turvy; trunks had been broken open, and chests of drawers and corner cupboards turned inside out, as in a time of general sack and pillage; but the most woeful sight was the widow of Yan Yost Vanderscamp, extended a corpse on the floor of the blue chamber, with the marks of a deadly grip on her windpipe.

All now was conjecture and dismay at Communipaw; and the disappearance of old Pluto, who was nowhere to be found, gave rise to all kinds of wild surmises. Some suggested that the negro had betrayed the house to some of Vanderscamp's buccaneering associates, and that they had decamped together with the booty; others surmised that the negro was nothing more nor less than a devil incarnate, who had now accomplished his ends, and made off with his dues.

Events, however, vindicated the negro from this last imputation. His skiff was picked up, drifting about the bay, bottom upward, as if wrecked in a tempest; and his body was found, shortly afterwards, by some Communipaw fishermen, stranded among the rocks of Gibbet Island, near the foot of the pirates' gallows. The fishermen shook their heads, and observed that old Pluto had ventured once too often to invite Guests from Gibbet Island.

MARVIN KAYE

Our Late Visitor

The narrator of the next piece does not pinpoint the location of the house in the woods that the titular late caller drops in on, but I know the author well enough to identify the site as Whitehall, a suburb of Allentown, Pennsylvania, where the Liberty Bell was hidden from British troops during the Revolution. I was in Whitehall one summer working on my second Hilary Quayle novel, The Grand Ole Opry Murders, *when I learned that my dear friend and singing mentor, the great tenor Robert Rounseville, suffered a fatal heart attack in his Carnegie Hall studio. That night I had a strange dream about Bob and the next afternoon I dashed off the following oddball tangent to my nightmare, the only story I ever wrote in a single unedited draft.*

Hearing an ascending tread upon the stairs leading to my work-room door, I peered out and saw Albert mounting the steps. I confess my first thoughts were completely selfish: *How the devil did he find us out here in the middle of the woods?*—and then, since he is often garrulous, *Now I shall never finish writing my chapter tonight!* But then my natural hospitality surfaced, and my conscience smote me fiercely for wishing away my closest friend. I resolutely set aside my petty problems—for, after all, I recollected, what were they compared to *his*, considering that he had died the previous week?

Of course, Jan and I only had the news second-hand, and we never put much faith in the *Times*. According to the obituary, rites were held in Albert's ancestral New England home, while a memorial ceremony was conducted in the city. But my own precarious health forbade me from attending it.

As he crossed the threshold of my den, I greeted Albert heartily and complimented him on the ruddiness of his complexion. He really looked the picture of health, and this made me something doubt the reliability of the newspaper accounts of his dissolution. I settled him in my easy chair, put a bottle of Majorska on the table by his side, and heartily pumped his cold hand. Despite the inconvenience of his visit (it was well past midnight), I was really quite pleased to see him, the more I thought of it. For several days, my spirits had been at their lowest ebb, and Albert's infectious *joie de vivre* seemed the fittest prescription for exorcising my *acedia*.

For several minutes, we exchanged hearty banalities. Naturally I was curious to learn the details of his interment, but I shrank from broaching the subject. I could not be sure whether it was proper etiquette to discuss so personal a topic, and besides, it was far too lugubrious when gaiety was what I craved!

We had scarce emptied the fifth when a sharp rap from the floor beneath quelled our festivities. Albert's voice is a big one that makes walls quake and furniture tremble. I feared its deep timbre had penetrated to the nursery below. Excusing myself, I descended the stairs and found Jan in our child's room, singing her back to sleep.

"You woke her!" she accused me, and I sheepishly explained that Albert had paid an unexpected call.

"How *dare* he?" she demanded. "He's supposed to be dead!"

"Hush! He'll hear you!"

"I don't care if he does. What right has he to intrude at this time of night and disturb the entire house? *Is he dead or not?*"

"Please," I implored, trying to quell her ire with a gesture, "what does it matter? After all, he *is* our friend!"

"He's your friend, not mine," Jan objected. "If he is *not* dead, it's too late for a social visit, and if he *is*, then he certainly has no business here! Hasn't he any sense of propriety?"

I did what I could to calm her, but to no avail. Her tenacity resembles nothing so much as a decapitated gila monster whose severed head still clings to the victim it has bitten. She positively insisted that I return to the attic and determine the precise state of Albert's health. I was reluctant to insult my guest, and told her so, but Jan would not be gainsaid.

"And while you're talking to him," she added, "see that he keeps quiet and doesn't waken Elania again. I had to sing her back to sleep, and you know how I hate music!"

"But isn't her musical turtle working?" I asked.

"*No.* It's broken! And it's not a turtle, as you know very well! It's a beetle—no matter *what* you tell Elania!"

The turtle was a long-standing toy of contention between Jan and me. It *was*, of course, a stuffed beetle with a music-box inside, but I detest crawling things, so I divested it of a few of its cloth legs and christened it "turtle," with which nomenclature our daughter heartily concurred.

"What harm is it," I repeatedly asked, "if Elania thinks of it as a turtle?"

"*Because,*" Jan insisted, "*it is a beetle!* A beetle is a beetle and a turtle is a turtle!"

I have often tried to reason with my wife. I have said again and again that if we *think* something is so, then it *is*, and have referred her to Pirandello for confirmation of my argument. But Jan's frame of reality is unshakably objective, and no internalization upon the mystery of things touches her. *I am*, she would have it, *therefore I think.*

I returned to the attic, and found Albert puffing on his clay pipe. A second fifth of vodka, half depleted, was at his elbow, and a merry smile played upon his thick lips.

"And now," he proclaimed as soon as I had shut the door, "I do believe it is time for a song!"

In vain, I tried to suppress his urge to carol forth, but I might as soon have harnessed the whirlwind. He has a well-trained voice. Once he carried spears at the Met, but in his maturer days, had graduated to the enviable role of torturer in "Samson and Delilah" and frequently had the privilege of burning out the strongman's eyes. Thus my friend was amply qualified to break into the refrain of "La Calunnia" at three o'clock in the morning.

My half-hearted protests forgotten, I sat at my work-table and listened, entranced.

He had scarce gotten halfway through the coda when a loud double-rap at the door of my den stopped him smack upon the final repetition of the word "flagello."

I had no opportunity to bid the knocker enter. Before the words could clear the roof of my mouth, the door slammed wide open and Jan strode in, fury in her eyes.

Albert rose and respectfully bowed to her. Then he drank her health and swallowed the rest of the vodka in his glass.

"I asked you to quiet him down!" she barked at me, then rounded on my friend. "And *you!!* What right have you to be here at this time of morning? Don't you know this is the only chance my husband has to work undisturbed?"

"I beg your pardon," Albert murmured, taking her hand in his and pressing her fingers to his lips, "but I so wished to see you all once more, and there simply was no opportunity to consider the niceties of timing."

She snatched back her hand, scarcely mollified. "That's the way you always *were*, Albert!" she accused. "My husband's welfare never concerned you, it's always been your convenience that has determined the scope of friendship—"

"Jan!" I pleaded, "you're insulting our guest!"

"I don't care, it's true! You're only an article of furniture to him. Whenever he wants to relax, he puts his feet up on you."

The situation was clearly impossible, and I turned to Albert with a shrug. My lips were sealed, but he knew what my pantomime meant right enough: *"We know what women are!"*

"Well, well," said Albert, walking to the door, "it is clear to me I have not timed my visit as conveniently as I might have, and so, I will say goodnight." He bowed, and turned to depart, but Jan, crossing her arms, fixed him with a stare.

"Not so fast, Albert!" she snapped. "You are *not* leaving until you answer one question!"

"Janice!" I begged, "Albert has come such a long way to visit us. Is it necessary to be so rude as—" but I got no further. She turned her baleful stare upon me, and my heart sank in a morass of cowardice.

"Well?" she asked in a threatening voice, glowering at me. Her foot tapped impatiently. "Will *you* ask him or shall I?"

I forestalled her with a resigned gesture and turned to Albert. His pudgy face wore his customary good-humored grin and he spread his hands apart in a gesture of amused bewilderment.

"What can you possibly ask," he inquired, "that would offend me? Despite what this good woman says, you are my dearest friend and I willingly open the secrets of my heart to your inspection. 'Speak, demand, I'll answer.' "

His words cheered me. After all, what wrong *could* my curiosity commit? It was neither a subject of embarrassment nor shame. I cleared my throat and resolved to hesitate no longer.

"Albert, *mon vieux,*" I said, smiling to prove that the matter was really of trifling consequence, "the fact is that Janice and I read some disturbing news in last Tuesday's *Times* . . ."

I paused, expecting him to catch my meaning. But he merely stared at me with a blank expression on his face.

"I am at a complete loss," he said at last, "to discover to what you allude. I do not recall any distressing articles in last week's papers—but perhaps you were not aware that I subscribe to the *Post?*"

"Well, then you see," I replied, flustered, "the *Times* . . . you know . . . that is . . . the fact is . . ." The words stuck in my throat, but Jan, grown weary of my dilatory approach, blurted out what I had tried to gently insinuate.

"The newspaper," she told Albert, *"positively stated you were dead."*

He stared at her amazed. Then he looked at me, and I cannot adequately describe the anguished expression that filled his eyes. Sorrow was the principal emotion, and pain, too. Yet there was something worse—a keen disappointment that exceeded the normal bounds of that mundane humor. All of Albert's inextinguishable zest for life had been suddenly, impossibly, but irrevocably quelled.

"I wish," he moaned in a daunted, mournful voice such as I have never heard him use before, "I wish most mightily that you *had never told me!*" And even as he spoke, the arch of his balding scalp caved inwards and his round skull turned into a hollow concavity. The lights within his eyes guttered and died, and the smile upon his lips flickered like a death's-head grin before the *labia* sucked in and disappeared. His arms and legs and trunk deflated, collapsed, as if they had been filled with Jell-O subjected to a bath of scalding water.

Where my friend had stood, there was nothing but a damp stain which oozed out of one of my daughter's oldest, most cruelly ravaged rag dolls that lay crumpled on the floor. Its face, half-obliterated by the devouring tooth of Time, soaked up the spreading liquid that poured from its body. I knelt beside the pool and, upon tasting it, identified it as Majorska vodka.

"For once," said Jan as she stripped off her nightdress and clambered into bed an hour later, "it appears as if the *Times* got its facts straight."

"Yes," I murmured sullenly, "but why did *we* have to bring it to his attention?"

"After all," she said, lightly caressing my cheek with her finger-tips, "he *had* to be told, sooner or later. Would you rather he'd heard it from a stranger instead of from his closest friends?"

I tried to argue about the necessity of telling him *at all*, but I could not make her see my point. Besides, her hands were busy beneath the covers, and soon I found myself preoccupied with other, more immediate concerns.

But before Janice permitted me to finish the business at hand, I had to promise her to tell Elania that her turtle was really a beetle.

BERNHARDT J. HURWOOD

The Girl with the Beckoning Eyes

BERNHARDT J. HURWOOD *wrote many anecdotal collections of factual and legendary ghosts, a humorously sexy vampire novel,* Dracutwig, *and the alternatively funny-racy "Man from O.R.G.Y." superspy novels under the pseudonym Ted Mark. Shortly before his premature death in 1987, I told Bernie that the following was my favorite story of his. This pleased him because it was one of his personal favorites, too. He explained, "I find a lot of my material through library research, but 'The Girl with the Beckoning Eyes' actually happened to my brother-in-law at a house in Brooklyn."*

When the De Simone family moved into the stately old house in the Bay Ridge section of Brooklyn in the early 1940's they regarded themselves as very fortunate. The place was large, light, and cheerful; the street on which it stood was broad and lined with gracious homes and tall shade trees. Probably the happiest member of the family was Peter De Simone. As the oldest son he had a room of his own and was not forced to share space with his two younger brothers, which he had done for so many years. He was a freshman at Brooklyn College and he was still under draft age, so that meant he had a good year or so to go before he was called into military service. With a room of his own he could study undisturbed when he felt like it.

When the family first moved in, it was early spring and Peter had no need to do any studying. He got along quite well with his brothers and sisters and his parents, and he spent little time alone in his room except when it was time to go to bed. At first he rarely shut the door and always left it open when he was out of the room.

The De Simones had been settled in the house for just about a month when the rest of the family noticed something strange about Peter. It wasn't anything big, but he began closing the door to his room and leaving it shut. At first no one said anything to him about it, but then he took to going up to his room every evening immediately after dinner and not appearing again until breakfast the next morning. Still no one said anything to him. The De Simones were people who believed in minding their own business, even among themselves, as long as no one did anything to hurt anyone else.

But then Peter's behavior became stranger still. Where he had been cheerful before, he began to grow moody and short-tempered. He snapped at everyone, and if the slightest thing displeased him he would storm from wherever he happened to be at the time, go straight to his room, and slam the door shut behind him. There was another thing. He was no longer eating the way he had been in the past. His cheeks were noticeably more hollow and there were deep, dark shadows under his eyes.

Since he wouldn't tell anyone what was wrong, his mother finally put her foot down and made him go to the doctor. But there was nothing physically wrong with him. The doctor gave him a tonic to improve his appetite and assured Mrs. De Simone that the only thing wrong with Peter was growing pains. He was passing from adolescence to adulthood, and he would soon snap out of it.

But he did not. He grew more gaunt, more sensitive, and almost frighteningly depressed. He barely spoke to anyone at meals and after eating only the barest essentials, he would retreat to his room—not only at night, but in the daytime as well. Worse yet, he now would not permit anyone to enter his room at all. What might have happened if the situation had continued like this is anyone's guess. What did happen is a matter of record.

On the first cool night of autumn the De Simones finished their dinner as usual and spent the evening doing all the ordinary

things they always did on an average week night. By eleven
o'clock they had all gone to bed. How it happened no one knows
for certain, but a gas leak in the cellar developed during the night
and the entire family was overcome by fumes. The smell was so
strong that a passing policeman on the beat noticed it and went to
investigate. When he realized what was happening he summoned
police and fire department emergency units. The De Simones
were taken out on stretchers and given oxygen, and they all
revived except for Peter and his oldest sister. Neither of them
showed any signs of life; nevertheless they were both rushed to
the hospital and administered shots of Adrenalin directly to the
heart and, by what could only be considered a miracle, they both
recovered.

Within days the De Simones found another place to live, this
time a large apartment in another section of Brooklyn. Once
more Peter had his own room, but unlike the house in Bay Ridge,
in the apartment he behaved just as he always did in the past; he
regained his appetite, and went back to being his old self. When
the family finally persuaded him to explain why he acted the way
he did in the house, it was enough to make the blood run cold.
There was no doubt about it. His room had been haunted.

One evening, shortly after moving into the Bay Ridge house,
Peter had gone to his room to look for something. While he was
sitting at his desk going through the drawers he heard a sound.
Looking up, he was astonished to see a beautiful girl about his
own age come out of the closet and smile at him. He rose up from
his chair and was about to say something when she put her finger
to her lips and nodded in the direction of the door. He understood at once. What would his family say if they saw him entertaining a strange girl in his bedroom? Winking in acknowledg-
ment, he went over and closed the door.

At the moment he was of the opinion that she was a neighbor
who had somehow found a secret means of entrance through the
closet, and when he asked her about it, she only smiled cryptically
and changed the subject. Well, he knew how girls were, and if she
wanted to keep a little secret from him that was all right. So they
sat and talked well into the night. She refused to tell him her full
name, saying only that she wanted him to call her Toddy. Another
thing that impressed him was that she would not let him touch

her, not even her fingertips; she said she had a phobia about being touched.

And so began a strange and ultimately terrifying friendship. For though Peter thoroughly believed at first that Toddy was a flesh-and-blood girl, he soon came to realize that she was an apparition, but he fell in love with her anyway, and he could not bring himself to face the reality of it and confront her with the question that really burned so fiercely in his heart. Then, too, a gradual change came about in their relationship. It was as if she knew that he knew what she really was, even though it remained an unspoken truth that they shared.

She became more demanding of his time, his presence. Although he longed to reach out to hold her in his arms, he somehow knew that if he did she would disappear and never return. And then there was that pleading, beckoning look in her eyes. Finally, toward the end, the barriers began to break down. Though she still did not admit what she was, she began suggesting that he come with her. Then she came right out with it and begged him to come away with her. He had begun dreaming about her, too, and he did not know whether she was really appearing to him in his dreams or whether during his sleeping hours she was just a figment of his imagination. There was never a doubt in his mind that she was real and there with him in the room when he was awake.

It began to dawn on Peter that his family had nothing more to offer him. School was a bore. And when he came to think of it, what did the future have to offer him? There was a war on. He would probably end up in the army soon and get killed on some foreign battlefield. If that happened he might never see Toddy again. He couldn't bear the thought of losing her. Finally he made up his mind: the next time she asked him he would go. He could hardly wait, because he had reached his decision very suddenly one afternoon while doing some homework, when everything seemed to be going wrong.

That night after dinner, when Toddy came, he was ready. She seemed to sense his feeling because for the first time since he had known her she held out her hands to him and murmured softly, "Come, Peter, take my hand and we'll go now." And he reached out and took her hand, and it was cool and soft, and as they started walking toward the closet he suddenly felt a tightness in his chest; it became impossible to breathe and he began gasping and choking. Toddy let go of his hand as he raised it to his throat, but she tried to grab his arm. "Hurry, Peter!" she screamed, her eyes blazing, a look of anguish on her face. He tried to stagger toward her, but then everything went black.

Strange as it seemed, when he woke up in the hospital he had a fleeting mental picture of Toddy crying and disappearing into the closet as she always did, but there was no great desire to see her. Although he didn't forget Toddy completely, he felt no sense of loss. Some months later, just out of curiosity, Peter De Simone went back to his old neighborhood and began asking questions of some of the people he had known while he lived there. They were the kinds of questions that most people either could not or would not answer. But there was one elderly man down the block who was anxious to talk, and when Peter asked him if there had been anything strange about the house he used to live in, the old man asked, "What kind of strange are you talking about, son?"

"You know," replied Peter. "Weird . . . spooky kind of strange, that sort of thing."

"I know," said the old man, lowering his voice and glancing around conspiratorily. "Most folks around here would tell you I was crazy to tell you a thing like this, but lemme tell you, before you people lived in that house no one ever stayed there for more'n two months. You know why?"

"Why?"

"Cause it was haunted, that's why!"

"What?"

"You heard me, I said, *haunted* . . ." Here he lowered his voice even more. "You see, ten years ago this family lived there . . . name of Hoyeson or Boyeson . . . I don't remember exactly. Well, they had a daughter, pretty girl too, but she was a wild one, got into some kind of trouble and hung herself in her bedroom closet one night. Well, they moved out pretty quick after that. But people who moved in after never stayed more'n two months, like I already told you. You see, *she* kept coming back, right out of that closet she hung herself in. I suppose she wanted company. Who knows, it might have been t'other way around—maybe she didn't like strangers sleeping in her bedroom . . ."

The old man checked himself, looked around again, and said to Peter, "Look, son, don't you go around telling anyone I told you about all this. They think I'm half-crazy as it is."

"Don't worry," Peter promised. "Besides," here he lowered his voice. "You see, I saw her too, and I'd just as soon you didn't tell anyone that, either."

Before he went home again, Peter De Simone took one last walk past the old house and he wondered if he would ever see Toddy again. Then he looked at his watch. It was late and he didn't want to be late for dinner.

don marquis

ghosts

Archy, author of the next piece, once was a free verse poet, but his soul transmigrated into an insect that lived in and around the newspaper desk of DON MARQUIS *(1878—1937), a native of Walnut, Illinois, who was a columnist for the New York* Sun *and later the New York* Tribune. *Imagine Marquis' amazement when one morning he found a manuscript he hadn't written in his typewriter roller. He investigated and learned that a cockroach named archy wrote it by jumping laboriously from letter to letter. The absence of capital letters was because archy weighed too little to work the shift key. Marquis shamelessly exploited archy, printing the bug's satirical verse in lieu of his own column. Archy and his friend Mehitabel the cat (who believed she was Cleopatra reincarnated) appeared in three book-length collections as well as a Broadway musical,* Shinbone Alley, *that was later made into a feature-length cartoon.*

you want to know
whether i believe in ghosts
of course i do not believe in them
if you had known
as many of them as i have
you would not
believe in them either
perhaps i have been

unfortunate in my acquaintance
but the ones i have known
have been a bad lot
no one could believe in them
after being acquainted with them
a short time
it is true that i have met
them under peculiar
circumstances
that is while they
were migrating into the
bodies of what human beings
consider a lower order
of creatures
before i became a cockroach
i was a free verse poet
one of the pioneers of the artless art
and my punishment for that
was to have my soul
enter the body of a cockroach
the ghosts i have known
were the ghosts of persons
who were waiting for a vacant
body to get into
they knew they were going
to transmigrate into the bodies of
lizards lice bats snakes
worms beetles mice alley cats
turtles snails tadpoles
etcetera
and while they were waiting
they were as cross as all get out
i remember talking to one of them
who had just worked his way
upward again he had been in the
body of a flea and he was going
into a cat fish
you would think he might be
grateful for the promotion

but not he
i do not call this much of an advance
he said why could i not
be a humming bird or something
kid i told him it will
take you a million years to work your
way up to a humming bird
when i remember he said
that i used to be a hat check boy
in a hotel i could
spend a million years weeping
to think that i should come to this
we have all seen better days i said
we have all come down in the world
you have not come down as far
as some of us
if i ever get to be a hat check boy
again he said i will sting
somebody for what i have had to suffer
that remark will probably cost you
another million years among
the lower creatures i told him
transmigration is a great thing
if you do not weaken
personally my ambition is to get
my time as a cockroach shortened for
good behavior and be promoted
to a revenue officer
it is not much of a step up but
i am humble
i never ran across any of this
ectoplasm that sir arthur
conan doyle tells of but it sounds
as if it might be wonderful
stuff to mend broken furniture with
                                        archy

ANONYMOUS

The Ghost of Washington

Most of the anonymous ghost stories in my personal book collection probably originated as journalistic reportage of local spooky legends, but the heightened literary tone of "The Ghost of Washington" suggests that it is wholly the product of its author's fertile imagination. This delightful trip back in time to Valley Forge, Pennsylvania, has a lighthearted flavor similar to Charles Dickens' "Tale of the Bagman's Uncle," an independent episode from The Pickwick Papers *that I included in my earlier anthology,* Ghosts.

It was early on Christmas morning when John Reilly wheeled away from a picturesque little village where he had passed the previous night, to continue his cycling tour through eastern Pennsylvania. To-day his intention was to stop at Valley Forge, and then to ride on up the Schuylkill Valley, visiting in turn the many points of historical interest that lay along his route. Valley Forge, his road map indicated, was but a short distance further on. All around him were the hills and fields and roads over which Washington and his half-starved army had foraged and roamed throughout the trying winter of 1777–8—one hundred and twenty-six years ago.

It was a beautiful Christmas day, truly, and, as he wheeled along, young Reilly's thoughts were almost equally divided between the surrounding pleasant scenery and the folks at home, who, he knew very well, were assembling at just about the present time around a heavily laden Christmas tree in the front parlor. The sun rose higher and higher and Reilly pedaled on down the valley, passing every now and then quaint, pleasant-looking farmhouses, many of which, no doubt, had been built anterior to the period which had given the vicinity its history.

Arriving, finally, at a place where the road forked off in two directions, Reilly was puzzled which way to go on. There happened to be a dwelling close by. Accordingly he dismounted, left his wheel leaning against a gate-post at the side of the road, and walked up a wretchedly flagged walk leading to the house, with the idea of getting instructions from its inmates.

Situated in the center of an unkempt field of rank grass and weeds, the building lay back from the highway probably one hundred and fifty feet. It was long and low in shape, containing but one story and having what is termed a gabled roof, under which there must have been an attic of no mean size. On coming close to the house, a fact Reilly had not noticed from the road became plainly evident. It was deserted. He saw that the roof and side shingles were in wretched condition; that the window sashes and frames as well as the doors and door frames were missing from the openings in the side walls where once they had been, and that the entire side of the house, including that part of the stone foundation which showed above the ground, was full of cracks and seams. At first on the point of turning back, he concluded to see what the interior was like anyway.

Accordingly he went inside. Glancing around the large dust-filled room he had entered his gaze at first failed to locate any object of the least interest. A rickety appearing set of steps went up into the attic from one side of the apartment and over in one corner was a large open fireplace, from the walls of which much of the brickwork had become loosened and fallen out. Reilly had started up the steps toward the attic, when happening to look back for an instant, his attention was attracted to a singular-looking, jug-shaped bottle no larger than a vinegar cruet, which lay upon its side on the hearth of the fireplace, partly covered up by debris of loose bricks and mortar. He hastened back down the steps and crossed the room, taking the bottle up in his hand and examining it with curiosity. Being partly filled with a liquid of some kind or other the bottle was very soon uncorked and held under the young man's nose. The liquid gave forth a peculiar, pungent and inviting odor. Without further hesitation Reilly's lips sought the neck of the bottle. It is hardly possible to describe the pleasure and satisfaction his senses experienced as he drank.

While the fluid was still gurgling down his throat a heavy hand was placed most suddenly on his shoulder and his body was given a violent shaking. The bottle fell to the floor and was broken into a hundred pieces.

"Hello!" said a rough voice almost in Reilly's ear. "Who are you, anyway? And what are you doing within the lines? A spy, I'll be bound."

As most assuredly there had been no one else in the vicinity of the building when he had entered it and with equal certainty no one had come down the steps from the attic, Reilly was naturally surprised and mystified by this unexpected assault. He struggled instinctively to break loose from the unfriendly grasp, and when he finally succeeded he twisted his body around so that he faced across the room. Immediately he made the remarkable discovery that there were four other persons in the apartment—three uncouth-looking fellows habited in fantastic but ragged garments, and a matronly-looking woman, the latter standing over a washtub which had been elevated upon two chairs in a corner near the fireplace. To all appearance the woman had been busy at her work and had stopped for the moment to see what the men were going to do; her waist sleeves were rolled up to the shoulders and her arms dripped with water and soapsuds. Over the tops of the tubs, partly filled with water, there were visible the edges of several well-soaked fabrics. To add to his astonishment he noticed that in the chimney-place, which a moment before was falling apart, but now seemed to be clean and in good condition, a cheerful fire burned, and that above the flames was suspended an iron pot, from which issued a jet of steam. He noticed also that the entire appearance of the room had undergone a great change. Everything seemed to be in good repair, tidy and neat; the ceilings, the walls and the door; even the stairway leading to the attic. The openings in the walls were fitted with window sashes and well-painted doors. The apartment had, in fact, evolved under his very eyesight from a state of absolute ruin into one of excellent preservation.

All of this seemed so weird and uncanny, that Reilly stood for a moment or two in the transformed apartment, utterly dumbfounded, with his mouth wide open and his eyes all but popping out of his head. He was brought to his senses by the fellow who had shaken him growling out:

"Come! Explain yourself!"

"An explanation is due me," Reilly managed to gasp.

"Don't bandy words with the rascal, Harry," one of the other men spoke up. "Bring him along to headquarters."

Thereupon, without further parley, the three men marched Reilly in military fashion into the open air and down to the road. Here he picked up at the gate-post his bicycle, while they unstacked a group of three old-fashioned-looking muskets located close by. When the young man had entered the house a few minutes before, this stack of arms had not been there. He could not understand it. Neither could he understand, on looking back at the building as he was marched off down the road, the mysterious agency that had transformed its dilapidated exterior, just as had been the interior, into a practically new condition.

While they trudged along, the strangers exhibited a singular interest in the wheel Reilly pushed at his side, running their coarse hands over the frame and handle-bar, and acting on the whole as though they never before had seen a bicycle. This in itself was another surprise. He had hardly supposed there were three men in the country so totally unacquainted with what is a most familiar piece of mechanism everywhere.

At the same time that they were paying so much attention to the wheel, Reilly in turn was studying with great curiosity his singular-looking captors. Rough, unprepossessing appearing fellows they were, large of frame and unshaven, and, it must be added, dirty of face. What remained of their very ragged clothing, he had already noticed, was of a most remarkable cut and design, resembling closely the garments worn by the Continental militiamen in the War of Independence. The hats were broad, low of crown, and three-cornered in shape; the trousers were buff-colored and ended at the knees, and the long, blue spike-tailed coats were flapped over at the extremities of the tails, the flaps being fastened down with good-sized brass buttons. Leather leggings were strapped around cowhide boots, through the badly worn feet of which, in places where the leather had cracked open, the flesh, unprotected by stockings, could be seen. Dressed as he was, in a cleanly, gray cycling costume, Reilly's appearance, most assuredly, was strongly in contrast to that of his companions.

After a brisk walk of twenty minutes, during which they occasionally met and passed by one or two or perhaps a group of men clothed and outfitted like Reilly's escorts, the little party followed the road up a slight incline and around a well-wooded bend to the left, coming quite suddenly, and to the captive, very unexpectedly, to what was without doubt a military encampment; a village, in fact, composed of many rows of small log huts. Along the streets, between the buildings, muskets were stacked in hundreds of places. Over in one corner, on a slight eminence commanding the road up which they had come, and cleverly hidden from it behind trees and shrubbery, the young man noticed a battery of field pieces. Wherever the eye was turned on this singular scene were countless numbers of soldiers all garmented in three-cornered hats, spike-tailed coats and knee breeches, walking lazily hither and thither, grouped around crackling fires, or parading up and down the streets in platoons under the guidance of ragged but stern-looking officers.

Harry stopped the little procession of four in front of one of the larger of the log houses. Then, while they stood there, the long blast from a bugle was heard, followed by the roll of drums. A minute or two afterward, several companies of militia marched up and grounded their arms, forming three sides of a hollow square around them, the fourth and open side being toward the log house. Directly succeeding this maneuver there came through the doorway of the house and stepped up the center of the square, stopping directly in front of Reilly, a dignified-looking person, tall and straight and splendidly proportioned of figure, and having a face of great nobility and character.

The cold chills chased one another down Reilly's back. His limbs swayed and tottered beneath his weight. He had never experienced another such sensation of mingled astonishment and fright.

He was in the presence of General Washington. Not a phantom

Washington, either, but Washington in the flesh and blood; as material and earthly a being as ever crossed a person's line of vision. Reilly, in his time, had seen so many portraits, marble busts and statues of the great commander that he could not be mistaken. Recovering the use of his faculties, which for the moment he seemed to have lost, Reilly did the very commonplace thing that others before him have done when placed unexpectedly in remarkable situations. He pinched himself to make sure that he was in reality wide awake and in the natural possession of his senses. He felt like pinching the figure in front of him also, but he could not muster up the courage to do that. He stood there trying to think it all out, and as his thoughts became less stagnant, his fright dissolved under the process of reasoning his mind pursued. To reason a thing out, even though an explanation can only be obtained by leaving much of the subject unaccounted for, tends to make one bolder and less shaky in the knees.

The series of strange incidents which he was experiencing had been inaugurated in the old-fashioned dwelling he had visited after information concerning the roads. And everything had been going along in a perfectly normal way up to the very moment when he had taken a drink from the bottle found in the fireplace. But from that precise time everything had gone wrongly. Hence the inference that the drinking of the peculiar liquid was accountable in some way or other for his troubles. There was a supernatural agency in the whole thing. That much must be admitted. And whatever that agency was, and however it might be accounted for, it had taken Reilly back into a period of time more than a hundred years ago, and landed him, body and soul, within the lines of the patriot forces wintering at Valley Forge. He might have stood there, turning over and over in his mind, pinching himself and muttering, all the morning, had not the newcomer ceased a silent but curious inspection of his person, and asked: "Who are you, sir?"

"John Reilly, at your pleasure," the young man replied, adding a question on his own account: "And who are you, sir?"

Immediately he received a heavy thump on his back from Harry's hard fist.

"It is not for you to question the general," the ragged administrator of the blow exclaimed.

"And it is not for you to be so gay," Reilly returned, angrily, giving the blow back with added force.

"Here, here!" broke in the first questioner. "Fisticuffs under my very nose! No more of this, I command you both." To Harry he added an extra caution: "Your zeal in my behalf will be better appreciated by being less demonstrative. Blows should be struck only on the battlefield." To Reilly he said, with a slight smile hovering over his face, "My name is Washington. Perhaps you may have heard of me?"

To this Reilly replied: "I have, indeed, and heard you very well spoken of, too." Emboldened by the other's smile, he ventured another question: "I think my reckoning of the day and year is badly at fault. An hour ago I thought the day was Christmas day. How far out of the way did my calculation take me, sir?"

"The day is indeed Christmas day, and the year is, as you must know, the year of our Lord one thousand seven hundred and seventy-seven."

Reilly again pinched himself.

"Why do you bring this man to me?" Washington now inquired, turning to Harry and his companions.

"He is a spy, sir," said Harry.

"That is a lie!" Reilly indignantly interpolated. "I have done nothing to warrant any such charge."

"We found him in the Widow Robin's house, pouring strong liquor down his throat."

"I had gone inside after information concerning the roads—"

"Which he was getting from a bottle, sir."

"If drinking from a bottle of necessity constitutes being a spy, I fear our camp is already a hotbed," Washington somewhat sagely remarked, casting his eye around slyly at his officers and men. "Tell me," he went on, with sudden sternness, looking Reilly through and through, as though to read his very thoughts, "is the charge true? Do you come from Howe?"

"The charge is not true, sir. I come from no one. I simply am making a tour of pleasure through this part of the country on my bicycle."

"With the country swarming with the men from two hostile armies, any kind of a tour, save one of absolute necessity, seems ill-timed."

"When I set out I knew nothing about any armies. The fact is, sir—" Reilly started to make an explanation, but he checked himself on realizing that the telling of any such improbable yarn would only increase the hazardousness of his position.

"Well?" Washington questioned, in a tone of growing suspicion.

"I certainly did not know that your army or any other army was quartered in this vicinity." Reilly hesitated for lack of something further to say. "You see," he finally added, prompted by a happy idea, "I rode my wheel from New York."

"You may have come from New York, though it is hard to believe you came on that singular-looking machine so great a distance. Where is the horse which drew the vehicle?"

Reilly touched his bicycle. "This is the horse, sir, just as it is; the vehicle," he said.

"The man is crazy!" Harry exclaimed. Washington only looked the incredulity he felt, and this time asked a double question.

"How can the thing be balanced without it be held upright by a pair of shafts from a horse's back, and how is the motive power acquired?"

For an answer Reilly jumped upon the wheel, and at a considerable speed and in a haphazard way pedaled around the space within the hollow square of soldiers. Hither and thither he went, at one second nearly wheeling over the toes of the line of astonished, if not frightened, militiamen; at the next, bearing suddenly down on Harry and his companions and making them dance and jump about most alertly to avoid a collision. Even the dignified Washington was once or twice put to the necessity of dodging hurriedly aside when his equilibrium was threatened. Reilly eventually dismounted, doing so with assumed clumsiness by stopping the wheel at Harry's back and falling over heavily against the soldier. Harry tumbled to the ground, but Reilly dexterously landed on his feet. At once he began offering a profusion of apologies.

"You did that by design!" Harry shouted, jumping to his feet. His face was red with anger and he shook his fist threateningly at the bicyclist.

Washington commanded the man to hold his peace. Then to Reilly he expressed a great surprise at his performance and a

desire to know more about the bicycle. The young man thereupon described the machine minutely, lifting it into the air and
spinning the wheels to illustrate how smoothly they rotated.

"I can see it is possible to ride the contrivance with rapidity. It
has been put together with wonderful ingenuity," Washington
said, when Reilly had replaced the wheel on the ground.

"And yet, sir, it is but a toy," an officer spoke up. "Put our
friend on his bundle of tin and race him against one of our
horsemen and he would make a sorry showing."

Reilly smiled. "I bear the gentleman no ill-will for his opinion,"
he said. "Still, I should like to show him by a practical test of the
subject that his ignorance of it is most profound."

"You would test the speed of the machine against that of a
horse?" Washington said, in amazement.

"I would, sir. You have a good road yonder. With your permission and a worthy opponent I would make the test at once."

"But, sir, the man is a spy," Harry broke in. "Would it not be
better to throw a rope around his neck and give him his deserts?"

"The charge is by no means proven," Washington replied.
"Nor can it be until a court martial convenes this afternoon. And
I see no reason why we may not in the meantime enjoy the unique
contest which has been suggested. It will make a pleasant break in
the routine of camp life."

A murmur of approval went up from the masses of men by
whom they were surrounded. While they had been talking it
seemed as though everybody in the camp not already on the
scene had gathered together behind the square of infantry.

"Then, sir," Harry said, with some eagerness, "I would like to
be the man to ride the horse. There is no better animal than mine
anywhere. And I understand his tricks and humors quite well
enough to put him to his best pace."

"I confess I have heard you well spoken of as a horseman,"
Washington said. "Be away with you! Saddle and bridle your
horse at once."

It was the chain of singular circumstances narrated above
which brought John Reilly into the most remarkable contest of
his life. He had entered many bicycle races at one time or other,
always with credit to himself and to the club whose colors he
wore. And he had every expectation of making a good showing

to-day. Yet a reflection of the weird conditions which had brought about the present contest took away some of his self-possession when a few minutes later he was marched over to the turnpike and left to his own thoughts, while the officers were pacing out a one mile straightaway course down the road.

After the measurements had been taken, two unbroken lines of soldiers were formed along the entire mile; a most evident precaution against Reilly leaving the race course at any point to escape across the fields. Washington came up to him again, when the preparations were completed, to shake his hand and whisper a word or two of encouragement in his ear. Having performed these kindly acts he left to take up a position near the point of finish.

The beginning of the course was located close to the battery of half concealed field pieces. Reilly was now conducted to this place. Shortly afterward Harry appeared on his horse. He leered at the bicyclist contemptuously and said something of a sarcastic nature partly under his breath when the two lined up, side by side, for the start. To these slights Reilly paid no heed; he had a strong belief that when the race was over there would be left in the mutton-like head of his opponent very little of his present inclination toward the humorous. The soldier's mount was a handsome black mare, fourteen and a half hands high; strong of limbs and at the flanks, and animated by a spirit that kept her prancing around with continuous action. It must be admitted that the man rode very well. He guided the animal with ease and nonchalance when she reared and plunged, and kept her movements confined to an incredibly small piece of ground, considering her abundance of action.

"Keep to your own side of the road throughout the race. I don't want to be collided with by your big beast," Reilly cautioned, while they were awaiting two signals from the starter.

To this Harry replied in some derision, "I'll give you a good share of the road at the start, and all of it and my dust, too, afterward." And then the officer who held the pistol fired the first shot.

Reilly was well satisfied with the conditions under which the race was to be made. The road was wide and level, smooth, hard and straight, and a strong breeze which had sprung up, blew squarely against his back. His wheel was geared up to eighty-four inches; the breeze promised to be a valuable adjunct in pushing it along. Awaiting the second and last signal, Reilly glanced down the two blue ranks of soldiers, which stretched away into hazy lines in the distance and converged at the termination of the course where a flag had been stuck into the ground. The soldiers were at parade rest. Their unceasing movements as they chatted to one another, turning their bodies this way and that and craning their heads forward to look toward the starting point, and then jerking them back, made the lines seem like long, squirming snakes. At the end of the course a thick bunch of militiamen clogged the road and overspread into the fields.

Crack! The signal to be off. Reilly shoved aside the fellow who had been holding his wheel upright while astride of it, and pushed down on the pedals. The mare's hoofs dug the earth; her great muscular legs straightened out; she sprang forward with a snort of apparent pleasure, taking the lead at the very start. Reilly heard the shout of excitement run along the two ranks of soldiers. He saw them waving their arms and hats as he went by. And on ahead through the cloud of dust there was visible the shadow-like outlines of the snorting, galloping horse, whose hoof beats sounded clear and sharp above the din which came from the sides of the highway. The mare crept farther and farther ahead. Very soon a hundred feet or more of the road lay between her and the bicyclist. Harry turned in his saddle and called out another sarcasm.

"I shall pass you very soon. Keep to your own side of the road!" Reilly shouted, not a bit daunted by the way the race had commenced. His head was well down over the handle-bars, his back had the shape of the upper portion of an immense egg. Up and down his legs moved; faster and faster and faster yet. He went by the soldiers so rapidly that they only appeared to be two streaks of blurry color. Their sharp rasping shouts sounded like the cracking of musketry. The cloud of dust blew against the bicyclist's head and into his mouth and throat. When he glanced ahead again he saw with satisfaction that the mare was no longer increasing her lead. It soon became evident even that he was slowly cutting down the advantages she had secured.

Harry again turned his head shortly afterward, doubtless expecting to find his opponent hopelessly distanced by this time. Instead of this Reilly was alarmingly close upon him. The man ejaculated a sudden oath and lashed his animal furiously. Straining every nerve and sinew the mare for the moment pushed further ahead. Then her pace slackened a bit and Reilly again crept up to her. Closer and closer to her than before, until his head was abreast of her outstretched tail. Harry was lashing the mare and swearing at her unceasingly now. But she had spurted once and appeared to be incapable of again increasing her speed. In this way they went on for some little distance, Harry using his whip brutally, the mare desperately struggling to attain a greater pace, Reilly hanging on with tenacity to her hind flanks and giving up not an inch of ground.

A mile is indeed a very short distance when traversed at such a pace. The finishing flag was already but a few hundred feet further on. Reilly realized that it was time now to go to the front. He gritted his teeth together with determination and bent his head down even further toward his front wheel. Then his feet began to move so quickly that there was only visible an indistinct blur at the sides of his crank shaft. At this very second, with a face marked with rage and hatred, Harry brought his horse suddenly across the road to that part of it which he had been warned to avoid.

It is hard to tell what kept Reilly from being run into and trampled under foot. An attempt at back pedaling, a sudden twist of the handlebar, a lurch to one side that almost threw him from his seat. Then, in the fraction of a second he was over on the other side of the road, pushing ahead of the mare almost as though she were standing still. The outburst of alarm from the throats of the soldiers changed when they saw that Reilly had not been injured; first into a shout of indignation at the dastardly attempt which had been made to run him down, and then into a roar of delight when the bicyclist breasted the flag a winner of the race by twenty feet.

As he crossed the line Reilly caught a glimpse of Washington. He stood close to the flag and was waving his hat in the air with the enthusiasm of a schoolboy. Reilly went on down the road slackening his speed as effectively as he could. But before it was possible to entirely stop his wheel's momentum the noisy acclamations in his rear ceased with startling suddenness. He turned in his saddle and looked back. As sure as St. Peter, he had the road entirely to himself. There wasn't a soldier or the ghost of a soldier in sight.

As soon as he could he turned his bicycle about and rode slowly back along the highway, now so singularly deserted, looking hither and thither in vain for some trace of the vanished army. Even the flag which had been stuck into the ground at the end of the one-mile race course was gone. The breeze had died out again and the air was tranquil and warm. In the branches of a nearby tree two sparrows chirped and twittered peacefully. Reilly went back to the place where the camp had been. He found there only open fields on one side of the road and a clump of woodland on the other. He continued on down the little hill up which Harry and his companions had brought him a few hours previously and followed the road on further, coming finally to the fork in it near which was located the old farmhouse wherein he had been taken captive. The house was, as it had been when he had previously entered it, falling apart from age and neglect. When he went inside he found lying on the brick hearth in front of the fireplace a number of pieces of broken glass.

DARRELL
SCHWEITZER

The Headless Horseman of Paoli

We just met "The Ghost of Washington" and now, in true egalitarian American style, we get to meet one of General George's soldiers—or part of him, at least. DARRELL SCHWEITZER, *fantasist and coeditor of the revenant* Weird Tales *magazine, proves that New York has not cornered the market on decapitated riders. Besides, Washington Irving's Sleepy Hollow spectre was a fake, whereas "The Headless Horseman of Paoli" (a Main Line community on the outskirts of Philadelphia) is a true phantom, albeit one with a paradoxically lively interest in the twentieth century.*

It was during the time when the Pennsylvania countryside ex-plodes with color, in the fall when the hills and fields are a riot of yellows and reds and fiery oranges, when the farmers come to harvest what spring and summer have left them—that was when I met him. That was when it all began.

I was late, of course. I was supposed to be at the Brandywine Museum for the first showing of a newly discovered series of paintings by an eighteenth-century Pennsylvania artist and repre-sent the Historical Society at that function, but somehow it didn't look like I was going to make it there on time. For one thing, I had taken back roads all the way, cruising slowly to let the local color sink in, savoring every minute away from the bloated monstrosity somebody had the gall to name "The City of Brotherly Love."

Besides that, I had stopped to talk with an Amish farmer. The Amish are very friendly people, really, and the guy waved, and as soon as he saw that I wasn't about to poke a camera in his face he called me over and we had a very pleasant conversation. That took time, though.

So there I was, late to a distinguished meeting but in no particular hurry, driving along a back country road between two cornfields, when I met the horseman. If I had been speeding I might have hit him. He seemed to just *appear* on the road in front of me. A little ways up ahead there was a grove of trees, and one of the fields ended for a while. He must have ridden out of that, but I certainly didn't see him. All of a sudden there he was, and that was all. I almost honked at him then, but from the way he was acting I knew something was going on. I paused cautiously, unsure of what to do. He sat still as a statue in front of me, mounted on a massive black stallion, holding out a leather bag in one hand as if he wanted me to take it.

I looked in my mirror and saw that no one was coming, put the car in neutral, set the emergency brake, and got out. It was then that I noticed how the fellow was dressed. He had knee breeches on, and huge white stockings. His shoes had brass buckles on them, and a sword hung at his side. I couldn't see his face, because there was a cape over it. He seemed to be sitting up straight, but I knew he had to be crouched under the cape because I couldn't see his head or even make out where his shoulders began.

There was absolute stillness about him. His horse didn't whinny or sputter, and he didn't say a word. There was no sound at all save for the purring of my auto engine. I wasn't sure what kind of gag this was, but I thought I'd might as well go through with it, now that we had gotten this far. So I took the bag. It was made of real leather and tied shut with a thong. Whatever was inside was round, about the size of a melon, and weighed a few pounds. I had a distinct feeling as I held it that something was very, very wrong.

Then the horseman suddenly sat up perfectly straight. He turned to me, threw back his cape, removed his ruffles, and unbuttoned the top of his collarless white shirt. I could see his chest then, and his neck, but not his head.

He didn't have any. It was gone, smoothly sliced off as if by an executioner's axe. The wound didn't look fresh. There was no blood.

He bowed to me, reined his horse, and galloped off in absolute silence. I didn't hear any hoofbeats. There was a strange, fluid-like quality to his movements, like something taken with a slow-motion camera. He rode across the fields and he was gone, and as soon as he was out of sight the birds started chirping again, and a dog barked somewhere nearby.

Like I said, I had this feeling that something was very wrong. I looked down at the bag I was holding, the thong-tied thing of very old leather, and I felt sick. And scared. I didn't *want* to know what was in it, although of course I already did. I half ran, half stumbled up the road until I came to the trees, and there I found a sluggish, marshy stream. I threw the bag into the water and hurried back to the car. I tore out of there doing ninety, trying not to even think about what had happened.

I wasn't late for the showing after all.

That was how it all began. I had hoped the affair was over, though I should have known that I couldn't get off the hook that easily. I was still shaky throughout the ceremonies, but I managed to get by. It was as I was driving home—on the highway this time and doing sixty—that I happened to glance down, and there on the seat beside me was the bag. It didn't even look wet.

I almost lost control of myself *and* the car right there, but I managed to pull off onto the shoulder before going completely to pieces.

"Now calm down there. There's nothing that's going to happen to you as long as you're not British." It was the bag talking. The state I was in I was willing to believe anything.

"Uh, I'm not British."

"Good, then let's get acquainted, shall we? I am Giles Hewlett, lately—although I'm not sure how lately, as I'll explain in a minute—of the Continental Army under General Washington, at your service, sir. And who might you be, who are to be my benefactor for this coming year?"

"David Styles. I'm with the Historical Society. What's this about the coming year?"

"Ah years, years, years. The good Lord knows how I try to keep track of them. How many has it been? You're an historical whatever, so you can tell me. I lost count a long time ago."

"How many years *since what?*"

"Since the *battle,* m'boy! Zounds, since I got killed! At Paoli. I trust you've heard of—"

"You mean the Paoli Massacre in the Revolution?"

"Massacre? You say it was a massacre? Too bad, those were all good lads. I wouldn't have known, because I got it myself too early to see much. Say, will you be a kind and Christian gentleman and take this bag off so I can see? I've been in the dark too long."

I jumped then, as if every muscle in my body decided it was time for a collective convulsion. I was almost able to accept the fact that I was talking to a leather bag, but to touch it, much less *open* it seemed more than I could stand.

"Well, come on! Come on! I won't bite ye!"

So I did. Giles Hewlett had a ruddy face with high cheekbones. His hair was long and tied behind his head with a ribbon, in the manner of his century. The color hadn't gone out of him, despite all he'd been through.

I felt sick again. I remembered an old legend I'd once written up as a filler for the Society's journal. It has to do with a soldier who'd had a dream the night before the Paoli Massacre and rushed to warn the Americans. He got there the same time the British did and got massacred himself. Ever since then he'd been riding around the countryside, giving his head to people every year on the anniversary of his death, and presumably reclaiming it once the terms of this ectoplasmic lend-lease were up. Or something like that. But there was one thing I was sure about. It was no story.

"That's better," the head/Giles continued. "Now, as I had asked, how many years has it been? It's been a while since anyone has taken me in like this, and I've been a little out of touch. You are a trusting soul, sir, and I appreciate it, though I do wish you would come out with the number of years."

"Well, this is 1980 and you died in, ah, when was it? We historians tend to forget dates sometimes. It's about two hundred years anyway."

"Two hundred years! And the world has changed so *marvelously*. If only Maggie could be here now."

"Who's Maggie?"

"A preacher's wife. Her husband was a very proper and strict man, and good to her I'm sure when he was around, but he was away a lot. He neglected her in favor of the pulpit so much that it was a sin, I daresay, a sin. I was, shall we say, setting matters right the night before the battle, and His Holiness showed up unexpectedly. I was just able to slip out the back window before he saw me. I rushed back to the camp, and as I got there the redcoats arrived. You know the rest."

"But I heard a different version of the story, about you having a vision—"

"Hellfire, lad! I didn't have any visions except one of Pastor You-Know-Who barging into the room before Maggie and I could make ourselves decent. Whatever you heard about me, put aside. I just told you what *really* happened."

"Some history will have to be rewritten."

"Lots of history will have to be rewritten with people like you writing it. But come on now, it's best we don't argue. We have twelve months of each other's company yet. There's nothing you can do to get rid of me, so why don't we become friends? I'll excuse you for throwing me in the swamp because you didn't know, but there had better not be any more incidents like that."

"Uh . . . okay, Mr. Hewlett."

"You can call me Giles. We'll be the best of chums before the year is out."

"Sure," I said as I restarted the car and pulled out into the traffic. A plan was forming in my mind. I knew what I had to do.

"Giles," I said after a minute, "wouldn't you like a better view? You can't see anything down there on the seat."

"I'd be most grateful. I do want to see what marvels man has wrought over the centuries."

I rolled down my window, picked the head up, and said, "Take a good look. Twelve months indeed!" And before he could answer I threw him out, then reached over and tossed the bag after him. I glanced briefly into my rearview mirror and saw him bounce once or twice before he disappeared behind me. I pressed the gas pedal all the way down and violated both speed limits and common sense the rest of the way home.

By the time I pulled into the apartment yard I was almost positive that I was crazy. I was seeing things. I needed a drink desperately and I remembered a fifth of brandy I had been saving for a rainy day. I hurried up the outside stairs, fumbled for my keys, and let myself in. I headed straight for the refrigerator and opened it.

Inside, Giles was waiting for me. Don't ask me how he got there, but he *was* in my refrigerator, lying on a platter among the leftovers, looking remarkably like John the Baptist. I slammed the door shut, but he called through it.

"It's no good. You can't get rid of me. Didn't I tell you that once before? You have been most rude to me, sir, most rude. You are trying my patience."

Then the refrigerator door opened by itself, and Giles glared at me. "I will forgive you once again, since it has been so long since anyone has taken me in. But I demand, sir, that you promise on your word of honor, that you will not cast me away again."

I looked toward the door, then to the telephone. I thought of calling the police, then realized how futile that would be. What exactly would I *tell* them?

"Okay," I said. "You win. Now what exactly do you want?"

"Why, Mr. Styles, I merely want to be your guest and your friend."

So, reluctantly at first, I allowed Giles to become my house guest. I got him a clean platter and continued to keep him in the refrigerator at nights. (I eventually found the bag behind the refrigerator.) He didn't seem to mind the cold, though, and it was as good a place for him to stay as any.

Things settled into a routine. Most of the time, Giles would watch television. He had wanted me to take him on a tour of Philadelphia, but with considerable difficulty I managed to dissuade him. It wouldn't do to carry a severed human head down a city street, I argued. It didn't matter if it could talk or not. The court would probably overlook that. People tend to ignore such things.

So my TV became his window to the world. He watched the news shows, movies, drama, and just about everything except situation comedies. Those he could not stand, despite the fact that we were living one.

No, I'm being unfair. I have to admit that Giles helped me a great deal in some of my research. His everyday knowledge of the eighteenth century proved invaluable, even though I sometimes had difficulty explaining where I got my information. He wouldn't leave the television until the test patterns came on, but after that he was willing to talk as long as I wanted. He didn't seem to need sleep. We were up at all hours of the night discussing little known historical facts. Did you know that Washington had a terrible fear of spiders? One night some of his men placed a bucket of them in his tent and he came running out in the middle of the night waving his sword and yelling, "The British are coming! The British are coming!" until his orderlies could calm him down and give him a few stiff jolts of homemade whiskey. *That* isn't in any of the history books.

Basically, Giles was an ideal house guest. Aside from his fondness for television he made few demands of me. It really didn't cost anything to keep him, either. So once I got used to him, and we made an unspoken agreement that I wouldn't try and dispose of him, we got along very well.

In fact things went splendidly until Pam showed up. Pamela Grey is my Maggie, only she isn't married to anyone. We've been friends for quite a while, and I may even love her, but I can't be sure. Somehow I hadn't thought of her when Giles came. I wasn't sure how I was going to introduce her to him, or even if I should. There are some things, after all, that Woman Is Not Meant to Know, and the presence of a severed head in her boyfriend's refrigerator is undoubtedly high up on the list.

Giles was watching an old Gary Cooper film when she drove up in her Toyota. Fortunately, I heard the gravel crunch and looked out just in time, and without saying anything more than, "My God! She's coming!" I turned off the western shootout that was on just then, and stuffed the protesting Giles into the refrigerator as Pamela began to ascend the stairs to the apartment. I had just slammed the refrigerator door shut when she burst in. The outside door wasn't locked.

"Hi, Dave. What's that you just put in the 'fridge?"

"Nothing. Nothing at all. I don't know what you're talking about."

"Oh, come on, Hon. I saw you rush over and shove something in like you didn't want me to see it."

"There's nothing there. Honest."

"You're lying."

"Would I lie to you?"

"With me, yes. To me, yes also."

"I'm offended."

She tried to get around me, but I blocked her. She feinted, dodged, and tried to get around the other side, but I stopped her again, keeping myself between her and the refrigerator.

"If there's nothing there, then why can't I see?" She draped herself over me, her hands folded behind my head. She started chewing on my arm. She does that when she wants something. Says all that black and blue means she loves me.

"Just a little peek?" she whined. Chomp, chomp. "Come on, what's so terrible?" Chomp.

"All right, you win. There's a lemon pie in there. I didn't want you to spoil your figure."

"I'll go on a diet." With that she stomped down hard on my right foot. She's a big girl, and it hurt. While I was hopping around in pain she forced her way past me, said, "Sorry, I was clumsy," and opened the refrigerator door.

And screamed.

And turned to me like I was some three-headed flesh-eating gargoyle and screamed again.

And ran out of the apartment shrieking, "Murder! Help! Police! Murder!"

Twenty minutes later the police arrived.

They certainly made a big enough production out of it. Sirens wailing and lights flashing, a patrol car skidded to a stop in the courtyard of the apartment complex, spewing gravel everywhere. Two cops came thundering up the rickety wooden steps.

"Giles! What can I do?"

"Just hold 'em off as long as you can. Act naturally, as if nothing had happened. I'll think of something."

"That's easy enough for you to say."

There was no use arguing. I had to go along with him, so I sat down at the kitchen table and pretended to read the newspaper. I glanced over the lead story—some grisly thing about a machete murderer. The officers knocked, and before I could yell, "It's unlocked!" they were inside. They were both big guys, the kind that must have been football stars in school. I didn't feel like tangling with either of them, let alone both. This would have to be a peaceful confrontation.

They stared down at me, as if from some unfathomable height. "Are you David Styles?"

"Yes I am. And what brings you here, may I ask? Care to sit down? May I get you something?" I had to be pretty nervous to rattle off lines like that.

"We have a complaint against you."

"*Really?* What's the problem?" I gave them my best shocked, I-have-nothing-to-hide-expression. God, I was so close to panic.

They looked at each other, unsure of how to phrase it.

"A head," said the shorter of the two after a pause.

"A head? A head indeed! It was probably attached to shoulders. They tend to go together, you know, for has it not been written that in the land of headless men the one-headed man is—?"

"Mr. Styles, we have a very serious charge against you. About the head, the lady said—"

"Head? What head? No heads here, except possibly myself." I reached over, took the top off the sugar bowl, handed it to the cop and said conspiratorially, "Hey, man. Wanna buy a lid?"

"I think we've got a psychopath on our hands, Nat," said the shorter policeman.

"Or else a wiseass," said Nat.

"Or a combination of both."

Then they turned serious, and the first one intoned in his very best Jack Webb voice, "Mr. Styles, a certain lady whose name shall remain confidential says she saw a severed human head in your apartment. We're here to look around, and maybe arrest you on suspicion of murder. Or more than that if you don't behave yourself."

"Murder? But I haven't murdered anyone in nearly three

weeks. Surely any arms, heads or whatever that I might have lying around would have gotten mighty putrid by now. Do you smell anybody—I mean anything?"

"She said it was in the refrigerator. I think we'll just have a look." Nat made for the refrigerator. I panicked and tried to get up, but a heavy hand on my shoulder forced me back into my seat. "Just you stay put," said the other policeman.

I knew I'd had it. I'd done my best but that wasn't good enough, and I was finished. They'd find Giles and that would be that. When they saw my reaction they knew they'd found what they came for. Nat opened the refrigerator while his partner, still standing over me, looked on.

"Gentlemen," said the thing on the platter, "I am Giles Hewlett, at your service. Pardon me if my host seemed a little ungracious, but due to the irregularity of the—"

They both left in a hurry. They made no attempt to charge me, arrest me, search me, or even close the door behind them. Their car screeched out far more furiously than it had come in, only this time there were no lights.

I really felt sorry for those two. I wonder what kind of report they handed in.

The weeks with Giles turned into months. I didn't see Pam any more, and I didn't miss her as much as I thought I would, so perhaps we weren't in love after all. Giles and I became the best of friends, or at least as close as we could considering the situation. Countless times I found myself wishing I had been born in his century, so I could have known him while he was, ah, living.

The following summer I overcame my fear of traveling with him, and the two of us went to Europe. I had some trouble getting him through customs, but I finally convinced the officials that he was made of plastic and a prop for my amateur ventriloquism act. ("Very realistic," someone remarked.) He was amazed by the way Paris looks now ("Where's the fat king?"), as he was with Rome, Madrid, Athens, and just about every other major European capital except London. He wouldn't go to Britain. I told him that the war had been over for a long time, and that America and the United Kingdom were allies now, but he was still one to hold a grudge.

"You're being ridiculous," I'd say.

"David, *you've* never rushed back from a lovely bounce between the sheets and then—swish!—off comes your head, or anything else. Now, have you?"

"Well, no . . ."

"Then who are you to judge?"

We flew back to New York without ever stopping in London. And the months followed one another, wonderful months, growing months, learning months, full of discovery. But they made up a year, eventually. The best year of my life, but a year nevertheless. Which was the catch. One part of the legend which I had come upon in my researches in the first week, but which I refused to believe, was very simply, that anyone who accepts the head of the Headless Horseman of Paoli will die within the year, frequently on the same day, a year later, when the horseman retrieves his head for another round of what I suppose you could call the old give-and-take.

I procrastinated incredibly. It was the day before our "anniversary" when I finally asked Giles.

"Yes, David, I'm afraid it's true. It does seem to happen that way."

"Well, why didn't you *tell* me?"

"Well, zounds, man! I thought you knew. Besides, you were having such a wonderful time I didn't want to spoil the fun."

I was silent for a long while after that. I paced back and forth in the kitchen. I banged my fists against the walls in frustration until the apartment shook. Giles could only follow me with his eyes, rolling them from side to side.

"Isn't there anything we can *do?*"

"Not that I know of," he said glumly.

"Can't we stop it, I mean him, I mean you? I'm confused. If you're you, then what's coming, in your body, I mean?"

"David, I have pondered that long and hard. I think I am on Earth still as a kind of purgatory, and the body is a demon or maybe some other kind of spirit sent to see me through it. Silent chap, really. Never said a word to me in all my two centuries."

"Your purgatory?"

"I was no saint, you'll recall."

"Well, how do you stop a spirit?"

"No idea."

"None?"

So I paced, and he rolled his eyes for a while. I looked at the clock on the wall. It was four-thirty. Was this my last afternoon, I asked myself? Was I doomed? What does a man do when a relentless demon is coming for his best friend's head (that being all of him there is to come for) and his own life?

"You could get an exorcist, I suppose," said Giles at last.

"A what?"

"Like on that weekday morning supernatural series, *Exorcise with Gloria.*"

"Gloria Grimm? I know her."

"You *know* her?"

"My mother went to her all the time to have her palm read. She was very superstitious. Believed in ghosts and all that—" I paused, unable to finish, staring at Giles, who gave me a strange look.

"Well, don't just stand there gawking like a moron! Do something!"

I looked at the clock again.

"Yes! Her shop closes in half an hour. Come on!"

I stuffed him into a shopping bag, raced down the stairs, and all but leapt into my car, pulling out of the driveway in a storm of dust and gravel and leaves. I drove crazier than I ever had before, and I really believed in guardian angels or whatever then because I didn't run over anybody or get flagged down by a cop, for all the fire hydrants I smashed into (three) or streets I one-wayed the wrong way.

But I made it. The Malvern Bargain Plaza stands in the middle of nowhere desperately trying to become somewhere. Fortunately, business is so bad the access roads are never clogged. At five of five I screeched into the parking lot, grabbed Giles, nearly *flew* out of the car before it had even come to a full stop, and raced breathlessly into the enclosed mall.

Gloria Grimm's little shop was between the shoe store and Gimbels. It had been there before the shopping plaza was even built. Rumor had it the developers had tried to run her out, but *something* had happened and they built the place around her. There she remained, doing a modest but steady business, driving

out devils, reading tea leaves, and the like. Above her door was a
blinking neon sign: GLORIA GRIMM, GYPSY WITCH.

She was a lot older than I'd remembered her, in her eighties at
least. There she sat behind a black satin covered table, frail and
wrinkle-faced, but stiff and tough-looking as an ancient oak, peering into a glowing crystal ball.

"Silence my son. Be calm. The spirits are about to speak.
Besides that, it's nearly closing time."

"Gloria—Miss Grimm. It's me, Davie Styles. Remember?"

She looked up, and a broad smile cracked her face.

"Yes! How you've grown! I remember when you sat on my
knee! You look so flustered. What's the rush?"

"You gotta help me!"

"Oh, but it's so late, and I'm tired. I'm not as young as I once
was, Davie. Couldn't you come by tomorrow morning, and we'll
have some nice hot chocolate, and you can tell me all about it?"

"It won't wait." And in a nearly incoherent fashion I tried to
explain it all in one sentence, which was garbled, as was the next
one, explaining that, and the next, and the next.

"If I could put in a word here," said Giles.

She looked at the bag in astonishment.

"You throwing your voice, Davie?"

I couldn't say anything, so I reached in and took Giles out.

"How do you do, Madame?" he said. "I watch you on the
television regularly."

She reached under the table for the switch to turn the crystal
ball off.

"My God! It's real! Oy vey. I just work here, you see. It's a
living. I want to retire to Florida like everybody else, but this!
Davie, what have you gotten yourself into?"

Giles explained it. All of it. Calmly, clearly.

"Well, well," she said, shaking her hands nervously. "I'll do
what I can. I . . . I have connections who might help."

"Please do whatever you can," said Giles. "And quickly, I pray
you."

"Yes . . . yes . . . Such a nice boy, too."

She took a telephone from under the table and dialed furiously.

A pause. "Oh damn . . . she died, and I haven't got the new

number." Dialed again. "Hello . . . What? Not until sundown?
Well, leave a message! It's Gloria Grimm. That's *G* as in Götter-
dämmerung, *L* as in Lilith . . . Yes, yes, okay . . . Damn answering service!" Another call and: "Yes, I'm fine. How are you?
And little Greymalkin? Oh, did you leave out a bowl of milk for
Nyarlathotep? He gets very angry if you don't. Look, I'm in a bit
of a sticky situation. You remember Davie Styles? Uh-huh . . .
Look, can you round up everybody and get them over here right
away? No, you don't have to file a flight plan! Thanks very much,
dearie."

So we waited. Gloria marveled at the sight of Giles and questioned him endlessly about ectoplasmic engrams, life beyond the
veil, and the like. They could have gone on all evening while I sat
there scared and forgotten, but then the guests began to arrive.

First there was another old, old lady, dressed all in black,
wearing a conical hat, who set a broom made of twigs against the
wall so gingerly you'd think it was a rare and delicate work of art.
Madame Midnight, Gloria called her. Then there was a teenaged
girl, barefoot and wearing jeans and a tee shirt, but with an owl
perched on either shoulder. A tall, thin woman in white didn't
seem to arrive. The air grew blurry for a second, and there she
was. An elderly, bearded man came in a box, which seemed to
float into the shop by itself. Three United Parcel men followed
with three more boxes, none larger than a violin case. They
adjourned to a back room. I heard scraping and dry rustling, then
the "Our Father" being recited backwards, after which they left,
taking the boxes with them. After which a tall, pale fellow in
evening dress joined us at the table. A dwarf dropped from the
ceiling.

At last there were twelve of them, including Gloria.

"We're all here," she said, "except the Black Man."

"No coven would be complete—" But before Gloria Grimm
could finish her sentence, an enormous black man, wearing top
hat, tux, tails and spats, with a cane over one arm and a monocle
in one eye, strolled in, shutting the door behind him. He smiled
broadly.

"Well, my children, all of us are present, I see."

He set a briefcase on the table. On the lid, printed in huge
letters was a comment:

THE GREAT JUMBOLO *IS* THE GREATEST.
THERE IS NO OTHER.
—BARON SAMEDI

On the inside was a rave review from the *New York Times* leisure and voodoo section.

"Shall we begin?" said The Great Jumbolo.

I have never seen such a sight in all my life. The black man shaped two lumps of wax into vague semblances of human heads. He placed Giles between them. He made me sit forward with my head down on the table, next to the other three.

Then he began a prayer or invocation. The others joined in, chanting, ranting, yelping, dancing around the table with their hands joined. At one point everybody was wearing black goatskins and rams' horns, but the air was so thick with incense I couldn't see much. It went on all night. I felt myself dozing off, but Jumbolo nudged me.

"No mon, you must stay awake, or else your soul turn into, how you say it? *Pretzel.*"

The shadows seemed alive. Some of them had wings and were flapping around above me. There was a flash of lightning and a clap of thunder. That's it, I told myself. Now the security guards hear us. This will be hard to explain. But they didn't come.

I only knew it was morning when the Muzak started and the fountains outside were turned on. It was a relatively quiet part of the ritual, and I could hear the water splashing.

"Oh dear," said Gloria. She fumbled under the table, got out her crystal ball, hooked an extension cord to it, and plugged it into a wall socket. "He's coming. He's crossing the parking lot now."

I turned and looked, and there, inside the crystal ball, was the image of the horseman gliding across the pavement between the lampposts.

"I hope we've done enough," said the dwarf. "It would be a shame to ruin such good work."

"I have the thing you need," said The Great Jumbolo. He took a flask out of his briefcase, opened it, and a wisp of white smoke floated in the air, not going anywhere. "It is a tame spirit," he said.

For some reason I *could* hear the horseman this time. His horse's hooves chattered on the polished floor. He was inside the mall now.

"Quick!" hissed Jumbolo. He touched my head, Giles, and the two wax models. He snapped a finger and pointed, and the white cloud drifted into the ear of one of the wax heads, and the thing began to melt and shift. I was too numb with astonishment to be surprised by anything at this point, so I took it in stride that the thing became a perfect replica of Giles, as did the other one. But I was upset, perturbed, and even terrified when I found myself looking down on my own body, seeing how I had slumped over the table unconscious. I was drifting among the winged shadows and incense fumes. I felt another presence. Somehow I knew it was Giles, drifting with me. I floated around the room, as if my head was weightless and I couldn't turn it. Sometimes I saw only the ceiling, but sometimes I was looking down.

I was looking down on myself, on Giles, Jumbolo, and the rest when the Horseman came in. He knocked once, and the latch on the door dropped away. The knob didn't turn, but the door swung open all by itself. In he came. Everybody except Jumbolo backed away from the table. Gloria hovered in a far corner, but the rest of them retreated into the back room. Only the black man faced the spectre face to . . . neck. He was magnificent.

"Looking for something, mon?"

The Horseman was silent. He approached the table. Suddenly the eyes of all three disembodied heads opened. They were so alike now it was hard to tell which was Giles and which were the imitations.

Which was exactly what was intended.

"I am the real Giles Hewlett," said the first. "Take me."

"No, *I* am the real Giles Hewlett."

"They're both lying. It's me."

The Horseman paused, and as he did, Jumbolo grinned a wide grin and shuffled the heads like nuts in a shell game.

"Which one, mon? You choose."

The Horseman stood there, put his hand to where his chin should have been, and puzzled the situation out. All the while I was drifting dizzily above, alternately looking down, up, and sideways.

At last he pointed to the middle head.

"It's yours," said the black man.

Then he went over and lifted me up by the hair. Even though I wasn't in my body, I felt the chill of his touch.

When I saw my face, I felt sick. I looked terrible. My eyes were rolled up so that only the whites showed. I was pale and slack-jawed. Drool ran down my chin.

"Dead," said the black man. "No soul in body."

The Horseman let go and my forehead banged against the tabletop. Without a word, he left.

"Come on out. He's gone," Jumbolo called, and soon the whole coven was seated at the table again. Two heads remained. One of them was turning into plain wax again. The other remained—Giles?

The incantations began. It was as if a sudden gust of wind blew through the place. Suddenly I was whirling all around. I was falling. The shop was gone, and I was high above a dark valley, swooping down between two snow-covered mountains which glowed from a sunset somewhere behind them. The crags below glowed a sullen furnace red. I was in the hereafter, beyond life. The landscape all around was so desolate. I wanted to cry out, but I was just a cloud without a voice.

But then a wrinkled, bony hand on the end of an arm a hundred miles long grabbed me by the scruff of the neck and dragged me back to this world. I saw the room again, blurry and swaying, and blacked out.

I awoke slowly, numb all over. I wanted to touch my face with my hand to assure myself I was still there, solid once more, but nothing touched.

I opened my eyes. At first I thought I was buried up to the chin in the middle of a vast plain of black velvety sand. Then, no, a hospital bed. With black sheets?

I saw the giants looming over me and I screamed.

"Hey! What is this? Help! You can't do this to me!"

And I saw *myself* sit up groggily, open my eyes, and look around in amazement.

"Zounds . . ."

The voice sounded terribly familiar.

"Giles!"

"David!"

"What are you doing in my body?"

"That's my head you're wearing!"

It was true.

"Oops," said The Great Jumbolo.

"Oops," said Gloria Grimm.

"Uh?" grunted the dwarf.

"I'm sorry, Davie," said Gloria Grimm. "These things happen. It's not our fault. We had to get you out, so you'd be dead and he'd leave you alone."

"Well, get me back *in!*" For the first time the odd thought came to me that a loose head should not be able to speak, lacking lungs, but by now I had faith in the supernatural. "Do what you did *again,* and put me back in my own body."

Jumbolo picked up the wax head, which was no more than a formless lump now.

"Too late," he said.

"Yes," said Gloria. "I'm afraid the new fitting has hardened. To undo one of these would take a long, long time."

"How long?"

"About a hundred years. But I'll work on it."

I believe she will. She's such a sweet old lady. As for the others, they left as unobtrusively as they'd come. I suppose I had to thank them for saving me, so I did, but in truth I wasn't too pleased with the lot of them. Unfortunately there are no malpractice suits in magic.

"Well," said Giles-in-my-body after they'd all left. "I shall enjoy being a whole man again. Really I shall!" And he walked over to the door.

I may have been scared before, but this was the one instant of hopeless, despairing terror.

"*Giles!* You can't . . . just leave me!"

He paused. He looked hurt and ashamed. I don't know what he was thinking, but he must have reconsidered, or understood what he was doing, or something.

"No, I *never*—! You're my friend!"

He put me in the shopping bag. Gloria Grimm drove us home in my car.

We had a hundred years to kill. Giles, an immortal spirit of sorts, cannot die. He sustains my body without aging it. In his head, made of ectoplasm or whatever, I can last forever, too.

The world gets stranger and stranger. He lacked so many of my everyday skills; he could never pass for me. He couldn't drive a car, do my job, sign my name to a check. So we had to give up the apartment, sell everything, and go on the road. He could have taken the money and run off, leaving me holding the bag (in the bag), so to speak, but he never did. We went on the road together. Our adventures were endless. Eventually we began working for a circus, traveling from town to town, giving "disconcertingly convincing" performances of ventriloquism, or so the press said.

Waiting a hundred years for Gloria Grimm, who will surely last that long, to set things right.

Did you know the shows keep logs, just like ships? They do. Topeka ahoy!

BERTHA RUNKLE

Artemisia's Mirror

In 1901, Small, Maynard & Company, a Boston publisher, printed A
House Party, *a bookful of twelve "stories told at a gathering of famous
American authors," but the identity of the contributors was kept secret.
Readers were invited to send in a coupon bound into the volume before
December 31 and try to name the writers. No one won the $1,000 grand
prize, though a Mrs. Horace Silsbee, of Seneca Falls, New York, got eleven
of them right. Eventually the publisher revealed who wrote what. The
following gentle ghost story, attributed to* BERTHA RUNKLE, *takes place in
the Greenwich Village section of New York City.*

Some sixty years ago, there lived in New York in a tiny frame
cottage in Greenwich village, a little girl who had three names. To
her mother and her grandfather, she was Pet; to her mates, she
was Arty; but on the record page of the family Bible, and, alack
and alas, on the sampler her mother had marked out for her, she
was Artemisia Vanderhooven.

In defiance of her Dutch name, she was dark-eyed and dark-
haired, quick and graceful in her motions as a kitten, quick, too,
in her temper, impatient, restless as quicksilver, fond of playing
with boys, hating everything quiet and dutiful. Such was the child
who was set down on summer afternoons to record in weary
stitches with a fine disregard of rhythm, that

> Artemisia Vanderhooven is my name
>   America is my nation
> New York is my dwelling place
>   And Christ is my salvation.

And furthermore, as if one stanza were not enough for mortal flesh to toil through,

> When I am dead and in my grave
>   And all my bones are rotten
> I leave these verses after me
>   That I be not forgotten.

It was Pet's miserable conviction that she should be in her grave before the very first line of the memorial was finished, so many times did the silk tangle and break, the needle rust in the little hot fingers, or the scissors take to themselves wings and fly away. Three times during the progress of that first line did her relentless mother make Pet rip out every stitch. Nor was the appearance of the sampler improved when used for wiping away tears.

The only drop of sweet in Pet's bitter cup was that sometimes on very hot days, when there was not a breath of air in the little house, she was allowed to take her sewing out into the garden, where Grandsir worked among his lilacs and May roses, his tulips and hyacinths, his hearts-ease and London pride. The garden was a haven of peace, for Grandsir never admonished one—on the contrary, he often seemed to forget one's presence. But to be forgotten was so far preferable to being remembered too strenuously, that Pet had no fault to find with him. She was his hot champion against all criticism—none the less ardent that the chief criticism—her mother's—was all unspoken. Never had Pet heard her mother say an unkind word of Grandsir; yet, with the keen intuition of childhood, she divined her mother's disapproval of his queer ways—his continual pottering over the flowers, his Indian-like silences. This tacit reproach it was impossible to combat, but when her playmate, Millie Kennedy, once said that her father said that old Mr. Vanderhooven was cracked, Pet, though by no means sure what cracked meant, slapped Millie, pulled her hair, and drove her home weeping. Pet was no Griselda.

Grandsir was trimming the box hedges one afternoon, looking, as he moved slowly about—a silent bowed figure, with long white beard and shining shears—rather like Father Time himself. Pet, sitting with her work-box on the step of the grape-arbour, was moved to help him. With her own little scissors she began snipping off box leaves, till, the scissors catching on a stiff twig, they flew out of her hand into the heart of the hedge. Pet jumped up to rescue them, when over went the work-box, its spools and skeins and needle books and emery and tape-measure all rolling about in the flowers and grass. She stamped her feet with rage; then, creeping about on her knees to pick up her work, she stained with loam the front of her white frock. Her one white frock had been put on to go to Millie's house to supper, and now Mother would never let her go. Unless perhaps, she should work so much and so diligently, all afternoon, that Mother would forgive her. With the fever of desperation, she bent over her sampler.

Presently Grandsir came nearer. Pet looked up and smiled as he approached—she always smiled when he came by, as one does at a baby. And now, for a miracle, Grandsir withdrew himself from the land of dreams where he walked alone, and put his hand on her flushed brow, and said:

"What's the matter with Grandsir's Pet?"

She would not tell him about the frock, for she knew she should cry, and lose time from the sampler, so she burst out, "I hate my name!"

"Artemisia?" said Grandsir softly, puzzledwise.

"Artemisia Vanderhooven!" cried that young person in accents of wrath.

"Twenty-one letters to work. Look at mother's little name, Jane Platt— Why didn't they call me Jane? Artemisia! I hate Artemisia!"

"But her name was Artemisia," said Grandsir, gently.

"My grandmother's?" Pet remembered the fact suddenly, and dropped her angry voice a key. She must have hurt Grandsir's feelings. Oh, day of misfortune! But he was never angry with her, and after a moment, she ventured—

"And did she like her name, Grandsir?"

"She liked it," said Grandsir, "and I liked it."

The haze that separated him from this world's doings came into his eyes again, and he spoke no more, and turned away to his work. But Pet was not done with the subject. The marvel of an Artemisia who liked the name absorbed her. She rose and slipped her hand into the old man's, rubbing against his side like a kitten.

"Why did she like it, Grandsir dear?"

Grandsir was that adorable being, a person who never joked. When others gave her an answer she could not understand, cruel experience had taught her to suspect witticisms at her expense; but Grandsir's mysterious replies always had sense in them, if you could only work it out. He was so old and could tell so much if he would. It often seemed when with him as if she stood on the very threshold of a store-house packed full of forgotten treasures; and never had she felt the explorer's thrill more vividly than now, when he answered at length, after a pause so long that she feared he would not answer at all—

"On account of the mirror, I think."

She paused an instant, almost afraid to breathe, lest the treasure-house door close upon her; but he did not speak again; and finally, very softly, as one who fears to frighten some shy wood-creature, she repeated, "The mirror, sir?"

This time the answer came at once:

"Cellini's mirror—Artemisia's mirror."

"Did the mirror belong to her, Grandsir?"

"Yes," he answered. And now a strange thing happened. The old man's placid face which, like the faces of the gods—or the dumb brutes—neither laughed nor wept, broke into a smile. His voice changed with it, and from an absent murmur as of one talking in a dream took on a louder, livelier, human tone. "At least, she took it, when she came with me. She said no one had a better right. Her name was on the frame."

Pet sighed with rapture. The past, the mysterious, the miraculous was unrolling before her.

"What did it look like, Grandsir?"

He seemed surprised.

"The child's seen it."

"No, Grandsir, never," she protested. Could it be that the

mirror existed? The mirror with her name—her own name, despised no longer—on the frame?

"It's put away for you," said Grandsir. "For little Artemisia."

She jumped up and down in joy.

"Oh, Grandsir, when can I have it? I don't hate the name now, I love it. Oh, when may I have it?"

The haze crept over Grandsir's face again. "Your mother—"

"Oh, no, Grandsir," the child cried. "It isn't mother's. It's just yours and mine. Oh, *please*, Grandsir. I'd be so careful of it. I love it so."

Mother never would have listened for a moment, but Grandsir, the only reasonable grown-up person whom Pet had ever seen, seemed to appreciate the justice of the argument.

"You would love it, wouldn't you?" he said. "She loved it too. She loved it dearly. She had it in her hand when he killed her."

"Oh, Grandsir!" the child cried, her eyes wide in horror. "Did some one kill your Artemisia?"

The cloud came over the old man's face; he frowned and clenched his fingers, in vain effort to think.

"I think they let him off," he muttered at length. "It was a long time ago. I presume," he added, with a pathetic struggle for self-respect, "I presume I never inquired just what happened." He turned away mechanically to his clipping, but Pet clutched his arm.

"But the mirror, Grandsir. Won't you let Artemisia have the mirror?"

He said never a word, but went straight into the house and got it for her.

It was a silver-framed glass, about twelve inches square, surrounded by a ring of laughing cupids, pelting one another with roses. Over the glass was a coat of arms; below, another, but quite different. On the right, running down the frame, was the name of Artemisia, and opposite, on the left, the name of Odoardo.

"But who was Odoardo?" cried Pet, as she took the treasure into her eager hands.

Then, bit by bit, day by day, the story of the mirror was revealed.

Somewhat to her surprise, Pet was allowed to keep the dear possession. Her mother feared it would make her a very vain little

girl. "But," said honest Pet, to whom had never occurred the
notion of using Artemisia's mirror to look at herself in, "I don't
care about it because it's a looking-glass; I care about it because it
has my name on it." And her mother, seeing the child hug it in
her arms, had not the heart to take it away.

Now were the sewing-hours, hours of joy. Pet would take her
little chair into the garden, plant it close to whatever flower-bed
was absorbing Grandsir, sit down with the sacred mirror on her
knees—for all her heedless ways she never once scratched or
dented it—and ply the old gentleman with questions. And from
what he told, and what her mother knew, and what, later, her own
imagination supplied to her, she constructed the history of the
mirror.

About 1527 I suppose, at all events, when the question of King
Henry VIII's divorce was first broached, and the king and his
Holy Father at Rome were the best friends in the world, a certain
young courtier named Edward Sutton was despatched to the
Vatican, to breathe privily into Clement's ear a moving account of
his Majesty's sufferings by reason of his unchurchly marriage.
That he, Edward, accomplished much for his master, history does
not show, but he did very well for himself when he married the
beauty and heiress, Artemisia Visconti. Jewels and plate and gold
coin he carried back to England in his wife's coffers, and, dearest
to Artemisia of all her gear, her father's gift, the mirror. The glass
was dull, to be sure, and flawed here and there, like a pond on a
gusty day; for mirror-making was an infant industry then, carried
on with infantile skill. But Artemisia, never having seen better,
was quite satisfied. And who indeed would think of defects in the
glass, when Cellini had made the frame? Artemisia never went
from London to Sutton House (the Dominican priory which the
King had wrenched from the Monks for his favourite Sir Edward)
without the loved mirror. It was unpacked and placed in her
bedchamber, even at the roadside inns where she passed a night,
and in the morning packed again, oh, so carefully, and strapped
to my lady's own saddle for the next day's ride. The mirror hung,
very epitome of worldliness, on the grey priory wall where never
mirror had hung before, and watched all the junketings of the
idle triflers that passed before it. The old walls, that never since
their building had beheld aught but black-gowned monks at their

sombre duties and bare refections, must have looked in horrified amaze on the feasts, the games, the dancing, the gay plumage of women and men. But the mirror, born, like its mistress, in mirth-loving Italy, beamed approval. From its high place, like a king on his dais, it presided over masque and rout, and gave smiling sanction to all. It felt, doubtless—how should a mirror guess otherwise?—that all passing and repassing before its glass, all actions within its sight, were but a pageant arranged for its pleasure. Like the King in his box at the play, it graciously rewarded the actors by giving back smile for smile when the piece was gay, and sympathetic frowns when lowering Tragedy showed her face. And, greatest tribute of all, the mirror paid the players the courtesy of unflagging attention. Day in, day out, season by season, year by year, be the piece gay or be the piece dull, absorbing drama or veriest farce, the mirror with unwearied patience, watched, watched, always watched. All the days of her life, it watched the lady of Sutton, and when at length the name of Artemisia Visconti was carved beside the English Kates and Elizabeths in Sutton church, it watched her children.

It almost forgot Benvenuto's workshop, or Artemisia's bridal chamber, overlooking the Tiber, so overlaid were those pictures by the swift, changing visions of the Priory. For two hundred years and more, the mirror hung in the great hall reflecting marriage feast and funeral breakfast, peace and war, retinues of Tudors, Stuarts, Brunswicks. It nearly lost its Priory home under Catholic Mary, only to have its right confirmed by Protestant Elizabeth. It saw the stately first Charles when once he spent a night at Sutton House; what it did not see—it was hidden in the cellars lest it should see or be seen—was the nag of a roundhead trooper tied to the very hook where itself had hung so long. But at length the land was at peace again, and Cellini's mirror took its old proud place. Where it had been for a hundred years, there it remained for a hundred more, and ought, so the Suttons aver, to be hanging to-day. But we Vanderhoovens hold otherwise. We maintain that the mirror is ours, on stronger testimony than that of the Suttons—the mirror's own.

At the beginning of the last century, there dwelt in Sutton House another Artemisia. Dark-haired she was, like her remote ancestress, with a clear skin, flushing and paling as she talked, and brown eyes looking out eagerly on life, demanding of it something more than the pompous comfort to which she had been born. A summer in London, a winter in Bath, marriage with a neighbouring squire, servants to manage, tenants to patronise, the still-room to order, music to copy, and accounts to keep—these satisfied her sisters, but Artemisia, lying wide-eyed in bed o'nights, had dreams of a wider world. The moment was ripe for the fairy prince, and lo, he appeared. His name was Hendrick Vanderhooven, and he came from the United States of America, from a place bearing the extraordinary name of Schenectady. He was young, handsome, a gentleman's son, but, above all, he was different. This difference was his conquering charm, assisted by the fact that from a parent's point of view he was utterly ineligible. In the first place he came from the rebellious colony, where hardly thirty years before, the Earl of Sutton's regiment had suffered grievous rout, the recollection of which stung Lord Sutton even now. And besides, rumours of a new war filled the air.

To the deadly crime of being an American, Hendrick added the unforgivable sin of being a younger son. In Lord Sutton's opinion, human depravity could no farther go. The sobbing Artemisia, told that her family blushed for her, retorted that they need not blush for her long. This was interpreted to be a threat of dying of a broken heart, and was pooh-poohed accordingly. The family mistook Artemisia.

One midnight, a little figure, clad in a kitchen-maid's homespun gown, stole from stair to stair with a lightness of tread no kitchen-maid ever attained. The hob-nailed shoes were in one hand; in the other she carried, tied together in a stout gray shawl, those worldly possessions which she had thought suitable to begin, with her, her new life on the new continent. Fifty years afterward, the man who had awaited her in the garden that night named over to her granddaughter every article that the English Artemisia carried in her shawl. The little garden in Christopher Street was as like as love and pains could make it, to the great garden at Sutton House; Hendrick Vanderhooven, who could not remember on Sunday the thing you had told him on Saturday, yet remembered every turn of the walks in Sutton House garden—and what flowers grew in every bed. He would forget his breakfast, if Pet did not lead him in to his place, but he knew after fifty years, the fashion of Artemisia's trousseau. First the skimp white satin gown in which she had been presented at court, and in which she hoped to conquer the hearts of her new and formidable kinsfolk, the feathered turban, the mitts, the silk stockings and white sandals. Then her prayer book, and Belinda Daphne, the doll given her on her third birthday, and her gold neck-chain and locket with her mother's picture in it; and a curl of her bosom friend Lady Betty Arminster's hair, and a copy of the Gentlemen's Magazine for February, 1811, containing *An Address* in *Rhyme* to Miss *A. S.* on her *Arrival* in *Bath;* and a water colour of Sutton House, executed by herself with much assistance from her drawing master. Also, four pounds, seven and four pence, in gold and silver, her India shawl that her uncle William had brought her from Calcutta, and a stuffed paroquet from the same source, which, all through her childish years, had been Belinda's rival in her deepest affections. She was afraid Hendrick might laugh at Belinda and the paroquet, but she could not steel her heart to the parting. Last of all, this practical young person insured Hendrick and herself from starvation on their road to Gretna, by providing half a loaf of plum-cake. Thus equipped, she felt herself competent to face stormy seas and even a stormy father-in-law. But as she stood in the little back hall, with her hand on the latch of the window, she came to a sudden pause, then, putting down her shoes and bundle, felt her way along the walls to the door at the end of the passage. Down another corridor she groped her noiseless way, and out into the old hall where the monks had eaten their black bread and lentils, and straight to the spot where hung Artemisia's mirror. For one moment she hesitated, conscience warring with desire, but when Hendrick rose from behind the holly bush to seize her, she panted, "There, take that," and thrust the mirror into his hands. It was rightly hers, she argued, since it bore her name. In the fair sweet evening at sea, as the ship sailed into the sunset, she confided to Hendrick, how she sometimes fancied herself that same Artemisia for whom the mirror was wrought, and who so long ago bore it when a bride over strange seas to her husband's home. In pursuit of the fancy, she loved to call Hendrick, Odoardo, or Sir Edward, Knight of St. George.

That early time was what Grandsir loved best to talk about, nor could Pet draw from him any but a vague and confused account of later happenings of how the young couple had gone to his father's home in Schenectady, and then to Hendrick's farm farther to the west, where they built a fair brick house and named it Sutton House, and laid out terraces and gardens after those at the old home in England. And there Pet's father was born and his mother called him the little lord of the manor.

"Why don't we live there now, Grandsir?" was Pet's natural question.

Grandsir's face clouded pitifully and the slow tears filled his old eyes, while he answered pitifully that he didn't know; Dirck had driven him away.

"But how could Dirck drive you and grandmother away?" the child persisted.

"She was dead," said the old man. "Artemisia was dead." He began to cry hopelessly and Pet climbed on his knees and comforted him, and asked him no more questions. But she asked her mother who was Dirck.

"Has your grandfather been talking to you about Dirck?" Mrs. Vanderhooven answered, a little startled, it seemed. "I never heard him so much as mention Dirck's name. I thought he'd forgotten. Dirck was his twin brother."

"He says Dirck drove him from his home!" Pet cried.

"I'll tell you the whole story, Artemisia," her mother said. "You're old enough to hear it now, and you couldn't understand it from Grandsir." Pet, with a fearful joy, composed herself to listen; fearful—for she knew the story concerned her grandmother's death, and her grandmother was killed, Grandsir had said; joyous—with the joy of childhood in stories and mysteries.

"Your grandfather's house—"

"Sutton House," Pet murmured to herself.

"—was burned down. One of the farm hands—his name was Edward Day—set it on fire for spite. Madam Vanderhooven ran into the house to save her mirror—that very mirror you make so much of—and she was burned to death."

"My grandmother Artemisia," whispered Pet, aghast.

"Yes, poor thing. She was so young, too—no more than thirty, and your father used to tell me, often, how pretty she was. He was ten years old at the time and he remembered her well. He used to say you'd grow up her very image."

"Was that why Grandsir left the farm, mother?"

"He had to go, for it wasn't his any longer. His father died in Schenectady only two days after the fire, and then it turned out that the title deeds that gave your Grandsir all his land had been burnt in the fire. It seems that your great grandfather had to leave Hendrick his share of the land in his will, but he deeded it to him earlier, when your grandfather brought his wife home. I presume Hendrick was the favourite son. And your grandfather always was kind of high-flown and heedless, and he never had the deeds recorded, as they call it, but when his father gave the papers to him, he threw them straight into his wife's lap and said, 'Take care of them, Artemisia, that's your fortune.' And she kept them, and he never took the trouble to know where they were, till they went up in smoke. So then Dirck got the place, because his father's will left him everything not already disposed of."

"But, mother, the place wasn't Grandsir's father's; it was Grandsir's," little Artemisia cried.

"Yes, but the papers to prove it were burnt," said her mother, with the calm of long submission. Artemisia, in tears, was jumping up and down with excitement over unbearable wrong.

"But didn't everybody know it was Grandsir's? Didn't Dirck know? Why didn't Grandsir tell him?" she sobbed.

"Oh, bless you, child, Dirck knew, and everybody knew. But the law wouldn't give your grandfather the place without the papers. He had no proof at all, so Dirck took it. It was the best land in your grandfather's estate, and Dirck had always been mad, so your father said, because Hendrick got it. He didn't offer to give it back, once he got it, Dirck didn't, and your Grandsir and your father were turned out, like beggars."

"Is Dirck alive?" Pet asked with visions of a just God striking him dead, like Ananias, for his iniquities. But her mother answered—

"Oh dear, yes. He comes to town every winter, and lives in one of the biggest houses in Lafayette Place. They're rolling in money, while your father clerked it all his days. But he'd sooner have starved than go to Dirck Vanderhooven for help."

"But don't we have any money at all, mother?" Pet asked.

"We've got what I earn," her mother told her. "Then there's the house, and a little besides. I couldn't take care of the three of us, all by myself. But I make every cent I can sewing. Your father couldn't say I don't try my best."

This, Pet's first glimpse into the ways of the great world, left her with a profound contempt for that machine of injustice known as the law, a Montague and Capulet hatred of the Lafayette Place Vanderhooven's, and a quite new respect for her hated needle. That mother worked to support her and Grandsir, had never occurred to her. Food was spread thrice a day, she had never questioned any more than Tim, the cat, whence it came. But now to help mother became her ardent ambition. The little devil that knotted the thread and ran off with the thimble was exorcised and triumphantly cast out, till on one proud day her mother said, "I do declare, Pet, you're a better hand with your needle than I am."

Pet was eighteen now, pretty and fresh and gay, working hard to ease mother, but finding time for play too, brooding little over the lost glories of her line, but finding life as pleasant to Pet Vanderhooven of the little cottage as it could be to her cousins, the young ladies of Lafayette Place. Grandsir was older, feebler, even more silent. When she went out, as she often did, to help his ineffective hands in the garden, there were no more stories of Artemisia. Save that he would sit for hours with the mirror in his hand, Pet could think that he had forgotten all, as she herself had well nigh forgotten it in the busy interests of her young life.

Then came the day when her mother fell ill. A slight cold, a mere nothing, they thought it, but in three days she was dying. Toward the last her eyes dwelt in a frightened way on Pet, and she seemed to long to speak, but could not, and passed in silence. Her going left Pet stunned with misery, but the ill fates had not done with her. The day her mother was buried came the lawyer through whom Mrs. Vanderhooven's little income had been paid, to tell Pet that Mr. Vanderhooven continued the free tenancy of the house, and the same allowance he had paid her mother.

"My grandfather?" Pet ejaculated, completely at a loss.

"Your great-uncle, Mr. Dirck Vanderhooven."

To her look of speechless amaze he went on.

"Didn't you know, Miss Vanderhooven, that Mr. Dirck Vanderhooven had made your mother an allowance of twenty dollars a month ever since your father's death, fifteen years ago?"

"Out of our own estate, the magnificent fortune of twenty dollars a month!" Pet blazed forth. "Convey my compliments, if you please, to Mr. Dirck Vanderhooven, and inform him that I have learned for the first time of his generosity and that from this hour I decline to be a beggar on his bounty."

"My dear Miss Vanderhooven," the lawyer protested, "think what you are doing."

"I do think," Pet retorted, though as a matter of fact she did not, she only felt. "I know what I am doing. I know Grandsir and I would rather starve than accept one penny from Mr. Dirck Vanderhooven. The money he has given us shall all be paid back, he may rest assured. I have no more to say to you, Mr. Cheever."

When Pet assumed the air that had won her grandmother the name of "the haughty madam," there was indeed no more to be said. The very next day, she and Grandsir were installed in two rooms in the very eaves of a narrow house in Bleecker Street, and Mr. Dirck Vanderhooven was richer by two hundred and forty dollars a year.

Heroism is seldom comfortable for the hero, my dears, but it is likely to bear even harder on the hero's family. Poor Grandsir could by no means understand why he must leave his garden plot, his work of fifteen years. He wept like a wronged child, and, with a child's obstinacy, clung by main force to the arbour-post and declined to budge. In despair, Pet told him they must go, because the house was Dirck's. Instantly Grandsir's lamentations ceased, while there came into his face both fear and cunning, a look even more pitiable than his tears.

"We must go, child; we must go this minute," he cried, clutching Pet's arm and peering round to see if perchance Dirck were lurking near. "We must go before Dirck finds us. He drove us away from Sutton House; he'll drive us out of the country if he can."

In the new abode, for weeks after, every time a board creaked, a step sounded in the hallway, Grandsir cringed and whispered "Dirck!" Pet's heart nearly broke for pity, but she was powerless to lay the ghost of the past she had raised.

Fortunately it was the depth of winter, so that Grandsir did not pine to be out in his garden, but was content with the pots of geraniums and pinks that Pet had brought from the old house.

Also, like a child with a loved toy, he played more and more with the mirror. Hour by hour, he would rub up to highest lustre its shining frame; hour by hour he would sit motionless gazing into its grey depths, and he told Pet that he could see Artemisia in the mirror; that she lived there, and when he was all alone she would come out of the glass and speak to him.

It was a pretty fancy, and Pet rejoiced to see that it made Grandsir happy. He talked again and more than ever of Artemisia, till her young grandmother seemed to Pet like one of the girls she knew, so familiar and real had her personality grown. Her presence filled the room; she seemed sometimes more alive than the two living beings who dwelt there.

Pet indeed felt herself by the ghost of her brilliant wilful triumphant namesake. All day long and all the evening, she sewed, sewed, sewed, for not only must she and Grandsir be kept respectable, but she must pay back that twenty dollars a month owed for fifteen years. A Herculean task, truly, but to it Pet set her slender strength with all the spirit of a Hercules.

Her life was a lonely one enough, for she would not spare time for visiting; but it was not unhappy; she was strung too keenly to her purpose to mind poverty or loneliness. She had no thought at all of herself; her life knew only two motives. Dirck Vanderhooven must be paid off, and Grandsir must be kept happy.

For Grandsir's sake, she put aside her work one spring day, and, leaving him in the care of a kindly neighbour, went out into the country even as far as Fiftieth Street, to dig him violets. She was tired out and the big market basket weighed a ton by the time she had trudged back to her own door. She set the basket down on the lowest step and sighed as she thought of the steep stairs. It was even at this moment that the hand of fate shoved toward her a young man who had recently come to lodge in the room next to Grandsir's. He was a nice looking young man whose eyes had a habit of following Pet.

"Mayn't I carry up your basket?" he now besought, hat in hand.

"Oh, thank you, sir, but it is *very* heavy." Pet protested ingenuously. The young man's bashfulness vanished before her confusion.

"Then I must certainly carry it," he replied. On the way up, Pet lifted the wet papers and showed him her treasures; he asked where they came from and she described her ramble. He remarked that he had seen her several times before; she answered carelessly that she thought she had seen him (she had encountered him on the stairs no longer ago than that morning). By the time they reached her door he had confided to her that he was a banker's clerk and his name was Eric Parker.

Pet, standing on the threshold, lifted her shy eyes to his. It struck her that the fear of Dirck's footstep might be lifted from Grandsir if he could be made to understand that it was this Mr. Eric Parker whose tread rang so often on the stairs.

"Would you like to come in and see my grandfather?" she asked. "Grandsir's quite old, Mr. Parker, and he doesn't always understand very well. But you won't appear to notice it?"

Eric promised eagerly, and she presented him to "my grandfather."

Grandsir, when visitors came, had but the one formula, whether to a stranger or to a friend of twenty years. "I don't know you, do I?" "Yes, Grandsir, it's Millie Kennedy," Pet would say. Then Grandsir would observe, with a recrudescence of former gallantry, "If you came oftener, my dear, I should know you better." But a moment later he would reiterate helplessly, "I don't know you, do I?"

He looked now at Eric Parker, in his old puzzled way. Then came a difference. He spoke with conviction, "I've *seen* you before."

"Very likely sir. I live in the house," Eric answered politely, though, for all chances of being seen by Grandsir, who never left his room, he might as well have lived in Kamtschatka.

"Why, of course I know you. You work on my farm," was Grandsir's amazing remark.

"No, Grandsir," interposed Pet, "Mr. Parker lives in New York. He was never on the farm."

"I beg your pardon, sir. I must have confused you with someone else," the old man apologised.

"A very natural mistake, I'm sure sir," said the courteous young man and the subject was dropped. But the next time Eric came (which was the following evening) Grandsir hailed him instantly as a messenger from the farm and asked how deep the snow was in the country, and how the stock were getting through the winter. And Eric, sitting down by the old man, fell into the game, answering as best he could all Grandsir's eager questions and inventing volumes of misinformation about the farm.

"That was very kind," Pet said to him in a low voice when he bade her good night. "It's a pious fraud, I'm sure, Mr. Parker. He did enjoy it so."

"Anything to save you, Miss Pet," Eric answered, ardently.

"Miss Vanderhooven," she corrected, blushing. Eric started.

"Vanderhooven? Are you kin to the Vanderhoovens in Lafayette Place?" he asked quickly.

Pet was ill-pleased at this eager interest in the rich Vanderhoovens. "Snob!" she cried inwardly, while replying with all the ancestral grand manner.

"We are the poor Vanderhoovens. We don't claim the slightest kinship with the Vanderhoovens of Lafayette Place."

The presumptuous youth declined to be crushed to earth by the Artemisian manner. On the contrary, he was delighted, he said, that she was not related to those Vanderhoovens.

What he had against the Lafayette Place Vanderhoovens she knew not, but the fact of his animosity endeared the youngster amazingly to Pet. The possession of common enemies is one of the dearest of all ties that bind—a tie far stronger than that of common friends. This, and his kindness to Grandsir, made Eric ever welcome, and Pet even allowed him to coax her out of doors on pleasant evenings. Before many weeks he and Pet, sitting on a secluded bench in Battery Park, concluded that they were made for each other. They had been repeating this with very slight variations for an hour or so when Eric asked Pet incidentally what her name was.

"Vanderhooven, the poor Vanderhooven," she answered, for he made fun of her fierce pride.

"Never mind, it shall be Parker soon. But I mean your first name dearest. I suppose your sponsors in baptism didn't christen you Pet, did they? Not that they could have found any name half so fit."

"Of course I have a name," Pet protested with dignity. "But it is too fine for every day, so Mother called me Pet. My real name is Artemisia."

He started away from her, dropping her hand.

"Artemisia Vanderhooven!"

"Yes, I was named for my grandmother, the Lady Artemisia Sutton." Pet's voice lingered lovingly on the name.

He sprang up, seeming to tower over her.

"Then your grandfather is Hendrick Vanderhooven. I might have guessed—But you told me you weren't related to those Vanderhoovens."

She rose too. Something, she knew not what, was hideously amiss.

"We have quarreled with them, and we have nothing to do with them. But my grandfather is Hendrick Vanderhooven."

"And my father was Edward Day."

"The man who killed my grandmother?"

The turf under her feet rose and fell like the waves in the bay, and the trees swayed like masts. Pet caught hold of the bench to steady herself.

"Eric, you're raving. Your name's Parker—"

"My father changed his name and left his home. But the stigma followed him everywhere till he died of the shame of it."

"Your father," Pet whispered, as if it were too hideous to say aloud. "And you came to me!"

"I didn't know—"

"The name of Vanderhooven should have been enough!"

"But I loved you before I knew your name, Pet."

Her anger melted like mist.

"O Eric! O my dear!"

He would have taken her in his arms but she cried passionately, "No, no! Don't touch me!" And then, as he stood chilled by her revulsion, her mood turned again, and she cried, "Eric, perhaps your father was innocent."

"Innocent?" his son repeated bitterly. "He was as innocent as I am—but for all that your grandfather put the rope round his neck to hang him to the nearest tree. And that's the man—that Hendrick Vanderhooven, to whom I've brought roses."

"Are you sorry you were kind to that old man?"

"No," answered Eric, probably untruthfully. "But I never would have darkened his door, had I known—Good-by, Pet."

Her love for him lent her patience that was not hers by nature.

"Wait, Eric," she said, as gently as the meekest of maidens. "If your father was innocent, we'll prove it."

"What, after forty years?"

"The truth must come out in the end, else one couldn't believe in God," answered Pet piteously.

"You know, Eric, I've been brought up to execrate your father's name. Then, if I, Artemisia Vanderhooven's granddaughter, can believe him innocent on your bare word, won't you help me prove it to others?"

His young spirit caught hope.

"God bless you, my darling. We will prove it."

They sat down again then, side by side like friends, while Eric told the story. He knew it but too well. He had heard it from his father many bitter times.

"Father was the son of a farmer living eight or ten miles from Sutton Place, and he hired out to your grandfather for the harvest. He was only twenty years old and he had never been away from home before, and he'd never been in a house where the family didn't eat with the hands. The Vanderhoovens didn't, though your grandfather worked beside the men in the fields; but he and Madam Vanderhooven and their little boy—that must have been your father, I suppose—had their meals in a parlour by themselves. Father didn't like that, and he began to comment on it to the men, and called it stuck-up and English, and he got into a regular spreadeagle speech against the English, when the madam came out and heard him. She took the wind out of his sails in a way that made him feel a fool and a booby before all the men, and then she told him he must apologise or go. He went, but he threatened her he'd get even with her.

"Father said he didn't mean anything in the world by that speech; he was so angry he didn't know what he was saying. Off he marched with his bundle over his shoulder, and he'd put five or six miles between him and Sutton House, when he remembered that he'd left his purse with every penny he had in the world, under the pillow. He turned round and went back to the house. It was noon by that time, and there wasn't a soul to be seen about the place. The men were working too far from home to return for dinner, and the women had all gone to carry it to them. He sneaked up to his room and found his purse, and he thought, coming down, he said, how easy it would be to take some of their silver, or spoil their pictures. But he swore he never touched one thing, but walked straight out of that house and on his way again.

"When he was about a mile from the house, he saw Madam Vanderhooven coming along with her son. Father said if she'd been alone he'd have faced her and asked her pardon, but he couldn't bear to humble himself before the boy, so he dropped down behind some bushes. She and the lad were busy talking, and they never saw him, and passed by. Afterward, he wished to God he had stopped her.

"He walked on another mile, to where the road went up over a hill, and on the crest he turned and looked back and saw flames bursting out of the windows of Sutton House. He knew one man would be powerless to help, so he raced along over the fields to the harvesters, shouting that Sutton House was on fire, and that Madam was there.

"While he was saying the words, up ran the boy from the other direction, to tell the same tale. He and his mother had seen the fire; she had run on to the house. When the men, father and everybody, came up, the whole place was in flames and no sign of Madam Vanderhooven. Her husband called for volunteers to find her—and the first to spring into the fire at his side was Edward Day. They were together when they found her lying on the floor in the little panelled parlour, with an old looking-glass clasped in her arms."

"Oh, poor lady," Pet breathed. "It was my mirror."

"The fire had spared her," he went on, "she seemed to have been suffocated by the smoke. They worked over her till finally she opened her eyes and said the one word *Edward*, and died.

"Instantly the cry rose that Edward Day had murdered her—he had fired the house. In the panelled room scattered straw, not quite destroyed, pointed to arson. Edward Day had quarrelled with the mistress and then had hung about the neighbourhood all day. Indeed the boy—your father—bore witness to seeing him hiding by the bushes in the road, though his mother had laughed at him for thinking it. Some one brought a rope, and Hendrick Vanderhooven put it round my father's neck.

"Nobody listened to a word father said. They were like mad wolves in their fury. But when that rope touched him, father with one plunge freed himself from the men who held him. The crowd was in a circle around him. He could not possibly escape, and they waited to see what he would do. He went over to where Madam Vanderhooven's body lay on the ground, and he lifted the cloth somebody had thrown over it. She wasn't disfigured, he said, and she looked just as quiet and pretty as if she were sleeping, except that her eyes were wide open, staring straight up at him.

"There was a sort of groan from the crowd when he went toward her, and they surged forward as if to stop him. But he knelt down by her, and put one hand on her forehead and one on her breast and said:

" 'I swear before God I never harmed her or her house. Boys, could I touch her if I'd brought her to her death?' "

"Oh, Eric," Pet cried. "They must have let him go then."

"They gave up the notion of lynching him. He was tried for arson, convicted, and served his term. I am a convict's son, Miss Vanderhooven."

"He was innocent, Eric," Pet cried quickly. "He must have been innocent." But after her brave assurance she shivered.

He broke a long silence. "Well, Pet?" She rose, with a strangled sob.

"I don't know, Eric—I don't know. Take me home."

It was late, and her first task was to help Grandsir to his bed. She kissed him with a mother's tenderness for his helplessness; and put out the light. Then as if she had no strength left, she sank down in Grandsir's chair, in misery none the less wretched that it made no sound. In Eric's presence, swayed by her love for him, by his own firm belief, she had not hesitated to champion his father's innocence. Now, alone in the dark, she wavered. Grandsir had thought him guilty, her father had thought him guilty, Artemisia herself had said in her dying breath *Edward*. Was it possible all of these, the court itself, had been wrong?

Whatever his father had been, she could never cease to love Eric. She could not blame him for his father's sin. But well she knew Grandsir would have no such charity. "I would never have darkened his doors, had I known," Eric had said, nor would Hendrick Vanderhooven, had he known, ever have received Eric Day. That Grandsir did not know, need never know, changed the

situation no whit. She should never tell him—of what use to open
old wounds?—but loyalty constrained her to act as if he knew.
Hendrick Vanderhooven's kin could be no wife, no friend even,
of Eric Day.

It made no difference in Pet's mind that the crime, if crime it
was, had happened forty years before; that neither Eric nor she
was born till the event was all but forgotten; that Eric and she
were guiltless of wrong, young, with their lives all before them.
Pet had lived all her days in the past; Sutton House was as much a
part of her life as if she had dwelt there in the flesh; her grandmother Artemisia's cause was her own. She could not separate
her fortunes from her family's; with a feudal loyalty she walked as
her forbears had walked. And Eric, too, nourished on the tale of
his father's wrongs; for him also was the dead past a living thing.
He, no more than the girl, could cut loose from the root whence
he had sprung. They had walked home in silence. Despite their
tenderness for each other, which no sin of others could kill, the
past had risen like a wall between them. They both felt it to be so,
and had parted without even touching hands.

And yet, and yet, Pet's heart yearned over him. She dropped on
her knees to pray for help, for light.

Where was light to come from after these forty years?

Before her, on the table where Grandsir had put it down, lay
Artemisia's mirror. The girl bent over it. In the dim starlight a
ghost of her face looked back at her, as Grandsir said his Artemisia looked at him. "Oh, grandmother, have pity on me and tell
me," Pet's heart implored. But the face had vanished from the
mirror. Nothing was there save the reflection of an empty room.
She lifted her hand to push away the glass, when of a sudden, with
a cry, she held still. For while the room about her was midnight
dark, the room in the mirror showed a band of sunshine across
the floor—while the real room was white-washed and furnished
with deal, the room in the mirror was panelled and beamed in
oak, and the furniture was all of teakwood. The polished floor
was covered with bear and panther skins. On the mantel-shelf
stood jars of roses. One side of the room showed a book-case; the
other a tall secretary with closed doors. The room was deserted,
yet even as she gazed the door opened for the hasty entrance of a
gentleman in riding dress. Some elusive yet insistent likeness

between the vigourous young face of the cavalier and that tremulous dim-eyed mask on the pillow behind her told the watcher that thus her grandfather had looked forty years before.

He moved straight to the secretary, flung open its unlocked doors, took out one by one every paper in its drawers and pigeon holes, examined it, and returned it to its proper place. Twice he went through the desk, patiently, carefully, minutely. With his riding crop he sounded for secret drawers, in vain. Then changing his field of search, he opened the book-case, removed book by book, ruffled the leaves over, shook them vainly, and put them back.

At first, his movements had been controlled, without haste and without nervousness. But as he continued his fruitless quest a feverish hurry overtook him. His hands shook. He started once or twice, as if at a noise without. The colour came and went in his cheeks. In a very frenzy of search, he tapped the walls for secret cubbies, fell on his knees to pry up the bricks of the hearth.

All at once he sprang up, opened the door a crack, and stood for several minutes listening. Then the danger, if such it were, passed. He flung the door wide and strode out and up the passage. For a time the room remained quiet. At length, the same visitor came back, empty-handed, scowling-browed. For what had Grandsir been looking, the loss of which had brought that look to his face?

For a moment he stood motionless, a sullen baffled figure whose despair suddenly before her eyes was changed to malevolent triumph. Abruptly he left the room and came back with an armful of straw, returning for more and again more. What was Grandsir doing? He was mad. No, the mirror was mad, lying. Grandsir was working in the fields that day; he did not fire the house.

As if she had heard it spoken aloud, the answer flashed to Pet. Dirck!

He had ridden from Schenectady with the news of his father's extremity. He found the house deserted, and he remembered the title deeds. Destroy them, and he was master of Sutton House. Even as the thought jumped into her brain the man knelt over the straw and struck a match. A second later, he leapt from the casement, leaving it open for the wind to fan the fire. Flames shot up licking the walls, then smoke rolled thick, hiding all. Pet sat sick and helpless. She must cry out, she must give warning—but this house had been burned forty years!

The smoke wreaths rolled aside as the door opened, admitting a blast of clearer air. Into the midst of the furnace rushed a little figure in a white frock, with dark curls flying, horrified dark eyes looking straight toward Pet. "Oh, my dear!" Pet cried in agony, starting forward with eager arms outstretched to save her—and found herself standing alone in the grey dawn, her cold hands clutching the grey glass of the mirror.

That it was a fevered dream she had no choice but to believe. Yet, unlike dreams, the memory of it did not fade as the hours went by, the impression did not blur. All day long the vision hung on Pet like an incubus, till at dusk it took her by the throat and forced her to Dirck Vanderhooven's door.

Sometimes Chance, ashamed of her slip-shod ways, rouses herself to outdo the very prince of diplomats. Mr. Dirck Vanderhooven was at home. The servant, a green country maid, more willing than discreet, conducted the visitor straight to his library door, murmured, "A lady to see you, sir," and left them alone together.

Mr. Dirck Vanderhooven was seated near the window, reading by the fading daylight. Pet saw how like he was to Grandsir, and how unlike. He was straight and vigourous—he looked twenty years younger than the bowed meek figure at home. Yet not so; on second glance there was no such look of youth about Dirck Vanderhooven as still shone from Hendrick's mild eyes. Dirck's face was lined, contracted with mean cares, old.

Evidently, he had not heard her.

But presently some finer sense than hearing told him of a presence in the room, and he lifted his eyes and saw her. He recoiled with the blanched face of one who sees death itself staring him in the face. His speechless lips shaped themselves to a name.

"Artemisia!"

"You fired Sutton House," said Artemisia's ghost to him.

"The house was empty. I never meant to kill you, Artemisia," he struggled to answer, and fell at Artemisia's feet.

She left his own people weeping over him and fled home like a criminal in the night. She had taken it upon herself to mete out punishment to the wicked; she had played at being God. And her punishment had come in the awful completeness of her success.

A little crowd of women hung about her own door, which broke into murmurs as she approached. "Ah, the poor young lady! The poor thing." Eric, quiet and pale, came out of Grandsir's room, and put his arm about her.

"He's gone, dear heart. I heard him through the wall of my room suddenly cry out, and fall. When I ran to him, he was dead."

Eric had laid Grandsir on the bed, covering him tenderly, all injuries forgotten. On the floor lay the mirror, shattered.

"He must have been holding it in his hand when he died," Eric said softly. "What I heard him cry was 'Artemisia.'"

Pet knelt and kissed the wan cheek. Eric lifted the mirror to put it in the dead hand when his eye fell on a folded paper, freed from its wall of glass when the mirror broke. "I Pieter Vanderhooven, make over and convey—." Safe, these fifty years, in Artemisia's mirror lay Artemisia's fortune!

He was at Pet's side, but before he could tell her, she lifted her eyes—eyes wet for present sorrows, but shining with hope of brightness to come.

"Eric, he died with her name on his lips, and don't you see, she died speaking his? 'Edward'—it's on the mirror in your hand, there. It was what she called her husband for his dearest name. She wasn't accusing anybody. She wasn't thinking of revenge. She was just thinking of love."

ISAAC ASIMOV

Unto the Fourth Generation

ISAAC ASIMOV—*the astoundingly prolific author of hundreds of science-fact books, articles, short stories, mysteries and science fiction—was having lunch with Robert P. Mills shortly after Anthony Boucher, beloved editor of* The Magazine of Fantasy and Science Fiction, *died and Mills had assumed the editorship of F&SF. Mills told Asimov he saw the name Lefkowitz several times that day on unrelated occasions and wondered whether Isaac could turn the curious coincidence into a story. Not only did Dr. A. do so, but he came up with one of his loveliest and least typical tales. "Unto the Fourth Generation" is a tribute to Boucher, who, Asimov explains, was a sincere Catholic who brought a faintly Catholic air to F&SF, "always a pleasant and liberal one, though, for that was the kind of man he was." The author wanted to recapture Boucher's editorial tone, but since Asimov is not Catholic, he mined his own heritage instead, penning "the only Jewish story it ever occurred to me to write, I think."*

At ten of noon, Sam Marten hitched his way out of the taxicab, trying as usual to open the door with one hand, hold his briefcase in another and reach for his wallet with a third. Having only two hands, he found it a difficult job and, again as usual, he thudded his knee against the cab-door and found himself still groping uselessly for his wallet when his feet touched pavement.

The traffic of Madison Avenue inched past. A red truck slowed its crawl reluctantly, then moved on with a rasp as the light changed. White script on its side informed an unresponsive world that its ownership was that of *F. Lewkowitz and Sons, Wholesale Clothiers.*

Levkowich, thought Marten with brief inconsequence, and finally fished out his wallet. He cast an eye on the meter as he clamped his briefcase under his arm. Dollar sixty-five, make that twenty cents more as a tip, two singles gone would leave him only one for emergencies, better break a fiver.

"Okay," he said, "take out one-eighty-five, bud."

"Thanks," said the cabbie with mechanical insincerity and made the change.

Marten crammed three singles into his wallet, put it away, lifted his briefcase and breasted the human currents on the sidewalk to reach the glass doors of the building.

Levkovich? he thought sharply, and stopped. A passerby glanced off his elbow.

"Sorry," muttered Marten, and made for the door again.

Levkovich? That wasn't what the sign on the truck had said. The name had read Lewkowitz, Loo-koh-itz. Why did he *think* Levkovich? Even with his college German in the near past changing the w's to v's, where did he get the "-ich" from?

Levkovich? He shrugged the whole matter away roughly. Give it a chance and it would haunt him like a Hit Parade tinkle.

Concentrate on business. He was here for a luncheon appointment with this man, Naylor. He was here to turn a contract into an account and begin, at twenty-three, the smooth business rise which, as he planned it, would marry him to Elizabeth in two years and make him a paterfamilias in the suburbs in ten.

He entered the lobby with grim firmness and headed for the banks of elevators, his eye catching at the white-lettered directory as he passed.

It was a silly habit of his to want to catch suite numbers as he passed, without slowing, or (heaven forbid) coming to a full halt. With no break in his progress, he told himself, he could maintain the impression of belonging, of knowing his way around, and that was important to a man whose job involved dealing with other human beings.

Kulin-etts was what he wanted, and the word amused him. A

firm specializing in the production of minor kitchen gadgets, striving manfully for a name that was significant, feminine, and coy, all at once—

His eyes snagged at the M's and moved upward as he walked. Mandel, Lusk, Lippert Publishing Company (two full floors), Lafkowitz, Kulin-etts. There it was—1024. Tenth floor. OK.

And then, after all, he came to a dead halt, turned in reluctant fascination, returned to the directory, and stared at it as though he were an out-of-towner.

Lafkowitz?

What kind of spelling was that?

It was clear enough. Lafkowitz, Henry J., 701. With an A. That was no good. That was useless.

Useless? Why useless? He gave his head one violent shake as though to clear it of mist. Damn it, what did he care how it was spelled? He turned away, frowning and angry, and hastened to an elevator door, which closed just before he reached it, leaving him flustered.

Another door opened and he stepped in briskly. He tucked his briefcase under his arm and tried to look bright alive—junior executive in its finest sense. He had to make an impression on Alex Naylor, with whom so far he had communicated only by telephone. If he was going to brood about Lewkowitzes and Lafkowitzes—

The elevator slid noiselessly to a halt at seven. A youth in shirtsleeves stepped off, balancing what looked like a desk-drawer in which were three containers of coffee and three sandwiches.

Then, just as the doors began closing, frosted glass with black lettering loomed before Marten's eyes. It read: 701—HENRY J. LEFKOWITZ—IMPORTER and was pinched off by the inexorable coming together of the elevator doors.

Marten leaned forward in excitement. It was his impulse to say: Take me back down to 7.

But there were others in the car. And after all, he had no reason.

Yet there was a tingle of excitement within him. The Directory *had* been wrong. It wasn't A, it was E. Some fool of a non-spelling menial with a packet of small letters to go on the board and only one hind foot to do it with.

Lefkowitz. Still not right, though.

Again, he shook his head. Twice. Not right for what?

The elevator stopped at ten and Marten got off.

Alex Naylor of Kulin-etts turned out to be a bluff, middle-aged man with a shock of white hair, a ruddy complexion, and a broad smile. His palms were dry and rough, and he shook hands with a considerable pressure, putting his left hand on Marten's shoulder in an earnest display of friendliness.

He said, "Be with you in two minutes. How about eating right here in the building? Excellent restaurant, and they've got a boy who makes a good martini. That sound all right?"

"Fine. Fine." Marten pumped up enthusiasm from a somehow-clogged reservoir.

It was nearer ten minutes than two, and Marten waited with the usual uneasiness of a man in a strange office. He stared at the upholstery on the chairs and at the little cubby-hole within which a young and bored switchboard operator sat. He gazed at the pictures on the wall and even made a half-hearted attempt to glance through a trade journal on the table next to him.

What he did not do was think of Lev—

He did *not* think of it.

The restaurant was good, or it would have been good if Marten had been perfectly at ease. Fortunately, he was freed of the necessity of carrying the burden of the conversation. Naylor talked rapidly and loudly, glanced over the menu with a practiced eye, recommended the Eggs Benedict, and commented on the weather and the miserable traffic situation.

On occasion, Marten tried to snap out of it, to lose that edge of fuzzed absence of mind. But each time the restlessness would return. Something was wrong. The name was wrong. It stood in the way of what he had to do.

With main force, he tried to break through the madness. In sudden verbal clatter, he led the conversation into the subject of wiring. It was reckless of him. There was no proper foundation; the transition was too abrupt.

But the lunch had been a good one; the dessert was on its way; and Naylor responded nicely.

He admitted dissatisfaction with existing arrangements. Yes, he had been looking into Marten's firm and, actually, it seemed to him that, yes, there was a chance, a good chance, he thought, that—

A hand came down on Naylor's shoulder as a man passed behind his chair. "How's the boy, Alex?"

Naylor looked up, grin ready-made and flashing. "Hey, Lefk, how's business?"

"Can't complain. See you at the—" He faded into the distance.

Marten wasn't listening. He felt his knees trembling, as he half-rose. "Who was that man?" he asked, intensely. It sounded more peremptory than he intended.

"Who? Lefk? Jerry Lefkovitz. You know him?" Naylor stared with cool surprise at his lunch companion.

"No. How do you spell his name?"

"L-E-F-K-O-V-I-T-Z, I think. Why?"

"With a V?"

"An F. . . . Oh, there's a V in it, too." Most of the good nature had left Naylor's face.

Marten drove on. "There's a Lefkowitz in the building. With a W. You know, Lef-COW-itz."

"Oh?"

"Room 701. This is not the same one?"

"Jerry doesn't work in this building. He's got a place across the street. I don't know this other one. This is a big building, you know. I don't keep tabs on every one in it. What is all this, anyway?"

Marten shook his head and sat back. He didn't know what all this was, anyway. Or at least, if he did, it was nothing he dared explain. Could he say: I'm being haunted by all manner of Lefkowitzes today.

He said, "We were talking about wiring."

Naylor said, "Yes. Well, as I said, I've been considering your company. I've got to talk it over with the production boys, you understand. I'll let you know."

"Sure," said Marten, infinitely depressed. Naylor wouldn't let him know. The whole thing was shot.

And yet, through and beyond his depression, there was still that restlessness.

The hell with Naylor. All Marten wanted was to break this up and get on with it. *(Get on with what?* But the question was only a whisper. Whatever did the questioning inside him was ebbing away, dying down . . .)

The lunch frayed to an ending. If they had greeted each other like long-separated friends at last reunited, they parted like strangers.

Marten felt only relief.

He left with pulses thudding, threading through the tables, out of the haunted building, onto the haunted street.

Haunted? Madison Avenue at 1:20 P.M. in an early fall afternoon with the sun shining brightly and ten thousand men and women bee-hiving its long straight stretch.

But Marten felt the haunting. He tucked his briefcase under his arm and headed desperately northward. A last sigh of the normal within him warned him he had a three o'clock appointment on 36th Street. Never mind. He headed uptown. Northward.

At 54th Street, he crossed Madison and walked west, came abruptly to a halt and looked upward.

There was a sign on the window, three stories up. He could make it out clearly: A. S. LEFKOWICH, CERTIFIED ACCOUNTANT.

It had an F and an EW, but it was the first "-ich" ending he had seen. The first one. He was getting closer. He turned north again on Fifth Avenue, hurrying through the unreal streets of an unreal city, panting with the chase of something, while the crowds about him began to fade.

A sign in a ground floor window, M. R. LEFKOWICZ, M.D.

A small gold-leaf semi-circle of letters in a candy-store window: JACOB LEVKOW.

(Half a name, he thought savagely. Why is he disturbing me with half a name?)

The streets were empty now except for the varying clan of Lefkowitz, Levkovitz, Lefkowicz to stand out in the vacuum.

He was dimly aware of the park ahead, standing out in painted motionless green. He turned west. A piece of newspaper fluttered at the corner of his eyes, the only movement in a dead world. He veered, stooped, and picked it up, without slackening his pace.

It was in Yiddish, a torn half-page.

He couldn't read it. He couldn't make out the blurred Hebrew letters, and could not have read it if they were clear. But one word was clear. It stood out in dark letters in the center of the page, each letter clear in its every serif. And it said Lefkovitsch, he knew, and as he said it to himself, he placed its accent on the second syllable: Lef-KUH-vich.

He let the paper flutter away and entered the empty park.

The trees were still and the leaves hung in odd, suspended attitudes. The sunlight was a dead weight upon him and gave no warmth.

He was running, but his feet kicked up no dust and a tuft of grass on which he placed his weight did not bend.

And there on a bench was an old man; the only man in the desolate park. He wore a dark felt cap, with a visor shading his eyes. From underneath it, tufts of gray hair protruded. His grizzled beard reached the uppermost button of his rough jacket. His old trousers were patched, and a strip of burlap was wrapped about each worn and shapeless shoe.

Marten stopped. It was difficult to breathe. He could only say one word and he used it to ask his question: "Levkovich?"

He stood there, while the old man rose slowly to his feet; brown old eyes peering close.

"Marten," he sighed. "Samuel Marten. You have come." The words sounded with an effect of double exposure, for under the English, Marten heard the faint sigh of a foreign tongue. Under the "Samuel" was the unheard shadow of a "Schmu-el."

The old man's rough, veined hands reached out, then withdrew as though he were afraid to touch. "I have been looking but there are so many people in this wilderness of a city-that-is-to-come. So many Martins and Martines and Mortons and Mertons. I stopped at last when I found greenery, but for a moment only— I would not commit the sin of losing faith. And then you came."

"It is I," said Marten, and knew it was. "And you are Phinehas Levkovich. Why are we here?"

"I am Phinehas ben Jehudah, assigned the name Levkovich by

the ukase of the Tsar that ordered family names for all. And we are here," the old man said, softly, "because I prayed. When I was already old, Leah, my only daughter, the child of my old age, left for America with her husband, left the knouts of the old for the hope of the new. And my sons died, and Sarah, the wife of my bosom, was long dead and I was alone. And the time came when I, too, must die. But I had not seen Leah since her leaving for the far country and word had come but rarely. My soul yearned that I might see sons born unto her; sons of my seed; sons in whom my soul might yet live and not die."

His voice was steady and the soundless shadow of sound beneath his words was the stately roll of an ancient language.

"And I was answered and two hours were given me that I might see the first son of my line to be born in a new land and in a new time. My daughter's daughter's daughter's son, have I found you, then, amidst the splendor of this city?"

"But why the search? Why not have brought us together at once?"

"Because there is pleasure in the hope of the seeking, my son," said the old man, radiantly, "and in the delight of the finding. I was given two hours in which I might seek, two hours in which I might find . . . and behold, thou art here, and I have found that which I had not looked to see in life." His voice was old, caressing. "Is it well with thee, my son?"

"It is well, my father, now that I have found thee," said Marten, and dropped to his knees. "Give me thy blessing, my father, that it may be well with me all the days of my life, and with the maid whom I am to take to wife and the little ones yet to be born of my seed and thine."

He felt the old hand resting lightly on his head and there was only the soundless whisper.

Marten rose.

The old man's eyes gazed into his yearningly. Were they losing focus?

"I go to my fathers now in peace, my son," said the old man, and Marten was alone in the empty park.

There was an instant of renewing motion, of the Sun taking up its interrupted task, of the wind reviving, and even with that first instant of sensation, all slipped back—

At ten of noon, Sam Marten hitched his way out of the taxicab, and found himself groping uselessly for his wallet while traffic inched on.

A red truck slowed, then moved on. A white script on its side announced: *F. Lewkowitz and Sons, Wholesale Clothiers.*

Marten didn't see it. Yet somehow he knew that all would be well with him. Somehow, as never before, he knew. . . .

THE SOUTH

New England's ghost stories principally were moral parables, while faintly iconoclastic laughter rang in the East, but many of the eerie tales in this section bear the stamp of verisimilitude, and anyone who has traveled through the Southern United States will understand why—for preternatural foreboding lurks in the lush, dismal bayous of Florida, Georgia and Mississippi, while the lonely mountain ridges, secret forests and fresh-running streams of the Carolinas, Kentucky and Tennessee seem to hide dark mysteries in their shut-away splendor.

Ghosts and even stranger things haunt these tales of the Old and New South.

AMBROSE BIERCE

The Spook House

AMBROSE BIERCE *(1842–1914?), a native of Ohio, was a successful journalist in his day, but now is best remembered for short savagely cynical fiction, much of it horrifying and some of it supernatural as well. The compendium volume,* Can Such Things Be?, *includes some of Bierce's most popular occult tales, among them "The Damned Thing," "The Death of Halpin Frayser," "Moxon's Master," "One Summer Night," and "Staley Fleming's Hallucination," as well as several lesser-known and presumably factual reports of hauntings, one of which is "The Spook House."*

On the road leading north from Manchester, in eastern Kentucky, to Booneville, twenty miles away, stood, in 1862, a wooden plantation house of a somewhat better quality than most of the dwellings in that region. The house was destroyed by fire in the year following—probably by some stragglers from the retreating column of General George W. Morgan, when he was driven from Cumberland Gap to the Ohio river by General Kirby Smith. At the time of its destruction, it had for four or five years been vacant. The fields about it were overgrown with brambles, the fences gone, even the few negro quarters, and outhouses generally, fallen partly into ruin by neglect and pillage; for the negroes and poor whites of the vicinity found in the building and fences an abundant supply of fuel, of which they availed themselves without hesitation, openly and by daylight. By daylight alone; after nightfall no human being except passing strangers ever went near the place.

It was known as the "Spook House." That it was tenanted by evil spirits, visible, audible and active, no one in all that region doubted any more than he doubted what he was told of Sundays by the traveling preacher. Its owner's opinion of the matter was unknown; he and his family had disappeared one night and no trace of them had ever been found. They left everything—household goods, clothing, provisions, the horses in the stable, the cows in the field, the negroes in the quarters—all as it stood; nothing was missing—except a man, a woman, three girls, a boy and a babe! It was not altogether surprising that a plantation where seven human beings could be simultaneously effaced and nobody the wiser should be under some suspicion.

One night in June, 1859, two citizens of Frankfort, Col. J. C. McArdle, a lawyer, and Judge Myron Veigh, of the State Militia, were driving from Booneville to Manchester. Their business was so important that they decided to push on, despite the darkness and the mutterings of an approaching storm, which eventually broke upon them just as they arrived opposite the "Spook House." The lightning was so incessant that they easily found their way through the gateway and into a shed, where they hitched and unharnessed their team. They then went to the house, through the rain, and knocked at all the doors without getting any response. Attributing this to the continuous uproar of the thunder they pushed at one of the doors, which yielded. They entered without further ceremony and closed the door. That instant they were in darkness and silence. Not a gleam of the lightning's unceasing blaze penetrated the windows or crevices; not a whisper of the awful tumult without reached them there. It was as if they had suddenly been stricken blind and deaf, and McArdle afterward said that for a moment he believed himself to have been killed by a stroke of lightning as he crossed the threshold. The rest of this adventure can as well be related in his own words, from the Frankfort *Advocate* of August 6, 1876:

"When I had somewhat recovered from the dazing effect of the transition from uproar to silence, my first impulse was to reopen the door which I had closed, and from the knob of which I was not conscious of having removed my hand; I felt it distinctly, still in the clasp of my fingers. My notion was to ascertain by stepping again into the storm whether I had been deprived of sight and hearing. I turned the door-knob and pulled open the door. It led into another room!

"This apartment was suffused with a faint greenish light, the source of which I could not determine, making everything distinctly visible, though nothing was sharply defined. Everything, I say, but in truth the only objects within the blank stone walls of that room were human corpses. In number they were perhaps eight or ten—it may well be understood that I did not truly count them. They were of different ages, or rather sizes, from infancy up, and of both sexes. All were prostrate on the floor, excepting one, apparently a young woman, who sat up, her back supported by an angle of the wall. A babe was clasped in the arms of another and older woman. A half-grown lad lay face downward across the legs of a full-bearded man. One or two were nearly naked, and the hand of a young girl held the fragment of a gown which she had torn open at the breast. The bodies were in various stages of decay, all greatly shrunken in face and figure. Some were but little more than skeletons.

"While I stood stupefied with horror by this ghastly spectacle and still holding open the door, by some unaccountable perversity my attention was diverted from the shocking scene and concerned itself with trifles and details. Perhaps my mind, with an instinct of self-preservation, sought relief in matters which would relax its dangerous tension. Among other things, I observed that the door that I was holding open was of heavy iron plates, riveted. Equidistant from one another and from the top and bottom, three strong bolts protruded from the beveled edge. I turned the knob and they were retracted flush with the edge; released it, and they shot out. It was a spring lock. On the inside there was no knob, nor any kind of projection—a smooth surface of iron.

"While noting these things with an interest and attention which it now astonishes me to recall I felt myself thrust aside, and Judge Veigh, whom in the intensity and vicissitudes of my feelings I had altogether forgotten, pushed by me into the room. 'For God's sake,' I cried, 'do not go in there! Let us get out of this dreadful place!'

"He gave no heed to my entreaties, but (as fearless a gentleman as lived in all the South) walked quickly to the center of the room, knelt beside one of the bodies for a closer examination and tenderly raised its blackened and shriveled head in his hands. A strong disagreeable odor came through the doorway, completely overpowering me. My senses reeled; I felt myself falling, and in clutching at the edge of the door for support pushed it shut with a sharp click!

"I remember no more: six weeks later I recovered my reason in a hotel at Manchester, whither I had been taken by strangers the next day. For all these weeks I had suffered from a nervous fever, attended with constant delirium. I had been found lying in the road several miles away from the house; but how I had escaped from it to get there I never knew. On recovery, or as soon as my physicians permitted me to talk, I inquired the fate of Judge Veigh, whom (to quiet me, as I now know) they represented as well and at home.

"No one believed a word of my story, and who can wonder? And who can imagine my grief when, arriving at my home in Frankfort two months later, I learned that Judge Veigh had never been heard of since that night? I then regretted bitterly the pride which since the first few days after the recovery of my reason had forbidden me to repeat my discredited story and insist upon its truth.

"With all that afterward occurred—the examination of the house; the failure to find any room corresponding to that which I have described; the attempt to have me adjudged insane, and my triumph over my accusers—the readers of the *Advocate* are familiar. After all these years I am still confident that excavations which I have neither the legal right to undertake nor the wealth to make would disclose the secret of the disappearance of my unhappy friend, and possibly of the former occupants and owners of the deserted and now destroyed house. I do not despair of yet bringing about such a search, and it is a source of deep grief to me that it has been delayed by the undeserved hostility and unwise incredulity of the family and friends of the late Judge Veigh."

Colonel McArdle died in Frankfort on the thirteenth day of December, in the year 1879.

MARY ELIZABETH
COUNSELMAN

The Shot-Tower Ghost

"The Shot-Tower Ghost," though rich in atmosphere and a sense of early American history, is one of the less familiar stories by the popular fantasist MARY ELIZABETH COUNSELMAN, *who contributed more than thirty short stories, including the popular "The Three Marked Pennies," to* Weird Tales *magazine during a period of nearly fifty years from 1933 to 1981.*

Most of us have nostalgic, so-dear-to-my-heart memories tucked into the back of our minds, our subconscious minds, to be coaxed out briefly now and then by some particular sound, some odor, some half-familiar sight . . .

As for me, I can not hear a whippoorwill crying at night but I go flying back through time and space to our old family "Homeplace" in Wythe County, Virginia. The ferry is no longer there—replaced by a coldly efficient steel bridge that the state built. Cars and wagons, herds of sheep and leisurely riders on horseback no longer pause at the brink of New River to call across: *"Hello-o-o!"* for the stocky, smiling ferryman to raft them over to where the road to Wytheville begins again. But on the east bank, the tall square fieldstone shot-tower still broods over the green-velvet countryside—a grim reminder of a day when Virginia was wracked with civil war, and brother turned against brother.

Yes; the shot-tower is still there, a historical landmark which my family at last turned over to the United Daughters of the Confederacy, for the edification of the passing tourist. The spiral staircase that winds up and up inside the tower is new—not rotten and precarious as it was when I was there, one of the scattered cousins who came "Back Home" every summer for a visit. The sturdy beamed floor of the single room, high up against the ceiling, used to be spattered with little hardened splashes of lead, spilled eighty-five years ago by determined Rebels and loyal sweating negroes frantically making ammunition for Lee's troops. The leaden souvenirs are probably gone by now; and the square hole in the floor is fenced in by chicken wire, lest the unwary tourist fall through it into that dark matching hole in the tower's dirt floor below. This leads, well-like, into the river. I am not sure about the huge iron cauldron which caught the shot. (Molten lead formed round rifle balls when it fell, hissing, into cold water.) The pot may yet be hanging down there into the river. Once, on a dare from another visiting cousin, I climbed halfway down the slimy ladder into that chill murmuring darkness. But something slithered against my arm, and I never finished the adventure . . . especially as it was almost nightfall, and time for the Shot-Tower Ghost to appear.

Let me say here, to your probable disappointment, that there never was a "shot-tower ghost." This gruesome family-spectre was nothing more than a product of my Great-uncle Robert's imagination. He is dead now, a white-bearded irascible old bachelor of the "hoss-racin' and cyard game" school. Dead, too, is Shadrach, his stooped and gray-haired "body-servant," last of the family slaves who accepted their "freedom" with a bored sniff as the impractical notion of "a passel o' po-white Yankees." To the last day of their lives—about two weeks apart—Uncle Robert and Shadrach, respectively, remained unreconstructed and un-freed. And the fact that one of my aunts married a Northerner, bore him a fine son, got rich, and came back to buy and remodel another old countryplace adjoining the Homeplace, was a great shock to both of them. I think they were convinced that "Yankees" are a roving tribe of gipsy marauders, and incapable of fathering offspring.

That son was my Cousin Mark, who had none of the gracious

charm of his mother's side of the family and all of the butt-headed stubbornness of his Connecticut father. But in those days just after World War I—"the war in Europe" as Uncle Robert verbally shrugged off any of our conflicts but the one between the States —I was a very young fluttery miss with a terrible crush on Francis X. Bushman, thence my Cousin Mark because he slightly resembled him.

This particular summer, however, another cousin of mine from the Georgia branch was also visiting the Homeplace, a red-headed minx named Adelia—she is fat and has five children now, may I add with vicious satisfaction. But she was two years older than I, and just entering the Seminary, so Cousin Mark's eyes were all for her, not for a gawky high school sophomore from Birmingham, Alabama.

Adelia was also popular with the younger set of Wytheville. Almost every night a squealing, laughing carful of young people would bear down on the ferryman, who had orders to ferry Miss Adelia's friends across free of charge. Uncle Robert and Shadrach would roll their eyes at each other and moan faintly, but a short while later my uncle would be grinning from ear to ear, seated in his favorite chair on the wide columned veranda with a bouquet of pretty girls clustered around him, begging for "ghost stories." Shadrach, his eyeballs and teeth the only white thing about his grinning ebony face, would circulate around, offering syllabub and tiny beaten-biscuits with baked ham between them, or calling "rounds" for an old-fashioned reel in the big living room where the Victrola played incessantly.

Cousin Mark was a member of this coterie more often than anyone else, and Uncle Robert always made him welcome in a formally polite manner that Adelia, giggling beside me later in our big featherbed upstairs, would mock outrageously. Mark and Uncle Robert seemed to clash as naturally as a hound and a fox, for Mark had a rather rude way of finding holes in Uncle Robert's tall tales, mostly about the supernatural.

"Did you ever actually *see* a ghost, sir?" Mark demanded once, sitting at ease on the front steps against a backdrop of gray dusk and twinkling fireflies . . . and the distant plaintive crying of whip-poor-wills.

"I have, suh!" my uncle lashed back at him stiffly. "With mah own two eyes . . . and if Ah may say so, Ah could pick off a Yankee sniper right now at fifty yards with a good rifle!"

"Unless he picked you off first," my cousin pointed out blandly. Then, with stubborn logic that seemed to infuriate my uncle: *"When* did you ever see a ghost, sir, may I ask?" he pursued. "And where? And how do you know it wasn't just an . . . an optical illusion?"

"Suh . . . !" Uncle Robert drew himself up, sputtering slightly like an old firecracker. "Suh, the Shot-Tower Ghost is no optical illusion. He is, and Ah give you mah word on it, a true case of psychic phenomena. You understand," Uncle slipped into his act—a very convincing one, in spite of Adelia's covert giggling, "you understand that, after some very dramatic or tragic incident in which a person dies suddenly, there may be left what is called . . . ah . . . I believe the American Society for Psychic Research calls it 'psychic residue.' An emanation, an . . . an ectoplasmic replica of the person involved. This replica is sometimes left behind after death occurs—the death of the body, that is. For, the circumstances under which the person died may have been so . . . so impossible to leave hanging, the ectoplasmic replica of that person lives on, repeating and repeating his last act or trying to finish some task that he strongly wishes to finish. . . ."

"Poppycock!" my cousin interrupted flatly. "I don't believe there's any such thing as an . . . 'ectoplasmic replica!' What a term!" he laughed lightly. "Where'd you dig that one up, sir? At some table-tapping séance—price ten bucks a spook?"

"No, suh, I did not." Uncle Robert was bristling now; Adelia punched me and giggled. We could all see how very much he wanted to take this young Yankee-born whippersnapper down a peg or two. "I find the term used often," Uncle drawled, "in Madame Blavatsky's four-volume work on the metaphysical. She was considered the foremost authority on the supernatural during the last century, the Nineteenth Century, when such notables as Arthur Conan Doyle were seriously studying the possibility of life after death. . . ."

"Blavatsky . . . Blavatsky," Mark murmured, then grinned and snapped his fingers. "Oh yes. I remember reading about her, something in *The Golden Bough.* Sir James Frazer says she's either the greatest authority . . . *or* the biggest fraud in the history of metaphysical study! I read that once in the library at Tech, just browsing around. . . ."

Uncle Robert choked. Most young people listened in wide-eyed awe to his erudite-sounding explanations of his "tower ghost" and certain other spook-yarns that he cooked up for our naive pleasure. But Mark was tossing his high-sounding phrases right back at him with great relish, and a covert wink at Adelia who was perched on the arm of Uncle's chair. His smug air seemed to annoy her, though, for:

"Oh, the shot-tower ghost isn't any fraud!" Adelia proclaimed tauntingly, with an affectionate pat for Uncle's gnarled old hand —at the moment gripping his cane as if he intended breaking it over Mark's head. "I've seen it, myself," she announced. "Lib has, too—haven't you, Lib?" she demanded, and I nodded solemnly.

"Now *you've* seen it!" Mark jeered, flipping a coin in the air and watching it glint softly in the mellow glow that slanted through the fan-light over the door. "Anybody else? Hmm? I've been hearing about this spook of Uncle Robert's ever since we moved here from Connecticut—but I've yet to catch a glimpse of him myself! A Confederate soldier with his legs cut off—how touching! Making shot for his comrades up to the day of Lee's surrender at Appomattox. And when the sad news comes, he throws himself off the tower into the river . . . Haha!" Mark chuckled suddenly, fastening a cold matter-of-fact young eye on Uncle Robert's face. "Come on, Unk. Didn't you make that one up out of whole cloth? It sounds like something out of one of those old paper-back dime novels I found in the attic. *Capitola, the Madcap, Or: Love Conquers All.* . . ."

"Young man!" Uncle Robert stood up abruptly, quivering. "Ah must ask you to mend yoah Yankee manners to yo' elders, suh! Are you havin' the . . . the temerity to dispute my word, you young . . . ?"

At that moment Shadrach took over, gently but firmly. Throwing a light shawl around his master's shoulders, he maneuvered around beside him, preparing to help him to his feet.

"Marse Robert, hit's yo' bedtime," the old darkey pronounced.

"Come along, now, Marse Robert. Tell de young folks good night, cause Ah'm fixin' to help you up to yo' room."

"Shadrach—damme, Ah'll take a hosswhip to yo' black hide!" My uncle roared petulantly, shrugging off the shawl and banging on the porch with his cane. "Quit babyin' me, confound it! Ah'll go to bed when Ah please! Get! Get away from me! Ah'll bend this cane over youah nappy head! Ah'll. . . ."

"Yassuh," said Shadrach imperturbably. "Hit's leb'm-thirty. Time you was asleep. Come on, now, Marse Robert. . . ." He tugged gently at my uncle's arm, finally wielding his heaviest weapon, the mention of my great-grandmother. "Miss Beth wouldn't like you settin' up so late, catchin' yo' death o' dampness. . . ."

"Oh, the devil!" Uncle snapped at him peevishly. "Ah'm comin', Ah'm comin'! Soon as Ah tell these pretty young ladies good night . . . and take a cane to this young smartalec!" He glared at Cousin Mark, who grinned back at him lazily. "It's not a wise thing," Uncle Robert intoned ominously, "to joke about the supernatural or regard it as a . . . parlor-game! And one of these days, young suh, you're going to find that out in a way you'll never forget!"

With that, and followed by a chorus of subdued giggles, he stamped into the house, leaving Adelia and me to bid our guests farewell. At the gate, after the carful of others had rolled away toward the ferry, Cousin Mark lingered, trying to persuade Adelia to kiss him good night. I would gladly have obliged, but my red-headed Georgia cousin switched away from him coolly, tossing her long auburn mop of curls.

"No, I won't!" she said shortly. "The idea, poking fun at Uncle Robert right to his face! You ought to be ashamed of yourself, Mark . . . and besides, you're such a smartalec, like Uncle said! How do *you* know there's no such thing as a ghost, just because you happen never to have seen one?"

Mark laughed softly, derisively. "And neither have you and Lib," he added. "I saw you wink at each other. Did you really think I'd swallow that silly yarn about the Confederate soldier?"

Adelia nudged me all at once, a signal to stand by and back up whatever mischief she had in mind.

"I've just remembered," she said quietly, "what tomorrow is!
Lib . . . it was a year ago that . . . that *we* saw the soldier throw
himself off that lookout porch at the top of the tower . . . Remember? You and I were riding horseback up the hill, just at
sundown. And you heard that awful scream, and we glanced up
just in time to . . . to see that shadow falling from the tower into
the river! On July 9, the date of Lee's surrender at Appomattox!"

"It was *April* 9!" I hissed in her ear. "You'll ruin everything . . . !"

"Sh-h!" Adelia hissed back, giggling. "A damyankee wouldn't
know *what* day it was, hardly the *year*! . . . . Oh, I'll never forget
that sight," she whispered, shuddering. "Not as long as I live!
The look of despair on that man's face, the glimpse I got of it as
he fell down, down. . . ."

"Bah!" Mark cut her off with a snort. "You're as big a liar as
your Uncle Robert! He and his ridiculous . . . ectoplasmic replica!"

"But it's true!" I chimed in solemnly. "When we told about it,
they dragged the river. But no body was ever found, and none
turned up at the Falls downstream. He was wearing a . . . a
shabby gray uniform. And . . . and a gray forage cap." I elabo-
rated, warming to our little hoax. "And he wasn't more than four
feet tall—his legs, you know; they'd been shot off by cannon-
fire. . . ."

Adelia punched me again sharply. "Don't overdo it!" she
hissed, then, with a grave frightened look turned on our cousin
from Connecticut: "Oh, Mark, you mustn't scoff at such things!
Tomorrow is the date of the surrender. Maybe if . . . if you
watch for him on the hill at sundown, you'll . . . you'll see him,
too!"

Mark snorted again, and strode toward the tethered horse he
had ridden across the fields to Uncle's house earlier. In tan riding
pants and sports shirt open at the neck, he was the handsomest
thing I had ever seen—barring, of course, Francis X. himself. I
sighed faintly as Adelia and I, arms about each other's waist,
watched him mount and start to ride away, then wheel his spirited
little bay back to face us.

"So tomorrow's the witching hour, huh?" he laughed. "Okay,

I'll be here—with bells on! But let's make this worth while, cuz!" he drawled tormentingly. "How about a little bet of . . . say, five bucks? You pay me if our ghost doesn't show up. If I see him, I'll pay you . . . and gladly!" he jeered.

Adelia stiffened. I saw her pretty chin set and her brown eyes flash, taking up the challenge Mark's cool blue eyes had thrown her.

"All right, Mr. Smartalec!" she snapped back. "It's a bet! Just be mighty sure you bring that five dollars!"

"Just you have yours in your hand!" Mark taunted, "Want to make a little side bet, huh? A kiss, maybe? That kiss you won't give me tonight?"

"That's a bet, too!" Adelia answered briskly. "That's how *sure* I am that there *is* a tower ghost, and that you'll see him tomorrow!"

"Okay, carrot-top!" our cousin laughed. "Remember, you're no Southern gentleman if you don't pay up!"

He galloped away with that, and we strolled back toward the house together, Adelia and I, listening to his lusty voice singing, out of sheer perversity, Sherman's "Marching Through Georgia." Adelia stamped her foot.

"I *hate* that . . . that . . . !" she burst out, unconvincingly. "Lib, we've just got to fix his wagon tomorrow!" Her eyes began to twinkle all at once, and she ran up the curving staircase to burst into Uncle's room, where Shadrach was trying to make him drink his hot milk instead of another whiskey.

Quickly she related the bet to Uncle Robert, whose mild old eyes lighted up also with mischief. He slapped his knee, chuckling.

"We'll fix him!" he promised. "Shadrach, get me young Saunders on the phone, Bill Saunders' boy in Wytheville. He's short enough to look . . . Hmm." He tugged at his white beard, grinning. "Where's that old ratty Confederate uniform that belonged to your Great-uncle Claud, Lib? In the attic, is it? Well, get it out. . . . That Saunders boy won the highdive contest at VMI last year, didn't he? Yes. Then, jumping off that lookout porch on the tower and landing in the river won't be much of a feat for him. Yes, hmm. Then he can swim underwater, and come up inside the shot well. Hide under the cauldron until young Mark stops looking for him to come up . . . !"

"Uncle Robert, you old faker—I *knew* you'd think of something!" Adelia burst out laughing, and hugged him, then went dancing around the high-ceiled bedroom where four generations of our kin had been born, made love, had babies, and died. "I can't wait to see that smarty's face!" she exulted. "I just can't wait!"

Shadrach, with his glass of hot milk, had been fidgeting around in the background, his wide negro-eyes flitting from one of our faces to the other. Suddenly he blurted:

"Marse Robert . . . s'posin' dey *is* a shot-tower ha'nt up yonder? Seem lak I reecollect dey *was* a little runty soldier what got one leg shot off at Murfreesboro. Name o' Jackson . . . and he *did* make shot up yonder in de tower. And he *did* jump off and git drownded!"

"Ah know that," Uncle Robert cut him short irritably. "Knew him personally; he was in my platoon. But he didn't jump. He . . ."

"Yassuh. Got drunk and *fell* off'n de lookout porch," the old darkey recalled uncomfortably. "But dat wouldn't stop his sperrit from comin' back, if'n he took a notion. . . ."

"Oh, balderdash!" Uncle Robert roared at him. "There's no such thing as . . . as a spirit! Ghost, haunt, call it whatever you like! You know very well Ah . . . Ah simply make up these yarns to amuse the young folks."

"Yassuh." Shadrach subsided meekly; but his eyes were large and troubled in his wrinkled black face.

Adelia and I giggled and whispered half the night about our practical joke on Cousin Mark. We gobbled our waffles and wild honey as early as Aunt Cornelia would cook them, and spent the rest of the morning on the phone. Everyone in our little crowd had to be told about Uncle Robert's hoax, and since most of them rather disliked Cousin Mark for his abrupt and opinionated manner, all were looking forward to seeing him "taken down a peg."

At noon Bill Saunders turned up, a small freckled youth. He made two or three "practice dives" off the tower porch, disappearing from sight each time mysteriously and reappearing through the shot well, slime-covered and draped with cobwebs.

"Splendid, splendid!" Uncle Robert applauded, chuckling.

"You're an excellent swimmer, my boy. . . . Well, Adelia?" His old eyes twinkled as my cousin stood with her arm about his waist, watching the performance from the point below the tower where she and I were supposed to have seen the ghost a year ago.

"It's perfect!" she laughed. "Mark doesn't know you can swim underwater and come up inside the shot well. He'll be skeptical, of course, until our spook disappears into the river! Oh, when he goes back to Connecticut to visit his father's people, he'll certainly have a tale that will curl their hair!"

The day passed slowly under the weight of our young impatience. After dinner our friends began to turn up, by twos and fours, laughing and whispering together, and winking at Uncle Robert, who was enjoying his little jest immensely. As the long Virginia twilight began to fall, Adelia and I, in fluffy organdy, proposed an innocent-looking game of croquet under the big leafy maples on the lawn. Fireflies were beginning to wink and dart among the hedges. The sun had gone down below the distant blue-gray mountains, but a queer flat light lingered in the sky, giving everything the look of a stereopticon picture.

"Don't anybody dare to snicker and give us away," Adelia ordered. "I want Mark to think this is just another evening of fun and dancing. Unrehearsed . . . Oh, I can't wait another minute!" she giggled, consulting the tiny wristwatch Uncle Robert had given her as a graduation present. "He's late! It'll be too dark in another half-hour for him to see Bill. But I've painted him all over with luminous paint. . . . You don't suppose Mark's got cold feet and backed out on his bet?"

"Not that hard-headed stubborn Yankee!" I scoffed. "An earthquake wouldn't keep him from . . . See?" I broke off, triumphant. "Here he comes now over the north hill!"

A solitary rider in white sport shirt and brown jodphurs was indeed coming, hell-for-leather, over the far hill that separated the Homeplace from my aunt's remodeled home. The little bay mare Mark always rode took the hill at a hard gallop and plunged down the other side without slackening speed. A narrow creek with a fence rambling along its farther bank divided the "bottom land" where the cows and horses grazed. As we watched, holding our breath, my cousin spurred his mount recklessly to take this precarious jump, ignoring the wide-open gate further down.

"Young idiot!" Uncle Robert muttered. "Rides like a damyan-kee. No consideration for the hoss. . . . Hah! He'll break his fool . . ."

Even as he spoke the words, the little bay, sailing over creek and fence, caught a hoof on the top rail and fell head over heels. Her rider went sprawling, and did not rise, even after the mare scrambled to her feet and went galloping back home through the open gate.

Adelia and I gasped, and started to run in that direction. But as we reached the orchard gate, we saw Cousin Mark striding to-ward us along the narrow path past the springhouse. We waved, he waved back, and Adelia sniffed.

"He's okay," she said, almost resentfully. "Nothing could make a dent in that rhinoceros hide!"

But as he approached us, I saw that he looked very pale and dazed. There was a great dark gash across his forehead at the temple, and he limped slightly. With a twinge of remorse we beckoned, ready to call off our little joke. But Mark shook his head mockingly, and pointed to the shot-tower, turning his steps in that direction before he reached the orchard. He shouted something, but wind must have blown the sound away from us, for we could hear nothing but the faint quavering cry of a whip-poorwill somewhere along the river.

Adelia stamped her foot. "See?" she exploded. "He's so smug, so sure of himself! Going to show us up for a bunch of supersti-tious nitwits! Just you wait . . . !"

We ran back through the orchard to join the others, lined up along the fence to watch Mark. Through the gathering dusk we could see his lone figure toiling up the hill toward the shot-tower, its bleak silhouette picked out sharply against the pale pink-and-gold of the western sky. White sheep dotted the green hillside, but as Mark picked his way among them, they did not start and run, but went on grazing, undisturbed.

We began to laugh and chatter excitedly as my cousin reached the point where the ghost could best be seen. Uncle Robert signaled surreptitiously with a flashlight, and instantly a fore-shortened figure, glowing with an eerie green radiance, appeared on the lookout porch. Laughing, we saw Mark stop short, staring up at the apparition.

Uncle Robert signaled again. Promptly a harsh quavering cry broke the evening stillness, heart-rending in its despair. The figure on the lookout porch, in gray Confederate uniform and forage cap, suddenly flung itself out into space. Screaming, it fell down, down, to disappear in the swirling river far below. We saw Mark standing on the riverbank, watching intently for the swimmer to bob up. When he did not, my cousin turned uncertainly, looking up and downstream, while we watched, bent double with mirth at his obvious bewilderment. He turned at last and entered the door of the shot-tower, evidently preparing to climb the spiral staircase and examine the lookout porch from which the spectre had jumped. We fell upon one another, rocked with laughter.

But abruptly my cousin's figure reappeared and started limping down the hill. He reached the front gate and stood there, swaying slightly, very pale and disheveled, but smiling in mocking triumph. As Adelia opened the iron gate for him, questioningly, trying to keep her face straight and solemn, Mark began to laugh silently—and held out his hand, palm up.

At that instant a second dripping figure, in soggy gray uniform and minus the forage cap, was seen slogging down the hill. Bill Saunders reached us and leaned on the fence, grinning disgustedly and coughing a bit as if strangled. Most of the phosphorescent paint had washed off, and he glowed ludicrously only in spots on Uncle Claud's faded uniform.

"Bill!" Adelia wailed, half-laughing. "Oh, shoot! What went wrong? How did Mark find out . . . ?"

"Aw-w!" Saunders ducked his head sheepishly. "I did it perfectly twice before! But *this* time I had to swim up under the wrong side of the shot cauldron! Got strangled and darn near drowned! Would have, if Mark hadn't heard me splashing around and caught me by the collar. . . ."

All eyes turned on my cousin Mark then, standing there quietly in the gathering dusk, looking oddly weak and pale but smiling with sardonic satisfaction. His hand was still held out mockingly, and Adelia flounced over to him, disgruntled.

"All right, General Grant!" she lashed out peevishly as Mark still did not speak. "Start rubbing it in, why don't you? You outflanked us! You won the bet . . . and I'm no welcher!" Her brown eyes twinkled suddenly. "But . . . I didn't say *where* you could kiss me—just on the cheek!" She turned her pretty face up to him, at the same time thrusting a crumpled bill into his hand; I gasped as I saw that it was a worthless piece of 1864 currency we had found in the attic, along with Uncle Claud's uniform. "And here's your five," Adelia jeered. "I didn't promise I wouldn't pay off . . . in Confederate money!"

Mark smiled at her, a one-sided ironic little smile of reluctant admiration. He shrugged and bent to kiss her on the cheek. But abruptly he swayed, an expression of pain and confusion crossing his handsome face, now only a white blur against the darkness. One hand groped for the money Adelia held out, the other went to the dark gash in his forehead. And I saw my pretty cousin's face soften with tenderness.

"Oh, Mark!" she cried out. "You *were* hurt when your horse threw you! Why didn't you tell us, instead of going on with this silly bet we . . . ?"

Someone screamed—a rasping high-pitched sound of utter terror. We all whirled toward the sound, startled. Shadrach, coming across the lawn gravely to find Uncle Robert, had halted abruptly. His darkey eyes were distended with horror, one black hand pointing shakily in our direction. We laughed, thinking he had seen Bill Saunders' glowing figure, and followed him into the house as he ran from us, still shrieking. But he locked himself in his room and no amount of coaxing would bring him out.

In the hallway we noticed the phone, off the hook. Uncle Robert picked it up, and was startled by the sound of sobbing coming over the wire.

It was my aunt, a rather hysterical woman. Mark's horse, she said, had returned, riderless, to the stable. She was sure something had happened to him. Was he all right? Was he there with us?

Uncle Robert soothed her, assured her that Mark was with us, quite uninjured, then called him to the phone to convince his mother.

There was no answer, other than the eerie cry of a distant

whippoorwill. Mark had vanished, left abruptly—after collecting, Adelia remarked in a covert tone of disappointment, only the money-half of their little bet. We'd phone and tease him about that when he reached home, she laughingly said. . . .

But an hour later, my aunt called back. Mark had not arrived. When she called again frantically around midnight, a search was instituted. Toward morning they found his body.

He was lying, all crumpled up, where his little bay mare had thrown him when she fell. A quick examination showed that his right leg had been broken in two places; but mercifully, he had not had to lie there suffering all night. A blow on the temple, when his head struck a rock, had killed him—instantly, the coroner said.

Mark had been dead all that time. The coroner jeered at the fantastic account we told of his saving Bill Saunders' life, then collecting that bet from Adelia. A case of mass-hypnotism, he called it, induced by the fact that we were all so anxious for Mark's presence to complete our little hoax about the shot-tower ghost. He quoted the illusion of the Indian rope-trick as an example; how a group of people in broad daylight can be made to "see" a small boy climb a rope rising in midair, and disappear before their very eyes. "Psychic residue" and "ectoplasmic replica" were terms he had never heard . . . nor did anyone ever hear of them again from Uncle Robert's lips. He and Shadrach were thereafter conspicuously silent, exchanging a long look, whenever the supernatural was mentioned. And as for me, the cry of a whippoorwill at dusk still makes me shiver uncontrollably. . . .

For there was one little item that the coroner could not explain. There was a crumpled five-dollar bill in my Cousin Mark's dead hand when they found him—a worthless piece of currency, printed by the Southern Confederacy in 1864.

EDGAR ALLAN POE

A Tale of the Ragged Mountains

EDGAR ALLAN POE *(1809–1849) was born in Boston, made his home in Philadelphia and also New York and died mysteriously in Baltimore. Father of the first modern detective stories, "The Purloined Letter," "The Mystery of Marie Roget," "The Gold Bug" and "The Murders in the Rue Morgue," Poe wrote such fantasy and horror classics as "The Tell-Tale Heart," "The Masque of the Red Death," "The Black Cat," "The Fall of the House of Usher" (parodied by Robert Bloch elsewhere in this book) and many other stories, poems and essays. Some of Poe's less familiar efforts require patience to read through nowadays, but the next selection is an exception that the late writer-editor Anthony Boucher once contended masqueraded as an occult tale but was really a murder mystery. Boucher's arguments were clever, but unconvincing. "A Tale of the Ragged Mountains" remains one of Poe's most unusual fantasies, the strange story of an out-of-body experience in the dense wooded mountains of Charlottesville, Virginia.*

During the fall of the year 1827, while residing near Charlottesville, Virginia, I casually made the acquaintance of Mr. Augustus Bedloe. This young gentleman was remarkable in every respect, and excited in me a profound interest and curiosity. I found it impossible to comprehend him either in his moral or his physical relations. Of his family I could obtain no satisfactory account.

Whence he came, I never ascertained. Even about his age—although I call him a young gentleman—there was something which perplexed me in no little degree. He certainly *seemed* young —and he made a point of speaking about his youth—yet there were moments when I should have had little trouble in imagining him a hundred years of age. But in no regard was he more peculiar than in his personal appearance. He was singularly tall and thin. He stooped much. His limbs were exceedingly long and emaciated. His forehead was broad and low. His complexion was absolutely bloodless. His mouth was large and flexible, and his teeth were more wildly uneven, although sound, than I had ever before seen teeth in a human head. The expression of his smile, however, was by no means unpleasing, as might be supposed; but it had no variation whatever. It was one of profound melancholy —of a phaseless and unceasing gloom. His eyes were abnormally large, and round like those of a cat. The pupils, too, upon any accession or diminution of light, underwent contraction or dilation, just such as is observed in the feline tribe. In moments of excitement the orbs grew bright to a degree almost inconceivable; seeming to emit luminous rays, not of a reflected but of an intrinsic lustre, as does a candle or the sun; yet their ordinary condition was so totally vapid, filmy, and dull, as to convey the idea of the eyes of a long-interred corpse.

These peculiarities of person appeared to cause him much annoyance, and he was continually alluding to them in a sort of half explanatory, half apologetic strain, which, when I first heard it, impressed me very painfully. I soon, however, grew accustomed to it, and my uneasiness wore off. It seemed to be his design rather to insinuate than directly to assert that, physically, he had not always been what he was—that a long series of neuralgic attacks had reduced him from a condition of more than usual personal beauty, to that which I saw. For many years past he had been attended by a physician, named Templeton—an old gentleman, perhaps seventy years of age—whom he had first encountered at Saratoga, and from whose attention, while there, he either received, or fancied that he received, great benefit. The result was that Bedloe, who was wealthy, had made an arrangement with Dr. Templeton, by which the latter, in consideration of a liberal annual allowance, had consented to devote his time and medical experience exclusively to the care of the invalid.

Doctor Templeton had been a traveller in his younger days, and at Paris had become a convert, in great measure, to the doctrine of Mesmer. It was altogether by means of magnetic remedies that he had succeeded in alleviating the acute pains of his patient; and this success had very naturally inspired the latter with a certain degree of confidence in the opinions from which the remedies had been educed. The Doctor, however, like all enthusiasts, had struggled hard to make a thorough convert of his pupil, and finally so far gained his point as to induce the sufferer to submit to numerous experiments. By a frequent repetition of these, a result had arisen, which of late days has become so common as to attract little or no attention, but which, at the period of which I write, had very rarely been known in America. I mean to say, that between Doctor Templeton and Bedloe there had grown up, little by little, a very distinct and strongly marked *rapport*, or magnetic relation. I am not prepared to assert, however, that this *rapport* extended beyond the limits of the simple sleep-producing power; but this power itself had attained great intensity. At the first attempt to induce the magnetic somnolency, the mesmerist entirely failed. In the fifth or sixth he succeeded very partially, and after long-continued effort. Only at the twelfth was the triumph complete. After this the will of the patient succumbed rapidly to that of the physician, so that, when I first became acquainted with the two, sleep was brought about almost instantaneously by the mere volition of the operator, even when the invalid was unaware of his presence. It is only now, in the year 1845, when similar miracles are witnessed daily by thousands, that I dare venture to record this apparent impossibility as a matter of serious fact.

The temperature of Bedloe was, in the highest degree sensitive, excitable, enthusiastic. His imagination was singularly vigorous and creative; and no doubt it derived additional force from the habitual use of morphine, which he swallowed in great quantity, and without which he would have found it impossible to exist. It was his practice to take a very large dose of it immediately after breakfast each morning,—or, rather, immediately after a cup of strong coffee, for he ate nothing in the forenoon,—and then set forth alone, or attended only by a dog, upon a long ramble among the chain of wild and dreary hills that lie westward and southward of Charlottesville, and are there dignified by the title of the Ragged Mountains.

Upon a dim, warm, misty day, toward the close of November, and during the strange *interregnum* of the seasons which in America is termed the Indian summer, Mr. Bedloe departed as usual for the hills. The day passed, and still he did not return.

About eight o'clock at night, having become seriously alarmed at his protracted absence, we were about setting out in search of him, when he unexpectedly made his appearance, in health no worse than usual, and in rather more than ordinary spirits. The account which he gave of his expedition, and of the events which had detained him, was a singular one indeed.

"You will remember," said he, "that it was about nine in the morning when I left Charlottesville. I bent my steps immediately to the mountains, and, about ten, entered a gorge which was entirely new to me. I followed the windings of this pass with much interest. The scenery which presented itself on all sides, although scarcely entitled to be called grand, had about it an indescribable and to me a delicious aspect of dreary desolation. The solitude seemed absolutely virgin. I could not help believing that the green sods and the gray rocks upon which I trod had been trodden never before by the foot of a human being. So entirely secluded, and in fact inaccessible, except through a series of accidents, is the entrance of the ravine, that it is by no means impossible that I was indeed the first adventurer—the very first and sole adventurer who had ever penetrated its recesses.

"The thick and peculiar mist, or smoke, which distinguishes the Indian summer, and which now hung heavily over all objects, served, no doubt, to deepen the vague impressions which these objects created. So dense was this pleasant fog that I could at no time see more than a dozen yards of the path before me. This path was excessively sinuous, and as the sun could not be seen, I soon lost all idea of the direction in which I journeyed. In the meantime the morphine had its customary effect—that of enduing all the external world with an intensity of interest. In the quivering of a leaf—in the hue of a blade of grass—in the shape of a trefoil—in the humming of a bee—in the gleaming of a dew-drop—in the breathing of the wind—in the faint odors that came from the forest—there came a whole universe of suggestion—a gay and motley train of rhapsodical and immethodical thought.

"Busied in this, I walked on for several hours, during which the mist deepened around me to so great an extent that at length I was reduced to an absolute groping of the way. And now an indescribable uneasiness possessed me—a species of nervous hesitation and tremor. I feared to tread, lest I should be precipitated into some abyss. I remembered, too, strange stories told about these Ragged Hills, and of the uncouth and fierce races of men who tenanted their groves and caverns. A thousand vague fancies oppressed and disconcerted me—fancies the more distressing because vague. Very suddenly my attention was arrested by the loud beating of a drum.

"My amazement was, of course, extreme. A drum in these hills was a thing unknown. I could not have been more surprised at the sound of the trump of the Archangel. But a new and still more astounding source of interest and perplexity arose. There came a wild rattling or jingling sound, as if of a bunch of large keys, and upon the instant a dusky-visaged and half-naked man rushed past me with a shriek. He came so close to my person that I felt his hot breath upon my face. He bore in one hand an instrument composed of an assemblage of steel rings, and shook them vigorously as he ran. Scarcely had he disappeared in the mist, before, panting after him, with open mouth and glaring eyes, there darted a huge beast. I could not be mistaken in its character. It was a hyena.

"The sight of this monster rather relieved than heightened my terrors—for I now made sure that I dreamed, and endeavored to arouse myself to waking consciousness. I stepped boldly and briskly forward. I rubbed my eyes. I called aloud. I pinched my limbs. A small spring of water presented itself to my view, and here, stooping, I bathed my hands and my head and neck. This seemed to dissipate the equivocal sensations which had hitherto annoyed me. I arose, as I thought, a new man, and proceeded steadily and complacently on my unknown way.

"At length, quite overcome by exertion, and by a certain oppressive closeness of the atmosphere, I seated myself beneath a tree. Presently there came a feeble gleam of sunshine, and the shadow of the leaves of the tree fell faintly but definitely upon the grass. At this shadow I gazed wonderingly for many minutes. Its character stupefied me with astonishment. I looked upward. The tree was a palm.

"I now arose hurriedly, and in a state of fearful agitation—for the fancy that I dreamed would serve me no longer. I saw—I felt that I had perfect command of my senses—and these senses now brought to my soul a world of novel and singular sensation. The heat became all at once intolerable. A strange odor loaded the breeze. A low, continuous murmur, like that arising from a full, but gently flowing river, came to my ears, intermingled with the peculiar hum of multitudinous human voices.

"While I listened in an extremity of astonishment which I need not attempt to describe, a strong and brief gust of wind bore off the incumbent fog as if by the wand of an enchanter.

"I found myself at the foot of a high mountain, and looking down into a vast plain, through which wound a majestic river. On the margin of this river stood an Eastern-looking city, such as we read of in the Arabian Tales, but of a character even more singular than any there described. From my position, which was far above the level of the town, I could perceive its every nook and corner, as if delineated on a map. The streets seemed innumerable, and crossed each other irregularly in all directions, but were rather long winding alleys than streets, and absolutely swarmed with inhabitants. The houses were wildly picturesque. On every hand was a wilderness of balconies, of verandas, of minarets, of shrines, and fantastically carved oriels. Bazaars abounded; and there were displayed rich wares in infinite variety and profusion —silks, muslins, the most dazzling cutlery, the most magnificent jewels and gems. Besides these things, were seen, on all sides, banners and palanquins, litters with stately dames close-veiled, elephants gorgeously caparisoned, idols grotesquely hewn, drums, banners, and gongs, spears, silver and gilded maces. And amid the crowd, and the clamor, and the general intricacy and confusion—amid the million of black and yellow men, turbaned and robed, and of flowing beard, there roamed a countless multitude of holy filleted bulls, while vast legions of the filthy but sacred ape clambered, chattering and shrieking, about the cornices of the mosques, or clung to the minarets and oriels. From the swarming streets to the banks of the river, there descended innumerable flights of steps leading to bathing places, while the river itself seemed to force a passage with difficulty through the vast fleets of deeply burdened ships that far and wide encountered its surface. Beyond the limits of the city arose, in frequent majestic groups, the palm and the cocoa, with other gigantic and weird trees of vast age; and here and there might be seen a field of rice, the thatched hut of a peasant, a tank, a stray temple, a gypsy camp, or a solitary graceful maiden taking her way, with a pitcher upon her head, to the banks of the magnificent river.

"You will say now, of course, that I dreamed; but not so. What I saw—what I heard—what I felt—what I thought—had about it nothing of the unmistakable idiosyncrasy of the dream. All was rigorously self-consistent. At first, doubting that I was really awake, I entered into a series of tests, which soon convinced me that I really was. Now, when one dreams, and, in the dream, suspects that he dreams, the suspicion *never fails to confirm itself,* and the sleeper is almost immediately aroused. Thus Novalis errs not in saying that 'we are near waking when we dream that we dream.' Had the vision occurred to me as I describe it, without my suspecting it as a dream, then a dream it might absolutely have been, but, occurring as it did, and suspected and tested as it was, I am forced to class it among other phenomena."

"In this I am not sure that you are wrong," observed Dr. Templeton, "but proceed. You arose and descended into the city."

"I arose," continued Bedloe, regarding the Doctor with an air of profound astonishment, "I arose, as you say, and descended into the city. On my way I fell in with an immense populace, crowding through every avenue, all in the same direction, and exhibiting in every action the wildest excitement. Very suddenly, and by some inconceivable impulse, I became intensely imbued with personal interest in what was going on. I seemed to feel that I had an important part to play, without exactly understanding what it was. Against the crowd which environed me, however, I experienced a deep sentiment of animosity. I shrank from amid them, and, swiftly, by a circuitous path, reached and entered the city. Here all was the wildest tumult and contention. A small party of men, clad in garments half Indian, half European, and officered by gentlemen in a uniform partly British, were engaged, at great odds, with the swarming rabble of the alleys. I joined the weaker party, arming myself with the weapons of a fallen officer, and fighting I knew not whom with the nervous ferocity of despair. We were soon overpowered by numbers, and driven to seek refuge in a species of kiosk. Here we barricaded ourselves, and, for the present, were secure. From a loop-hole near the summit of the kiosk, I perceived a vast crowd, in furious agitation, surrounding and assaulting a gay palace that overhung the river. Presently, from an upper window of this palace, there descended an effeminate-looking person, by means of a string made of the turbans of his attendants. A boat was at hand, in which he escaped to the opposite bank of the river.

"And now a new object took possession of my soul. I spoke a few hurried but energetic words to my companions, and, having succeeded in gaining over a few of them to my purpose, made a frantic sally from the kiosk. We rushed amid the crowd that surrounded it. They retreated, at first, before us. They rallied, fought madly, and retreated again. In the meantime we were borne far from the kiosk, and became bewildered and entangled among the narrow streets of tall, overhanging houses, into the recesses of which the sun had never been able to shine. The rabble pressed impetuously upon us, harassing us with their spears, and overwhelming us with flights of arrows. These latter were very remarkable, and resembled in some respects the writhing creese of the Malay. They were made to imitate the body of a creeping serpent, and were long and black, with a poisoned barb. One of them struck me upon the right temple. I reeled and fell. An instantaneous and dreadful sickness seized me. I struggled—I gasped—I died."

"You will hardly persist *now*," said I, smiling, "that the whole of your adventure was not a dream. You are not prepared to maintain that you are dead?"

When I said these words, I of course expected some lively sally from Bedloe in reply; but, to my astonishment, he hesitated, trembled, became fearfully pallid, and remained silent. I looked toward Templeton. He sat erect and rigid in his chair—his teeth chattered, and his eyes were starting from their sockets. "Proceed!" he at length said hoarsely to Bedloe.

"For many minutes," continued the latter, "my sole sentiment —my sole feeling—was that of darkness and nonentity, with the consciousness of death. At length there seemed to pass a violent and sudden shock through my soul, as if of electricity. With it came the sense of elasticity and of light. This latter I felt—not saw. In an instant I seemed to rise from the ground. But I had no bodily, no visible, audible, or palpable presence. The crowd had departed. The tumult had ceased. The city was in comparative repose. Beneath me lay my corpse, with the arrow in my temple, the whole head greatly swollen and disfigured. But all these things I felt—not saw. I took interest in nothing. Even the corpse seemed a matter in which I had no concern. Volition I had none, but appeared to be impelled into motion, and flitted buoyantly out of the city, retracing the circuitous path by which I had entered it. When I had attained that point of the ravine in the mountains at which I had encountered the hyena, I again experienced a shock as of a galvanic battery; the sense of weight, of volition, of substance, returned. I became my original self, and bent my steps eagerly homeward—but the past had not lost the vividness of the real—and not now, even for an instant, can I compel my understanding to regard it as a dream."

"Nor was it," said Templeton, with an air of deep solemnity, "yet it would be difficult to say how otherwise it should be termed. Let us suppose only, that the soul of the man of to-day is upon the verge of some stupendous psychal discoveries. Let us content ourselves with this supposition. For the rest I have some explanation to make. Here is a water-color drawing, which I should have shown you before, but which an unaccountable sentiment of horror has hitherto prevented me from showing."

We looked at the picture which he presented. I saw nothing in it of an extraordinary character; but its effect upon Bedloe was prodigious. He nearly fainted as he gazed. And yet it was but a miniature portrait—a miraculously accurate one, to be sure—of his own very remarkable features. At least this was my thought as I regarded it.

"You will perceive," said Templeton, "the date of this picture —it is here, scarcely visible, in this corner—1780. In this year was the portrait taken. It is the likeness of a dead friend—a Mr. Oldeb —to whom I became much attached at Calcutta, during the administration of Warren Hastings. I was then only twenty years old. When I first saw you, Mr. Bedloe, at Saratoga, it was the miraculous similarity which existed between yourself and the painting which induced me to accost you, to seek your friendship, and to bring about those arrangements which resulted in my becoming your constant companion. In accomplishing this point, I was urged partly, and perhaps principally, by a regretful memory of the deceased, but also, in part by an uneasy, and not altogether horrorless curiosity respecting yourself.

"In your detail of the vision which presented itself to you amid the hills, you have described, with the minutest accuracy, the Indian city of Benares, upon the Holy River. The riots, the combat, the massacre, were the actual events of the insurrection of Cheyte Sing, which took place in 1780, when Hastings was put in imminent peril of his life. The man escaping by the string of turbans was Cheyte Sing himself. The party in the kiosk were sepoys and British officers, headed by Hastings. Of this party I was one, and did all I could to prevent the rash and fatal sally of the officer who fell, in the crowded alleys, by the poisoned arrow of a Bengalee. That officer was my dearest friend. It was Oldeb. You will perceive by these manuscripts," (here the speaker produced a note-book in which several pages appeared to have been freshly written) "that at the very period in which you fancied these things amid the hills, I was engaged in detailing them upon paper here at home."

In about a week after this conversation, the following paragraphs appeared in a Charlottesville paper:

"We have the painful duty of announcing the death of MR. AUGUSTUS BEDLO, a gentleman whose amiable manners and many virtues have long endeared him to the citizens of Charlottesville.

"Mr. B., for some years past, has been subject to neuralgia, which has often threatened to terminate fatally; but this can be regarded only as the mediate cause of his decease. The proximate cause was one of especial singularity. In an excursion to the Ragged Mountains, a few days since, a slight cold and fever were contracted, attended with great determination of blood to the head. To relieve this, Dr. Templeton resorted to topical bleeding. Leeches were applied to the temples. In a fearfully brief period the patient died, when it appeared that, in the jar containing the leeches, had been introduced, by accident, one of the venomous vermicular sangsues which are now and then found in the neighboring ponds. This creature fastened itself upon a small artery in the right temple. Its close resemblance to the medicinal leech caused the mistake to be overlooked until too late.

"N.B.—The poisonous sangsue of Charlottesville may always be distinguished from the medicinal leech by its blackness, and especially by its writhing or vermicular motions, which very nearly resemble those of a snake."

I was speaking with the editor of the paper in question, upon the topic of this remarkable accident, when it occurred to me to ask how it happened that the name of the deceased had been given as Bedlo.

"I presume," said I, "you have authority for this spelling, but I have always supposed the name to be written with an *e* at the end."

"Authority?—no," he replied. "It is a mere typographical error. The name is Bedlo with an *e*, all the world over, and I never knew it to be spelt otherwise in my life."

"Then," said I mutteringly, as I turned upon my heel, "then indeed has it come to pass that one truth is stranger than any fiction—for Bedlo, without the *e*, what is it but Oldeb conversed! And this man tells me it is a typographical error."

FRANCES GARFIELD

Come to the Party

Anyone who ever saw FRANCES GARFIELD *in the loving company of her late husband, Manly Wade Wellman (whose own eerie story immediately follows), would agree with my friend and former editor Pat LoBrutto, who once remarked to me, "Those two are the best advertisement for monogamy in the whole world." Some of this autobiographical affection may be felt in the following partly true story, which reportedly takes place in the vicinity of the writer's home in Chapel Hill, North Carolina.*

Dusk was fast overcoming the autumn twilight. Nora felt no closer to Steve Thomas's country house than they'd been half an hour earlier. She snuggled closer to big Jeff in the back seat and tried to see the road ahead. The headlights bravely probed a path, but the darkness seemed to nestle nearer and gloomier to either side.

Willie, in the front seat beside Sam, bent her ginger head above a crude, penciled map, which the four had begun to fear was false.

"Steve just doesn't know how to draw maps," Willie half moaned. "And he promised to put up signals to show where to turn off onto his private road. Why ever did I pick a publisher who throws his parties on the far side of nowhere?"

"But, my dear, this publisher picked you out," reminded silver-haired Sam at the wheel. "A dozen others turned you down—"

"Please. Why bring that up?" Willie appealed. But he went on.

"Here was Steve with his little regional publishing house, pretty much on the far side of nowhere itself, a county away. Regional, and he wanted a regional novel for the Christmas trade. And he liked yours very much. And here we are, on our way to cheer you on while you autograph a thousand or so flyleaves."

Sam loved his writer wife, and showed it by his teasing. Nora knew he smiled his special smile of affectionate amusement, blue eyes slanted and twinkling.

"He said there might be about a dozen guests," protested Willie. "He said he'd invited some special friends who might like my book and buy it. And tell all their friends—so they'd buy it too. For Christmas gifts. Word-of-mouth advertising, Steve called it."

"Yes. Cheaper than published advertising," remarked Sam.

"There's that little white church again," said Jeff, big and trying to sound cheerful. "How many times have we passed it? Three? Or maybe four?"

"Four, I'm sure," put in Nora. "And there's the little gray house that keeps following us."

"Damn," said Sam. "This curve looming ahead is boringly familiar. We seem to be in orbit—"

A grotesquely painted van charged into the glare of headlights, squarely in the center of the road. Sam cursed and wrenched the wheel. The car swayed onto the grassy shoulder. The tremendous van shot past, its driver goggling out, blocky white teeth gleaming from a dark thicket of beard. Then he was gone, and Sam twisted back onto the road.

"Whew," gasped Willie. "Thank God you were driving, Sam, not me."

Nora tossed her thick, black hair out of her eyes. Her hand tingled where Jeff had gripped it so powerfully. She could still see that staring, shaggy face.

"It'll be a great party if we ever get there," she said in a feeble attempt at humor. "Look, isn't that the church again?"

"I wonder if anybody will find the place," ventured Willie.

"Pessimist," chuckled Sam. He loved everything about Willie, including her novel about a woman's passion for both her husband and her husband's brother. Nora had overheard a neighbor woman ask Sam which of the characters he was supposed to be. "A little of both," he had said, with a perfectly straight face, slant blue eyes twinkling as usual.

"There'll be people there all right," promised burly Jeff. "And Nora and I are here to give you moral support, Willie." He, too, admired the book, had helped Willie read proof on it. The four were close friends, always enjoyed each other, never bored together.

"That van looks better behind us than in front of us," said Sam. "Maybe he's lost out here, too, rolling round and round. Look, a mist is coming up."

An owl hooted in the distance, strangely loud and clear above the motor's purr. No houses showed now, only great twisted trees crowded at the sides of the road, branches laced overhead. Willie gave a sudden, happy squeak.

"Look—a bit of tinsel on a post," she cried. "That's bound to be Steve's signal."

"And a driveway just past it," said Sam, turning deftly. "A long one, too."

They followed turns, rises, and falls in the bumpy road. Dark thickets massed to right and left. They heard nothing, no sound but the motor. Nora saw a grotesquely hunched tree that reminded her of a cedar of Lebanon she remembered from Winchester Cathedral. Weird.

"Turn there," directed Willie, pointing ahead. And Sam turned.

"Geez, how well you obey Willie," laughed Nora. "One word from me and Jeff does the exact opposite."

Jeff said nothing. He stared out of the window, lips clamped; his cheek had a taut crease where there should be a dimple.

Sam bumped the car over the coarse outflung roots of a great oak, and stopped on the tall grass. Ahead of them showed a great, bleakly drab house. Wavering lights from the tall windows tinted the dim evening. A broad chimney, rosy in the dusk, climbed the side wall. Large pillars rose along a wide porch.

"Okay." Jeff touched Nora's shoulder, and she felt his great hand tremble. "Let's go on in."

Willie smoothed her cap of ginger curls and freshened her

lipstick. Nora shook her long, dark hair and moved to follow Jeff. "Odd," she said. "I don't see any other cars."

"They've probably been and gone," joked Sam, coming along behind with Willie. "It took us long enough to find the place."

They mounted the steps. A dark, heavy door loomed. Sam swung the huge knocker, and the door opened.

"Come in. Come in," came a booming voice.

They went in.

The man at the door was outrageously handsome, blond and tall, dressed in a tuxedo, shirtfront all foamy with lace, self-consciously cordial. "Glad you came," he greeted them.

"We had some problems," said Nora. "Where's Steve?"

"Oh, never mind Steve for a moment. My name's Patrick. Come on in and join the crowd."

The hubbub inside was unbelievable. Nora took hold of Jeff's coat, seeking reassurance. For what reason she didn't know. They had come into a huge, swarming room, a multitude of bodies. All kinds—tall, thin, short, fat, every one of them completely strange to her. Maybe Willie knew some of them, she thought. They could be part of Steve's publishing company. She stepped back to let Willie lead the way.

"Keep straight ahead," Patrick advised from behind. He was dismayingly handsome, and Nora speculated for a moment whether his hair had been permanented. "Food and drink over there," he smiled. "You'll find some friends there, probably."

"With my sort of friends, that's just where I'll find them," said Jeff, grinning now.

The four wove in and out among packed groups. Everybody was talking to everybody else and nobody seemed to notice them. A dull red fire glowed on a broad hearth, but did not seem to send out any heat. Several extremely thin men stood there and listened to a grossly heavy man. His face was bearded, toothy. Nora remembered the driver of that killer van. High along an inner wall ran a balcony. Faces looked down, the faces, perhaps, of children. One gnawed on what might have been a chicken wing.

"It's positively unreal," Nora whispered to Jeff, and it was. They seemed to walk through people, as though people dissolved from in front of them. "My imagination's going haywire," she said, and squeezed his hand for comfort.

Willie's brilliant, curly head had led the way to a butler's pantry. It, too, thronged with people, filling trays with barbecued chicken, cold cuts, sliced cheese. Baskets of crackers and little cakes sat here and there. In the midst of everything, a gigantic glass bowl of rosy liquid.

"Pink wine," whispered Sam, crinkling his nose. "The cheapest."

For a moment, they thought they saw Steve Thomas's beautiful wife balancing an empty tray toward a rear door, perhaps the kitchen. "Hey, Florence," Willie called out. But whoever it was didn't turn. She vanished so abruptly, they couldn't be sure if they'd seen her.

Sam picked up a plate and piled it high with salad and meat. "Let's dig in," he said. "That ride would give a skeleton an appetite. I'll even try this sorry wine—it's not worthy of Steve. Or is it? I think he outdid himself this time."

"There's Em Selden, there by the fireplace," said Nora to Jeff. "Where?"

"No, she's gone. Maybe it wasn't Em. Anyway, let's stick together. What a strange bunch of people."

As she spoke, she thought she heard singing somewhere. A radio, a record player? It died away as she wondered.

"Look," said Willie, putting down her plate. "At the end of the hall. It looks like Patrick, summoning me. I'd better go see— maybe it's time for me to autograph some books."

Briskly she headed for the long hallway, striding fast on green high-heeled sandals and swinging the skirt of her flowered green dress. There were chairs lining the hall. They seemed to be heaped with mink coats. "Hmm," Nora heard her murmur as she left. "None of Steve's authors could afford those."

Nora chewed on a strangely tasteless slice of sausage as she watched Willie out of sight. "I hope she sells enough books to make this trip worthwhile."

"You're not having fun?" worried Sam.

"That means you aren't happy, either." Nora looked from platter to platter. "What happened to the chicken wings? They're my favorite food."

"If I had a pair of chicken wings, I might just fly out of here," said Jeff. Nora laughed, but Jeff didn't join her.

The crowd had grown thicker, noisier. The air seemed damp and close; it had a smell like a roomful of old clothes. Sam frowned and brushed back his silver hair.

"Let's go somewhere quiet," he said.

"How about up on the balcony with the kids?" suggested Nora.

But the balcony seemed empty, lost in dark shadows. Maybe a hint of movement. Or maybe not.

"How much of this putrid wine did you drink, Jeff?" asked Sam.

"No more than I could help. I hope Willie's in her element, autographing books."

"I'm going to go see," said Sam.

He moved toward the hallway where Willie had vanished. The crowd let him through without seeming to make way.

"At least Steve had the sense to stay away from his own party," growled Jeff. "Look there in the corner. Isn't that Genevieve and Joe?"

Nora peered. "Let's go see."

They pressed their way through a huddle of people, who made a path for them. Nobody looked familiar. Except, against a far wall—the bearded van driver? The voices, all s's and all loud, hurt their ears. The air thickened, and was hard to breathe.

"Here we are," said Jeff, reaching the corner.

But nobody stood there. Nobody. Only a flicker from the fireplace that did not seem to give off heat.

"I'll be damned," Jeff muttered. "Do we have a single friend in this room?"

They looked around. Halfway across the room drifted a face, wan as lemon custard, peering from under the brim of a worn, shapeless felt hat. The body seemed lost in foggy darkness—they imagined a long black caftan. Behind him, or it, there grimaced the bearded driver.

"Jeff," said Nora, "I don't like it here."

"It's just that you don't know anybody," said Jeff. But his dimples did not show. "But you're right. The whole thing's a crashing bore. Let me go check with Willie and Sam. Maybe we can sneak out if they're through."

"Yes, go look for them." Nora tried to smile.

"I'll be right back."

Away he tramped, huge among the others. She watched him enter the hallway between the piled fur coats. Watched his dark head disappear. Then she stood alone, nobody noticing her, nobody talking to her. She felt dull, sticky, as though she hung in a mass of warm jelly.

Haze crawled in the air of the crowded room. It smelled, not like tobacco, not like that other familiar-grown marijuana smell. Nora did not belong there. She knew it. She hadn't been invited, really; she and Jeff had only come with Willie and Sam. For moral support. She wished they had stayed at home. Or wished, anyway, she had gone along with Jeff to find the others.

I'll follow them, she said to herself. Follow them. Maybe they're ready to go.

The hallway seemed to narrow as she entered. Those piles of furs closed in around her. Maybe the little white rabbit in the Alice book had felt closed in like that. And the hallway was shadow-barred, with open doorways shedding light along the side.

Nora looked in at a door. Music seeped out. Something in there like a little old-fashioned organ. It seemed to be playing, all by itself, a tune like a hymn, but dissonant, repelling. Voices echoed through the next doorway. Nora went there.

"Come in," somebody called. "We've been waiting."

A man in a very dark suit put out a very white hand to her. His chalky face grinned with dark, narrow teeth. His hand was clammy as it touched hers. "Come in," he said again.

Staring past him, she saw dull paneled walls, a hanging lamp that sprouted a shaky flame, a closely drawn knot of people. They, too, wore dark clothes, tight-fitted to gaunt bodies. They seemed to have faces of pale clay. Their eyes looked little and beady. They spoke from thick red lips, unintelligibly.

But on the floor lay three others, instantly recognizable—a bit of green cloth. Jeff's great, limp body. The red curls of Willie, the silver hair of Sam. None of them moved.

"Come in," a chorus, bidding.

All hands rose toward her, beckoning.

Nora screamed thinly and whirled to run.

Run anywhere, away from that little room, anywhere. A door stood at the end of the hallway. Escape. That was all she could think of. She gasped stranglingly. At the door, she clawed for the knob. She strove hard against the panel, and the door grumbled open.

She filled her lungs with fresh air. Somehow, miraculously, she was outside. Where to go? It didn't matter. Only get away.

She ran in the dark night, stumbling over the heavy coiled roots of trees, tearing her sheer hose. A slipper came off and desperately she kicked the other away. She kept running. Stones hurt her bare feet, biting painfully at her ankles. A mockingbird sang, strangely comforting. She was escaping. Away from that house.

A broad, open lawn loomed ahead of her. A beautiful house, standing tall and proud against sentinel pines. She floundered to one knee, dragged herself up again and to the door, beating at it with her fists.

"Why, Nora!"

There stood Steve Thomas, opening to her. Steve was slim, impeccable. His curled black hair was carefully groomed, a smile was on his face.

"For heaven's sake. Where have you been? Where are the others?"

She flung herself into his arms, and he held her close to quiet her trembling. "Where are they?" he asked again.

"I don't know," she chattered. "I saw them on the floor—over there at your party—"

"What are you talking about?"

She fought her choking sobs. "Over in that big house, right over there—"

"My God, Nora, there hasn't been a house there for years." Steve held her closer. "You're imagining things. No house. It burned down, long before I came here."

"B-burned down?"

"I've heard a crazy story. A bunch of far-out people, who had a belief of some sort about human sacrifice. And one night, when they celebrated it, lightning struck and burned the place to the ground, with everybody inside."

"But—"

"Look, Nora. There's nothing there. Nothing whatever."

Nora made herself look.

There *was* nothing there. Nothing whatever.

MANLY WADE WELLMAN

Nobody Ever Goes There

MANLY WADE WELLMAN *(1903–1986), late husband of Frances Gar-field, whose ghost story immediately precedes this selection, won the World Fantasy Award, the Mystery Writers of America's fact-crime "Edgar" and was once a Pulitzer Prize nominee. For more than half a century he contrib-uted many works of fiction to* Weird Tales, *including the following "John the Ballad Singer" tale, which appeared in the third issue of the Zebra Books* Weird Tales *revival edited by Lin Carter. The narrator of this story positions its setting southeast of Tennessee and northwest of Asheville, North Carolina, but since those states are contiguous, the little town of Trimble must rest smack on the borderline between them.*

That was what Mark Banion's grandparents told him when he was a five-year-old with tousled black hair, looking from the porch and out across Catch River to a big dark building and some small dark ones clumped against the soaring face of Music Mountain, rank with its gloomy huddles of trees.

His grandparents towered high to tell him, the way grownups do when you're little, and they said, "Nobody ever goes there," without explaining, the way grownups do when you're little. Mark was a good, obedient boy. He didn't press the matter. And he sure enough didn't go over.

The town had been named Trimble for somebody who, a hundred and forty-odd years ago, had a stock stand there, entertainment for man and beast. In those old days, stagecoaches and trading wagons rolled along the road chopped through the mountains, and sometimes came great herds of cattle and horses and hogs. Later there had been the railroad that carried hardly anything anymore. Trucks rumbled along Main Street and on, northwest to Tennessee or southeast to Asheville. Trimble was no great size for a town. Maybe that was why it stayed interesting to look at. It had stores on Main Street, and Mark's grandfather's chair factory, the town hall and the *Weekly Record.* On side streets stood the bank, the high school where students came by bus from all corners of the rocky county, and three churches. All those things were on this side of Catch River.

But over yonder where nobody went, loomed the empty-windowed old textile mill, like the picture of a ruined castle in an outlawed romantic novel. Once it had spun its acres of cloth. People working there had lived in the little house you could barely see from this side. Those houses had a dusky, secret look, bunched against Music Mountain. When Mark asked why it was called Music Mountain, his grandparents said, "We never heard tell why." So once, in his bed at night, Mark thought he heard soft music from across Catch River to his window. When he mentioned that next day, they laughed and said he was making it up.

He stopped talking about that other side of the river, but he kept his curiosity as he grew older. He found out a few things from listening to talk when he played in town. He found out that a police car did cruise over there two or three times a week on the rattly old bridge that nobody else used, and that the cruise was made only by daylight. When he was in high school, tall and tanned and a hot-rock tight end on the football team, he and two classmates started to amble across one Saturday. They were nearly halfway to the other side when a policeman came puffing after them and scolded them back. That night, Mark's grandparents told him never to let them hear of doing such a fool thing again. He asked why it was foolish, and his grandmother said, "Nobody ever goes there. Ever." And shut up her mouth with a snap.

One who did tell Mark something about it was Mr. Glover Shelton, the oldest man in Trimble, who whittled birds and bear cubs and rabbits in his little shop behind the Worley Café. Once a month he sold a crate of such whittlings to a man who carried them to a tourist bazaar off in another county. Mr. Glover was lamed so that he had an elbow in one knee, like a cricket. He wore checked shirts and bib overalls and a pointed beard as white as dandelion fluff. And he had memories.

"Something other happened there round about seventy-five years back," he said. "I was another sight younger than you then. There was the textile mill, and thirty-forty folks a-living in them company houses and a-working two shifts. Then one day, they was all of a sudden all gone."

"Gone where?" Mark asked him.

"Don't rightly know how to answer that. Just gone. Derwood Neidger the manager, and Sam Brood the foreman, and the whole crew on shift—gone." Mr. Glover whittled at the bluejay he was making. "One night just round sundown, the whistle it blowed and blowed, and folks over here got curiosed up and next day some of 'em headed over across the bridge. And nair soul at the mill, nor neither yet in the houses. The wives and children done gone, too. Everbody."

"Are you putting me on, Mr. Glover?"

"You done asked me, boy, and I done told you the thing I recollect about it."

"They just packed up and left?"

"They left, but they sure God nair packed up. The looms was still a-running. Derwood Neidger's fifty-dollar hat was on the hook, his cigar burnt out in a tray on his desk. Even supper a-standing on the stoves, two-three places. But nair a soul to be seen anywheres."

Mark looked to see if a grin was caught in the white beard, but Mr. Glover was as solemn as a preacher. "Where did they go?" Mark asked.

"I just wish you'd tell me. There was a search made, inquiries here and yonder, but none of them folks air showed theirself again."

"And now," said Mark, "nobody ever goes there."

"Well now, a couple-three has gone, one time another . . . from here, and a hunter or so a-cooning over Music Mountain from the far side. But none air come back no more. Only them policemen that drives over quick and comes back quick—always by daylight, always three in the car, with pistols and sawed-off shotguns. Boy," said Mr. Glover, "folks just stays off from that there place, like a-staying off from a rocky patch full of snakes, a wet bottom full of chills and fever."

"And now it's a habit," said Mark. "Staying out."

"Likewise a habit not to go a-talking about it none. Don't you go a-naming it to nobody I told you this much."

Mark played good enough football to get a grant in aid at a lowland college, about enough help to make the difference between going and not going. Summers, he mostly worked hard to keep in condition, in construction and at road mending. By the time he graduated, his grandparents had sold the chair factory and had retired to Florida. Mark came back to Trimble, where they hired him to coach football and baseball and teach physical education at his old high school.

And still nobody ever went across Catch River. He felt the old interest, but he quickly became more interested in Ruth Covell, the history teacher.

She was small and slim, and her hair was blond with a spice of red to it. She wore it more or less the length Mark wore his own black mane. She came up to about his coat lapel. Her face was round and sweet. She gave him a date, but wanted to sit and talk on the porch of the teacherage instead of driving to an outdoor movie. It was a balmy October night. She fetched them out two glasses of iced tea, flavored with lemon juice and ginger. They sat on bark-bottomed chairs, and Ruth said it was good to be in Trimble.

"I've liked it here from the first," she said, "I've thought I might write a history of this town."

"A history of Trimble?" Mark repeated, smiling. "Who'd read that?"

"You might, when I finish it. This place has stories worth putting on record. I've been to the town hall and the churches. I've found out lots of interesting things, but one thing avoids me."

"What's that, Ruth?" Mark asked, sipping.

"Why nobody ever goes across the river, and why everybody changes the subject when I bring it up."

From where they sat they could see a spattery shimmer of

moonlight on the water, but Music Mountain beyond was as black as soot.

"Ruth," Mark said, "you're up against a story that just never is told in Trimble."

"But why not?" Her face hung silvery in the moonglow.

"I don't know. I never found out, and I was born here. Old Mr. Glover Shelton told me a few things, but he's dead now." He related the old man's story. "I'm unable to tell you why things are that way about the business," he wound up. "It's just not discussed, sort of the way sex didn't used to be discussed in polite society. I suspect that most people have more or less forgotten about it, pushed it to the back of their minds."

"But the police go over," she reminded him. "The chief said it was just a routine check, a tour in a deserted area. Then he changed the subject, too."

"If I were you, I'd not push anyone too hard about all this," said Mark. "It's a sort of rule of life here, staying on this side of the river. As an athletic coach, I abide by rules."

"As a historian, I look for the truth," she said back, "and I don't like to have the truth denied me."

He changed the subject. They talked cheerfully of other things. When he left that night, she let him kiss her and said he could come back and see her again.

Next Saturday evening, Ruth finished grading a sheaf of papers and just before sundown she walked out in the town with Mark. She wore snug jeans and a short, dark jacket. They had a soda at Doc Roberts's drugstore and strolled on along Main Street. Mark told her about his boyhood in Trimble, pointed out the massive old town hall (twice burned down, once by accident, and rebuilt both times inside its solid brick walls), and led her behind Worley's Café to show her where Glover Shelton once had worked. The door of the little old shop was open. A light gleamed through it, and a voice from inside said, "Hidy."

A man sat at the ancient work bench, dressed in a blue hickory shirt and khaki pants and plow shoes, carefully shaping a slip of wood with a bright, sharp knife. He was lean, and as tall as Mark, say six feet. His long, thoughtful face was neither young nor old. In his dark hair showed silver dabs at the temples and in a brushed-back lock on top.

"Glover Shelton and I were choice friends, years back," he said. "I knew the special kinds of wood he hunted out and used here, and his nephew loaned me a key so I could come work me out a new bridge for my old guitar."

It was an old guitar indeed, seasoned as dark brown as a nut. The man set the new bridge in place, with a dab of some adhesive compound. "That'll dry right while we're a-studying it," he said. Then he laid the strings across, threaded them through the pegs, and tightened them with judicious fingers. He struck a chord, adjusted the pegs, struck and struck again. "Sounds passable," he decided.

"Those strings shine like silver," offered Ruth.

"It just so happens that silver's what they are," was the reply, with a quiet smile. "Silver's what the oldest old-timers used. Might could be I'm the last that uses it."

He achieved a chord to suit him. Tunefully, richly, he sang:

> She came down the stair,
> Combing back her yellow hair,
> And her cheek was as red as the rose . . .

Mark had made up his mind to something.

"Sir," he said, "I knew Mr. Glover Shelton when I was a boy. This young lady wishes he had lived for her to talk to. Because he was the only man I ever heard speak of the far side of Catch River yonder, the Music Mountain side."

"I know a tad of something about that," said the guitar-picker, while the strings whispered under his long, skilled fingers. "An old Indian medicine man, name of Reuben Manco—he mentioned about it to me one time."

"Nobody here in Trimble talks about it," said Mark. "They just stay away from over there. Nobody ever goes there."

"I reckon not, son. The way Reuben Manco had it, the old Indians more or less left the place alone, too. What was there didn't relish to be pestered."

"Some other kind of men than Indians?" suggested Ruth.

"Better just only call them things. The way the old story comes down, they didn't truly look like aught a man could tell of at first. And they more or less learnt from a-studying men—Indians— how to get a little bitty bit like men, too."

"They sound weird," said Mark, interested.

"I reckon that's a good word for them. The Indians were scared of how they made themselves to look. So sometimes the Indians got up on the top of the mountain yonder and sang to the things, to make sure they wouldn't try to come out and make trouble." The long, thoughtful face brooded above the guitar's soft melody. "I reckon that's how it come to be named Music Mountain. The Indians would sing those things back off and into their place, time after time. I reckon all the way up to when the white men came in."

"Came in and took the Indians' land," said Mark. "That happened here."

"Shoo, it happened all over America—the taking of the land. All right, I've given you what Reuben Manco gave me. Music Mountain for the music the Indians used against those things."

"Why won't anybody in town tell about this?" Ruth asked.

"I don't reckon folks in town much heard of it. Especially when they might not want to hear tell of it."

"I'm glad to hear it," declared Ruth. "I'm someone who wants to know things."

"There's always a right much to get to know, ma'am," was the polite rejoinder.

Mark sat down on the work bench. "Music," he repeated. "Could the Indians control something like that—something frightening, you said—with music?"

"Well, son, with Indians the right song can make the rain to fall. An Indian hunter sings to bring him luck before he goes after game. Medicine sing to cure a sick man or a hurt man. One time another, music's been known to do the like of such things."

Mark asked for the story of the mill that had been built under Music Mountain. It seemed that Derwood Neidger had interested some Northern financiers and had built his mill, with Trimble's townspeople shaking their heads about it. But there was good pay, and families came from other places to live in the houses built for them and to spin the cloth. Until the night they all vanished.

"What if there had been music at the mill?" Mark wondered. "In the houses?"

"Doesn't seem like as if there was much of that, so we can't rightly tell. And it's too late to figure on it now."

The sun sank over the western mountains. Dusk slid swiftly down into the town. Mark listened as his companion struck the silver strings and sang again:

> She came down the stair,
> Combing back her yellow hair . . .

He muted the melody with his palm. "Sounds like that beauty-looking young girl that came here with you. Where's she gone off to?"

Mark jumped up from where he sat. Ruth was nowhere in sight. He hurried out of the shop, around the café and out into the street.

"Ruth, wait—"

Far along the sidewalk, in the light of a shop window, he saw her as she turned off and out of view, where the old alley led to where the bridge was.

"Wait!" he yelled after her, and started to run.

It was a long sprint to the alley. One or two loungers gazed at Mark as he raced past. He found the alley, headed into it, stumbled in its darkness and went to one knee. He felt his trousers rip where they struck the jagged old cobbles. Up again, he hurried to the bridge.

It was already too dim to see clearly, but Ruth must be there. She must be moving along, almost as fast as he. "You damned fool," he wheezed into the darkening air as he ran. "You damned little fool, why did you do this?" And in his heart her voice seemed to answer him, *I'm someone who wants to know things.*

The old, old boards of the bridge rattled under his feet. He heard the soft, purling rush of Catch River. There she was now, at the far end, a darker point in the night that came down on them. "Ruth," he tried to call her once more, but his breath wasn't enough to carry it. He ran on after her.

Now he had come out on the other bank, where nobody ever went. He turned to his left. A road of sorts had been there once, it seemed. Its blotchy stones were rank between with grass. His shoe skidded on what must have been slippery moss and he nearly went down again. To his right climbed the steep face of

Music Mountain, huddled with watching trees as black as ink. On ahead of him, small, dark houses clung together at the roadside. Farther beyond them rose the sooty pile of the old mill. He stood for a moment and wheezed to get his breath. Something came toward him. He quivered as he faced it.

"I knew you'd come too, Mark," said Ruth's merry voice.

At that moment, the moon had scrambled clear of the mountain and flung pale light around them. He saw that Ruth smiled.

"Why ever did you—" he began to say.

"I told you, Mark, I want to find things out. Nobody else here wants to. Dares to."

"You come right back to town with me," he commanded.

She laughed musically.

On into the sky swam the round, pallid moon, among a bright sprinkling of stars. Its light picked out the mill more clearly. It struck a twinkle from the glass of a window; or could there be a stealthy light inside? Ruth laughed again.

"But you came across, at least," she said, as though happy about it.

The glow of the moon beat upon her, making her hair pale. And something else moved on the road to the mill.

He hurried toward Ruth as the something drifted from between those dubious houses, a murky series of puffs, like foul smoke. He thought, for a moment hoped, that it might be fog; but it gathered into shapes as it emerged, shadowy, knobby shapes. Headlike lumps seemed to rise, narrow at the top, with, Mark thought, great loose mouths. Wisps stirred like groping arms.

"Let's get out of here," he said to Ruth, and tried to catch her by the hand.

But then she, too, saw those half-shaped things that now stole into groups and advanced. She screamed once, like an animal caught in a trap, and she lost her head and ran from them. She ran toward the mill in the moonlight that flooded the old paving stones.

Mark rushed after her because he must, because she had to be caught and hustled back toward the bridge. As the two of them fled, the creatures from among the houses slunk, stole after them, made a line across the road, cut off escape in that direction.

Ruth ran fast in her unreasoning terror, toward where a great squat doorway gaped in the old mill. But then she stopped, so suddenly that Mark nearly blundered against her as he hurried from behind.

"More—" she whimpered. "More of them—"

And more of them crept out through that door. Many more of them, crowding together into a grotesque phalanx.

Ruth pressed close against Mark. She trembled, sagged, her pert daring was gone from her. He gathered his football muscles for a fight, whatever fight he could put up. They came closing in around him and Ruth, those shapes that were only half-shapes. They churned wispily as they formed themselves into a ring.

He made out squat bodies, knobs of craniums, the green gleam of eyes, not all of the eyes set two and two. The Indians, those old Indians, had been right to fear presences like these. Everything drew near. Above the encircling, approaching horde, Mark saw things that fluttered in the air. Bats? But bats are never that big. He heard a soft mutter of sound, as of panting breath.

Even if Ruth hadn't been there to hold on her feet, Mark could never have run now. The way was cut off. It would have to be a battle. What kind of battle?

Just then, abrupt music rang out in the shining night.

And that was a brave music, a flooding burst of melody, like harps in the hands of minstrels. A powerful, tuneful voice sang words to it:

> The cross in my right hand,
> That I may travel open land,
> That I may be charmed and blessed,
> And safe from any man or beast . . .

The pressing throng ceased to press around Mark and Ruth. It ebbed away, like dark water flowing back from an island.

The song changed, the guitar and the voice changed:

> Lights in the valley outshine the sun,
> Lights in the valley outshine the sun,
> Lights in the valley outshine the sun—
> Look away beyond the blue.

Those creatures, if they could be called creatures, fell back.
They fell back, as though blown by the wind. The singing voice
put in words of its own, put in a message, a guidance:

> Head for the bridge and I'll follow you,
> Head for the bridge and I'll follow you,
> Head for the bridge and I'll follow you—
> Look away beyond the blue.

Ruth would have run again. Mark held her tightly by the arm,
kept her to a walk. Running just now might start something else
running. They stumbled back along the rough stones with the
grass between the edges. The moonlight blazed upon them. Behind them, like a prayer, another verse of the song:

> Do, Lord, oh do, Lord, oh do remember me,
> Do, Lord, oh do, Lord, oh do remember me,
> Do, Lord, oh do, Lord, oh do remember me—
> Look away beyond the blue.

But this time, a confident happiness in that appeal. Mark felt
like joining in and singing the song himself, but he kept silent and
urged Ruth along by her arm. He thought, though he could not
be sure, that soft radiances blinked on and off in the shantylike
old houses strung along the road. He did not stop to look more
closely. He peered ahead for the bridge, and then the bridge was
there and thankfully they were upon it, their feet drumming the
planks.

Still he panted for breath, as they reached the other side. He
held Ruth to him, glad that he could hold her, glad for her that he
was there to hold her. He looked across. There on the bridge
came something dark. It was the guitar-picker, moving at a slower
pace than Mark and Ruth had moved. He sang, softly now, softly.
Mark could not make out the song. He came and joined them at
last. He stood tall and lean with his hair rumpled, holding his
guitar across himself like a rifle at the port.

"You all can be easy now," he said gently. "Looky younder,
they can't come over this far."

Over there, all the way over there at the far bridge head, a dark
cluster of forms showed under the moon, standing close together
and not coming.

"The fact about it is," said the guitar-picker, "they don't seem to be up to making their way across a run of water."

Mark was able to speak. "Like *Dracula*," he said numbly. "Like the witches in *Tam O'Shanter*."

"Sure enough, like them. Now, folks," and the voice was gentler than ever, "you all see they'd best be left alone on their side yonder, the way folks have mostly left them alone, all the way back to when the whole crew of the mill went off to nowhere. Old ways can be best."

"Mark, I was such a fool," Ruth mumbled against Mark's shirt.

"I told you that, dear," he said to her.

"Did you call me dear?"

"Yes."

"It makes me feel right good to hear talk like that with nice young folks like you two," said the guitar-picker.

Mark looked up above Ruth's trembling golden head. "You were able to defeat them," he said. "You knew music would hold them back."

"No, I nair rightly knew that." The big hand swept a melody from the silver string. "I hoped it, was all, and the hope wasn't vain."

Mark held out a shaking hand. "We'll never be able to thank you, Mr.—I don't even know your name."

"My name's John."

"John what?" Mark asked.

"Just call me John."

ARNOLD M. ANDERSON

Ghost
of Buckstown Inn

One of the scarcer items in the serious fantasy collector's library is a perishable paperback, Twenty-Five Ghost Stories, *that Avon Books issued in 1941 as the second half of a fat book that began with an obscure Wilkie Collins novel,* The Haunted Hotel. *Most of the stories in the collection are by anonymous writers, but the following bit of Americana is attributed to* ARNOLD M. ANDERSON, *a name unfamiliar to me, though his style suggests he may have been a professional reporter. Journalists tend to be well educated in libel law, which may account for the absence of any place named Buckstown in Arkansas . . . although there is a Buckner in the southwestern part of the state.*

Several travel-worn drummers sat in the lobby exchanging yarns. It was Rodney Green's turn, and he looked wise and began his tale.

"I don't claim, by any means, that the belief in ghosts is a general thing in Arkansas, but I do say that I had an experience out there a few years ago.

"It was late in the fall, and I happened to be in the village of Buckstown, which desecrates a very limited portion of the State. The town is about as small and dirty a place as ever I saw, and the Buckstown Inn is not much above the general character of the place. The region is inhabited by natives who still cling to all sorts of foolish superstitions. The inn, in the ante-bellum days, was kept by one who was said to be the meanest and most crabbed of mortals. The old demon was as miserly as he was mean, and all his narrow life he hoarded his filthy lucre with fiendish greed. Report had it also that he had even murdered his patrons in their beds for their money. What the facts actually were I don't know, but even to this day the old inn is held in suspicion. A lingering effect of former horrors still clouds its memory.

"The present proprietor, Bunk Watson—his real name is Bunker, I believe—is an altogether different sort of chap—a Southern type, in fact—one of those shiftless, heedless, happy-go-lucky mortals who loves strong whiskey and who chews an enormous quid of black tobacco and smokes a corncob pipe at the same time.

"When the former keeper 'shuffled off,' his property fell to a distant relative, the present keeper, who, with his family, immediately moved in from a neighboring hamlet and took possession. It was well known that the old proprietor had accumulated considerable wealth during his sojourn among the living, but all efforts to discover any treasure upon the premises had failed, and now the idea of ever finding it was practically given up. As far as Bunk was concerned, the matter troubled him little. He had a hard-working wife who ran things the best she could under the circumstances, and saw that his meals were forthcoming at their respective intervals. What more could he wish? Why should he care if there was a treasure buried upon his place? Indeed, it would have been a sore puzzle for him to know what to do with a fortune unless perhaps his wife came to his aid.

"Among the stories that hovered in the history of the Buckstown Inn was one which involved a ghost. In the room where the former keeper had died peculiar noises were heard at unearthly hours: sighing, moaning, and, in fact, all the other indications which point to the existence of ghosts, were said to be present. On account of this the chamber had long since been abandoned.

"I listened with keen interest to the wonderful tales about the haunted room, and then suddenly resolved to investigate—to sleep in that chamber that very night and see for myself all that was to be seen. I told Buck of my purpose. He shook his head, shrugged his shoulders, but instead of warning me and offering a flood of protests, as I expected, he merely took his pipe from his mouth, let fly a quart or so of yellowish juice from between a pair of brown-stained lips, and, opening one corner of his wide mouth, lazily called out: 'Jane.' His wife appeared, and he intimated that I should settle the matter with the 'old woman.' The prospect of a fee persuaded the wife, and off she went to arrange for my bed in that ill-fated room.

"At nine o'clock that evening I bid the family good-night, took my candle, ascended the rickety stairs and entered the chamber of horrors. The atmosphere was heavy and had a peculiar odor that was not at all pleasing. However, I latched the door and was soon in bed. Having propped myself up with pillows, I was prepared to await the coming of the ghost.

"Overhead the dusty rafters, which once had experienced the sensation of being whitewashed, but which were now a dirty, yellowish color, were hung with a fantastic array of cobwebs. The flickering light of the candle reflected upon the walls and against the ceiling a pyramid of grotesque shapes, and with this effect being continually disturbed by the swaying cobwebs, the whole caused the room to appear rather ghostly after all, and especially so to an imaginative mind.

"I waited and waited for hours, it seemed, but still no ghost. Perhaps it was afraid of my candle light, so I blew it out. No sooner had I done this and settled back in bed again than a white hand appeared through the door, then a whole figure—at last the ghost had come, a white and sheeted ghost!

"It had come right through the door, although it was locked, and now it advanced toward the bed. Raising its long, white arm, it pointed a bony finger at me, and then commanded: 'Come with me!' Thereupon it turned to the door, while instantly I jumped out of bed to follow. Some unseen power compelled me to obey. The door flew open and the ghost led me down the stairs, through long halls into the cellar, through mysterious underground corridors, upstairs again, in and out rooms which I never dreamed were to be found in that old rambling inn. Finally, through a small door in the rear, we left the house. I was in my sleeping garments, but no matter, I had to follow.

"The white form, with a slow and measured tread and as silent as death, led the way into the orchard. There, under a tree at the farther end, it pointed to the ground, and in the same ghostly tones before used, said:

" 'Here you will find a great treasure buried.'

"The ghost then disappeared, and I saw it no more. I stood dazed and trembling. Upon recovering my wits I started to dig, but the chill of the night air and the scantiness of my night robes made such labor impracticable. So I decided to leave some mark to identify the place and come around again at daybreak. I reached up and broke off a limb. Overcome with my night's exertions I slept the next morning until a loud rapping on my door and a croaking voice warned me that it was noon.

"I had intended to leave Buckstown Inn that day, but, prompted by curiosity and anxious to investigate, I unpacked my gripsack for a comfortable stay.

"You must understand that this was my first experience with a ghost, and I feared I might never see another.

"At breakfast my landlady waited on me in silence, though once I detected her eyes following me with a peculiar expression. She wanted to ask me how I enjoyed the night, but I would not gratify her by volunteering a word.

"My host was more outspoken.

" 'Reckon ye didn't get much sleep,' said he, with a queer smile.

" 'Did you hear anything?' I asked.

" 'Well, I did—ye-es,' he said, with a drawl. 'But ye didn't disturb me any. I knew ye'd hev trouble when ye went in thet room ter sleep.'

"That afternoon I slipped out to the tree. But to my amazement I found that the twig I had broken from the branches was gone. Finally I found under the lower trunk of an apple tree an open place from which a small branch had evidently been wrested. But on looking further, I discovered that every apple tree in the orchard had been similarly disfigured.

" 'More mysterious than ever,' I said; 'but tonight shall decide.'

"That night I pleaded weariness, which no one seemed inclined to question, and sought my couch earlier.

" 'Goin' ter try it again?' asked my host.

" 'Yes; and I'll stay all winter but what I'll get even with that ghost,' I said.

"That night I kept the candle burning until midnight, when I blew it out.

"Instantly the room was flooded with a soft light, and at the foot of the bed stood my ghost, the identical ghost of last night.

"Again the bony finger beckoned and a sepulchral voice whispered, 'Follow me!' I sprang from the bed, but the figure darted ahead of me. It flew through the doorway and down the stairs, and I after it. At the foot of the staircase an unseen hand reached forward and caught my foot and I fell sprawling headlong.

"But in a second I was on my feet and pursuing the ghost. It had gained on me a few yards, but I was quicker, and just as we reached the outside door I nearly touched its robes. They sent a chill through my frame, and I nearly gave up the pursuit.

"As it passed through the doorway it turned and gave me one look, and I caught the same malignant light in its eyes that I remembered from the night before.

"In the open orchard I felt sure I could catch it.

"But my ghost had no intention of allowing me any such opportunity. To my disgust, it darted backward and into the house, slamming the door in my face.

"In my frenzy of fear and chagrin I threw myself against the oaken door with such force that its rusty old hinges yielded and I landed in the big front room of the inn just in time to see the white skirts of the ghost flit up the stairs.

"Upstairs I flew after it, and into an old chamber. There, huddled in a corner, I saw it. In the minute's delay it had secured a lighted candle and, as I entered, it advanced to daunt me with bony arm upraised to a great height.

" 'Caught!' I cried, throwing my arms around the figure. And I had made the acquaintance of a real live ghost.

"The white robes fell, and I saw revealed my hostess of Buckstown Inn.

"Next morning, when I threatened to call the police, she confessed to me that she masqueraded as a ghost to draw visitors to the out-of-the-way old place, and that she found its tale of being haunted highly profitable to her."

L. FRANK BAUM

The Stuffed Alligator

If Homo sapiens believes its own species is capable of returning from the dead, why not other animals as well? Here is a not-too-serious "animal fairy tale" about a resurrected Southern alligator by L. FRANK BAUM (1856–1919), author of The Wonderful Wizard of Oz *and many other beloved children's classics. "The Stuffed Alligator" first appeared in 1905 in* The Delineator, *a popular American woman's magazine of that time.*

When mothers are worried they are apt to be cross; and that explains why Mum'r Alligator spoke so sharply to her son Wolly.

"See here! Don't you dare swim into the swift current," she said, fretfully, as Wolly crossed to the end of the old log, which lay half buried in the marsh, and dropped into shallow water. "Keep to the warm pools and swim there as much as you like; but if you go near the river for a single instant I'll—I'll—I'll go to the Red-Eyed One and tell him how bad you are!"

It was a terrible threat. The Red-Eyed One was the mighty magician of the Alligator people; the most wise, the most powerful, the most fearful creature of all the inhabitants of the Swamps. He could not be deceived by ordinary 'gators—the simple mud-wallowers that refused to think as they lay blinking in the sun—and it was known that the Red-Eyed One dealt out sharp punishment for disobedience. At least, this was what mothers told their children, when mothers were worried and cross; and the children were willing to believe anything of the mighty magician who dwelt in the Hidden Cavern.

Wolly Alligator had no thought of being disobedient when he swam away from home and left Dad'n Alligator asleep on a bank of mud and Mum'r Alligator taking her daily sun-bath on her log. Young Alligators are apt to become restless, and aged Alligators love peace and quiet. Moreover, Wolly was hungry.

Dad'n Alligator could be content a week longer on the meal of Spring lamb he had eaten a fortnight before; but Wolly had only been given part of a leg, and that was no satisfaction at all to a young and growing 'gator.

So he started with a firm though secret intention to discover a dinner, for in the stagnant pools of the marsh, where Alligators abounded, it was not likely a dinner would escape the hundreds of vigilant eyes that were watching on every side. Therefore he crossed the pools, crawled over the intervening bank of mud (which was the danger line) and came at last to where the broad river wandered away upon its crooked course.

At the other side of the river were green fields and pasture lands, showing above the embankment. On this side the water of the river blended into the mud-bank and the marsh, with scarce any other distinction to mark its path beyond the steady flow of the current.

Here, at the river's edge, Wolly halted, and looked longingly across. Many dinners wandered on those green banks. Why should his mother forbid him to stalk his prey? How should the Red-Eyed One know if he seized a fat sheep or a calf and returned with the morsel inside him?

It was the hunger that drove him to disobedience; for without stopping to consider either warnings or commands he swam slowly across the river and raised his nose above the edge of the green bank.

What happened at that moment Wolly could never explain clearly. A rope flew through the air and settled around his neck, gripping close to the scales. With a movement quick as a light-ning flash he pounded his tail upon the bank and tried to turn; but the rope drew taut and threw him half a length farther upon the grass. Then, quivering, he lay still and darted a glance along the rope. The far end was wound about a tree, and a Man clung to the last fold. A Man! Anger swelled in Wolly's breast. An enemy and a dinner in one—and seemingly very near.

Like the wind was his rush upon the foe; but, alas! he had merely dashed to destruction. The folds of the line about the tree held him close prisoner and the Man was a safe distance away, still calmly holding in his hands the end of the rope.

Wolly was but half grown, yet he struggled for his life with a desperation worthy the Red-Eyed One himself. To be sure it was unavailing; but he always had the satisfaction of knowing he had done his best.

The last that he remembered was lying helpless amid the coils of rope and watching with upturned eyes the flash of a knife. Then his eyes saw blackness; his brain ceased to think; he lay still.

The Man was proud of his conquest. There was now one less Alligator to steal his lambs. He carried the thick, tough skin home to his bungalow and carefully cured it, the head being left on. Then he stuffed both head and body very artistically, and sent to the City for some glass eyes, which he fastened into the head.

After this Wolly lay, in a very life-like attitude, under a bench at the back of the porch; and when friends of the Man came to visit him he showed them his stuffed Alligator with considerable pride.

Mum'r Alligator became worried when Wolly did not return. Dad'n Alligator only thought she was getting fretful again, and blinked one eye after the other without budging from his mud-bank or replying with a single word.

This apathy made Mum'r indignant. She tossed her tail and wriggled about until the muddy water that circled around her log was churned into a foam that showed silver under the moon's rays. For night had come, but no Wolly.

In the morning she could bear the anxiety no longer. So she slipped into the water and made her way through the swamps until she reached a place where a cluster of great rocks broke the flatness of the landscape. Here she paused, made a dive into deep water, and came to the surface within a cavern hollowed out of the centre of the rock.

The cavern was not lighted; but, as Mum'r lay with her chin upon the rocky edge of the pool, she could dimly perceive an immense dark form lying outstretched before her.

The mighty magician was asleep.

Then a red light glowed in the dusk, flooding her with its rays. And now another light flashed beside it. The Red-Eyed One had unclosed his eyelids.

Mum'r was awed in the silence that followed. She felt the terrible gaze full upon her, reading her every thought. She wanted to speak, but could not.

Finally the magician coughed; and the sound was so warning, and at the same time so sympathetic, that Mum'r Alligator knew at once her worst fears were realized.

"Oh, my poor boy! my Wolly!" she moaned, the big tears rolling from her eyes and splashing into the pool.

"I'm sorry," remarked the magician; and he moved slightly his great body, so that the reflected light rippled from scale to scale until it died away at the far tip of his tail.

"What has happened?" implored Mum'r Alligator, mournfully; "tell me—what has happened?"

"The Man has captured your son," said the Red-Eyed One, slowly. "He has taken poor Wolly's skin and head, and has carried them to the house wherein he dwells."

With a wild sob Mum'r sank deep into the pool, swam back to the marsh, and dragged her weary, heart-sick body to the log she called her home.

Dad'n 'Gator opened both eyes at once when he heard the sad story; but he didn't move. Two hours later he remarked:

"Wolly was careless."

It wasn't much comfort to Mum'r; but she didn't expect comfort. Probably Dad'n felt sad and miserable in his own way; but he was old, and he had learned that words cure no ills and mend no breaks.

Afterward Mum'r Alligator went again to the Red-Eyed One, who told her that Wolly had been stuffed and now lay upon the Man's porch, looking as beautiful and lifelike as ever.

That was a great comfort to Mum'r, and she lay many days upon her log and dreamed of Wolly, and longed for him in her motherly way, until one morning a happy thought came to her.

The thought sent her hurrying at a rapid pace to the rocky cavern in which the Red-Eyed One dwelt, where she asked him:

"Are you really a magician?"

"I am," was the reply, while the two eyes glared upon her as if resenting the inquiry.

"Then, can you not restore my Wolly to life?" demanded Mum'r, her voice trembling with eagerness she could not suppress.

"I can," said the Red-Eyed One, calmly.

"And will you—will you?" asked Mum'r, anxiously.

The magician paused. He was thinking. Presently he answered: "If you will promise that I receive from your family one fat sheep a month, for twelve months to come, and if you dare venture to the Man's house to restore Wolly to life, I will give you a charm that will work the transformation."

"I promise, and I dare!" cried Mum'r Alligator, without hesitation.

"Good!" said the magician. Then he paused again, thoughtfully.

Mum'r was so excited she could scarcely wait for him to continue. But it was several minutes before he said, speaking the words slowly and impressively:

"Under my left claw lies a magic gem which, if placed upon your son Wolly's head, will restore him to life. But if light falls upon this gem its virtue will depart. Therefore you must go at night to the house of the Man, and carry the gem in your mouth, so that even the moon cannot shine upon it."

Mum'r heard this with a shiver of dread; for Alligators never move in the dark if they can avoid it. But the rescue of Wolly had now become the one ambition of her life.

"Give me the magic gem," she said, firmly; "I will make the journey at night that no light may fall upon the talisman and destroy its charm."

"Wait until I close my eyes," returned the magician. "Then feel under my left claw for the gem, and conceal it in your mouth."

The red lights vanished, and the cavern became dark. Mum'r felt for the gem, placed it in her mouth and closed her huge jaws tight around it. Then she sank into the pool, swam from the cavern, and emerged in the Swamp which lay steaming under the hot rays of the afternoon sun.

It filled her with uneasiness to see the glaring sunshine all around her, and to know that if she coughed, or even yawned, Wolly would never be restored to her. But she kept her jaws fast closed and returned slowly to her log.

For a wonder, Dad'n Alligator was awake and stirring.

"Where's that file I sharpen my teeth on?" he demanded, as soon as Mum'r came near. "I want it. I'm hungry again, and I'm going hunting. Where have you put the file I sharpen my teeth on?"

Mum'r Alligator did not reply, of course. She dared not open her mouth while the sun beat down so brilliantly upon the marsh. Dad'n must find the file himself.

But hungry Alligators are cross Alligators. Dad'n stormed and raved and flopped around and wanted his file—which was nothing more than a sliver of rock, if the truth must be told. And Mum'r wouldn't answer a word.

I'm really ashamed to tell of Dad'n's actions. He lashed the shallow water into a sea of mud, and spattered it all over Mum'r's clean scales. Usually she would have lashed Dad'n in return with her sharp tongue; but now she remained meekly quiet, although there was a look in her half-closed eyes that boded future trouble, if her husband hadn't been too much excited to take notice of it.

Dad'n capped the climax of his evil deeds by actually pushing Mum'r off her log and calling her a fish—which is a terrible term of reproach among Alligators—and then floundered away to the river to seek his dinner before it got too dark, caring little in his rage whether his teeth were sharpened or not.

Mum'r's lips curled in a vengeful smile that was half a yard long; but she did not part them. Her jaws were locked over the precious gem, and she intended to keep them locked. Time enough to punish Dad'n when her great task had been accomplished.

She crawled out of the water into which she had been thrust and resumed her place upon the log, patiently waiting for the sun to set.

Toward evening Dad'n returned. His features wore a contented look, and as he rolled to his place on the bank Mum'r noticed a big lump just below his front paws—where his stomach was located. Dad'n was a mighty hunter; there was no doubt of that. But he had been selfish, and had eaten his dinner alone. Mum'r wouldn't forget.

He looked at her rather uneasily, and tried to make his peace before he went to sleep.

"Perhaps I was a little rough with you this afternoon when I couldn't find my file," he ventured to say; but Mum'r's grim look never relaxed. "Well, well; let bygones be bygones," he continued, carelessly, as he closed his eyes.

Mum'r said nothing. She could wait.

When night came she slipped from the log and began her journey. Over the mud-banks, through the swamps, across the broad river she travelled, and crawled up the steep bank to the meadow. By this time the moon was shining, and she paused to look around her.

A beaten path wound inland from the river. It had been worn by the feet of sheep and men, and Mum'r crawled slowly along it. Beetles chirped in the tall grass, and in the far distance a dog barked; but no other sounds broke the stillness. For the sheep were in the fold and the cows in the barnyard.

Mum'r crept slowly on. Never had Alligator ventured before so near the abode of Man. Her presence in such a place at such an hour was all unexpected.

Now the dim outlines of the bungalow came into view. Its windows were dark, for time had drifted toward midnight. Mum'r drew nearer and nearer, creeping as noiselessly as possible. She came to the steps of the porch, hesitated an instant, and climbed up them.

She could see very well in the dark, and one glance showed her the motionless form of her stuffed darling lying underneath a bench at the back of the porch. She was tempted to cry out, to utter a wail of anguish; but her steadfast courage enabled her to resist the temptation.

Now was the supreme moment of her adventure. She crept forward and noted that Wolly's head was raised so high that there was not room under the bench for her to drop the gem from her mouth upon his head. So with her nose she lifted an end of the bench and thrust it gently aside. The next moment her jaws rested over her darling's head and the precious talisman slipped from her mouth.

So dark were the shadows at the back of the porch that no ray of light penetrated them, and the magic gem instantly sank into Wolly's head and disappeared. Mum'r had faithfully performed her mission!

She felt the form beside her stir. Then it thrust its nose against her shoulder, and a voice said wonderingly:

"Mum'r dear—is it you?"

Her heart gave a bound of joy; but she realized they were still in danger. Man is a terrible foe; and Man was very near to mother and son, although he lay asleep.

"Hush!" she whispered; "follow me!"

Then she turned and crept down the steps to the path; and Wolly, bewildered and understanding nothing of what had happened since the knife flashed long ago, followed obediently. Mum'r retraced her steps along the path to the river. Often she turned her head to watch Wolly, who crept close after her.

It was a great triumph, this bringing to life a stuffed Alligator by means of magic, and Mum'r had never respected the mighty Red-Eyed One so much as now.

When they reached the river bank and slid into the water the new day was breaking. They swam to the other side and lay half hidden in the marsh to rest. There Wolly told his mother of his capture; and she told him of her visit to the Red-Eyed One, and of her bargain to bring him one fat sheep each month.

"That is a small price, indeed," said the child; "and it shall be my task to pay it. Wait here a moment, Mum'r. I hear a sheep-bell tinkle. Let us take the great magician a fat lamb this very morning, to show our gratitude."

"But think of the danger!" she cried.

"There is no danger," returned Wolly. "Being stuffed, I need fear neither gun nor knife-thrust; for not even Man can kill again the body that has been made to live by the magic of the Red-Eyed One."

That seemed reasonable; so Mum'r let him go back to the meadow.

The first lamb that Wolly brought into the marsh he made his mother eat; and then he captured the fattest sheep that came to the river to drink and bore it in his jaws toward the cavern of the magician. Often, on the way, they had to fight to retain this luscious morsel of food; for dozens of hungry Alligators attempted to rob them. But Wolly, small though he was, soon made himself feared; for nothing seemed to injure his stuffed body, and the snap of his jaws was as powerful as that of a steel trap.

So they made the first payment to the Red-Eyed One, and then returned to their home.

Dad'n lay sunning himself upon his mud-bank in a state of great contentment. Lazily he remembered the ease with which he had subdued Mum'r. Usually she scolded him. Now he had scolded her, and she had not dared utter a word. He was master now! If he had but ventured to push her off her log long ago he would have been master then, undoubtedly. That push had quite conquered her. Dad'n smiled to himself as he recalled her meekness and submission. He had been both brave and wise; he had—

Whack!

His brain suddenly reeled, and his eyes saw a multitude of stars.

Whack!

What had happened? Dad'n wondered. Was it an earthquake? Or had he been struck by a lightning-bolt?

Whack! Whack! Whack!

Dad'n's head was driven flat into the mud-bank. His tail lashed in terror and anguish; but it merely fanned the air or churned the water into a dingy foam. He managed to pull his head from the mud and open his eyes just as the angry sweep of a huge tail, bristling with hard scales, fell once more with terrific force upon his forehead.

He saw stars again; but he also understood. Mum'r had returned. Mum'r was not so meek as he had suspected. Mum'r was being revenged for every slight to her dignity. Mum'r was probably vexed, or—

Whack! Whack!

Dad'n stopped thinking and began to act. Though dazed and half blinded, he rolled and floundered into deep but muddy water, dove to the right, swam to the left, wiggled around in a circle, and came to the surface to breathe only when he had put a good bit of water between himself and his angry wife.

Wolly lay on the log beside his mother, who panted from her exertions.

"Those were splendid blows," he remarked; "and well aimed. I am sure Dad'n is sufficiently punished."

An hour later a black nose rose from the water a few yards away and two black eyes looked pleadingly at the log.

"My head aches," said Dad'n.

"Oh, does it?" inquired Mum'r, a mischievous twinkle in her eyes. "Then, who do you suppose, my dear Dad'n, is a fish?"

Dad'n looked longingly at his mud-bank, and decided to purchase peace at any price.

"If there is a fish in this marsh," he announced, sadly, "it is certainly me."

Then he crawled upon the bank and presently forgot his troubles in sleep.

Wolly never grew to be a big Alligator, but he came to be a terror to the farmers across the river. For once every month he captured a fat sheep and carried it to the cave of the Red-Eyed One to keep the promise Mum'r had made the mighty magician. Again and again the Man shot at him, but so tough was his tanned skin that a bullet could seldom penetrate it, and even those that got through did the stuffed Alligator no harm. He was also clever enough to avoid a lasso since his first terrible experience with the rope; so that Wolly soon became famed as a mighty hunter.

One night, about a year after Wolly's rescue from the bungalow, an earthquake shook all that country about the Swamp. Mum'r was thrown from her log and Dad'n was so scared that he slipped from his trembling mud-bank into the water and stayed there all through the night.

But in the morning everything seemed peaceful again; so Wolly swam away at early dawn and captured the last sheep he was obliged to carry to the magician. And when he reached the place where the Red-Eyed One's cave had been, he found nothing left but a heap of jumbled rocks; for the earthquake had not only buried the ancient magician, but had erected above him a monument that to this day is regarded with veneration by every Alligator in the swamp.

So Wolly carried his sheep home to Dad'n and Mum'r; and thereafter he devoted himself to the task of providing a plentiful supply of food for his parents, so that they grew in time to be the biggest and fattest Alligators ever known. Dad'n, who was something of a joker, would often say to his friends and gossips:

"There are three stuffed Alligators in our family. The Man stuffed Wolly, you know; and now Wolly stuffs us!"

EDWARD LUCAS WHITE

The House of the Nightmare

The precise locale of "The House of the Nightmare" is difficult to pinpoint, but the combination of hickory furniture, ailanthus trees and country vernacular persuades me to include it in the Southern part of Haunted America. EDWARD LUCAS WHITE, *author of the often anthologized horror story "Lukundoo," claimed that he actually dreamed the nightmare in the following tale. It frightened him so badly that he woke up midway through it and "my wife had to quiet and soothe me as if I had been a scared child; and then I went to sleep again and* finished the dream!"

I first caught sight of the house from the brow of the mountain as I cleared the woods and looked across the broad valley several hundred feet below me, to the low sun sinking toward the far blue hills. From that momentary viewpoint I had an exaggerated sense of looking almost vertically down. I seemed to be hanging over the checkerboard of roads and fields, dotted with farm buildings, and felt the familiar deception that I could almost throw a stone upon the house. I barely glimpsed its slate roof.

What caught my eyes was the bit of road in front of it, between the mass of dark-green shade trees about the house and the orchard opposite. Perfectly straight it was, bordered by an even row of trees, through which I made out a cinder side path and a low stone wall.

Conspicuous on the orchard side between two of the flanking trees was a white object, which I took to be a tall stone, a vertical splinter of one of the tilted limestone reefs with which the fields of the region are scarred.

The road itself I saw plain as a box-wood ruler on a green baize table. It gave me a pleasurable anticipation of a chance for a burst of speed. I had been painfully traversing closely forested, semi-mountainous hills. Not a farmhouse had I passed, only wretched cabins by the road, more than twenty miles of which I had found very bad and hindering. Now, when I was not many miles from my expected stopping-place, I looked forward to better going, and to that straight, level bit in particular.

As I sped cautiously down the sharp beginning of the long descent the trees engulfed me again, and I lost sight of the valley. I dipped into a hollow, rose on the crest of the next hill, and again saw the house, nearer, and not so far below.

The tall stone caught my eye with a shock of surprise. Had I not thought it was opposite the house next the orchard? Clearly it was on the left-hand side of the road toward the house. My self-questioning lasted only the moment as I passed the crest. Then the outlook was cut off again; but I found myself gazing ahead, watching for the next chance at the same view.

At the end of the second hill I only saw the bit of road obliquely and could not be sure, but, as at first, the tall stone seemed on the right of the road.

At the top of the third and last hill I looked down the stretch of road under the overarching trees, almost as one would look through a tube. There was a line of whiteness which I took for the tall stone. It was on the right.

I dipped into the last hollow. As I mounted the farther slope I kept my eyes on the top of the road ahead of me. When my line of sight surmounted the rise I marked the tall stone on my right hand among the serried maples. I leaned over, first on one side, then on the other, to inspect my tires, then I threw the lever.

As I flew forward I looked ahead. There was the tall stone—on the left of the road! I was really scared and almost dazed. I meant to stop dead, take a good look at the stone, and make up my mind beyond peradventure whether it was on the right or the left—if not, indeed, in the middle of the road.

In my bewilderment I put on the highest speed. The machine leaped forward; everything I touched went wrong; I steered wildly, slewed to the left, and crashed into a big maple.

When I came to my senses I was flat on my back in the dry ditch. The last rays of the sun sent shafts of golden green light through the maple boughs overhead. My first thought was an odd mixture of appreciation of the beauties of nature and disapproval of my own conduct in touring without a companion—a fad I had regretted more than once. Then my mind cleared and I sat up. I felt myself from the head down. I was not bleeding; no bones were broken; and, while much shaken, I had suffered no serious bruises.

Then I saw the boy. He was standing at the edge of the cinder-path, near the ditch. He was stocky and solidly built; barefoot, with his trousers rolled up to his knees; wore a sort of butternut shirt, open at the throat; and was coatless and hatless. He was tow-headed, with a shock of tousled hair; was much freckled, and had a hideous harelip. He shifted from one foot to the other, twiddled his toes, and said nothing whatever, though he stared at me intently.

I scrambled to my feet and proceeded to survey the wreck. It seemed distressingly complete. It had not blown up, nor even caught fire; but otherwise the ruin appeared hopelessly thorough. Everything I examined seemed worse smashed than the rest. My two hampers alone, by one of those cynical jokes of chance, had escaped—both had pitched clear of the wreckage and were unhurt, not even a bottle broken.

During my investigations the boy's faded eyes followed me continuously, but he uttered no word. When I had convinced myself of my helplessness I straightened up and addressed him:

"How far is it to a blacksmith shop?"

"Eight mile," he answered. He had a distressing case of cleft palate and was scarcely intelligible.

"Can you drive me there?" I inquired.

"Nary team on the place," he replied; "nary horse, nary cow."

"How far to the next house?" I continued.

"Six mile," he responded.

I glanced at the sky. The sun had set already. I looked at my watch: it was going—seven thirty-six.

"May I sleep in your house to-night?" I asked.

"You can come in if you want to," he said, "and sleep if you can. House all messy; ma's been dead three year, and dad's away. Nothin' to eat but buckwheat flour and rusty bacon."

"I've plenty to eat," I answered, picking up a hamper. "Just take that hamper, will you?"

"You can come in if you're a mind to," he said, "but you got to carry your own stuff." He did not speak gruffly or rudely, but appeared mildly stating an inoffensive fact.

"All right," I said, picking up the other hamper; "lead the way."

The yard in front of the house was dark under a dozen or more immense ailanthus trees. Below them many smaller trees had grown up, and beneath these a dank underwood of tall, rank suckers out of the deep, shaggy, matted grass. What had once been, apparently, a carriage-drive left a narrow, curved track, disused and grass-grown, leading to the house. Even here were some shoots of the ailanthus, and the air was unpleasant with the vile smell of the roots and suckers and the insistent odor of their flowers.

The house was of gray stone, with green shutters faded almost as gray as the stone. Along its front was a veranda, not much raised from the ground, and with no balustrade or railing. On it were several hickory splint rockers. There were eight shuttered windows toward the porch, and midway of them a wide door, with small violet panes on either side of it and a fanlight above.

"Open the door," I said to the boy.

"Open it yourself," he replied, not unpleasantly nor disagreeably, but in such a tone that one could not but take the suggestion as a matter of course.

I put down the two hampers and tried the door. It was latched, but not locked, and opened with a rusty grind of its hinges, on which it sagged crazily, scraping the floor as it turned. The passage smelt moldy and damp. There were several doors on either side; the boy pointed to the first on the right.

"You can have that room," he said.

I opened the door. What with the dusk, the interlacing trees outside, the piazza roof, and the closed shutters, I could make out little.

"Better get a lamp," I said to the boy.

"Nary lamp," he declared cheerfully. "Nary candle. Mostly I get abed before dark."

I returned to the remains of my conveyance. All four of my lamps were merely scrap metal and splintered glass. My lantern was mashed flat. I always, however, carried candles in my valise. This I found split and crushed, but still holding together. I carried it to the porch, opened it, and took out three candles.

Entering the room, where I found the boy standing just where I had left him, I lit the candle. The walls were whitewashed, the floor bare. There was a mildewed, chilly smell, but the bed looked freshly made up and clean, although it felt clammy.

With a few drops of its own grease I stuck the candle on the corner of a mean, rickety little bureau. There was nothing else in the room save two rush-bottomed chairs and a small table. I went out on the porch, brought in my valise, and put it on the bed. I raised the sash of each window and pushed open the shutters. Then I asked the boy, who had not moved or spoken, to show me the way to the kitchen. He led me straight through the hall to the back of the house. The kitchen was large, and had no furniture save some pine chairs, a pine bench, and a pine table.

I stuck two candles on opposite corners of the table. There was no stove or range in the kitchen, only a big hearth, the ashes in which smelt and looked a month old. The wood in the wood-shed was dry enough, but even it had a cellary, stale smell. The ax and hatchet were both rusty and dull, but usable, and I quickly made a big fire. To my amazement, for the mid-June evening was hot and still, the boy, a wry smile on his ugly face, almost leaned over the flame, hands and arms spread out, and fairly roasted himself.

"Are you cold?" I inquired.

"I'm allus cold," he replied, hugging the fire closer than ever, till I thought he must scorch.

I left him toasting himself while I went in search of water. I discovered the pump, which was in working order and not dry on the valves; but I had a furious struggle to fill the two leaky pails I had found. When I had put water to boil I fetched my hampers from the porch.

I brushed the table and set out my meal—cold fowl, cold ham, white and brown bread, olives, jam, and cake. When the can of soup was hot and the coffee made I drew up two chairs to the table and invited the boy to join me.

"I ain't hungry," he said; "I've had supper."

He was a new sort of boy to me; all the boys I knew were hearty eaters and always ready. I had felt hungry myself, but somehow when I came to eat I had little appetite and hardly relished the food. I soon made an end of my meal, covered the fire, blew out the candles, and returned to the porch, where I dropped into one of the hickory rockers to smoke. The boy followed me silently and seated himself on the porch floor, leaning against a pillar, his feet on the grass outside.

"What do you do," I asked, "when your father is away?"

"Just loaf 'round," he said. "Just fool 'round."

"How far off are your nearest neighbors?" I asked.

"Don't no neighbors never come here," he stated. "Say they're afeared of the ghosts."

I was not at all startled; the place had all those aspects which lead to a house being called haunted. I was struck by his odd matter-of-fact way of speaking—it was as if he had said they were afraid of a cross dog.

"Do you ever see any ghosts around here?" I continued.

"Never see 'em," he answered, as if I had mentioned tramps or partridges. "Never hear 'em. Sort o' feel 'em 'round sometimes."

"Are you afraid of them?" I asked.

"Nope," he declared. "I ain't skeered o' ghosts; I'm skeered o' nightmares. Ever have nightmares?"

"Very seldom," I replied.

"I do," he returned. "Allus have the same nightmare—big sow, big as a steer, trying to eat me up. Wake up so skeered I could run to never. Nowheres to run to. Go to sleep, and have it again. Wake up worse skeered than ever. Dad says it's buckwheat cakes in summer."

"You must have teased a sow some time," I said.

"Yep," he answered. "Teased a big sow wunst, holding up one of her pigs by the hind leg. Teased her too long. Fell in the pen and got bit up some. Wisht I hadn't 'a' teased her. Have that nightmare three times a week sometimes. Worse'n being burnt out. Worse'n ghosts. Say, I sorter feel ghosts around now."

He was not trying to frighten me. He was as simply stating an opinion as if he had spoken of bats or mosquitoes. I made no reply, and found myself listening involuntarily. My pipe went out. I did not really want another, but felt disinclined for bed as yet, and was comfortable where I was, while the smell of the ailanthus blossoms was very disagreeable. I filled my pipe again, lit it, and then, as I puffed, somehow dozed off for a moment.

I awoke with a sensation of some light fabric trailed across my face. The boy's position was unchanged.

"Did you do that?" I asked sharply.

"Ain't done nary thing," he rejoined. "What was it?"

"It was like a piece of mosquito-netting brushed over my face."

"That ain't netting," he asserted; "that's a veil. That's one of the ghosts. Some blow on you; some touch you with their long, cold fingers. That one with the veil she drags acrosst your face— well, mostly I think it's ma."

He spoke with the unassailable conviction of the child in "We Are Seven." I found no words to reply, and rose to go to bed.

"Good night," I said.

"Good night," he echoed. "I'll set out here a spell yet."

I lit a match, found the candle I had stuck on the corner of the shabby little bureau, and undressed. The bed had a comfortable husk mattress, and I was soon asleep.

I had the sensation of having slept some time when I had a nightmare—the very nightmare the boy had described. A huge sow, big as a dray horse, was reared up on her forelegs over the foot-board of the bed, trying to scramble over to me. She grunted and puffed, and I felt I was the food she craved. I knew in the dream that it was only a dream, and strove to wake up.

Then the gigantic dream-beast floundered over the foot-board, fell across my shins, and I awoke.

I was in darkness as absolute as if I were sealed in a jet vault, yet the shudder of the nightmare instantly subsided, my nerves quieted; I realized where I was, and felt not the least panic. I turned over and was asleep again almost at once. Then I had a real nightmare, not recognizable as a dream, but appallingly real—an unutterable agony of reasonless horror.

There was a Thing in the room; not a sow, nor any other namable creature, but a Thing. It was as big as an elephant, filled the room to the ceiling, was shaped like a wild boar, seated on its haunches, with its forelegs braced stiffly in front of it. It had a hot, slobbering, red mouth, full of big tusks, and its jaws worked hungrily. It shuffled and hunched itself forward, inch by inch, till its vast forelegs straddled the bed.

The bed crushed up like wet blotting-paper, and I felt the weight of the Thing on my feet, on my legs, on my body, on my chest. It was hungry, and I was what it was hungry for, and it meant to begin on my face. Its dripping mouth was nearer and nearer.

Then the dream-helplessness that made me unable to call or move suddenly gave way, and I yelled and awoke. This time my terror was positive and not to be shaken off.

It was near dawn: I could descry dimly the cracked, dirty window-panes. I got up, lit the stump of my candle and two fresh ones, dressed hastily, strapped my ruined valise, and put it on the porch against the wall near the door. Then I called the boy. I realized quite suddenly that I had not told him my name or asked his.

I shouted "Hello!" a few times, but won no answer. I had had enough of that house. I was still permeated with the panic of the nightmare. I desisted from shouting, made no search, but with two candles went out to the kitchen. I took a swallow of cold coffee and munched a biscuit as I hustled my belongings into my hampers. Then, leaving a silver dollar on the table, I carried the hampers out on the porch and dumped them by my valise.

It was now light enough to see to walk, and I went out to the road. Already the night-dew had rusted much of the wreck, making it look more hopeless than before. It was, however, entirely undisturbed. There was not so much as a wheel-track or a hoof-print on the road. The tall, white stone, uncertainty about which had caused my disaster, stood like a sentinel opposite where I had upset.

I set out to find that blacksmith shop. Before I had gone far the sun rose clear from the horizon, and almost at once scorching. As I footed it along I grew very much heated, and it seemed more like ten miles than six before I reached the first house. It was a new frame house, neatly painted and close to the road, with a whitewashed fence along its garden front.

I was about to open the gate when a big black dog with a curly tail bounded out of the bushes. He did not bark, but stood inside the gate wagging his tail and regarding me with a friendly eye; yet I hesitated with my hand on the latch, and considered. The dog might not be as friendly as he looked, and the sight of him made me realize that except for the boy I had seen no creature about the house where I had spent the night; no dog or cat; not even a toad or bird. While I was ruminating upon this a man came from behind the house.

"Will your dog bite?" I asked.

"Naw," he answered; "he don't bite. Come in."

I told him I had had an accident to my automobile, and asked if he could drive me to the blacksmith shop and back to my wreckage.

"Cert," he said. "Happy to help you. I'll hitch up foreshortly. Wher'd you smash?"

"In front of the gray house about six miles back," I answered.

"That big stone-built house?" he queried.

"The same," I assented.

"Did you go a-past here?" he inquired astonished. "I didn't hear ye."

"No," I said; "I came from the other direction."

"Why," he meditated, "you must 'a' smashed 'bout sunup. Did you come over them mountains in the dark?"

"No," I replied; "I came over them yesterday evening. I smashed up about sunset."

"Sundown!" he exclaimed. "Where in thunder've ye been all night?"

"I slept in the house where I broke down."

"In that there big stone-built house in the trees?" he demanded.

"Yes," I agreed.

"Why," he quavered excitedly, "that there house is haunted! They say if you have to drive past it after dark, you can't tell which side of the road the big white stone is on."

"I couldn't tell even before sunset," I said.

"There!" he exclaimed. "Look at that, now! And you slep' in that house! Did you sleep, honest?"

"I slept pretty well," I said. "Except for a nightmare, I slept all night."

"Well," he commented, "I wouldn't go in that there house for a farm, nor sleep in it for my salvation. And you slep'! How in thunder did you get in?"

"The boy took me in," I said.

"What sort of a boy?" he queried, his eyes fixed on me with a queer, countrified look of absorbed interest.

"A thick-set, freckle-faced boy with a harelip," I said.

"Talk like his mouth was full of mush?" he demanded.

"Yes," I said; "bad case of cleft palate."

"Well!" he exclaimed. "I never did believe in ghosts, and I never did half believe that house was haunted, but I know it now. And you slep'!"

"I didn't see any ghosts," I retorted irritably.

"You seen a ghost for sure," he rejoined solemnly. "That there harelip boy's been dead six months."

FRANK BELKNAP LONG

The Elemental

The next story begins in Louisville, home of the Kentucky Derby, but then the action and its hero move swiftly, very *swiftly, to the Virginia coast!* FRANK BELKNAP LONG, *born in 1903 in New York City, contributed prolifically to* Weird Tales *magazine and was one of H. P. Lovecraft's closest personal friends.*

Wheeler thought it was a coincidence at first. Ebony Lady was losing steadily in the sunlight. She was falling back to fourth place, passing Radio Crooner in reverse and galloping steadily in the wrong direction over the nut-brown track.

Or so it seemed to the grandstand and the cheering crowds beyond the finish line. Actually Ebony Lady's retrogressive spurt was an optical illusion. With no mist in her nostrils, the fastest wet-weather colt in all the Blue Grass was emulating a telegraph pole glimpsed from an express train.

Then came the "coincidence." Ebony Lady stopped passing horses in reverse, and recaptured the lead again. She retook the lead in less than five seconds spurting past three horses like a jet of liquid petrolatum.

Wheeler rubbed his eyes. Had he turned an also-ran into a winner with one little thought? For several hours now he had been aware of a strange, new power in himself. Just by concentrating he could push people aside when he walked. In a crowd, when he needed elbow room he could clear a path for himself. But Ebony Lady was thundering over the turf a quarter of a mile away! And in his mind there was no awareness of strain. He was merely thinking, "I want that horse to go faster. I want that horse to *win.*"

Push, push. A little purposeful thought, moving about in his mind!

Someone was tugging at his sleeve. "Well, for crying out loud! Look at that horse go!"

Wheeler did not like to be touched. He scowled resentfully, and withdrew his gaze from the track. Standing beside him was a bald-headed stout man in a checkered suit, his heavy-jowled face studded with sweat, his eyes jiggling in his head.

"Nothing can stop her now! Look at her go!"

Wheeler rasped, "It's barely possible that I can stop her, mister."

The fat man let go of Wheeler's arm and edged nervously away along the paddock rail.

"A screw loose," he muttered.

Wheeler brushed his sleeve as though a contamination had descended upon it, and returned his gaze to the track. Ebony Lady was bearing down on the finish line with flying hoofs, her long neck outthrust, her jockey bent double in an ecstasy of anticipation.

Wheeler did not want Ebony Lady to lose. He desperately needed the five dollars he had placed on Ebony Lady to win. But —well, he *had* to find out. It was vital to his peace of mind.

Could he slow up Ebony Lady with a thought? Was the new power as tremendous as he feared?

He thought, "I want that horse to go slower. I want that horse to fall back."

Like jets of liquid petrolatum three horses, including Radio Crooner, spurted past Ebony Lady.

The man in the checkered suit gasped. He swung about and stared at Wheeler with startled eyes.

Wheeler said tremulously, "I did it, you see."

Something about the fat man repelled Wheeler. But he was horribly shaken. He had to discuss it with someone.

The fat man said, "You did *what?* Slowed Ebony Lady? You expect me to swallow that?"

Wheeler's lips were white. "I'm not trying to convince you," he said. "I'm simply stating a fact."

"A fact, eh?" jeered the other. "Then suppose you put that wet horse back in the lead again. It ought to be easy—on a dry track!"

Wheeler sighed. "Very well," he said. "Watch Ebony Lady."

He allowed the thought to form. "I want that horse to win." Push, push. A little purposeful thought directed across the turf to where bright hoofs were thundering.

Ebony Lady seemed to leave the ground as she came abreast of Radio Crooner, and thundered into high again. Now she was third, now second, now a length off the leader. Now she was passing the leader two furlongs from the finish line.

The people in the grandstand were shouting themselves hoarse. Like some demoniac hippogriff Ebony Lady flashed past the judge's stand, wrenching a blare from the loudspeaker: "Ebony Lady it is, ladies and gentlemen. Ebony Lady wins the Derby!"

The fat man was visibly stunned. "It's—it's uncanny," he muttered.

Wheeler nodded. "I don't understand it myself," he said.

The fat man thrust his face forward, a rapacious light gleaming behind his pupils.

"Could you do it again?" he ventured.

"What do you mean?"

"At another race? Anytime?"

Wheeler nodded. "I am sure that I could," he said.

The fat man edged closer. "Where are you headed for, buddy?"

"Wheeler said, "I've got to collect ten dollars from a bookie."

The fat man took out a mammoth roll of bills, and peeled off one.

"Chicken feed," he said. "Take this and come with me. I'm staking you to a drink."

Wheeler hesitated. He thought, "I don't want liquor. But I could order a glass of milk and get him to taste it."

The fat man was tugging at his sleeve. "Come on, buddy. One little drink won't hurt you."

Five minutes later they were seated at the circular counter of a trackside soft drink concession. Outside in the sunlight the crowd was slowly dispersing, streaming north, south and west over the dappled turf.

Wheeler was holding a glass of milk, his thin fingers coiled tightly about whiteness. His companion was attached to a whisky and soda.

He was scowling at Wheeler. *"Milk,"* he said contemptuously.

Wheeler said, "It's against the law to serve liquor at the track, Mr. Sheed. This concession is violating the law."

"Call me Ted," said the fat man. "Look, Harry, why can't you relax and be human? We could help each other. I have plenty of what it takes to cash in on a sure thing."

Wheeler said, "I'll admit it's a temptation. I've been out of work for two months. I've stood in breadlines, bunked in flop houses—"

Suddenly he shivered. He was forgetting about the milk. He raised the glass to his lips and sipped at it fearfully. A look of horror came into his face.

Sheed said, "Well, what do you say?"

Tremulously Wheeler set down the glass and pushed it toward his companion. "I wish you'd just taste that milk," he said.

Sheed grimaced. "Why in hell should I? I don't like milk. It strangles me."

"Just taste it, please," insisted Wheeler.

"Oh, all right."

Sheed raised the glass and took a reluctant sip. Instantly he set the beverage down with such violence that the counter shook.

"Sour!" he exclaimed. "Sour as a rancid herring."

All the color drained from Wheeler's face. "Then it's true," he groaned. "I haven't been imagining it."

"What are you talking about?"

"Every time I taste milk it turns sour," said Wheeler.

Sheed growled impatiently. "So what? You got acidosis or something. It happens all the time."

"No, it doesn't," insisted Wheeler. "You see, I know something about acid diathesis. I used to work in a pathological testing laboratory. You can't turn milk sour simply by tasting it. I mean, if you had a rheumatic or gouty diathesis, which is a very acid condition, you could gargle with milk, and it wouldn't turn sour."

Sheed was becoming exasperated. "You can speed up the horses," he growled, "and you're worrying about a little thing like that. Goaty die teasers. Bah!"

Suddenly Wheeler seized his companion's glass and drained it at a gulp.

"Hey, wait a minute," protested Sheed. "You didn't have to do that. I'll order you a man's drink."

"Make it a double Scotch and soda," said Wheeler.

The high brown beverage did things to Wheeler. His despair receded and a wave of moral indignation surged up in him. He began to see his companion in a less favorable light. He leaned forward across the table.

"You mean, it's a gold mine?" he inquired.

"A regular gold mine, sure. I'll pick the horses and you'll speed 'em up. We'll be living off the fat, my lad."

Wheeler said, "You're distinctly slimy, Sheed. I don't like you."

"What's that?"

"I don't like your fat, smirking face!"

Sheed's face turned scarlet. He ceased to smirk. He leaped to his feet and stood glaring down at Wheeler. "I've a good mind to sock you," he said.

The thought formed quickly: "Push him fast and far."

Sheed screamed. Something lifted him up, twisted him around. He went sailing erratically across the little soft drink concession, his body rotating about his knees.

There was a splintering of glass. Out through the window of the concession Sheed spun. He sailed over the paddock rail and crashed to the turf on his face.

Wheeler smiled, rose and laid four quarters beside his drained whisky and soda. "Now that was distinctly worthwhile," he said.

Swiftly he slipped from the concession and mingled with the dispersing crowd.

People brushed against him. He laughed and sent them lightly spinning. The human throng divided as he walked. Being a man of kindly instincts, he did not abuse his power. There was no animosity in his mind. It simply amused him to watch people spin away from him, and whirl about like leaves in a dry wind. He felt like an Israelite walking through the Red Sea.

He kept on walking, ignoring startled and resentful glances. He lifted a woman six feet in the air and sent her sailing like a feather across the track. She landed thirty feet away, screaming hysterically. A crowd converged about her. Wheeler pushed the entire congregation of appalled men, women and children fifty feet along the track.

Instantly he reproached himself: "That was shameful. I shouldn't have done that."

In contrition he took to levitating his own body. He rose into the air and sailed lightly over the turf. In little aerial spurts he progressed above the heads of the dispersing throng. Once he descended on the shoulders of a fat man who tottered and yelled.

"Sorry," he apologized and rose into the air again.

He was thinking, "I've always wanted to fly. Now I am truly flying."

He flapped his arms as though they were wings. "I should like to soar," he thought.

Instantly he rose high into the air. He rose two thousand feet and soared like a condor high above the grandstand. Far below him he saw little specks dispersing. Here and there the specks coalesced into wriggling, dark clumps with agitated peripheries.

People in terror. Dozens of tiny people flocking together under the stress of a shared horror.

He rose higher, flew more audaciously. Presently he was "winging" his way toward the east. Flap, flap, flap.

Beneath him stretched fields of blue grass. He saw cows at pasture, winding country lanes, brooks glimmering in the sunlight. He saw a meadow starred with white-flowered asphodels.

He thought, "I must remain calm. I must not allow myself to become excited."

Kentucky was a beautiful state. Now he was flying high above an old Southern mansion. He saw people moving about in the vicinity of the great house, sleekly groomed horses galloping on a private bridle path, plantation workers toiling in the bright noon-day glare.

He passed swiftly eastward, soaring over the Black Mountains into Virginia, winging his way across the Blue Ridge and the Coastal Plain.

He thought, "This is more exhilarating than traveling in box cars," and swooped low to observe a yellow-crowned night heron which was rising from the somber cypress-hung Dismal Swamp and winging its way toward the bright waters of Chesapeake Bay.

He followed the heron in a kind of trance. In the depths of his mind terror churned, but it did not flow into his consciousness— except occasionally in little eddies.

He had moments of sudden, terrible doubt, of perplexity and fright. But so entranced was he by his gift of flight that he shivered in rapture and ignored the dark misgivings which occasionally assailed him.

Flap, flap, flap. He was flying now above Pokomoke Sound, the coast of Virginia a glimmering blue line far to the west. The heron had vanished, and he was alone under the sun.

He had been flying steadily for hours but he was not fatigued. Or was he? It was barely possible that he was getting a little tired. He had to keep repeating to himself: "I am flying effortlessly now. I am as buoyant as a feather."

The sense of buoyancy receded a little when he ceased to concentrate and then he found himself descending toward the bright gleaming waters of the Sound.

The waters were reddening when fatigue crept unmistakably upon him. Flying became an effort. But resolutely he kept flapping his arms and assuring himself that he was lighter than air.

He was flying low above big and little islands when his buoyancy ebbed disastrously. His legs became leaden, inert. Horror engulfed him as he stared downward. He had ceased to mount and the level expanse of water beneath him was ascending like a rising floor.

For a thousand feet he fell like a plummet, flailing the air with his arms. He was almost level with the waves when something seemed to burst in his chest. He spun about and zoomed erratically, spurting eastward over a little island, and whirling about high in the air.

The little island was barely forty feet in diameter, a pinnacle of jagged rock emerging precariously from the wine-dark sea.

Whirligigging like a Mayfly, Wheeler descended toward it. He swirled over a menacing spire of granite and came jarringly to rest on a sloping ledge where barnacles clustered. For an instant he stood swaying above the sea, his eyes wide with terror.

Something like a cloud was settling down beside him. He felt for an instant like a jellyfish on stilts. Then his legs turned to water, and he sank down on the spray-lashed granite.

The cloud became denser, coalescing into an upright cone that shimmered with a pale luminescence. Wheeler groaned and raised himself on his hands.

A voice said, "You are less intelligent than an idiot child."

All the blood seeped from Wheeler's face, leaving it ashen. Swirling beside him on the spray-drenched rock was a conical mass of spray, its summit rainbow-hued, two iridescent orbs gleaming in its tenuous bulk.

The blood-red disk of the sun was slipping below the rim of the bay, but there was still sufficient illumination to mingle the shadows of Wheeler and the cone. The shadow of the cone was wolfishly devouring the shadow of Wheeler, consuming its human outlines with evident relish.

Wheeler's flesh congealed. He started to back away across the rock, but directly he moved the cone swirled closer.

"Be careful, you fool," it warned. "That rock is slippery."

The cone's voice was resonant but expressionless. It bumped against Wheeler and swiftly rebounded, its rainbow-hued bulk glistened in the spray.

Wheeler's teeth were chattering. "What . . . what are you?" he moaned.

The cone said, "An elemental. A force elemental. I have no intention of harming you. I am as much to blame as you are for this . . . this calamity."

"But how did you get here?"

"You brought me here," replied the cone. "When you exhausted my energies I couldn't sustain you any longer."

"You mean you came with me?"

"Of course. I've been inhabiting your body for several days. It was an experiment which I now regret."

"You've been inhabiting my—"

"I took possession of your body temporarily. You know what an elemental is, don't you?"

Wheeler hesitated for an instant. "I . . . I think I do," he said, finally. "A nature spirit. A spirit of earth, air, fire or water."

"That is substantially correct," said the cone. "I am glad you did not say a *force* of nature. I am not a force in a scientific sense. I am a true spirit."

"A true *spirit?*"

"Yes. I am as real as an elf or goblin. Your scientists deny that spirits exist. Right under their noses we inhabit the bodies of idiot children. We raise tables into the air, break crockery, send objects spinning and they deny that we exist!"

"You mean you're a poltergeist," exclaimed Wheeler, his jaw gaping.

"You may call me that if you wish. Each age has a different name for us. The Greeks preferred to think of us simply as nature spirits who could curdle milk, ride the night wind, set mysterious fire and wreck ships at sea."

Wheeler stammered. "But why . . . why did you pick on me?"

"It was sheer madness," said the elemental, "but . . . well, you are a *new frontier.* No elemental has ever dared to inhabit an adult mortal before. Children, yes—idiot children. Their imbecile rages are of brief duration and do not exhaust us. But adult mortals have minds of their own."

"You mean you are subject to the whims of my mind?"

"In a sense, yes. When you think of something you want to do I am compelled to assist you. Helping you at the racetrack was tiring, but this flight has drained me completely."

"It was your presence within me that made me reckless," said Wheeler. "I wanted to fly because I was sure that I could."

"I know," said the elemental. "We are caught in a vicious circle. I give you ideas and a sense of power, and you exhausted me. So long as I am bound to you I am compelled to satisfy the demands of your will."

"But you could leave me, couldn't you?"

"No. I can pour out of you and move objects at a distance, or I can move about close to you as I am doing now. But I cannot leave you. Have you ever watched a caterpillar spin a cocoon? It draws the threads continuously tighter about itself until it is completely imprisoned."

"But you are outside your prison now," protested Wheeler.

"Merely as a penumbral projection," explained the elemental. "My matrix is still inhabiting your body. We elementals are beings of a complex structure. If you could see me as I really am you would understand."

The black shadows of night were closing in swiftly now. There were little, rubescent glints on the dark water, but the sun had vanished from view. Far out in the bay a gull wheeled and dipped. The elemental seemed to be shivering.

"I am exhausted . . . ill," it said. "I wish it were morning."

Wheeler stared at it in sudden apprehension. "You mean you can't levitate me in the darkness? We . . . we won't be able to fly back?"

The elemental said, "You fool! Did you have to fly out over the sea?"

"I intended to return," said Wheeler. "I didn't know your power would fail me."

"Well, it has failed," said the elemental. "I am close to death."

Wheeler paled. *"You mean you can die?"*

"Of course. Elementals are not immortal. When our energies expire we burst into flames. We die in bursts of glory."

"Good God!" exclaimed Wheeler.

The elemental drew close to him, bounced against him and ascended into the air. It flew a swift circle about the little island and descended in a shower of sparks.

Wheeler cried out in horror. He recoiled backward and nearly toppled into the sea.

The elemental swirled toward him across the rock. "Careful, you fool! I was just testing my strength."

Wheeler pulled himself to safety again, his shoes dripping brine. Sharp barnacles tore at his clothes as he dragged himself to the summit of the rock. He sat with his feet dangling a yard above the water, staring at the elemental with resentful eyes.

"Did you have to frighten me like that?"

"I'm sorry," apologized the elemental. "Would my death distress you so much?"

"If you die, I'll freeze to death," muttered Wheeler. "I'll starve. I'll die of thirst. We're on one of the little rock islands south of Cape Charles. No ships pass this way at all."

"I see," said the elemental coldly. "A purely selfish reaction."

Wheeler groaned and fumbled in his pocket for a cigarette. "Why did this have to happen to me?" he muttered.

He was lighting the cigarette when the elemental swirled toward him like a devouring entity. It tore the match from his fingers and whirled it about in the air. The flame spurted in all directions. It rayed through the elemental from base to summit, bathing it in an unearthly refulgence.

"Ah, that is good," murmured the spirit as the glow subsided. "I feel better now."

Wheeler gasped. "You mean you can draw energy from a flame."

"From light, you fool. Tomorrow when the sun rises I shall suck in energy and be strong again. The sun is the source of all my strength."

A great wave of relief surged up in Wheeler. He fumbled for another match, lit it, held it up. Instantly it was snatched from his fingers. For fifteen minutes he fed the elemental matches.

He had one match left when he said, "Can I smoke now?"

"Go ahead," said the elemental.

Wheeler felt better as soon as the soothing smoke entered his lungs. He inhaled deeply, sighed and assumed a more comfortable position on the rock.

"I suppose we shall be here until morning," he said, with resignation.

He did not see the wave coming. It rose up behind him, crashed against the rock and drenched him with spray from head to foot. The spray was ice cold and so was the little eel that plopped against his neck and slithered down under his collar behind.

Wheeler began cursing softly in the semi-darkness, his fingers clutching in despair a charred cylinder that dripped.

The elemental said, "I must be fairly strong even now, if I can raise a wave."

The night passed wretchedly for Wheeler. The cold crept into his bones and filled his throat with phlegm. He dozed and woke in fitful starts.

Once he awoke suddenly and saw the elemental bobbing about in the sea. Once he saw it standing amidst shadows with its back to a cloud. The moon was veiled in a mist, but the luminosity which poured from the eternally vigilant cone bathed the little island in a spectral radiance.

Toward morning Wheeler fell into a heavy sleep. He slept dreamlessly at first, but when light touched his eyelids he began to stir and dream about the sun. He dreamed that he was flying about the solar disk, his body revolving like a planet, his arms flapping in the dawn. Beside him raced the planet Mercury, its orbit coinciding with his own. Within him surged boundless power; a sense of kinship with the great orb of life. Now he was passing little Mercury in his flight above the sun.

He awoke with a start. The air about him was bright and cold. It was a grayish brightness. The island and the sea were enshrouded in a bright, grayish fog!

A fog! It swirled above the water and, rising in little eddies, flowed mistily about the rock upon which he lay. He was aware of a wailing, a hideous sobbing immediately beneath him.

"I am dying. Oh, I am dying. The sun has failed me."

The silver-gray passenger seaplane was winging its way over Chesapeake Bay. The pilot was gazing downward at the long, bright coast-line of a mighty peninsula that reached outward with eager arms into the sea. He was passing directly over a group of little islands when he saw the light. A sudden, blinding flare that lit up all the sea beneath him, and ascended to the sky, brightening the clouds. A terrific flare in daylight, amidst a dispersing fog.

His hands trembled on the controls. He turned to the assistant pilot beside him, issued swift commands.

"We must descend immediately. That was an emergency flare. A plane is down, perhaps."

Beside him a grim boy nodded. "Yes, I understand. It came from one of those little islands, didn't it?"

The plane descended in a slow arc above Chesapeake Bay. It descended competently, for its pilots were Mineola-trained experts who knew how to approach the sea with foresight in a region where islands clustered thickly.

Swiftly downward the plane swooped, a great behemoth of the skyways that trembled not at all as its silvery bulk descended above the fog-wreathed water. The fog still clung tenuously to the still water in ghostlike filaments.

Nebulously the little rock island loomed out of the bay, seeming to increase in height as the plane swooped level with the waves and scudded to rest in a swirl of foam.

"You're sure that was the island," said the pilot who had first sighted the flare. He stared across the filmy water, squinting through filtering sunlight at a jagged pinnacle of rock.

"I'm positive," said the grim boy. "There's someone on it, too. Shall we hail him?"

"Wait a minute," said the other. "We're drifting closer."

The plane was within fifty feet of the little island when the castaway came distinctly into view. The two pilots stared incredulously. The grim boy was wearing spectacles. Swiftly he took them off, wiped them and put them on again.

"Good God!" he exclaimed. "How do you suppose *that* got there?"

Clinging tenaciously to the rock was a frail little man in shabby clothes, a crushed derby adhering to his skull, his shoes and trouser legs flaked with crystals of snow-white salt. Red sunlight was pouring revealingly on his upturned face, clotting at the corners of his mouth and filling his eye cavities with a lambent radiance.

His face in the thin, dispersing fog resembled a skull suspended above a lake of brimstone, with the lurid vapors of Hades swirling up above it.

Getting that frail, half-frozen little man off the rock and into the passenger cabin was a task as complicated as it was hazardous, but the Mineola-trained pilots were equal to the emergency. And once inside the cabin the little man was no longer a problem. The passengers took over.

They fussed over him, and graciously endeavored to make him as comfortable as possible. There was something about him that appealed to the maternal instinct of the women passengers. But the men were kind to him, too.

They screened him from view while they helped him into dry clothes, offering him underwear and outer garments which were warm and expensive. One stout man opened a suitcase and presented him with a hand-tailored shirt. Another made him a gift of neatly pressed trousers. They helped him don a yellow Angora golf sweater and a tweed sport coat.

But despite everything they could do for him his face kept

straining against the light. He stood shivering and gazing out the cabin window at the sea, as though he were looking at a picture under glass. A picture that terrified and appalled him.

He stood rigid in his expensive but ill-fitting clothes, beads of sweat on his thin face to which a two days' growth of beard gave something of an ascetic cast.

"You'd better sit down," said a tall, elderly woman in a tailormade suit whose severity of manner was redeemed by kindly eyes. "Better sit down there by the window in the sun. You've been through a terrible ordeal, my poor man."

Wheeler passed a hand across his brow. He shuddered, convulsively. "Thank you," he murmured. "It was awful, *feeling* it die. It seemed to wrench at me."

The passengers were all staring at him in concern. One of the pilots shook his head sadly, and made a rotary motion with his forefinger close to his temple.

The little man said suddenly, "But the dazzle saved me, didn't it? The dazzle brought you down. It died in a burst of glory, didn't it?"

"Yes," said the stout man to humor him. "I guess it did."

"Twelve hours in the thick fog, without sunlight, and toward the end I could feel it dying."

Suddenly he sat up straight in his chair. "Could I . . . could I have a glass of milk?" he asked.

"Why, of course," said the pilot.

The milk was cold, and there were little bubbles at the edge of the glass. It was just an ordinary glass of milk, but as Wheeler held it he was shaken to the depths of his being. His first and most powerful feeling was that he was about to free himself of a hideous dread. He was about to prove to himself that he was no longer possessed.

But he had also a feeling of loss and desolation. He was about to sound the knell of something almost godlike. The gift of flight, the power to move and shake.

Slowly he raised the glass, slowly he drank.

"Well," said the pilot, smiling down at him. "Feel better now?"

Wheeler did not reply. He sat staring up at the pilot in consternation, his lips tremulous, his eyes wide with horror.

"I can't taste this milk at all," he gasped. "It . . . it has absolutely no taste. It doesn't even feel cool on my tongue!"

A tall man with a grizzled Vandyke arose from a seat near the aisle and crossed to Wheeler's chair.

"Shock anesthesia," he explained patiently. "It lasts for hours sometimes."

Then he perceived how perturbed Wheeler was and smiled reassuringly. "Nothing to get alarmed about. By this time tomorrow you'll be fit as a fiddle. Able to move mountains, my lad. Able to move mountains."

There is such a thing as expecting too much of a man. Wheeler paled, groaned, dropped his glass, and slid from the chair in a dead faint.

HENRY KUTTNER

We Are the Dead

Our final Southern selection takes place in Arlington (Virginia) National Cemetery, just across the Potomac River from Washington, D.C. This forgotten but unfortunately still timely story from the April 1937 issue of Weird Tales *was written by* HENRY KUTTNER *(1915–1958), who began his career as a literary agent and went on to write such highly regarded works of fantasy and science fiction as "The Graveyard Rats," "Masquerade," "Dr. Cyclops," "The Twonky" and* Chessboard Planet.

Senator Kennicott was grateful for the cool night wind on his flushed face. He wished Hobson, walking slowly at his side, would stop his interminable argument about the bill. The man's high-pitched, rather unpleasant voice seemed out of place, incongruous in the peaceful hush of Arlington Cemetery.

Hobson was panting a little, his fleshy, well-massaged face creased in annoyance. The walk through the cemetery had been no hardship to the slim, whipcord body of the Senator, but Hobson was not used to walking. Kennicott had felt that a stroll homeward from the banquet would calm his turbulent thoughts, excited by the innumerable activities of Memorial Day; and Hobson, anxious to settle the matter of the bill, had rather unwillingly decided to accompany him.

"It may bring us closer to war," the Senator said, breaking in sharply on Hobson's involved explanation.

"Not at all. It's merely preparedness." Hobson's sharp little eyes searched the other's face. "We must protect American interests in foreign countries. Surely—"

"But this is very—aggressive," Kennicott objected. "After all, we don't want the hatred of other countries."

"Oh, come now! That's going it a bit strong. I've already explained how—"

"But—war," the Senator said, looking absently at a tombstone in the distance.

"There'll be no war," Hobson insisted somewhat shrilly. "If I thought this bill were really dangerous I'd be the first to demand its withdrawal."

"How much do you stand to make out of it?" the Senator asked abruptly. "Well—never mind. That's scarcely a fair question. Can't we let this go till tomorrow, Hobson? I'm so utterly tired!"

Hobson stared at him for a moment. Then, choosing his words with care, he said, "The bill really should go through, Senator. I think it will—assure your securing the nomination next year."

Kennicott looked at him keenly, little lines bracketing his mouth. Hobson's support was valuable—in fact, indispensable. If he were to withdraw it—

Glancing sideways at his companion, the Senator almost walked into a shadowy, slim figure that stood quietly in the darkness beneath a tall elm.

A drawn, white face was turned to Kennicott, and he felt a sudden sense of shock at the agony in the dark, brooding eyes. It was a young man, almost a boy, with deep lines of pain etched in his face.

"I'm sorry," the Senator said quickly, glancing at the boy's faded, worn khaki uniform. "I didn't see you."

The boy made no answer, and the Senator made a tentative movement to pass on. Abruptly the youthful, haggard face was turned away, and the boy said in a muffled tone, "I can't sleep."

"Eh?" Kennicott stared.

"I say I can't sleep," the boy repeated, his voice dull with pain.

Hobson made a clucking sound of commiseration and glanced at the Senator.

Kennicott felt a surge of sympathy. The obvious youthfulness of the boy was so incongruous with his taut face, the white tortured line of his lips.

"I know," Kennicott said. "It can be terrible. I had insomnia for almost a week once."

"A week," the other said scornfully. "That's nothing. It's been ages—"

Kennicott was scribbling something on the back of an envelope. "Be with you in a minute," he said under his breath to Hobson, who was chafing at the delay. "Here—any druggist can fill this," he said, giving the paper to the boy. "It will fix you up if anything can. I know how you feel," he ended sympathetically.

The youth took it skeptically and thrust it into a pocket. "Thanks just the same," he said oddly. "It's always like this on Memorial Day—it's worse then, you know."

Hobson moved impatiently, his pale eyes flickering uneasily over the boy's form.

"Oh," the Senator said understandingly. "I see—but—look here, aren't you rather young to—"

"Am I?" the youth asked. "I'm not so young as I look. I was in the war, all right."

Hobson gave a grunt of disbelief. Even the Senator felt that the boy was lying. True, his face was worn, haggard—but he couldn't be over twenty-five at most. Probably he didn't mean the World War. There were always battles going on—Manchuria, South America, Africa.

"Well—you get those powders," the Senator said after an awkward pause. "I'm sure they'll do the trick." He cleared his throat. "Can you use—" He drew out his wallet rather hesitantly, but the boy was not offended.

"No, thanks," he said, a boyish grin suddenly appearing on his face. Then it was gone, replaced by that strained expression of pain. He suddenly seemed to notice a low, gray tombstone nearby, and took a few slow steps toward it. "Poor fool," he murmured very softly.

The Senator looked away quickly. It was a shock to hear Hobson's high-pitched, rasping voice. Had the man no intelligence,

no decency? Kennicott put up a restraining hand, but it was too
late.

"Oh—come, come," Hobson was saying. "Don't say a thing
like that, son. It isn't right."

"Come on," Kennicott urged under his breath, but the boy
interrupted him.

"Why not?" he asked, a sharp note in his tired young voice.
"Wasn't he a fool?"

Hobson would try to argue with the boy, the Senator thought
hopelessly. Couldn't he see that—

"You're too young. You don't understand what he died for—
what his comrades died for," Hobson said, his plump face very
earnest.

"Does it matter?" the boy asked very quietly. "They—died."

"They died for something very real," Hobson plowed on. "If
they could—"

"For God's sake, come on," Kennicott snapped, grasping Hobson's arm. "Leave him alone. Can't you see—"

"All right," the boy said suddenly. "Maybe you're right. But—
let me tell you a little story." He came closer, his eyes dark and
tortured. "About a fellow who went over to France in '17. Just an
ordinary fellow, I guess—who was scared stiff when the shells
started bursting around, and the machine-guns were making
their racket in the dark. But he was like the rest of the fellows. He
didn't dare show how much he was afraid. A sniper got him in
'18."

The Senator was uncomfortable and showed it, but to his disgust he saw that Hobson was preparing to answer the boy.

"Wait—let me finish. A sniper got him, I said, and that was fine.
He didn't hear the bullets screaming over the trench, or the
groaning of dying men; all the horrors were gone, and he was
resting, forgetting. The darkness was kind . . . and then one
day he awoke."

"Eh?" That was Hobson, frankly staring.

"I say he woke up. Glory woke him up—splendor and a stone
monument that was very heavy. Bitter glory and squalid splendor," the boy went on fiercely. "They tortured and shamed him.
You see, he was awake now, and he wanted—God!—how he
wanted to *forget!*"

There were tears in the tortured eyes, and the boy brushed them away roughly with his sleeve. Then, catching his breath in a little gasp, he turned suddenly and began to walk quickly away.

For a heartbeat the Senator stood silent, unmoving, staring at that slim khaki figure receding into the gloom. "Wait," he called.

"Let him go," Hobson said, an angry undercurrent in his voice. "You can't—"

But Kennicott was remembering that white, drawn face, those brooding eyes from which all the youthfulness had been drained. "No—I've got to—" he said in an inarticulate aside to Hobson and took a few hasty steps forward. He saw the pale blur that was the boy's face turned toward him briefly, and the slender figure increased its pace. Ignoring Hobson's remonstrances, the Senator began to hurry after the boy.

Kennicott had to exert himself to overtake his quarry, and was glad that his muscles were still firm and elastic. He saw the boy turn hastily down a side path, and broke into a run. For a hundred feet or so the path was very dark, and then it broadened out into a large clearing. At its edge Kennicott swept a searching glance around, and jerked abruptly to a halt. His jaw dropped.

A moment later Hobson pounded up, wheezing a little. He paused, scrutinizing Kennicott's face. "What's the matter?" he asked quickly.

The Senator did not answer, and Hobson repeated his question. Then Kennicott turned a startled, almost frightened face to his companion. "Did—did you see that?" he asked unsteadily.

"What?" Hobson glanced around. "The boy? He's gone."

"He's—yes, he's gone. Hobson, I—I saw—" He brushed a hand across his eyes. "Hobson—can a man *vanish?*"

"What?" Hobson stared, his mouth open. "A—a man—"

"But I saw it!" the Senator said earnestly, as though pleading for belief. "That boy—wasn't—" He pointed toward a great white block in the center of the clearing. "It was right there—I—I— saw—" He could not finish.

"What are you talking about?" Hobson's voice was purposely crisp and peremptory. "You're all unnerved. Come on—the boy's gone. We can't stay here."

"You go on," Kennicott said suddenly. "I'm going to—stay here for a while."

Hobson hesitated. Then, making up his mind, he drew a paper from his pocket, held it out. "Here's the bill, then. I'll phone you tomorrow."

Kennicott made no move. He said dully, "The bill. No, no, I can't—"

"Look here," Hobson said furiously. "You're not going to act like a damned fool, are you? What the devil's the matter?"

The Senator turned to him a face of white marble and said nothing.

Hobson hesitated, and then his rage pushed aside his diplomacy, his caution. "Because—by Heaven, I can break you," he snarled. "You're not President yet! I can ruin your career, and you know it."

"I know it," the Senator said quietly. "But that bill won't pass while I'm in the Senate." He turned his back on Hobson and stood silently gazing at the gaunt white mausoleum in the clearing. He had spoken patriotically and at length there not six hours before.

It was the tomb of the Unknown Soldier.

THE WEST

Sagebrush, sixshooters and superstition? At first glance, America's hard-riding cowboys seem unlikely sidekicks for spooks, but at the end of a long day on the cattle range, campfire crooning under a lonely prairie moon often had an eerie tinge—a fact that Vaughn Monroe cashed in on in the 1940s with his hit single, "Ghost Riders in the Sky," and its less familiar followup, "The Phantom Stagecoach." Both songs were rooted in authentic Western folklore.

Though fully a fifth of America's population—more than fifty million people—lives in Alaska, Arizona, California, Colorado, Hawaii, Idaho, Montana, Nevada, New Mexico, Oklahoma, Oregon, Texas, Utah, Washington and Wyoming, the vastness of the land is equivalent to a population density of only twenty-five persons per square mile. That's a lot of isolated range for our Western ghosts to wander about in. Appropriately, this section covers plenty of territory, from the high plains of "Injun country" and the California desert to the eerie mountains of New Mexico and the tropical forests of Hawaii. But since progress pushes back every frontier, modern bogeys from Los Angeles, San Francisco and Seattle also rattle their respective chains.

ALGERNON BLACKWOOD

The Destruction of Smith

U.S. writers naturally dominate Haunted America, *but the next story has a convincingly Western "feel" to it, even though its author is the great English fantasist* ALGERNON BLACKWOOD *(1869–1951). Much of Blackwood's supernatural fiction is set in the Canadian woods, but "The Destruction of Smith" is an exception. This chillingly original ghost story takes place round a campfire at the edge of wooded mountain slopes (probably Arizona's Kaibab National Forest) and "the desolate alkali plains of Arizona where tufts of sage-brush are the only vegetation till you reach the lips of the Colorado Canyons."*

Ten years ago, in the western States of America, I once met Smith. But he was no ordinary member of the clan: he was Ezekiel B. Smith of Smithville. He *was* Smithville, for he founded it and made it live.

It was in the oil region, where towns spring up on the map in a few days like mushrooms, and may be destroyed again in a single night by fire and earthquake. On a hunting expedition Smith stumbled upon a natural oil well, and instantly staked his claim; a few months later he was rich, grown into affluence as rapidly as that patch of wilderness grew into streets and houses where you could buy anything from an evening's gambling to a tin of Boston baked pork-and-beans. Smith was really a tremendous fellow, a sort of human dynamo of energy and pluck, with rare judgment in his great square head—the kind of judgment that in higher walks of life makes statesmen. His personality cut through the difficulties of life with the clean easy force of putting his whole life into anything he touched. "God's own luck," his comrades called it; but really it was sheer ability and character and personality. The man had power.

From the moment of that "oil find" his rise was very rapid, but while his brains went into a dozen other big enterprises, his heart remained in little Smithville, the flimsy mushroom town he had created. His own life was in it. It was his baby. He spoke tenderly of its hideousness. Smithville was an intimate expression of his very self.

Ezekiel B. Smith I saw once only, for a few minutes; but I have never forgotten him. It was the moment of his death. And we came across him on a shooting trip where the forests melt away towards the vast plains of the Arizona desert. The personality of the man was singularly impressive. I caught myself thinking of a mountain, or of some elemental force of Nature so sure of itself that hurry is never necessary. And his gentleness was like the gentleness of women. Great strength often—the greatest always —has tenderness in it, a depth of tenderness unknown to pettier life.

Our meeting was coincidence, for we were hunting in a region where distances are measured by hours and the chance of running across white men very rare. For many days our nightly camps were pitched in spots of beauty where the loneliness is akin to the loneliness of the Egyptian desert. On one side the mountain slopes were smothered with dense forest, hiding wee meadows of sweet grass like English lawns; and on the other side, stretching for more miles than a man can count, ran the desolate alkali plains of Arizona where tufts of sage-brush are the only vegetation till you reach the lips of the Colorado Canyons. Our horses were tethered for the night beneath the stars. Two backwoodsmen were cooking dinner. The smell of bacon over a wood fire mingled with the keen and fragrant air—when, suddenly, the horses neighed, signalling the approach of one of their own kind. Indians, white men—probably another hunting party—were within scenting distance, though it was long before my city ears caught any sound, and still longer before the cause itself entered the circle of our firelight.

I saw a square-faced man, tanned like a redskin, in a hunting shirt and a big sombrero, climb down slowly from his horse and move towards us, keenly searching with his eyes; and at the same moment Hank, looking up from the frying-pan where the bacon and venison spluttered in a pool of pork-fat, exclaimed, "Why, it's Ezekiel B.!" The next words, addressed to Jake, who held the kettle, were below his breath: "And if he ain't all broke up! Jest look at the eyes on him!" I saw what he meant—the face of a human being distraught by some extraordinary emotion, a soul in violent distress, yet betrayal well kept under. Once, as a newspaper man, I had seen a murderer walk to the electric chair. The expression was similar. Death was *behind* the eyes, not in them. Smith brought in with him—terror.

In a dozen words we learned he had been hunting for some weeks, but was now heading for Tranter, a "stop-off" station where you could flag the daily train 140 miles south-west. He was making for Smithville, the little town that was the apple of his eye. Something "was wrong" with Smithville. No one asked him what —it is the custom to wait till information is volunteered. But Hank, helping him presently to venison (which he hardly touched), said casually, "Good hunting, Boss, your way?"; and the brief reply told much, and proved how eager he was to relieve his mind by speech. "I'm glad to locate your camp, boys," he said. "That's luck. There's something going wrong"—and a catch came into his voice—"with Smithville." Behind the laconic statement emerged somehow the terror the man experienced. For Smith to confess cowardice and in the same breath admit mere "luck," was equivalent to the hysteria that makes city people laugh or cry. It was genuinely dramatic. I have seen nothing more impressive by way of human tragedy—though hard to explain why—than this square-jawed, dauntless man, sitting there with the firelight on his rugged features, and saying this simple thing. For how in the world could he know it—?

In the pause that followed, his Indians came gliding in, tethered the horses, and sat down without a word to eat what Hank distributed. But nothing was to be read on their impassive faces. Redskins, whatever they may feel, show little. Then Smith gave us another pregnant sentence. "*They* heard it too," he said, in a lower voice, indicating his three men; "they saw it jest as I did." He looked up into the starry sky a second. "It's hard upon our trail right now," he added, as though he expected something to drop upon us from the heavens. And from that moment I swear we all felt creepy. The darkness round our lonely camp hid terror in its folds; the wind that whispered through the dry sage-brush brought whispers and the shuffle of watching figures; and when the Indians went softly out to pitch the tents and get more wood for the fire, I remember feeling glad the duty was not mine. Yet this feeling of uneasiness is something one rarely experiences in the open. It belongs to houses, overwrought imaginations, and the presence of evil men. Nature gives peace and security. That we all felt it proves how real it was. And Smith, who felt it most, of course, had brought it.

"There's something gone wrong with Smithville" was an ominous statement of disaster. He said it just as a man in civilised lands might say, "My wife is dying; a telegram's just come. I must take the train." But how he felt so sure of it, a thousand miles away in this uninhabited corner of the wilderness, made us feel curiously uneasy. For it was an incredible thing—yet true. We all felt *that.* Smith did not imagine things. A sense of gloomy apprehension settled over our lonely camp, as though things were about to happen. Already they stalked across the great black night, watching us with many eyes. The wind had risen, and there were sounds among the trees. I, for one, felt no desire to go to bed. The way Smith sat there, watching the sky and peering into the sheet of darkness that veiled the desert, set my nerves all jangling. He expected something—but what? It was following him. Across this tractless wilderness, apparently above him against the brilliant stars, Something was "hard upon his trail."

Then, in the middle of painful silences, Smith suddenly turned loquacious—further sign with him of deep mental disturbance. He asked questions like a schoolboy—asked them of me too, as being "an edicated man." But there were such queer things to talk about round an Arizona camp-fire that Hank clearly wondered for his sanity. He knew about the "wilderness madness" that attacks some folks. He let his green cigar go out and flashed me signals to be cautious. He listened intently, with the eyes of a puzzled child, half cynical, half touched with superstitious dread. For, briefly, Smith asked me what I knew about stories of dying men appearing at a distance to those who loved them much. He had read such tales, "heard tell of 'em," but "are they dead true, or are they jest little feery tales?" I satisfied him as best I could with one or two authentic stories. Whether he believed or not I cannot say; but his swift mind jumped in a flash to the point. "Then, if that kind o' stuff is true," he asked, simply, "it looks as though a feller had a dooplicate of himself—sperrit maybe—that gits loose and active at the time of death, and heads straight for the party it loves best. Ain't that so, Boss?" I admitted the theory was correct. And then he startled us with a final question that made Hank drop an oath below his breath—sure evidence of uneasy excitement in the old backwoodsman. Smith whispered it, looking over his shoulder into the night: "Ain't it jest possible then," he asked, "seeing that men an' Nature is all made of a piece like, that places too have this dooplicate appearance of theirselves that gits loose when they go under?"

It was difficult, under the circumstances, to explain that such a theory *had* been held to account for visions of scenery people sometimes have, and that a city may have a definite personality made up of all its inhabitants—moods, thoughts, feelings, and passions of the multitude who go to compose its life and atmosphere, and that hence is due the odd changes in a man's individuality when he goes from one city to another. Nor was there any time to do so, for hardly had he asked his singular question when the horses whinnied, the Indians leaped to their feet as if ready for an attack, and Smith himself turned the colour of the ashes that lay in a circle of whitish-grey about the burning wood. There was an expression in his face of death, or, as the Irish peasants say, "destroyed."

"That's Smithville," he cried, springing to his feet, then tottering so that I thought he must fall into the flame; "that's my baby town—got loose and huntin' for me, who made it, and love it better'n anything on Gawd's green earth!" And then he added with a kind of gulp in his throat as of a man who wanted to cry but couldn't: "And it's going to bits—it's dying—and I'm not thar to save it—!"

He staggered and I caught his arm. The sound of his frightened, anguished voice, and the shuffling of our many feet among the stones, died away into the night. We all stood, staring. The darkness came up closer. The horses ceased their whinnying. For a moment nothing happened. Then Smith turned slowly round and raised his head towards the stars as though he saw something. "Hear that?" he whispered. "It's coming up close. That's what I've bin hearing now, on and off, two days and nights. Listen!" His whispering voice broke horribly; the man was suffering atrociously. For a moment he became vastly, horribly animated—then stood still as death.

But in the hollow silence, broken only by the sighing of the wind among the spruces, we at first heard nothing. Then, most curiously, something like rapid driven mist came trooping down the sky, and veiled a group of stars. With it, as from an enormous distance, but growing swiftly nearer, came noises that were beyond all question the noises of a city rushing through the heavens. From all sides they came; and with them there shot a reddish, streaked appearance across the misty veil that swung so rapidly and softly between the stars and our eyes. Lurid it was, and in some way terrible. A sense of helpless bewilderment came over me, scattering my faculties as in scenes of fire, when the mind struggles violently to possess itself and act for the best. Hank, holding his rifle ready to shoot, moved stupidly round the group, equally at a loss, and swearing incessantly below his breath. For this overwhelming certainty that Something living had come upon us from the sky possessed us all, and I, personally, felt as if a gigantic Being swept against me through the night, destructive and enveloping, and yet that it was not one, but many. Power of action left me. I could not even observe with accuracy what was going on. I stared, dizzy and bewildered, in all directions; but my power of movement was gone, and my feet refused to stir. Only I remember that the Redskins stood like figures of stone, unmoved.

And the sounds about us grew into a roar. The distant murmur came past us like a sea. There was a babel of shouting. Here, in the deep old wilderness that knew no living human beings for hundreds of leagues, there was a tempest of voices calling, crying, shrieking; men's hoarse clamouring, and the high screaming of women and children. Behind it ran a booming sound like thunder. Yet all of it, while apparently so close above our heads, seemed in some inexplicable way far off in the distance—muted, faint, thinning out among the quiet stars. More like a *memory* of turmoil and tumult it seemed than the actual uproar heard at first hand. And through it ran the crash of big things tumbling, breaking, falling in destruction with an awful detonating thunder of collapse. I thought the hills were toppling down upon us. A shrieking city, it seemed, fled past us through the sky.

How long it lasted it is impossible to say, for my power of measuring time had utterly vanished. A dreadful wild anguish summed up all the feelings I can remember. It seemed I watched, or read, or dreamed some desolating scene of disaster in which human life went overboard wholesale, as though one threw a hatful of insects into a blazing fire. This idea of burning, of thick suffocating smoke and savage flame, coloured the entire experience. And the next thing I knew was that it had passed away as completely as though it had never been at all; the stars shone down from an air of limpid clearness, and—there was a smell of burning leather in my nostrils. I just stepped back in time to save my feet. I had moved in my excitement against the circle of hot ashes. Hank pushed me back roughly with the barrel of his rifle.

But, strangest of all, I understood, as by some flash of divine intuition, the reason of this abrupt cessation of the horrible tumult. The Personality of the town, set free and loosened in the moment of death, had returned to him who gave it birth, who loved it, and of whose life it was actually an expression. The Being of Smithville was literally a projection, an emanation of the dynamic, vital personality of its puissant creator. And, in death, it had returned on him with the shock of an accumulated power impossible for a human being to resist. For years he had provided it with life—but *gradually*. It now rushed back to its source, thus concentrated, in a single terrific moment.

"That's him," I heard a voice saying from a great distance as it seemed. "He's fired his last shot—!" and saw Hank turning the body over with his rifle-butt. And, though the face itself was calm beneath the stars, there was an attitude of limbs and body that suggested the bursting of an enormous shell that had twisted every fibre by its awful force yet somehow left the body as a whole intact.

We carried "it" to Tranter, and at the first real station along the
line we got the news by telegraph: "Smithville wiped out by fire.
Burned two days and nights. Loss of life, 3000." And all the way
in my dreams I seemed still to hear that curious, dreadful cry of
Smithville, the shrieking city rushing headlong through the sky.

HENRY SLESAR

The Return
of the Moresbys

This nasty little "guignol" from the prolific Emmy and Edgar–award-winning writer HENRY SLESAR *is set in Southern California, haven of gimcrack religions. When Mrs. Moresby came under the spell of the Temple of Metempsychosis, it was more than a transplanted Vermonter like her husband could tolerate. . . .*

One drop of blue dye in a gallon of water would have made the precise color of Moresby's eyes. Framed by the white bandages, their hue was only slightly more intense, and as the hospital hours passed, the blue faded, faded, in an eerie synchronization with his ebbing life.

Three hours before Moresby's end came, there was a burst of stubborn vitality in the dying man, a sudden spell of clarity, and a desire to talk. The interns would have restrained him, except for one word that Moresby used. It was the word "murder."

That word made Moresby's fate a police matter, and a lieutenant named Gardner was summoned to the bedside. He was the last man Moresby spoke to on earth, and he could have done worse. Lieutenant Gardner was a good listener. . . .

I like Southern California (Moresby began). I was born in Vermont and never knew the time I was warm enough. I came west when I was twenty, and soon discovered that sunlit indolence was the only way of life that I truly enjoyed. I lived on beaches. I became bronzed and muscular, a superb swimmer, an incorrigible loafer.

It was on a beach in Southern California that I met Una, the white-skinned, bony, bountiful woman who would become my beloved, my wife—and the support of my lazy sunshine hours.

Our honeymoon lasted a whole year—on the beaches of the Caribbean and the French Riviera. Una got freckled. Finally we returned to our home in Los Angeles and settled down to a quiet, companionable marriage. Una's financial resources were without end, and so was her ingenuousness. I took advantage of neither. I was not a spendthrift, nor an unfaithful husband. I was too intelligent to spoil a lifelong holiday because of petty indulgences.

No, it was Una who spoiled it—Una in search of an anchor. For some people, money would have been anchor enough. But Una had been born to her wealth, and felt the need of something more. For a time, marriage supplied this. Then she made a pitiful attempt at Art—with a capital A. It was laughable. Then she tried a career. That too failed. Then she tried religion. It bored her.

Most religion, that is. But finally she discovered the amusing variety that abounds in Southern California. She met Dr. Archibald Sing, the high priest of the Temple of Metempsychosis.

Una was not a brilliant woman, but neither was she a complete fool. There was a case for Dr. Sing. He was an eye-stopping man, tall as a tower and hugely shouldered, cleverly bearded for an effect of wisdom and youth combined. He avoided the usual pretensions of esoteric cults, and maintained a simple meeting place of almost monastic restraint. He wore well-tailored everyday clothes, delivered his sermons in conversational English, and conducted his services without incense, idols, or theatrics. But he preached a doctrine intensely interesting to poor Una—a doctrine of eternal life and the love of small animals.

Una first visited the Temple in the company of a cocktail companion. On her second visit she insisted that I come along. I was ironically hostile to the whole thing, of course, but I still remember Dr. Sing's little speech.

"The soul is immortal," he said. "The soul cannot die. The soul, upon leaving the body, must make its passage elsewhere.

The science of eschatology—dealing with the last four things of death, judgment, heaven, and hell—is the most ancient of all sciences, and from its wisdom has come the inescapable certainty of the transmigration of souls.

"And where does it go? The soul, according to all the wise men of past generations, departs from the mouth of the dying, and is consequently a small thing, given to seeking a home in the body of a small thing. A bird, a snake, a mouse; a dove or a hawk; a dog, a cat, an insect. For these small creations of God are empty vessels, placed on Earth to house the departing souls of humanity, so they need not wander forever in a trackless eternity."

Pure rot, of course, and the fact that Una didn't immediately recognize it as such was the most surprising thing I ever learned about my wife. The second surprising thing was the amount of devotion she gave to Dr. Sing and his gospel. The third surprising thing was the money.

To be honest, I really didn't mind Una taking up a faith. After all, the transmigration of souls has had quite a few adherents in the history of gullible man and is no sillier a concept than I've heard expressed in more Westernized religions. If she wanted to end up as a homing pigeon instead of an angel, that was strictly her business, and I made no attempt to interfere. But the money. That was different. Damn it, how that money went out!

Most of it, of course, went to the Temple. Dr. Archibald Sing had the deepest collection plate in the spiritual kingdom, and Una seemed determined to keep it filled. Thousands more went as donations to various institutions for the care and comfort of cats, dogs, and birds. Una has always been fond of furry, romping, and flying things, but now she had an additional incentive: she was Preventing Cruelty to Souls. Fortunately, there was no Home for Underprivileged Insects, or she would have given money to that, too.

Then came the final blow. I learned that Una had decided to further Dr. Sing's good work by a gesture that would prove her absolute faith in his mission. She was altering her will to leave the bulk of her fortune to the Temple.

Her announcement one Friday of this intent was the cause of our first real quarrel. I told her in detail what I thought of Dr.

Archibald Sing. I also made some candid remarks on her belief in transmigration. The truth is, I was very rude.

She cried a great deal, and the very next morning she made a Monday appointment with her attorney. This gave me one weekend to move around in. It's amazing how fast one can think—when Necessity is in the driver's seat.

On Saturday night I overdosed her milk with sleeping powders, and then put on an enormous pot of coffee with which I would attempt to wake her. The coffee wasn't yet perking when the police arrived and found her dead. They were most sympathetic.

At the inquest the testimony concerning Una's preoccupation with a Religion of Death was considered meaningful. The verdict was suicide.

But I should mention one more thing about that fateful night. Una did not die immediately. She fell into a state halfway between sleep and wakefulness, and she knew what I had done to her and why. In a terrible voice that I can summon all too easily to recollection, she swore revenge. It was mere raving, of course, but Una had a special reason for believing in vengeance from beyond the grave.

"I'll come back, Richard," she said. "You'll see. I'll come back just as Dr. Sing says, . . ."

Well, I had never liked animals much. Fangs, claws, wings, and tails had little attraction for me. As a matter of fact, I had always been slightly fearful of dogs, and the word had spread among the canine population. They say it's olfactory; perhaps it is. At any rate, I didn't take Una's threat seriously. I was not a convert to Dr. Sing's belief in metempsychosis, and when that gentleman came to pay me a dutiful condolence call, and spoke solemnly of Una's transported soul, I could not resist an open snicker.

By sheer coincidence I was chased by a mongrel on the very day of Una's interment. One of those things. I was driving home from the funeral, and this belligerent cur decided to bark at the tires of my Ferrari. I would have gladly run the creature over, but a smudgy-mouthed lad came along and cradled it in his arms.

"Sorry, mister," he said. "He always barks at foreign cars."

"Patriotic little beast, isn't he?" I snarled.

That night I had terrible nightmares.

Two days later some sort of shiny-winged bird, an immense

thing that might have been a pheasant, slammed against the picture window of my living room. I jumped out of my chair with a start, spilling the Balkan Sobranie out of my pipe. It was really nothing new—birds sometimes hit that window, mistaking it for open highway; usually, they dashed their brains out and that was that. This beggar was only stunned.

It lay on the patio tiles, feebly flapping its damned glossy wings. I have to admit I was terrified. I ran upstairs and called the game warden, a beefy, unimaginative man who laughed at my discomfort and ultimately removed the bird from the premises. He said something about dinner. Ugh! What if it *had* been Una? Cannibal!

That night there was a fly in my library—a big buzzing bluebottle of a fly. It was still early in spring, and that fly was surely ahead of its flight schedule. When it swooped into my vicinity, I swatted at it mightily with a copy of *Fortune* and it brushed my forehead. The touch of the thing was so revolting that I actually screamed the name of my dead wife.

You can see the state I was in. I finally got the thing with a bug bomb.

I felt a little better the next day. I went to the beach and lay under the loving warmth of the sun and forgot about Una and her deathbed promise. I lay there and listened to the swish-swash of the tide, the comforting sound of distant laughter, the shrill cries of the gulls.

The gulls.

The sharp beaks. Swooping creatures, diving for prey. Stabbing, pecking, tearing . . . I thought of Prometheus and his liver.

The sun turned suddenly cold. I left the beach hastily and went to have dinner at a pleasant club I knew. When I left, I discovered a lunar moth as big as a child's fist on my rear window. I was driving when it flew off and fluttered around the car's interior, and that was when I had my accident.

Only a minor one—I skidded over a curb, knocking down a newspaper boy. My ribs were bruised and my fender crumpled. Small damage, but enough, so I decided it was time to have a little chat with Dr. Archibald Sing. Not that I believed, you understand. But he was a doctor in a way, wasn't he?

When I told him of my experiences he was greatly reassuring.

"Come now," he smiled. "Do you think so little of your poor departed wife as to suspect her of such petty malice? Why should Una torment you?"

"Well, we had our little disagreements," I said.

"And besides, do you really think Una would be transmigrated into the forms you mention? No, no, Mr. Moresby, the process is surely not so random or so cruel."

"No?" I said.

"Certainly not. It is my sincere belief that our souls are weighed and judged by Higher Powers before the transformation takes place, and each of us is given the vessel which best conforms to the human personality we have left behind. Una a car-chasing dog? Never. A bird, perhaps—but not an ungainly pheasant. A fly, a gull, a moth? No, Mr. Moresby, you may take my word for it. That soft, gentle woman would never be so unjustly rewarded in her after-life. These encounters of yours are pure coincidences."

"Well," I sighed, "I thought as much myself. But in your opinion—if Una did come back—what sort of animal *would* she be?"

"You know your wife best," Dr. Sing smiled.

That night I heard the noise in the cellar.

I was not accustomed to paying attention to house sounds. The bang of a shutter, the clank of a pipe, the knock of the furnace—these rarely bothered me. But this soft padded sound, coming at a time of such highly nervous agitation, was irritating. I simply had to investigate its source.

I tiptoed down the cellar steps and found the lighting system—one stark bulb—insufficient for a thorough search. I got a flashlight and probed the shadows. In the beginning I had no success. Whatever had caused the noise—a mouse?—was frozen into inactivity because of my investigation.

I flicked off the light, held my breath, and waited. My strategy was rewarded. An empty oil can toppled over, and my flashlight beam picked out the culprit. A mouse? No, a cat.

I don't like cats—never have. They're skulking, cynical, malicious creatures. This alley denizen, its white fur shaggy, its eyes baleful in the spotlight, was monstrously big and yet strangely bony and fleshless. Like all cats, it had iridescent pupils that stared with a curious mixture of fear, hostility, and resentment.

"Scat!" I said.

It didn't scat. It made a soft mewling sound and then came toward me. *Toward* me.

"Una," I said.

I made a cowardly dash for the cellar door. It stuck for one hideous moment, then yielded to pressure.

Once I had reached the other side of the door, I remembered the hunting rifle that Una had given me for Christmas, thinking it would remind me of Vermontian pleasures. It stood unused in an upstairs closet. I found it, loaded it, and brought it back to the cellar.

I hadn't fired a rifle since boyhood. But I stood on the top step of the cellar stairway, and when my flashlight beam picked out the ghostly white feline haunching in a corner, I put down the light, raised the weapon, and squeezed the trigger, aiming blindly.

The report was deafening, but the recoil was worse. My precarious balance on the top step was lost, and I fell backward, crashing through the flimsy railing and dropping ten feet to the concrete floor.

When I tried to lift myself, the pain in my right leg was agonizing. I had fractured or broken a bone, and I was unable to move. There was a heavy mist of plaster in the room, and when it cleared I saw just how bad my aim had been. The cat was still alive, and it was regarding me at this new level, its body sprinkled with plaster dust, its eyes now filled with hatred.

I can't describe the gruesome thoughts that raced through my mind, or what exaggerations of horror troubled my brain. I began to crawl toward the fallen rifle, gasping with pain. My fingers touched the barrel. I looked backward at my adversary, and saw it advancing toward me.

"Una!" I screamed, and strained to retrieve the rifle. My fingers closed on the center of the weapon and I pulled it toward me, grasping too quickly in my panic.

My fingers were on the trigger; the rifle went off again, and the bullet struck me in the chest. . . .

The faded blue eyes dimmed once more. The lips paled, and closed. The hands, twitching over the sheets, became still.

"Enough for now," the intern said.

Lieutenant Gardner agreed. He stood up.

"Was it worth anything?"

"Something," Gardner said. "He confessed to killing his wife. Think he can manage to sign a statement?"

"Not likely," the intern said.

An hour later Moresby died.

The following morning Lieutenant Gardner drove out to the Moresby home. It was a brilliant, sunshiny day, perfect for the beach. He thought of Moresby.

He spoke briefly to the uniformed patrolman who had been posted the previous night at the scene of the tragedy. The officer reported a quiet night.

"Think I'll take a look at that cellar," the Lieutenant said.

Nothing had been touched. The flashlight was still on the top step. There was a gaping hole in the corner where the bullet had shattered the plaster. The floor showed white dust, except for the grim area where Moresby had fallen.

There was one window in the cellar—a narrow one at the top of the long wall, permitting a thin rectangle of sunlight to enter the room. The window was open, and a faint breeze stirred dust motes.

Lieutenant Gardner went upstairs and the patrolman offered him a cup of coffee.

"Pretty sad," the officer said. "Two deaths in less than a month. Happens that way sometimes."

"It happens," the Lieutenant agreed. "When you were here last night, did you see any sign of a cat in the basement?"

"A cat? No, sir, nothing like that."

A moment later Lieutenant Gardner lowered his cup.

"Did you hear something?"

"No."

"Sort of a scratching noise?"

He went to the cellar door and opened it.

"I hear it now," the cop said. "Should we take a look, sir?"

The Lieutenant went into the cellar, the officer behind him.

"For the love of Mike," the patrolman chuckled. "Take a look at that."

In the center of the basement the great shaggy white cat sputtered at them, dropping the squirming object in its mouth. Its outspread claw pinned it again, replaced it between eager jaws, and the cat dined.

When its hasty meal was over, the cat bounded from one packing case to another until it reached the open window. Then it was gone, with one quick backward glance at its audience, a look composed of satiety and triumph.

"There goes your cat," the officer said. "We almost interrupted its dinner."

"Never mind that," Lieutenant Gardner said. "Did you see its eyes—the rat's eyes?"

"Eyes?"

"Yes, its eyes!" the Lieutenant said. "Maybe I'm nuts, but they were blue. Did you ever see a rat with pale blue eyes?"

HELEN EUSTIS

The Rider on the Pale Horse

The finely crafted, evocative prose of HELEN EUSTIS *is an excellent anti-dote to today's endless spate of bestselling pulp-mentality fiction. Mystery buffs still recall* The Horizontal Man *with pleasure and her borderline fantasy* The Fool Killer, *one of the most highly praised novels of 1954, was favorably compared with J. D. Salinger's* The Catcher in the Rye *and Davis Grubb's* The Night of the Hunter. *"The Rider on the Pale Horse," also known as "Mr. Death and the Redheaded Woman," was dramatized during the early days of television with the virtuoso husband-wife dance team of Marge and Gower Champion starring as Maude Applegate and Mr. Death.*

Mister Death come aridin' in from the plains on his pale stallion, ashootin' off his pistols, bangety-bang-bang, till you'd 'a' thought some likkered-up Injun was on a spree. Hoo-ee! We was scared, all us little uns, and the grown folks, too, only to them he seemed more familiar.

But he never touched nary a soul that day but Billy-be-damn Bangtry, the one the girls was all crazy for. An' Mister Death no more'n just laid a finger on him, so he didn't die right off, but lay there cold and sweatin', dyin' of a bullet in his belly which was shot off by a drunken cowpoke in a wild euchre game.

Now, many a girl in our town wet the pillow with her tears when she heard how young Billy was like to die, for he was a handsome man and drove all women wild; but the one that cried and carried on the worst was pretty little Maude Applegate with the freckles and the red hair.

Old Injun Mary was anursin' Billy with poultices and healin' herbs, and wouldn't let no other woman near his door, so there wasn't nary a thing Maude Applegate could do for him. But you can't expect a redheaded woman to jest sit around and fret, like you would another color girl, an' Maude was no exception to that rule. Though she cried and carried on for a while, she pretty soon decided something had to be done, so she dried her eyes on her pettiskirt, saddled up her daddy's pinto pony and took out across the plains after Mister Death.

Maude Applegate, she rode high and she rode low; she rode through the cow country into the sheep country; through the sheep country into the Injun country; through the Injun country to the far mountains, and there at last she caught up with Mister Death, jest about a mile down the trail from the little ole shack where he lived with his granny, up above the timber line.

When Maude Applegate spied his pale stallion, she was mighty tired and mighty weary; her red hair was all tumbled down her back, and her daddy's pinto wasn't no more'n skin and bone.

But she caught her breath and sang out loud, "Oh, wait up, Mister Death! Wait up for me!"

Mister Death, he pulled up his pale stallion and looked around, surprised-like, for there isn't many that call out to halt him.

"Why, what you want, missy?" he asked Maude Applegate as she rode up alongside. "Jumpin' Jehoshaphat, if you don't look like you rode clean through the brier patch!"

"Oh, Mister Death," Maude panted out, "I rode high and I rode low after you! I rode through cow country into sheep country; through sheep country into Injun country; through Injun country to the far mountains, and all to ask you would you spare Billy-be-damn Bangtry, my own true love!"

At that, Mister Death throwed back his head so's his black sombrero slipped off and hung round his neck by the strings, and he laughed loud.

"Now ain't that cute!" said Mister Death. "Honey, I reckon you're jest about the cutest thing I'm likely to see!"

But Maude Applegate, she'd rode high and she'd rode low, she'd stood thirst and she'd stood hunger, she'd like to killed her daddy's pretty little pinto; furthermore, she was a redheaded woman, and she wasn't goin' to be laughed at so. She took and cussed out Mister Death good. She tole him that where she come from, no gentleman laughed at no lady in her true trouble, and she'd thank him to mind his manners with her, and she'd like to know who brought him up anyhow? Why, she knew dirty nekkid Injun bucks acted better'n him. She'd lay his mammy's aspinnin' in her grave, an' so on.

Well, Mister Death, he sobered down shortly and set up straight in his saddle and listened real still, with only his eyes ablinkin'. When Maude give out of breath, he took out his 'baccy bag, licked a paper an' rolled him a smoke.

"What'll you give me for Billy-de-damn Bangtry?" said he.

But Maude Applegate, she was really wound up. She tossed her red hair like a pony's mane and made a sassy mouth. "I ain't agonna talk business until I've washed my face and had me a bite to eat," said she. "I've rode high and I've rode low—"

"All right, all right!" said Mister Death. "Ride along now, and I'll take you to my cabin, where my ole granny'll take care of you."

So Maude and Mister Death they rode up the slope, Mister Death reinin' in his pale stallion to keep down to the pore tired pinto, until presently they come to a little ole shack with smoke comin' out of the stovepipe. There was Mister Death's granny astandin' in the door, as pleased as Punch to see some company.

"Why, you're right welcome, missy!" she sang out, soon's they were within callin' distance. "The pot's on the stove and the kettle's abilin'. Come right in and rest yourself a while!"

So they pulled up, and Mister Death swung down off his pale stallion, come around by Maude and lifted her right down to the ground, with his two big hands ameetin' around her little waist.

"Oh, ain't she the purty little thing?" his granny kept asayin' all the while, and hobblin' around the dooryard on her crutch like a bird with a broken wing. Then she taken Maude inside and give her warm water, and a ivory comb, and a pretty white silk wrapper from out of her ole brass-bound chest, and when Mister Death come in from seein' to the hosses, there's Maude Applegate asettin' like a redheaded angel, drinkin' tea.

Maude, she perked up soon's she got some vittles inside her, and presently she had Mister Death and his granny laughin' fit to bust with her comical tales of the folks back home.

Soon Mister Death, he set in to yawnin' and gapin'. "I've rode a far piece today," he said to his granny. "I been twice around the world and back, and I think I'll lay my head in your lap and catch forty winks." And shortly he was asnorin'.

Then Death's granny begun to talk low to Maude Applegate, questionin' her all about herself, and where she come from, and why she come. So Maude tole her all about how Billy-be-damn Bangtry, her own true love, lay adyin' of a bullet in his belly, so what could she do but take out after Mister Death to beg him to stay his hand? When Death's granny had heard the whole story, she fetched a great sigh.

"Well," she said, "it's a great pity to me you got your heart set, for you're like the girl I once was, and if I had my way, you're the girl I'd choose for my grandson to marry, for I'm ole and tired and would like to see him settled before I go to my rest. You're young, and you're purty, and you don't stand for no sass, and if my ole eyes don't deceive me, you can do a bit of witchin' too. Now ain't that true?"

"Well," Maude answered her modestly, "jest a little of the plain."

"Like what now?" said Death's granny. "White or black?"

"Little o' both," said Maude. "Witched my little brother into passin' his arithmetic, and I also witched the preacher's wife so she tripped on her shoestring and fell in the horse trough."

Once more Death's granny fetched a sigh. "That's a good start for a young'un," said she. "Don't look to me like a girl like you ought to waste herself on no drunken gamblin' cowhand gets hisself shot up in some fool card game. Howsomever, if you got your heart set, I'll help you. Whenever Death catnaps this way, he shortly begins to talk in his sleep, and when he talks, he'll answer three questions truly, and then wake up. What shall I ask him for you?"

"Ask him," said Maude right away, "what is his price to let off Billy-be-damn Bangtry."

"That's one," said Death's granny. "You got three questions. What else?"

At this, Maude had to think, and presently she said, "Ask him why he took my baby sister from her cradle."

"Very well, chile," said Granny. "And one more."

Then Maude Applegate bent her red head near to the red fire and was still, but at last she said, kinda low and slow, "Ask him what he does when he's lonesome."

To this, Death's granny answered nothing at all, and so they set in quiet until shortly Death begun to mumble in his sleep. Then his granny took aholt of a lock of his coal-black hair and tweaked it, gentle-like.

"Yes?" Death said, but without wakin' up. "Yes?"

"Tell me, son," Death's granny said, bendin' over his ear. "What will you take to let off Billy-be-damn Bangtry?"

At this, Death twitched and turned in his sleep. "Oh, granny," he said, "she's such a pretty girl! If it was some, I'd make it an eye. An' if it was others, I'd make it ten years o' life. But for her, I'll make it that she must ride with me two times around the world and give me a kiss on the lips."

At this, Maude drawed a great deep breath and leaned back in her chair.

"Well, son," said granny, "here's another question she asks of you. Why did you take her baby sister from the cradle?"

Then Death twisted and turned in his sleep again. "She was sick," he said. "She was full of pain. I took her so she need never cry no more."

At this, Maude bowed her head and hid her cheek in her hand.

"Well, son," said Death's granny, "an' here's the last. What is it you do when you're lonesome?"

At this, Death give a regular heave and a great groan, and turned his face from the light of the fire. For a long time he whispered and mumbled, and finally he said real low, "I peep through the windows at how the human bein's sleep in each other's arms."

And with this last, he woke up with a jerk, give a mighty yawn, sayin', "My stars, I must of dropped off!"

Now Mister Death and his granny was cheerful folks in spite o' his profession, and that evenin' they gave Maude Applegate such a high ole time that she was almost glad she come. Death's granny, she tole some mighty edifyin' stories about her young days, and furthermore, she got out a jug of her blackberry wine, and Death, he played such merry tunes on his fiddle that Maude Applegate got right out of her chair, picked up her skirts and danced. It was late that night when Death's granny showed Maude to the little trundle bed all made up fresh beside her own four-poster.

In the mornin', Death's granny had Maude's own dress all mended and pressed for her, and a fine breakfast of coffee and ham and grits to stay their stomachs for their long trip, and when Mister Death brought round his pale stallion, all saddled and bridled to go, the tears was standin' in his granny's eyes as she kissed Maude Applegate good-by.

"Good-by," Maude said. "I thank you for your fine hospitality, and if it wasn't for Billy-be-damn Bangtry, my own true love, I'd be right sorry to go."

Mister Death, he lifted Maude up to his big stallion and leaped astride; then away they rode, right up the snowy mountaintop into the sky, and Maude Applegate was surprised to find herself warm and comfortable, ridin' pillion with her arms wrapped around Mister Death's waist.

Then didn't they have a ride! Mister Death, he rode his pale stallion up the mountains of the storm to the pastures of the sky, where the little clouds was grazin' beside their big fat white mammies, and the big black daddy clouds kept watch around the edge. And he rode right up in the fields where the stars grow, and let Maude Applegate pluck a few to wear in her red hair. He rode past the moon, and when Maude Applegate reached out and touched it, it was cold as snow, and slippery too. They couldn't go too near the sun, Mister Death said, lest they might get burned.

But Mister Death, he had his business to tend to, so pretty soon they set out across the wide ocean on their way to twice around the world. Mister Death, he wrapped Maude in his cloak of invisibility, and he took her to all sorts of houses in all sorts of climes—

houses where Chinee folks lived, and Rooshian, and Japanee, and African, and folks that never spoke a word of English since the day they was born. He showed her castles and dirty little huts the like of which she never seen in all the state of Texas; he showed her kings and princes and poor folks and all, and maybe she didn't just open her eyes! But in one respect she noticed they was all alike: when Mister Death come, the living couldn't see him, and wept and wailed, but the folks that was dyin' rose up to greet him, and smiled at him on their way, like they knew him for a friend. She was right glad to see that everybody didn't take him for such a bad fellow after all. While they rode, Mister Death, he tole Maude Applegate many a pretty tale about his far travels, and it was plain to see he was a man knew more'n likker and women and ridin' herd.

And when they was on their last lap round and on their way home, Mister Death, he rode out over the ocean and showed Maude Applegate where the whales played—she saw 'em just as plain, aplowin' through the clear green water like a herd of buffalo on a grassy plain. And he rode over the North Pole, for her to see the polar bears, which was all white but for their noses, and he showed her the crocodiles of Egypt driftin' down the Nile, and the tigers of India, too, and every strange creature with his mate. And at last Maude Applegate couldn't help feeling sorry for Mister Death, that he was the only one who had to be alone in all the whole wide world.

But at last they was lopin' back over the plain toward our town; they seen the smoke arisin' from the stovepipes and chimleys into the pale blue sky; they rode right down the main street past Tarbell's Emporium, past the Wells Fargo office, and reined up before the Blue Bird Saloon.

"Why, what you pullin' up here for?" Maude Applegate asked of Mister Death, feelin' surprised, but Mister Death only answered, "Ne'mind; you'll see," and swung down out of the saddle.

Then he reached up and lifted Maude down from off his pale stallion, and he wrapped her once more in his cloak of invisibility, and he said to her, "Now fer the rest of the bargain."

So Maude stood there with her eyes shut, kinda stiff, and steelin' herself for his kiss, but nothin' happened at all, so she opened 'em again, and Mister Death said to her, "No, Maude, the bargain was that you was to kiss me."

So Maude, she was obliged to ask Mister Death to lean down his head, which he did, and she was obliged to reach up and put her mouth on his. Now maybe she thought it would be cold, and maybe she thought it would be fearful to kiss Mister Death—I don't know, I'm sure—but it surely come as a great surprise to her when she found her two arms around his neck without her knowin' how they got there, and her own two lips on his, and the truth of the matter is, it was Mister Death stepped away the first, and tole her, soft and low, "Run along now, Maude. Billy-be-damn Bangtry, your own true love, is settin' right in there in the Blue Bird Saloon."

Then Mister Death unwrapped her from his cloak of invisibility, so's she couldn't see him no more—only hear his spurs jinglin' as he walked away—and Maude Applegate was left standin' by herself before the Blue Bird Saloon, where, inside the window, she could see Billy-be-damn Bangtry, her own true love, settin' at a table drinkin' whisky with a bunch of fly young women of a kind doesn't mind settin' in saloons. Oh, then Maude Applegate's bosom was so full of a thousand feelin's she thought she would bust, and she didn't know whether what she wanted most was to wrench up the hitchin' rail, bust into the Blue Bird Saloon and lambaste her own true love, or whether she'd simply like to melt of shame and sink through the ground. Then she noticed that her daddy's pinto, all groomed and saddled, was tied up by the Blue Bird door. She was jest about decided to mount him and gallop off home before anybody seen her, when Billy-be-damn Bangtry caught a sight of her through the window, and come pushin' out the swingin' doors, swaggerin' and hitchin' his pants like he'd never been half dead in his life.

"Why," he sings out, "if it ain't little Maude Applegate waitin' for me outside the Blue Bird Saloon! Where you been, honey? Heared you was away."

Maude Applegate, she felt the red comin' up in her face. She snapped back at him, "Heared you was mighty sick."

"Mighty sick," Billy said, shakin' his head. "Mighty sick and like to die, but ole Injun Mary, she doctored me good as new with her poultices and herbs!"

Now this was the last straw to Maude Applegate. She'd rode high and she'd rode low; she'd rode through cow country to sheep country; through sheep country to Injun country; through Injun country to the far mountains, all to stay the hand of Mister Death from taking Billy-be-damn Bangtry, her own true love; she'd rode twice around the world and back and give a kiss on the lips to a strange man, and all to save a feller which turned out to be this horse-smellin', whisky-breathin', tobaccer-chewin', loose-livin', gamblin', no-good cow hand standin' here lookin' at her like she was a ripe peach an' all he had to do was shake the tree. Maude Applegate was so mad she could of cried, but she didn't do no such of a thing, since she was a redheaded woman, and besides, somethin' better come to her mind.

Just then she seen ole Pap Tarbell lean outen the upstairs winder of Tarbell's Emporium, and Maude, she took and witched a spell. When Pap let fly with his tobaccer juice, Maude, she witched it straight into Billy-be-damn Bangtry's eye. And while he was still standin' there acursin' and aswearin' in such language as no lady cares to hear, Maude unhitched her daddy's little pinto pony and leaped astride. She dug in her heels and set the dust aflyin' as she galloped down the street out of town. She rode through cow country into sheep country, through sheep country into Injun country, through Injun country to the far mountains, until she caught sight of Mister Death on his pale stallion.

Then she sung out, "Oh, wait up, Mister Death! Wait up for me!"

And when Mister Death heard her he turned and rode back down the trail—though he is one who turns back for no man—and he snatched her off her little pinto and onto his pale stallion, he held her close and he kissed her good and pretty soon he said, "I guess granny'll be mighty proud to see you."

And Maude Applegate said to him, "Jest don't let me hear no talk about peepin' through folks' windows never no more."

Now Maude Applegate she lived long and happy with Mister Death, and from all I hear, she's with him yet. Fact is, she took to helpin' him with his work, and when we was little uns, and cross at bedtime, and startin' to cry, our mammies'd tell us, "Hush, now, honey, close your eyes, and pretty soon Maude Applegate'll sit by your bed and sing you a lullaby."

And she used to too. Heard her myself.

FRITZ LEIBER, JR.

The Glove

FRITZ LEIBER, JR., *is the prolific author of such science fiction and fantasy as the novels* The Green Millenium *and the thrice-filmed* Conjure Wife, *as well as the popular Grey Mouser swords-and-sorcery tales. Leiber's byline appeared on several occasions in* Weird Tales *magazine, so when Stuart David Schiff published a special* Weird Tales *issue of his award-winning periodical,* Whispers, *one of the stories he featured in it was "The Glove," a hard-hitting modern ghost story set in San Francisco.*

My most literally tangible brush with the supernatural (something I can get incredibly infatuated with yet forever distrust profoundly, like a very beautiful and adroit call girl) occurred in connection with the rape by a masked intruder of the woman who lived in the next apartment to mine during my San Francisco years. I knew Evelyn Mayne only as a neighbor and I slept through the whole incident, including the arrival and departure of the police, though there came a point in the case when the police doubted both these assertions of mine.

The phrase "victim of rape" calls up certain stereotyped images: an attractive young woman going home alone late at night, enters a dark street, is grabbed . . . or, a beautiful young suburban matron, mother of three, wakes after midnight, feels a nameless dread, is grabbed . . . The truth is apt to be less romantic.

Evelyn Mayne was 65, long divorced, neglected and thoroughly detested by her two daughters-in-law and only to a lesser degree by their husbands, lived on various programs of old age, medical and psychiatric assistance, was scrawny, gloomy, alcoholic, waspish, believed life was futile, and either overdosed on sleeping pills or else lightly cut her wrists three or four times a year.

Her assailant at least was somewhat more glamorous, in a sick way. The rapist was dressed all in rather close-fitting gray, hands covered by gray gloves, face obscured by a long shock of straight silver hair falling over it. And in the left hand, at first, a long knife that gleamed silver in the dimness.

And she wasn't grabbed either, at first, but only commanded in a harsh whisper coming through the hair to lie quietly or be cut up.

When she was alone again at last, she silently waited something like the ten minutes she'd been warned to, thinking that at least she hadn't been cut up, or else (who knows?) wishing she had been. Then she went next door (in the opposite direction to mine) and roused Marcia Everly, who was a buyer for a department store and about half her age. After the victim had been given a drink, they called the police and Evelyn Mayne's psychiatrist and also her social worker, who knew her current doctor's number (which she didn't), but they couldn't get hold of either of the last two. Marcia suggested waking me and Evelyn Mayne countered by suggesting they wake Mr. Helpful, who has the next room beyond Marcia's down the hall. Mr. Helpful (otherwise nicknamed Baldy, I never remembered his real name) was someone I loathed because he was always prissily dancing around being neighborly and asking if there was something he could do —and because he was six foot four tall, while I am rather under average height.

Marcia Everly is also very tall, at least for a woman, but as it happens I do not loathe her in the least. Quite the opposite in fact.

But Evelyn Mayne said I wasn't sympathetic, while Marcia (thank goodness!) loathed Mr. Helpful as much as I do—she thought him a weirdo, along with half the other tenants in the building.

So they compromised by waking neither of us, and until the

police came Evelyn Mayne simply kept telling the story of her rape over and over, rather mechanically, while Marcia listened dutifully and occupied her mind as to which of our crazy fellow-tenants was the best suspect—granting it hadn't been done by an outsider, although that seemed likeliest. The three most colorful were the statuesque platinum-blonde drag queen on the third floor, the long-haired old weirdo on six who wore a cape and was supposed to be into witchcraft, and the tall, silver-haired, Nazi-looking lesbian on seven (assuming she wore a dildo for the occasion and was nuttier than a five-dollar fruit cake).

Ours really is a weird building, you see, and not just because its occupants, who sometimes seem as if they were all referred here by mental hospitals. No, it's eerie in its own right. You see, several decades ago it was a hotel with all the rich, warm inner life that once implied: bevies of maids, who actually used the linen closets (empty now) on each floor and the round snap-capped outlets in the baseboards for a vacuum system (that hadn't been operated for a generation) and the two dumb-waiters (their doors forever shut and painted over). In the old days there had been bellboys and an elevator operator and two night porters who'd carry up drinks and midnight snacks from a restaurant that never closed.

But they're gone now, every last one of them, leaving the halls empty-feeling and very gloomy, and the stairwell an echoing void, and the lobby funereal, so that the mostly solitary tenants of today are apt to seem like ghosts, especially when you meet one coming silently around a turn in the corridor where the ceiling light's burnt out.

Sometimes I think that, what with the smaller and smaller families and more and more people living alone, our whole modern world is getting like that.

The police finally arrived, two grave and solicitous young men making a good impression—especially a tall and stalwart (Marcia told me) Officer Hart. But when they first heard Evelyn Mayne's story, they were quite skeptical (Marcia could tell, or thought she could, she told me). But they searched Evelyn's room and poked around the fire escapes and listened to her story again, and then they radioed for a medical policewoman, who arrived with admirable speed and who decided after an examination that in all probability there'd been recent sex, which would be confirmed by analysis of some smears she'd taken from the victim and the sheets.

Officer Hart did two great things, Marcia said. He got hold of Evelyn Mayne's social worker and told him he'd better get on over quick. And he got from him the phone number of her son who lived in the city and called him up and threw a scare into his wife and him about how they were the nearest of kin, God damn it, and had better start taking care of the abused and neglected lady.

Meanwhile the other cop had been listening to Evelyn Mayne, who was still telling it, and he asked her innocent questions, and had got her to admit that earlier that night she'd gone alone to a bar down the street (a rather rough place) and had one drink, or maybe three. Which made him wonder (Marcia said she could tell) whether Evelyn hadn't brought the whole thing on herself, maybe by inviting some man home with her, and then inventing the rape, at least in part, when things went wrong. (Though I couldn't see her inventing the silver hair.)

Anyhow the police got her statement and got it signed and then took off, even more solemnly sympathetic than when they'd arrived, Officer Hart in particular.

Of course, I didn't know anything about all this when I knocked on Marcia's door before going to work that morning, to confirm a tentative movie date we'd made for that evening. Though I was surprised when the door opened and Mr. Helpful came out looking down at me very thoughtfully, his bald head gleaming, and saying to Marcia in the voice adults use when children are listening, "I'll keep in touch with you about the matter. If there is anything I can do, don't hesitate . . ."

Marcia, looking at him very solemnly, nodded.

And then my feeling of discomfiture was completed when Evelyn Mayne, empty glass in hand and bathrobe clutched around her, edged past me as if I were contagious, giving me a peculiarly hostile look and calling back to Marcia over my head, "I'll come back, my dear, when I've repaired my appearance, so that people can't say you're entertaining bedraggled old hags."

I was relieved when Marcia gave me a grin as soon as the door was closed and said, "Actually she's gone to get herself another drink, after finishing off my supply. But really, Jeff, she has a reason to this morning—and for hating any man she runs into." And her face grew grave and troubled (and a little frightened too) as she quickly clued me in on the night's nasty events. Mr. Helpful, she explained, had dropped by to remind them about a tenants' meeting that evening and, when he got the grisly news, to go into a song and dance about how shocked he was and how guilty at having slept through it all, and what could he do?

Once she broke off to ask, almost worriedly, "What I can't understand, Jeff, is why any man would want to rape someone like Evelyn."

I shrugged. "Kinky some way, I suppose. It does happen, you know. To old women, I mean. Maybe a mother thing."

"Maybe he *hates* women," she speculated. "Wants to punish them."

I nodded.

She had finished by the time Evelyn Mayne came back, very listless now, looking like a woebegone ghost, dropped into a chair. She hadn't got dressed or even combed her hair. In one hand she had her glass, full and dark, and in the other a large, pale gray leather glove, which she carried oddly, dangling it by one finger.

Marcia started to ask her about it, but she just began to recite once more all that had happened to her that night, in an unemotional, mechanical voice that sounded as if it would go on forever.

Look, I didn't like the woman—she was a particularly useless, venomous sort of nuisance (those wearisome suicide attempts!) —but that recital got to me. I found myself hating the person who would deliberately put someone into the state she was in. I realized, perhaps for the first time, just what a vicious and sick crime rape is and how cheap are all the easy jokes about it.

Eventually the glove came into the narrative naturally: ". . . and in order to do that he had to take off his glove. He was particularly excited just then, and it must have got shoved behind the couch and forgotten, where I found it just now."

Marcia pounced on the glove at once then, saying it was important evidence they must tell the police about. So she called them and after a bit she managed to get Officer Hart himself, and he told her to tell Evelyn Mayne to hold onto the glove and he'd send someone over for it eventually.

It was more than time for me to get on to work, but I stayed until she finished her call, because I wanted to remind her about our date that evening.

She begged off, saying she'd be too tired from the sleep she'd lost and anyway she'd decided to go to the tenants' meeting tonight. She told me, "This has made me realize that I've got to begin to take some responsibility for what happens around me. We may make fun of such people—the good neighbors—but they've got something solid about them."

I was pretty miffed at that, though I don't think I let it show. Oh, I didn't so much mind her turning me down—there were reasons enough—but she didn't have to make such a production of it and drag in "good neighbors." (Mr. Helpful, who else?) Besides, Evelyn Mayne came out of her sad apathy long enough to give me a big smile when Marcia said "No."

So I didn't go to the tenants' meeting that night, as I might otherwise have done. Instead I had dinner out and went to the movie—it was lousy—and then had a few drinks, so that it was late when I got back (no signs of life in the lobby or lift or corridor), and gratefully piled into bed.

I was dragged out of the depths of sleep—that first blissful plunge—by a persistent knocking. I shouted something angry but unintelligible and when there was no reply made myself get up, feeling furious.

It was Marcia. With a really remarkable effort I kept my mouth shut and even smoothed out whatever expression was contorting my face. The words one utters on being suddenly awakened, especially from that matchless first sleep that is never recaptured, can be as disastrous as speaking in drink. Our relationship had progressed to the critical stage and I sure didn't want to blow it, especially when treasures I'd hoped to win were spread out in front of my face, as it were, under a semi-transparent nightgown and hastily-thrown-on negligee.

I looked up, a little, at her face. Her eyes were wide.

She said in a sort of frightened little-girl voice that didn't seem at all put on, "I'm awfully sorry to wake you up at three o'clock in the morning, Jeff, but would you keep this 'spooky' for me? I can't get to sleep with it in my room."

It is a testimony to the very high quality of Marcia's treasures that I didn't until then notice what she was carrying in front of her —in a fold of toilet paper: the pale gray leather glove Evelyn Mayne had found behind her couch.

"Huh?" I said, not at all brilliantly. "Didn't Officer Hart come back, or send someone over to pick it up?"

She shook her head. "Evelyn had it, of course, while I was at my job—her social worker did come over right after you left. But then at supper time her son and daughter-in-law came (Officer Hart did scare them!) and bundled her off to the hospital, and she left the glove with me. I called the police, but Officer Hart was off duty and Officer Halstead, whom I talked to, told me they'd be over to pick it up early in the morning. Please take it, Jeff. Whenever I look at it, I think of that crazy sneaking around with the silver hair down his face and waving the knife. It keeps giving me the shivers."

I looked again at her "spooky" in its fold of tissue (so that she wouldn't have to touch it, what other reason?) and, you know, it began to give *me* the shivers. Just an old glove, but now it had an invisible gray aura radiating from it.

"Okay," I said, closing my hand on it with an effort, and went on ungraciously, really without thinking, "Though I wonder you didn't ask Mr. Helpful first, what with all his offers and seeing him at the meeting."

"Well, I asked *you,*" she said a little angrily. Then her features relaxed into a warm smile. "Thanks, Jeff."

Only then did it occur to me that here I was passing up in my sleep-soddenness what might be a priceless opportunity. Well, that could be corrected. But before I could invite her in, there came this sharp little cough, or clearing of the throat. We both turned and there was Mr. Helpful in front of his open door, dressed in pyjamas and a belted maroon dressing gown. He came smiling and dancing toward us (he didn't really dance, but he gave that impression in spite of being six foot four) and saying, "Could I be of any assistance, Miss Everly? Did something alarm you? Is there . . . er? . . ." He hesitated, as if there might be something he should be embarrassed at.

Marcia shook her head curtly and said to me quite coolly, "No thank you, I needn't come in, Mr. Winter. That will be fine. Good night."

I realized Baldy *had* managed to embarrass her and that she was making it clear that we weren't parting after a rendezvous, or about to have one. (But to use my last name!)

As she passed him, she gave him a formal nod. He hurried back to his own door, a highlight dancing on the back of his head. (Marcia says he shaves it; I, that he doesn't have to.)

I waited until I heard her double-lock her door and slide the bolt across. Then I looked grimly at Baldy until he'd gone inside and closed his—I had that pleasure. Then I retired myself, tossed the glove down on some sheets of paper on the table in front of the open window, threw myself into bed and switched out the light.

I fully expected to spend considerable time being furious at my hulking, mincing, officious neighbor, and maybe at Marcia too, before I could get to sleep, but somehow my mind took off on a fantasy about the building around me as it might have been a half century ago. Ghostly bellboys sped silently with little notes inviting or accepting rendezvous. Ghostly waiters wheeled noiseless carts of silver-covered suppers for two. Pert, ghostly maids whirled ghostly sheets through the dark air as they made the bed, their smiles suggesting they might substitute for non-arriving sweethearts. The soft darkness whirlpooled. Somewhere was wind.

I woke with a start as if someone or something had touched me, and I sat up in bed. And then I realized that something *was* touching me high on my neck, just below my ear. Something long, like a finger laid flat or—oh God!—a centipede. I remembered how centipedes were supposed to cling with their scores of tiny feet—and *this* was clinging. As a child I'd been terrified by a tropical centipede that had come weaving out of a stalk of new-bought bananas in the kitchen, and the memory still returned full force once in a great while. Now it galvanized me into whirling my hand behind my head and striking my neck a great brushing swipe, making my jaw and ear sting. I instantly turned on the light and rapidly looked all around me without seeing anything close to me that might have brushed off my neck. I thought I'd felt something with my hand when I'd done that, but I couldn't be sure.

And then I looked at the table by the window and saw that the glove was gone.

Almost at once I got the vision of it lifting up and floating through the air at me, fingers first, or else dropping off the table and inching across the floor and up the bed. I don't know which was worse. The thing on my neck *had* felt leathery.

My immediate impulse was to check if my door was still shut. I couldn't tell from where I sat. A very tall clothes cabinet abuts the door, shutting the view of it off from the head of the bed. So I pushed my way down the bed, putting my feet on the floor after looking down to make sure there was nothing in the immediate vicinity.

And then a sharp gust of wind came in the window and blew the last sheet of paper off the table and deposited it on the floor near the other sheets of paper *and the glove* and the tissue now disentangled from it.

I was so relieved I almost laughed. I went over and picked up the glove, feeling a certain revulsion, but only at the thought of who had worn it and what it had been involved in. I examined it closely, which I hadn't done earlier. It was rather thin gray kid, a fairly big glove and stretched still further as if a pretty big hand had worn it, but quite light enough to have blown off the table with the papers.

There were grimy streaks on it and a slightly stiff part where some fluid had dried and a faintly reddish streak that might have been lipstick. And it looked old—decades old.

I put it back on the table and set a heavy ashtray on top of it and got back in bed, feeling suddenly secure again.

It occurred to me how the empty finger of a gray leather glove is really very much like a centipede, some of the larger of which are the same size, flat and yellowish gray (though the one that had come out of the banana stalk had been bright red), but these thoughts were no longer frightening.

I looked a last time across the room at the glove, pinioned under the heavy ashtray, and I confidently turned off the light.

Sleep was longer in coming this time, however. I got my fantasy of hotel ghosts going again, but gloves kept coming into it. The lissom maids wore work ones as they rhythmically polished piles of ghostly silver. The bellboys' hands holding the ghostly notes were gloved in pale gray cotton. And there were opera gloves, almost armpit length, that looked like spectral white cobras, especially when they were drawn inside-out off the sinuous, snake-slender arms of wealthy guesting ladies. And other ghostly gloves, not all hotel ones, came floating and weaving into my fantasy: the black gloves of morticians, the white gloves of policemen, the bulky fur-lined ones of polar explorers, the trim dark gauntlets of chauffeurs, the gloves of hunters with separate stalls only for thumb and trigger finger, the mittens of ice-skaters and sleigh riders, old ladies' mitts without any fingers at all, the thin, translucent elastic gloves of surgeons, wielding flashing scalpels of silver-bright steel—a veritable whirlpool of gloves that finally led me down, down, down to darkness.

Once again I woke with a start, as if I'd been touched, and shot up. Once again I felt something about four inches long clinging high on my neck, only this time under the other ear. Once again I frantically slashed at my neck and jaw, stinging them painfully, only this time I struck upward and away. I *thought* I felt something go.

I got the light on and checked the door at once. It was securely shut. Then I looked at the table by the open window.

The heavy ashtray still sat in the center of it, rock firm.

But the rapist's glove that had been under it was gone.

I must have stood there a couple of minutes, telling myself this could not be. Then I went over and lifted the ashtray and carefully inspected its underside, as if the glove had somehow managed to shrink and was clinging there.

And all the while I was having this vision of the glove painfully humping itself from under the ashtray and inching to the table's edge and dropping to the floor and then crawling off . . . almost anywhere.

Believe me, I searched my place then, especially the floor. I even opened the doors to the closet and the clothes cabinet, though they had been tightly shut, and searched the floor there. And of course I searched under and behind the bed. And more than once while I searched, I'd suddenly jerk around thinking I'd seen something gray approaching my shoulder from behind.

There wasn't a sign of the glove.

It was dawn by now—had been for some time. I made coffee and tried to think rationally about it.

It seemed to boil down to three explanations that weren't wildly farfetched.

First, that I'd gone out of my mind. Could be, I suppose. But from what I'd read and seen, most people who go crazy know damn well ahead of time that something frightening is happening to their minds, except maybe paranoiacs. Still, it remained a possibility.

Second, that someone with a duplicate or master key had quietly taken the glove away while I was asleep. The apartment manager and janitor had such keys. I'd briefly given my duplicate to various people. Why, once before she got down on me, I'd given it to Evelyn Mayne—matter of letting someone in while I was at work. I *thought* I'd got it back from her, though I remember once having a second duplicate made—I'd forgotten why. The main difficulty about this explanation was motive. Who'd want to get the glove?—except the rapist, maybe.

Third, of course, there was the supernatural. Gloves are ghostly to start with, envelopes for hands—and if there isn't a medieval superstition about wearing the flayed skin of another's hand to work magic, there ought to be. (Of course, there was the Hand of Glory, its fingers flaming like candles, guaranteed to make people sleep while being burgled, but there the skin is still on the dried chopped-off hand.) And there are tales of spectral hands a-plenty—pointing out buried treasure or hidden graves, or at guilty murderers, or carrying candles or daggers—so why not gloves? And could there be a kind of telekinesis in which a hand controls at a distance the movements and actions of a glove it has worn? Of course that would be psionics or whatnot, but to me the parapsychological is supernatural. (And in that case what had the glove been trying to do probing at my neck?—strangle me, I'd think.) And somewhere I'd read of an aristocratic Brazilian murderess of the last century who wore gloves woven of spider silk, and of a knight blinded at a crucial moment in a tourney by a lady's silken glove worn as a favor. Yes, they were eerie envelopes, I thought, gloves were, but I was just concerned with one of them, a vanishing glove.

I started with a jerk as there came a measured *knock-knock*. I opened the door and looked up at the poker faces of two young policemen. Over their shoulders Mr. Helpful was peering down eagerly at me, his lips rapidly quirking in little smiles with what I'd call questioning pouts in between. Back and a little to one side was Marcia, looking shocked and staring intently at me through the narrow space between the second policeman and the door jamb.

"Jeff Winters," the first policeman said to me, as if it were a fact that he was putting into place. It occurred to me that young policemen look very *blocky* around their narrow hips with all that equipment they carry snugly nested and cased in black leather.

"Officer Hart—" Marcia began anxiously.

The second policeman's eyes flickered towards her, but just then the first policeman continued, "Your neighbor Miss Everly says she handed you a glove earlier this morning," and he stepped forward into the private space (I think it's sometimes called) around my body, and I automatically stepped back.

"We want it," he went on, continuing to step forward, and I back.

I hesitated. What was I to say? That the glove had started to spook me and then disappeared? Officer Hart followed the first policeman in. Mr. Helpful followed *him* in and stopped just inside my door, Marcia still beyond him and looking frantic. Officer Hart turned, as if about to tell Mr. Helpful to get out, but just then Officer Halstead (that was the other name Marcia had mentioned) said, "Well, you've still got it, haven't you? She gave it to you, didn't she?"

I shook and then nodded my head, which must have made me look rattled. He came closer still and said harshly and with a note of eagerness, "Well, where is it, then?"

I had to look up quite sharply at him to see his face. Beyond it, just to one side of it, diagonally upward across the room, was the top of the tall clothes cabinet, and on the edge of that there balanced that damned gray glove, flat fingers dripping over.

I froze. I could have sworn I'd glanced up there more than once when I was hunting the thing, and seen nothing. Yet there it was, as if it had flown up there or else been flicked there by me the second time I'd violently brushed something from my face.

Officer Halstead must have misread my look of terror, for he ducked his head toward mine and rasped, "Your neighbor Mr. Angus says that it's *your* glove, that he saw you wearing gray gloves night before last! What do you say?"

But I didn't say anything, for at that moment the glove slid off its precarious perch and dropped straight down and landed on Mr. Helpful's (Angus's) shoulder close to his neck, just like the hand of an arresting cop.

Now it may have been that in ducking his head to look at it, he trapped it between his chin and collarbone, or it may have been (as it looked to me) that the glove actively clung to his neck and shoulder, resisting all his frantic efforts to peel it off, while he reiterated, his voice mounting in screams, "It's not my glove!"

He took his hands away for a moment and the glove dropped to the floor.

He looked back and forth and saw the dawning expressions on the faces of the two policemen, and then with a sort of despairing sob he whipped a long knife from under his coat.

Considerably to my surprise I started toward him, but just then Officer Hart endeared himself to us all forever by wrapping his arms around Mr. Angus like a bear, one hand closing on the wrist of the hand holding the knife.

I veered past him (I vividly recall changing the length of one of my strides so as not to step on the glove) and reached Marcia just in time to steady her as, turned quite white, she swayed, her eyelids fluttering.

I heard the knife clatter to the floor. I turned, my arms around Marcia, and we both saw Mr. Angus seem to shrink and collapse in Officer Hart's ursine embrace, his face going gray as if he were an empty glove himself.

That was it. They found the other glove and the long silver wig in a locked suitcase in his room. Marcia stayed frightened long enough, off and on, for us to become better acquainted and cement our friendship.

Officer (now Detective) Hart tells us that Mr. Angus is a model prisoner at the hospital for the criminally insane and has gone very religious, but never smiles. And he—Hart—now has the glove in a sort of Black Museum down at the station, where it has never again been seen to move under its own power. If it ever did.

One interesting thing. The gloves had belonged to Mr. Angus's father, now deceased, who had been a judge.

C. H. SHERMAN

Kaena Point

Hawaii, that exotic tropical chain of islands in the Pacific Ocean, is approximately as far away from the continental United States as New York is from California. The only place in America where one may visit a former royal palace, Hawaii has its own language, culture and superstitions, all of which figure in the strangely moving plot of "Kaena Point," a story about the wild westernmost tip of Oahu by C. H. SHERMAN, *whose earlier stories "Tapestry" and "Doll-Baby" appeared respectively in my collections* Devils and Demons *and* Witches and Warlocks. *Under another name, Sherman is an actor who plays a recurring role on a popular CBS-TV daytime drama and is frequently seen on national television commercials.*

Dan Lomax's spirits fell when all he saw on the way to the Mauna Hotel were pizza parlors and more hotels. After the ugliness of the past year with Denise, soon to be the ex-Mrs. Lomax, he was desperate to surround himself with the exotic beauty of Hawaii. But he needn't have despaired; Oahu's beauty revived him despite civilization's interference. He lay on the beach the first two days, allowing the pineapple-scented sea breezes to relax, then invigorate him. By the third day he was ready to cleanse himself with adventure.

He answered a corny ad by a Captain Cook, Jr., but it was the only one that offered off-the-beaten-track day trips. Dan paid extra for a private trip, so the guide picked him up in a purple army-surplus jeep early Thursday morning. Cook was right out of Central Casting, sixtyish with scraggly silver hair, an eye patch and, of all things, a black derby. Definitely not a native islander. He chewed stick after stick of Dentyne and talked with a distinct New Jersey accent about the wonders of his Hawaiian paradise.

"Yes sir, you got everything you need on the islands. You got the beach, you got the mountains, you got the nightclubs, you got the hula girls, you got the best damn Chinese food I ever ate excepting maybe Hong Fat's in Chinatown—I'm talking New York now, not San Francisco, you know I'm saying?—but hey, you got tours and you got tours. Now anybody can take you to see the Arizona or the Dole Pavilion or Queen Emma's Summer Palace, but you want something different, you want a little excitement, you want something to get old Pele all hot and bothered, you come with Cookie here. I'll give you a vacation you'll never forget, you know I'm saying?"

"Pele? The soccer player?"

Cook roared. "No kiddo, Pele is a goddess. The natives here always try to stay on her good side. They think she makes the volcanoes erupt when she blows a gasket. Don't make no difference what the scientists say, it's Pele's fault, you know I'm saying? You got to abide by her rules or she'll clobber you."

Just then Dan's hat blew off. It was an expensive new Panama he'd bought specifically for the trip. He had quite a selection of hats and was always adding to it. At fifty-one he was well on the way to total baldness. His hair had been thinning since his early twenties but over the last three years what little hair he had finally decided to fall out. Just a few sturdy strands graced his scalp. He had considered growing the sides long and sweeping them across to camouflage the old billiard ball, but he couldn't stand the possibility of looking like a lopsided fool in the wind and rain. If he could change one thing in his life, it would be his hairline. It might have saved his marriage. Dan was only a year older than Denise, the demure half of the Dynamic Duo of Danbury, but as things got more strained between them she made it worse by referring to him as the old man and an old fart. Jokingly, of course. The last time she did it Dan smashed her box of seashells that she'd been collecting since college. The next day she moved in with her sister.

Cook pulled off the road so Dan could run back to get his hat. He was red-faced and out of breath when he climbed back into the jeep.

"Don't want you getting sunstroke on me," laughed Cook as he popped a few more sticks of Dentyne into his mouth. "Hold onto your hats!" He gunned the engine and they took off. "We're headed for Kaena Point, big fella. You won't find another guide who'll even tell you about it. Legend has it that it's the cliff where the souls of the dead jump off into eternal night. We'll have to do some heavy-duty hiking, though, you know I'm saying? No cars near the top. You game?"

"Is it safe?"

"As long as it's daylight we're fine. 'Course, I don't plan on being up there at night. Too remote. But we'll be there and back by late afternoon. If we keep moving."

It wasn't exactly what Dan had in mind when he said he wanted adventure. Was it possible to have adventure without danger? He was in pretty good shape, physically at least, and this was definitely different. Besides, Cook never said it would be dangerous.

"I'm game."

It didn't take them very long to get to the end of the paved road. The jeep rattled through scruffy underbrush until Cook took mercy on both the jeep's suspension and his passenger's kidneys. He aimed for a giant palm and let the car stall at its base. Beginning to question his guide's sense of humor, Dan opted for a Rolaids tablet instead of Cook's offer of Dentyne.

The sun beat down with an amazing fierceness. Dan was tempted to take off everything except his hat and L. L. Bean hiking shorts but he knew his skin would blister within minutes. He gratefully followed Cook into an overgrown jungle. What a difference between the Hawaii most tourists see and this throwback to some prehistoric era. Even the blazing sun couldn't break through the lushness. The heavy air misted around them. Dan brushed aside sticky lime-green vines dangling overhead from tops of trees too high up to be seen. Giant leafy ferns blocked their paths and scraped against their legs as they waded through the undergrowth. Invisible birds made strange music.

After an hour Dan was winded and thinking about ways to convince Cook to head back without admitting to his weakness. Breathing was getting harder and he was very aware that fifty-one was indeed fifty-one. He didn't want to collapse in some godforsaken jungle and have to be hauled out by a real old fart. He had just made a pact with himself to hang on for another fifteen minutes when they came to a clearing.

The sun spotlighted a narrow, rickety bridge about twenty-five feet long, suspended from two giant trees over a wide pool of dark water. The far side was rocky, mountainous, with much less vegetation. Nailed to a post near the foot of the bridge was a sign: CROSS AT YOUR OWN RISK. THIS BRIDGE HAS NOT BEEN BLESSED. Underneath someone had scratched in pencil: KAPU! THE GODS COMMAND!

Dan stopped short. He felt an overwhelming sense of dread as he stared at the lagoon. Too many scary movies as a child haunted him even now. Middle-aged unease played its part as well.

Cook turned and watched him. "It'll be easier on the other side. You game?"

Dan tried to remember why he had come and what he was looking for.

"There's no other way to cross?"

"Okay, we'll head back. No sense doing something if it scares the hell out of you."

"Wait!" shouted Dan, still trying to catch his breath. "I'm just wondering about the sign. What does 'kapu' mean?"

"It just means warning. There's nothing to worry about. They're Hawaiian gods, right? Hawaiian superstitions, right? You and me ain't Hawaiian so there's no problem, you know I'm saying?" Still Dan hesitated. "Okay, I can drop you off at Queen Emma's before it closes." Cook brushed past him with a disgusted look on his face.

"Wait a minute, I'll go across. The bridge just doesn't seem all that safe, blessed or not." Dan was embarrassed by his need to be back in the older man's good graces. "I'm not dressed for a swim, you know I'm saying?"

"It's stronger than it looks, trust me. You game?"

"Yeah, I'm game."

The guide grinned. He slapped Dan on the back and pushed him towards the bridge. Cook, chuckling like an old little boy, took out his wad of gum and plopped it on top of the warning sign. Together they stepped onto the wooden slats and crossed gingerly to the middle while the bridge swayed and creaked.

"See? Strong enough for ten men. Hold onto the sides so you won't get seasick."

With that, Cook started bouncing up and down. Dan grabbed for the rope supports but fell to his knees. Cook hooted and hollered. He jumped as high as he could and yelled a banshee cry that made the unseen birds screech.

"Buzz off, you pitiful gods!"

He squealed with laughter and danced a crazy dance as the bridge swayed more strongly. Dan stared at his guide gone mad. Cook clumped back and forth in his noisy army boots, oblivious to his charge's discomfort. Dan wavered, afraid to move, afraid of Cook's bizarre behavior. Cook pranced the length of the bridge, climbing on the ropes and cackling like a hyena. At the far end he cocked his derby at a jaunty angle and turned back to Dan, who was still on his knees.

"What are you doing? Praying?"

Still midway on the swinging bridge, Dan glared at Cook lounging safely on the other side. When he got close enough he would punch the old buzzard in the nose. Slowly he stood up. The rocking of the bridge actually made him nauseous. Cook hollered to him.

"Come on, sport, it ain't gonna fall!"

Still laughing, Cook bounded back across the bridge. Dan started to wave him away but lost his footing and fell flat. Suddenly, he heard a ripping sound and looked up in time to see the ropes closest to him spiral down. The bridge twisted and tilted as the planks groaned. Cook, frozen like a strung-up marionette, mirrored Dan's own disbelief and fear. He reached for Dan seconds before the bridge crashed into the water, spilling both of them into the lagoon.

The boards Dan was clutching wrenched out of his hands when he hit the icy water. The shock of the impact stunned him. His chest heaved; he struggled to hold onto what little air he had left. A board bashed his head. Blinding pain. Something clawed his ankle, pulling him down. He kicked in terror at it as his lungs screamed for air. His foot connected with something both pulpy and scaly. The hold on him released.

An eternity later Dan broke surface. He gagged and choked and gulped air into his lungs. The sunlight dazzled him. Never a good swimmer, he splashed his way desperately to the shore, dragged himself onto land and crawled over rocks and spiky grass to get as far away as possible from the lagoon and the thing that had grabbed him. Only when his legs gave out did he stop and turn around. Though he felt the sun beating down on him, he couldn't stop shivering. His ankle was scraped and bruised. His head throbbed. Blood gushed from a deep cut above his eyebrow. Dan retched again and again, throwing up breakfast and pond water.

Shaking and sweating in his muck, he suddenly remembered Cook. Where was he? Had he escaped? He tried to call out, but his voice cracked. He hacked and spat until he could make sounds, then called again. There was no answer. He thought of the thing that gripped his ankle. Could it have been Cook? He didn't want to go back into the water and see Cook's mangled body or bloated face, but the chance that he might be trapped alive in the debris made Dan crawl back to the edge of the lagoon to look.

The collapsed bridge dangled brokenly from one last support rope on the opposite bank where the warning sign still stood. The water was deeper than Dan realized; the bridge's other end was totally submerged. He splashed in the shallows and shouted for Cook to please God be alive, but there was no answer. Then Dan saw the old guide's battered derby floating near some loose planks on the other side. . . .

Cook was gone and Dan was too afraid to go back into the water to look for him. He felt like a coward. Hugging himself, rocking back and forth, Dan began to cry. Finally, he passed out in pure exhaustion.

When he woke up, dizzy and sore, a stiff wind was blowing and it was almost dark. He was chilled in his damp clothes. His ankle felt swollen and his head ached; when he touched his forehead, dried blood flaked onto his fingertips.

Dan had no idea how long he'd slept, but he knew he had to get away from there and get help. Stumbling to his feet, he tried to find a path. The vegetation was rough. He needed a way down, but the only clear areas were above. Maybe, he thought, he could circle around and come down on the other side of the bridge. He started off. Dark clouds hung overhead. The only sound he heard was the whistling of the wind.

Then Dan saw a movement in the shadows off to his right. He squinted and caught a glimpse of silver hair. It was Cook! His scraggly hair was plastered to his head and his clothes were dripping wet. Dan called his name.

Cook stopped and slowly turned around. His left arm was bent backwards, obviously badly broken. His eye patch was gone. A gaping hole stared blankly where an eye had been. A jagged gash in his neck oozed black blood. The old man saw Dan and smiled crookedly. "You game?" he asked. "Trust me."

Dan jerked back from the gnarled hand Cook offered him. He couldn't bear to touch it. The old man winked his good eye, then turned away as a sudden wind knocked Dan to the ground. Rain gushed down and pelted him with drops the size of pebbles. Thunder cracked overhead. He felt, rather than heard, Cook calling to him, urging him on.

With the wind and rain slashing at him, Dan began to crawl painfully through the underbrush. Lightning ripped the sky. Ahead of him he saw Cook working his way up an incline. Dazed, Dan rose to his feet and followed, limping. Raindrops stung his face and heavy air clogged his chest, but Dan hobbled on, unable to turn back. In his mind, over and over again, a mantra repeated itself soundlessly—Cook is dead, Cook is dead, Cook is dead. Now he knew where the old man was headed, where he must follow.

Kaena Point. The cliff where dead souls jump off into . . . *what? The dark? Eternal night? Hell?*

Thunder and lightning shattered the sky.

All the petty stupidities of his life came back to him—the memory of each ugly thing he'd ever said to his wife and family, all the things he'd never done, the unfulfilled dreams, missed opportunities—all the selfish, destructive, miserable ways he had ruined his life bore down on him, making each step unbearably heavy. He threw himself to the ground, moaning. He wanted to drown in the storm, to let the mud fill his mouth, to let the rain tear the skin from his bones.

A high-pitched inhuman wail pierced his brain, and his body was yanked forward. He caught at a jutting boulder, dug his fingers deep into the ground and scraped his feet against slippery rocks but he couldn't resist the force dragging him to Kaena Point to join Cook. Their destiny was sealed on that cursed bridge. Only—*I'm not dead yet!*

The black and green sky burst into flame and Dan saw Cook's ghost floating ahead of him near the edge of the cliff. Smiling, the battered, crushed old man motioned for Dan to follow. "It'll be easier on the other side. Trust me," he grinned, blood dribbling from his mouth.

"No! I'm alive, you son-of-a-bitch!"

A powerful gust of wind shoved Dan closer to the cliff. Cook laughed as Dan scrambled desperately for something to hold onto. His chin scraped a jagged rock. The invisible power suffocated him. Lightning flashed again and he saw he was on the very edge. Dan jammed his knee into a crevice and dangled on the ledge as Cook's spirit leapt off Kaena Point, falling end over end until it disappeared in the oily blackness. The roar of the ocean drowned its last horrifying wail.

Dan closed his eyes against the horror, against the awful power that was sucking his life away. He saw his wife's face, the face of the woman he had sworn to love so long ago. The emptiness of his soul cried out. Another chance! One more chance to make it right! He didn't want death, not yet, not this way. If he were allowed to live, he would change. He swore it!

"I don't want to die!"

"Then you shall not."

A woman's voice whispered in his ear and strong arms lifted him away from the edge of the cliff. Muscles still taut with fear, Dan felt himself cradled against the woman's soft breasts. She was warm and dry. His body vibrated as she began to croon a strange low melody. Incredibly, the storm quietened and died. Like a child, he lay in her arms while the moon slipped out from behind the clouds. The moonlight shone on the woman's delicately beautiful face, the most wonderfully beautiful woman Dan had ever seen. He reached up and wrapped a strand of her wild pale hair between his fingers. She smiled and stroked his face as she sang. His breathing slowed. The tension drained from his body. He inhaled her musky fragrance and stared at the curves of her mouth as she spoke.

"You here are a stranger. I know already that this is not your time. But you have trifled with the gods and now see you their power. Implore their forgiveness and I will see that you return with safety."

Dan managed to croak weakly, "Please, I beg their forgiveness. But what about Cook?"

"In death his spirit is the same as it was in life. Sleep now, haole. I protect you." She kissed the top of his head.

He must have fallen asleep immediately because he didn't remember anything until he was awakened in daylight by a jitney driver who found him lying alongside Farrington Highway. When Dan told him about the strange woman, the driver questioned him carefully as to whether or not he had shown her respect. Dan explained that he owed his life to her. The jitney driver beamed.

"You have great fortune. The Goddess Pele is not always so gracious."

The driver made a great to-do over Dan and told everyone they saw back at the hotel how the American-Stateside had seen Pele. Even the police who questioned Dan about Cook's disappearance were eager to hear about the mysterious woman. With the help of other guides Dan was able to show the authorities where the collapsed bridge was. They found Cook's body the second day, pinioned beneath splintered boards, his left arm bent backward and his eye patch missing.

Dan was cleared of any wrongdoing and flew back home the next day. His mind reeled from his brush with death but visions of ghosts were tempered by visions of goddesses. Eventually, the nightmares of falling into the blackness with Cook disturbed his sleep less often. And every time he looked in the mirror he said a prayer of thanks to Pele, if indeed that was she, for the kiss that gave him a full head of hair.

Second chances should be benefit enough.

JESSICA AMANDA SALMONSON

Atrocities

JESSICA AMANDA SALMONSON *publishes* Fantasy Macabre, *which well may be America's most sophisticated "little magazine" devoted to supernatural literature. She has also written such superbly idiomatic fiction as the* Tomoe Gozen Saga, *"The Trilling Princess" (which appeared in my earlier anthology,* Devils and Demons*) and the following Pirandellian nightmare set in Seattle, Washington. It comes from Salmonson's 1989 Ace Books short story collection,* A Silver Thread of Madness.

> ". . . a tiny morsel in a dish of night."
> —GERTRUDE KOLMAR

Lucifer, to see what it was like to be a man, removed all vestiges of power from himself, and limped through the world, helpless for seven days. Tired, hungry, observing cruelty, badly treated, arrested, tortured, and terrified, on the seventh day he obtained a horrible vengeance, then retired to his dark pit with the knowledge that in Evil, as in everything, he was second-rate, and Hell was nothing compared to God's Earth.

That is a story I believe is true. No greater evil can be found than on God's Earth. Lucifer could not do anything more terrible than God has already done, or we have done to each other.

I believe in the supernatural. Anyone who believes in God

believes in the supernatural. I have particular reason to believe, as I have seen the things that I have seen; I know what I have learned. And I have felt the pain of small, crippled beings and seen their spirits wander. The ghosts of dogs and all manner of animals struck by automobiles huddle along the highway margins. The ghosts of hundreds of thousands of rats, poisoned or dissected in the gutters or laboratories, continue their desperate quest to end their hunger and their pain. Children, dead of neglect, still wail from their beds and sniffle in their cellars. Ours is a haunted planet. It is haunted by misery and injustice. It is haunted by confusion and prejudice and hate.

Once I saw the sick ghost of a mother. She was emaciated and her breast was bared but could not give milk. She carried the shade of a dead infant, as pathetic as herself, dark their eyes, thin their faces. The ghost-mother saw that I noticed her existence and she said, "Don't look at me. I'm too ugly." All that I could do to ease her pain was to look away. She did not wish to be seen.

I have this ability to see the things that others cannot see. For years I thought I was mad. I hid it well. No one but myself knew of my madness. But as I observed this war-torn world and its material horrors, I realized that I alone was rational. The rest of the world was insane and I was not. I began slowly to accept the unique qualities of my mind. I accepted the things I saw, the ghostly things. There is the ghost of an old synagogue not far from where I live in Seattle. Nobody knows it is there but me. I am used to such things. My ability is a painful ability, a sacred ability, an ability of no crucial value to me, but still, it is my ability.

Resigned as I am to living in a world that is different from the world others believe they live in, it is hard for me to be made nervous or afraid. I have adjusted too well to everything. I'm cynical about everything. I'm sorry for everything I see. It is hard for me to be surprised. But one day I was badly upset. It was when my friend of many years came to see me and he told me about a horrible dream. He had dreamed about a world that only I knew to be real. Let me tell you in his own words what he said: "I dreamed about a world that only you know to be real." It was a very odd choice of phrasing, and his words terrified me. I felt that he had dreamed about my secret, for how else could he have known that I knew the things he dreamed about were real? "What is more," he said, "I have not yet awakened. I am still dreaming of this world, of you, of the terrible things that you alone know to be true."

I consoled him and convinced him it was all a dream, but since that time, I have not myself been convinced. Am I even now in this old friend's nightmare? Are all the tragedies the fault of my friend for dreaming so fierce a dream?

This made more sense than people always killing people, building machines of war, governments of war, human beings dying in such vast numbers, only to wander about in a perpetual daze asking, "Why am I dead? Why has this happened? Why is the world like this?"

A few days later I went to my friend's house to wake him up.

"It's no use," he said, fixing me some breakfast tea. "I cannot actually awaken. You cannot get out of the nightmare to get to me in my real life. I can only imagine that I am in a coma someplace. Perhaps I am in a hospital and they are keeping me alive. If you knew where that hospital was, and could reach it, you could perform a mercy killing. It would be a mercy to this whole world, for at the moment my nightmare ends, everything is over."

I began to visit all the hospitals far and wide to see if my friend were in two places at once, in his old home and in some hospital, but none of the hospitals knew about him or had anyone answering to his description.

"Surely you can change the nature of your dream," I said to him one evening as we sat in the park looking at the reservoir. The park was crowded with unhappy ghosts, people who had died in the park, or had been killed somewhere else but wandered into the park. A lot of transparent pigeons were being fed by a transparent old woman. Some living pigeons moved in and out among the ghosts of pigeons past. The reservoir had many floating bodies. My friend whose nightmare it was could not see any of it. Only I knew the truth of what he dreamed.

"Who can change their dream?" he asked of me. "I cannot. I do not even know all the parts of my dream. What is going on in Bangkok at this moment? What is going on inside those houses along that hill beyond the reservoir? I, for one, haven't the least idea. My dream has taken on a ghostly life of its own. It does as it pleases. Even I am but its pawn."

"You must struggle with your dream nonetheless," I said. "Think about a kind world, a world filled with generosity and goodwill, a world of gentle people."

"It would be murder!" he exclaimed.

"What? How so?"

"Should I do away with all these people who are already here? They must change themselves. I cannot change them. It would be murder. I cannot dream a better world upon the blood of their destruction."

"I see."

We left the park and walked along the avenue. The street was cluttered with thousands upon thousands of classic and vintage cars, mostly ruined, piled one atop the other and for as far as my eyes could see. But only my eyes could see them. Those automobiles that still functioned rushed down the street and through the ghosts of cars as though they were not there.

"If I were to kill you," I suggested, "it would end your dream."

"It would remove me physically from my dream," he said, "but I would still be dreaming."

"Then I must find some way out of this dream," I surmised. "I must make it somehow into the world where you are dreaming."

"How can you get there?"

"In a dream of my own," I said. "I know a great hypnotist. I will tell him the exact nature of the dream I must dream."

"But won't it be only a dream within my dream?"

"I will tell the great hypnotist to plant the dream in my mind in such a way as to establish irreconcilable contradictions. Have you studied Zen? No? Well. Thoughts are like mirrors. There will be two opposing thoughts in my dream. It will be impossible to say who reflects who and into whose infinity. Both directions, both possibilities, will be as one. I will find you in my dream and wake you up. If you are comatose, lying in some hospital as you have supposed, I will destroy you."

"Wouldn't it be suicide for you?" he asked. "It will end everything to end my dream."

"Will it? I wonder. Will I cease to be a dreamer dreaming that I killed the dreamer who dreamed me? Might I become the new dreamer, hypnotically compelled to dream a world of a better kind? Won't I have escaped from this world that you have made, at the moment it ceases to exist, and live in the dream of my own making instead? Think of the complexity of the situation! We cannot know a definite answer."

We had gone into a diner. All the cows and chickens that had been eaten in that establishment were crowded all around, but I alone could see them.

"Perhaps I won't die willingly," he hypothesized. "Suppose that I return to my home and fall into a sound rest and dream, without intending to do so, that I have gone into the other world to stop you from killing me? You will be standing as above a vampire, ready to put the stake into my heart, and suddenly I will appear to stay your hand! If I can be in two places at once, here and where I'm sleeping, surely I can be in three places, dreaming myself dreaming myself . . ."

Suddenly my friend stopped in mid-sentence and his eyes glazed over. He seemed to have short-circuited his brain and gotten stuck on his idea.

"I thought you hadn't studied Zen," I said, thinking to break his peculiar concentration.

At that moment he fell backward with a ferocious spasm, tumbling away from the table with a great clatter, scattering the chickens that perched on the backs of the diner's many chairs. The owner rushed out shouting, "What is the matter? What has happened?"

"He has had a heart attack," I said, feeling my friend's pulse. "Please call an ambulance."

But already it was too late. He was dead. I crouched over him, waiting, waiting, waiting to see if everything would dissolve. The chickens and cows watched, too. A little ghostly lamb said "bah, bah," for no ear but my own. Out of the corner of my eye I caught a glimpse of my friend's spirit slipping out the diner's front door, passing through the glass and into the street. Nothing dissolved. It was all still the same, still terrible.

I remain obsessed by the idea that he is sleeping in some other world. I have been to the hypnotist many times to reinforce my alternative creation. In my dreams, I search for my friend, meaning his destruction. I dream of a better world, a world where there is no war and no terror, and all the ghosts are laid. It is the opposite of this world. In my waking world, I alone am rational. I alone see how things really are and that killing is bad. In the other world, the world of my dream, there is no killing, but I stalk through the nights searching for my friend.

It is a good dream.

WILLIAM F. NOLAN

Gibbler's Ghost

I first met WILLIAM F. NOLAN *in 1989 at a horror film seminar in Detroit where we both were invited as lecturers. I was already familiar with him through his affiliation with the excellent, short-lived* Gamma *science-fiction magazine, an index he prepared of his friend Ray Bradbury's work as well as two SF anthologies,* A Sea of Space *and* Man Against Tomorrow, *and a volume of his own science-fantasy,* Impact-20. *Bill has written many genre screenplays for the movies and TV, including a fine BBC adaptation of Henry James's "The Turn of the Screw." Nolan claims that the Hollywood haunting in the following risible story (also known as "Full of, Mostly, Bagels and Cream Cheese") truly happened in Pennsylvania to a certain randy movie star whose appropriate real name unfortunately must remain undisclosed.*

Plippity-plop.

A girl a night.

Rainbow chicks: blonde on Monday, brunette on Tuesday, red-head on Wednesday. Falling like soft, ripe plums into Des Cahill's bed. Des shook the tree, and down they came.

Plippity-plop.

Ole Des, the Makeout King. Cahill the Cool. Mr. Codpiece. Remember how it was? Every young stud in the country envied him—walked like Des in his Gucci buckle-clips, wore his hair with the same cruel curl over one eye, thumb-crushed his cigs after three quick puffs the same savage way Des did.

Sure. Who could forget?

But now he's gone. No more movies or TV specials or Broadway guest shots in the nude. Women (and a lot of men) paid scalpers up to a hundred bucks to get a front-row peek at Cahill's equipment, and they were never disappointed.

So what happened? How come, at the top of the ladder, he walks, does the big fade, and is seen no more? I can tell you. I figure his public deserves to have the real rap laid down on Des Cahill.

I was his best friend—if he ever had one. My name is Albert. I took care of his income tax problems and lent him my shoulder. For crying on. And believe me, Des had plenty to cry about.

It begins with a ghost.

Des liked to swing high. His pad was in Benedict Canyon. Rafters, crackling fire, mile-deep rugs, a bear's head on the wall. Cozy. I was working in the back of the house, late one night, on a capital gains tax dodge for Des—my first time over to his place—when I hear this agonized female shriek of fear from the master bedroom. As I rush toward the room, out the door comes this pneumatic blonde wearing Midnight Hush eye makeup and a really terrified expression. She snake-shakes into her clothes, looking great doing it, and does a quick exit. Then she misses three gears on her MG going down the hill.

Des is standing by the bed, wearing a rumpled pair of Tiger's Eye shorts and looking bereft. That's the only word for how he looked. Bereft.

"It was him again," he says softly.

"Who's him?"

"The frigging ghost. Who the hell else would I have in there?"

Right away, I take his word.

"Then you've seen this spook before?"

At my question, Des chuckles. He laughs. He throws back his head and howls. He falls down on the rug, breaking up. Then he stops and looks at me.

"Albert," he says. "I am going to tell you something I have never told anybody else in this living world. I'm twenty-five, loaded with bread, up to my ass in fame, with maybe ten thousand cuddly little numbers ready to make the sex scene any time I lift a pinky—and you know what?"

"What?"

"Albert, I am a virgin."

We have a drink. Two drinks. We're on our third (vodka martinis with hair on their chests) when Des lays it out for me.

"First time I tried to make it all the way with a chick, I was fifteen—and that's when I saw him. The ghost. In broad daylight, at the beach on a Saturday afternoon. An old geezer dressed in full armor, looming right above us with this horse over his head."

I stop Des there and he tells me that whenever the ghost appears, he is always holding up a horse—holding it in the air.

"Like he's about to throw it at you," says Des. "Anyhow, the chick fainted and I was very disturbed. It happened again the following Friday, with me and the mayor's daughter. And that's the way it's been ever since. I get a chick into the hay and we are at the absolute moment of truth, you know . . ."

"I know."

". . . and *that's* when the ghost comes on with the horse. Naturally, it scares the shit out of my date."

"Naturally."

"No matter where I am, it happens. On location down in Pennsylvania last summer for the coal mine flick, I had every precious young available female in town panting at my motel door. So I took 'em on, one per night, and always got up to the grand moment, you know . . ."

"I know."

". . . when out he pops with his goddamn overhead horse, and the scene is blown. Thirty-six days on location, thirty-six chicks, thirty-six blowups." He knuckles his eyes, rolls his head. "Albert, I cannot go on. I've got the hottest sex rep in show biz, and I haven't made it once." He sobs—a broken, terrible sound. "Not *once!*"

That's when I give him my shoulder.

To cry on.

Later, I give him advice. Hire a class ghost-breaker, who knows his spooks, and go after the bastard with the horse.

This he does. The ghost-breaker is a nervous, kinky little guy, but he guarantees his work. There will no longer be a ghost when he is through. This we can bank on.

He goes the full route. With powders that flash and explode. With chalked circles around the bed and invocations and curses and lots of arm-waving. With incense that really stinks and hand-clapping and plenty of yelling.

But each time, just as Des and the particular lady of his choice reach the ultimate moment, WHAP! the ghost is there. Naturally, all the stinking incense and exploding powders and yelling and hand-clapping don't exactly delight the young thing who happens to be sharing the sheets with Des, and she always demands to know just what the hell is going on with this creepy guy hopping nervously around their bed. But Des is able to calm her down, and she's usually okay until the ghost shows. At which point she bolts, like they all bolt—straight out of the room, shrieking.

This goes on for three weeks, with Des getting thinner and more bereft-looking by the week. Finally, I ask him if he'd mind if I joined the group—to kind of size up the ghost for myself and maybe come in with some fresh ideas. Sure, he says, and that night there's Des and the uneasy ghost-breaker and a redhead with an immense heaving bosom and me, all of us in the master bedroom.

Sex, under these conditions, is never good—but Des manages to thrash himself into a damned remarkable performance until, ZAMBO! there's the ghost, right on the ole button.

I give him the careful once-over. A seedy old gink, scowling inside a cheapsie suit of backlot armor, with a crazy-eyed palomino above his head. I concentrate on the face. Suddenly, I let out a whoop.

"I *know* the bum! That's Joey Gibbler. It's Gibbler, I tell you!"

The ghost looks startled and vanishes, but, by then, the girl is shrieking and the nervous ghost-breaker is exploding more powders and Des is in no real condition to listen to me.

After, when things are more settled, I spell it out.

"Gibbler was an extra back in the days of the silents," I tell Des. "I remember reading about how he and this palomino horse both broke their necks doing a battle sequence for *The Queen's Cute*

Question, one of those slapstick historicals they used to grind out at Monarch."

Des shoots up an eyebrow. "Dad directed that one—I know he did. It was his last picture."

"Exactly! And he died of a stroke the following week. Which explains everything."

"Not to me, it doesn't."

"Joey was sore over getting his neck broke, and he blamed your pop for it. But he didn't have time to haunt him. The stroke beat him out. So Gibbler decides to haunt *you* instead. He waits until you're old enough to taste the sweet fruits of life and then he cunningly denies them to you. And he'll keep on until we placate him."

"But how? How do you placate a sore spook?"

"The key is Joey Gibbler, Jr. The kid must be about thirty by now. Not bad-looking, I've seen his name in the trades."

"An extra trying to make it as an actor?"

"Right. So set it up for him. Throw around some weight at the studio and get him into a picture. Junior clicks, and his old man stops haunting you out of sheer gratitude. You can do it."

"Albert," he says, "I can do it."

He does it. Joey winds up with a fat part in *The Big Bottom* and overnight, the way it can happen, Joey Gibbler, Jr. is a star.

And, overnight, Des makes it all the way through the moment of truth. No ghost. Ole Des Cahill is devirginized.

He hugs me, dances me around the room, thrusts signed checks at me, insists that I accept his mother's wedding ring. It is a tearful, joyous occasion.

The next night, I get a jingle at my place. Des on the horn. Sounding terribly bereft.

"What's wrong?" I ask.

"A new one showed," he says.

"Another ghost?"

"Albert, it can't be—but it is. It's Joey Jr."

I buzz over to Benedict Canyon in my Porsche. Des meets me at the door, crazy-eyed like the palomino.

We get it all on the eleven o'clock news: "Actor dies in freak set accident. Rising star Joey Gibbler, Jr. suffers a broken neck when

a delicatessen set falls on him during a Jewish film sequence."
Wow.

Des signs. "That accounts for the white butcher's apron he's
wearing and what he holds above his head."

"Which is?"

"A display case full of, mostly, bagels and cream cheese."

I'm sorry to tell you, but this story had no happy ending. Des,
who swears he'll never resign himself to celibacy, has quit the
acting game and is on the move. Last I heard, he'd covered most
of Europe, Asia, and the Middle East, and was in the Australian
back country.

What he's looking for is a very brave chick, well-stacked, eighteen to twenty-five, who isn't afraid of seeing, each night, a scowling spook in a butcher's apron with a display case full of, mostly,
bagels and cream cheese above his head.

And they just don't hardly *make* that kind anymore.

ANTHONY BOUCHER

They Bite

ANTHONY BOUCHER *(1911–1968) is a pen name for William Anthony Parker White, the co-founding editor of* The Magazine of Fantasy and Science Fiction. *Boucher was the mystery and science-fiction critic for two major New York City newspapers and he also wrote such excellent mystery novels as* The Case of the Baker Street Irregulars, The Case of the Crumpled Knave, The Case of the Seven Sneezes, Nine Times Nine *and* Rocket to the Morgue, *as well as several short fantasy tales, some of which were collected in* The Compleat Werewolf. *Most of Boucher's fiction is light and amusing in tone, but not "They Bite." It is (literally) a full-blooded horror story set in the Rockies.*

There was no path, only the almost vertical ascent. Crumbled rock for a few yards, with the roots of sage finding their scanty life in the dry soil. Then jagged outcroppings of crude crags, sometimes with accidental footholds, sometimes with overhanging and untrustworthy branches of greasewood, sometimes with no aid to climbing but the leverage of your muscles and the ingenuity of your balance.

The sage was as drably green as the rock was drably brown. The only color was the occasional rosy spikes of a barrel cactus.

Hugh Tallant swung himself up onto the last pinnacle. It had a deliberate, shaped look about it—a petrified fortress of Lilliputians, a Gibraltar of pygmies. Tallant perched on its battlements and unslung his field glasses.

The desert valley spread below him. The tiny cluster of buildings that was Oasis, the exiguous cluster of palms that gave name to the town and shelter to his own tent and to the shack he was building, the dead-ended highway leading straightforwardly to nothing, the oiled roads diagramming the vacant blocks of an optimistic subdivision.

Tallant saw none of these. His glasses were fixed beyond the oasis and the town of Oasis on the dry lake. The gliders were clear and vivid to him, and the uniformed men busy with them were as sharply and minutely visible as a nest of ants under glass. The training school was more than usually active. One glider in particular, strange to Tallant, seemed the focus of attention. Men would come and examine it and glance back at the older models in comparison.

Only the corner of Tallant's left eye was not preoccupied with the new glider. In that corner something moved, something little and thin and brown as the earth. Too large for a rabbit, much too small for a man. It darted across that corner of vision, and Tallant found gliders oddly hard to concentrate on.

He set down the bifocals and deliberately looked about him. His pinnacle surveyed the narrow, flat area of the crest. Nothing stirred. Nothing stood out against the sage and rock but one barrel of rosy spikes. He took up the glasses again and resumed his observations. When he was done, he methodically entered the results in the little black notebook.

His hand was still white. The desert is cold and often sunless in winter. But it was a firm hand, and as well trained as his eyes, fully capable of recording faithfully the designs and dimensions which they had registered so accurately.

Once his hand slipped, and he had to erase and redraw, leaving a smudge that displeased him. The lean, brown thing had slipped across the edge of his vision again. Going toward the east edge, he would swear, where that set of rocks jutted like the spines on the back of a stegosaur.

Only when his notes were completed did he yield to curiosity, and even then with cynical self-reproach. He was physically tired, for him an unusual state, from this daily climbing and from clearing the ground for his shack-to-be. The eye muscles play odd nervous tricks. There could be nothing behind the stegosaur's armor.

There was nothing. Nothing alive and moving. Only the torn and half-plucked carcass of a bird, which looked as though it had been gnawed by some small animal.

It was halfway down the hill—hill in Western terminology, though anywhere east of the Rockies it would have been considered a sizable mountain—that Tallant again had a glimpse of a moving figure.

But this was no trick of a nervous eye. It was not little nor thin nor brown. It was tall and broad and wore a loud red-and-black lumberjacket. It bellowed, "Tallant!" in a cheerful and lusty voice.

Tallant drew near the man and said, "Hello." He paused and added, "Your advantage, I think."

The man grinned broadly. "Don't know me? Well, I daresay ten years is a long time, and the California desert ain't exactly the Chinese rice fields. How's stuff? Still loaded down with Secrets for Sale?"

Tallant tried desperately not to react to that shot, but he stiffened a little. "Sorry. The prospector getup had me fooled. Good to see you again, Morgan."

The man's eyes had narrowed. "Just having my little joke," he smiled. "Of course you wouldn't have no serious reason for mountain climbing around a glider school, now, would you? And you'd kind of need field glasses to keep an eye on the pretty birdies."

"I'm out here for my health." Tallant's voice sounded unnatural even to himself.

"Sure, sure. You were always in it for your health. And come to think of it, my own health ain't been none too good lately. I've got me a little cabin way to hell-and-gone around here, and I do me a little prospecting now and then. And somehow it just strikes me, Tallant, like maybe I hit a pretty good lode today."

"Nonsense, old man. You can see—"

"I'd sure hate to tell any of them Army men out at the field some of the stories I know about China and the kind of men I used to know out there. Wouldn't cotton to them stories a bit, the Army wouldn't. But if I was to have a drink too many and get talkative-like—"

"Tell you what," Tallant suggested brusquely. "It's getting near sunset now, and my tent's chilly for evening visits. But drop around in the morning and we'll talk over old times. Is rum still your tipple?"

"Sure is. Kind of expensive now, you understand—"

"I'll lay some in. You can find the place easily—over by the oasis. And we . . . we might be able to talk about your prospecting, too."

Tallant's thin lips were set firm as he walked away.

The bartender opened a bottle of beer and plunked it on the damp-circled counter. "That'll be twenty cents," he said, then added as an afterthought, "Want a glass? Sometimes tourists do."

Tallant looked at the others sitting at the counter—the redeyed and unshaven old man, the flight sergeant unhappily drinking a Coke—it was after Army hours for beer—the young man with the long, dirty trench coat and the pipe and the new-looking brown beard—and saw no glasses. "I guess I won't be a tourist," he decided.

This was the first time Tallant had had a chance to visit the Desert Sport Spot. It was as well to be seen around in a community. Otherwise people begin to wonder and say, "Who is that man out by the oasis? Why don't you ever see him anyplace?"

The Sport Spot was quiet that night. The four of them at the counter, two Army boys shooting pool, and a half-dozen of the local men gathered about a round poker table, soberly and wordlessly cleaning a construction worker whose mind seemed more on his beer than on his cards.

"You just passing through?" the bartender asked sociably.

Tallant shook his head. "I'm moving in. When the Army turned me down for my lungs, I decided I better do something about it. Heard so much about your climate here I thought I might as well try it."

"Sure thing," the bartender nodded. "You take up until they started this glider school, just about every other guy you meet in the desert is here for his health. Me, I had sinus, and look at me now. It's the air."

Tallant breathed the atmosphere of smoke and beer suds, but did not smile. "I'm looking forward to miracles."

"You'll get 'em. Whereabouts you staying?"

"Over that way a bit. The agent called it 'the old Carker place.'"

Tallant felt the curious listening silence and frowned. The bartender had started to speak and then thought better of it. The young man with the beard looked at him oddly. The old man fixed him with red and watery eyes that had a faded glint of pity in them. For a moment, Tallant felt a chill that had nothing to do with the night air of the desert.

The old man drank his beer in quick gulps and frowned as though trying to formulate a sentence. At last he wiped beer from his bristly lips and said, "You wasn't aiming to stay in the adobe, was you?"

"No. It's pretty much gone to pieces. Easier to rig me up a little shack than try to make the adobe livable. Meanwhile, I've got a tent."

"That's all right, then, mebbe. But mind you don't go poking around that there adobe."

"I don't think I'm apt to. But why not? Want another beer?"

The old man shook his head reluctantly and slid from his stool to the ground. "No thanks. I don't rightly know as I—"

"Yes?"

"Nothing. Thanks all the same." He turned and shuffled to the door.

"Tallant smiled. "But why should I stay clear of the adobe?" he called after him.

The old man mumbled.

"What?"

"They bite," said the old man, and went out shivering into the night.

The bartender was back at his post. "I'm glad he didn't take that beer you offered him," he said. "Along about this time in the evening I have to stop serving him. For once he had the sense to quit."

Tallant pushed his own empty bottle forward. "I hope I didn't frighten him away."

"Frighten? Well, mister, I think maybe that's just what you did do. He didn't want beer that sort of came, like you might say, from the old Carker place. Some of the old-timers here, they're funny that way."

Tallant grinned. "Is it haunted?"

"Not what you'd call haunted, no. No ghosts there that I ever heard of." He wiped the counter with a cloth and seemed to wipe the subject away with it.

The flight sergeant pushed his Coke bottle away, hunted in his pocket for nickels, and went over to the pinball machine. The young man with the beard slid onto his vacant stool. "Hope old Jake didn't worry you," he said.

Tallant laughed. "I suppose every town has its deserted homestead with a grisly tradition. But this sounds a little different. No ghosts, and they bite. Do you know anything about it?"

"A little," the young man said seriously. "A little. Just enough to—"

Tallant was curious. "Have one on me and tell me about it."

The flight sergeant swore bitterly at the machine.

Beer gurgled through the beard. "You see," the young man began, "the desert's so big you can't be alone in it. Ever notice that? It's all empty and there's nothing in sight, but there's always something moving over there where you can't quite see it. It's something very dry and thin and brown, only when you look around it isn't there. Ever see it?"

"Optical fatigue—" Tallant began.

"Sure. I know. Every man to his own legend. There isn't a tribe of Indians hasn't got some way of accounting for it. You've heard of the Watchers? And the twentieth-century white man comes along, and it's optical fatigue. Only in the nineteenth century things weren't quite the same, and there were the Carkers."

"You've got a special localized legend?"

"Call it that. You glimpse things out of the corner of your mind, same like you glimpse lean, dry things out of the corner of your eye. You encase 'em in solid circumstance and they're not so bad. That is known as the Growth of Legend. The Folk Mind in Action.

You take the Carkers and the things you don't quite see and you put 'em together. And they bite."

Tallant wondered how long that beard had been absorbing beer. "And what were the Carkers?" he prompted politely.

"Ever hear of Sawney Bean? Scotland—reign of James First, or maybe the Sixth, though I think Roughead's wrong on that for once. Or let's be more modern—ever hear of the Benders? Kansas in the 1870s? No? Ever hear of Procrustes? Or Polyphemus? Or Fee-fi-fo-fum?

"There are ogres, you know. They're no legend. They're fact, they are. The inn where nine guests left for every ten that arrived, the mountain cabin that sheltered travelers from the snow, sheltered them all winter till the melting spring uncovered their bones, the lonely stretches of road that so many passengers traveled halfway—you'll find 'em everywhere. All over Europe and pretty much in this country too before communications became what they are. Profitable business. And it wasn't just the profit. The Benders made money, sure; but that wasn't why they killed all their victims as carefully as a kosher butcher. Sawney Bean got so he didn't give a damn about the profit; he just needed to lay in more meat for the winter.

"And think of the chances you'd have at an oasis."

"So these Carkers of yours were, as you call them, ogres?"

"Carkers, ogres—maybe they were Benders. The Benders were never seen alive, you know, after the townspeople found those curiously butchered bodies. There's a rumor they got this far west. And the time checks pretty well. There wasn't any town here in the eighties. Just a couple of Indian families, last of a dying tribe living on at the oasis. They vanished after the Carkers moved in. That's not so surprising. The white race is a sort of super-ogre, anyway. Nobody worried about them. But they used to worry about why so many travelers never got across this stretch of desert. The travelers used to stop over at the Carkers', you see, and somehow they often never got any farther. Their wagons'd be found maybe fifteen miles beyond in the desert. Sometimes they found the bones, too, parched and white. Gnawed-looking, they said sometimes."

"And nobody ever did anything about these Carkers?"

"Oh, sure. We didn't have King James Sixth—only I still think it was First—to ride up on a great white horse for a gesture, but twice Army detachments came here and wiped them all out."

"Twice? One wiping-out would do for most families." Tallant smiled.

"Uh-uh. That was no slip. They wiped out the Carkers twice because, you see, once didn't do any good. They wiped 'em out and still travelers vanished and still there were gnawed bones. So they wiped 'em out again. After that they gave up, and people detoured the oasis. It made a longer, harder trip, but after all—"

Tallant laughed. "You mean to say these Carkers were immortal?"

"I don't know about immortal. They somehow just didn't die very easy. Maybe, if they were the Benders—and I sort of like to think they were—they learned a little more about what they were doing out here on the desert. Maybe they put together what the Indians knew and what they knew, and it worked. Maybe Whatever they made their sacrifices to understood them better out here in Kansas."

"And what's become of them—aside from seeing them out of the corner of the eye?"

"There's forty years between the last of the Carker history and this new settlement at the oasis. And people won't talk much about what they learned here in the first year or so. Only that they stay away from that old Carker adobe. They tell some stories— The priest says he was sitting in the confessional one hot Saturday afternoon and thought he heard a penitent come in. He waited a long time and finally lifted the gauze to see was anybody there. Something was there, and it bit. He's got three fingers on his right hand now, which looks funny as hell when he gives a benediction."

Tallant pushed their two bottles toward the bartender. "That yarn, my young friend, has earned another beer. How about it, bartender? Is he always cheerful like this, or is this just something he's improvised for my benefit?"

The bartender set out the fresh bottles with great solemnity. "Me, I wouldn't've told you all that myself, but then, he's a stranger too and maybe don't feel the same way we do here. For him it's just a story."

"It's more comfortable that way," said the young man with the beard, and he took a firm hold on his beer bottle.

"But as long as you've heard that much," said the bartender, "you might as well— It was last winter, when we had that cold spell. You heard funny stories that winter. Wolves coming into prospectors' cabins just to warm up. Well, business wasn't so good. We don't have a license for hard liquor, and the boys don't drink much beer when it's that cold. But they used to come in anyway because we've got that big oil burner.

"So one night there's a bunch of 'em in here—old Jake was here, that you was talking to, and his dog Jigger—and I think I hear somebody else come in. The door creaks a little. But I don't see nobody, and the poker game's going, and we're talking just like we're talking now, and all of a sudden I hear a kind of a noise like *crack!* over there in that corner behind the juke box near the burner.

"I go over to see what goes and it gets away before I can see it very good. But it was little and thin and it didn't have no clothes on. It must've been damned cold that winter."

"And what was the cracking noise?" Tallant asked dutifully.

"That? That was a bone. It must've strangled Jigger without any noise. He was a little dog. It ate most of the flesh, and if it hadn't cracked the bone for the marrow it could've finished. You can still see the spots over there. The blood never did come out."

There had been silence all through the story. Now suddenly all hell broke loose. The flight sergeant let out a splendid yell and began pointing excitedly at the pinball machine and yelling for his payoff. The construction worker dramatically deserted the poker game, knocking his chair over in the process, and announced lugubriously that these guys here had their own rules, see?

Any atmosphere of Carker-inspired horror was dissipated. Tallant whistled as he walked over to put a nickel in the jukebox. He glanced casually at the floor. Yes, there was a stain, for what that was worth.

He smiled cheerfully and felt rather grateful to the Carkers. They were going to solve his blackmail problem very neatly.

Tallant dreamed of power that night. It was a common dream with him. He was a ruler of the new American Corporate State that would follow the war; and he said to this man, "Come!" and he came, and to that man, "Go!" and he went, and to his servants, "Do this!" and they did it.

Then the young man with the beard was standing before him, and the dirty trench coat was like the robes of an ancient prophet. And the young man said, "You see yourself riding high, don't you? Riding the crest of the wave—the Wave of the Future, you call it. But there's a deep, dark undertow that you don't see, and that's a part of the Past. And the Present and even your Future. There is evil in mankind that is blacker even than your evil, and infinitely more ancient."

And there was something in the shadows behind the young man, something little and lean and brown.

Tallant's dream did not disturb him the following morning. Nor did the thought of the approaching interview with Morgan. He fried his bacon and eggs and devoured them cheerfully. The wind had died down for a change, and the sun was warm enough so that he could strip to the waist while he cleared land for his shack. His machete glinted brilliantly as it swung through the air and struck at the roots of the brush.

When Morgan arrived his full face was red and sweating.

"It's cool over there in the shade of the adobe," Tallant suggested. "We'll be more comfortable." And in the comfortable shade of the adobe he swung the machete once and clove Morgan's full, red, sweating face in two.

It was so simple. It took less effort than uprooting a clump of sage. And it was so safe. Morgan lived in a cabin way to hell-and-gone and was often away on prospecting trips. No one would notice his absence for months, if then. No one had any reason to connect him with Tallant. And no one in Oasis would hunt for him in the Carker-haunted adobe.

The body was heavy, and the blood dripped warm on Tallant's bare skin. With relief he dumped what had been Morgan on the floor of the adobe. There were no boards, no flooring. Just the earth. Hard, but not too hard to dig a grave in. And no one was likely to come poking around in this taboo territory to notice the grave. Let a year or so go by, and the grave and the bones it contained would be attributed to the Carkers.

The corner of Tallant's eye bothered him again. Deliberately he looked about the interior of the adobe.

The little furniture was crude and heavy, with no attempt to smooth down the strokes of the ax. It was held together with wooden pegs or half-rotted thongs. There were age-old cinders in the fireplace, and the dusty shards of a cooking jar among them.

And there was a deeply hollowed stone, covered with stains that might have been rust, if stone rusted. Behind it was a tiny figure, clumsily fashioned of clay and sticks. It was something like a man and something like a lizard, and something like the things that flit across the corner of the eye.

Curious now, Tallant peered about further. He penetrated to the corner that the one unglassed window lighted but dimly. And there he let out a little choking gasp. For a moment he was rigid with horror. Then he smiled and all but laughed aloud.

This explained everything. Some curious individual had seen this, and from his accounts had burgeoned the whole legend. The Carkers had indeed learned something from the Indians, but that secret was the art of embalming.

It was a perfect mummy. Either the Indian art had shrunk bodies, or this was that of a ten-year-old boy. There was no flesh. Only skin and bone and taut, dry stretches of tendon between. The eyelids were closed; the sockets looked hollow under them. The nose was sunken and almost lost. The scant lips were tightly curled back from the long and very white teeth, which stood forth all the more brilliantly against the deep-brown skin.

It was a curious little trove, this mummy. Tallant was already calculating the chances for raising a decent sum of money from an interested anthropologist—murder can produce such delightfully profitable chance by-products—when he noticed the infinitesimal rise and fall of the chest.

The Carker was not dead. It was sleeping.

Tallant did not dare stop to think beyond the instant. This was no time to pause to consider if such things were possible in a well-ordered world. It was no time to reflect on the disposal of the body of Morgan. It was a time to snatch up your machete and get out of there.

But in the doorway he halted. There, coming across the desert, heading for the adobe, clearly seen this time, was another—a female.

He made an involuntary gesture of indecision. The blade of the machete clanged ringingly against the adobe wall. He heard the dry shuffling of a roused sleeper behind him.

He turned fully now, the machete raised. Dispose of this nearer one first, then face the female. There was no room even for terror in his thoughts, only for action.

The lean brown shape darted at him avidly. He moved lightly away and stood poised for its second charge. It shot forward again. He took one step back, machete arm raised, and fell headlong over the corpse of Morgan. Before he could rise, the thin thing was upon him. Its sharp teeth had met through the palm of his left hand.

The machete moved swiftly. The thin dry body fell headless to the floor. There was no blood.

The grip of the teeth did not relax. Pain coursed up Tallant's left arm—a sharper, more bitter pain than you would expect from the bite. Almost as though venom—

He dropped the machete, and his strong white hand plucked and twisted at the dry brown lips. The teeth stayed clenched, unrelaxing. He sat bracing his back against the wall and gripped the head between his knees. He pulled. His flesh ripped, and blood formed dusty clots on the dirt floor. But the bite was firm.

His world had become reduced now to that hand and that head. Nothing outside mattered. He must free himself. He raised his aching arm to his face, and with his own teeth he tore at that unrelenting grip. The dry flesh crumbled away in desert dust, but the teeth were locked fast. He tore his lip against their white keenness, and tasted in his mouth the sweetness of blood and something else.

He staggered to his feet again. He knew what he must do. Later he could use cautery, a tourniquet, see a doctor with a story about a Gila monster—their heads grip too, don't they?—but he knew what he must do now.

He raised the machete and struck again.

His white hand lay on the brown floor, gripped by the white teeth in the brown face. He propped himself against the adobe wall, momentarily unable to move. His open wrist hung over the deeply hollowed stone. His blood and his strength and his life poured out before the little figure of sticks and clay.

The female stood in the doorway now, the sun bright on her thin brownness. She did not move. He knew that she was waiting for the hollow stone to fill.

CAROLE BUGGÉ

Miracle at Chimayo

CAROLE BUGGÉ *is a professional actor-singer and one of the hilariously inventive stars of the New York improvisational comedy ensemble Chicago City Limits. Her story "Miracle at Chimayo," partly inspired by a visit to Taos, New Mexico, is a conscientiously crafted pastiche of a peasant folktale.*

In all his twelve years as prelate of the parish of Chimayo, Father José Guarrez del Río had never slept so badly. Several times during the night he rose from his bed and, throwing the sheets off, walked restlessly to his bedroom window, which overlooked the high road to Taos from Santa Fe, with the hills swelling up on either side of it. "Breasts of Mother Nature" was what the Indians called these hills, and Father José mused that once again the Indians had said it exactly right. The mountains were like breasts, soft and full, and mysterious as Nature herself.

As he stood barefoot at the window, he saw a singularly bright flash of lightning off in the hills, followed by an enormous clap of thunder that made him jump. The lightning continued for some time, a dazzling display of jagged streaks, all ending at the same point off in the hills. The strange thing, he was to recall later, was that the night sky remained perfectly cloudless—throughout this entire disturbance he could see all the constellations perfectly. As

Father José stood at his window, the words of a prayer formed themselves in his mind of their own accord, and as they did Father José whispered them softly to himself.

"Preserve, O Lord, Thy son who walks tonight in peril—shield him from the Evil One and let him walk in love. . . . Amen," he added, when no more words came.

Manuel Gutiérrez needed a miracle. It was not for himself, but for someone else that he needed this miracle, and that was why he was so certain he could get it. Because it was not for him, not even for his family, he was sure that the famous black *Cristo* of Chimayo would grant him this miracle. So Manuel decided to go on a pilgrimage to see the holy *Cristo* in person, to ask him to make Marissa Sánchez well again. No one knew what exactly was wrong with Marissa Sánchez, not even the tall Anglo doctor from Santa Fe who came to see her in his big shiny black car; all they knew was that for three weeks now she had lain in her bed, pale and exhausted, refusing all food but the thick broth Manuel's grandmother made her. At night she woke with the fever, sweating and shivering in her long white bed, and sometimes at twilight she would see visions of the Virgin Mary or Saint Anthony, patron saint of lost things.

"I must be a lost soul," she would say after these visions, "or why would Saint Anthony come to visit me?"

Manuel went to see her every day, bringing her hot soup straight from his grandmother's kitchen. He would walk carefully across the dirt lot that separated their houses, holding the soup tureen out in front of him so as not to spill a drop; he even developed a superstitious feeling that if he did spill any soup it would delay Marissa's recovery. And Manuel was convinced she would recover, even though his grandmother shook her head and sighed whenever they talked about it. Manuel had known Marissa all his life; they were the exact same age, born on the same day in the year of the great rains. That was a heady year for their village, his grandmother told him, a year when all the crops doubled their harvest and many of the ewes bore twin lambs—a strange and portentous year. It was also the year that brought the death of Manuel's mother—she lived to see him born, but died less than an hour later. A death from childbirth was not unusual in the village, but her loss was obscene in that year of opulence and plenty. Manuel's father, an earnest, deliberate man, could not seem to grasp that she was really gone, and it was said that he wandered from room to room clutching the nightgown in which she had died, humming softly to himself an Andalusian folk song which she used to sing. One night he just wandered right out of the village and towards the mountains and was never seen again. The Tewa Indians of the region went on "spirit walks" in these hills, on which they claimed to commune with ghosts of their dead ancestors, but everyone in Manuel's village feared going into the mountains, especially alone. Juan Valdez was the only other person in Manuel's tiny village of Tesuque who had ever gone into the mountains alone; a few months after the disappearance of Manuel's father he wandered in drunk one night and he had returned not quite right in the head, claiming that he had joined an Indian spirit walk and spoken to many shades from the other world. Some people in the village whispered that Manuel's father was one of the spirits Valdez saw.

Manuel's grandmother had been running the household since his mother's death, and after his father's disappearance she just had one less man to look after. Now she and Manuel lived alone together in the low adobe house with its red tiled clay roof. They were never lonely; Manuel's grandmother was a masterful story-teller, so good that the children in the village could recite many of her tales by heart: there was the story of Juan Gonzalez of Taos, the great horseman who raced the devil and won eternal life, or the story of Jesús Ortiz of Madrid, who could understand the language of birds and so saved his village from the devastation of a tornado—all of these were true stories, of course, and on the first Tuesday of every month the children of the village would gather to hear Manuel's grandmother tell a new one. Sitting under the grape arbor in her garden, her skirts billowing out around her, she was like a brooding hen surrounded by her chicks. Marissa was always there, the first to arrive and the last to leave; but then Marissa was always there most evenings, and she and Manuel would play in the garden until the sun sank behind the mountains and his grandmother called them in for soup and beans.

But now Marissa was sick, and Manuel didn't know what to do

with himself in the evenings. When he brought the soup over to Marissa, her mother, a long, pale woman who always appeared to be wincing, would take the steaming pot from him and tell him Marissa had said this or that during her fever last night, and Manuel would nod gravely, kicking gently at the yellow kernels of chicken feed that lay in the dusty front yard of Marissa's house, waiting for her mother to tell him he could go in and visit Marissa. Sometimes she was "too sick" to see him; her mother was afraid he would wear her out, but sometimes her mother would just shrug her thin shoulders and motion him into the house. He would walk quietly, carefully across the smooth stone kitchen floor and into the little back room where Marissa's bed stood, under the window with the flowering mimosa tree outside. Sometimes she was dozing when he came in, and he would sit in the leather-backed chair next to her bed for a long time before she woke up, and seeing him sitting there, she would smile and brush with her hand at the damp wisps of hair that clung to her forehead.

They never talked about her illness, as if talking about it might empower it; they just ignored it as one might ignore a *duende*, a goblin, lurking in the corner of dark rooms at night. Manuel would tell her his grandmother's latest story, or tell her about how Juan Romero's mule escaped from his pen and ate several bags of chicken feed before being spotted, or about how Jorges Cardoso had challenged Carmen Silveira to a duel but then got so drunk in the back of his brother's rusting pickup truck that he never showed up and now, disgraced, muttered his revenge into his beer mug, but nobody took him seriously anymore. Marissa liked to hear these stories, and she would laugh softly and tell Manuel he had inherited his grandmother's talent. But now, after three weeks, Marissa was paler and weaker, and her hands lay folded on the white sheets while Manuel told his stories, and she often stared out at the mimosa tree, which was losing its blossoms.

On the third Friday of Marissa's illness Manuel stood in his bedroom looking at the pictures that sat on his thick old oak dresser. Manuel kept two pictures in his room: one was of his father, wearing a battered old sombrero and squinting into the bright sunlight. The other was a yellowed postcard of the Santuario at Chimayo that his father brought to his mother while she was carrying Manuel. He had no picture of his mother; she was superstitious like her mother and believed that cameras evidenced the hand of Satan and that if you possessed the image of someone you had power over them.

Manuel gazed at the picture of the Santuario. He thought of the many stories his grandmother had told about the powers of the miraculous church, powers celebrated since the day of its erection upon ground long sacred to the Tewa Indians of the region. The legend of the Santuario was well known: on a Good Friday early in the 1800s, the head of a local family saw a burst of light which fell on the spot where the church now stands. Something compelled him to dig at the place in the ground where the light fell, and when he did he found a crucifix with a dark green cross and a darkened Christ figure. The "Black Christ" is worshiped all over South America, and this one, some said, resembled the crucifixes carved in Esquipulas, Guatemala. News of the miraculous discovery traveled quickly, and the man, believing the crucifix had helped him recover from a lingering illness, financed the building of a church on the very spot.

The Santuario was constructed near springs that the Tewa Indians felt had healing properties. In the floor of the back room of the church, to the left of the altar, is the Well of Miraculous Healing, a deep hole in the ground filled with clay soil. Every year thousands of visitors come to take small bits of dirt from the well, which they rub on injured or diseased areas of the body; some actually eat the dirt. Some carry the precious dirt, carefully wrapped in pouches, for thousands of miles to sick friends or relatives. The people of Chimayo claim that the well stands on the exact spot where the *Cristo* was dug up, and they believe that one day the well will refill itself, and that this will be proof of its miraculous powers. Manuel's father once visited the Santuario at Chimayo to get some dirt from the Well of Miraculous Healing to ensure that the baby when it was born would be a healthy one. Manuel had been a robust baby, brown and fat; only his mother had languished, worn out by the long struggle of birth.

As Manuel stood there in his bedroom an idea came to him, as suddenly as a summer thunderstorm: he would go to Chimayo!

He would ask the famed black *Cristo* to make Marissa well again. If he left the next morning he could be there by Sunday, in time for the early service, and he reasoned that the *Cristo* would be most in the mood to grant miracles on the Sabbath. As he stepped across the hot, hard dirt lot, carrying the soup, a fresh chicken broth with *posole,* he made up his mind that he would tell Marissa. She should know, and he would be very firm and explain that nothing she could say would change his mind. When he got to the front door, it was so quiet inside that at first he thought no one was home. He knocked softly, cradling the soup under one arm. Around him, the mourning doves began to coo softly in the bushes. There was no sound from inside the house.

Manuel peered into the cool, dark interior and could make out the tall, thin form of Marissa's mother gliding from room to room. He knocked again, a little louder. The form stopped, then began to move toward him, as noiselessly as a shadow. She appeared at the door and nodded to Manuel, reaching for the soup dish. Manuel spoke hastily, almost choking in his eagerness.

"Can I speak to Marissa?"

Her mother shook her head slowly.

"She's asleep, and she didn't sleep well last night. Could you come back tomorrow?"

Manuel paused, deciding how much of his plan he should reveal.

"I will be away for a while," he said, lowering his eyes. "Tell her I'll see her Monday."

Her mother looked at him, her eyes narrowing with puzzlement. Except for these past three weeks, Manuel and Marissa had not gone a day of their lives without seeing each other; Manuel's abrupt, unexplained pronouncement had no precedent. For a moment she looked as though she were going to question him, but then she shrugged, her characteristic gesture, and turned back into the silent house.

Manuel stood in the yard and felt the evening closing in on the village. His belly began to tingle with the anticipation of travel. Tomorrow he would be on the road to Chimayo, on a journey that would change everything. He turned towards his house just as Paloma Rodriguez's cock, who always crowed at dusk instead of dawn, began a series of high, hoarse shrieks. He turned back to look at Marissa's house. The kitchen light glowed briefly and then went off. Somewhere in the hills a dog howled.

The next morning Manuel woke up as the first streak of daylight began to creep across the sky. He had packed clothes the night before and now, creeping past his grandmother's room, laid his pack softly on the kitchen table and pulled a loaf of bread, a few corn tortillas, some goat cheese and a can of beans from the cupboard, and stuffed them into his bag.

He went back into his room to see if he had forgotten anything. As he stepped into the room the picture of his father fluttered off the dresser and onto the floor right in front of him. He bent to pick it up and then, without knowing why, he slipped it into his breast pocket. Then Manuel returned to the kitchen and laid a carefully worded note to his grandmother in the middle of the kitchen table where she could not miss it. In it he apologized for not telling her but was afraid she would have tried to stop him.

"I'm sorry," he wrote, "for taking food without asking."

Manuel knew perfectly well that his grandmother would gladly starve for his sake; this last was merely a tactic to make his note appear more contrite.

He shouldered his pack and walked into the yard. The day was breaking, clear and hot, over the Sangre de Cristo mountains. He walked to where Negrito, their ugly black horse, was tethered. Negrito, his head hanging low on his scrawny neck, either was asleep or pretending to be. Negrito was the ugliest horse in the village. He was also the best: smart, strong and surefooted, his only flaw was a certain willfulness which emerged from time to time. Many people had offered Manuel's grandmother good money for Negrito; she refused all offers, saying a horse like that had no price. Even Orlando Ortega, who already owned six horses, wanted to buy Negrito. "He is a very good horse," Orlando had proclaimed. "He is a very ugly horse, but a very good horse." Besides being fast, Negrito could count to ten, dance on his hind legs, and—so Manuel's grandmother claimed—he possessed the ability to see spirits. One of her more famous stories concerned the time he saw a swarm of *diablos rojos* hovering over Old Man Díaz's roof. Manuel remembered the day she told it:

they were all sitting out by the flowering yucca bush in the garden, Marissa with her head leaning on Manuel's shoulder, Manuel's grandmother sitting on her stool, her skirt spread out like a sail in a gusty wind.

"Juan Díaz had not taken a drop of drink in twenty years," she said in a low voice rich with foreboding, "and everyone knew he avoided the bottle as though it were Death itself. Well, your father, Manuel, went riding by the Díaz house one night and Negrito was so upset by something he saw—he began to rear and paw the ground, and nearly threw your father—that your father went to speak to Díaz about it the next day. And what do you think?" She paused for effect, and the only sound in the garden was the buzzing of the black flies and the quick, light scurry of an occasional lizard. They all leaned closer in to Manuel's grandmother.

"He was found the next day with a nearly empty bottle of whiskey, muttering about *diablos rojos* on his roof causing his delirium. Three days later he died of alcohol poisoning. Now that's a talented horse."

But now this talented animal stood with his lower lip almost touching the ground, his ratty-looking tail hanging limply. Manuel walked up to him and whispered softly into his ear.

"Negrito," he said, "would you like to go on a journey?"

The horse opened one eye and regarded Manuel languidly. He seemed to be considering the question. Manuel went on talking as he threw a saddle blanket over Negrito's back.

"We will travel through the mountains," he said in a soothing voice, "and we will see the famous black *Cristo* in person." Manuel then quickly saddled and bridled Negrito, who stood patiently and took the bit without even sticking his tongue out as he sometimes did. Manuel untied him, strapped his pack to the saddle and mounted. He touched the horse's sides lightly; Negrito gave a disgusted snort and stepped out onto the main road which led out of the village and towards the mountains.

As Negrito ambled along, Manuel took out the map he had brought from his pack. There was only one road to Chimayo, but Manuel intended to leave it and take a shorter route through the mountains. His grandmother would certainly have disapproved of this plan.

"Spirits roam those hills at dusk," she would say, tilting her head so that her intense black eyes gazed straight into Manuel's. "There is no doubt that your father was carried away by a *duende* —a goblin!"

Manuel did not believe in these things and thought his grandmother's superstition a sign of weakness.

As horse and rider walked along, the sun rose higher in the sky. It felt hot on Manuel's back. The baked earth was yellow and cracked; dried-up arroyos snaked off into the distance on either side of the road. The map, spread out across the pommel of the saddle, reflected the hot sun onto Manuel's face. He began to feel sleepy. Negrito walked as though he were indeed still asleep, carrying his head low and only flicking occasionally with his tail at the black flies that darted around his ears and eyes.

The sun had started its afternoon descent when they came to the point in the road where Manuel planned to turn off into the mountains. He pulled slightly on the reins. Negrito was extremely sensitive to the wishes of his rider; at times you only had to think about where you wanted to go and Negrito would head there—but to Manuel's surprise, Negrito ignored him and kept on walking. Manuel pulled the reins again, this time a little harder. Still Negrito did not alter his course or even break stride. Exasperated, Manuel called his name sharply.

"Negrito!" The word broke the still air. Negrito stopped abruptly and turned his head to look at Manuel, as if urging him to reconsider. "Are you sure you want to do this?" his large, intelligent eyes seemed to say. Manuel felt irritated. A strange feeling had begun to creep up his spine, but he ignored it and jabbed at Negrito's sides. Negrito hated being kicked; it was an indignity for such an intelligent horse. With a snort he turned off the road at a trot.

They headed west toward the setting sun, across a flat scrub plain which soon gave way to the foothills of the Sangre de Cristo mountains. High above them, a red-tailed hawk circled the sky. The air began to grow cooler, and Manuel, feeling the evening chill on his skin, realized he had not eaten all day. They were in the woods now, and he could hear the slow trickle of a brook through the trees. He pulled back on the reins and Negrito stopped under a tall Douglas fir. Manuel got off, feeling very stiff from the long ride. He led Negrito to the stream—they were both very thirsty and drank for a long time. Then he spread out a cloth on the ground and sat to eat his meal of bread and cheese. Negrito grazed around him. It was cool in the forest, and the slanting rays of the dying sun cast long shadows all around them, making the trees look even taller than they really were. The moss they call old-man's beard hung like grey lace from the tree branches.

Manuel finished eating and lay down on the blanket to rest. He could hear Negrito munching grass close by. The only other sounds were the forest birds, the rippling brook, and the wind high in the trees. He fell into a deep sleep and dreamed: a man roaming through woods very like these was calling his name, but no sound came out of his mouth. His lips formed "Manuel" over and over again, but the air itself sucked up the sound of his voice. He looked sad. Manuel strained to make out the features of his face but couldn't. The man raised his hand as if in warning. Manuel tried to call to him, but a shadow fell over his eyes and he could not see him anymore.

A change in the air made Manuel shiver slightly in his sleep. He did not see a tall form approaching through the underbrush, walking slowly with heavy steps. Negrito saw, however, and began to paw the ground and toss his head. He whinnied—a low, rumbling sound of alarm. Manuel stirred in his sleep but did not wake. The dark figure approached and bent over him. A long, thin hand extended from beneath his long cape. Negrito, whinnying loudly, stood on his hind legs and pawed the air near the stranger's head, causing him to cringe momentarily. Manuel awoke with a start. Standing over him was a tall, gaunt man with hollow cheeks and white, bloodless skin. He was dressed in a long flowing cape and high, polished black boots. He bowed politely, holding a wide black hat in his long, pale hands.

"A thousand pardons if I startled you, good sir," he said in a dry, rasping voice, "but I chanced to come upon you slumbering by your trusty steed here"—with this he indicated Negrito, who snorted and tossed his head—"and it occurred to me that we might join forces and travel together, if indeed our journeys lie along the same path."

Manuel rubbed his eyes and stared at the man. He wondered at his formal, curiously archaic speech.

"May I inquire whither you are headed, my good sir?" the man went on, fingering his hat and cautiously moving away from Negrito, who had fixed his eye on him.

"To Chimayo, to the Santuario," answered Manuel. "I am on a pilgrimage there."

"Ah! A fine thing, a pilgrimage," cried the man. "We should all take pilgrimages . . . tell me, is it then possible, good countryman, that I might join you? I have traveled these woods many"— here he smiled strangely—"years . . . and I might be of some assistance."

"Are you too on a pilgrimage?" Manuel asked.

"Some might call it that," the tall stranger replied, "but if you'll forgive me, I must say that I find definitions"—here he paused as if searching for the right word—"confining. It is, perhaps, one of my quirks." He smiled broadly, showing a gold tooth.

The sun had set while Manuel was sleeping and now the moon was rising above the firs and quaking aspen, casting its pallid white light on the little group in the clearing. The stranger pointed to the moon. As he did, a shadow flicked across its surface and then was gone. "The moon is full tonight," said the man amiably. "We might travel by its light awhile, if you are game."

Manuel rubbed his hand through his hair and stretched. He did feel rested after his nap—he felt he had never slept so deeply. "All right," he said, stooping to pick up his blanket.

"If you wish I will help you pack," said the stranger, and with that he began carefully to fold Manuel's blanket. As he did, Negrito pranced about nervously, kicking at the ground, neighing softly. He nudged Manuel with his nose.

"What is it, Negrito?" Manuel wondered at his horse's strange behavior. Meanwhile, the stranger carefully walked around Negrito, staying far from his hooves. He handed the blanket to Manuel, who strapped it to the saddle and climbed up.

"Would you like to take turns riding and walking?" he asked the man.

"Oh, thank you kindly but I never got along with—horses," the man said smoothly. "They frighten me, and besides, I am a good walker and don't tire easily.

"By the way," he said as they started off through the moonlit forest, "allow me to introduce myself. I am Señor Theda."

"My name is Manuel Gutiérrez."

"It is my pleasure to make your acquaintance," said Señor Theda, bowing his low, formal bow, "the more so as I had the pleasure of knowing your father." Manuel thought he chuckled slightly to himself. He wanted to ask Señor Theda how he had known his father but something stopped his tongue and again he felt a creeping sensation up his spine.

They walked on through the moonlit forest for a long time, hardly speaking. Señor Theda led the way—he was indeed a good walker, and after several hours seemed even less tired than Manuel, though he rode Negrito. The hypnotic motion of the horse's rolling gait made Manuel so sleepy he felt he must lie down. They came to another clearing, where pine needles on the ground made a soft bed to lie on, and there they stopped. Manuel unrolled his blanket and lay down. It was then he noticed that Señor Theda had no baggage, not even a back pack.

"Would you like to share my blanket?" he asked.

"Oh, thank you, but I require little sleep; I will sit here and keep watch while you sleep," answered Señor Theda, sitting on the root of a tall corkbark fir. Manuel shrugged and lay down; he was too tired to wonder further. Within seconds he was asleep. Again he fell into a deep slumber, and again he dreamed. This time he dreamed he was alone in this same clearing in the woods and saw Señor Theda approaching through the trees. Manuel walked to meet him. The shadows of the trees fell over the tall man's face, though, and he could not make out the features under the wide-brimmed hat. But then, when he was only a few feet away from Señor Theda, a gust of wind blew off the hat to reveal a horrible grinning death's head that laughed as bony arms reached for Manuel's throat. Manuel tried to run but could not move—his limbs had turned to ice. The long skeletal fingers encircled his neck—the black, vacant eye holes in the skinless face glowed red and again the creature laughed, a raucous, hollow sound that echoed through the branches and was carried away by the wind.

Manuel cried out and woke suddenly, bathed in sweat. His hand instinctively reached for the picture of his father in his breast pocket, but it was gone. He looked around him wildly. Señor Theda was gone, and so was Negrito. Manuel jumped up.

"Negrito!" he shouted. "Negrito! Where are you?" He stumbled through the underbrush, calling Negrito over and over. He heard the horse's frantic whinny, farther on through the trees. He ran, disregarding the brambles that scratched his face and arms. Vines clung to his ankles, tripping him, but still he ran. There ahead in a clearing was Negrito, rearing and stamping at something on the ground.

"Negrito!" Manuel cried. The horse stopped abruptly and backed away, shivering and panting. Manuel walked to the spot where the horse had been and saw, lying on the ground, Señor Theda's black, silk-lined cape. He bent to pick it up. As his hand closed on it he felt the air suddenly grow colder. A feeling of terror engulfed him and he let the cape drop to the ground. Then suddenly, behind him, he heard the terrible, chilling laughter of his dream. He whirled around. There, at the edge of the clearing, stood Señor Theda.

"You thought you could cheat me of the girl," he said in a voice as parched and dry as yellowed leaves of paper. "Where is your magic *Cristo* now? I'll get your little girlfriend, and now I've got you!"

Señor Theda started towards Manuel, laughing, and as he did, his face dissolved into the horrible skeletal mask of Manuel's dream. His bony claws reached for Manuel's throat. He threw back his head and laughed and again the taunting sound echoed through the forest. Manuel shut his eyes and waited helplessly for the terrible fingers to close around his neck. . . .

But just as Manuel felt he was about to faint from fear, another sound pierced the air of the forest. It rose above Señor Theda's mocking laughter, above the roaring in Manuel's ears. It was a voice, a human voice, a cry of rage and pain. "Noooooo!" the voice wailed. "Noooooo!" Manuel opened his eyes. The thing that had been Señor Theda stopped and looked around wildly. Manuel saw the one who had made the sound running through the trees. It was the same sad man who wordlessly tried to call to Manuel in his dream, but now he had a voice and Manuel could make out his features—it was his father! He ran with great long strides and leapt into the clearing.

"Stop! I forbid it!" he cried, raising his arms.

"You!" snarled Death. "What makes you think you can defeat me?"

"You have no power over me now," said Manuel's father, "and I know your weakness."

"Ha!" sneered Death. "Try and stop me!" With that he brandished a small bit of paper in his terrible twisted claw. It was the photograph of Manuel's father. "Back!" cried Death in his hideous, raspy voice.

Manuel saw his father stagger and clutch his head. Unable to contain himself any longer, Manuel cried out. His father turned toward him. His face expressed infinite suffering and tenderness.

"Get—the—picture!" he gasped. Before Death could turn toward him, Manuel sprang up behind him and grabbed the photograph. With a howl, Death spun around to face Manuel, his ghastly skeletal face a mask of fury and rage. He lunged at Manuel, who staggered back towards Negrito, rearing and pawing the air with his hooves.

"Run, Manuel," cried his father. "Fly! Walk in love always, and DO NOT LOOK BACK! "

With that, he leapt with a roar upon the figure of Death. An unearthly light enveloped the struggling figures. Manuel froze for a second and started towards them to help his father, but his father shouted in an anguished voice.

"Go! Keep love in your heart and go! Go now!"

Without thinking, Manuel stumbled towards Negrito, who stood with flared nostrils and wild eyes. Manuel climbed on his back and immediately the horse lunged forward and galloped out of the clearing through the woods. Manuel clung to his mane as trees whizzed past them. Behind him, he heard an inhuman cry of fury and rage. He wanted to turn and look, but his father's words still echoed in his ears, so Manuel hugged Negrito's neck and buried his face in his mane.

"Chimayo, Negrito," he whispered. "Go to Chimayo!" And so they raced through the black night. Streaks of lightning pierced the sky and thunderclaps rolled above them. Still Negrito ran, with Manuel clinging to his charging neck.

It seemed to Manuel as if they raced on for hours, but he had lost all sense of time and space. The wood stretched out in front of them, the night seemed endless. Manuel could hear Negrito's breath coming in thick gasps and felt his own aching ribs were about to crack. Trees swirled in front of him like dark phantoms, their branches grotesque, twisted fingers that seemed to reach towards him as Negrito pounded by, his hooves kicking up clods of soft black soil.

As he rode, Manuel drifted into an exhausted semiconsciousness in which he saw vague images of people: Marissa's pale face loomed before his eyes; he saw his grandmother, and then his father, who was smiling with a weary, loving smile. Then Manuel in his delirious state thought he saw his father's face dissolve into another, the face of a young priest with straight black hair and a serious expression. His eyes, though, were the eyes of Manuel's father.

Negrito emerged from the trees into a wide field of tall grass. The sky was growing light—dawn was approaching. On the other side of the field Manuel could see, snaking through the hills, the road to Chimayo. Negrito stopped and Manuel climbed off, exhausted. His knees failed him; his legs folded under him and he collapsed on the ground, weeping.

"Father," he said. "Oh, Father . . . Thank you . . ."

Negrito stood beside him, panting heavily. Around them the birds of the field began their busy chatter as dawn threw its fingers of light across the sky.

"Preserve, O Lord, Thy son who walks tonight in peril—shield him from the Evil One and let him walk in love. . . . Amen."

Father José stood before his bedroom window shivering slightly in the night air. As he peered into the blackness, the moon, which had been obscured by a thick grey cloud, suddenly emerged and shone over the valley, lighting up the fields of Chimayo with its cool white light. Father José thought about the prayer which he had just recited. This was not the first time that prayers had come to him unbidden; in fact, this phenomenon began when he became prelate of the Santuario. Often he would meet, a day or a week later, the person for whom the prayer must have been intended; most often it was someone he had never met, and someone who had come to the Santuario for a miracle, or just for comfort, as many people came every day. Sometimes he would never meet the person, but a letter would appear in the next few days thanking him and the holy Santuario for a healing, a piece of good news, unexpected good luck. If he were a vain man he would have ascribed these powers to his own holiness, but as he was a humble, modest man, he believed himself to be acting on behalf of the strange powers of the miraculous Santuario.

As he stood by the open window with the cool night air rustling the white curtains, Father José remembered the day twelve years ago he had come to Chimayo from his monastery. He had intended to become a monk, but when he was still a novice he dreamed three nights in a row of a chapel by a stream under the shadow of tall mountains, and his Father Superior told him that this dream meant he was not meant for the sequestered life and that he must go to Chimayo; that the old priest there had just died and he was needed there. When Father José saw Chimayo, he instantly felt he had been there before, and that he had come back home. He looked across the open field to the flashing lightning in the hills and crossed himself.

As suddenly as it began, the lightning and thunder stopped. All was silent, and Father José could hear the soft coo of a night owl in the garden below him. Crossing himself again, he turned from the window and went back to bed. This time he fell asleep immediately and slept a dreamless sleep until daybreak. Somewhere in the hills a wolf howled.

Father José awoke feeling refreshed and without the depression which had visited him the night before. He rose early as he always did, and as it was Sunday, went to his kitchen table to put the finishing touches on his sermon. He sat down with his breakfast—a cup of hot, strong coffee and sopapillas with honey which his housekeeper María had made the night before—when something, some movement outside the window, caught his eye.

Out across the field behind the church, the field from which the mountains rose so steeply and majestically, he saw what at first he thought to be an apparition—a small figure on a scrawny black horse, walking slowly out of the mist toward him. Everything about the sight—the boy's bent shoulders and drooping head, the labored, dragging walk of the horse—suggested utter physical and spiritual exhaustion.

Father José immediately rose from the table and ran out the door toward them. He jumped across the small stream that separated the open field from the churchyard and ran full tilt across the field, his cassock flapping about him like useless brown wings. Reaching the pair, Father José, without saying a word, grabbed the bridle of the horse, who stopped immediately, gratefully. Father José reached up to the boy, gently pulled him out of the saddle and carried him in his arms. He led the horse across the stream to the soft, shady lawn of the outdoor chapel. The boy, insensate in his arms, had fallen asleep at once. Father José put him in his own bed and closed the curtains.

It was not until he sat back down to his coffee that Father José paused to reflect and realized that he had just encountered the reason for his impromptu prayer of the previous night. He did not question this or spend much time wondering about it—he was accustomed by now to accepting things he could not fully understand.

After he finished writing his sermon, Father José got up and went to the church with a pail of sand to refill the hole. He could not have said he felt something was different, and yet his heart began to beat hard against his ribs as he entered the Santuario.

The Santuario itself is an old adobe structure with high vaulted ceilings with the characteristic *lattias,* or crossbeams, dark wooden floors and *santos,* or portraits of the saints, on its walls. On the altar is a replica of the famed black *Cristo* dug up by the founder of the church. Softly burning candles light the cool chamber from within as the sun streaming in through the stained-glass windows lights it from without.

It is in the rear alcoves of the church that the spirit of the Santuario is most evident. Lining the walls of the two dark, cramped chambers are curios, *bultos,* or statues of the saints, cards and letters, crutches, and maudlin pictures of the bleeding, tortured Christ, a touching testimony to human suffering and hope. In the tiny rearmost room is the renowned Well of Miraculous Healing. The room's only light comes from one small window and scores of constantly burning votive candles. In this tiny back room, on a wall overlooking the well, is the actual black Christ dug up by the founder of the church.

The interior of the Santuario was cool and quiet; filtered sunlight streamed in through the stained-glass windows. Father José shivered as the heavy wooden door closed behind him. His steps echoed on the stone floor as he approached the altar. As he did, the *bulto* of Saint James, known locally as Señor Santiago de Chimayo, caught his eye. The statue depicts Saint James of Compostela (who was so revered that Spanish soldiers sometimes cried "Santiago!" when riding into battle) as a *caballero* with boots, straw hat and sword, astride a horse. Father José thought he saw a glint of sunlight reflecting off the statue's glass case. Again he shivered. He turned to enter the rear room, and stopped at the entrance, took a deep breath. . . .

The room was still. Light flickering from the single window fell across the threshold onto the stones at his feet. He peered around the corner, half expecting to see something terrible, and then—

The well of dirt was filled!

At first Father José stood there motionless, trying to collect his thoughts; then he raced to the church bell and began ringing it madly, shouting, "Miracle! It's a miracle—a true miracle!"

Everyone who was in the town that day heard the bells ringing long before the scheduled service, and everyone dropped what they were doing and came running. They found Father José on his knees kissing the dirt. He showed everyone what had happened, blessing them all, laughing and crying all at once.

Some say that Father José carried on his shoulders a small black-haired boy of about twelve whom no one had ever seen before, and that the priest cried, "He has brought a miracle. He is holy!" Some even claim this boy was the Christ Child returned to earth and that all the people fell to their knees, blessing him. It is well documented, though, that a huge celebration took place that day in Chimayo, with feasting and thanksgiving, and that a week later the Bishop himself paid a visit to Father José.

Of the disappearance of the boy not much is known: some say they saw him, astride a horrible-looking black horse, riding off into the hills at dusk. Others say he simply vanished into the valley mist which descends quickly in the evenings. But it is also said that a week later Father José received a letter with no postmark, a letter he keeps in his dresser drawer. In it is a picture of a small dark-haired boy and a thin, pale-looking girl. They are sitting together on the steps of a low adobe building, smiling in the bright sunshine.

The letter ends with the words, "Dear Father, walk in love always."

RICHARD MATHESON

Slaughter House

RICHARD MATHESON *is, in my opinion, America's greatest living horror writer. He is the author of many grim tales and novels, including "Night-mare at 20,000 Feet" (one of* Twilight Zone's *most popular episodes), "Blood Son,"* What Dreams May Come, A Stir of Echoes, *two twice-filmed books,* I Am Legend *and* The Incredible Shrinking Man, *and the haunted house novel,* Hell House. *Here is another grim Matheson tale of a ghost-ridden mansion. The location of Slaughter House is not mentioned anywhere in the story, but I couldn't bear to omit it from* Haunted America, *so I included it in the West because the author resides in California.*

I submit for your consideration the following manuscript which was mailed to this office some weeks ago. It is presented with neither evidence nor judgment as to its validity. This determination is for the reader to make.

SAMUEL D. MACHILDON,
Associate Secretary, Rand Society for Psychical Research

This occurred many years ago. My brother Saul and I had taken a fancy to the old, tenantless Slaughter House. Since we were boys the yellow-edged pronouncement—*For Sale*—had hung lopsided in the grimy front window. We had vowed with boyish ambition that, when we were old enough, the sign must come down.

When we had attained our manhood, this aspiration somehow remained. We had a taste for the Victorian, Saul and I. His painting was akin to that roseate and buxom transcription of nature so endeared by the nineteenth-century artists. And my writing, though far from satisfactory realization, bore the definite stamp of prolixity, was marked by that meticulous sweep of ornate phrase which the modernists decry as dullness and artifice.

Thus, for the headquarters of our artistic labors, what better retreat than the Slaughter House, that structure which matched in cornice and frieze our intimate partialities? None, we decided, and acted readily on that decision.

The yearly endowment arranged by our deceased parents, albeit meager, we knew to suffice, since the house was in gross need of repair and, moreover, without electricity.

There was also, if hardly credited by us, a rumor of ghosts. Neighborhood children quite excelled each other in relating the harrowing experiences they had undergone with various of the more eminent specters. We smiled at their clever fancies, never once losing the conviction that purchase of the house would be wholly practical and satisfactory.

The real estate office bumbled with financial delight the day we took off their hands what they had long considered a lost cause, having even gone so far as to remove the house from their listings. Convenient arrangements were readily fashioned and, in a matter of hours, we had moved all belongings from our uncommodious flat to our new, relatively large house.

Several days were then spent in the most necessary task of cleaning. This presented itself as far more difficult a project than first anticipated. Dust lay heavy throughout the halls and rooms. Our energetic dusting would send clouds of it billowing expansively, filling the air with powdery ghosts of dirt. We noted in respect to that observation that many a spectral vision might thus be made explicable if the proper time were utilized in experiment.

In addition to dust on all places of lodgment, there was thick grime on glass surfaces ranging from downstairs windows to silver-scratched mirrors in the upstairs bath. There were loose banisters to repair, door locks to recondition, yards of thick rugging out of whose mat to beat decades of dust, and a multitude of other chores large and small to be performed before the house could be deemed livable.

Yet, even with grime and age admitted, that we had come by an obvious bargain was beyond dispute. The house was completely furnished, moreover furnished in the delightful mode of the early 1900's. Saul and I were thoroughly enchanted. Dusted, aired, scrubbed from top to bottom, the house proved indeed a fascinating purchase. The dark luxurious drapes, the patterned rugs, the graceful furniture, the yellow-keyed spinet; everything was complete to the last detail, that detail being the portrait of a rather lovely young woman which hung above the living-room mantel.

When first we came upon it, Saul and I stood speechless before its artistic quality. Saul then spoke of the painter's technique and finally, in rapt adulation, discussed with me their various possibilities as to the identity of the model.

It was our final conjecture that she was the daughter or wife of the former tenant, whoever he had been, beyond having the name of Slaughter.

Several weeks passed by. Initial delight was slaked by full-time occupancy and intense creative effort.

We rose at nine, had our breakfast in the dining room, then proceeded to our work, I in my sleeping chamber, Saul in the solarium, which we had been able to improvise into a small studio. Each in our places, the morning passed quietly and effectively. We lunched at one, a small but nourishing meal and then resumed work for the afternoon.

We discontinued our labors about four to have tea and quiet conversation in our elegant front room. By this hour it was too late to go on with our work, since darkness would be commencing its surrounding pall on the city. We had chosen not to install electricity both for reasons of monetary prudence and the less sordid one of pure aesthetics.

We would not, for the world, have distorted the gentle charm of the house by the addition of blatant, sterile electric light. Indeed we preferred the flickering silence of candlelight in which to play our nightly game of chess. We needed no usurping of our silence by noxious radio bleatings, we ate our bakery bread unsinged and found our wine quite adequately cooled from the old icebox. Saul enjoyed the sense of living in the past and so did I. We asked no more.

But then began the little things, the intangible things, the things without reason.

Walking on the stairs, in the hallway, through the rooms, Saul or I, singly or together, would stop and receive the strangest impulse in our minds; of fleeting moment yet quite definite while existent.

It is difficult to express the feeling with adequate clarity. It was as if we heard something although there was no sound, as though we saw something when there was nothing before the eye. A sense of shifting presence, delicate and tenuous, hidden from all physical senses and yet, somehow, perceived.

There was no explaining it. In point of fact we never spoke of it together. It was too nebulous a feeling to discuss, incapable of being materialized into words. Restless though it made us, there was no mutual comparison of sensation nor could there be. Even the most abstract of thought formation could not approach what we were experiencing.

Sometimes I would come upon Saul casting a hurried glance over his shoulder, or surreptitiously reaching out to stroke empty air as though he expected his fingers to touch some invisible entity. Sometimes he would catch me doing the same. On occasion we would smile awkwardly, both of us appreciating the moment without words.

But our smiles soon faded. I almost think we were afraid to deride this unknown aegis for fear that it might prove itself actual. Not that my brother or I were superstitious in the least degree. The very fact that we purchased the house without paying the slightest feasance to the old wives' tales about its supposed anathema seems to belie the suggestion that we were, in any manner, inclined toward mystic apprehensions. Yet the house did seem, beyond question, to possess some strange potency.

Often, late at night, I would lie awake, knowing somehow that Saul was also awake in his room and that we both were listening and waiting, consciously certain about our expectation of some unknown arrival which was soon to be effected.

And effected it was.

II

It was perhaps a month and a half after we had moved into Slaughter House that the first hint was shown as to the house's occupants other than ourselves.

I was in the narrow kitchen cooking supper on the small gas stove. Saul was in the dining alcove arranging the table for supper. He had spread a white cloth over the dark, glossy mahogany and, on it, placed two plates with attendant silver. A candelabrum of six candles glowed in the center of the table casting shadows over the snowy cloth.

Saul was about to place the cups and saucers beside the plates as I turned back to the stove. I twisted the knob a trifle to lower the flame under the chops. Then, as I began to open the icebox to get the wine, I heard Saul gasp loudly and something thumped on the dining-room rug. I whirled and hurried out of the kitchen as fast as I could.

One of the cups had fallen to the floor, its handle snapping off. I hurriedly picked it up, my eyes on Saul.

He was standing with his back to the living-room archway, his right hand pressed to his cheek, a look of speechless shock contorting his handsome features.

"What is it?" I asked, placing the cup on the table.

He looked at me without answering and I noticed how his slender fingers trembled on his whitening cheek.

"Saul, what *is* it?"

"A hand," he said. "A hand. *It touched my cheek.*"

I believe my mouth fell open in surprise. I had, deep within the inner passages of my mind, been expecting something like this to happen. So had Saul. Yet now that it had, a natural sense of oppressive impact was on both of our shoulders.

We stood there in silence. How can I express my feeling at that moment? It was as though something tangible, a tide of choking air, crept over us like some shapeless, lethargic serpent. I noticed how Saul's chest moved in convulsive leaps and depressions and my own mouth hung open as I gasped for breath.

Then, in an added moment, the breathless vacuum was gone, the mindless dread dissolved. I managed to speak, trusting to break this awesome spell with words.

"Are you sure?" I asked.

His slender throat contracted. He forced a smile to his lips, a smile more frightened than pleasant.

"I hope not," he replied.

He reinforced his smile with some effort.

"Can it really be?" he went on, his joviality failing noticeably, "Can it really be that we've been duped into buying ourselves a haunted house?"

I maintained an effort to join in with his spirit of artificial gusto for the sake of our own minds. But it could not long last nor did I feel any abiding comfort in Saul's feigned composure. We were both exceptionally hypersensitive, had been ever since our births, mine some twenty-seven years before, his twenty-five. We both felt this bodiless premonition deep in our senses.

We spoke no more of it, whether from distaste or foreboding I cannot say. Following our unenjoyable meal, we spent the remainder of the evening at pitifully conducted card games. I suggested, in one unguarded moment of fear, that it might be worth our consideration to have electrical outlets installed in the house.

Saul scoffed at my apparent submission and seemed a little more content to retain the relative dimness of candlelight than the occurrence before dinner would have seemed to make possible in him. Notwithstanding that, I made no issue of it.

We retired to our rooms quite early as we usually do. Before we separated, however, Saul said something quite odd to my way of thinking. He was standing at the head of the stairs looking down, I was about to open the door to my room.

"Doesn't it all seem familiar?" he asked.

I turned to face him, hardly knowing what he was talking about.

"Familiar?" I asked of him.

"I mean," he tried to clarify, "as though we'd been here before. No, more than just been here. Actually *lived* here."

I looked at him with a disturbing sense of alarm gnawing at my mind. He lowered his eyes with a nervous smile as though he'd said something he was just realizing he should not have said. He stepped off quickly for his room, muttering a most uncordial good night to me.

I then retired to my own room, wondering about the unusual restlessness which had seemed to possess Saul throughout the evening manifesting itself not only in his words but in his impatient card play, his fidgety pose on the chair upon which he sat, the agitated flexing of his fingers, the roving of his beautiful dark eyes about the living room. As though he were looking for something.

In my room, I disrobed, effected my toilet and was soon in bed. I had lain there about an hour when I felt the house shake momentarily and the air seemed abruptly permeated with a weird, discordant humming that made my brain throb.

I pressed my hands over my ears and then seemed to wake up, my ears still covered. The house was still. I was not at all sure that it had not been a dream. It might have been a heavy truck passing the house, thus setting the dream into motion in my upset mind. I had no way of being absolutely certain.

I sat up and listened. For long minutes I sat stock still on my bed and tried to hear if there were any sounds in the house. A burglar perhaps or Saul prowling about in quest of a midnight snack. But there was nothing. Once, while I glanced at the window, I thought I saw, out of the corner of my eye, a momentary glare of bluish light shining underneath my door. But, when I quickly turned my head, my eye saw only the deepest of blackness and, at length, I sank back on my pillow and fell into a fitful sleep.

III

The next day was Sunday. Frequent wakings during the night and light, troubled sleep had exhausted me. I remained in bed until ten-thirty although it was my general habit to rise promptly at nine each day, a habit I had acquired when quite young.

I dressed hastily and walked across the hall, but Saul was already up. I felt a slight vexation that he had not come in to speak to me as he sometimes did nor even looked in to tell me it was past rising time.

I found him in the living room eating breakfast from a small table he had placed in front of the mantelpiece. He was sitting in a chair that faced the portrait.

His head moved around quickly as I came in. He appeared nervous to me.

"Good morning," he said.

"Why didn't you wake me up?" I said. "You know I never sleep this late."

"I thought you were tired," he said. "What difference does it make?"

I sat down across from him, feeling rather peevish as I took a warm biscuit from beneath the napkin and broke it open.

"Did you notice the house shaking last night?" I asked.

"No. Did it?"

I made no reply to the flippant air of his counter-question. I took a bite from my biscuit and put it down.

"Coffee?" he said. I nodded curtly and he poured me a cup, apparently oblivious to my pique.

I looked around the table.

"Where is the sugar?" I asked.

"I never use it," he answered. "You know that."

"*I* use it," I said.

"Well, you weren't up, John," he replied with an antiseptic smile.

I rose abruptly and went into the kitchen. I opened up one side of the cabinet and retrieved the sugar bowl with irritable fingers.

Then, as I passed it, about to leave the room, I tried to open the other side of the cabinet. It would not open. The door had been stuck quite fast since we moved in. Saul and I had decided in facetious keeping with neighborhood tradition that the cabinet contained shelf upon shelf of dehydrated ghosts.

At the moment, however, I was in little humor for droll fancies. I pulled at the door knob with rising anger. That I should suddenly insist on that moment to open the cabinet only reflected the ill-temper Saul's neglect could so easily create in me. I put down the sugar bowl and placed both hands on the knob.

"What on earth are you doing?" I heard Saul ask from the front room.

I made no answer to his question but pulled harder on the

cabinet knob. But it was as if the door were imbedded solidly into the frame and I could not loosen it the least fraction of an inch.

"What were you doing?" Saul asked as I sat down.

"Nothing," I said and the matter ended. I sat eating with little if any appetite. I do not know whether I felt more anger than hurt. Perhaps it was more a sense of injury since Saul is usually keenly sensitive to my responses, but that day he seemed not the slightest particle receptive. And it was that blasé dispassion in him, so different from his usual disposition, that had so thoroughly upset me.

Once, during the meal, I glanced up at him to discover that his eyes were directed over my shoulder, focusing on something behind me. It caused a distinct chill to excite itself across my back.

"What are you looking at?" I asked of him.

His eyes refocused themselves on me and the slight smile he held was erased from his lips.

"Nothing," he replied.

Nonetheless I twisted about in my chair to look. But there was only the portrait over the mantel and nothing more.

"The portrait?" I asked.

He made no answer but stirred his coffee with deceptive composure.

I said, "Saul, I'm talking to you."

His dark eyes on me were mockingly cold. As though they meant to say, Well, so you are but that is hardly a concern of mine, is it?

When he would not speak I chose to attempt an alleviation of this inexplicable tension which had risen between us. I put down my cup.

"Did you sleep well?" I asked.

His gaze moved up to me quickly, almost, I could not avoid the realization, almost suspiciously.

"Why do you ask?" he spoke distrustingly.

"Is it such an odd question?"

Again he made no reply. Instead he patted his thin lips with his napkin and pushed back his chair as though to leave.

"Excuse me," he muttered, more from habit than politeness, I sensed.

"Why are you being so mysterious?" I asked with genuine concern.

He was on his feet, ready to move away, his face virtually blank. "I'm not," he said. "You're imagining things."

I simply could not understand this sudden alteration in him nor relate it to any equivalent cause. I stared incredulously at him as he turned away and began walking toward the hallway with short, impatient steps.

He turned left to pass through the archway and I heard his quick feet jumping up the carpeted steps. I sat there unable to move, looking at the spot from which he had just disappeared.

It was only after a long while that I turned once more to examine the portrait more carefully.

There seemed nothing unusual about it. My eyes moved over the well-formed shoulders to the slender, white throat, the chin, the cupid-bowed red lips, the delicately upturned nose, the frank green eyes. I had to shake my head. It was only the portrait of a woman and no more. How could this affect any man of sense? How could it affect Saul?

I could not finish my coffee but let it stand cold on the table. I rose, pushed back my chair and started upstairs. I went directly to my brother's room and turned the knob to enter, then felt a stiffening in my body as I realized he had locked himself in. I turned away from his door, tight-lipped and thoroughly annoyed, disturbed beyond control.

As I sat in my room most of the day, sporadically reading, I listened for his footsteps in the hall. I tried to reason out the situation in my mind, to resolve this alien transformation in his attitude towards me.

But there seemed no resolution save that of assuming headache, imperfect sleep or other equally dissatisfying explanations. They served not at all to decipher his uneasiness, the foreign way in which his eye regarded me, his marked disinclination to speak civilly.

It was then, against my will I must state clearly, that I began to suspect other than ordinary causes and to yield a momentary credence to local accounts of the house in which we lived. We had not spoken of that hand he had felt, but was it because we believed it was imagination or because we knew it wasn't?

Once during the afternoon, I stood in the hallway with closed
eyes, listening intently as though I meant to capture some particular sound and ferret it out. In the deep quiet I stood wavering
back and forth on the floor, the very stillness ringing in my ears.

I heard nothing. And the day passed with slow, lonely hours.
Saul and I had a morose supper together during which he rejected all extended conversation and multiple offers of card
games and chess during the later evening.

After he had finished his meal, he returned immediately to his
room and I, after washing the dishes, returned to mine and soon
retired.

The dream returned again, yet not in certainty a dream, I
thought lying there in the early morning. And had it not been a
dream only a hundred trucks could have made such a vibration as
that which shook the house in my fancy. And the light which
shone beneath the door was too bright for candlelight, a glaring
blue lucency of illumination. And the footsteps I heard were very
audible. Were they only in my dream however? I could not be
sure.

IV

It was nearly nine-thirty before I rose and dressed, strongly irritated that my work schedule was being thus altered by concern. I
completed my toilet quickly and went out into the hall, anxious to
lose myself in occupation.

Then, as I looked automatically toward Saul's room I noticed
that the door was slightly ajar. I immediately assumed he was
already up and at work above in the solarium, so I did not stop to
see. Instead, I hurried downstairs to make myself a hasty breakfast, noticing as I entered the kitchen that the room was just as I
had left it the night before.

After a moderate breakfast I went upstairs again and entered
Saul's room.

It was with some consternation that I found him still on his bed.
I say "on" rather than "in" since the blankets and sheets had
been, and violently so, it appeared, thrown aside and were hanging down in twisted swirls upon the wooden floor.

Saul lay on the bottom sheet, clad only in a pajama trousers, his chest, shoulders and face dewed with tiny drops of perspiration.

I bent over and shook him once, but he only mumbled in sleep-ridden lethargy. I shook him again with hardened fingers and he rolled over angrily.

"Leave me alone," he spoke in thickened irritability. "You know I've been . . ."

He stopped, as though, once more, he was about to speak of something he should not.

"You've been what?" I inquired, feeling a rising heat of aggravation in my system.

He said nothing but lay there on his stomach, his face buried in the white pillow.

I reached down and shook him again by the shoulder, this time more violently. At this he pushed up abruptly and almost screamed at me.

"Get out of here!"

"Are you going to paint?" I asked, shaking nervously.

He rolled on his side and squirmed a little, preparatory to sleeping again. I turned away with a harsh breath of anger.

"You make your own breakfast," I said, feeling yet more fury at the senseless import of my words. As I pulled shut the door in leaving, I thought I heard Saul laughing.

I went back to my room and started to work on my play though hardly with success. My brain could not grasp concentration. All I could think of was the uncommon way in which my pleasant life had been usurped.

Saul and I had always been exceptionally close to one another. Our lives had always been inseparable, our plans were always mutual plans, our affections invariably directed primarily upon each other. This had been so since our boyhood when in grade school other children laughingly called us The Twins in contraction of our fuller title—The Siamese Twins. And, even though I had been two years ahead of Saul in school we were always together, choosing our friends with a regard to each other's tastes and distastes, living, in short, with and for each other.

Now this; this enraging schism in our relationship. This harsh severance of comradely association, this abrupt, painful transmutation from intimacy to callous inattention.

The change was of such a gravity to me that almost immediately I began to look for the most grave of causes. And, although the implied solution seemed at the very least tenuous, I could not help but entertain it willingly. And, once more entertained, I could not remove myself from the notion.

In the quiet of my room, I pondered of ghosts.

Was it then possible that the house was haunted? Hastily I mulled over the various implications, the various intimations that the theory was verifiable.

Excluding the possibility that they were dream content, there were the heaving vibrations and the weird, high-pitched humming which had assailed my brain. There was the eerie blue light I had dreamed or actually seen beneath my door. And, finally, the most damning of evidence, there was Saul's statement that he had felt a hand on his cheek. *A cold, damp hand!*

Yet, despite all, it is a difficult thing to admit the existence of ghosts in a coldly factual world. One's very instincts rebel at the admission of such maddening possibility. For, once the initial step is made into the supernatural, there is no turning back, no knowing where the strange road leads except that it is quite unknown and quite terrible.

So actual were the premonitions I began to feel that I put aside my unused writing tablet and pen and rushed into the hall and to Saul's room as though something were awry there.

The ludicrous, unexpected sound of his snoring set me momentarily at ease. But my smile was short-lived, vanishing instantly when I saw the half-empty liquor bottle on his bedside table.

The shock of it made my flesh grow cold. And the thought came—he is corrupted, although I had no knowledge of its source.

As I stood there above his spread-eagled form, he groaned once and turned on his back. He had dressed, but his slept-in attire was now dishevelled and crumpled. His face, I noted, was unshaven and extremely haggard and the bloodshot gaze he directed at me was that of one stranger to another.

"What do you want?" he asked in hoarse, unnatural tones.

"Are you out of your mind?" I said. "What in God's name . . . ?"

"Get out of here," he said again to me, his brother.

I stared at his face and, although I knew it could be only the result of drink distorting his unshaven features, I could not dispel the apprehension that he was, somehow, coarse, and a shudder of strange revulsion ran through me.

I was about to take the bottle away from him when he swung at me, a wildly inaccurate flinging of the arm, his sense of direction blunted by a drink-thickened brain.

"I said, get *out* of here!" he shouted in a fury, streaks of mottled red leaping into his cheeks.

I backed away, almost in fright, then turned on my heel and hurried into the hall, trembling with the shock of my brother's unnatural behavior. I stood outside his door for a long time, listening to him toss restlessly on his bed, groaning. And I felt close to tears.

Then, without thought, I descended the darkening stairway, moved across the living room and dining alcove and entered the small kitchen. There, in the black silence, I held aloft a spluttering match and then lit the heavy candle I retrieved from the stove.

My footsteps, as I moved about the kitchen, seemed oddly muffled, as though I were hearing them through thick, cotton padding in my ears. And I began to get the most incongruous sensation that the very silence was drumming roughly in my ears.

As I passed the left-hand side of the cabinet I found myself swaying heavily as though the dead, motionless air had suddenly become mobile and were buffeting me about. The silence was a roaring now and, suddenly, I clutched out for support and my twitching fingers knocked a dish onto the tile floor.

A positive shudder ran through me then because the sound of the breaking dish had been hollow and unreal, the sound of something greatly distant. If I had not seen the porcelain fragments lying on the dark tile I might have sworn the dish had not shattered at all.

With a sense of mounting restlessness I pushed my index fingers into my ears and twisted them around as if to ease what seemed an obstruction. Then I clenched my fist and struck the fastened cabinet door, almost desperate for the comfort of logical sound. But no matter how strong my blows, the sound came to my ears no louder than that of someone far away knocking at some door.

I turned hastily to the small icebox, very anxious now to make my sandwiches and coffee and be out of there, up in my room once more.

I put the bread on a tray, poured a cupful of the steaming black coffee and put the coffee pot down on its burner again. Then, with distinct trepidation, I bent over and blew out the candle.

The dining alcove and living room were oppressively dark now. My heart began to thud heavily as I moved across the rug, my footsteps muffled as I walked. I held the tray in stiff, unfeeling fingers, my gaze directed straight ahead. As I moved, my breath grew more harsh, bursting from my nostrils as I held my lips pressed tightly together lest they begin shaking with fright.

The blackness and the dead, utter silence seemed to crush in on me like solid walls. I held my throat stiff, my every muscle suspended by will for fear that relaxation would cause me to shake without control.

Halfway to the hall I heard it.

A soft, bubbling laughter which seemed to permeate the room like a cloud of sound.

A swamping wave of coldness covered my body and my footsteps halted abruptly as my legs and body stiffened.

The laughter did not cease. It continued, moving about me as if someone—or some *thing*— circled me on soundless tread, its eyes always on me. I began to tremble and, in the stillness, I could hear the rattling of the cup on my tray.

Then, suddenly, a damp, cold hand pressed against my cheek!

With a terrified howl of fear I dropped the tray and ran wildly into the hall and up the stairs, my weakening legs propelling me forward in the blackness. As I ran there was another gush of liquid laughter behind me, like a thin trail of icy air in the stillness.

I locked the door to my room and hurled my self on the bed, pulling the bedspread over myself with shaking fingers. My eyes tightly shut, I lay there with heart pounding against the mattress. And, in my mind, the hideous cognition that all my fears were justified was a knife stabbing at delicate tissues.

It was all true.

As actually as if a living human hand had touched me, I had felt that cold and soggy hand on my cheek. But what living person was down there in the darkness?

For a short time I belied to tell myself it had been Saul executing a cruel and vicious joke. But I knew it had not been, for I would have heard his footsteps and I had heard none, either before or now.

The clock was chiming ten when I was at last able to summon the courage to throw off the spread, scrabble for the box of matches on my bedside table and light the candle.

At first the guttering light assuaged fear slightly. But then I saw how little it illuminated the silent darkness and I avoided, with a shudder, the sight of huge and shapeless walls. I cursed the old house for its lack of electricity. Fear might be eased in blazing lamplight. As it was, the imperfect flickering of that tiny flame did nothing to allay my fears.

I wanted to go across the hall and see if Saul were all right. But I was afraid to open my door, imagining hideous apparitions lurking there in the blackness, hearing once more in my mind the ugly, viscid laughter. I hoped that Saul was so hopelessly under alcoholic influence that nothing short of an earthquake could awaken him.

And, though I yearned to be near him even if he were treating me faithlessly, I felt no courage whatsoever. And, quickly undressing, I hastened to my bed and buried my head beneath the blankets again.

V

I woke suddenly, shivering and afraid. The bedclothes were gone from my body, the black silence as awful as it had been earlier in the night.

I reached for the blankets anxiously, my fingers groping for them. They had fallen from the edge of the bed. I rolled on my side hurriedly and reached down, my fingers recoiling as they came in contact with the icy floorboards.

Then, as I reached for the blankets, I saw the light beneath the door.

It remained in sight only the fragment of a second but I knew I had seen it. And, as it passed abruptly from my eyes, the throbbing began. My room seemed filled with the humming pulsations. I could feel the bed shaking beneath me and my skin growing taut and frigid; my teeth chattering together.

Then the light appeared again and I heard the sound of bare feet and knew it was Saul walking in the night.

Driven more by fear for his safety than by courage, I threw my legs over the side of the bed and padded to the door, shuddering at the iciness of the flooring beneath my soles.

Slowly I opened the door, my body held tight in anticipation of what I might see.

But the hall was pitch black and I walked out and over to the door of Saul's room, listening to see if I could hear the sound of his breathing. But before I could judge anything, the hall below was suddenly illumined with that unearthly blue glow and I turned and rushed, again instinctively, to the head of the stairs and stood there clutching the old banister, staring down.

Below, an aura of intense brilliant blue light was passing through the hall moving in the direction of the living room.

My heart leaped! Saul was following it, arms ahead of him in the familiar pose of the somnambulist, his eyes staring ahead and glittering in the shapeless blue effulgence.

I tried to call his name but found that my voice could make no utterance. I tried to move for the stairs to wrest my Saul away from this terror. But a wall, invisible in the blackness, held me back. It grew close and airless. I struggled violently but it was to no avail. My muscles were strengthless against the horrible, impossible power that clutched me.

Then, suddenly, my nostrils and brain were assaulted by a pungent, sickly odor that made my senses reel. My throat and stomach burned with almost tangible fire. The darkness grew more intense. It seemed to cling to me like hot, black mud, constricting my chest so that I could hardly breathe. It was like being buried alive in a black oven, my body bound and rebound with heavy grave wrappings. I trembled, sobbing and ineffectual.

Then, abruptly, it all passed and I stood there in the cold hallway soaked with perspiration, weak from my frantic efforts. I tried to move but could not, tried to remember Saul, but was incapable of preventing the thought of him from slipping from my numbed brain. I shivered and turned to go back to my room but, at the first step, my legs buckled and I pitched forward heavily on the floor. The icy surface of it pressed against my flesh and, my body wracked by shivering, I lost consciousness.

When my eyes opened again I still lay crumpled on the cold floor.

I rose to a sitting position, the hall before my eyes wavering in alternate tides of light and darkness. My chest felt tight and a remorseless chill gripped my body. I pulled myself up to a bent-over stance and staggered to Saul's room, a cough burning in my throat as I stumbled across the floor and against his bed.

He was there and looked emaciated. He was unshaved and the dark wiry growth on his skin seemed like some repugnant growth. His mouth was open and emitting sounds of exhausted slumber and his smooth, white chest rose and fell with shallow movements.

He made no motion as I tugged weakly at his shoulder. I spoke his name and was shocked at the hoarse, grating sound of my own voice. I spoke it again, and he stirred with a grumble and opened one eye to look at me.

"I'm sick," I muttered, "Saul, I'm sick."

He rolled on one side, turning his back to me. A sob of anguish tore at my throat.

"Saul!"

He seemed to snap his body around insanely then, his hands clenched into bony, white fists at his sides.

"Get out of here!" he screamed. "Leave me alone or I'll kill you!"

The body-shaking impact of his words drove me back from the bed to where I stood dumbly staring at him, breath stabbing at my throat. I saw him toss his body back over as if he wanted to break it. And I heard him mutter to himself miserably, *"Why does the day have to last so long?"*

A spasm of coughing struck me then and, my chest aching with fiery pains, I struggled back to my own room and got into bed with the movements of an old man. I fell back on the pillow and pulled up the blankets, then lay there shivering and helpless.

There I slept all day in spasmodic periods offset by waking moments of extreme pain. I was unable to rise to get myself food or water. All I could do was lie there, shaking and weeping. I felt beaten as much by Saul's cruelty to me as by the physical suffering. And the pain in my body was extremely severe. So much so that during one seizure of coughing it was so awful I began to cry like a child, hitting the mattress with weak, ineffective fists and kicking my legs deliriously.

Yet, even then, I think I wept for more than the pain. I wept for my only brother who loved me not.

It seemed that night came more swiftly than I had ever seen it come before. I lay alone in the darkness praying through mute lips that no harm should come to him.

I slept awhile and then, abruptly, I was awake, staring at the light beneath the door, hearing the high-pitched humming in my ears. And I realized in that moment that Saul still loved me but that the house had corrupted his love.

And from this knowledge came resolution, from despair I gained amazing heart. I struggled to my feet and swayed there dizzily until the streaks before my eyes dispersed. Then I put on my robe and slippers, went to the door and threw it open.

What made things happen as they did I cannot say. Perhaps it was my feeling of courage that caused the black obstruction in the hall to melt before me. The house was trembling with the vibrations and the humming. Yet they seemed to lessen as I moved down the stairway and, all of a sudden, the blue light vanished from the living room and I heard loud and furious rumblings there.

When I entered, the room was in its usual order. A candle was burning on the mantel. But my eyes were riveted to the center of the floor.

Saul stood there, half naked and motionless, his body poised as though he were dancing, his eyes fastened to the portrait.

I spoke his name sharply. His eyes blinked and, slowly, his head turned to me. He didn't seem to comprehend my presence there for, suddenly, his glance flew about the room and he cried out in despairing tones:

"Come back! Come back!"

I called his name again and he stopped looking around but directed his gaze at me. His face was gaunt and cruelly lined in the flickering candlelight. It was the face of a lunatic. He gnashed his teeth together and started to move toward me.

"I'll kill you," he muttered in liquid tones, "I'll *kill* you."

I backed away.

"Saul, you're out of your mind. You don't—"

I could say no more for he rushed at me, his hands extended as if he would clutch at my throat. I tried to step aside but he grabbed hold of my robe and pulled me against him.

We began to struggle, I begging him to throw off this terrible spell he was under, he panting and gnashing his teeth. My head was being shaken from side to side and I saw our monstrous shadows heaving on the walls.

Saul's grip was not his own. I have always been stronger than he but, at that moment, his hands seemed like cold iron. I began to choke and his face blurred before my eyes. I lost balance and we both fell heavily to the floor. I felt the prickly rug against my cheek, his cold hands tightening on my throat.

Then my hand came in contact with something cold and hard. It was the tray I had dropped the night before, I realized. I gripped it and, realizing that he was out of his mind and meant to kill me, I picked it up and drove it across his head with all the power I had remaining.

It was a heavy metal tray and Saul sank to the floor as if struck dead, his hands slipping from my bruised throat. I struggled up, gasping for breath, and looked at him.

Blood was running from a deep gash in his forehead where the edge of the tray had struck.

"Saul!" I screamed, horrified at what I'd done.

Frantically I leaped up and rushed to the front door. As I flung it open I saw a man walking by in the street. I ran to the porch railing and called to him.

"Help!" I cried. "Call an ambulance!"

The man lurched and looked over at me with startled fright.

"For God's sake!" I beseeched him. "My brother has struck his head! Please call an ambulance!"

For a long moment he stared at me, open-mouthed, then broke into a nervous flight up the street. I called after him but he would not stop to listen. I was certain he would not do as I'd asked.

As I turned back, I saw my bloodless face in the hall mirror and realized with a start that I must have frightened the wits out of the man. I felt weak and afraid again, the momentary strength sapped from me. My throat was dry and raw, my stomach on edge. I was barely able to walk back to the living room on trembling stalks of legs.

I tried to lift Saul to a couch but dead weight was too much for me and I sank to my knees beside him. My body slumped forward and, half crouched, half lay by the side of my brother. The harsh sound of my breathing was the only sound I could hear. My left hand stroked Saul's hair absently and quiet tears flowed from my eyes.

I cannot say how long I had been there when the throbbing began again; as if to show me that it hadn't really gone away.

I still crouched there like a dead thing, my brain almost in coma. I could feel my heart beating like some old clock in my chest, the dull-edged and muffled pendulum hitting against my ribs with a lifeless rhythm. All sound registered with similar force, the clock on the mantel, my heart and the endless throbbing; all blending into one horrible beat that became a part of me, that became *me*. I could sense myself sinking deeper and deeper as a drowning man slips helplessly beneath the silent waters.

Then I thought I heard a tapping of feet through the room, the rustling of skirts and, far off, a hollow laughter of women.

I raised my head abruptly, my skin tight and cold.

A figure in white stood in the doorway.

It began to move toward me and I rose with a strangled cry on my lips only to collapse into darkness.

VI

What I had seen had been not a ghost but an interne from the hospital. The man I had called in the street had, apparently, done what I'd asked. It will give some indication of the state I was in when I reveal that I heard neither the ringing of the front door-bell not the pounding of the interne's fist on the half-open door. Indeed, had the door not been open, I am certain that I would be dead now.

They took Saul to the hospital to have his head cared for. There being nothing wrong with me but nervous exhaustion, I remained in the house. I had wanted to go with Saul, but was told that the hospital was overcrowded and I would do more good by staying home in bed.

I slept late the next morning, rising about eleven. I went downstairs and had a substantial breakfast, then returned to my room and slept a few hours more. About two, I had some lunch. I planned to leave the house well before darkness to make sure nothing further happened to me. I could find a room in a hotel. It was clear that we would have to desert the place regardless of whether we sold it or not. I anticipated some trouble with Saul on that point but made up my mind to stand firm on my decision.

About five o'clock I dressed and left my room, carrying a small bag for the night. The day was almost gone and I hurried down the stairs, not wishing to remain in the house any longer. At the bottom of the staircase I stepped across the entry hall and closed my hand over the doorknob.

The door would not open.

At first I would not allow myself to believe this. I stood there tugging, trying to combat the cold numbness that was spreading itself over my body. Then I dropped my bag and pulled at the knob with both hands but to no avail. It was as securely fastened as the cabinet door in the kitchen.

Suddenly, I turned from the door and ran into the living room but all the windows were jammed fast into their frames. I looked around the room, whimpering like a child, feeling unspoken hate for myself for letting myself be trapped again. I cursed loudly and, as I did, a cold wind lifted the hat from my head and hurled it across the floor.

Abruptly, I placed my shaking hands over my eyes and stood there trembling violently, afraid of what might happen any second, my heart hammering against my chest. The room seemed to chill markedly and I heard that grotesque humming noise again that came as if from another world. It sounded like laughter to me, laughter that mocked me for my poor, feeble efforts to escape.

Then, with equal suddenness, I remembered Saul again, remembered that he needed me and I pulled away my hands from my eyes and screamed aloud,

"Nothing in this house can harm me!"

Sudden cessation of the sound gave me added courage. If my will could successfully defy the ungodly powers of the place, then perhaps it could also destroy them. If I went upstairs, if I slept in Saul's bed, then I too would know what he had experienced and thus be enabled to help him.

I felt no lack of confidence in my will to resist, never once stopping to think that my ideas might not be my own.

Quickly, two steps at a time, I rushed up the stairs and into my brother's room. There I quickly removed my hat, overcoat and suitcoat, loosened my tie and collar and sat down on the bed. Then, after a moment, I lay down and looked up at the darkening ceiling. I tried to keep my eyes open but, still fatigued, I soon fell asleep.

It seemed only a moment before I was fully awake, my body tingling with sensations of not unpleasant character. I could not understand the strangeness of it. The darkness seemed alive. It shimmered under my gaze as I lay there, warm with a heat that betokened sensualism although there was hardly any apparent cause for such a feeling.

I whispered Saul's name without thinking. Then the thought of him was taken from my brain as if invisible fingers had plucked it away.

I remember rolling over and laughing to myself, behavior most extraordinary if not unseemly for a person of my steady inclinations. The pillow felt like silk against my face and my senses began to fade. The darkness crept over me like warm syrup, soothing my body and mind. I muttered senselessly to myself, feeling as if my muscles were sucked dry of all energy, heavy as rock and lethargic with a delicious exhaustion.

Then, when I had almost slipped away, I felt another presence in the room. To my incredulous realization, it was not only familiar to me but I had absolutely no fear of it. Only an inexplicable sense of languorous expectation.

Then she came to me, the girl in the portrait.

I stared at the blue haze about her for only a moment for this quickly faded and, in my arms, was a vibrantly warm body. I remember no one feature of her behavior for everything was lost in overall sensation, a sensation mixed of excitement and revulsion, a sense of hideous yet overpowering rapacity. I hung sus-

pended in a cloud of ambivalence, my soul and body corroded
with unnatural desire. And in my mind and echoing on my tongue
I spoke a name over and over again.

The name *Clarissa.*

How can I judge the number of sick, erotic moments I spent
there with her? Sense of time completely vanished from the
scheme of things. A thick giddiness enveloped me. I tried to fight
it but it was no use. I was consumed as my brother Saul had been
consumed by this foul presence from the grave of night.

Then, in some inconceivable fashion, we were no longer on the
bed but downstairs, whirling about in the living room dancing
wildly and closely. There was no music, only that incessant, beating rhythm I had heard those nights before. Yet now it seemed
like music to me as I spun about the floor holding in my arms the
ghost of a dead woman, entranced by her stunning beauty yet, at
the same time, repelled by my uncontrollable hunger for her.

Once I closed my eyes for a second and felt a terrible coldness
crawling in my stomach. But when I opened them it was gone and
I was happy once more. *Happy?* It seems hardly the word now. Say
rather hypnotized, torpid, my brain a numbed vessel of flesh
unable to remove me one iota from this clutching spell.

Dancing went on and on. The floor was filled with couples. I am
sure of that and yet I recall no aspect of their dress or form. All I
remember is their faces, white and glistening, their eyes dull and
lifeless, their mouths hanging open like dark, bloodless wounds.

Around and around and then a man with a large tray standing
in the hallway arch and sudden immersion in the dark; empty and
still.

VII

I awoke with a sense of complete exhaustion.

I was soaked with perspiration, dressed only in my bottom
undergarment. My clothes lay scattered across the floor, apparently thrown about in a frenzy. The bedclothes also lay in disordered heaps on the floor. From all appearances, I had gone
insane the night before.

The light from the window annoyed me for some reason and,
quickly, I shut my eyes, reluctant to believe it was morning again.

I turned over onto my stomach and put my head beneath the pillow. I could still remember the enticing odor of her hair. The memory of it made my body shudder with odious craving.

Then a warmth began to cover my back and I raised myself up with a muttering frown. The sunlight was streaming through the windows onto my back. With a restless movement I pushed myself up, threw my legs over the side of the bed and got up to draw the shades.

It was a little better without the glare. I threw myself on the bed again, closed my eyes tightly and crowded the pillow over my head. I felt the light.

It sounds incredible, I know, but I felt it as surely as do certain creeper plants that climb towards the light without ever seeing it. And, in feeling light, I yearned all the more for darkness. I felt like some nocturnal creature somehow forced into brightness, repelled and pained by it.

I sat on the bed and looked around, a sound of unremitting complaint in my throat. I bit my lips, clenched and unclenched my hands, wanting to strike out violently at something, at anything. I found myself standing over an unlit candle, blowing sharply on it. I knew, even then, the senselessness of the act and yet I did it nevertheless, trying, inanely, to make an invisible flame go out so that night could return through its dark roads. Bringing back Clarissa.

Clarissa.

A clicking sound filled my throat and my body positively writhed. Not in pain or pleasure but in a combination of the two. I put my brother's robe over my body and wandered out into the silent hallway. There were no physical wants, no hunger, thirst, or other needs. I was a detached body, a comatose slave to the tyranny which had shackled me and now refused to let me go.

I stood at the head of the stairway, listening intently, trying to imagine her gliding up to meet me, warm and vibrant in her mist of blue. *Clarissa.* I closed my eyes quickly, my teeth grated together and, for a split second, I felt my body stiffen with fright. For a moment I was returned to myself.

But then, in another breath, I was enslaved again. I stood there, feeling myself a part of the house, as much a portion of it as the beams or the windows. I breathed its breath, felt its soundless heartbeat in my own. I became at one with an inanimate body, knowing its past life, sensing the dead hands that had curled their fingers on the arms of the chairs, on banisters, on doorknobs, hearing the labored tread of invisible footsteps moving through the house, the laughter of long-consumed humor.

If, in those moments, I lost my soul, it became a part of the emptiness and stillness that surrounded me, an emptiness I could not sense nor a stillness feel for being drugged. Drugged with the formless presence of the past. I was no longer a living person. I was dead in all but those bodily functions which kept me from complete satisfaction.

Quietly, and without passion, the thought of killing myself drifted through my mind. It was gone in a moment but its passage had stirred no more in me than apathetic recognition. My thoughts were on the life beyond life. And present existence was no more than a minor obstruction which I could tumble with the slightest touch of razored steel, the minutest drop of poison. I had become the master of life for I could view its destruction with the most complete apathy.

Night. Night! When would it come? I heard my voice, thin and hoarse, crying out in the silence.

"Why does the day have to last so long!"

The words shocked me back again, for Saul had spoken them. I blinked, looked around me as if just realizing where I was. What was this terrible power over me? I tried to break its hold but, in the very effort, slipped back again.

To find myself once more in that strange coma which suspends the very ill in that slender portion of existence between life and death. I was hanging on a thread over the pit of everything that was hidden to me before. Now I could see and hear and the power to cut the thread was in my hands. I could let myself hang until the strands parted one by one and lowered me slowly down. Or I could wait until driven beyond endurance, then end it suddenly, cut myself loose and plunge down into the darkness; that signal darkness where she and hers remained always. Then I would have her maddening warmth. Maybe it was her coldness. Her comfort then. I could pass eternal moments with her and laugh at the robot world.

I wondered if it would help to get dead drunk and lose all consciousness till night.

I descended the stairs on unfeeling legs and sat for a long time before the mantel looking up at her. I had no idea what time it was nor did I care. Time was relative, even forgotten. I neither knew of it nor cared about it. Had she smiled at me then? Yes, her eyes glowed, how they glowed in the dimness. That smell again. Not pleasant yet something excitingly musky and pungent about it.

What was Saul to me? The idea filled my mind. He was no relation of mine. He was a stranger from another society, another flesh, another life. I felt complete dispassion toward him. You hate him, said the voice in my mind.

That was when it all collapsed like a flimsy house of cards.

For those words caused such a rebellion in my innermost mind that, suddenly, my eyes were cleared as though scales had fallen from them. I looked about, my head snapping crazily. What in God's name was I doing, still here in the house?

With a shiver of angry fear I jumped to my feet and ran upstairs to dress. As I passed the hall clock I saw with a start that it was past three in the afternoon.

As I dressed, normal sensations returned one by one. I felt the cold floor beneath my bare feet, became aware of hunger and thirst, heard the deep silence of the house.

Everything flooded over me. I knew why Saul had wanted to die, why he loathed the day and waited for the night with such angry impatience. I could explain it to him now and he would understand because I had been through it myself.

And, as I ran down the stairs, I thought about the dead of Slaughter House, so outraged at their own inexplicable curse that they tried to drag the living down into their endless hell.

Over, over!—exulted my mind as I locked the front door behind me and started through the misty rain to the hospital.

I did not see the shadow behind me, crouching on the porch.

VIII

When the woman at the hospital desk told me that Saul had been discharged two hours before my arrival, I was too stunned to speak. I clutched at the counter, staring at her, hearing myself tell her that she must be mistaken. My voice was hoarse, unnatural. The woman shook her head.

I sagged against the counter then, all the drive gone out of me. I felt very tired and afraid. A sob broke in my throat as I turned away and I saw people staring at me while I moved across the tile floor with unsteady motions. Everything seemed to swirl about me. I staggered, almost fell. Someone clutched my arm and asked me if I were all right. I muttered something in reply and pulled away from the person without even noting if it were a man or a woman.

I pushed out through the door and into the gray light. It was raining harder and I pulled up my coat collar. Where was he? The question burned in my mind and the answer to it came quickly, too quickly. Saul was back in the house. I felt sure of it.

The idea made me start running up the dark street toward the trolley-car tracks. I ran for endless blocks. All I remember is the rain driving against my face and the gray buildings floating by. There were no people in the streets and all the taxicabs were full. It was getting darker and darker.

My legs almost buckled and I was thrown against a lamppost and clung to it, afraid of falling into the streaming gutter.

An ugly clanging filled my ears. I looked up, then chased after the trolley car and caught it at the next block. I handed the conductor a dollar and had to be called back for my change. I stood hanging from a black strap, swaying back and forth with the motion of the car, my mind tormented by thoughts of Saul alone in that house of horror.

The warm, stale air of the car began to make me sick to the stomach. I could smell the raincoats and the wet clothes of the people caught in the rain as well as the smell of dripping umbrellas and packages soaked. I closed my eyes and stood there, teeth clenched, praying that I would get home before it was too late.

I got off the car at last and ran up the block as fast as I could. The rain sprayed over my face and ran into my eyes, almost blinding me. I slipped and went sprawling on the sidewalk, skinning my hands and knees. I pushed up with a whine, feeling the clothes soaked against me. I kept running wildly, only sensing the direction by instinct until I stopped and saw through the thick veil of rain, the house in front of me, high and dark.

It seemed to crawl over the ground toward me and clutch me to itself for I found myself standing and shivering on the wooden porch. I coughed and felt the chill through my flesh.

I tried the door. At first I could not believe it. It was still locked and Saul had no key! I almost cried in gratitude. I ran down from the porch. Where was he then? I had to find him. I started down the path.

Then, as surely as if I had been tapped on the shoulder I whirled about and stared up at the porch. A flash of lightning illuminated the darkness and I saw the broken, jagged-edged window. My breath caught and I stared at it, my heart pounding like a heavy piston in my chest.

He *was* in there. Had she come already? Was he lying upstairs in bed smiling to himself in the blackness, waiting for her luminous self to come and envelop him?

I had to save him. Without hesitation I ran up on the porch and unlocked the door, leaving it wide open so that we could escape.

I moved across the rug and onto the steps. The house was quiet. Even the storm seemed apart from it. The rushing sound of the rain seemed to grow less and less distinct. Then I turned with a gasp as the front door slammed shut behind me.

I was trapped. The thought drove barbs of fear into me and I almost ran down to try and escape. But I remembered Saul and fought to quicken resolution. I had conquered the house once and I could do it again. I had to. For him.

I started up the stairs again. Outside the flashes of lightning were like false neon trying to invade the austerity of the house. I held onto the banister tightly, muttering beneath my breath to keep attention from degrading into fright, afraid to let the spell of the house beset me again.

I reached the door to my brother's room. There I stopped and leaned against the wall, eyes closed. What if I found him dead? I knew the sight would unnerve me. The house might defeat me then, taking me in that moment of utter despair and twisting my soul from my grip.

I would not let myself conceive of it. I would not allow myself the realization that without Saul life was empty, a meaningless travesty. He *was* alive.

Nervously, my hands numbed with fright, I pushed open the door. The room was a stygian cave. My throat contracted and I took a deep breath. I clenched tight fists at my sides.

"Saul?" I called his name softly.

The thunder roared and my voice disappeared beneath the swell. A flash of lightning brought a split second of daylight into the room and I looked around quickly, hoping to see him. Then it was dark again and silent except for the endless rain falling on the windows and roof. I took another step across the rug, cautiously, my ears tense, trying to hear. Every sound made me start. I twitched and shuffled across the floor. Was he here? But he must be. If he were here in the house, this was the room he would be in.

"Saul?" I called, louder. "Saul, answer me."

I began to walk toward the bed.

Then the door slammed behind me and there was a rushing sound behind me in the darkness. I whirled to meet it. I felt his hand clamp on my arm.

"Saul!" I cried.

Lightning filled the room with hideous light and I saw his twisted white face, the candlestick held in his right hand.

Then he struck me a violent blow on the forehead, driving a wedge of agonizing pain into my brain. I felt his hand release me as I slumped to my knees and my face brushed against his bare leg as I fell forward. The last sound I heard before my mind fell into the darkness was laughing and laughing and laughing.

I X

I opened my eyes. I was still lying on the rug. Outside it was raining even harder. The sound of it was like the crashing of a waterfall. Thunder still rolled in the sky and flashes of lightning made the night brilliant.

In one flash I looked at the bed. The sight of the covers and sheets all thrown about insanely made me push up. Saul was downstairs with *her!*

I tried to get to my feet but the pain in my head drove me back to my knees. I shook my head feebly, running trembling hands over my cheeks, feeling the gouged wound in my forehead, the dried blood which had trickled down across one temple. I swayed back and forth on my knees, moaning. I seemed to be back in that void again, struggling to regain my hold on life. The power of the house surrounded me. The power which I knew was her power. A cruel and malignant vitality which tried to drink out the life force from me and draw me down into the pit.

Then, once more, I remembered Saul, my brother, and the remembrance brought me back the strength I needed.

"No!" I cried out as if the house had told me I was now its helpless captive. And I pushed to my feet, ignoring the dizziness, stumbling through a cloud of pain across the room, gasping for breath. The house was throbbing and humming, filled with that obnoxious smell.

I ran drunkenly for the door, found myself running into the bed. I drew back with almost a snarl at the numbing pain in my shins. I turned in the direction of the door and ran again. I did not even hold my arms ahead of me and had no chance to brace myself when I ran into the door dizzily.

The excruciating pain of my nose being near broken caused a howl of agony to pass my lips. Blood immediately began gushing down across my mouth and I had to keep wiping it away. I jerked open the door and ran into the hall, feeling myself on the border of insanity. The hot blood kept running down across my chin and I felt it dripping and soaking into my coat. My hat had fallen off but I still wore my raincoat over my suit.

I was too bereft of perception to notice that nothing held me back at the head of the stairs. I half ran, half slid down the stairs, goaded on by that humming, formless laughter which was music and mockery. The pain in my head was terrible. Every downward step made it feel as if someone drove one more nail into my brain.

"Saul, Saul!" I cried out, running into the living room, gagging as I tried to call his name a third time.

The living room was dark, permeated with that sickly odor. It made my head reel but I kept moving. It seemed to thicken as I moved for the kitchen. I ran into the small room and leaned against the wall, almost unable to breathe, pinpoints of light spinning before my eyes.

Then, as lightning illumined the room I saw the left cupboard door wide open and, inside, a large bowl filled with what looked like flour. As I stared at it, tears rolled down my cheeks and my tongue felt like dry cloth in my mouth.

I backed out of the kitchen choking for breath, feeling as if my strength were almost gone. I turned and ran into the living room, still looking for my brother.

Then, in another flash of lightning, I looked at her portrait. It was different and the difference froze me to the spot. Her face was no longer beautiful. Whether it was shadow that did it or actual change, her expression was one of vicious cruelty. The eyes glittered, there was an insane cast to her smile. Even her hands, once folded in repose, now seemed more like claws waiting to strike out and kill.

It was when I backed away from her that I stumbled and fell over the body of my brother.

I pushed up to my knees and stared down in the blackness. One flash of lightning after another showed me his white, dead face, the smile of hideous knowledge on his lips, the look of insane joy in his wide-open eyes. My mouth fell open and breath caught in me. It seemed as if my world was ending. I could not believe it was true. I clutched at my hair and whimpered, almost believing that in a moment, Mother would wake me from my nightmare and I would look across at Saul's bed, smile at his innocent sleep and lie down again secure with the memory of his dark hair on the white pillow.

But it did not end. The rain slapped frenziedly at the windows and thunder drove deafening fists against the earth.

I looked up at the portrait. I felt as dead as my brother. I did not hesitate. Calmly I stood and walked to the mantel. There were matches there. I picked up the box.

Instantly, she divined my thoughts for the box was torn from my fingers and hurled against the wall. I dove for it and was tripped by some invisible force. Those cold hands clutched at my throat. I felt no fright but tore them away with a snarl and dove for the matches again. Blood began running faster and I spat out some.

I picked up the box. It was torn away again, this time to burst and spray matches all over the rug. A great hum of anguish seemed to rock the house as I reached for a match. I was grabbed.

I tore loose. I fell to my knees and slapped at the rug in the darkness as lightning ceased. My arms were held tightly. Something cold and wet ran around in my stomach.

With maniacal fury I pressed my teeth against a match I saw in the lightning and bit at the head. There was no rewarding flare. The house was trembling violently now and I heard rustlings about me as if she had called them all to fight me, to save their cursed existence.

I bit at another match. A white face stared at me from the rug and I spat blood at it. It disappeared. I tore one arm loose and grabbed a match. I jerked myself to the mantel and dragged the match across the rough wood. A speck of flame flared up in my fingers and I was released.

The throbbing seemed more violent now. But I knew it was helpless against flame. I protected the flame with my hand though, lest that cold wind come again and try to blow it out. I held the match against a magazine that was lying on a chair and it flared up. I shook it and the pages puffed into flame. I threw it down on the rug.

I went around in that light striking one match after another, avoiding the sight of Saul lying there. She had destroyed him but now I would destroy her forever.

I ignited the curtains. I started the rug to smoldering. I set fire to the furniture. The house rocked and a whistling sigh rose and ebbed like the wind.

At last I stood erect in the flaming room, my eyes riveted on the portrait. I walked slowly toward it. She knew my intentions for the house rocked even harder and a shrieking began that seemed to come from the walls. And I knew then that the house was controlled by her and that her power was in that portrait.

I drew it down from the wall. It shook in my very hands as if it were alive. With a shudder of repugnance I threw it on the flames.

I almost fell while the floor shuddered as if an earthquake were striking the land. But then it stopped and the portrait was burning and the last effect of her was gone. I was alone in an old burning house.

I did not want anyone to know about my brother. I did not want anyone to see his face like that.

So I lifted him and put him on the couch. I do not understand to this day how I could lift him up when I felt so weak. It was a strength not my own.

I sat at his feet, stroking his hand until the flames grew too hot. Then I rose. I bent over him and kissed him on the lips for a last good-bye. And I walked from the house into the rain. And I never came back. Because there was nothing to ever come back for.

This is the end of the manuscript. There seems no adequate evidence to ascribe the events recounted as true. But the following facts, taken from the city's police files, might prove of interest.

In 1901, the city was severely shocked by the most wholesale murder ever perpetrated in its history.

At the height of a party being held at the home of Mr. and Mrs. Marlin Slaughter and their daughter Clarissa, an unknown person poisoned the punch by placing a very large amount of arsenic in it. Everyone died. The case was never solved although various theories were put forth as to its solution. One thesis had it that the murderer was one of those who died.

As to the identity of this murderer, supposition had it that it was not a murderer but a murderess. Although nothing definite exists to go by, there are several testimonies which refer to "that poor child Clarissa" and indicate that the young woman had been suffering for some years from a severe mental aberration which her parents had tried to keep a secret from the neighbors and the authorities. The party in mention was supposed to have been planned to celebrate what her parents took for the recovery of her faculties.

As to the body of the young man later supposed to be in the wreckage, a thorough search has revealed nothing. It may be that the entire story is imagination, fabricated by the one brother in order to conceal the death of the other, said death probably being unnatural. Thus, the older brother knowing the story of the house tragedy may have used it for a fantastic evidence in his favor.

Whatever the truth, the older brother has never been heard of again either in this city or in any of the adjacent localities.

And that's the story. S.D.M.

THE MIDWEST

We have followed the perimeter of the United States from the Atlantic seaboard around the Gulf of Mexico, over the Mexican border and up the Pacific coast (with a side trip to Hawaii) and now it is time to penetrate into the heartland of America.

The twelve states that make up the Midwest account for one fifth of the nation's total area—765,000 square miles of dramatically variegated terrain stretching westward from densely populated Ohio and Chicago-dominated Illinois to the sparsely settled badlands of the Dakotas, with the thousand-plus lakes apiece of Michigan, Minnesota and Wisconsin in the north, the great plains of Kansas and Nebraska to the southwest and Mark Twain's Missouri river country in the southeast.

Perhaps because it borders on Eastern, Southern and Western states, the Midwest is a fascinating chameleon, sometimes urban, sometimes bucolic, and the same may be said of its "night life"— for in the following nine tales, the reader will encounter spooks both primitive and modern.

ROBERT E. HOWARD

The Dead Remember

Our first Midwestern story might have been included in the West, since it begins in Texas, but this haunting follows the route of the old cattle drives and ends up in Dodge City, Kansas, home of Wyatt Earp and Bat Masterson and site of the original Boot Hill Cemetery. ROBERT E. HOWARD *(1906–1936), author of the Solomon Kane series and the "Conan" stories popularized in comic books and films, sold "The Dead Remember" to* Argosy *the same year he committed suicide.*

Dodge City, Kansas
November 3, 1877

Mr. William L. Gordon,
Antioch, Texas.

Dear Bill:

I am writing you because I have got a feeling I am not long for this world. This may surprise you, because you know I was in good health when I left the herd, and I am not sick now as far as that goes, but just the same I believe I am as good as a dead man.

Before I tell you why I think so, I will tell you the rest of what I have to say, which is that we got to Dodge City all right with the herd, which tallied 3,400 head, and the trail boss, John Elston, got twenty dollars a head from Mr. R. J. Blaine, but Joe Richards, one of the boys, was killed by a steer near the crossing of the Canadian. His sister, Mrs. Dick Westfall, lives near Seguin, and I wish you'd ride over and tell her about her brother. John Elston is sending her his saddle and bridle and gun and money.

Now, Bill, I will try to tell you why I know I'm a goner. You remember last August, just before I left for Kansas with the herd, they found that Old Joel, that used to be Colonel Henry's slave, and his woman dead—the ones that lived in that live-oak thicket down by Zavalla Creek. You know they called his woman Jezebel, and folks said she was a witch. She was a high-yellow gal and a lot younger than Joel. She told fortunes, and even some of the white folks were afraid of her. I took no stock in those stories.

Well, when we was rounding up the cattle for the trail drive, I found myself near Zavalla Creek along toward sundown, and my horse was tired, and I was hungry, and I decided I'd stop in at Joel's and make his woman cook me something to eat. So I rode up to his hut in the middle of the live-oak grove, and Joel was cutting some wood to cook some beef which Jezebel had stewing over an open fire. I remember she had on a red and green checked dress. I won't likely forget that.

They told me to light and I done so, and set down and ate a hearty supper, then Joel brought out a bottle of tequila and we had a drink, and I said I could beat him shooting craps. He asked me if I had any dice, and I said no, and he said he had some dice and would roll me for a five-cent piece.

So we got to shooting craps, and drinking tequila, and I got pretty full and raring to go, but Joel won all my money, which was about five dollars and seventy-five cents. This made me mad, and I told him I'd take another drink and get on my horse and ride. But he said the bottle was empty, and I told him to get some more. He said he didn't have no more, and I got madder, and begun to swear and abuse him, because I was pretty drunk. Jezebel come to the door of the hut and tried to get me to ride on, but I told her I was free, white and twenty-one, and for her to look out, because I didn't have no use for smart high-yellow gals.

Then Joel got mad and said, yes, he had some more tequila in the hut, but he wouldn't give me a drink if I was dying of thirst. So I said, "Why, damn you, you get me drunk and take my money with crooked dice, and now you insult me. I've seen nigras hung for less than that."

He said, "You can't eat my beef and drink my licker and then call my dice crooked. No white man can do that. I'm just as tough as you are."

I said, "Damn your black soul, I'll kick you all over this flat."

He said, "White man, you won't kick nobody." Then he grabbed up the knife he'd been cutting beef with, and ran at me. I pulled my pistol and shot him twice through the belly. He fell down and I shot him again, through the head.

Then Jezebel come running out screaming and cursing, with an old muzzle-loading musket. She pointed it at me and pulled the trigger, but the cap burst without firing the piece, and I yelled for her to get back or I'd kill her. But she run in on me and swung the musket like a club. I dodged and it hit me a glancing lick, tearing the hide on the side of my head, and I clapped my pistol against her bosom and jerked the trigger. The shot knocked her staggering back several foot, and she reeled and fell down on the ground, with her hand to her bosom and blood running out between her fingers.

I went over to her and stood looking down with the pistol in my hand, swearing and cursing her, and she looked up and said, "You've killed Joel and you've killed me, but by God, you won't brag about it. I curse you by the big snake and the black swamp and the white cock. Before this day rolls around again you'll be branding the devil's cows in hell. You'll see, I'll come to you when the time's ripe and ready."

Then the blood gushed out of her mouth and she fell back and I knew she was dead. Then I got scared and sobered up and got on my horse and rode. Nobody seen me, and I told the boys next day I got that bruise on the side of my head from a tree branch my horse had run me against. Nobody never knew it was me that killed them two, and I wouldn't be telling you now, only I know I have not got long to live.

That curse has been dogging me, and there is no use trying to dodge it. All the way up the trail I could feel something following me. Before we got to Red River I found a rattlesnake coiled up in my boot one morning, and after that I slept with my boots on all the time. Then when we was crossing the Canadian it was up a little, and I was riding point, and the herd got to milling for no reason at all, and caught me in the mill. My horse drowned, and I would have, too, if Steve Kirby hadn't roped me and dragged me out from amongst them crazy cows. Then one of the hands was cleaning a buffalo rifle one night, and it went off in his hands and blowed a hole in my hat. By this time the boys was joking and saying I was a hoodoo.

But after we crossed the Canadian, the cattle stampeded on the clearest, quietest night I ever seen. I was riding nightherd and didn't see nor hear nothing that might have started it, but one of the boys said just before the break he heard a low wailing sound down amongst a grove of cottonwoods, and saw a strange blue light glimmering there. Anyway, the steers broke so sudden and unexpected they nearly caught me and I had to ride for all I was worth. There was steers behind me and on both sides of me, and if I hadn't been riding the fastest horse ever raised in South Texas, they'd have trampled me to a pulp.

Well, I finally pulled out of the fringe of them, and we spent all next day rounding them up out of the breaks. That was when Joe Richards got killed. We was out in the breaks, driving in a bunch of steers, and all at once, without any reason I could see, my horse gave an awful scream and rared and fell backward with me. I jumped off just in time to keep from getting mashed, and a big mossy horn give a bellow and come for me.

There wasn't a tree bigger than a bush anywhere near, so I tried to pull my pistol, and some way the hammer got jammed under my belt, and I couldn't get it loose. That wild steer wasn't more than ten jumps from me when Joe Richards roped it, and the horse, a green one, was jerked down and sideways. As it fell, Joe tried to swing clear, but his spur caught in the back cinch, and the next instant that steer had drove both horns clean through him. It was an awful sight.

By that time I had my pistol out, and I shot the steer, but Joe was dead. He was tore up something terrible. We covered him up where he fell, and put up a wood cross, and John Elston carved on the name and date with his bowie knife.

After that the boys didn't joke any more about me being a hoodoo. They didn't say much of anything to me and I kept to myself, though the Lord knows, it wasn't any fault of mine as I can see.

Well, we got to Dodge City and sold the steers. And last night I dreamt I saw Jezebel, just as plain as I see the pistol on my hip. She smiled like the devil himself and said something I couldn't understand, but she pointed at me, and I think I know what that means.

Bill, you'll never see me again. I'm a dead man. I don't know how I'll go out but I feel I'll never live to see another sunrise. So I'm writing you this letter to let you know about this business and I reckon I've been a fool but it looks like a man just kind of has to go it blind and there is not any blazed trail to follow.

Anyway, whatever takes me will find me on my feet with my pistol drawed. I never knuckled down to anything alive, and I won't even to the dead. I am going out fighting, whatever comes. I keep my scabbard-end tied down, and I clean and oil my pistol every day. And, Bill, sometimes I think I am going crazy, but I reckon it is just thinking and dreaming so much about Jezebel; because I am using an old shirt of yours for cleaning rags, you know that black and white checked shirt you got at San Antonio last Christmas, but sometimes when I am cleaning my pistol with them rags, they don't look black and white any more. They turn to red and green, just the color of the dress Jezebel was wearing when I killed her.

Your brother,

JIM

STATEMENT OF JOHN ELSTON, NOVEMBER 4, 1877

My name is John Elston. I am the foreman of Mr. J. J. Connolly's ranch in Gonzales County, Texas. I was trail boss of the herd that Jim Gordon was employed on. I was sharing his hotel room with him. The morning of the third of November he seemed moody and wouldn't talk much. He would not go out with me, but said he was going to write a letter.

I did not see him again until that night. I came into the room to get something and he was cleaning his Colt's .45. I laughed and jokingly asked him if he was afraid of Bat Masterson, and he said:

"John, what I'm afraid of ain't human, but I'm going out shooting if I can." I laughed and asked him what he was afraid of, and he said: "A high-yeller gal that's been dead four months." I thought he was drunk, and went on out. I don't know what time that was, but it was after dark.

I didn't see him again alive. About midnight I was passing the Big Chief saloon and I heard a shot, and a lot of people ran into the saloon. I heard somebody say a man was shot. I went in with the rest, and went on back into the back room. A man was lying in the doorway, with his legs out in the alley and his body in the door. He was covered with blood, but by his build and clothes I recognized Jim Gordon. He was dead. I did not see him killed, and know nothing beyond what I have already said.

STATEMENT OF MIKE O'DONNELL

My name is Michael Joseph O'Donnell. I am the bartender in the Big Chief saloon on the night shift. A few minutes before midnight I noticed a cowboy talking to Sam Grimes just outside the saloon. They seemed to be arguing. After awhile the cowboy came on in and took a drink of whiskey at the bar. I noticed him because he wore a pistol, whereas the others had theirs out of sight, and because he looked so wild and pale. He looked like he was drunk, but I don't believe he was. I never saw a man who looked just like him.

I did not pay much attention to him after that because I was very busy tending bar. I suppose he must have gone on into the back room. At about midnight I heard a shot in the back room and Tom Allison ran out saying that a man had been shot. I was the first one to reach him. He was lying partly in the door and partly in the alley. I saw he wore a gun belt and a Mexican carved holster and I believed it to be the same man I had noticed earlier. His right hand was torn practically off, being just a mass of bloody tatters. His head was shattered in a way I had never seen caused by a gunshot. He was dead by the time I got there and it is my opinion he was killed instantly. While we were standing around him a man I knew to be John Elston came through the crowd and said, "My God, it's Jim Gordon!"

STATEMENT OF DEPUTY GRIMES

My name is Sam Grimes, I am a deputy sheriff of Ford County, Kansas. I met the deceased, Jim Gordon, before the Big Chief saloon, at about twenty minutes until twelve, November 3rd. I saw he had his pistol buckled on, so I stopped him and asked him why he was carrying his pistol and if he did not know it was against the law. He said he was packing it for protection. I told him if he was in danger it was my business to protect him, and he had better take his gun back to his hotel and leave it there till he was ready to leave town, because I saw by his clothes that he was a cowboy from Texas. He laughed and said, "Deputy, not even Wyatt Earp could protect me from my fate!" He went into the saloon.

I believed he was sick and out of his head, so I did not arrest him. I thought maybe he would take a drink and then go and leave his gun at his hotel as I had requested. I kept watching him to see that he did not make any play toward anybody in the saloon, but he noticed no one, took a drink at the bar, and went on into the back room.

A few minutes later a man ran out, shouting that somebody was killed. I went right to the back room, getting there just as Mike O'Donnell was bending over the man, who I believed to be the one I had accosted in the street. He had been killed by the bursting of the pistol in his hand. I don't know who he was shooting at, if anybody. I found nobody in the alley, nor anybody who had seen the killing except Tom Allison. I did find pieces of the pistol that had exploded, together with the end of the barrel, which I turned over to the coroner.

STATEMENT OF TOM ALLISON

My name is Thomas Allison. I am a teamster, employed by McFarlane & Company. On the night of November 3rd, I was in the Big Chief saloon. I did not notice the deceased when he came in. There was a lot of men in the saloon. I had had several drinks but was not drunk. I saw "Grizzly" Gullins, a buffalo hunter, approaching the entrance of the saloon. I had had trouble with him, and knew he was a bad man. He was drunk and I did not want any trouble. I decided to go out the back way.

I went through the back room and saw a man sitting at a table with his head in his hands. I took no notice of him, but went on to the back door, which was bolted on the inside. I lifted the bolt and opened the door and started to step outside.

Then I saw a woman standing in front of me. The light was dim that streamed out into the alley through the open door, but I saw her plain enough to tell she was a Negro woman. I don't know how she was dressed. She was not pure black but a light brown or yellow. I could tell that in the dim light. I was so surprised I stopped short, and she spoke to me and said, "Go tell Jim Gordon I've come for him."

I said, "Who the devil are you and who is Jim Gordon?" She said, "The man in the back room sitting at the table; tell him I've come!"

Something made me turn cold all over, I can't say why. I turned around and went back into the room, and said, "Are you Jim Gordon?" The man at the table looked up and I saw his face was pale and haggard. I said, "Somebody wants to see you." He said, "Who wants to see me, stranger?" I said, "A high-yellow woman there at the back door."

With that he heaved up from the chair, knocking it over along with the table. I thought he was crazy and fell back from him. His eyes were wild. He gave a kind of strangled cry and rushed to the open door. I saw him glare out into the alley, and thought I heard a laugh from the darkness. Then he screamed again and jerked out his pistol.

There was a flash that blinded me and a terrible report, and when the smoke cleared a little, I saw the man lying in the door with his head and body covered with blood. His brains were oozing out, and there was blood all over his right hand. I ran to the front of the saloon, shouting for the bartender. I don't know whether he was shooting at the woman or not, or if anybody shot back. I never heard but the one shot, when his pistol burst.

CORONER'S REPORT

We, the coroner's jury, having held inquest over the remains of James A. Gordon, of Antioch, Texas, have reached a verdict of death by accidental gunshot wounds, caused by the bursting of the deceased's pistol, he having apparently failed to remove a cleaning rag from the barrel after cleaning it. Portions of the burnt rag were found in the barrel. They had evidently been a piece of a woman's red and green checked dress.

Signed:

> J. S. Ordley, Coroner
> Richard Donovan
> Ezra Blaine
> Joseph T. Decker
> Jack Wiltshaw
> Alexander V. Williams

JAMES THURBER

The Night the Ghost Got In

JAMES THURBER *(1894–1961) contributed cartoons and humorous essays to* The New Yorker *magazine and wrote* Fables for Our Time, The Great Quillow, Many Moons, The Middle-Aged Man on the Flying Trapeze *and many other books and short pieces, including the famous "The Catbird Seat" and "The Secret Life of Walter Mitty," filmed in 1947 with my boyhood hero Danny Kaye (no relationship) in the title role. I myself portrayed Mitty at the 1989 Edinburgh (Scotland) International Festival in a production of* A Thurber Carnival *starring William Windom. Bill, who played Thurber on the TV series* My Life and Hard Times *and in his own successful touring road shows, opened our* Carnival *performances at the Royal Scots Club with the hilarious "The Night the Bed Fell" from* My Life and Hard Times, *Thurber's recollections of his early family life in Columbus, Ohio. "The Night the Ghost Got In," another chapter from that book, though not as familiar as the earlier tale, is in my opinion even funnier.*

The ghost that got into our house on the night of November 17, 1915, raised such a hullabaloo of misunderstanding that I am sorry I didn't just let it keep on walking, and go to bed. Its advent caused my mother to throw a shoe through a window of the house next door and ended up with my grandfather shooting a patrolman. I am sorry, therefore, as I have said, that I ever paid any attention to the footsteps.

They began about a quarter past one o'clock in the morning, a rhythmic, quick-cadenced walking around the dining-room table. My mother was asleep in one room upstairs, my brother Herman in another; grandfather was in the attic, in the old walnut bed which, as you will remember, once fell on my father. I had just stepped out of the bathtub and was busily rubbing myself with a towel when I heard the steps. They were the steps of a man walking rapidly around the dining-room table downstairs. The light from the bathroom shone down the back steps, which dropped directly into the dining-room; I could see the faint shine of plates on the plate-rail; I couldn't see the table. The steps kept going round and round the table; at regular intervals a board creaked, when it was trod upon. I supposed at first that it was my father or my brother Roy, who had gone to Indianapolis but were expected home at any time. I suspected next that it was a burglar. It did not enter my mind until later that it was a ghost.

After the walking had gone on for perhaps three minutes, I tiptoed to Herman's room. "Psst!" I hissed, in the dark, shaking him. "Awp," he said, in the low, hopeless tone of a despondent beagle—he always half suspected that something would "get him" in the night. I told him who I was. "There's something downstairs!" I said. He got up and followed me to the head of the back staircase. We listened together. There was no sound. The steps had ceased. Herman looked at me in some alarm: I had only the bath towel around my waist. He wanted to go back to bed, but I gripped his arm. "There's something down there!" I said. Instantly the steps began again, circled the dining-room table like a man running, and started up the stairs toward us, heavily, two at a time. The light still shone palely down the stairs; we saw nothing coming; we only heard the steps. Herman rushed to his room and slammed the door. I slammed shut the door at the stairs top and held my knee against it. After a long minute, I slowly opened it again. There was nothing there. There was no sound. None of us ever heard the ghost again.

The slamming of the doors had aroused mother: she peered out of her room. "What on earth are you boys doing?" she demanded. Herman ventured out of his room. "Nothing," he said, gruffly, but he was, in color, a light green. "What was all that running around downstairs?" said mother. So she had heard the steps, too! We just looked at her. "Burglars!" she shouted, intuitively. I tried to quiet her by starting lightly downstairs.

"Come on, Herman," I said.

"I'll stay with mother," he said. "She's all excited."

I stepped back onto the landing.

"Don't either of you go a step," said mother. "We'll call the police." Since the phone was downstairs, I didn't see how we were going to call the police—nor did I want the police—but mother made one of her quick, incomparable decisions. She flung up a window of her bedroom which faced the bedroom windows of the house of a neighbor, picked up a shoe, and whammed it through a pane of glass across the narrow space that separated the two houses. Glass tinkled into the bedroom occupied by a retired engraver named Bodwell and his wife. Bodwell had been for some years in rather a bad way and was subject to mild "attacks." Most everybody we knew or lived near had *some* kind of attacks.

It was now about two o'clock of a moonless night; clouds hung black and low. Bodwell was at the window in a minute, shouting, frothing a little, shaking his fist. "We'll sell the house and go back to Peoria," we could hear Mrs. Bodwell saying. It was some time before mother "got through" to Bodwell. "Burglars!" she shouted. "Burglars in the house!" Herman and I hadn't dared to tell her that it was not burglars but ghosts, for she was even more afraid of ghosts than of burglars. Bodwell at first thought that she meant there were burglars in his house, but finally he quieted down and called the police for us over an extension phone by his bed. After he had disappeared from the window, mother suddenly made as if to throw another shoe, not because there was further need of it but, as she later explained, because the thrill of heaving a shoe through a window glass had enormously taken her fancy. I prevented her.

The police were on hand in a commendably short time: a Ford sedan full of them, two on motorcycles, and a patrol wagon with about eight in it and a few reporters. They began banging at our front door. Flashlights shot streaks of gleam up and down the walls, across the yard, down the walk between our house and

Bodwell's. "Open up!" cried a hoarse voice. "We're men from Headquarters!" I wanted to go down and let them in, since there they were, but mother wouldn't hear of it. "You haven't a stitch on," she pointed out. "You'd catch your death." I wound the towel around me again. Finally the cops put their shoulders to our big heavy front door with its thick beveled glass and broke it in: I could hear a rending of wood and a splash of glass on the floor of the hall. Their lights played all over the living-room and crisscrossed nervously in the dining-room, stabbed into hallways, shot up the front stairs and finally up the back. They caught me standing in my towel at the top. A heavy policeman bounded up the steps. "Who are you?" he demanded. "I live here," I said. "Well, whattsa matta, ya hot?" he asked. It was, as a matter of fact, cold; I went to my room and pulled on some trousers. On my way out, a cop stuck a gun into my ribs. "Whatta you doin' here?" he demanded. "I live here," I said.

The officer in charge reported to mother. "No sign of nobody, lady," he said. "Musta got away—whatt'd he look like?" "There were two or three of them," mother said, "whooping and carrying on and slamming doors." "Funny," said the cop. "All ya windows and doors was locked on the inside tight as a tick."

Downstairs, we could hear the tromping of the other police. Police were all over the place; doors were yanked open, drawers were yanked open, windows were shot up and pulled down, furniture fell with dull thumps. A half-dozen policemen emerged out of the darkness of the front hallway upstairs. They began to ransack the floor: pulled beds away from walls, tore clothes off hooks in the closets, pulled suitcases and boxes off shelves. One of them found an old zither that Roy had won in a pool tournament. "Looky here, Joe," he said, strumming it with a big paw. The cop named Joe took it and turned it over. "What is it?" he asked me. "It's an old zither our guinea pig used to sleep on," I said. It was true that a pet guinea pig we once had would never sleep anywhere except on the zither, but I should never have said so. Joe and the other cop looked at me a long time. They put the zither back on a shelf.

"No sign o' nuthin'," said the cop who had first spoken to mother. "This guy," he explained to the others, jerking a thumb at me, "was nekked. The lady seems historical." They all nodded but said nothing; just looked at me. In the small silence we all heard a creaking in the attic. Grandfather was turning over in bed. "What's 'at?" snapped Joe. Five or six cops sprang for the attic door before I could intervene or explain. I realized that it would be bad if they burst in on grandfather unannounced, or even announced. He was going through a phase in which he believed that General Meade's men, under steady hammering by Stonewall Jackson, were beginning to retreat and even desert.

When I got to the attic, things were pretty confused. Grandfather had evidently jumped to the conclusion that the police were deserters from Meade's army, trying to hide away in his attic. He bounded out of bed wearing a long flannel nightgown over long woolen underwear, a nightcap, and a leather jacket around his chest. The cops must have realized at once that the indignant white-haired old man belonged in the house, but they had no chance to say so. "Back, ye cowardly dogs!" roared grandfather. "Back t' the lines, ye goddam lily-livered cattle!" With that, he fetched the officer who found the zither a flat-handed smack alongside his head that sent him sprawling. The others beat a retreat, but not fast enough; grandfather grabbed Zither's gun from its holster and let fly. The report seemed to crack the rafters; smoke filled the attic. A cop cursed and shot his hand to his shoulder. Somehow, we all finally got downstairs again and locked the door against the old gentleman. He fired once or twice more in the darkness and then went back to bed. "That was grandfather," I explained to Joe, out of breath. "He thinks you're deserters." "I'll say he does," said Joe.

The cops were reluctant to leave without getting their hands on somebody besides grandfather; the night had been distinctly a defeat for them. Furthermore, they obviously didn't like the "layout"; something looked—and I can see their viewpoint—phony. They began to poke into things again. A reporter, a thin-faced, wispy man, came up to me. I had put on one of mother's blouses, not being able to find anything else. The reporter looked at me with mingled suspicion and interest. "Just what the hell is the real lowdown here, Bud?" he asked. I decided to be frank with him. "We had ghosts," I said. He gazed at me a long time as if I were a slot machine into which he had, without results, dropped a nickel. Then he walked away. The cops followed him, the one grandfather shot holding his now-bandaged arm, cursing and blaspheming. "I'm gonna get my gun back from that old bird," said the zither-cop. "Yeh," said Joe. "You—and who else?" I told them I would bring it to the station house the next day.

"What was the matter with that one policeman?" mother asked, after they had gone. "Grandfather shot him," I said. "What for?" she demanded. I told her he was a deserter. "Of all things!" said mother. "He was such a nice-looking young man."

Grandfather was fresh as a daisy and full of jokes at breakfast next morning. We thought at first he had forgotten all about what had happened, but he hadn't. Over his third cup of coffee, he glared at Herman and me. "What was the idee of all them cops tarryhootin' round the house last night?" he demanded. He had us there.

HENDERSON STARKE

Dumb Supper

Though The Magazine of Fantasy and Science Fiction (F&SF, *as it is commonly known) was the training ground for many of America's most important science-fiction writers in the 1950s, the first several issues were more heavily weighted towards fantasy. The third issue included one of the chilliest little tales I've ever read, "Dumb Supper," set in the real town of Carthage in southwestern Missouri.* HENDERSON STARKE, *who in 1950 was perhaps* F&SF's *oldest contributor, lived in the Ozarks where, Starke said, "the ladies in my neighborhood know all about dumb suppers—but none of 'em will ever admit to cooking one!"*

("Why shucks, everybody *knows* black is the color of death. If you see something black coming at you in your dreams, you may just as well give up, 'cause you ain't long for *this* world.")

Rosalynn twisted in her chair and picked at a bit of lint on her wool skirt as she looked at the speaker.

("You should have seen the dress Nellie bought over in Joplin; the *cutest* thing.")

Rosalynn extended her legs and looked down at them.

("They say it cost fifty dollars. My!")

Rosalynn hooked her toe under the rocker of the chair before her and set it in motion.

"Oh! Don't do that, dear," Marsha said. "A chair that's empty rocked, its owner will with ills be stocked."

Rosalynn looked up. "I'm sorry," she said.

("Of course it may be a little too low for her, you know. She doesn't have the *figure.*")

Jean Towers came over and sat down by Rosalynn. "Don't mind Marsha. She's just superstitious."

"I didn't mind," Rosalynn said.

"I guess you think we're unfriendly?"

"No," said Rosalynn.

("And they say they're gonna get married next month. And about time, too, if you ask me.")

"I don't think you're unfriendly. I'll just need a little time to get to know you, and then I'll be all right."

("Well, I certainly wish Jude would hurry up and ask me.")

"Amy told me your family just moved in last week."

"Yes," Rosalynn said. "From California. Fresno."

"What do you think of Carthage?"

"Oh," Rosalynn said, "it's—I mean, I think I'll like it. I mean, I'm *sure* I'll like it."

"Sure you will."

"It's just that now—at first, I mean—everybody is talking about people I don't know and places I—"

("And me too!" someone said, and it sent some of the girls off into peals of laughter.)

Jean Towers smiled sympathetically. "You'll get caught up in the swing of things."

"Uh-huh. Ah—could you tell me—" But Jean Towers had left her side.

("And I said to him, 'If you think for a minute that—' ")

Rosalynn picked at the lint again. This was a new town and this was her first party and she wanted—oh, so very badly—to make a good impression; or they maybe wouldn't ask her again. And it was really her place, she knew, to be friendly.

("You girls better have a dumb supper.")

"What would you think of a dumb supper, Rosalynn?" Jean Towers asked.

Rosalynn said, "A dumb supper? Why—I guess, I mean—sure, if you girls want to. I think I'd like something like that."

"Do you have dumb suppers, ever, where you come from?" Amy asked.

Rosalynn said, "It's a game, isn't it?"

"Not exactly—well, I guess you might say it was a game, too, sort of."

"Then I guess we have something like it back in Fresno," Rosalynn said and laughed. For the first time she was included in the general conversation and she was happy. "Why don't you tell me just what it is and then I'll tell you if we had anything like it."

"Well," Jean Towers said, "it's a kind of a legend. Nobody believes in it anymore. Except some of the peckerwood people back in the hills. And maybe one or two of the old timers, like Uncle Alvin down on the river bottom." She made a deprecating little gesture. " 'Course there *are* stories. . . ."

"Maybe you ought to tell her the one Grandma Wilson's always telling."

"I don't know—well— Would you like to listen to it, Rosalynn?"

Rosalynn said, "Yes."

"It all happened in the Rush family. (They're—the Rushes, that is—they're all over this section now; there's a lot of them around Pierce City, and the Roberts of Webb City are first cousins—but this was a long time ago, maybe a hundred years, when they'd just moved in from Kentucky.) There was a girl in the family, young, name of Sarah. A pretty little thing, friendly, the way Grandma Wilson tells it."

Rosalynn stared down at her shoe tops, wishing she were pretty, trying to believe what her mother told her, "It's not what you look like, honey, that's important; it's the kind of a person you are," and remembering, too, how she looked to herself in the mirror, wondering where she could find a husband for a face like that.

Jean Towers said, "One night at a party—a party like this, I imagine, when the old people were gone—somebody suggested that they have a dumb supper; just like you do suggest things, half joking, half serious: that way. Sarah thought it was a good idea (they used to do things like that back in Kentucky), and she wasn't afraid at all."

Sarah had been a friendly girl; Rosalynn wondered how people got to be that way; how they learned to say the right things and do the right things and make people like them.

"Of course, you understand, a dumb supper isn't really a *supper*. It's just a halfway supper. Nobody eats anything—and there isn't anything to eat, except two little pieces of corn bread."

Rosalynn wondered why she always was half frightened by people; why she had to screw her courage down tight even to come to a party like this. She really wanted to like people and have them like her. And after all, everyone here was friendly—and they'd wanted her to come: or Amy wouldn't have asked her. They were nice enough, too, a little different from the girls back home, but nice in their way, and she'd stop feeling like an outsider in a little while.

"Well, Sarah began to fix for the dumb supper. Now, fixing for a dumb supper has to be done in a special way."

At first Rosalynn thought they had resented her—maybe because her clothes were nicer than theirs, or maybe because her father had a better job than their fathers, or maybe because she lived in the big house out on South Main, or maybe because she didn't have an accent like they had and talked faster. But now, with them gathered around her, listening, she saw that they really didn't hate her and it had only been in her imagination all along.

"Everything has to be done *backwards*. Everything, like mixing the batter, striking the match, even walking. Everything opposite from usual."

Maybe she was afraid of people because she thought they all wanted to hurt her. (In her second year of high school—she could still remember burningly what she had heard her best friend say.) Her father had explained it all: "You see, people aren't really as bad as you think; they may be thoughtless, but they're very seldom cruel. Most people aren't like your friend Betty. They'd rather be friendly than unfriendly, if you'll only give them the chance."

"Sarah cooked her corn bread, doing everything backwards, the way it's supposed to be done. And then she set out the plates. Two of them. One for herself and one for her husband."

Rosalynn was going to be a different girl. She was going to make all kinds of new friends (like Jean and Amy and Marsha—the superstitious one). And she would have the best times talking to them, and parties at her big house—and maybe dates (for she wasn't *that* ugly; only she always seemed to scare the few boys off because she was so timid, but it would be different this time). Then maybe—

"You see, if you do everything just right, according to the story, at least, when you set down at your plate with the backward corn bread on it, your husband will come in (not *really*, I mean, but like a ghost) and set down at *his* plate so you can see his face and that way you get to find out who your husband is going to be."

"Oh," said Rosalynn, resolving to listen more carefully, for if she wanted to make friends, she must remember not to feel sorry for herself, but to be very polite and listen very closely whether or not she was interested.

"At each plate Sarah put down a knife. (They had funny knives in those days with bone handles: and the one she put at her husband's plate had a big, star-shaped chip knocked off of it.)

"By this time the wind was coming up in the north (as it always does at a dumb supper), and you could hear it moan in the trees. It was very quiet in the house, for you mustn't talk—not anyone—at a dumb supper.

"Sarah put a piece of corn bread on each plate and then she sat down, as calm as anything, to wait.

"Everybody was holding their breath, and you could hear the wind blowing louder and louder."

Rosalynn shivered; she really didn't want to hear the rest of the story.

"And then—bang!—the front door flew open and slammed back against the wall, hard, making the house shake. And the wind blew in and made the candles flicker. (This was long ago, before electricity.)

"And just as the candles went out, a figure all in white came rushing in to set down beside Sarah."

Jean Towers paused, and Rosalynn could hear her own heart beating in the stillness.

"When the candle was lit again, the figure was gone. And the knife that had lain by its plate was gone too."

"Is—is that all?" Rosalynn asked.

"No. No, that's just the first part. You see, she really got to see its face. (Or so she said.)

"Well, some time after that, maybe a year or two, a stranger came to town; name was Hall. Young man, handsome, good worker, although a quiet sort, not given to talking too much. When Sarah saw him, she knew that was the man who was going to be her husband, for his face was the face of the figure in white.

"She married him and they went to live in a little cabin on her father's property.

"Things went along fine for a year, for he was a good farmer and a sober, loving husband. But one day—

"Well, her father went down to see them, and when he got up to the top of the ridge (the cabin was down in a valley, like), he could see that there wasn't any sign of smoke in the chimney; which wasn't right, for it was a chilly autumn day. The cabin was still, as if there wasn't anyone around. (You know, sometimes you can tell when you see a house that there isn't anybody at home.) Well, he knew immediately that there was something wrong. So he hurried down.

"And what do you think he found in the cabin? . . . Sarah. Lying on the floor. She was lying there with her eyes closed and a knife sticking out between her breasts.

"She wasn't dead, though (but it was just a lucky thing that her father came along when he did or she would have been). And she didn't die, either. But it was quite a while before she could get up and around (the doctors didn't know as much in those days).

"Finally, she told everybody what had happened.

"That morning, when her father found her lying there in the cabin almost dead, she had told her husband (for the first time) about how she had seen his face there at the dumb supper.

"At first he didn't say anything at all—just sort of stared at her. Then he got up and went to a little box he always kept—he wore the key around his neck and wouldn't let anyone see what was in it —and opened it. He took out the knife that was there on a velvet cushion.

"And he turned back to Sarah.

" 'So you're the witch that sent me through that night of hell!' he screamed, and then he plunged the knife into her.

"It was the knife with the star-shaped chip out of the bone handle.

"And she never saw her husband again."

Rosalynn swallowed. "That—that was—awful," she said.

Marsha laughed thinly.

"You mean that you actually still have dumb suppers?" Rosalynn asked.

"Well," Jean Towers said, "not very often. Oh, maybe once in a while. I mean there's nothing *in* it. Though some of the peckerwoods would say it was witchcraft. Just for a laugh, you know. We don't *believe* it. But it does give you a funny, creepy feeling."

"I think we ought to have one," Amy said. "Then Rosalynn can see—the kind of games we play."

"Yes, let's."

"Let's even let Rosalynn cook it."

"How about it, Rosalynn?"

Rosalynn said, "All right, I mean, if you want to. But let somebody else cook it, why not? I—I'm afraid I never learned how to cook—not even corn bread."

"If *that's* all. We can show you how that's done."

"Well," Rosalynn said slowly, "I'll do it if somebody will too." She turned to Marsha. "You?"

"I wouldn't do it for the *world*," Marsha said.

"Be still!" Jean told her. And then to Rosalynn: "She doesn't believe anything would happen of course. She—she just doesn't believe in taking chances. All of us here have cooked dumb suppers before."

"Yes," said Marsha. "We have."

"Well, how about you, Amy?"

"Me? It's—more fun if only one person cooks the supper."

"Oh . . . I mean, I guess, if you really *want* me to, of course . . ." Rosalynn realized vaguely that it was probably just an ordinary prank they were in on; trying to scare her. Maybe like an initiation stunt. And if she wanted them to be her friends she'd have to go through with it. And not show that she was scared.

"All right," she said, "I'll do it."

Before, it seemed a million times, Rosalynn had wished she wasn't so easy to frighten. Even when she was little the parents had to stay in the room until she was asleep; and now and then, still, she would turn on the light at night (which took all her courage) just to be sure nothing was there.

She told herself something that usually worked; she told herself, "They will all be laughing about it next week, and then I can tell them how scared I was and they won't mind at all."

She looked at the wall clock.

There was no help there. Mr. and Mrs. Pierce, Amy's parents, wouldn't get back from Carthage until midnight.

The house was a farmhouse, four miles out of town. And Rosalynn had no way to leave, even if she wanted to, for she was depending on the Pierces to take her home when they came back.

"Come on," Jean said.

They went into the kitchen where Amy got the proper ingredients; there were three little cups of them, already set out. Rosalynn knew, then, that they had prepared for this.

"Flour," Amy said, pointing. "Corn meal. Baking powder." She drew a glass of water from the tap. "Mix the stuff all together and add the water until it's doughy."

"Salt?" Rosalynn asked.

"I thought you said you didn't know how to make corn bread."

"I—I don't: I just thought it ought to have salt in it—I mean, most things ought to have salt in them."

"Not *this* corn bread, Rosalynn. There isn't supposed to be any salt in *it*."

"Oh! I—see."

"Now. How would you mix these things together?"

"I'd—I'd put the baking powder and the corn meal in the flour and—shake them up, I guess. And then I'd add the water."

"Good. Now listen: Put the flour, the corn meal and the baking powder in the water. Then stir them up. Backwards, you see. And if you usually stir clockwise, be sure to stir counterclockwise this time. And walk backwards. And strike the match for the oven away from you if you usually strike it towards you. Everything backwards."

"All right, I will, Amy. Don't worry."

Amy went on explaining all the details and Rosalynn listened, trying to remember, trying to play the game, so they would ask her to parties all the time.

It was only a silly superstition, and, contemplating the whole thing in the brightly lit kitchen of a farm house, she began to decide it was really nothing to be afraid of. . . . Just a silly, childish prank, that's all.

"You're ready, then?"

"Yes, I guess so."

"All right, now. Remember this: no matter what happens, don't talk. None of us can talk. That's the *most* important thing of all. None of us can talk until it's all over."

"I won't say a word," Rosalynn said.

"Okay. Then you're ready?"

"Yes . . . Only first—I mean, I know it sounds silly, but look— You don't really believe anything's going to happen—I mean, my husband come, or anything like that?"

Amy looked levelly at her; she paused a moment before answering.

"No," she said.

"No more talking," Jean Towers said.

And there was silence.

Rosalynn did everything the way she had been told—everything, that is, but about striking the match. She always struck the match toward herself; and this time, in the spirit of a little girl crossing her fingers before telling one of the little fibs little girls tell, she struck the match in the usual way.

After the corn bread was in the oven, she walked backward into the living room and sat down to wait for the ten minutes before it came time to set the table.

The other girls, silently as ghosts, had arranged themselves around the room; their eyes were upon her and she felt uncomfortable—like the first time she—well, she had felt everybody watching her then, too. It was something like that. As if they were waiting for something to give.

She thought Jean Towers' face was tense, and Marsha's eyes were—but she was letting her imagination run away with her.

Absolute silence. But for the clock.

She began to feel the vague, uneasy fingers of fear again.

The strangest thing was: None of the girls giggled. They were very still, waiting. They were—serious.

She heard the monotonous tick-tock, tick-tock of the clock.

There was the picture of the Indian, looking hopelessly into the chasm, there on the wall. Drooping spear.

(Tick-tock)

There were the goldfish, over in the corner. Slowly circling.

(Tick-tock)

There was—

Her heart leaped toward her throat.

The clock had stopped!

Rosalynn choked back a scream and her nails dug into her palms.

Slowly she relaxed. Only a clock had stopped, and clocks often stop; every minute, day and night, somewhere in the world, a clock stops.

Maybe the girls had arranged for that too, although it was a little difficult to imagine how they—

She looked at first one and then the other, and tension began to mount within her again. Their eyes were bright and they seemed to be leaned forward, tense, watching her.

Her father had said, "People aren't really as bad as you think: they're very seldom cruel." She tried to believe that.

It was time to begin setting the table. She had to fight with herself to stand; the eyes shifted upward with her.

Even if they hated her, she wasn't going to quit . . . to show she was afraid . . . not now.

(But they would all laugh about it tomorrow.)

She began to walk backward toward the kitchen. Hair along her neck bristled.

Silence.

She began the slow, awkward process of setting the table for herself and for a guest.

And then from far away! She tried to close her ears to it.

The second plate clattered loudly on the table.

She felt tears form, and her nose wrinkled and tingled. She could not scream.

She could only move toward the drawer, take two knives.

The expression on their faces. And she knew now. They *did* hate her, each of them. They were straining, listening, holding their breaths to hear it, and it grew louder!

They hated her—maybe because her father had a better job than their fathers, or maybe because she didn't have an accent and talked faster. *But they hated her!*

Rosalynn forgot about them. She was at the table again, and

her movements were forced from her. She wanted to run and scream and cry.

She put the second knife before the second plate. (It had a good, stainless steel handle.)

Wind in winter! Wind from the north, moaning in the trees: wind in winter in southern Missouri.

("It always comes up at a dumb supper," Jean Towers had said.)

. . . Mr. Pierce had said, that evening, that it was going to be a hard winter. But wind in winter? . . .

Marsha's eyes were glassy, and her breath came short.

Screaming wind, tearing at the house, gripping it, shaking it. In winter?

She took out the corn bread, using a pot holder to keep from burning her hands. She cut it into two pieces. The corn bread was soggy: she should have baked it longer.

She put the large piece on *his* plate.

She felt herself sitting down. There was nothing else she could do; she tried to fight but her muscles were caught in a clammy vise.

There was terror in her mind, overflowing it.

(The three goldfish, in the living room, were still circling slowly.)

The icy wind seemed all around her—caressing her, *kissing* her, muttering, muttering, like an obscene lover.

Weak. She was weak. Her skin crawled.

Something—from Outside.

Outside what?

Just Outside. That's all—Outside of—everything.

The girl-faces, now: blank, wide-eyed, drained. Waiting, waiting.

She tried to move her lips and the wind stopped them with a frozen kiss.

And the wind was everywhere; a laughing, insane fury, a cold, musty breath.

Frozen. Everything was frozen. Time stood still. Waiting for her husband to come.

He came.

She looked up from her plate and saw him.

A shadowy figure, unreal, tenuous, flowing into the room. Flowing toward her.

Her heart beat, beat, beat.

He was going to sit down beside her—her bridegroom!

Wind, evil wind.

The lights faded, growing weaker and weaker. And the white wrapped figure, settling into the chair prepared for it. It turned its head and stared full into Rosalynn's face.

She found that she could scream now; her voice was shrill, and it went on and on and on in the darkness. . . .

Finally the lights came back on.

The girls were circled tightly around her, their faces tense.

"What did he look like?" Marsha asked.

"He—he—it had no face. It wasn't my husband. It was—only—only blackness; awful black, blacker than the blackest night. . . ." She was sobbing.

"There, there, now," Jean Towers said, "you mustn't cry. Take my handkerchief. It's nothing to cry about."

"No," said Marsha, "you mustn't cry."

Suddenly the girls were bustling around her, wonderfully sweet and nice, drying her eyes, saying soft words to her, leaning over backward to be helpful.

Rosalynn was shaking. "Let me alone," she begged. *"Please* let me alone. You *hate* me. I know you do."

"Shucks, no, we don't either," Marsha said.

For a long moment the words seemed to echo in her mind; and then they began to call up new echoes.

Slowly she came to remember it—an overheard scrap of conversation. She knew the meaning of black, and why they were being so nice to her. For Marsha had said, "Black is the color of Death."

And she knew, too, who was ultimately to be her only true Friend and bridegroom.

WILLA CATHER

The Fear That Walks by Noonday

WILLA CATHER (1873–1947), born in Virginia and raised in Nebraska, began her literary career as a teacher, journalist and poet and later became an important American novelist and short-story writer of such works as My Ántonia, O Pioneers!, Death Comes for the Archbishop *and the memorably tragic "Paul's Case." She was fond of ghost stories and wrote a few in her youth. Of these, perhaps the most remarkable is the following brash mixture of the occult and the all-American sport of football told in sincere stylistic imitation of Henry James and written while Cather matriculated at the University of Nebraska at Lincoln, the state capital. One afternoon after a football game, Cather's fellow student Dorothy Canfield (later the writer Dorothy Canfield Fisher) suggested the basic plot of "The Fear That Walks by Noonday," which Cather wrote for the 1895 edition of the school's periodical,* Sombrero. *When the story won a prize of ten dollars, Willa promptly paid half of it to her friend Dorothy.*

"Where is my shin guard? Horton, you lazy dog, get your duds off, won't you? Why didn't you dress at the hotel with the rest of us? There's got to be a stop to your blamed eccentricities some day," fumed Reggie, hunting wildly about in a pile of overcoats.

Horton began pulling off his coat with that air of disinterested deliberation he always assumed to hide any particular nervousness. He was to play two positions that day, both half and full, and he knew it meant stiff work.

"What do you think of the man who plays in Morrison's place, Strike?" he asked as he took off his shoes.

"I can tell you better in about half an hour; I suppose the 'Injuns' knew what they were about when they put him there."

"They probably put him there because they hadn't another man who could even look like a full back. He played quarter badly enough, if I remember him."

"I don't see where they get the face to play us at all. They would never have scored last month if it hadn't been for Morrison's punting. That fellow played a great game, but the rest of them are light men, and their coach is an idiot. That man would have made his mark if he'd lived. He could play different positions just as easily as Chum-Chum plays different roles—pardon the liberty, Fred—and then there was that awful stone wall strength of his to back it; he was a mighty man."

"If you are palpitating to know why the 'Injuns' insist on playing us, I'll tell you; it's for blood. Exhibition game be damned! It's to break our bones they're playing. We were surprised when they didn't let down on us harder as soon as the fellow died, but they have been cherishing their wrath, they haven't lost an ounce of it, and they are going into us to-day for vengeance."

"Well, their sentiments are worthy, but they haven't got the players."

"Let up on Morrison there, Horton," shouted Reggie, "we sent flowers and sympathies at the time, but we are not going to lose this game out of respect to his memory: shut up and get your shin guard on. I say, Nelson, if you don't get out of here with that cigarette I'll kick you out. I'll get so hungry I'll break training rules. Besides, the coach will be in here in a minute going around smelling our breaths like our mammas used to do, if he catches a scent of it. I'm humming glad it's the last week of training; I couldn't stand another day of it. I brought a whole pocket full of cigars, and I'll have one well under way before the cheering is over. Won't we see the town to-night, Freddy?"

Horton nodded and laughed one of his wicked laughs. "Training has gone a shade too far this season. It's all nonsense to say that nobody but hermits and anchorites can play foot ball. A

Methodist parson don't have to practice half such rigid abstinence as a man on the eleven." And he kicked viciously at the straw on the floor as he remembered the supper parties he had renounced, the invitations he had declined, and the pretty faces he had avoided in the last three months.

"Five minutes to three!" said the coach, as he entered, pounding on the door with his cane. Strike began to hunt frantically for the inflater, one of the tackles went striding around the room seeking his nose protector with lamentations and profanity, and the rest of the men got on their knees and began burrowing in the pile of coats for things they had forgotten to take out of their pockets. Reggie began to hurry his men and make the usual encouraging remarks to the effect that the universe was not created to the especial end that they should win that foot ball game, that the game was going to the men who kept the coolest heads and played the hardest ball. The coach rapped impatiently again, and Horton and Reggie stepped out together, the rest following them. As soon as Horton heard the shouts which greeted their appearance, his eyes flashed, and he threw his head back like a cavalry horse that hears the bugle sound a charge. He jumped over the ropes and ran swiftly across the field, leaving Reggie to saunter along at his leisure, bowing to the ladies in the grand stand and on the tally-hos as he passed.

When he reached the lower part of the field he found a hundred Marathon college men around the team yelling and shouting their encouragement. Reggie promptly directed the policemen to clear the field, and, taking his favorite attitude, his feet wide apart and his body very straight, he carelessly tossed the quarter into the air.

"Line 'em up, Reggie, line 'em up. Let us into it while the divine afflatus lasts," whispered Horton.

The men sprang to their places, and Reggie forgot the ladies on the tally-hos; the color came to his face, and he drew himself up and threw every sinew of his little body on a tension. The crowd outside began to cheer again, as the wedge started off for north goal. The western men were poor on defensive work, and the Marathon wedge gained ground on the first play. The first impetus of success was broken by Horton fumbling and losing the ball. The eleven looked rather dazed at this, and Horton was the most dazed looking man of them all, for he did not indulge in that kind of thing often. Reggie could scarcely believe his senses, and stood staring at Horton in unspeakable amazement, but Horton only spread out his hands and stared at them as though to see if they were still there. There was little time for reflection or conjecture. The western men gave their Indian yell and prepared to play; their captain sang out his signals, and the rushing began. In spite of the desperate resistance on the part of Reggie's men, the ball went steadily south, and in twelve minutes the "Injuns" had scored. No one quite knew how they did it, least of all their bewildered opponents. They did some bad fumbling on the five-yard line, but though Reggie's men fell all over the ball, they did not seem to be able to take hold of it.

"Call in a doctor," shouted Reggie; "they're paralyzed in the arms, every one of 'em."

Time was given to bandage a hurt, and half a dozen men jumped over the ropes and shot past the policemen and rushed up to Reggie, pitifully asking what the matter was.

"Matter! I don't know! They're all asleep or drunk. Go kick them, pound them, anything to get them awake." And the little captain threw his sweater over his shoulder and swore long and loud at all mankind in general and Frederick Horton in particular. Horton turned away without looking at him. He was a younger man than Reggie, and, although he had had more experiences, they were not of the kind that counted much with the men of the eleven. He was very proud of being the captain's right-hand man, and it cut him hard to fail him.

"I believe I've been drugged, Black," he said, turning to the right tackle. "I am as cold as ice all over and I can't use my arms at all; I've a notion to ask Reggie to call in a sub."

"Don't, for heaven's sake, Horton; he is almost frantic now; believe it would completely demoralize the team; you have never laid off since you were on the eleven, and if you should now when you have no visible hurt it would frighten them to death."

"I feel awful, I am so horribly cold."

"So am I, so are all the fellows; see how the "Injuns" are shivering over there, will you? There must be a cold wave; see how Strike's hair is blowing down in his eyes."

"The cold wave seems to be confined to our locality," remarked Horton in a matter-of-fact way; but in somewhat strained tones. "The girls out there are all in their summer dresses without wraps, and the wind which is cutting our faces all up don't even stir the ribbon on their hats."

"Y-a-s, horribly draughty place, this," said Black blankly.

"Horribly draughty as all out doors," said Horton with a grim laugh.

"Bur-r-r!" said Strike, as he handed his sweater over to a substitute and took his last pull at a lemon, "this wind is awful; I never felt anything so cold; it's a raw, wet cold that goes clear into the marrow of a fellow's bones. I don't see where it comes from; there is no wind outside the ropes apparently."

"The winds blow in such strange directions here," said Horton, picking up a straw and dropping it. "It goes straight down with force enough to break several camels' backs."

"Ugh! it's as though the firmament had sprung a leak and the winds were sucking in from the other side."

"Shut your mouths, both of you," said Reggie, with an emphatic oath. "You will have them all scared to death; there's a panic now, that's what's the matter, one of those quiet, stupid panics that are the worst to manage. Laugh, Freddie, laugh hard; get up some enthusiasm; come, you, shut up, if you can't do any better than that. Start the yell, Strike, perhaps that will fetch them."

A weak yell that sounded like an echo rose from the field and the Marathon men outside the ropes caught it up and cheered till the air rang. This seemed to rouse the men on the field, and they got to their places with considerable energy. Reggie gave an exultant cry, as the western men soon lost the ball, and his men started it north and kept steadily gaining. They were within ten yards of the goal, when suddenly the ball rose serenely out of a mass of struggling humanity and flew back twenty, forty, sixty, eighty yards toward the southern goal! But the half was versed in his occupation; he ran across and stood under the ball, waiting for it with out-stretched arms. It seemed to Horton that the ball was all day in falling; it was right over him and yet it seemed to hang back from him, like Chum-Chum when she was playing with him. With an impatient oath he ground his teeth together and bowed his body forward to hold it with his breast, and even his knees if need be, waiting with strength and eagerness enough in his arm to burst the ball to shreds. The crowd shouted with delight, but suddenly caught its breath; the ball fell into his arms, between them, through them, and rolled on the ground at his feet. Still he stood there with his face raised and his arms stretched upward in an attitude ridiculously suggestive of prayer. The men rushed fiercely around him shouting and reviling; his arms dropped like lead to his side, and he stood without moving a muscle, and in his face there was a look that a man might have who had seen what he loved best go down to death through his very arms and had not been able to close them and save. Reggie came up with his longest oaths on his lip, but when he saw Horton's face he checked himself and said with that sweetness of temper that always came to him when he saw the black bottom of despair,

"Keep quiet, fellows, Horton's all right, only he is a bit nervous." Horton moved for the first time and turned on the little captain, "You can say anything else you like, Reggie, but if you say I am scared I'll knock you down."

"No, Fred, I don't mean that; we must hang together, man, every one of us, there are powers enough against us," said Reggie, sadly. The men looked at each other with startled faces. So long as Reggie swore there was hope, but when he became gentle all was lost.

In another part of the field another captain fell on his fullback's neck and cried, "Thomas, my son, how did you do it? Morrison in his palmiest days never made a better lift than that."

"I-I didn't do it, I guess; some of the other fellows did; Towmen, I think."

"Not much I didn't," said Towmen, "you were so excited you didn't know what you were doing. You did it, though; I saw it go right up from your foot."

"Well, it may be," growled the "Injun" half, "but when I make plays like that I'd really like to be conscious of them. I must be getting to be a darned excitable individual if I can punt eighty yards and never know it."

"Heavens! how cold it is. This is a great game, though; I don't believe they'll score."

"I don't; they act like dead men; I would say their man Horton was sick or drunk if all the others didn't act just like him."

The "Injuns" lost the ball again, but when Reggie's men were working it north the same old punting scheme was worked somewhere by someone in the "Injuns'" ranks. This time Amack, the right half, ran bravely for it; but when he was almost beneath it he fell violently to the ground, for no visible reason, and lay there struggling like a man in a fit. As they were taking him off the field, time was called for the first half. Reggie's friends and several of his professors broke through the gang of policemen and rushed up to him. Reggie stepped in front of his men and spoke to the first man who came up, "If you say one word or ask one question I'll quit the field. Keep away from me and from my men. Let us alone." The paleness that showed through the dirt on Reggie's face alarmed the visitors, and they went away as quickly as they had come. Reggie and his men lay down and covered themselves with their overcoats, and lay there shuddering under that icy wind that sucked down upon them. The men were perfectly quiet and each one crept off by himself. Even the substitutes who brought them lemons and water did not talk much; they had neither disparagement nor encouragement to offer; they sat around and shivered like the rest. Horton hid his face on his arm and lay like one stunned. He muttered the score, 18 to 0, but he did not feel the words his lips spoke, nor comprehend them. Like most dreamy, imaginative men, Horton was not very much at home in college. Sometimes in his loneliness he tried to draw near to the average man, and be on a level with him, and in so doing made a consummate fool of himself, as dreamers always do when they try to get themselves awake.

He was awkward and shy among women, silent and morose among men. He was tolerated in the societies because he could write good poetry, and in the clubs because he could play foot ball. He was very proud of his accomplishments as a half back, for they made him seem like other men. However ornamental and useful a large imagination and sensitive temperament may be to a man of mature years, to a young man they are often very like a deformity which he longs to hide. He wondered what the captain would think of him and groaned. He feared Reggie as much as he adored him. Reggie was one of those men who, by the very practicality of their intellects, astonish the world. He was a glorious man for a college. He was brilliant, adaptable, and successful; yet all his brains he managed to cover up by a pate of tow hair, parted very carefully in the middle, and his iron strength was generally very successfully disguised by a very dudish exterior. In short, he possessed the one thing which is greater than genius, the faculty of clothing genius in such boundless good nature that it is offensive to nobody. Horton felt to a painful degree his inferiority to him in most things, and it was not pleasant to him to lose ground in the one thing in which he felt they could meet on an equal footing.

Horton turned over and looked up at the leaden sky, feeling the wind sweep into his eyes and nostrils. He looked about him and saw the other men all lying down with their heads covered, as though they were trying to get away from the awful cold and the sense of Reggie's reproach. He wondered what was the matter with them; whether they had been drugged or mesmerized. He tried to remember something in all the books he had read that would fit the case, but his memory seemed as cold and dazed as the rest of him; he only remembered some hazy Greek, which read to the effect that the gods sometimes bring madness upon those they wish to destroy. And here was another proof that the world was going wrong—it was not a normal thing for him to remember any Greek.

He was glad when at last he heard Reggie's voice calling the men together; he went slowly up to him and said rather feebly, "I say, a little brandy wouldn't hurt us, would it? I am so awfully cold I don't know what the devil is the matter with me, Reggie, my arms are so stiff I can't use 'em at all."

Reggie handed him a bottle from his grip, saying briefly, "It can't make things any worse."

In the second half the Marathon men went about as though they were walking in their sleep. They seldom said anything, and the captain was beyond coaxing or swearing; he only gave his signals in a voice as hollow as if it came from an empty church. His men got the ball a dozen times, but they always lost it as soon as they got it, or, when they had worked it down to one goal the "Injun" would punt it back to the other. The very spectators sat still and silent, feeling that they were seeing something strange and unnatural. Every now and then some "Injun" would make a run, and a Marathon man would dash up and run beside him for a long distance without ever catching him, but with his hands hanging at his side. People asked the physicians in the audience what was the matter; but they shook their heads.

It was at this juncture that Freddie Horton awoke and bestirred himself. Horton was a peculiar player; he was either passive or brilliant. He could not do good line work; he could not help other men play. If he did anything he must take matters into his own hands, and he generally did; no one in the northwest had ever made such nervy, dashing plays as he; he seemed to have the faculty of making sensational and romantic situations in foot ball just as he did in poetry. He played with his imagination. The second half was half over, and as yet he had done nothing but blunder. His honor and the honor of the team had been trampled on. As he thought of it the big veins stood out in his forehead and he set his teeth hard together. At last his opportunity came, or rather he made it. In a general scramble for the ball he caught it in his arms and ran. He held the ball tight against his breast until he could feel his heart knocking against the hard skin; he was conscious of nothing but the wind whistling in his ears and the ground flying under his feet, and the fact that he had ninety yards to run. Both teams followed him as fast as they could, but Horton was running for his honor, and his feet scarcely touched the earth. The spectators, who had waited all afternoon for a chance to shout, now rose to their feet and all the lungs full of pent-up enthusiasm burst forth. But the gods are not to be frustrated for a man's honor or his dishonor, and when Freddie Horton was within ten yards of the goal he threw his arms over his head and leaped into the air and fell. When the crowd reached him they found no marks of injury except the blood and foam at his mouth where his teeth had bitten into his lip. But when they looked at him the men of both teams turned away shuddering. His knees were drawn up to his chin; his hands were dug into the ground on either side of him; his face was the livid, bruised blue of a man who dies with apoplexy; his eyes were wide open and full of unspeakable horror and fear, glassy as ice, and still as though they had been frozen fast in their sockets.

It was an hour before they brought him to, and then he lay

perfectly silent and would answer no questions. When he was stretched obliquely across the seats of a carriage going home he spoke for the first time.

"Give me your hand, Reggie; for God's sake let me feel something warm and human. I am awful sorry, Reggie; I tried for all my life was worth to make that goal, but—" he drew the captain's head down to his lips and whispered something that made Reggie's face turn white and the sweat break out on his forehead. He drew big Horton's head upon his breast and stroked it as tenderly as a woman.

II

There was silence in the dining room of the Exeter house that night when the waiters brought in the last course. The evening had not been a lively one. The defeated men were tired with that heavy weariness which follows defeat, and the victors seemed strained and uneasy in their manners. They all avoided speaking of the game and forced themselves to speak of things they could not fix their minds upon. Reggie sat at the head of the table correct and faultless. Reggie was always correct, but to-night there was very little of festal cheer about him. He was cleanly shaved, his hair was parted with the usual mathematical accuracy. A little strip of black court plaster covered the only external wound defeat had left. But his face was as white as the spotless expanse of his shirt bosom, and his eyes had big black circles under them like those of a man coming down with the fever. All evening he had been nervous and excited; he had not eaten anything and was evidently keeping something under. Every one wondered what it was, and yet feared to hear it. When asked about Horton he simply shuddered, mumbled something, and had his wine glass filled again.

Laughter or fear are contagious, and by the time the last course was on the table every one was as nervous as Reggie. The talk started up fitfully now and then but it soon died down, and the weakly attempts at wit were received in silence.

Suddenly every one became conscious of the awful cold and inexplicable downward draught that they had felt that afternoon. Every one was determined not to show it. No one pretended to even notice the flicker of the gas jets, and the fact that their breath curled upward from their mouths in little wreaths of vapor. Every one turned his attention to his plate and his glass stood full beside him. Black made some remarks about politics, but his teeth chattered so he gave it up. Reggie's face was working nervously, and he suddenly rose to his feet and said in a harsh, strained voice,

"Gentlemen, you had one man on your side this afternoon who came a long journey to beat us. I mean the man who did that wonderful punting and who stood before the goal when Mr. Horton made his run. I propose the first toast of the evening to the twelfth man, who won the game. Need I name him?"

The silence was as heavy as before. Reggie extended his glass to the captain beside him, but suddenly his arm changed direction; he held the glass out over the table and tipped it in empty air as though touching glasses with some one. The sweat broke out on Reggie's face; he put his glass to his lips and tried to drink, but only succeeded in biting out a big piece of the rim of his wine glass. He spat the glass out quickly upon his plate and began to laugh, with the wine oozing out between his white lips. Then everyone laughed; leaning upon each other's shoulders, they gave way to volleys and shrieks of laughter, waving their glasses in hands that could scarcely hold them. The negro waiter, who had been leaning against the wall asleep, came forward rubbing his eyes to see what was the matter. As he approached the end of the table he felt that chilling wind, with its damp, wet smell like the air from a vault, and the unnatural cold that drove to the heart's center like a knife blade.

"My Gawd!" he shrieked, dropping his tray, and with an inarticulate gurgling cry he fled out of the door and down the stairway with the banqueters after him, all but Reggie, who fell to the floor, cursing and struggling and grappling with the powers of darkness. When the men reached the lower hall they stood without speaking, holding tightly to each other's hands like frightened children. At last Reggie came down the stairs, steadying himself against the banister. His dress coat was torn, his hair was rumpled down over his forehead, his shirt front was stained with wine, and the ends of his tie were hanging to his waist. He stood looking at the men and they looked at him, and no one spoke.

Presently a man rushed into the hall from the office and shouted "McKinley has carried Ohio by eighty-one thousand majority!" and Regiland Ashton, the product of centuries of democratic faith and tradition, leaped down the six remaining stairs and shouted, "Hurrah for Bill McKinley."

In a few minutes the men were looking for a carriage to take Regiland Ashton home.

CARL JACOBI

The Chadwick Pit

CARL JACOBI, *one of the most respected and admired contributors to American adventure and supernatural periodicals, was the prolific author of "Carnaby's Fish," "Mive," "Portrait in Moonlight," "Revelations in Black" and many other memorable stories.* Lost in the Rentharpian Hills, *R. Dixon Smith's excellent study of Jacobi's life and work, reveals that the following story, shorn of its fantasy elements and titled "McIver's Fancy," was first published in* Mike Shayne Mystery Magazine. *Lin Carter eventually restored it to its original length and genre and published it as "The Pit" in the first issue of the short-lived Zebra Books revival of* Weird Tales. *The inspiration for "The Chadwick Pit" (the author's title) was an old Indian burial mound near Chaska, Minnesota, the Carver County seat not far from a summer cabin where Jacobi used to vacation.*

The country of Sleep has no borders, but many roads and the Dream Traveler needs no visa.

Images and Fancies
GILES BALINTON

Chadwick walked slowly up the lane and gazed with satisfaction at his property. The more he saw of it, the more he considered it a stroke of luck. It wasn't often that one could buy ten acres of land and a house of his particular needs for the small amount he had paid. He had wanted a house, modern, yet with an architecture of the past, in an isolated location where he could continue the recluse-like existence he had led in the city.

Owego House answered all those wants. Owego. It was an Indian name, he had been told.

Seen through a copse of cedars, the house looked friendly and inviting, with a wide veranda, oversized burgundy shutters and a new substantial roof tile. Then Chadwick's gaze turned fifty yards east. If Owego was an odd name for a house, Dead Man's Pit was an appropriate name for the great sink hole that marked the end of his property.

Here were rank weeds, thorn bushes and ragged outcroppings. In the center of this wasteland was a deep depression filled with water so black it didn't even reflect the sky. The borders were strewn with rocks.

Sight of the place depressed Chadwick, and he turned back down the lane toward his house. In the driveway his parked station wagon reminded him that his weekly trip to town for supplies was overdue. He got into the car and headed toward Blacktop 3.

In Chaska he parked and went to several shops, where he talked very little to the tradespeople. In the hardware store, however, he found conversation pressed upon him.

"How do you like your new place?" the hardware man said as he packaged the nails Chadwick had purchased.

"I like it all right," Chadwick said.

"It's a nice house," the man said, "considering that it's been there close to a hundred years."

"I thought a hundred years ago this was all Indian country."

The man rang up the register. "Farther north, mebbe. Not here. But that Pit on your place was once an old Indian burial mound. The first two owners dug it all up, looking for treasure or somethin'."

"Did they find any?" Chadwick asked.

"I don't think so. The first was before my time, but he's supposed to have shot himself. Accidentally. The second just went away and never came back. Nobody ever saw or heard of him."

Chadwick turned to go. "Well, it's an eyesore," he said. "I suppose I'll have it filled up one of these days."

The man's face darkened perceptibly. "I don't think I'd do that," he said. "If I were you, I'd just leave it alone."

Chadwick went out to his car, musing over the merchant's words. He tossed his packages into the rear seat. The August street was hot and sultry, and by contrast the library on the opposite corner a block away, shaded by a couple of elms, looked cool and inviting. On impulse, he crossed the street, walked the block and climbed the steps. Inside, to the girl behind the desk, he said,

"I'd like some information on the building of a summer house. Plans . . . pictures . . . anything you have."

She was gone almost ten minutes. When she returned, she looked at Chadwick with interest.

"You rarely hear of such things anymore. Are you planning to build one yourself?"

She was attractive in a fragile way, with long dark hair and lustrous eyes. It had been a long time since Chadwick had been attracted to a girl, but now he felt himself talking without restraint. She was a ready listener. Before leaving, he learned her name, Emily Hunter. With a lighter step than he had known in years, he went out again into the blazing street.

Chaska was an old town, built along the Minnesota River. A German settlement with the characteristic neatness evident on all sides, its streets were redolent with the summer musk from the bottomlands. The county seat courthouse faced the center park, and as Chadwick strode past, a heavy set, redfaced man with a wide brimmed hat came out and hailed him. It was the sheriff, Tom Blunt.

"Just wondered how you were gettin' along," Blunt said, lighting a cigar with a kitchen match.

"I'm okay," Chadwick said.

"You figgerin' on stayin' in your new place alone?"

"I don't suppose there's any law that says a man has to have a regiment around him," Chadwick replied testily.

Blunt grinned. "No law. Only your place is pretty far out."

"I'm used to being alone."

"What are you figgerin' on doin' with the Pit?"

"What do you mean, what am I going to do with it?"

"Well, it's a dangerous place. The Caston boy drowned there a year ago. He'd been studyin' anthropology and he was lookin' for relics."

All this talk about what he considered the one disagreeable feature of his property irritated Chadwick. "I suppose I'll have it filled up," he said.

It was the second time that day he had made that statement, and for the second time it prompted an odd reply.

"I don't think it's necessary to do that," Blunt said quickly. "Why don't you just fence it off and put up a few warning signs?"

Chadwick said that he would consider the matter and as soon as he decently could, he broke away, returned to his car and headed back for home.

For several weeks after that he busied himself repairing the veranda railing, some of the rungs had rotted out—tidying up the grounds and poring over the construction books that Emily had selected for him. It was true that he had wanted a summer house for a long time. Such a building had lingered in his memories since childhood, and it was the desire for one that had been a major reason behind his move from the city.

He decided to build a conventional structure with a stonework lower portion and a screened upper part open to the air. Most of the material he could obtain in Chaska. The stones for the lower portion were available close at hand—in the Pit.

He went to the sink hole, selected the stones with care and trundled them in a barrow to the house grounds. The work was hard and he was disconcerted to find himself so completely exhausted. Not only did he have tired muscles, but the task, particularly while he was in the Pit, for some reason affected his eyes. Once he fancied he saw a head-shaped rock in the center come to life and move toward him, and once, when he peered down into the black water, he thought he saw an elongated shadow like a sea serpent writhe and twist just below the surface.

But all his troubles vanished several weeks later when the summer house, with the aid of two Chaska youths, was finally completed. Quickly the building molded itself into his life. He began to spend the long summer afternoons there. A strange quality of contentment fell over him as he sat at the little iron table in the circular room, drinking juleps from a frosty glass. He installed a couch and passed the sultry nights stretched out upon it. To his surprise he found that sleep, which had always been a problem with him, now came with ease.

His sleep, however, was marred by dreams.

Like all men, Chadwick had had his share of dreams since childhood. And as with most persons, these dreams were usually disconnected, distorted and marked by complete lack of logic. Now, however, they were different.

Though he could remember no details, he now retained three impressions upon awakening: search, flight, and pursuit by persons or things unknown. What he was searching for was not clear. Sometimes it was for a jungle beast, sometimes a composite, always female. The "flight" followed immediately, whether the search was successful or not. He fled panic-stricken with leaden feet, unable to run or hurry. The "pursuit" was a relentless thing that followed him, and constituted a horror from which he knew there was no escape. These dreams formed a cohesive unit, too. That is, the action continued chronologically from one night to another.

But the aspect that was incredible, which he could not at first make himself believe, was the fact that these dreams came only when he slept in the summer house. On those occasions when he spent the night in the house bedroom, the sequence was broken, and he either did not dream at all or his sleeping fantasies were the usual bland meaningless affairs of before.

Sometimes he awoke in the middle of the night, bathed in perspiration, shaking with fear, to discover odd things: the door unlocked or his clothes piled in a disorderly heap in the middle of the floor. Yet the very anticipation of those dreams affected him like an opiate and he could not force himself to stay away from the summer house.

On a morning following several nights when the dreams had been particularly enervating, Chadwick was on his veranda when Sheriff Blunt drove up.

"In the neighborhood," Blunt said, "so I thought I'd stop by. Seen any strangers around?"

"I haven't seen anybody," Chadwick said.

"Then you haven't heard what's happened the last few days?"

Chadwick shook his head. "I haven't been to town in more than a week."

"We've had a murder," Blunt said. "And a disappearance which might well be a second."

Chadwick stared.

"We found Jim Evans' wife—he's the Chaska jeweler—strangled in a ditch along 41. And Irene Trask hasn't been seen since Wednesday night.

"I've got two deputies working around the clock," Blunt continued, "but so far we haven't come up with anything. You'd better keep an eye out, living all alone out here."

Chadwick got up and walked to the end of the veranda. He came back slowly and sat down again. A distant look entered his eyes.

"A long time ago," he said haltingly, "it must have been around '55, I did a hitch on the Chicago police force. That's ancient history, of course, but I'd be glad to help in any way I can."

Blunt nodded. "I may take you up on that," he said. "Did you know a detective sergeant named Fallon? I think he was in Chicago about that time."

"I don't recall the name."

In spite of the police background that he had mentioned, Chadwick was disturbed by the sheriff's warning. After Blunt had gone, he began a search of his grounds, although he had no idea what he was looking for. The doom which had seemed to lie in wait for him in his dreams now became almost a reality. He was chagrined to find himself glancing over his shoulder at every wind-tossed clump of foliage.

In the back of the house, facing the direction of the Pit, he found one of the lower windows open. But there were no footprints near, so he attributed it to his own negligence. There were, however, footprints leading to the driveway where he parked his car. Not far away was a little pile of cigarette stubs, as if someone had stood there a long time. Then he saw that they were his brand and realized that he must have forgotten being there. His car gave him more concern. Though he couldn't be sure, the gas supply seemed less and the odometer reading more than when he had last driven. But it would have been impossible for anyone to have taken the car without awakening him, even though the driveway was some distance from the house. He had a vague impression of night driving and of walking in the darkness. But this, he knew, was only a residue of his summer-house dreams. For years he had never gone anyplace after sundown. The loneliness of his property began to weigh on him. He had the unpleasant feeling of being watched by unseen eyes.

On Friday he drove to Chaska. The town was in a state of excitement. The body of the missing girl, Irene Trask, had been found strangled and there was another disappearance. Sheriff Blunt stood on the courthouse steps talking to his deputies and a state police officer.

Chadwick went into the library to return the construction books. He found Emily Hunter almost in a state of hysteria. She told him the missing girl, Mary Philbin, was one of her closest friends.

"I can't understand why anyone would want to harm her," she said. "She was liked by everybody."

"A tall, thin girl with reddish hair?"

"Yes. Do you know her?"

He shook his head. "I've probably seen her around town." In an effort to calm her, he changed the subject and talked of casual things. She quieted and smiled a little.

"Anyone would know you're a bachelor," she said. "You're wearing one black sock and one brown. And you really should stay out of the mud, Mr. Chadwick. Tell me, did you finish your summer house?"

Chadwick nodded. "Yes, but I'm afraid the job was a little too much for me. I had help on all except the stonework."

"Where did you get the stones?"

"In the Pit. That's a sort of sink hole on my property."

Her face clouded. "Yes, I know the Pit. You shouldn't have taken the stones from there, Mr. Chadwick."

"Why not?"

She fingered her pendant. "Let's just say it isn't a healthy place. It . . . has an evil reputation."

"Yes, I know," Chadwick said. "The Caston boy drowned there a year ago, but he was. . . ."

"Billy Caston was one of the finest swimmers in Carver County."

Back home Chadwick tried to think more of his days as a police officer. He had told Blunt that he was on the Chicago force in '55. But he could recall little of that work save a few trips in a prowl car, and even these were hazy, like the recollection of an old gangster movie.

It now occurred to him that there were still some parts of his house that he had not fully examined. It seemed to him as good a time as any to do a little exploring. He took a flashlight and descended to the cellar. There were actually two cellars, one opening off the other, but there was nothing in either except a plenitude of cobwebs and some empty boxes. He went up to the second floor and prowled down the corridor. Toward the rear he came upon a room he had not entered before. Here a wan shaft of sunlight filtered through a dirty pane to reveal a few pieces of discarded furniture and a carpet gray with dust. About to leave, he saw a large cabinet, almost hidden by a pile of drapery. It was filled with books.

Chadwick stepped closer and ran his eyes over the titles. They were a curious assortment. Many were cheap novels of a generation ago, but there were also a few authoritative volumes on psychology, psychic research, strange myths and primitive beliefs. One of the last bore the title *The Prehistoric Hopewell Culture*.

Chadwick riffled through the pages. He stopped at a passage marked with a pencil check:

"An utterly strange culture preceded the North American Indian by several thousand years. It was unique for its complex burial mounds and its so-called 'Cult of the Dead'.

"It is the warnings of this Cult of the Dead which have come down to us through the mists of the past. Defilers of the burial mounds were promised all the avenging horrors of the culture's diabology."

Chadwick closed the book thoughtfully. He selected several psychology volumes which, at the moment, were of more interest to him and carried them downstairs. He had become increasingly concerned with dreams the last few days, and each of the books had one or more chapters on this subject. For his nightmares in the summer house had grown more and more disturbing. Although he still could remember no specific details upon awakening, the three impressions—search, flight and pursuit—continued. Now the "search" was intensified, a powerful urge to seek out something. The "flight" too was more frantic. And the "pursuit" was a nameless terror that followed him relentlessly.

These dreams were debilitating too. They left Chadwick exhausted, almost as if he had not slept at all. Yet though he knew that he had only to move from the summer house to end them, somehow he couldn't do that. It was as if he were taking a stimulant, sweet, bitter, unpleasant, habit-forming.

Late on a cheerless morning, three days after his trip to Chaska, he was awakened by a distant pistol shot. Ten minutes later Sheriff Blunt appeared at the edge of his grounds, followed by one of his deputies.

"Thought we saw him," Blunt said disgustedly. "But it was only this jacket hanging on a bush."

"We traced him across Barlow's Swamp," Blunt continued. "He seemed to be heading for the Pit. Then Jake here saw the jacket and took a shot. But the trail was cold. Have you seen anyone?"

"Not a soul," Chadwick said. "Have there been any more killings?"

Blunt looked at his deputy and frowned. "No," he said, "no more murders. But another disappearance. I believe you know her. The Hunter girl."

Chadwick's jaw went slack. "Not Emily!" he cried. "The girl who works in the library?" He made fists of his hands. "Blunt," he said after a long moment of silence, "you've got to deputize me. If you don't I'll go on my own."

The sheriff nodded sympathetically. "All right," he said. "I understand."

After Blunt had gone, Chadwick went into his house and looked for his revolver. He found a gun; it wasn't a police special but an old Webley Scott automatic. Outside, he got into his station wagon and drove fast to Blacktop 3. There were a thousand places he could search. Emily Hunter lived close to Chaska on 41, but almost automatically he headed in the opposite direction, toward the Victoria cutoff. He didn't know why he did this. He had never driven the cutoff, yet a recollection of this road seemed to come to him. His mind seethed. If only it had been someone else. The thought struck him that his actions now were repetitive, like scenes from a movie run many times. And then abruptly the spell was broken. He looked upon his surroundings with complete unfamiliarity. Puzzled, he turned the car and headed for home.

In the central room he buried his head in his hands. He must do something. . . . He must think. . . .

From the table he took up one of the psychology books he had brought down from the little room upstairs. As if it had been read many times at that place, the book fell open to the chapter on dreams. Half unconsciously, Chadwick began to read:

"The dream is the least understood part of the human psyche. The distortion, irrationality and lack of logical coherence which characterize many of them is no doubt the result of a multitude of subliminal perceptions and is almost impossible to explain."

He turned a page:

"No interpretation of the dream can be made without liberal references to mythology, folklore and primitive beliefs such as witchcraft, lycanthropy, etc. It is a curious fact that the dreamer need have no prior knowledge of these cabala. They are universal in their distribution."

Chadwick discarded the book and took up another. It too opened of its own accord to the dream chapter:

"In 1945 the Belgian, Anatole Arman, quoted the case of a man who, while asleep, not only noctambulated a considerable distance but also lived a life completely divorced from his waking hours. Yet he had no knowledge of that life. To offset this, he created for himself a fantasy past. Such cases are extremely rare, and it is thought that only some malignant influence could induce such a condition."

Chadwick's eyes drifted from the page to the table. There, where he had emptied his pockets upon coming in from outside, were a couple of objects he didn't remember seeing before: a length of window sash cord with each end carefully bound with tape to prevent fraying, and a short piece of rounded wood with a wide, deep notch cut about six inches from one end. He looked at them, puzzled, for the moment unable to explain their presence.

It was now several hours since Sheriff Blunt had told him about Emily Hunter, and he suddenly realized he had done absolutely nothing. A confused picture flashed before his inner eye of her, standing at his side, now running before him. He gathered up his things from the table, went back out to his car and headed for Chaska. He seemed to be viewing his surroundings through a prism, with everything strange and out of proportion. At the town outskirts a car suddenly pulled diagonally across the road in front of his, blocking the way.

The sheriff emerged and approached. "Oh, it's you. We're stoppin' all cars. Where you headin', Chadwick?"

Chadwick spread his hands on the wheel.

"Well, there's no sense to our drivin' two cars," Blunt said. "I'll go along with you."

He walked back, drove his car onto the side of the road, and a moment later climbed in beside Chadwick.

Uncertainly, Chadwick shifted gears. For some time he drove in silence. Then he burst into speech.

"We can't just go blind! You must have some idea. . . ."

"No, I haven't." The sheriff's face was immobile. "We don't know if Emily Hunter is alive or dead. We do know that with the other two victims there was an interlude of about forty hours between the time of their disappearance and their death. We know that both were kept alive in one place and then taken somewhere else to be murdered. I'm hoping the killer will keep to the same schedule. If he does, we may have a small margin of time left."

"Why would he do that?" Chadwick heard himself ask.

The sheriff shrugged. "There's no explaining a psychotic killer. I figure he can go just so far in his lust for blood, then he cools. When the urge comes upon him again, he goes back and finishes the job."

"But why forty hours?"

"After a day and a night. I suppose he's got to sleep."

Blunt was a fool, Chadwick thought. A busybody and a fool. Not even a good sheriff. The car swung past Houseman's Woods. When another fork appeared, he swung into it.

"Now you're going in a circle."

"I know." Chadwick did not say that a strange compulsion was guiding his movements.

"When you were in Chicago, did you ever run into a case of this kind?" The sheriff seemed to be talking only to pass the time.

"No."

"Know anything about fingerprints?"

"I know Bertillion discovered them."

"How about ballistics?"

Chadwick shook his head.

"Most premeditary criminals don't use guns anymore. They use too much noise and bullets can be traced. They prefer a knife."

"Knives can be traced, too," Chadwick said.

"I suppose so," Blunt said. "But that pretty well exhausts the field."

"There's the garotte." Chadwick's words were automatic.

"Oh, yes. The garotte. But I'd hardly call that a weapon, would you?"

"Yes, I would," Chadwick said. "It goes back to the fifteenth century. In Spain it was a method of injuring the spinal cord at the base of the brain."

"I didn't know that. Have you done much reading along those lines?"

"It used to be my hobby," Chadwick said.

Blunt expelled a mouthful of smoke. "Where are we? Oh, yes, the old Lake Virginia road."

"It comes to the Pit from the other side," Chadwick said: "Nobody uses it anymore."

The road was deep rutted and the willows along the narrow shoulders pressed close. Presently the forlorn wasteland that was the Pit opened before them.

It was a different view than Blunt was accustomed to seeing. From this angle, the loneliness of the place was more pronounced. The piles of rock were larger and the black water left only a thin corridor for the car to pass. Then this too ended and Blunt understood why the road was no longer used. It should be posted "Dead End," he thought.

Chadwick stopped the car. He got out and like an automaton,

body stiff, muscles unflexed, began to pace slowly along the water's edge. His gait was shambling, uneven. He stared straight ahead with all the fixed intensity of a sleepwalker.

Quietly, Blunt began to follow a few steps behind.

And now, what seemed like Chadwick's destination looked up, an ugly cairn of black boulders fashioned by nature into a grotto-like structure with a jagged opening on one side and a roof formed by an uptilted rock slab.

Suddenly with a hoarse cry, Chadwick stopped and turned. "Over there!" he cried. "Behind you! Back of that rock!"

Even as Blunt spun around in obedience to the command, he realized his mistake. But before he could move, a rope encircled his throat, twisted tight with lightning rapidity and choked off his windpipe. The garotte!

He jerked both hands upward in vain effort to tear it away. His throat constricted as his breath was shut off. With the wooden fulcrum turning, exerting double strength, he felt his senses begin to leave him, blackness rise up to shroud his vision. His legs buckled.

But with a final lunge born of desperation, his right hand reached down and grasped his holstered revolver. He clawed the weapon free, twisted his body sideways, spun the gun barrel down and back, and fired.

The shot echoed across the Pit. Behind him, Chadwick uttered a low cry and released his grip. The garotte fell free. Blunt swiveled, brought back his left arm and delivered a final blow. Chadwick fell, almost at the opening of the cairn.

In that opening a third figure now became visible, a girl bound hand and foot, her mouth gagged with a wad of cloth. The sheriff gave a sigh of relief as he saw that she was still alive. And minutes later he assured himself that Emily Hunter was unharmed. He carried her across to the car and lifted her gently into the seat.

"Take it easy, Miss," he said. "I'll have you out of here in a moment."

With Chadwick he was not so gentle. He saw that his bullet had struck the other man's thigh and although not serious, was completely incapacitating. Nevertheless he snapped on handcuffs and half dragged him to the car. He turned the car around and headed up the Virginia road. At the fork he swung left toward Chaska.

"You've been a busy man," he said to Chadwick. "And you'll pay, one way or another, even though you didn't know what you were doing."

AUGUST W. DERLETH AND MARK SCHORER

The Return of Andrew Bentley

Here is a shivery collaborative effort from the pen of the late AUGUST DERLETH *(1909–1971), who wrote well over a hundred supernatural tales as well as the Conan Doyle–inspired Solar Pons mystery stories. Derleth, who cofounded Arkham House Publishers in his home town of Sauk City, Wisconsin, was a key member of that circle of writers who admired and imitated the crypto-science-fictional fiction of H. P. Lovecraft (represented elsewhere in this volume). "The Return of Andrew Bentley," one of Derleth's most successful Lovecraftian compositions, takes place in the vicinity of Sac Prairie, which a former Wisconsin resident tells me is another name for Sauk City.*

It is with considerable hesitation that I here chronicle the strange incidents which marked my short stay at the old Wilder homestead on the banks of the Wisconsin River not far from the rustic village of Sac Prairie. My reluctance is not entirely dispelled by the conviction that some record of these events should emphatically be made, if only to stop the circulation of unfounded rumors which have come into being since my departure from the vicinity.

The singular chain of events began with a peremptory letter from my aging uncle, Amos Wilder, ordering me to appear at the homestead, where he was then living with a housekeeper and a caretaker. Communications from my Uncle Amos were not only exceedingly rare, but usually tinged with biting and withering comments about my profession of letters, which he held in great scorn. Previous to this note, we had not seen each other for over four years. His curt note hinted that there was something of vital importance to both of us which he wished to take up with me, and though I had no inkling of what this might be, I did not hesitate to go.

The old house was not large. It stood well back in the rambling grounds, its white surface mottled by the shadows of leafy branches in the warm sunlight of the day on which I arrived. Green shutters crowded upon the windows, and the door was tightly closed, despite the day's somnolent warmth. The river was cerulean and silver in the immediate background, and farther beyond, the bluffs on the other side of the river rose from behind the trees and were lost in the blue haze of distance to the north and south.

My uncle had grown incredibly old, and now hobbled about with the aid of a cane. On the morning of my arrival he was dressed in a long, ragged black robe that trailed along the floor; beneath this garment he wore a threadbare black jersey and a pair of shabby trousers. His hair was unkempt, and on his chin was a rough beard, masking his thin, sardonic mouth. His eyes, however, had lost none of their fire, and I felt his disapproval of me as clearly as ever. His expression was that of a man who is faced with an unpleasant but necessary task.

At last, after a rude scrutiny, he began to speak, having first made certain that no one lurked within earshot.

"It's hardly necessary for me to say I'm not too certain I've done a wise thing in choosing you," he began. "I've always considered you somewhat of a milksop, and you've done nothing to change my opinion."

He watched my face closely as he spoke, to detect any resentment that I might feel; but I had heard this kind of speech from him too often before to feel any active anger. He sensed this, apparently, for he went on abruptly.

"I'm going to leave everything I've got to you, but there'll be a condition. You'll have to spend most of your time here, make this your home, of course, and there are one or two other small things you'll have to see to. Mind, I'm not putting anything in my will; I want only your word. Do you think you can give it? Think you can say, 'Yes' to my terms?"

He paused, and I said, "I see no reason why I shouldn't—if you can guarantee that your terms won't interfere with my writing."

My uncle smiled and shook his head as if in exasperation. "Nothing is easier," he replied curtly. "Your time for writing will be virtually unlimited."

"What do you want me to do?" I asked.

"Spend most of your time here, as I said before. Let no day go by during which you do not examine the vault behind the house. My body will lie there, and the vault will be sealed; I want to know that I can depend upon you to prevent anything from entering that vault. If at any time you discover that some one has been tampering, you will find written instructions for your further procedure in my library desk. Will you promise me to attend to these things without too much curiosity concerning them?"

I promised without the slightest hesitation, though there were perplexing thoughts crowding upon my mind.

Amos Wilder turned away, his eyes glittering. Then he looked through the window directly opposite me and began to chuckle in a curiously guttural tone. At last he said, his eyes fixed upon a patch of blue sky beyond the tree near the window, "Good. I'll block him yet! Amos Wilder is still a match for you—do you hear, Andrew?"

What his words might portend I had no means of knowing, for he turned abruptly to me and said in his clipped, curt way, "You must go now, Ellis. I shall not see you again." With that, he left the room, and as if by magic, old Jacob Kinney, the caretaker, appeared to show me from the grounds, his lugubrious face regarding me with apologetic eyes from the doorway through which his master had so abruptly vanished but a moment before.

My uncle's strange words puzzled me, and it occurred to me that the old man was losing his mind. That I then did him an injustice I subsequently learned, but at the time all evidence pointed to mental derangement. I finally contented myself with this explanation, though it did not account for the old man's obvious rationality during most of the conversation. Two points struck me: my uncle had put particular stress upon the suggestion that something might enter his vault. And secondly, what was the meaning of his last words, and to whom was my uncle referring when he said, "I'll block him yet!" and "Amos Wilder is still a match for you—do you hear, Andrew?" Conjecture, however, was futile; for, since I knew very little of my uncle's personal affairs, any guesses I might have made as to his obscure references, if indeed he was not losing his mind, would be fruitless.

I left the old homestead that day in May only to find myself back there again within forty-eight hours, summoned by Thomas Weatherbee of Sac Prairie, my uncle's solicitor, whose short telegram apprising me of Amos Wilder's death reached me within three hours of my return to the St. Louis apartment which served me as my temporary home. My shock at the news of his sudden death was heightened when I learned that the circumstances surrounding his decease indicated suicide.

Weatherbee told me the circumstances of my uncle's singular death. It appeared that Jacob Kinney had found the old man in the very room in which he and I had discussed his wishes only a day before. He was seated at the table, apparently asleep. One hand still grasped a pen, and before him lay a sheet of note-paper upon which he had written my name and address, nothing more. It was presumed at first that he had had a heart attack, but a medical examination had brought forth the suspicion that the old man had made away with himself by taking an overdose of veronal. There was, however, considerable reluctance to presume suicide, for an overdose of veronal might just as likely be accident as suicide. Eventually a coroner's jury decided that my uncle had met his death by accident, but from the first I was convinced that Amos Wilder had killed himself. In the light of subsequent events and of his own cryptic words to me, "I shall not see you again," my suspicion was, I feel, justified, though no definite and conclusive evidence emerged.

My uncle was buried, as he had wished, in the long-disused family vault behind the house, and the vault was sealed from the outside with due ceremony and in the presence of witnesses. The reading of the will was a short affair, for excepting bequests made to the housekeeper and caretaker, I inherited everything. My living was thus assured, and as my uncle had said, I found the future holding many hours of leisure in which to pursue letters.

And yet, despite the apparent rosiness of the outlook, there was from the first a peculiar restraint upon my living in the old homestead. It was indefinable and strange, and numerous small incidents occurred to supplement this odd impression. First old Jacob Kinney wanted to leave. With great effort I persuaded him to stay, and dragged from him his reason for wanting to go.

"There've been mighty strange things a-goin' on about this house, Mr. Wilder, all the time your uncle was alive—and I'm afraid things'll be goin' on again after a bit."

More than that cryptic utterance I could not get out of him. I took the liberty shortly after to repeat Kinney's words to the housekeeper, Mrs. Seldon. The startled expression that passed over her countenance did not escape me, and her immediate assurance that Jake Kinney was in his dotage did not entirely reassure me.

Then there was the daily function of examining the seal on the vault. The absurdity of my uncle's request began to grow on me, and my task, trivial as it was, became daily more irritating. Yet, having given my promise, I could do no more than fulfill it.

On the third night following my uncle's interment, my sleep was troubled by a recurrent dream which gave me no little thought when I remembered its persistence on the following day. I dreamed that my Uncle Amos stood before me, clad as I had last seen him on the visit just preceding his strange death. He regarded me with his beady eyes, and then abruptly said in a mournful and yet urgent voice, "You must bring Burkhardt back here. He forgot to protect me against them. You must get him to do so. If he will not, then see those books on the second shelf of the seventh compartment of my library."

This dream was repeated several times, and it had a perfectly logical basis, which was briefly this: My uncle was buried by Father Burkhardt, the Sac Prairie parish priest, who was not satisfied with the findings of the coroner's jury, and consequently, in the belief that Amos Wilder had killed himself, had refused to bless the grave of a suicide. Yet, what the dream-shape of the night before had obviously meant when he spoke of what Father Burkhardt had forgotten to do, was the blessing of the grave.

I spent some time mulling over this solution of the dream, and at length went to see the priest. My efforts, however, were futile. The old man explained his attitude with great patience, and I was forced to agree with him.

On the following night the dream recurred, and in consequence, since a visit to Father Burkhardt had already failed to achieve the desired effect, I turned, impelled largely by curiosity, to the books on the second shelf of the seventh compartment indicated by the dream-figure of my uncle. From the moment that I opened the first of those books, the entire complexion of the occurrences at the homestead changed inexplicably, and I found myself involved in a chain of incidents, the singularity of which continues to impress me even as I write at this late date. For the books on the second shelf of the seventh compartment in my dead uncle's library were books on black magic—books long out of print, and apparently centuries old, for in many of them the print had faded almost to illegibility.

The Latin in which most of the books were written was not easily translated, but fortunately it was not necessary for me to search long for the portions indicated by my uncle, for in each book paragraphs were marked for my attention. The subjects of the marked portions were strangely similar. After some difficulty I succeeded in translating the first indicated paragraph to catch my eye. "For Protection from Things That Walk in the Night," it read. "There are many things stalking abroad by darkness, perhaps ghouls, perhaps evil demons lured from outer space by man's own ignorance, perhaps souls isolated in space, havenless and alone, and yet strongly attached to the things of this earth. Let no bodies be exposed to their evil wrath. Let there be all manner of protection for vaults and graves, for the dead as well as the living; for ghouls, incubi, and succubi haunt the near places as well as the far, and seek always to quench the fire of their unholy desire. . . . Take blessed water from a church and mix it with the blood of a young babe, be it ever so small a measure, and with this cross the grave or the door of the vault thrice at the full of the moon."

If this was what my Uncle Amos desired me to do, I knew at once that the task had devolved upon the wrong man; for I could certainly not see myself going about collecting holy water and the blood of a young child and then performing ridiculous rites over the vault with an odious mixture of the two. I put the books aside and returned to my work, which seemed suddenly more inviting than it had ever been before.

Yet what I had read disturbed me, and the suggestion that my uncle had come to believe in the power of black magic—perhaps even more than this, for all I knew—was extremely distasteful to me. In consequence, my writing suffered, and immediately after my supper that evening, I went for a long walk on the river bank.

A half-moon high in the sky made the countryside bright and clear, and since the night was balmy and made doubly inviting by the sweet mystery of night sounds—the gasping and gurgling of the water, the splashing of distant fish, the muted cries of night-birds, particularly the *peet, peet* of the nighthawk and the eery call of the whippoorwill, and the countless mysterious sounds from the underbrush in the river bottoms—I extended my walk much farther than I had originally intended; so that it was shortly after midnight when I approached the house again, and the moon was close upon the western horizon.

As I came quietly along in the now still night, my eye caught a movement in the shadowy distance. The movement had come from the region of the large old elm which pressed close upon the house near the library window, and it was upon this tree that I now fixed my eyes. I had not long to wait, for presently a shadow detached itself from the giant bole and went slowly around the house toward the darkness behind. I could see the figure quite clearly, though I did not once catch sight of its face, despite the fact that the man, for man it was, wore no hat. He walked with a slight limp, and wore a long black cape. He was near medium height, but quite bent, so that his back was unnaturally hunched. His hands were strikingly white in the fading light of the moon, and he walked with a peculiar flaffing motion, despite his obvious limp. He passed beyond the house with me at his heels, for I was determined to ascertain if possible what design had brought him to the old house.

I lost sight of him for a few moments while I gained the shelter of the house, but in a minute I saw him again, and with a gasp of astonishment realized that he was making directly for the vault in which my Uncle Amos lay buried. I stifled an impulse to shout at him, and made my way cautiously in the shadow of a row of lilac bushes toward the vault, before which he was now standing. The darkness here was intense, owing to the fact that the trees from the surrounding copse pressed close upon this corner of the estate; yet I could see from my crouching position that the mysterious intruder was fumbling with the seals of the vault. My purpose in following him so closely was to collar him while he was engaged with the seals, but this design was now for the moment thwarted by his stepping back to survey the surface of the vault door. He remained standing in silence for some while, and I had almost decided that it might be just as easy to capture him in this position, when he moved forward once more. But this time he did not fumble with the seals. Instead, he seemed to flatten himself against the door of the vault. Then, incredible as it may seem, his figure began to grow smaller, to shrink, save for his gaunt and gleaming white fingers and arms!

With a strangled gasp, I sprang forward.

My memory at this point is not quite clear. I remember seizing the outstretched fingers of the man at the vault door, feeling something within my grasp. Then something struck me at the same moment that the intruder whirled and leaped away. I had the fleeting impression that a second person had leaped upon me from behind. I went down like a log.

I came to my senses not quite an hour later, and lay for a moment recalling what had happened. I remembered having made a snatch at the intruder's fingers, and being struck. There was an appreciable soreness of the head, and a sensitive bruise on my forehead when finally I felt for it. But what most drew my attention was the thing that I held tightly in my left hand, the hand which had grasped at the strangely white fingers of the creature pressed against the door of the Wilder vault. I had felt it within my grasp from the first moment of consciousness, but from its roughness, I had taken it for a small twig caught up from the lawn. In consequence, it was not until I reached the security of the house that I looked at it. I threw it upon the table in the dim glow of the table lamp—and almost fell in my utter amazement; for the thing I had held in my hand was a fragment of human bone—the unmistakable first two joints of the little finger!

This discovery loosed a flood of futile conjectures. Was it after

all a man I had surprised at the vault, or was it—something else?
. . . That my uncle was in some way vitally concerned now became apparent, if it had not been entirely so before. The fact that
Amos Wilder had looked for some such interruption of his repose in the old vault led me to believe that whatever he feared
derived from some source in the past. Accordingly, I gave up all
conjecture for the time, and promised myself that in the morning
I would set on foot inquiries designed to make me familiar with
my secluded uncle's past life.

I was destined to receive a shock in the morning. Determined
to prosecute my curiosity concerning my uncle without loss of
time, I summoned Jacob Kinney, whose surliness had noticeably
increased during the few days I had been at the old Wilder house.
Instead of asking directly about my uncle, I began with a short
account of the figure I had seen outside the preceding night.

"I was out quite late last night, Jake," I began, "and when I
came home I noticed a stranger on the grounds."

Kinney's eyebrows shot up in undisguised curiosity, but he said
nothing, though he began to exhibit signs of uneasiness which
did not escape my notice.

"He was about five feet tall, I should say, and wore no hat," I
went on. "He wore a long black cape, and walked with a slight
limp."

Abruptly Kinney came to his feet, his eyes wide with fear.
"What's that you say?" he demanded hoarsely. "Walked with a
limp—wore a cape?"

I nodded, and would have continued my narrative, had not
Kinney cut in.

"My God!" he exclaimed. "Andrew Bentley's back!"

"Who's Andrew Bentley?" I asked.

But Kinney did not hear. He had whirled abruptly and run from
the room as fast as his feeble legs would allow him to go. My
astonishment knew no bounds, nor did subsequent events in any
way lessen it; for Jacob Kinney ran not only from the house, but
from the grounds, and his flight was climaxed shortly after by the
appearance of a begrimed youth representing himself as the old
man's nephew, who came for "Uncle Jake's things." From him I
learned that Kinney was leaving his position at once, and would

forfeit any wages due him, plus any amount I thought fit to recompense me for his precipitate flight.

Kinney's unaccountable action served only to sharpen my already keen interest, and I descended upon Mrs. Seldon posthaste. But the information which she was able to offer me was meager indeed. Andrew Bentley had arrived in the neighborhood only a few years back. He and my uncle had immediately become friends, and the friendship, despite an appearance of strain, had ended only when Bentley mysteriously disappeared about a year ago. She confirmed my description of the figure I had seen as that of Bentley. Mrs. Seldon, too, was inexplicably agitated, and when I sought to probe for the source of this agitation she said only that there were some very strange stories extant about Bentley, and about my uncle as well, and that most of the people in the neighborhood had been relieved of a great fear when Bentley disappeared from the farm adjoining the Wilder estate. This farm, which he had inhabited for the years of his residence, but had not worked, and had yet always managed to exist without trouble, was now uninhabited. This, together with a passing hint that Thomas Weatherbee might be able to add something, was the sum of what Mrs. Seldon knew.

I lost no time in telephoning Weatherbee and making an appointment for that afternoon. On the way to the attorney's office I had ample time to think over the events of the last ten days. That it was Andrew Bentley whom my Uncle Amos had referred to when he spoke so cryptically with me before his death, I had no longer any doubt. Evidently then, he, too, feared his strange neighbor, but how he hoped to thwart any attempt that Bentley might make to get the body—for what reason he might want it I could not guess—with black magic, was beyond my comprehension.

Thomas Weatherbee was a short and rather insignificant man, but his attitude was conducive to business, and he made clear to me that he had only a limited time at my disposal. I came directly to the matter of Andrew Bentley.

"Andrew Bentley," began Weatherbee with some reluctance, "was a man with whom I had no dealings, with whom I cared to have none. I have seldom met any one whose mere presence was so innately evil. Your uncle took up with him, it is true, but I believe he regretted it to the end of his days."

"What exactly was wrong with Bentley?" I cut in.

Weatherbee smiled grimly, regarded me speculatively for a moment or two, and said, "Bentley was an avowed sorcerer."

"Oh, come," I said; "that sort of thing isn't believed in any more." But a horrible suspicion began to grow in my mind.

"Perhaps not generally," replied Weatherbee at once. "But I can assure you that most of us around here believe in the power of black magic after even so short an acquaintance as ours with Andrew Bentley. Consider for a moment that you have spent the greater part of your life in a modern city, away from the country-side where such beliefs flourish, Wilder."

He stopped with an abrupt gesture, and took a portfolio from a cabinet. From this he took a photograph, looked at it with a slight curl of disgust on his lips, and passed it over to me.

It was a snapshot, apparently made surreptitiously, of Andrew Bentley, and it had been taken evidently at considerable risk after sunset, for the general appearance of the picture led me to assume that its vagueness was caused by the haziness of dusk—a supposition which Weatherbee confirmed. The figure, however, was quite clear, save for blurred arms, which had evidently been moving during the exposure, and for the head. The view had been taken from the side, and showed Andrew Bentley, certainly identified for me by the long cape he wore, standing as if in conversation with some one. Yet it struck me as strange that Bentley could have stood quietly during the exposure with no incentive to do so, and I commented upon it at once.

Weatherbee looked at me queerly. "Wilder," he said, "there was another person there—or should I say *thing?* And this thing was directly in line with the lens, for he was standing very close to Bentley—and yet, there is nothing on the snapshot, nor is there any evidence on the exposed negative itself that any one stood there; for, as you can see, the landscape is unbroken."

It was as he said.

"But this other person," I put in. "He was seen, and yet does not appear. Apparently the camera was out of focus, or the film was defective."

"On the contrary. There are logical explanations for the non-appearance of something on a film. You can't photograph a dream. And you can't photograph something that has no material form—I say *material* advisedly—even though our own eyes give that thing a physical being."

"What do you mean?"

"Father Burkhardt would call it a familiar," he said, clipping his words. "A familiar, in case you don't know, is an evil spirit summoned by a sorcerer to wait upon his desires. That tall, gaunt man was never seen by day—always by night, and never without Bentley. I can give you no more of my time now, but if you can bring yourself to accept what I have to say at face value, I'll be glad to see you again."

My interview with Thomas Weatherbee left me considerably shaken, and I found myself discarding all my previously formed beliefs regarding black magic. I went immediately to my late uncle's store of books, and began to read through them for further information, in the hope that something I might learn would enable me to meet Andrew Bentley on more equal footing, should he choose to call.

I read until far into the night, and what inconceivable knowledge I assimilated lingers clearly in my mind as I write. I read of age-old horror summoned from the abyss by the ignorance of men, of cosmic ghouls that roamed the ether in search of prey, and of countless things that walk by night. There were many legends of familiars, ghastly demons called forth from the depths at the whims of long-dead sorcerers; and it was significant that each legend had been heavily scored along the margins, and in one case the name "Andrew Bentley" was written in my uncle's hand. In another place my uncle had written, "We are fools to play with powers of whose scope even the wisest of us has no knowledge!"

It was at this point that it occurred to me that my uncle had left a letter of sealed instructions for me in case the vault was tampered with. This letter was to be in the library desk, where I found it with little trouble, a long, legal-looking envelope with my name inscribed very formally. The handwriting was undoubtedly my uncle's, and the letter within was the thing that finally dispelled all doubt from my mind as to the reality of the sorcery that had been and was still being practiced near the Wilder homestead; for it made clear what had happened between my uncle and Andrew Bentley—and that other.

My Dear Ellis:

If indeed they have come for me, as they must have if you read this, there is but one thing you can do. Bentley's body must be found and utterly destroyed; surely there cannot be much left of it now. Perhaps you have seen him in the night when he walks—as I have. He is not alive. I know, because I killed him a year ago—stabbed him with your grandfather's hunting-knife—which must yet lie in his black skeleton.

I think both Burkhardt and Weatherbee suspected that I aided Bentley to his black rites, but that was long before I dreamed of what depths of evil lurked in his soul. And when he began to hound me so, when he brought forward that other, that hellish thing he had conjured up from the nethermost places of evil—could I do otherwise than rid myself of his evil presence? My mind was at stake—and yes, my body. When you read this, only my body is at stake. For they want it—conceive if you can the ghastly irony of my lifeless body given an awful new existence by being inhabited by Bentley's familiar!

The body—Bentley's body—I put it in the vault, but that other removed it and hid it somewhere on the grounds. I have not been able to find it, and this past year has been a living hell for me—they have hounded me nightly, and though I can protect myself from them, I cannot stop them from appearing to taunt me. And when I am dead, my protection must come from you. But I hope that Burkhardt will have closed his eyes and blessed the vault, for this I think will be strong enough to keep them away—and yet, I cannot tell.

And perhaps even this is being read too late—for if once they have my body, destroy me, too, with Bentley's remains—by fire.

AMOS WILDER

I put down this letter and sat for a moment in silence. But what thoughts crowded upon my mind were interrupted by an odd sound from outside the window, a sound that was unnaturally striking in the still night. I glanced at my watch; it was one o'clock in the morning. Then I turned out the small reading-lamp and moved quietly toward the window, immediately beyond which stood the giant elm beneath which on the previous night I had first seen the ghostly figure of Andrew Bentley—for since he had been killed a year before, what I had seen could have been none other than his specter.

Then a thought struck me that paralyzed me with horror. Suppose I had been struck by *that other?* It seemed to me that the blow which had knocked me out had been struck from behind. At the same instant my eyes caught sight of the faintest movement beyond the window. The moon hung in a hazy sky and threw a faint illumination about the tree, despite the fairly heavy shadow of its overhanging limbs. There was a man pressed close to the bole of the tree, and even as I looked another seemed to rise up out of the ground at his side. And the second man was Andrew Bentley! I looked again at the first, and saw a tall, gaunt figure with malevolent red eyes, *through* whom I could see the line of moonlight and shadow on the lawn beyond the tree. They stood there together for only a moment, and then went quickly around the house—toward the vault!

From that instant events moved rapidly to a climax.

My eyes fixed themselves upon that place in the ground from which the figure of Andrew Bentley had sprung, and saw there an opening in the trunk of the old tree—for the elm was hollow, and its bole held the remains of Andrew Bentley! Small wonder that my uncle had been haunted by the presence of the man he had killed, when his remains were hidden in the tree near the library window!

But I stood there only for a fraction of a minute. Then I went quickly to the telephone, and after an agonizing delay got Weatherbee on the wire and asked him to come out at once, hinting enough of what was happening to gain his assent. I suggested also that he bring Father Burkhardt along, and this he promised to do.

Then I slipped silently from the house into the shadowy garden. I think the sight of those two unholy figures hovering about the door of the vault was too much for me, for I launched myself at them, heedless of my danger. But realization came almost instantly, for Andrew Bentley did not even turn at my appearance. Instead, the other looked abruptly around, fixed me with his red and fiery eyes, smiled wickedly so that his leathery face was weirdly creased, and leisurely watched my approach. Instinct, I believe, whirled me about and sent me flying from the garden.

The thing was somewhat surprised at my abrupt bolt, and this momentary hesitation on its part I continue to believe is responsible for my being alive to write this. For I knew that I was flying for my life, and I ran with the utmost speed of which I was capable. A fleeting glance showed me that the thing loped after me, a weirdly flaffing shape seeming to come with the wind in the moonlight night, and struck shuddery horror into my heart.

I made for the river, because I remembered reading in one of my uncle's old books that certain familiars could not cross water unless accompanied by those whose sorcery had summoned them to earth. I leaped into the cold water, tense with the hope that the thing behind could not follow.

It could not.

I saw it raging up and down along the river bank, impotent and furious at my fortunate escape, while I kept myself afloat in mid-current. The current carried me rapidly downstream, and I kept my eyes fixed upon the thing I had eluded until it turned and sped back toward the vault. Only when I was completely out of its sight did I make for the bank once more.

I ran madly down the road along which Weatherbee and the priest must come, flinging off some of my wet clothes as I went. What was happening at the vault I did not know—at the moment my only thought was temporary safety from the thing whose power I had so thoughtlessly challenged.

I had gone perhaps a half-mile beyond the estate when the headlights of Weatherbee's car swept around a curve and outlined me in the road. The car ground to an emergency stop, and Weatherbee's voice called out. I jumped into the car, and explained as rapidly as I could what had happened.

Father Burkhardt regarded me quizzically, half smiling.

"You've had a narrow escape, my boy," he said, "a very narrow escape. Now if only we can get to the vault before they succeed in their evil design. Such a fate is too harsh a punishment even for the sins of Amos Wilder."

He shuddered as he spoke, and Weatherbee's face was grim.

None of us wasted a moment when the car came to a stop near the house. Father Burkhardt, despite his age, led the way, marshaling us behind him, for he went ahead with a crucifix extended.

But even he faltered at the horrifying sight that met our eyes when we rounded the house and came into the garden. For the vault was open, and from it emerged the skeletal Bentley and his familiar, and between them they dragged the lifeless body of my Uncle Amos! Burkhardt's hesitation, however, was only momentary, for he ran forward immediately; nor were Weatherbee and I far behind.

At the same moment the two at the vault caught sight of us. With a shrill scream, the tall, gaunt thing loosed his hold of the corpse and launched himself forward. But the crucifix served us well, for the thing fell shuddering away from it. Father Burkhardt immediately pressed his advantage, and following his sharp command, Weatherbee and I rushed at Bentley, who had up to this moment remained beside the corpse, still keeping hold of one dead arm.

But at our advance, Bentley wavered a moment, and then turned and took flight, dodging nimbly past us and running for the house. We were at his heels, and saw him when he vanished in the deep shadows of the tree near the library window.

Father Burkhardt presently made his appearance, walking warily, for the thing was still at bay but eager to attack.

"Find the bones," directed the priest. "They're in the tree, I suspect."

I bent obediently, and presently my searching hand encountered a scooped-out hollow in the trunk just above the opening at the base of the tree. In this lay the skeleton of Andrew Bentley, together with the weapon by which he had met his death, and here it had lain ever since the thing Bentley had summoned from the depths had removed the sorcerer's body from the old vault. Small wonder that it had never been discovered!

Father Burkhardt stood protectingly close while Weatherbee and I prepared a pyre to consume the remains of the sorcerer.

"But what can we do about that?" I asked once, pointing to the familiar that now raged in baffled fury just beyond us.

"We need not bother about that," said the priest. "He is held to earth only by the body of the man who summoned him from below. When once that body is destroyed, he must return. That's why they were after your uncle's body. If the familiar could inhabit a body fresh from a new grave, he could walk by day as well as by night, and need have no fear of having to return."

Once or twice the thing did rush at us—but each time its charge was arrested by the power of that crucifix held unfalteringly aloft by Father Burkhardt, and each time the thing shrank away, wailing.

It was over at last, but not without a short period of ghastly doubt. The remains of Andrew Bentley were reduced to ashes, utterly destroyed, and yet the thing Bentley had called from outside lingered beyond us, strangely quiet now, regarding us malevolently.

"I don't understand," admitted Father Burkhardt at last. "Now that Bentley's ashes alone remain, the thing should go back into the depths."

But if the priest did not understand, I did. Abruptly I ran to the library window, raised it as far as it would go, and scrambled into the room. In a moment I emerged, bearing the fragment of Bentley's little finger which I had snatched from the skeletal hand the night before. I threw it into the flames already dying down in the shadow of the tree.

In a moment it had caught fire, and at the same instant the thing hovering near gave a chilling scream of pain and fury, pushed madly toward us, and then abruptly shot into space and vanished like the last fragment of an unholy, ghastly nightmare.

"*Requiescat in pace,*" said Father Burkhardt softly, looking at the ashes at our feet. But the dubious expression in his eyes conveyed his belief that for the now-released spirit of Andrew Bentley a greater and longer torture had just begun.

BARRY N. MALZBERG

Away

The bleating politician in BARRY MALZBERG's "Away" is a melancholy reminder that all too many of those who boast of their American citizenship neither uphold nor believe in the humanitarian principles on which our country was founded. Malzberg's spectral narrator is based on a true historical personage, Josiah Bushnell Grinnell, a New England attorney, businessman and clergyman who indeed paid heed to Horace Greeley and moved west to Iowa. There he established a town bearing his name that once was a stop on the antislavery movement's Underground Railroad and is now the site of Grinnell College, a highly rated liberal arts school founded in 1846.

My name is Josiah Bushnell Grinnell. In 1853, responding to the invocation of the famous Horace Greeley, publisher of the New York Tribune, I take myself to the new state of Iowa and thereupon establish both a town and a college. "Go west, young man, go west and grow with the country," Greeley has said, and solemn young fellow that I am, I take him seriously. What a surprise, what a disappointment to learn only after I am established where the tall corn grows that Greeley stole this from an obscure Indiana newspaperman named Soule and has appropriated the statement as his own. If I had known this, I might have gone to Indiana.

Instead, here I am in Iowa. What an unusually solemn man I am! I have always taken the invocations of my elders seriously, which is why the college I establish, the town to be named after me, the entire state itself takes on a somewhat sectarian whiff. A century later it is impossible for citizens to enter upon our interstates without murmuring prayers. In 1857, Sioux Indians massacre men, women, and children at Spirit Lake, the last massacre by Indians in the midwest and the released souls, the violated spirits add their pain and terror to the general chatter. On a hot May afternoon, the dead sun sprawling low in the panels of sky, the sounds of the cattle rising toward the dusk, it is possible to imagine oneself if one were a small man lying in a field, gazing, that one had entered upon the outer regions of the landscape painted by the honorable John Calvin. It is a difficult state, a difficult time.

I, Josiah Bushnell Grinnell, know this; know of all the interstices and difficulties of the sovereign state of Iowa. Cleaved from the Wisconsin territory, admitted to statehood on December 28, 1846, Iowa sprawls, flatland, on the way to the west. There are ways around it—there are ways around everything the good Lord knows—but once on the interstate, it is hard to find the way.

Here it is. It is 1954. I have been deceased for many decades, however, my spirit—no less than those massacred at Spirit Lake —lives on. Iowa is the possessor of its inhabitants, no one who has ever lived in this state has known true release. We hang around. This may seem an unlikely statement, a remarkable condition, but wait your turn, enjoy the common passage before you act in judgment. Here in 1954 the senior senator from this great state, the honorable, if that is quite the term I am seeking, Bourke B. Hickenlooper is inveighing against the Communists at a Fourth of July picnic. Hickenlooper, with McCarthy, with Jenner, is the pride of what may be called the conservative wing. To Hickenlooper it is an insult when the first Negro set the first Negro foot on the Negro shores of the first Negro city in this country, uttering incoherent Negro chants. It is not that Hickenlooper is a racist, you understand. It is merely that he is still linked to Spirit Lake by ancestry and blood, still sees the frame of the assassin arched against the moonlight. "We must expel the Communists from our shores," Hickenlooper says. He is on a podium, at some remove from the crowd, screaming without benefit of microphone. Fourth of July picnics are still important in the Iowa of this time. Politicians are expected to make speeches, to invoke Americana. Hickenlooper is merely doing his duty. Of his true thoughts of the matter we know not. He may or may not have an interior. Most politicians do not. "McCarran Act!" Hickenlooper screams. "Joseph McCarthy! Millard Tydings! Eighty-seven hundred card-carrying Communists!" And so on. The crowd reacts stiffly. It is very hot. A band plays in the distance, raucous parade ground arias of the kind soon enough to be popularized by Meredith Willson (born in Mason City) in *The Music Man.* "Who promoted Peress?" Hickenlooper asks. The crowd mutters. Their mood is not hostile but they are tired.

My name is Josiah Bushnell Grinnell. It is hard to explain exactly what I am doing at this picnic or what I expect to come of it. We Iowans (or transplanted Iowans) as I have said, our spirits live on. Even after death. Relegated to some limbo we come in and out, reincarnates or observers, bound to some flatland of the spirit, replicating our history, moving in and out of time. Screams of the settlers at Spirit Lake. Bullshit of Greeley. Moving ever west. From this limbo I emerge at odd times, strange moments, find myself at Iowa State Events. Such seems to be the case now. I am jammed in with this crowd, listening to Bourke B. Hickenlooper. To my left and right are Iowans of various sexes and ages, most of them young, in a burst of color, standing at parade rest, listening to the rantings of the honorable senator. Now and then a baby yowls or a young woman faints, her parasol preceding her on a graceless slide to the ground. Men leap to the rescue of the women, the babies are pacified in other ways. The huge bowl of the sky presses. It is indecently hot, even for a spirit, even for the gullible sectarian spirit of a man who would listen to Horace Greeley (at least I never knew of Horatio Alger; it is impossible to say to what state he might have sent me.) "Hickenlooper!" I shout. "Hey, Hickenlooper!"

The crowd stares at me. Sometimes I can be heard and sometimes not; sometimes I am visible and at other times invisible. Reincarnation, like life itself, is a chancy business. At this time it would appear that I can be seen. Yards down range the senator stares at me, his stride momentarily broken. "Hey, Senator!" I shout. Hickenlooper removes his enormous hat, peers at me. I stride forward, closing the ground between us.

"You're all wrong, don't you know that?" I say. "Listen to me!" I say, turning around, gesturing at the farmers, their wives, the beaus and beauxettes in their holiday undress who look at me incuriously. "This man is not telling the truth. We lived to open frontiers, he is closing them!"

I am stared at incomprehendingly. One could, after all, envision no other possibility. Politics may be entertainment but metaphysics is unendurable in the Hawkeye State. "He speaketh with forked tongue!" I point out.

There are a forest of shrugs around me. I turn back toward the podium, find Hickenlooper in brisk conference with several aides who have jumped to the sides of the platform. He cups an ear, listens intently. They gesture at me. "Answer the charge!" I yell. "Don't hide behind the others, explain yourself. Tell why you are breeding fear, why you are seeking to close off that which will be opened."

Hickenlooper points at me. The hand is commanding, enormous. At my side, suddenly, are two earnest, honest Iowa state police; they seize me by the elbows. "If you will, sir," one says, "if you'll just come along."

"Don't arrest me," I say, struggling in their grasp, "arrest that man. That man is the assassin. I am Josiah Bushnell Grinnell, the founder of Grinnell College. I am a man of substance—"

"Card-carrying!" I hear Hickenlooper shout and then, this is the truth, I hear no more; speedily, forcibly, forcefully, I am carried from the grounds. Beaus and beauxettes, farmers and their daughters, little towheaded children and Iowa cattle, they all look at me mournfully. The troopers are insistent. "Don't you understand?" I say to them. "This isn't the end, this is just the passage, it's going to happen again, again and *again*—"

"Stay calm, sir," one says, "everything will be all right. Just don't struggle, understand the situation—"

I close my eyes. Again and again and it is too late. In the sudden, cool rushing darkness ninety-seven years are taken from me as if by death itself and I am at Spirit Lake once more, oh God, I am at Spirit Lake and in the sudden, clinging, rushing, tumultu-

ous darkness, I hear the sound of the Sioux closing in around us;
one high wail coming then, concentrating them, poised—

I scream then, try once more to give the alarm. But I cannot;
my throat is dry, my lungs are cut out, my fate is darkness; in the
night, eleven years after union, three years before the Civil War,
they are coming, they are coming and the stain will leach outward, ever outward—

Go west, young man, go west—

I listened, I came. I propagated, and I could not save them.
And in the face of the Hickenloopers, through to dissolution
itself, I never, never will. Until by something that is, at last,
beyond me, I too will be cut off.

ANONYMOUS

The Strange Guests

"The Strange Guests," allegedly based on an American Indian legend, was published anonymously in 1837. It is a simple, yet eloquently moving ghost story set near Lake Superior, whose shores border Michigan, Minnesota and Wisconsin.

Many years ago there lived, near the borders of Lake Superior, a noted hunter, who had a wife and one child. His lodge stood in a remote part of the forest, several days' journey from that of any other person. He spent his days in hunting, and his evenings in relating to his wife the incidents that had befallen him in the chase. As game was very abundant, he seldom failed to bring home in the evening an ample store of meat to last them until the succeeding evening; and while they were seated by the fire in his lodge partaking the fruits of his day's labour, he entertained his wife with conversation, or by occasionally relating those tales, or enforcing those precepts, which every good Indian esteems necessary for the instruction of his wife and children. Thus, far removed from all sources of disquiet, surrounded by all they deemed necessary to their comfort, and happy in one another's society, their lives passed away in cheerful solitude and sweet contentment. The breast of the hunter had never felt the compunctions of remorse, for he was a just man in all his dealings. He had never violated the laws of his tribe by encroaching upon the hunting-grounds of his neighbours, by taking that which did not belong to him, or by any act calculated to displease the village chiefs or offend the Great Spirit. His chief ambition was to support his family with a sufficiency of food and skins by his own unaided exertions, and to share their happiness around his cheerful fire at night. The white man had not yet taught them that blankets and clothes were necessary to their comfort, or that guns could be used in the killing of game.

The life of the Chippewa hunter peacefully glided away.

One evening during the winter season, it chanced that he remained out later than usual, and his wife sat lonely in the lodge, and began to be agitated with fears lest some accident had befallen him. Darkness had already fallen. She listened attentively to hear the sound of coming footsteps; but nothing could be heard but the wind mournfully whistling around the sides of the lodge. Time passed away while she remained in this state of suspense, every moment augmenting her fears and adding to her disappointment.

Suddenly she heard the sound of approaching footsteps upon the frozen surface of the snow. Not doubting that it was her husband, she quickly unfastened the loop which held, by an inner fastening, the skin door of the lodge, and throwing it open she saw two strange women standing before it. Courtesy left the hunter's wife no time for deliberation. She invited the strangers to enter and warm themselves, thinking, from the distance to the nearest neighbours, they must have walked a considerable way. When they were entered she invited them to remain. They seemed to be total strangers to that part of the country, and the more closely she observed them the more curious the hunter's wife became respecting her guests.

No efforts could induce them to come near the fire. They took their seats in a remote part of the lodge, and drew their garments about them in such a manner as to almost completely hide their faces. They seemed shy and reserved, and when a glimpse could be had of their faces they appeared pale, even of a deathly hue. Their eyes were bright but sunken: their cheekbones were prominent, and their persons slender and emaciated.

Seeing that her guests avoided conversation as well as observation, the woman forbore to question them, and sat in silence until her husband entered. He had been led further than usual in the pursuit of game, but had returned with the carcass of a large and fat deer. The moment he entered the lodge, the mysterious women exclaimed:

"Behold! what a fine and fat animal!" and they immediately ran and pulled off pieces of the whitest fat, which they ate with avidity.

Such conduct appeared very strange to the hunter, but supposing the strangers had been a long time without food, he made no remark; and his wife, taking example from her husband, likewise restrained herself.

On the following evening the same scene was repeated. The hunter brought home the best portions of the game he had killed, and while he was laying it down before his wife, according to custom, the two strange women came quickly up, tore off large pieces of fat, and ate them with greediness. Such behaviour might well have aroused the hunter's displeasure; but the deference due to strange guests induced him to pass it over in silence.

Observing the parts to which the strangers were most partial, the hunter resolved the next day to anticipate their wants by cutting off and tying up a portion of the fat for each. This he did: and having placed the two portions of fat upon the top of his burden, as soon as he entered the lodge he gave to each stranger the part that was hers. Still the guests appeared to be dissatisfied, and took more from the carcass lying before the wife.

Except for this remarkable behaviour, the conduct of the guests was unexceptionable, although marked by some peculiarities. They were quiet, modest, and discreet. They maintained a cautious silence during the day, neither uttering a word nor moving from the lodge. At night they would get up, and, taking those implements which were then used in breaking and preparing wood, repair to the forest. Here they would busy themselves in seeking dry branches and pieces of trees blown down by the wind. When a sufficient quantity had been gathered to last until the succeeding night they carried it home upon their shoulders. Then carefully putting everything in its place within the lodge, they resumed their seats and their studied silence. They were always careful to return from their labours before the dawn of day, and were never known to stay out beyond that hour. In this manner they repaid, in some measure, the kindness of the hunter, and relieved his wife from one of her most laborious duties.

Thus nearly the whole year passed away, every day leading to some new development of character which served to endear the parties to each other. The visitors began to assume a more hale and healthy aspect; their faces daily lost something of that deathly hue which had at first marked them, and they visibly improved in strength, and threw off some of that cold reserve and forbidding austerity which had kept the hunter so long in ignorance of their true character.

One evening the hunter returned very late after having spent the day in toilsome exertion, and having laid the produce of his hunt at his wife's feet, the silent women seized it and began to tear off the fat in such an unceremonious manner that the wife could no longer control her feelings of disgust, and said to herself:

"This is really too bad. How can I bear it any longer?"

She did not, however, put her thought into words, but an immediate change was observed in the two visitors. They became unusually reserved, and showed evident signs of being uneasy in their situation. The good hunter immediately perceived this change, and, fearful that they had taken offence, as soon as they had retired demanded of his wife whether any harsh expression had escaped her lips during the day. She replied that she had uttered nothing to give the least offence. The hunter tried to compose himself to sleep, but he felt restive and uneasy, for he could hear the sighs and lamentations of the two strangers. Every moment added to his conviction that his guests had taken some deep offence; and, as he could not banish this idea from his mind, he arose, and, going to the strangers, thus addressed them:

"Tell me, ye women, what is it that causes you pain of mind, and makes you utter these unceasing sighs? Has my wife given you any cause of offence during the day while I was absent in the chase? My fears persuade me that, in some unguarded moment, she has forgotten what is due to the rights of hospitality, and used expressions ill-befitting the mysterious character you sustain. Tell me, ye strangers from a strange country, ye women who appear not to be of this world, what it is that causes you pain of mind, and makes you utter these unceasing sighs."

They replied that no unkind expression had ever been used towards them during their residence in the lodge, that they had received all the affectionate attention they could reasonably expect.

"It is not for ourselves," they continued, "it is not for ourselves that we weep. We are weeping for the fate of mankind; we are weeping for the fate of mortals whom Death awaits at every stage of their existence. Proud mortals, whom disease attacks in youth and in age. Vain men, whom hunger pinches, cold benumbs, and poverty emaciates. Weak beings, who are born in tears, who are nurtured in tears, and whose whole course is marked upon the thirsty sands of life in a broad line of tears. It is for these we weep.

"You have spoken truly, brother; we are not of this world. We are spirits from the land of the dead, sent upon the earth to try the sincerity of the living. It is not for the dead but for the living that we mourn. It was by no means necessary that your wife should express her thoughts to us. We knew them as soon as they were formed. We saw that for once displeasure had arisen in her heart. It is enough. Our mission is ended. We came but to try you, and we knew before we came that you were a kind husband, an affectionate father, and a good friend. Still, you have the weaknesses of a mortal, and your wife is wanting in our eyes; but it is not alone for you we weep, it is for the fate of mankind.

"Often, very often, has the widower exclaimed, 'O Death, how cruel, how relentless thou art to take away my beloved friend in the spring of her youth, in the pride of her strength, and in the bloom of her beauty! If thou wilt permit her once more to return to my abode, my gratitude shall never cease; I will raise up my voice continually to thank the Master of Life for so excellent a boon. I will devote my time to study how I can best promote her happiness while she is permitted to remain; and our lives shall roll away like a pleasant stream through a flowing valley!' Thus also has the father prayed for his son, the mother for her daughter, the wife for her husband, the sister for her brother, the lover for his mistress, the friend for his bosom companion, until the sounds of mourning and the cries of the living have pierced the very recesses of the dead.

"The Great Spirit has at length consented to make a trial of the sincerity of these prayers by sending us upon the earth. He has done this to see how we should be received—coming as strangers, no one knowing from where. Three moons were allotted to us to make the trial, and if, during that time, no impatience had been evinced, no angry passions excited at the place where we took up our abode, all those in the land of spirits, whom their relatives had desired to return, would have been restored. More than two moons have already passed, and as soon as the leaves began to bud our mission would have been successfully terminated. It is now too late. Our trial is finished, and we are called to the pleasant fields whence we came.

"Brother, it is proper that one man should die to make room for another. Otherwise, the world would be filled to overflowing. It is just that the goods gathered by one should be left to be divided among others; for in the land of spirits there is no want, there is neither sorrow nor hunger, pain nor death. Pleasant fields, filled with game spread before the eye, with birds of beautiful form. Every stream has good fish in it, and every hill is crowned with groves of fruit-trees, sweet and pleasant to the taste. It is not here, brother, but there that men begin truly to live. It is not for those who rejoice in those pleasant groves but for you that are left behind that we weep.

"Brother, take our thanks for your hospitable treatment. Regret not our departure. Fear not evil. Thy luck shall still be good in the chase, and there shall ever be a bright sky over thy lodge. Mourn not for us, for no corn will spring up from tears."

The spirits ceased, but the hunter had no power over his voice to reply. As they had proceeded in their address he saw a light gradually beaming from their faces, and a blue vapour filled the lodge with an unnatural light. As soon as they ceased, darkness gradually closed around. The hunter listened, but the sobs of the spirits had ceased. He heard the door of his tent open and shut, but he never saw more of his mysterious visitors.

The success promised him was his. He became a celebrated

hunter, and never wanted for anything necessary to his ease. He became the father of many boys, all of whom grew up to manhood, and health, peace, and long life were the rewards of his hospitality.

LARRY SIEGEL

Another Chance
for Casey

*Who says sports and the supernatural don't mix? Willa Cather's occult
football game appeared earlier in this section, while baseball has had more
than its share of fantasies, e.g., Douglas Wallop's deal-with-the-devil novel,*
The Year the Yankees Lost the Pennant, *better known in its musical
incarnation,* Damn Yankees, *and Bernard Malamud's borderline fantasy,* The Natural, *basis of a 1984 Robert Redford film. Ernest L.
Thayer's famous baseball poem, "Casey at the Bat," was the inspiration for*
LARRY SIEGEL'S *wonderfully funny and heartwarming sequel, "Another
Chance for Casey," which was published in 1950 by the* American Legion Magazine. *Thayer's Mudville is a mythical town, but Siegel's revenant batter is mistaken for a new player expected to arrive from Evansville,
and since there are real Evansvilles in Illinois, Indiana, Minnesota and
Wisconsin, it's reasonable to assume that Casey's infamous strikeout happened somewhere in the Midwest.*

Casey walked slowly across the cloud and went up to the big
golden gate. He took his bat off his shoulder, and for the
12,123rd time he rapped loudly with his fist. Nobody answered
and he stepped back. He looked up at the hand-lettered sign over
the gate and read for the 12,123rd time—

WITHIN THESE SACRED PORTALS DWELL THE SPIRITS OF THE SHINING
LIGHTS OF BASEBALL. NO TRESPASSING!

SIGNED, A. DOUBLEDAY, C.O.

Casey knocked on the gate again. Suddenly he heard someone approaching from inside. A few seconds later the door was thrown open, and a chunky figure poked his head out. "Well, well, if it ain't old Casey again," the figure said. "What do you want this time—as if I didn't know?"

"Mr. McGraw," said Casey, "I want in."

"Oh you do, do you?" said McGraw, cocking his head and grinning sarcastically. "Look, Casey, I been telling you for the past twenty years and the guy before me at the gate told you for another twenty years that we don't want failures in here. Do you see what that sign up there says? 'Shining light.' You ain't a shining light. What right has a flop to come in here and play ball with guys like Matty, the Babe, and the Big Train?"

"I ain't a flop," said Casey.

"Oh, you ain't?" McGraw came back. "What do you call that day in Mudville when you whiffed—V-Day? *And somewhere men are laughing, and somewhere children shout, but there is no joy in . . .*"

"Can it, Mr. McGraw," said Casey sensitively. "That damn poem is driving me nuts. Look, I been upstairs for around forty years now. I like it pretty much. But if I can't get inside *this* gate, I might as well be stationed downstairs in the other place."

"Look, Casey," said McGraw, "when anybody mentions your name, what do they think of? A big bust, right? Now how would it look to anyone if I brought a big bust inside these gates?"

"Mr. McGraw," said Casey, "didn't any of the guys inside ever flop once?"

"I suppose so," said McGraw, "but nobody made a fuss about it."

"That's what I'm driving at," said Casey. "Nobody looks at my overall record. All they think about is that single lousy day in Mudville. In case you didn't know it, I was a shining light up till then, but I never got another chance after that strikeout. I think it's time I got another chance—right now."

"What do you mean, 'right now'?" asked McGraw.

"Well," said Casey, "today I spoke to some guy who just arrived up here from the U.S.A. He told me about some moving pictures he's been seeing—whatever *they* are—and in them there are stories about guys from up here who get a chance to go downstairs to earth to take care of unfinished business. Now, I got unfinished business in Mudville. If you could fix me up with a little pass, maybe I . . ."

"Don't be nuts, Casey," said McGraw. "It's too much trouble to get those passes. And even if I could get one, why should I give it to *you?*"

"Because you guys owe it to me," said Casey. "Every man who gets a rough deal should get another break."

"Supposing," said McGraw, "that I got you a pass and you flopped again, would you swear that you'd never bother me again?"

"I swear," said Casey.

"On this?" asked McGraw, holding out a faded copy of *The Sporting News.*

"On this," said Casey solemnly, as he dropped his bat, removed his cap, and placed his left hand on *The Sporting News* and his right hand in the air.

"Wait here," said McGraw, "I'll be right back."

Casey whistled softly as he paced the cloud. He tugged at the large square peak on his woolen cap. He fidgeted with his black stockings. He kicked star dust out of his spikes, and he swung his big bat back and forth.

An hour later McGraw opened the gate again. "Casey," he said, "you'll never know what I went through for you. They don't give these passes to just anybody, you know; and I had to speak to everybody all the way up before I got any place. Even then I didn't do too well. The best I could get was a one-hour pass with an extra six minutes for traveling."

"If there's a game on at Mudville, that's all the time I need," said Casey.

"Yeah, there's one going on now," said McGraw. "One of the spotters inside gave me the dope. Right now it's three minutes to three, Mudville time. You gotta be back here three minutes after four, their time, and I wouldn't be A.W.O.L. if I was you. The elevator operator will give you an hour and six minutes worth of mortal fluid. Don't try to connive for more 'cause the officers up here are strict about those things. Oh yeah, before I forget, don't be coming back with wild stories because somebody'll be watching every move you make."

With that, McGraw gave Casey the pass and closed the gate.

Casey went to the elevator on East Astral Street, took his proper amount of fluid, and in a short while he was zooming through space with unbelievable speed.

A minute later the elevator stopped, and Casey got out. He found himself in a dark corridor. He looked around and up ahead he saw a light. He followed the light, came to a few steps, went up the steps, and discovered that he was standing in a dugout. About a dozen men were sitting around on a long bench peering intently at the field in front of them. They didn't see him. What strange outfits these guys wear, Casey thought. They had the word "Mudville" written across their shirt fronts, just as he did, but everything else was different.

Casey turned and looked out on the field. An electric shock shot through him. Old familiar memories stirred within him. The sight of uniformed men battling on a diamond. The sound of horsehide hitting against wood. The chatter in the stands. The scent of earth and sweat. All these things made him feel as if he were back home after an eternity in prison.

Casey saw a squat, elderly man sitting nearby, and he sat down next to him. "What's the score?" asked Casey.

"One all, top of the 7th," the man said, without looking at Casey.

"Who you playing?" Casey asked.

"Fallsburgh," the man said.

"Old Casey could break the tie," Casey said nonchalantly, as he leaned back and propped his feet up against the wall.

The man stiffened like a cut of frozen meat. His mouth opened and closed five times, but he didn't speak. Then he turned and looked at Casey for the first time. "Holy mackerel!" he said. "Who are you? Where'd you get that circus suit? And what's the idea of cursing in this dugout?"

Casey locked his hands behind his head and pushed his cap over his eyes lazily. "All I said is that old Casey could break the tie."

The man jumped to his feet. "Look, Mac," he said, "I'm Pete Morgan. I been managing this outfit for ten years. This town ain't hard to get along with, but what you just said is like swearing in church around here. Do you know that we refused to play the New York Yankees an exhibition game here last year because their manager's first name is the name you just said? Do you know we don't allow people from Kansas City in here? Do you know what the initials of Kansas City are? Don't say it! Do you know . . . say, who the hell are you, anyway?"

"Well," said Casey, unaffected by the speech, "I just got in from . . ."

"Evansville!" Morgan broke in. "That's it! You're the new guy Sanders was supposed to send me from Evansville. But you ain't a young kid, and we didn't expect you till Wednesday. Let's see, Sanders told me your name, but I forgot it."

Casey started to say something, but all of a sudden Morgan let out a moan. The Mudville pitcher just threw a home run ball. "Damn!" said Morgan. "Can't that guy go one game without a gopher ball? Look, Mac, why don't you go inside and have Charley fix you up with a good uniform. I don't know where you got the thing you're wearing, but those outfits went out with the Stanley Steamer."

"I don't have any time to change," said Casey.

"Oh, I see," said Morgan, regarding Casey strangely.

Mudville finally got Fallsburgh out and came into the dugout for the last half of the 7th. When the players saw the oddly-dressed figure who was relaxing on the bench, they turned to Morgan for an explanation. "Fellahs," said Morgan, "this here is a prima donna that Sanders sent us from Evansville. He picked up that suit he's wearing from a junk dealer in town. Now don't go annoying him or telling him to change into another uniform. You see, he doesn't have too much time." With that, Morgan winked at the men.

Casey lifted his cap from his face and said, "Hi, men." Then he got up, stretched, and said to Morgan, "When do I bat?"

"Well," said Morgan, "it's still early in the game. You can lean back and take it easy for a while. When the bases are loaded in the 9th with two out, I'll call for you."

"Thanks," said Casey. "I'd rather go in at a crucial spot. It'll look better upstairs."

"Oh, it sure will look better upstairs," said Morgan, glancing at the men and making a rotating motion around his ear.

Mudville went down in the 7th, and nothing happened in both

halves of the 8th. It was 2–1, in favor of Fallsburgh, as the top of the 9th began.

"What time is it?" asked Casey.

"Twenty to four," said Morgan.

"I still got time," said Casey, loosening his shoulder muscles.

The first two Fallsburgh men singled. Morgan sprang to his feet and, leaning out of the dugout, he waved to the bull-pen.

"What are you doing?" Casey asked, chewing on a piece of grass.

"My wife just came in the park, and I want her to know where I'm sitting," said Morgan. "What the hell do you *think* I'm doing? I'm telling the relief pitchers to warm up. Tulley's about ready for the showers."

"What are relief pitchers?" asked Casey.

Morgan looked at him wearily. "Relief pitchers," he said, "relieve other pitchers."

"Oh, you got more than one pitcher?" Casey asked.

"Heavens, yes," said Morgan sarcastically. "We got all kinds of pitchers. Great big ones. Little skinny ones. And then we got . . ."

"Seems like a waste of money," said Casey, interrupting him. "We never had more than two. Sometimes only one."

"Now ain't that nice," said Morgan. "Strong-armed pitchers, just like in the old days. And how were their spitters working?"

"Well," said Casey, "McGowan only used his in spots, but Thompson threw his a couple of times an inning."

"Oh, my Lord!" said Morgan. "How long is this insane talk gonna go on?"

Tulley managed to put out the fire, and it was still 2–1, Fallsburgh, as Mudville came in for the last of the 9th. "Let's go, damn it!" said Morgan to the men as they came into the dugout. "Let's get back into this ball game."

The first two men made out. Then the next man singled, and the following man walked. It was now Tulley's turn to bat.

Casey got up off the bench, picked up his bat, and said to Morgan, "I think there's a chance that the bases won't be loaded this inning. I think maybe I better get up there now. It's getting kind of late, you know."

With that, he stretched and started climbing out of the dugout.

"Now where do you think *you're* going?" asked Morgan, seizing Casey by the leg.

"I told you it's getting kind of late," said Casey. "Besides, I think they want action upstairs."

He broke loose from Morgan and ambled toward the plate. "The fool's actually gonna do it!" a player shouted at Morgan. "Do something!"

"The guy's nuts," said Morgan. "He's absolutely and completely goofy."

"Should I go out and drag him back?" another player asked Morgan.

"No," said Morgan, "let him bat. The guy's got more guts than brains. He'd be just crazy enough to . . ."

Casey was almost up to the plate. A curious buzz swept through the stands. Fans were leaning forward to get a better look at this quaint, picturesque figure who moved with a confident stride. Was it a gag? Who was he?

Suddenly in the stands old Doc Walker, number one baseball fan in Mudville—and still active for his 80 years, leaped to his feet. "If I wasn't sure," he said, "if I wasn't absolutely and positively sure that . . . that . . ."

"What is it, Doc?" somebody asked.

"No," said Doc. "Forget it. I felt like I was goin' loco for a minute."

Casey was now rubbing dirt on his hands. The umpire, a gigantic figure, went over to him, and bending down to dust off the plate, he asked, "You pinch-hitting?"

"That's right," said Casey. "It's getting late, and I figure this is a good enough spot."

The umpire walked to the screen and picked up his megaphone. He came back and asked, "What's your name, bud?"

"Casey. Why?" Casey said, taking a firm stance.

"Now batting for Mudville," the umpire bellowed, "CASEY! . . . Casey?" he said, dropping his megaphone and double-taking. "Casey? Well, I'll be—"

For a fleeting moment there was silence in the Mudville ball park. . . .

Then from that stricken multitude went up a maddened yell, like the sound of tortured devils a-screaming down in hell! The teeming stands were raging; there was chaos everywhere. How dare the name of Casey contaminate this air!

Pete Morgan in the dugout and all the Mudville herd were petrified like statues; they didn't say a word. Their necks were strained like stallions that are ready at the post. Their eyes bulged from their sockets as if they'd seen a ghost.

And now the roaring hundreds came moving from the stands, like groups of stalking panthers, but with weapons in their hands. Their prey was at the plate; on his shoulder was a bat. His crime? His name was Casey. What bigger crime than that?

But then the masses halted on their trip out to the plate. The umpire stood and faced them—a massive wall of weight. Six feet six inches tall he stood, and weighed three hundred pounds. And he made it clear he wanted no strangers on his grounds.

With a loud and booming voice he addressed the seething throng. And every word he uttered rang clearly like a gong. "Whoever lays a hand upon this batter's head, will have to deal with me. Now let's play ball," he said.

Casey heaved a little sigh as he stepped into his place. A funny little smile started playing on his face. Four thousand angry eyes watched him blow into his hands. Two thousand hostile tongues hissed venom from the stands. And when responding to their jeers he lightly tipped his hat, no stranger in the crowd could doubt 'twas Casey at the bat!

And now the rival pitcher got his sign and slowly rocked. And Casey's figure tensed, and his bat was set and cocked. And then the ball came winging—a whizzing blur of white. A whirling blob of fire, a lightning flash in flight. Close by the form of Casey the blazing horsehide sped. "Too high for me," said Casey. "That's a strike," the umpire said.

"Kill him! Kill the batter!" screamed an overheated fan. "Let's put an end forever to this flubbing, whiffing clan!" Calmly, Casey called for time and rubbed his bat with dirt. And then he smiled again as he fiddled with his shirt. "It was much too high," said Casey. "Two feet above my head." "It was right across your shoulders," the mammoth umpire said.

The Mudville stands were boiling like a pot upon a stove. They cursed the name of Casey and the fiendish spell it wove. But Casey took a toehold and signaled to the mound. And then the

pitch came flying with a chilling, whistling sound. "Kind of low,"
said Casey. "Right around my shoe." "Your eyes are telling stories," the umpire said. "Strike two!"

"Fake!" roared the irate hundreds, and the echo answered,
"Fake! Let's throw him in the river or burn him at the stake!"

Then Casey dropped his smile, and his lips were firm and tight.
He had to do it now or spend eternity in night. He hitched his
weary shoulders and dug his feet in earth. The next pitch would
determine just what his name was worth.

And then the pitcher had his sign, and then began his rock.
And somewhere in the distance it was tolling four o'clock. And
now the ball came shooting from its gun upon the mound. It was
heading far outside, just a foot above the ground. The batter took
a lunge as he quickly arched his back. And then there was a gust
of wind and then there was a crack! Away up in the stratosphere a
leather horsehide flew. It danced up in the sunlight and it disappeared from view.

SOMEWHERE IN THIS FAVORED LAND THE CLOUDS BEGIN TO FORM.
SOMEWHERE WINDS ARE HOWLING AND SOMEWHERE THERE'S A
STORM. BUT THERE'S A DIAMOND FAR ABOVE, JUST WITHIN A GOLDEN
GATE—WHERE THE SHINING LIGHTS OF BASEBALL TAKE THEIR TURNS
UP AT THE PLATE. AND STANDING UP THERE NOW, BRUSHING STAR
DUST FROM HIS SUIT, IS A HAPPY, SMILING FIGURE—CASEY, THE NEW
RECRUIT!

APPENDIX

The Midnight Tourist's Guide to Haunted America

Ghosts usually tend to be shyer than the paradoxically lively set whose nocturnal exploits are chronicled in *Haunted America*. This probably suits most readers just fine, but those (fool-?) hardy exceptions who relish the notion of standing face-to-sheet with a genuine spook may find the following supplement useful in tracking down phantoms.

This appendix is an extension of "A Baedeker of Favorite U.S. Haunts," a roster of some fifty allegedly haunted locales in nineteen states that appeared in *Ghosts: A Treasury of Chilling Tales Old and New* (Doubleday, 1981). While the original list has been retained, many new places situated throughout all fifty American states have been added. In a handful of instances where no specific paranormal activity could be found for a given area, one or more popular tourist spots that have promisingly eerie and/or grisly local histories have been recommended.

Sources consulted in preparation of this expanded "Baedeker" include nearly sixty books (half a dozen of them by the eminently readable Hans Holzer), many newspaper and magazine articles, tourism manuals, promotional pamphlets, a brochure from the U.S. Department of Commerce, the *Rand McNally Road Atlas*, a student term paper and a few letters from "pen pals."

Caveat lector! The reliability and probability of these supposed hauntings vary widely. It would be burdensome to preface each item with "alleged," but it should be understood that some are pure folklore. Others may be hard to find because local names change. It also should be remembered that towns and houses sometimes burn down or succumb to the wrecker's ball—although that does not always spell *finis* to a good ghost story. Still, if one intends to visit a problematical area, a letter or phone call to the local chamber of commerce and/or library might save time, expense and disappointment. Another caveat: some sites are on private property and may only be viewable from an automobile window *en passant*.

An asterisk (*) designates a public place or tourist attraction open to the public. (It is advisable to check visiting hours to make sure the place is not closed for the season or for repairs.) Some undesignated sites also may be open to the public.

ALABAMA

FLORENCE   Smithsonia, an abandoned four-story house overlooking the Tennessee River, was supposedly haunted by an angry woman. Smithsonia burned down in 1969.

HUNTSVILLE   In *Some of My Best Friends Are Ghosts,* Hans Holzer reports a *new* house in this city that produced strange noises and an atmosphere of unwelcomeness for one young couple. A ghost showed up on a photo taken in the house.

MONTGOMERY   An empty residence on South Court Street was troubled by mysterious ringing bells and spectral visages appearing on photographs. The house has been torn down and a motel put up in its place.

PRATTVILLE   Gurney Manufacturing Co., a venerable textile firm near an Alabama River damsite, is, according to Richard Winer's book *Houses of Horror,* haunted by a floating woman in black and also a dye mixer named Moe.

ALASKA

*SKAGWAY   Town museums recall the violent days of the Klondike Gold Rush. The spot may be visited where "honest Frank Reid" dueled to the death with desperado Soapy Smith. Both are buried in the Gold Rush Cemetery.

ARIZONA

*OATMAN   The Oatman Hotel in this small ex-mining town near the Colorado River has been cited by tabloids as being haunted by Clark Gable and Carole Lombard. Arthur Myers' *Ghosts of the Rich and Famous* effectively explodes that notion, but still reports considerable poltergeist activity and an isolated sighting of a spectral chambermaid at the hotel.

ARKANSAS

HOLLY GROVE   According to Hans Holzer, a piano-playing Indian woman haunts Mulls House, a private home situated off a highway (probably U.S. 49) halfway between Holly Grove and the eastern border town of Helena.

CALIFORNIA

HOLLYWOOD   The ghost of Harry Cohn, the controversial head of Columbia Pictures, is said to haunt his old office suite, which, according to Peter Underwood's *The Ghost Hunter's Guide,* is now occupied by other firms.

KING CITY   While on an archaeological dig several years ago, Richard Senate saw a ghostly monk in the San Antonio de Padua Mission near here. Senate got so interested in ghosts, he began studying them in earnest, and has subsequently taught a course in the History of Ghosts and Ghost Hunting at Ventura Community College.

MILLBRAE   A poltergeist in a new house situated on a hill of this small town near San Francisco was investigated by Hans Holzer, who tells the story in his book *Ghosts of the Golden West.*

*SAN DIEGO   The Whaley House (Old Town, 2482 San Diego Avenue, San Diego 92110) was built in 1865 by Judge Thomas Whaley. San Diego's first brick mansion and the seat of local government through the 1870s, Whaley House is said to be haunted by the ghost of a hanged man.

*SAN JOSE   The Winchester Mystery House (525 South Winchester Boulevard, San Jose 95128) is one of the strangest mansions ever built. It has more than 160 rooms, secret chambers, stairs that lead nowhere, rooms within rooms, a ballroom inscribed with mysterious mottoes and many other bizarre features. Stories conflict on why Sarah Winchester kept workmen busy day and night for decades building and rebuilding her house; the most popular legend has it that she feared those killed by the Winchester firearms manufactured by her late husband's firm would haunt her unless she gave the gentler ghosts a home; the confusing network of chambers and passages supposedly was meant to prevent the angrier spirits from following her about the house. Before an earthquake in 1906 leveled part of the upper stories, the mansion numbered some 700 rooms!

*SONOMA VALLEY   Writer Jack London employed more than a score of workmen to construct Wolf House, a gargantuan castle that fire destroyed before it was completed. The extant ruins in Jack London State Park are claimed to be vigorously haunted.

COLORADO

*GRAND LAKE   This village adjacent to Arapaho National Park is near Grand Lake, which the Ute Indians avoid because a raftful of their squaws and children once were lost in its glacial depths. The tribe believes that the fog drifting over the water is really the ghosts of the drowned.

CONNECTICUT

*NEW LONDON   Monte Cristo Cottage (325 Pequot Avenue, New London) was the childhood home of the Nobel Prize-winning playwright Eugene O'Neill. Sudden temperature changes and inexplicable noises have been attributed to O'Neill's mother's ghost.

*STONY CREEK   According to a hearsay report in the September 1, 1885, issue of the New York *Sun*, a decaying summer hotel on Frisbie Island was often seen with strange lights in its windows late at night. Frisbie is one of the Thimble Islands in Long Island Sound just south of Stony Creek.

STRATFORD   The same newspaper article cited in the preceding item also reported rappings, footsteps, moans and groans in the home of one Elihu Osborn, whose house was the scene a dozen years earlier of a murder and suicide.

DELAWARE

*DOVER   Woodburn, the state governor's mansion, is viewable on a limited basis. Its ghost (reminiscent of one of the spooks in the film *Ghostbusters*) supposedly empties wine decanters in the dining room.

DISTRICT OF COLUMBIA

*THE CAPITOL   According to an article in the October 2, 1898, edition of the Philadelphia *Press,* at least fifteen spectres walk the marble halls, including Woodrow Wilson in the Senate wing and John Quincy Adams in the House wing. Mysterious footsteps have been reported in Statuary Hall. But the most horrific phantom is a Demon Cat that swells from normal feline size to the dimensions of an elephant! Reportedly seen by security officers in 1862 and 1898, it disappeared when one of the watchmen shot at it.

*DECATUR HOUSE   The early American naval hero Stephen Decatur died in a duel but may still frequent his old Washington home across Lafayette Park from the White House.

EIGHTEENTH STREET & NEW YORK AVENUE   When the British torched the White House, President James Madison and his wife Dolly resided for a time in an old mansion at this address. An invisible presence that trips people on its stairs was reported in the 1898 Philadelphia *Press* article cited above.

GEORGETOWN   In *Ghosts I've Met,* Hans Holzer reports paranormal activities at 3400 Prospect Street. Built in 1783 by Benjamin Stoddert, the first U.S. Secretary of the Navy, Halcyon House once was owned by Harvard University and later was bought by Georgetown University for use as a dormitory.

*THE OCTAGON   Built in the 1700s, Octagon House at 1799 New York Avenue, N.W., is a frequently discussed Washington treasure trove of occult phenomena.

*NATIONAL BUILDING MUSEUM   According to Arthur Myers in

Ghosts of the Rich and Famous, faces have appeared in the huge Corinthian columns of this old Washington building and as recently as 1972 a guard saw an eyeless man who "smelled of the stench of the dead."

*POTOMAC RIVER   According to an article by Maureen Dowd in the *New York Times,* there are in Washington "regular sightings of Chessie, the Potomac's answer to the Loch Ness monster."

*THE WHITE HOUSE   One of the responsibilities of our Chief Executive is to put up with the ghostly inhabitants of the presidential residence at 1600 Pennsylvania Avenue—among them, according to tradition, the spirits of Abraham Lincoln and James Garfield.

FLORIDA

MIAMI   The Halloween 1982 issue of the Miami *Herald* labeled the Villa Paula at 5811 North Miami Avenue the city's most haunted house. Built in 1925, the villa was once Miami's first Cuban embassy. The newspaper reported poltergeist activity, a female ghost and a sinister iron gate where several cats were found strangled to death.

TALLAHASSEE   In *More Haunted Houses,* Richard Winer discusses nocturnal screams and "presences" in the records division of the state's Department of Corrections, housed in what was once the local jail.

GEORGIA

PLAINS   A home lived in by President Jimmy Carter and his wife, Rosalynn, from 1956 to 1960 reportedly has a room Mrs. Carter was afraid to enter alone. The house, dating back to 1850, has the local reputation of being haunted by a woman in a long white dress.

SAVANNAH   Author Hans Holzer seldom reveals addresses. A rare exception is the haunted house at 507 East St. Julian Street.

HAWAII

*Maui   Kula o Ka Maomao, the isthmus joining the eastern and western portions of "the valley isle," is, according to local tradition, "the plain of spirits and mirages."

*Molokai   Many battles were once fought on this central Hawaiian island. One such site at Maunaloa is reputedly haunted by spirits of the dead warriors.

Kauai   Not far from Captain Cook's landing place on this northern island is the village of Waimea, whose firehouse is reportedly haunted by a seven-foot-tall headless ghost.

IDAHO

*Idaho City   This once-bustling gold rush city is now a tiny village with a violent past. Boot Hill Cemetery is mainly filled with the victims of gun battles.

ILLINOIS

Belleville   A suicide's ghost was seen in a two-story brick house near the intersection of Seventeenth and Main streets.

*Hardin   According to the September 18, 1888, St. Louis *Globe-Democrat*, a callow group of investigators went to Diamond Island about two miles from here and had their boat commandeered by the fiery spectre of a murdered man. Residents on the far shore heard screams and rescued the foolhardy youths.

*Woodstock   According to legend, Elvira was an actress who leaped from the Woodstock Opera House bell tower. Her ghost often sits—where else?—in seat No. 113. It is risky for actresses to visit the tower. Elvira urges them to jump.

INDIANA

*Benton   A story in the September 13, 1896, Philadelphia *Press* recounts the harrowing tale of a farmer named James A. French and his wife who, while riding by a country church cemetery near Benton one night, saw a gigantic club-carrying ghost beckoning to them in the roadway. The horses shied; the ghost began to approach the wagon. At last the terrified farmer turned the horses around and dashed back the way they came. The apparition was identified as a man murdered ten years earlier.

INDIANAPOLIS   Hannah House on Madison Avenue, once part of the Underground Railroad, is the focus of ghostly activity, including phantom fleeing slaves.

IOWA

*WATSON   This town is not far from the promisingly named Spook Cave and Effigy Mounds National Monument, where prehistoric Indian burial mounds carved in the shape of animals and birds may be found on cliffs near the Mississippi River.

KANSAS

*COFFEYVILLE   A Western street shootout with the Dalton Boys left eight dead. The Dalton Museum retells the bloody story.

*SALINA   Nearly one hundred and fifty Indian skeletons were dug from a pre-Columbian burial pit four miles east of town.

KENTUCKY

FRANKFORT   The ghost of a frightened woman runs through the gardens of Liberty Hall, a historic Georgian mansion here.

*OWENSBORO   *Fate* magazine claims a ghostly woman changes into an equally ethereal dog at Wilson's Ferry on the Ohio River.

LOUISIANA

*FRANKLIN   Oaklawn Manor, a white-pillared mansion with marble floors and fine imported antiques, was often visited by statesman Henry Clay. It still is.

*NEW ORLEANS   The heart of Dixieland jazz is also a hub of

superstition. The ghost of a tortured slave haunts LaLaurie House, now an apartment building. The following are open to the public: Beauregard House (also called LeCarpentier House), 1113 Chartres Street, is haunted by Civil War General P. G. T. Beauregard; Pharmacie Française, 514 Chartres Street, displays voodoo artifacts, as does the Voodoo Museum at 739 Bourbon Street; St. Louis Cemetery No. 1, 334 Royal Street, has aboveground tombs because of the soil's dampness. Alleged voodoo queen Marie Levaux's grave is still visited by residents for "spiritual guidance."

*NEW ROADS   A beautiful young woman is thought to haunt Parlange Plantation, an early Louisiana estate on Route 1.

*ST. FRANCISVILLE   The Cottage Plantation on Route 5, the remnant of a picturesque Southern mansion, was a showcase often visited by American politicians and the Marquis de Lafayette. It is uncertain which of them still lingers. Not far away is Louisiana's oldest, biggest plantation, The Myrtles, where sleepers have complained that a ghostly French governess wakes them by staring into their faces.

*ST. MAURICE   St. Maurice Plantation is a huge estate troubled by poltergeists and the ghost of a child.

*VACHERIE   Ruined Valcour Aime Plantation, once the "Versailles of Louisiana," is haunted by a nameless spirit.

MAINE

DAMARISCOTTA   Mary Howe was a medium who in 1882 (according to one faction) entered a state of suspended animation for more than a month. But the sheriff sided with the physician who claimed she was dead because he could find no heartbeat. Though her body was still warm and showed no signs of deterioration, authorities buried her, not without stiff (sorry) local opposition. Some Damariscotta citizens think Mary haunts her still-standing house.

*WISCASSET   The Marine Antique Shop used to be a restaurant where employees claimed chairs and tables moved unnaturally. Nearby, the Musical Wonder House is a museum with hundreds of mechanical music machines and its share of ghosts.

MARYLAND

*BALTIMORE   USF *Constellation,* America's oldest naval vessel still under commission, is tied up to Pier 1, Constellation Dock, at Baltimore's Inner Harbor. A brochure issued by the U.S. Department of Commerce claims the ghost of a sailor tried for cowardice haunts the ship, but according to Will Eisner (appropriately, the cartoonist who draws The Spirit) in his *Spirit Casebook of True Haunted Houses and Ghosts,* Seaman Neil Harvey fell asleep during his watch and was executed by Captain Thomas Truxton. Tourists have spotted the ghosts of both Harvey and Truxton below decks. Another tourist attraction about ten miles north of town is haunted Hampton Mansion, a historic site operated by the National Park Service. Local legend also refers to the spectral Peg Alley who, according to the May 1866 *Baltimore American,* was murdered by her spouse on a two-mile-long wooded peninsula near the Miles River. Her ghost was seen by rail workers. The place was once known as Peg Alley's Point.

MASSACHUSETTS

*BOSTON   The ferocious phantom of a "lady in black" roams the ramparts of Fort Warren on Georges Island outside of Boston Harbor. She was executed as a spy after her unsuccessful attempt to rescue her imprisoned husband. On numerous occasions, her angry ghost has reportedly tried to strangle soldiers stationed at the fort.

CAMBRIDGE   One of the classroom buildings at Lesley College on Avon Hill in North Cambridge is allegedly haunted.

*CAPE ANN   Not far from the village of Rockport is now-deserted Dogtown Common, where early settlers once lived, many of them allegedly in league with dark powers. The area is said to be haunted by witches and pirates.

CAPE COD   In the November 1934 *Harper's Monthly,* the pseudonymous Harlan Jacobs (actually a Columbia University professor) recounted a series of frightening happenings during a four-month "vacation" in a Cape Cod summer house.

CONCORD   Orchard House, where Louisa May Alcott wrote *Little Women*, is troubled by the spectre of Louisa's sister May.

MARBLEHEAD   An eighteenth-century fisherman's cottage here is said to be haunted by a formidable man and a gentle woman.

*SALEM   The Salem Witch Museum on Washington Square North recreates the horrors of the 1692 persecutions in what *Amtrak Express* magazine calls "a multi-sensory presentation." The Witch House on Essex House is the restored haunted home of witch trial judge Jonathan Corwin.

MICHIGAN

*COPPER HARBOR   Sail from here or from Houghton, Michigan, to Isle Royale National Park, one of North America's wildest spots. Moose and wolves roam the thick forests and old pathways lead to ancient copper pits, an old lighthouse and perhaps a ghost or two.

MINNESOTA

*MILLES LACS KATHIO STATE PARK   Research failed to turn up a single Minnesota ghost, but Milles Lacs, site of an ancient Dakota Indian village, promises fascinating native lore. One might also try Tower-Soudan State Park, an *underground* state park with the state's deepest iron mine. Riding an elevator half a mile into the earth sounds like pretty scary stuff.

MISSISSIPPI

FRIARS POINT   According to local oral tradition, a forty-acre farm known as "the Key place" three miles out of town was where a black preacher found buried treasure but was scared away from digging it up by ghosts. The apocryphal story is told in Richard M. Dorson's *American Negro Folktales*.

MISSOURI

*JACKSON   Reported in the October 6, 1887, St. Louis *Globe-Democrat:* salesmen traveling an old turnpike road four miles out of Cape Girardeau, going toward Jackson, saw a white, diaphanous object rise into the air where the highway rounds a high bluff. The place was named Spooks Hollow.

ST. LOUIS　　Lemp Mansion was the home of a rich brewer named William Lemp who killed himself in the house. His two sons also committed suicide there. The dead men are still there.

WEBSTER GROVES　　Wispy entities flit through a two-story home on the 300 block of Plant Avenue.

MONTANA

*AGENCY　　Custer Battlefield National Monument marks Custer's Last Stand. The site of the Sioux massacre on the banks of the Little Bighorn River is supposedly haunted.

NEBRASKA

*TRENTON　　The aptly named Massacre Canyon here is the site of a bloody Indian battle in which Sioux slaughtered hundreds of the Pawnee tribe, which fled to Oklahoma. Another grisly Nebraska site, Fort Robinson, now in a state park, was the place where Chief Crazy Horse came for peace talks a year after he defeated General Custer. Angry soldiers stabbed the defenseless Indian to death.

NEVADA

VIRGINIA CITY　　The rich vein of silver and gold known as the Comstock Lode created several boom towns, including this one. In 1874, the townspeople saw flame erupting from an abandoned mine shaft; when they investigated they saw no fire but an eerie light at the bottom of the shaft, and they heard a miner's pick and strange laughter. One brave young man descended but returned swiftly, pursued by the ghost of Henry Comstock, the prospector for whom the lode was named.

NEW HAMPSHIRE

HENNIKER   Mary Wilson was born aboard a ship attacked by buccaneers, but the pirate chief spared the lives of all on board in exchange for the baby being named after his mother. In after years, Mary settled on a farm on a hill overlooking Contocook River near Henniker and took care of the pirate after he retired from the sea. He was murdered in the vicinity and buried at the house. Mary later died, but continues to materialize at her home, which is now known as Ocean-Born Mary House, also haunted by the old brigand.

NEW JERSEY

CAMDEN   522 North Fifth Street is allegedly haunted by a child and a woman who suffered a fatal fall on the steps of this railroad-flat home.

*MANAHAWKIN   There was once a haunted hotel somewhere on the sand dunes of Long Beach near this small town ten miles north of Atlantic City, that has since burned down.

*THE PINE BARRENS   This vast, desolate stretch of forest is haunted by a dragonlike monster known as the Leeds Devil.

TRENTON   Mercer County Community College reputedly has a haunted room in a fraternity house on a Trenton side street. Mediums claim a brother and a sister murdered each other there.

NEW MEXICO

FORT UNION   During pioneer days, a young woman at this military post told her fiancé, a lieutenant, that if he was killed on an upcoming expedition against the Apaches, she would never wed another. But after he was long missing, she changed her mind. On her wedding night, the hatchet-scarred ghost of the lieutenant showed up to claim his faithless lover. She died in his arms after they danced a macabre waltz together.

NEW YORK

ALBANY　A ghost walks the terrace at Cherry Hill, South Pearl Street, a mansion that may have been the scene of a murder.

GLENS FALLS　American and European folklore sometimes claims that the dead hold services at midnight in empty churches. This town's St. Mary's Church may be one such place; mysterious lights and choirs have been observed and heard.

MONTAUK　One of Bernhardt J. Hurwood's books describes a vampire cat that haunts a tourist house at this resort.

*NEW YORK CITY　Where so many millions live, there are bound to be plenty of haunts, and there certainly are. Here are an unlucky thirteen places where spectres supposedly abide: (1) The Belasco Theatre at 111 West Forty-fourth Street is haunted by producer David Belasco, who sometimes drops in at the business office but usually clanks around the deserted ten-room apartment he used to live in at the top of the building. (2) According to an October 28, 1983, article in the New York *Post*, the ghosts of millionaire sisters Janet and Rosetta Van der Voort, who during the 1880s lived in a mansion on Fourteenth Street, still ice skate sometimes at the Wollman rink near the southern end of Central Park. (3) Out on Staten Island, the "Conference House" is where a colonial delegation that included John Adams and Benjamin Franklin met in 1776 with the British commander Lord Howe. Miscellaneous poltergeist phenomena have occurred in it. (4) Back in Manhattan, the Cloisters in Fort Tryon Park houses a medieval museum and art gallery that consists of many antique European buildings reassembled stone by stone in an impressive wooded setting. It is rich in atmosphere, by turns peaceful and eerie. (5) Further downtown, the Dakota, a grand apartment building at Seventy-second Street and Central Park West, has had many shuddery legends whispered about it—hardly surprising, since Boris Karloff once lived in it. The Dakota is said to be the model for the setting of Ira Levin's *Rosemary's Baby*. (6) Eleven Bank Street, near the Greenwich Village studio where Uta Hagen teaches acting, has an amiable ghost. (7) The Jan Hus

Playhouse, 351 East Seventh-fourth Street, home of the excellent improvisational comedy company Chicago City Limits, is haunted by an unfriendly spirit. (This is one haunting I can personally vouch for. In 1973, I was public relations director for the performing troupe that used to play there. One night while working late after the performance, I was frightened away by the Jan Hus phantom. For details, see page 623 of *Ghosts: A Treasury of Chilling Tales Old and New.*) (8) The Morris-Jumel Mansion, Edgecombe Avenue at One Hundred Sixtieth Street, home of Colonel Roger Morris, served as General George Washington's headquarters during the Revolutionary War's Battle of Long Island and is now a museum. Visitors to the mansion have sometimes seen a spectral woman in blue, a colonial soldier and a third nondescript resident ghost. (9) A chapel built in 1660 by Peter Stuyvesant has been replaced by the venerable St. Mark's-in-the-Bouwerie Episcopal Church at Tenth Street and Second Avenue. Worshipers have occasionally seen the ghost of a praying woman and a few spectral gentlemen, one of whom, like Stuyvesant, walks with a cane. (10) Twelve Gay Street was the Greenwich Village townhouse of New York Mayor "Gentleman" Jimmy Walker. Ghosts have been encountered inside and even on the front steps. (11) 27 Jane Street, an historic Greenwich Village address that by now may have succumbed to progress, was the home of the doctor who treated Alexander Hamilton after his fatal duel with Aaron Burr. Hamilton actually died in his physician's house and supposedly remains there in spirit. (12) 278 West One Hundred Thirteenth Street, home of Harry Houdini, is rumored to be haunted by the world-famous magician. (13) During the Civil War, so the legend goes, Confederate General Samuel E. McGowan sneaked behind enemy lines to spend some time with his mistress, who lived at 226 Fifth Avenue. He found her in another lover's arms; a fight broke out and McGowan was killed. His body was hidden in the house, but McGowan's spectre walked its halls until 1953, when psychic investigator Hans Holzer claims he helped release the soldier's ghost.

RYE   Seven Oaks, a colonial Westchester County mansion, is the haunted residence of an actress friend of mine. I visited once and though I did not see, hear or feel any spectral presences, a bizarre event did take place. My hostess complained that one of the titular oaks was dying and she wished lightning would strike it and save her the cost of clearing it away. Within minutes, a thunderstorm sprang up and lightning struck and decimated that tree. Perhaps the house should be renamed Six Oaks?

WEST POINT   A pre-Civil War soldier was reportedly seen in 1972 by a cadet in his dormitory room (#4714) at the military academy. His commanding officer also "felt a presence" there.

*YOUNGSTOWN   Old Fort Niagara has a tourable castle haunted by a French soldier, Henri LeClerc, who was beheaded in a duel with one of his comrades.

NORTH CAROLINA

*OCRACOKE   A ghostly burning pirate ship supposedly appears "on the first night of the new moon" every September, according to Charles Harry Whedbee's delightful book, *The Flaming Ship of Ocracoke & Other Tales of the Outer Banks.*

NORTH DAKOTA

*FORT ABERCROMBIE   This 1857 stockade was built to help protect wagon trains and shipping. The Sioux Indians attacked it many times during that nation's 1862 uprising. Part of the fort has been restored and made into a museum.

OHIO

CLEVELAND   Franklin Castle is a large, gloomy, gaslit four-story manor with secret passages and sliding panels. At least two murders are thought to have happened here and at least one phantom woman in black has been seen.

DAYTON   A report in the March 25, 1884, Philadelphia *Press* claims that a great many townspersons went to Miamisburg Cemetery near Dayton to "catch" a female ghost who appeared every night at 9 P.M. Billy clubs, brouhaha, even pistol shots caused her to vanish—possibly out of indignation?

OKLAHOMA

*LAWTON   The Apache chief Geronimo was captured and imprisoned here till he died and was buried in the Apache Cemetery just north of Fort Sill, now part of the U.S. Army Artillery and Missile Center. Another place possibly haunted by Indians is Tahlequah, once capital of the Cherokee nation.

OREGON

HECETA HEAD   This remote part of the Pacific coastline has a lighthouse that was recently fully automated. Ever since the keepers left, the adjoining house has been plagued by poltergeist activity and the appearance of a woman in grey.

PENNSYLVANIA

ALTOONA   Anna Baker died in 1914, an embittered spinster. She still haunts her family's local home.

*DOYLESTOWN   This Bucks County municipality has several haunted houses. Aldie Manor has an old clock that still sometimes mysteriously moves. Fonthill (available for tours) is tended by a ghostly housekeeper. Tyler Hall, part of the community college complex, was named for Stella Tyler, who students say still wanders the halls.

DYERSTOWN   The Marquis de Lafayette visited the site that is now the Water Wheel Inn. He still supposedly shows up there once a year.

*HUNTINGTON   Lincoln Caverns on U.S. Route 22 three miles west of town hosts a ghost tour in what one brochure redundantly calls "Pennsylvania's most unique haunted house."

*LEVITTOWN   Pennsbury, on the Delaware River near here, was once the home of state founder William Penn. It has a haunted guest chamber.

MILLVALE   At least two sources report that a painter (variously named Maxo Vanka and Maxim Hvatka) commissioned to do religious frescoes in the chapel of the Millvale Croatian Catholic church was terrified by the literally chilling presence of a ghostly priest, who is thought to be a Father Ranzinger, spiritual leader of an earlier church that stood on the same site but burned down.

*NORTHUMBERLAND   The Joseph Priestley House at the juncture of the north and west branches of the Susquehanna River is the restored home and museum of the famous freethinker and scientist. "Joseph still potters about in his laboratory," a descendant once told a *Grit* reporter.

*PHILADELPHIA   Loudoun Mansion, 4650 Germantown Avenue, is the restored home of a nineteenth-century merchant and also an antique-filled museum. A little boy reputedly haunts it.

*POTTSTOWN   Local legend has it that a phantom hitchhiker thumbs rides and vanishes from back seats . . . but there is a ghostly hitchhiker myth in every state of the union, and sociologist Louis C. Jones points out in *Things That Go Bump in the Night* that the hitchhiker is a recurrent folk tale that may be traced back to Europe and the days of horse-drawn wagons.

RHODE ISLAND

*BLOCK ISLAND   Eleven miles off the coast of Rhode Island, Block Island is the site of a ghostly offshore light that has been explained by a variety of natural causes. But Austin N. Stevens' anthology, *Mysterious New England,* states that one local resident says she saw the cause of the glow: a ghostly ship that like the one at Ocracoke, North Carolina (q.v.), is all in flames.

*NEWPORT   The Breakers, an 1895 mansion once owned by Cornelius Vanderbilt, is a tourist attraction allegedly haunted by Mrs. Vanderbilt's shade. Another Newport house said to be haunted is at 25 Greenough Place.

SOUTH CAROLINA

*COLUMBIA   Two male ghosts were twice seen watching football games here at the University of South Carolina.

*PAWLEYS ISLAND   A man in a grey fishing cap and work clothes frequents the sand dunes of this little Atlantic seaboard community about twenty-five miles south of Myrtle Beach.

SOUTH DAKOTA

RAPID CITY   When my Texas friend and correspondent Iva Riddle belonged to the U.S. Air Force, she was taken on an inspection tour at Ellsworth Air Force Base near here. She wondered why one of the antenna buildings was staffed by four, since all the others only had one serviceman on duty. She was told that strange things happened there: inanimate objects moved, coffeepots plugged and unplugged, lights went on and off, strange shadows appeared and, Iva writes, "several times eyes could be seen, watching. No face, just dark brown eyes." While there, Iva experienced bone-chilling cold and on her way out received a "fresh" pat from an invisible hand. "I got to talking to some of the other women in the squadron later and it was common knowledge that you didn't go there alone, and the WAF didn't go there AT ALL."

TENNESSEE

*CHATTANOOGA   Chickamauga, one of the bloodiest battlefields of the American Civil War, may be visited at Chattanooga National Military Park. It is said to be haunted by many spectres, the most frightening being "Old Green Eyes," who, according to one legend, is the spirit of a beheaded Confederate. A more chilling theory is that "Old Green Eyes" is an older, not-necessarily-human apparition that Civil War soldiers saw prowling amongst the corpses.

*NASHVILLE   Old City Cemetery, a historic and atmospheric graveyard, features a large lamplit "avenue of the dead." Particularly notable is the memorial for Ann Rawlings Sanders, a young woman who drowned herself in the nearby Cumberland River after a lovers' quarrel. Her grief-stricken boyfriend put an eternal light on her tomb to quiet her troubled ghost, for Ann had always been afraid of the dark.

*NATCHEZ   Glenburnie, the mayor's residence, is reputedly haunted by a previous owner, who was murdered in 1932 but still roams the woods nearby. Neighbors have heard ghostly piano music coming from Glenwood, the house next door, where the chief murder suspect once lived. Other haunted spots in Natchez include the restored plantation Longwood and King's Tavern, which may be the town's oldest building.

TEXAS

*ALPINE   Chinati Mountain, situated just off U.S. Highway 67/90 between Alpine and Marfa to the west, is the site of a mysterious blue light that motorists have seen glowing high up on the cliff. Locals say it is a ghostly Indian's campfire. Investigations have proven fruitless; the light vanishes when approached.

*HENDERSON   In 1851, Sam Houston's cousin James L. Howard built a mansion on South Main Street that is now a museum allegedly haunted by the original Mrs. Howard.

*HOUSTON   The public library is allegedly haunted by a former janitor's violin-playing ghost.

UTAH

SALT LAKE CITY   A formally clad gentleman has been seen haunting a house that is now used as a storage facility by the Bailey Feed Company.

VERMONT

*BRISTOL   Outside town is an area called Bristol Notch where villagers dug countless shafts futilely looking for Spanish silver said to have been hidden there. A small boy fell into one of these holes and died. His dog, who would not leave the spot, also perished. Locals have named the pit the Ghost Shaft because of the eerie cries and howls heard there.

*CUTTINGSVILLE   On Route 103 near here is the Haunted Mansion Bookshop, situated on the premises of a great estate and adjacent to a cemetery once owned by John P. Bowman, a farmer-turned-tanner whose will left a large sum for the upkeep of the grounds and house. Bowman House is said to be a very grim place: footsteps have been heard, a woman's ghost was seen there once and there is a dark spot at the top of one staircase that no one likes to linger by. Once a small girl tourist stuck out her tongue at one of the portraits; several witnesses claim they saw it fly off the wall and strike her. The bookshop owners depart promptly at sundown and allow nobody to remain on the premises at night.

VIRGINIA

*ALEXANDRIA This lovely community near Washington, D.C., has several ghost-ridden houses. One, at 607 Oronoco Street, was once owned by Robert E. Lee's father and is haunted by a young boy. It is a tourist attraction, as is Ramsay House, residence of the city's first mayor, William Ramsay, who still appears occasionally at an upstairs window.

*AMELIA Many ghostly manifestations are supposed to haunt Haw Branch Plantation, a 1745 Georgian-Federal residence, including a limping man in the attic; a cavalier in riding boots calling for help; phantom cowbells; the odor of fresh oranges and roses; and an invisible heavy object that sometimes falls outside near the moat. In 1969, a charcoal portrait hung over the library fireplace gradually changed to pastel hues. Its subject, Florence Wright, never visited Haw Branch while she was alive but is thought to be the woman in white one family member saw admiring the portrait before disappearing.

*BEAVERDAM Scotchtown was once the home of Dolly Madison as well as patriot Patrick Henry. One of its legends is that a duel fought in its hall left bloodstains and spectres.

*CHARLES CITY Ancestral home of the King Carter family, Shirley Plantation is filled with architectural and antique treasures. A portrait of an "Aunt Pratt" is said to emit ghostly noises if hung improperly.

*FREDERICKSBURG This city is particularly rich in haunted houses. Chatham, on a hill overlooking the Rappahannock River, once had such illustrious guests as George Washington, the Marquis de Lafayette and Abraham Lincoln, but it is supposedly haunted by a lovelorn English "lady in white" who shows up every seven years. Her next scheduled appearances will be in 1993 and the year 2000. Another haunted mansion, Chimneys, built in 1772, was the childhood home of Nell

Herndon, who became President Chester A. Arthur's First Lady. Chimneys is the hangout of an active, unidentified girl ghost who sings and plays the piano. Fall Hill, allegedly haunted by Katina, a Sioux Indian princess, and Federal Hill, where former Governor Alexander Spotswood still walks, are private residences not open to the public. But nearby Kenmore is tourable: a Georgian estate rumored to be haunted by Colonel Fielding Lewis, an officer in the Revolutionary War and organizer of the Virginia Militia. Next to the local country club is a third unvisitable private home, Mansfield. It served as a Civil War hospital, and Confederate soldiers supposedly still haunt it. The Rising Sun Tavern is a tourist "must" that dates back to 1792. It no longer has a liquor license, but there is a mischievous spook who likes to turn lights on and off and who once literally pulled a rug out from under a tour guide. Finally, there is St. George's Episcopal Church, where a sad woman in white was once seen by a choir member.

*HAMPTON   Fort Monroe is America's oldest continually garrisoned fortress. It has at least ten phantoms.

*MIDDLETOWN   Nestled in the Shenandoah Mountains is Belle Grove, a former plantation that is now a museum. A murder that happened there left ghosts lurking by the smokehouse.

*PETERSBURG   The Trapezium House at 244 Market Street is one of America's great architectural oddities and may be the one place to go to *escape* from ghosts. Its builder, Charles O'Hara, had a West Indian servant who convinced him that phantoms and evil spirits only inhabit right angles, so O'Hara built a home that contains no ninety-degree angles: the walls are not parallel, the windows, doors and stairs are all skewed and every floor board was cut on a slant! Trapezium House is a brick three-story Federal-style building that the City of Petersburg acquired in 1972 and restored in time to open nine years later as "The Ghost Story Telling House of Virginia."

*RICHMOND   Westover Plantation harbors the spirit of Evelyn Byrd, who died of grief when her father forbade her engagement to a British nobleman.

*WILLIAMSBURG   This popular tourist haven has 173 acres of restored Early American buildings. One of them, Wyeth House, is haunted by a woman clad in a colonial ball gown.

WASHINGTON

SEATTLE   A story in the January 10, 1892, Seattle *Press-Times* claims that a phantom train runs along a portion of Northern Pacific track at Eagles Gorge near Seattle.

WEST VIRGINIA

*GRANTSVILLE   A section of Calhoun County some three miles out of town is said to be haunted by a ghost who will make life unpleasant for farmers living within a rather large radius, not to mention anyone traveling the roads after dark. But this is an old haunting—reported in the September 30, 1884, edition of the Cincinnati *Enquirer.*

WISCONSIN

SUMMERWIND   This decaying mansion near a lake in the northern woods, once the residence of a U.S. Secretary of Commerce, is haunted by Jonathan Carver, an eighteenth-century explorer. A family of eight who moved there in 1970 left after a year. Ghostly phenomena drove their father mad, and their mother tried to kill herself.

WYOMING

*DEVILS TOWER   Anyone who saw Steven Spielberg's science-fiction film *Close Encounters of the Third Kind* will recall the monolithic Devils Tower, which President Theodore Roosevelt declared as America's first national monument in 1906. Indians believe that ghosts live on top of the 865-foot-high column of rock.

Acknowledgments

"Come to the Party" copyright © 1983 by Stuart David Schiff for *Whispers IV*. Reprinted by arrangement with the author's agent, Kirby McCauley.

"Nobody Ever Goes There" copyright © 1981 Manly Wade Wellman. First published in *Weird Tales*, Vol. 48, No. 3. Reprinted by arrangement with the author's agent, Kirby McCauley.

"The Elemental" copyright © 1939 by Street & Smith Publications, Inc., for *Unknown*, July 1939. Reprinted by arrangement with the author's agent, Kirby McCauley.

"We Are the Dead" copyright 1937, © renewed 1965 by Catherine Reggie. Reprinted by permission of Don Congdon Associates, Inc.

"The Return of the Moresbys" copyright © 1963 Davis Publications, Inc. Reprinted by permission of the author.

"The Rider on the Pale Horse" copyright © 1950 Helen Eustis. Published in *Saturday Evening Post*, February 11, 1950. Reprinted by permission of William Morris Agency, Inc., on behalf of the author.

"The Glove" copyright © 1975 by Stuart David Schiff for *Whispers* Nos. 6–7. Reprinted by permission of the author's agent, Richard Curtis.

"Kaena Point" copyright © 1990 C. H. Sherman. Printed by permission of the author.

"Atrocities" copyright © 1989 Jessica Amanda Salmonson, from *A Silver Thread of Madness*. Reprinted by permission of the author.

"Gibbler's Ghost" copyright © 1974 William F. Nolan. Originally printed in *Alien Horizons*. Reprinted by permission of the author.

"They Bite" copyright 1943, © renewed 1971 by Phyllis White. Reprinted by permission of Curtis Brown, Ltd.

"Miracle at Chimayo" copyright © 1990 Carole Buggé. Printed by permission of the author.

"Slaughter House" copyright 1953, © renewed 1981 by Richard Matheson. Reprinted by permission of Don Congdon Associates, Inc.

"The Dead Remember" copyright © 1936 by the Frank A. Munsey Co. for *Argosy*, Aug. 15, 1936; © renewed 1964. Reprinted by permission of Glenn Lord.

"The Night the Ghost Got In" copyright 1933, © 1961 James Thurber. From *My Life and Hard Times*, published by Harper & Row. Reprinted by permission of Rosemary A. Thurber.

"Dumb Supper" copyright 1950 Fantasy House Inc.; © renewed 1978. Reprinted by permission of the author's agent, Forrest J Ackerman, 1495 Glendower Ave., Hollywood CA 90027.

"The Chadwick Pit" copyright © 1980 Carl Jacobi. Reprinted by arrangement with the author's agent, R. Dixon Smith.

"The Return of Andrew Bentley" copyright © 1966 August Derleth. Reprinted by permission of April Jacobs.

"Away" copyright © 1985 Martin H. Greenberg. Originally appeared in *American Horror Stories*. Reprinted by permission of the author.

"Another Chance for Casey" copyright © 1950 *The American Legion Magazine*. Reprinted by permission of *The American Legion Magazine*.